MAJORITY

MAJORITY

TORTH BOOK ONE

ABBY GOLDSMITH

Podium

This series is dedicated to everyone who has read it all the way through to the ending, and especially to my extraordinary husband and alpha reader, Adam Robert Thompson.

Cover design by Podium Publishing

ISBN: 978-1-0394-4272-6

Published in 2023 by Podium Publishing, ULC
www.podiumaudio.com

Podium

MAJORITY

PROLOGUE
THE LION WITHIN

Cherise ghosted through the recreation room. She might as well be no one, easily ignored.

The scissors hidden in her pocket were razor-sharp.

The teens in this cluttered game room had said hello to her when the social worker was introducing her to them. Now that adults were absent? Cherise was a shadow hidden behind curtains of black hair. She was a stir of air beneath the war zone sounds of their video game. No one would bother to speak to a girl who never said a word out loud.

A fat teenager glanced away from the TV and suddenly caught sight of Cherise. He waggled his tongue, as if to imply that the new girl might be enticed by disgusting sights.

Cherise tightened her grip on the hidden scissors she had stolen from an unguarded sewing kit. This group home was a lot less vigilant than the mental institution had been.

"Huey?" a small boy said. "That guy looks like your dad."

The fat teen looked toward the TV screen. It was full of violence, with macho guys slamming their fists into each other's faces.

"Oh, so funny, Thomas." The fat teen sneered at the small one.

The object of his sourness was severely disabled. Not only was Thomas small and prepubescent, but he sat in a powered wheelchair. Judging by his stunted, withered limbs, he could not walk at all. He held a lightweight laptop balanced across his bony knees. How could such a frail kid feel safe challenging someone so much larger?

Oh, well. It was not Cherise's problem.

She exited the recreation room before anyone else took notice of her. It was always a good idea to avoid fellow victims. Abused children absorbed cruel lessons from their parents, Cherise knew. She herself had learned all kinds of selfish cruelty from her ma.

Not that she could have protected her baby sister. Nobody could have.

Still, she should have put up a fight. That was what a good person would have done.

The kitchen smelled like ramen noodles. Mrs. Hollander stood by the stove, stirring a pot, making dinner for her eight wards. Cherise sneaked past her new foster mother, unnoticed. That rickety door, over there, must lead to the backyard of this house.

Cherise unlatched the decrepit door. Hinges creaked as she slipped into the night, although she tried to be quieter than the rain hissing upon leaves. She eased the door shut behind her.

The back porch was soft with rot.

Cherise sat on a bench that looked battered and eroded. She pushed up her sleeve and poked the sharp end of the scissors against her dark skin.

Slice.

She dragged the blade, wishing it would scratch out her hatred, wishing she could release her pent-up screams.

She sliced again.

And again.

Again.

Maybe she ought to cut herself out of the world?

Mrs. Hollander seemed pleasant. No doubt she would appreciate having one less broken teenager to include around the dinner table.

The flimsy door creaked open.

Cherise froze, ready to hide the scissors or else stab someone. Who had dared follow her into the rainy night?

It was the ultra-disabled kid.

Thomas powered his wheelchair through the doorway, and the door clattered shut behind him. "Hi," he said in a friendly voice. "I'm your suicide watch."

Cherise raised the bloody scissors in an unspoken threat. The kid must be lying. No one sane would put this little pipsqueak in charge of a suicide watch. His limbs looked as fragile as twigs, and his squeaky voice could never raise an alarm.

Only extraordinarily messed-up kids ended up in foster care, Cherise felt sure. Had Thomas's father or mother beaten him until he couldn't walk? He must contain a volcano of rage. No doubt he was here to torment the new kid. Would he make fun of her baggy clothes?

"You're Cherise." Thomas fumbled for the notebook tucked by his side and painstakingly tore out a sheet. "I don't mind that you're silent. I can hear your thoughts."

What crap was this?

Cherise narrowed her eyes at the disabled kid. Thomas was white, his hair the color of wet sand, like many people in Appalachia. No doubt he would zero in on how different she looked and bludgeon her with it. Maybe he would quiz her on what ethnicity she was. Latina? Native American? Why did she have a French name?

"I know you're not physically mute," Thomas said. "You have a legit phobia of speech." He folded the sheet of paper, this way and that. "Everyone misjudges me, also. I know what that's like."

He actually sounded sympathetic.

Okay, so he planned to reel her in with false pity. Ha. Cherise knew that game. Everyone wanted to trick the mute girl into saying something. This kid would slam her with a harsh joke the instant she let her guard down.

"You're afraid that if you start speaking," Thomas said, "you'll scream. And you won't be able to stop."

That was accurate.

Cherise ignored the throbbing of her cut arm. It was as if Thomas saw who she truly was, beneath her glasses and thick hair. But that was impossible.

"Your mother punished you every time you spoke." Thomas fluffed the paper, sculpting it. "For your entire life, up until recently, you were unable to speak without suffering a punishment. That's why your throat closes up whenever you try."

Cherise smelled the dirty gag stuffed in her mouth, as if she'd just begged for something to eat. Ma hated complaints.

Could her silence really be due to Ma? Cherise assumed that she'd been born defective and pathetic, just like Ma said.

But hadn't Ma said the same things about the baby?

The baby who wouldn't shut up.

Glitzy kept wailing, drowning out the flies that buzzed around their trailer. She must have been very hungry. Ma kept punishing her until that final time, when Glitzy went silent forever.

I hate Ma. I hate her. The pain in Cherise's torn skin was nothing next to her searing fury. She wanted to stab Ma in the gut. Stab her until she screamed and then keep stabbing until she went silent. Stab her eyes out. Stab her throat.

Surely no one else seethed with such feral, animalistic rage? If other people felt this way, they would never be able to laugh or smile.

They would not have kind eyes, like this boy.

Cherise's inner hatred and rage was how she knew that her ma was right, after all. She was a defective freak.

"Your ma never knew you." Thomas made more creases in the paper. "She never tried to get to know you. And your feelings are rightfully earned. Rage and hatred are not a sign of being defective. It's all completely normal, given your situation."

The way he answered her exact thoughts… Cherise wanted to ask how he'd guessed what was inside her mind.

She opened her mouth, but her throat thickened until she could no longer smell the rain. She couldn't make a sound.

"You associate speaking with pain." Thomas studied her with unabashed interest.

His curiosity should have made him look childlike. But his eyes were strange, and not just in color. Somehow, Thomas looked as if he had witnessed a thousand lifetimes. He looked like a grizzled old man stuffed inside the skin of a disabled child.

"Your phobia is so ingrained," Thomas went on, "knowing the cause won't help you much. But time will. You don't have to be mute forever."

Cherise wanted to ask how Thomas could be so certain.

Words stuck in her throat, aching. She would never be able to speak.

"You're speaking right now," Thomas said. "We're having a conversation."

Thomas seemed to hear her thoughts as clearly as she heard the song of crickets. He seemed to truly see who she was. Not just a victim. Not just a target. Not just a lonely girl, or a tragic news story, but the actuality of *her*, Cherise Chavez, without embellishments or labels.

Do you hear my thoughts? Cherise wondered.

"Yes." Thomas answered exactly as if she'd spoken aloud. "I'm a mind reader."

The impossible statement was as stark and undeniable as the rainwater that dripped from the gutters and the blood dripping from her arm.

Wow.

Cherise could not imagine why a uniquely powerful psychic wanted to talk to the likes of her. Was he trying to save an unwanted teenager whose mother was in prison for murder? Why? Cherise was a girl who lacked friends. She lacked a future.

Maybe Thomas simply felt compelled to reach out? Was he some sort of disabled superhero? Cherise was pretty sure she had read about a character like him in some *X-Men* comics.

"I'm not a superhero." Thomas faced her with a pained expression. "My pain is as real as yours. Mostly, I work on staving off my own early death." He gestured at his frail body. "Everyone has problems, especially in a place like this. I have plenty of my own. Time is valuable to me. I don't waste it. I only came out here because…well, because I judged that you're worth talking to."

Cherise had never been so sincerely complimented. "…Why?"

She paused at the sound of her own voice, quavering like an old lady's. Her voice!

She felt no fear of speaking in front of Thomas. None at all. There was no danger of misunderstanding. He would know what she meant, no matter if she tripped up on words, no matter whether or not she used her voice.

Why do you believe I'm worthwhile? She asked the question inside her mind, because that was more comfortable for her.

Thomas made more folds in the paper. "Cherise, I absorb memories." He looked ashamed. "I've glimpsed what you survived, the home where you grew up, and I'm certain that it would have killed me, or sent me to a loony bin. Very few people could grow up in that household and still see beauty in the world. You're one in a billion. You have a resilience that I want to…well…be around."

Cherise had the impression that he meant every word.

His sincerity made her smile a little. The expression felt brittle, as if her face was made of clay.

Thomas faced her squarely. "Let's get something straight. I'm not trying to force a friendship. We're both lonely—there's no point in treading around that issue—but I came out here because I'd rather not see your particular mind vanish."

She swallowed. His compliment defied everything her ma had ever said about her.

"I have some first aid stuff in the back pocket of my wheelchair." Thomas indicated her wounded forearm. "Would you please bandage that up? No one has to know. I've absorbed several lifetimes worth of medical knowledge, so I can make sure it doesn't get infected."

He was offering to save her.

"If you refuse," Thomas said, "then I'll stop bothering you. I promise." He seemed hesitant. "I just figured I'd ask."

The more Cherise studied Thomas, the more she realized how ancient he looked, despite his childishness. His body was frail and prepubescent. But his gaze? That belonged on a war veteran.

"You see me." Thomas sounded grateful. "Your perceptiveness is a lot like mind reading. You have insights into everyone, but no one understands you."

Cherise held her bleeding arm away from her clothing. She rummaged in the back pocket of Thomas's wheelchair, one-handed, until she found the adhesive bandage roll.

Once she was done bandaging her cut, Thomas handed her the notebook paper. It was transformed into a perfect origami lion.

"For you," he said.

Cherise marveled at the crisp folds.

"Squeeze his mane," Thomas said, "and he'll roar."

Cherise tried it. The lion roared silently.

"There's a lion inside you," Thomas said. "When you rip your mother's grip off your throat, everyone will listen."

PART ONE

In the void where stray atoms float and time is relative, all is frozen and silent. Nothing lives in deep space. There are no voices.

Except for the silent transmissions of the Torth galactic collective.

Have You heard about the rogue child on that primitive wilderness planet?

Huh?

Which planet?

Here is what it looks like ( ).

Its natives call it "Earth" (or "dìqiú") (or "bhūmi") (the indigenous sapients lack a unified language).

Disembodied thoughts converged. Stars remained eternal and uncaring, pins in cosmic space-time. But abstractions crisscrossed the dark energy matrix of the galactic spiral faster than light speed. They formed an ever-shifting kaleidoscope of silent conversations.

The originators of the news shared and swapped mental snapshots of a boy in a wheelchair. *Here is the rogue child's corporeal form*, they explained. *The local natives gave him a spoken name: "Thomas."*

!?

The vast majority of minds had never heard of anyone living lawlessly among primitives. This was news. This was something to talk about.

How remarkable, many commented.

Has anything like this ever happened before (in galactic history)?

Hmm. Wait. How do (You) We know that this child is actually one of Us?

Indeed. The physical similarities between Our corporeal forms and that of (those primitives) humans are uncanny.

That's because the indigenous primitives of Earth are an evolutionary offshoot of Our own predecessors.

Oh, really? I didn't know that.

Yes. (I am a relic specialist; I know all kinds of obscure ancient history.)

Anyway. So isn't it possible that this child is merely a precocious human?

Dissenters changed the direction of millions of conversations. *BUT HE HEARS THOUGHTS.*

Everyone shifted, like kelp bowing to an oceanic current.

Primitives (humans) who regularly interact with this child claim that he is a mind reader.

Primitives (humans) who work with this child praise him as an unparalleled genius.

The primitives deem his accomplishments to be superhuman.

The indigenous natives (humans) are cognizant of the vast gulf in intelligence between him and them.

That did seem like evidence.

Well.

Well, well.

How did (one of Us) this rogue child end up alone and unsupervised?

Why isn't he safely confined on a baby farm?

Relevant memories got swapped in the voids between space dust. The replays hinted at an answer to the most popular questions.

Oh. Her.

The Servant of All who failed to serve All.

The one who went rogue.

!!!

She birthed an illegal child?

!!!!!!

Fresh listeners joined the silent conversations, attracted by the waves of *(!!!)* surprise that signified breaking news.

Everyone was eager to insert their own opinions. Conversational clouds grew as large as nebulas.

Is that rogue child even aware of Us?

Does he even know that Torth exist?

What mayhem is he causing?

Does he actually believe that he is a mere primitive (a human)?

Who cares? That is not germane.

Right. That rogue child is a menace to the native population of Earth.

He might speed up their development of (unspoken communications) their internet.

Or he might gift them with other technological boons.

That would transform them (the natives of Earth) into a potential threat.

Which We would then have to eliminate (destroy) (or enslave).

He would ruin the natural innocence of the natives.

Opinions rolled together, gathering into a unified conclusion as dominant and inescapable as a nebula.

We ought not leave him there.

Agreed.

The Majority decision led to debates. Not everyone agreed on how to remove the rogue child from Earth.

Let Us dispose of (kill) him.

!?

He is too wild (a feral child). He is unlikely to adapt to (Us) civilization. Plus, he is a hybrid.

He is not worthy of being introduced to Us (civilization).

Right. He is probably too primitive.

Right. He is not fully Torth.

Other minds pulled away in disagreement.

Surely he should be given a chance?

His mind may yet be malleable.

He is young, barely ripe.

And while We collect him, can't We use this as an opportunity to finish the task his mother failed to complete?

Oh, you mean kill that dangerous hybrid?

Yes. Kill the Giant.

Oh, come on. What a wasted opportunity! Why can't We collect the Giant instead?

Bring the Giant to My city. I'll make his execution a public spectacle.

No, My city should host the event.

No, Mine!

Lesser conversations eddied past the topic of the rogue child, discussing how best to slay the dangerous hybrid known as the Giant. The main conversation, however, recentered on what to do about Thomas.

Have You heard about his invention?

???

Yes. The rogue child invented an effective medical treatment for his own congenital illness using only primitive tools.

At a very young age.

Oh, wow.

He must have astronomical potential.

He must be a supergenius—a very useful mutant.

A silent chorus formed, upholding one suggestion above all others. A Majority decision coalesced.

Give him a chance.

Yes.

Bring "Thomas" to civilization.

Agreed.

Let him ascend.

Give him a chance to become ONE OF US.

CHAPTER 1

SORTING SECRETS

"Thank you for coming," Thomas told the well-dressed audience.

Their wants and desires saturated the air, more pungent than perfume. Thomas tried not to wrinkle his nose with distaste. Instead, he made himself sound pleasant.

"And again," he said, "if you make a donation to Rasa Biotech, you'll receive a full-length recording of me explaining my breakthrough with ubiquitin-inhibiting enzymes."

He suppressed a sigh of relief as one of his adult colleagues leaned into her microphone to offer her own closing remarks. The press conference was over. Soon, Thomas would be able to escape the cloying moods all around him.

His fellow panelists were distinguished molecular biologists and neuroscientists. All had gray hair. For them, college was decades ago. Middle school was even farther in the rearview mirror. Thomas was painfully aware of what he looked like to the biochem majors and journalists in the audience.

A gimmick.

A poster boy.

He forced himself to smile as the audience clapped, aiming extra applause his way. He always got extra attention for being underage and visibly disabled. He wasn't a typical neuroscientist.

Reporters surged toward Thomas, and he braced himself for a maelstrom of unwanted thoughts. His colleagues from Rasa Biotech gave him sympathetic looks, but they were free to leave, and they wisely trotted away.

"Thomas!" A microphone nearly smacked him in the face. "Thomas Hill! Can you confirm that you're scheduled to speak at Harvard next month?"

—Like a trained monkey.

Another microphone. "Do you have any school-aged friends, Thomas?"

Even if he is a smart kid, there's no way a thirteen-year-old—

Another microphone. "What do kids your age say about you working as a consultant for a leading biotech company?"

Answer my question first, you smug brat.

"How does your foster mother handle your busy schedule, Thomas?"

Doubt he'll live to adulthood. Even if he's in on clinical trials—

Thomas attempted to power his wheelchair through the crowd, but reporters shoved past each other like vultures around fresh carrion. The barrage of thoughts blended into a screaming whirlwind of mood-laced nonsense.

The attention had been tolerable earlier, when the vast majority of people sat beyond his range of telepathy. Thomas didn't mind one or two people within his range. Even four or five was okay. He was used to living in crowded group homes.

But thirty-plus?

The nonstop babble gave him a pounding headache. He could not lift his underdeveloped arms high enough to shove the microphones away.

All he dared say was "Thank you for coming." Otherwise, he might accidentally answer someone's unspoken thought.

His caretaker, Vy, pushed through the crowd. "I'm so sorry," Vy said with an apologetic smile as she squeezed past a cameraman. "Sorry." She pulled on her winter coat, whacking a reporter in the process. "Whoops! Did I hit you? I'm really sorry."

At six feet tall, Vy could take up a lot of space. People tended to forgive her. She was a natural redhead with a sweet, kindhearted face.

Vy got behind Thomas's wheelchair and plowed toward the off-stage ramp. The reporters could overlook his determination to leave, but not hers. All they could do was try to keep up.

Cameras flashed. The babble echoed against the high ceiling. The remaining audience crowded the aisles, eager for a close-up glimpse of the phenomenal child whom newspapers touted as the "next Einstein" or a "young da Vinci." Headlines screamed that Thomas had an immeasurable IQ score.

The testers had no idea that he cheated.

Thomas feared that if his secret ever leaked into the public, today's mob would be a trite little blip. He would cease to be a biotechnology consultant. He would no longer get opportunities to guide scientific research in an advantageous direction. Instead, he would become an unwilling research subject, locked up in a government facility and poked and prodded until he died.

He dared not let the world learn what he could do.

—poor kid—

—should get going if I'm going to pick up dinner for—

All he can do is study, since he's so—

—would think that his birth mother would come out of the woodwork, just *to claim him—*

The cacophony of thoughts went on and on. Thomas realized tiredly that most of them were not actually talking.

"Can I have an aspirin?" he asked.

"You just had one before the panel," Vy pointed out. Even so, she kindly opened the bottle of baby aspirin and shook out a pill. She put it into his mouth, then held a bottle of water for him to drink from.

... ( ) ...

That was a strange mind.

Thomas halted his wheelchair, causing Vy to bump into him.

That woman wearing sunglasses, just beyond his four-yard range of telepathy, seemed to contain countless millions of minds instead of just one.

But she was no longer in his range. She had stepped back.

Thomas figured he must be more exhausted than he'd realized. Nobody had a mind like that. He contained a few thousand extra lifetimes' worth of knowledge, but they were not all whispering inside him at once, like a sinister audience. He only had one consciousness. It was his own.

Anyway, he had never met anyone with a mind like his. Not even close.

Rather than attempt to explain why he had stopped, Thomas pushed the button on his armrest and moved forward again. That woman looked like a normal graduate student, or perhaps a professor. He had likely hallucinated a microsecond of weirdness.

Why was she wearing sunglasses indoors?

He glanced back. Sure enough, her eyes remained completely hidden. Her skin had a plastic artificiality to it. Perhaps she was a burn victim?

"What's wrong?" Vy asked. "Did you forget something back there?"

"No." Thomas faced forward, embarrassed by his own lapse in judgment, or his perceptual error. People misjudged him all the time. He didn't want to do it to some innocent bystander. "Let's just get home."

"Can't wait."

Winter turned travel into a process. Before they exited the college building, Vy had to wrap Thomas in a knit scarf and a thermal blanket. Once he was bundled up, she opened the door for him, and he powered his wheelchair into the icy parking lot.

Gray-white asphalt matched the overcast sky. This time of year in New Hampshire, everything seemed to be different shades of gray.

Stragglers streamed past. "Great talk," people told Thomas. Or they gave him a thumbs-up sign.

It was all fake, exaggerated praise. He heard their unspoken doubts.

Whoever coached him did an amazing job.

Well-rehearsed lines.

As long as they talked positively about Rasa Biotech, their unspoken opinions about Thomas shouldn't matter. Thomas kept reminding himself of that.

Vy loaded his wheelchair into the minivan. While she operated the lift, he overheard her personal thoughts. Vy was holding an inner debate on whether or not to pick up Cherise, who was three years older than Thomas and a sophomore in high school. Vy detested driving in heavy traffic. But her mom— Thomas's foster mother—would appreciate the kindness, since it would help some of the kids get a much-needed early start on their homework.

"Can we pick up Cherise on our way home?" Thomas asked.

Vy gave him one of her troubled looks, and Thomas sensed her mood fuzz with frustration. *How does he always manage to make on-target comments about what's on my mind?* she wondered. *It can't be a coincidence. He has to be a mind reader.*

Thomas had lived in the Hollander home with Vy for nearly three years. They knew each other well.

He gave her a beneficent smile.

"Sure." Vy strapped his wheelchair into its usual place, so it wouldn't roll if the van hit a pothole. "That's a nice thought."

She secured Thomas into place with more straps. Sitting upright was hard work for his atrophied muscles, so he needed the support.

He listened to Vy's thoughts without trying to listen. He had no choice. She was nearby, and his telepathy range was roughly thirteen feet in a radius from his head. That range fluctuated only a tiny bit. It narrowed when he was hungry or in pain, like now. It widened when he was feeling good.

...Scholarship.

Vy was considering ways to secure a scholarship. She had a love affair with meteorology, but apparently, she had failed to get the internship at the local weather channel. It conflicted with her job as an emergency room nurse.

"Sorry you didn't get the internship," Thomas said.

"Thanks." Vy eyed him with unease. "I just got the rejection email while your panel was going on. How did you know?"

Thomas knew far more than he wanted to know about Violet Hollander, his primary caretaker and foster sister. Storms thrilled her the way roller coasters thrilled other people. As she climbed into the driver's seat, he vicariously experienced the weight of her corkscrew earrings. He felt the loose ripple of hair that brushed her cheek. Everything Vy experienced, Thomas felt in a lighter way, as phantom sensations.

"I could just tell," Thomas said. "By your mood." That wasn't exactly a lie.

Soon they were on their way, off the college campus and cruising down the highway. Vy tapped her thumbs on the steering wheel, enjoying music. Thomas felt each tap.

Other cars passed them in other lanes. Their occupants ghosted through Thomas's range, just long enough for him to catch a whiff of cigarette smoke or a phantom burst from a radio tune. He couldn't block foreign perceptions and moods and thoughts. The best he could do was pretend to be ignorant.

Other people's thoughts were the background of his life.

CHAPTER 2
STRAPPED IN PLACE

Teenagers made Thomas feel like a xeno-anthropologist immersed in an alien society. Their moods shifted so fast, they seemed iridescent, like butterfly wings.

"Do you ever miss going to school?" Vy asked as they pulled into the crowded high school parking lot.

"Nope." Thomas had spent much of his life convincing adults that homework was nothing but a waste of his time. Once he absorbed a tidbit of information, he never forgot it. His memory was as flawless as a digital recorder. He could replay any experience he had absorbed and study it frame by frame.

That was how he cheated his way through life.

That, and his secret telepathic ability.

A couple of athletic boys walked close enough for Thomas to overhear the mental gist of their conversation. They were concerned about an upcoming basketball game, and girls.

Thomas sensed their satisfied exhaustion from basketball practice. That was nothing that he could relate to. His neuromuscular disease prevented his muscles from gaining strength. He was skeletal and underdeveloped below his neck.

"There's Cherise," Vy said.

Thomas peered through Vy's perceptions. He saw Cherise standing at a curb, waiting for a school bus and failing to blend in with the crowd of white kids. Thick bangs and glasses did little to shield her face.

Vy rolled down a window and waved. "Hey! Cherise!"

Their dented red minivan, with its handicap plate, was easy to recognize. Cherise adjusted her backpack and hurried toward them.

A gangly, smug-looking teenager followed her. He leaned close to speak in Cherise's ear. She sped up, eager to get away from him.

She wasted no time in climbing into the passenger seat of the minivan.

As soon as she was within Thomas's range of telepathy, he sensed her mood, prickly with humiliation. She knew—and therefore Thomas knew—that the gangly kid had acted fake friendly. "*See ya tomorrow, hottie,*" he had said to Cherise. "*Maybe you'll learn to say hi to me.*"

No one else seemed to notice Roy's cruelty.

Thomas absorbed memories from Cherise so often, he knew her life. He knew exactly how it felt to eat alone in the school cafeteria. Sometimes Roy stared at Cherise from another table. Sometimes he slammed her sketchbook shut without warning.

And today?

Today Roy had followed Cherise down a crowded hallway between classes. He had lurched at her like an attack dog, and he'd laughed at her flinching reaction.

Everyone knew that Cherise hardly ever talked. Roy must feel safe. She wouldn't report him.

"Stop the van." Thomas could not reach the toggle button for the window, so he had to add, "Roll down my window."

Vy had no intention of stopping.

But fate intervened. A group of teenagers crossed her path, and Vy was forced to stop anyway.

She used the driver's door controls to roll down his window, letting in a flow of icy air. "What's up?"

"Hey, Roy!" Thomas called.

!!!

Panic spiked from Cherise.

"Roy!" Thomas called, making sure the asshole heard him. "Come here!"

"What are you doing?" Vy asked.

The bully ambled toward Thomas's open window with an expression of private amusement. "What's up?" His gaze flicked from Thomas to Cherise, then back again. "Sweet handicap van."

The cold wind made Thomas's eyes water. He ignored it and probed Roy's mind.

Like planets, minds had ecosystems and biomes. Emotions gave them texture. Memories comprised their structure. Thomas found an eddy of vulnerability in Roy's mind, and he followed it downward, toward a deep chasm of buried humiliations.

"I saw a YouTube video of you." Roy smirked. "Baby Einstein, right? Hey, Latina! Your little boyfriend is adorbs."

"Who are you?" Vy asked, her tone a threat.

Thomas studied the worst memories of Roy's life. "Roy," he said. "I wonder if your mom would pour her vomit bucket over you again if she saw how you treat Cherise?"

Roy looked as if he'd been punched.

Thomas imitated the shrill, drunken tone of Roy's mother. "You've got to clean your underwear better, baby Roy!" He laughed, imitating Roy's cruelty.

That caused something like an earthquake of rage.

"Drive!" Thomas said, a split second before Roy's hands reached through the window to strangle him.

The minivan rolled forward. Roy fell away with a short scream of pain.

"What the hell?" Vy radiated anger. It was partly aimed at Roy, but Thomas sensed that she was also angry at him, for starting a fight.

Cherise, though...

Her unspoken inner voice felt as delicate as snowflakes. *That was awesome.*

Behind them, Roy jumped to his feet, roaring mad. "I know where you freaks live!"

"Oh? You'd better be careful in that new Audi you're so proud of," Thomas called through the open window. "Your reckless driving is likely to get you killed."

"What?" Vy said.

Roy seemed just as shocked. He jogged to catch up with the slowly rolling minivan, his eyes wild with rage and sudden fear.

"Yeah. I'm sorry, Roy." Thomas made himself sound sympathetic. "I can't help knowing things. Knowledge just comes to me." He held his weak hands apart. "A bend in the road, and..." He smacked his hands together, although he was too weak for that to make any noise.

Roy looked stricken with terror. Teenagers gathered to watch, curious.

"Sorry." Thomas let his hands fall. "If your mom gets wasted at your funeral, I hope she doesn't puke on your coffin."

Vy stomped on the brake. She radiated fury like a boiling cauldron.

"You lying freak." Roy looked ugly with fear.

"I never lie," Thomas said.

Roy's face contorted. "If—"

"—if you were really psychic..." Thomas spoke in mocking sync with the bully. "...it would be world news or something."

He could speak in precise sync with anyone. He had sensed every word welling up in Roy's mind.

The window began to slide closed, controlled by Vy.

"Hey!" Thomas glared at her.

"You've made your point," Vy said.

Their minivan rolled toward the road. Behind them, Roy shouted something in a pleading tone. The crowd of teenagers whispered and used their phones to record the scene. One said, "...like Professor X?" in a hushed tone.

"I wasn't done," Thomas said.

"Yes, you are." Vy signaled a turn onto the street. "I don't know who that kid is, or what he did to you. Or to Cherise." She glanced at their foster sister. "But

Thomas? Death threats aren't okay. You can't go around threatening people."

As if he needed a lecture.

Thomas curled his fingers into weak imitations of fists. He wasn't strong enough to toggle the window button, let alone win an argument with his caretaker, but he was sick of being treated like a disabled child.

Most people saw his withered limbs, his concave chest, and his sagging spine, and they assumed he was helpless.

Even Vy.

He supposed it was difficult to respect someone who needed help using a toilet. Vy saw him in his weakest moments. She would never take him seriously.

"That kid deserved worse," Thomas said. "He was threatening Cherise."

"How do you know that?" Vy glanced at him in the rearview mirror, frustrated and suspicious. "Are you just guessing?"

Thomas growled. Sometimes he thought he should just tell Vy about his ability. She probably wouldn't tell the whole world. Probably not.

Thank you. Appreciation glowed from Cherise. She felt safer, as if a weight had been lifted off her shoulders. *I don't know what I'd do without you.*

Thomas relaxed. He could bask in that glow forever. Moments like this made everything else worthwhile.

Their minivan passed the familiar chain-link fences, dilapidated houses, and rusting auto parts of their neighborhood. Thomas saw poverty, and he knew that Vy saw poverty as well. But Cherise?

Cherise noticed a cheerfully painted sled.

She saw a harvest wreath that defied the wintry frost.

She had a way of seeing beauty just about anywhere. Whenever Thomas saw the world filtered through Cherise, everything seemed nice. He loved that.

If only she could stay with him at home, while he used his laptop to fine-tune the medicine he was developing with the Rasa Biotech team. She didn't deserve to suffer the indignities of school.

Vy cleared her throat. "You said you never lie."

"Yup," Thomas admitted.

It was true. He might say misleading things, but he only spoke facts. He had been born with an enormous advantage over other people. As far as he knew—and he knew a lot—no one else in the world could read minds. If he resorted to telling direct lies, then he would be a bully. He would be no different than a natural athlete shoving disabled children out of wheelchairs.

"You told that kid that he'll die in a car wreck," Vy stated flatly.

Her unspoken accusation was loud and clear. She believed that Thomas had lied.

"No," Thomas said, correcting her. "If you paid attention to my wording, I was only speculating out loud. I used words such as *if* and it's *likely*. I never said he'll die. He just inferred the worst-case scenario from what I said."

Vy groaned.

Thomas pretended he couldn't hear her low opinion of him. So what if his caretaker believed he was some sort of bully? Vy was wrong.

Most people were wrong.

Not Thomas. He saw the truths behind fake expressions and casual fibs.

I saw kids recording that scene on their phones, Cherise thought. *It will get passed around the whole school. Might go viral on social media.*

"People will assume it was staged," Thomas said, answering her unspoken concern for him. "No one believes kids."

He tried not to sound too bitter. Even if his medical breakthrough saved a million lives, people would continue to assume he was a hoax.

He needed to get past puberty. In order to do that, he needed to live to adulthood.

Painful spinal injections of nusinersen might get him there. But that drug was more expensive than the Hollander home could afford, and its side effects might kill him anyway. NAI-12, his neuronal apoptosis inhibitor, was a much better option. It was what he needed—whether or not it got approved for clinical trials.

"Anyway," Thomas said to Cherise, "you don't deserve to be treated like that. It was worth a risk."

Vy eyed them both with unease, but she refrained from making a comment. She was familiar with their half-verbal conversations.

Everyone in the Hollander home knew about the friendship between Thomas and Cherise. Well, they knew that Cherise spent hours in Thomas's bedroom, anyway. Was she doing homework, or drawing in one of her sketchbooks, or…?

No one quite dared to ask.

And Thomas didn't mind their unspoken suspicions. He liked to keep people guessing. Their unanswered questions imbued him with an aura of mystique, which gave him a little bit of power.

He used to be truly helpless. He had always been a disabled child in the foster care system, and that meant some bitter and sad years before he'd gained any scientific credibility. He never wanted to feel that way again.

"What on Earth?" Vy braked the minivan.

A woman stood in their gravel driveway.

Thomas switched his focus to Vy's perceptions for a better view. It was someone from the audience of his Rasa Biotech panel—the woman with dark sunglasses and plastic-looking skin. Her breath made puffs in the frosty air. She wore a black overcoat, which contrasted sharply against her curly blond hair.

"She's not moving out of my way," Vy said. "Weird. I wonder what she wants?"

Cherise said nothing. However, Thomas was close enough to overhear her thoughts, and he sensed Cherise's speculation that this woman looked like Thomas.

She had his coloring. The same narrow chin. Also, his wide forehead. Was she an unknown, unanticipated family member?

Like…his birth mother?

Thomas's heartbeat sped up. He tried to smooth down his excitement, reminding himself that his birth parents seemed uninterested in claiming him. Ever since he had begun to speak in public, garnering funding for his project at Rasa Biotech, journalists and other celebrity-chasers wanted a piece of his meager fame. He got invited to sell products. Idiots invited him to endorse their ideas or their pitiful college projects.

A CIA think tank had even approached him, covertly.

That federal agent had pretended to be a friendly journalist, and Thomas had likewise pretended. He had done his best to act ignorant and childishly innocent, misleading the "journalist" without outright lying to her.

Sometimes he felt like a performer balancing on a tightrope. He needed to maintain just enough credibility to manage a team of neuroscientists. Only that, and no more. Too much hype would put him under a magnifying glass, and if the world found out how he cheated…well, everyone who'd praised him would reduce him to a lab rat.

Might this strange woman be an undercover agent for some think tank?

Or she might be a con artist trying to cash in on Thomas's fame. Maybe she hoped to trick him into believing that she was his birth mother?

Or…

She might be the real deal.

A memory haunted Thomas. It was so faded that it might be only a dream, but he had carried it with him for as long as he'd existed.

Frigid cold. Falling snow. A twinned glow from distant headlights. And a woman with curly blond hair, walking away from him, beneath snow-laden pines.

She had left him—a newborn infant—to die alone in the woods.

She never glanced back. No matter how he yearned for her to turn around, he never saw her face.

"I'd like to meet her." Thomas eyed the stranger without actually looking at her. He peered through the eyes of Cherise and Vy, shifting from one foster sister to the other. "Can we just park here and find out what she wants?" He fidgeted, signaling to Vy that he wanted someone to undo his straps and lower his wheelchair.

CHAPTER 3
THE MANY

Thomas waited impatiently for his wheelchair to touch the ground. The mystery of his birth mother had troubled him all his life. If she had truly not wanted her newborn infant, well, then why hadn't she killed him? Infants were easy to dispose of. Such crimes often went unsolved. Why had his birth mother granted him a meager chance to survive?

She had wrapped him in a dish towel, as if that could protect the baby from subzero temperatures.

She had left him near a roadside in the predawn hours of the darkest night of the year. That gave him a chance to be seen by passing cars.

A surgeon on his commute to work had noticed the discarded bundle. That was how Thomas got his name: Thomas, for the surgeon who had rescued him, and Hill, because he'd been found on Liberty Hill Road. He was an orphan in the truest sense of the word. No family had ever stepped forward to claim him.

He wanted answers.

"Ma'am, can I help you?" Vy stepped between Thomas and the stranger.

The blonde woman spoke in a cultured, clipped voice. "I have a matter to discuss with your resident supergenius." She sidestepped Vy and walked into Thomas's range of telepathy.

Thomas prepared to soak up her name and personal information. No one could prevent him from learning whatever secrets he was determined to learn. He anticipated revelations and weird secrets...but this...

You.

Her mind was unlike any he had ever encountered.

Boldly, defiantly, unlike any mind on Earth.

Cherise and Vy had moods. Everyone had moods, erupting like volcanoes or lapping like ocean waves, yet this woman felt dead inside. Her mood was as smooth as glass.

You.

Thousands of distant individuals seemed to whisper inside the woman's mind. Their wordless attention pointed at Thomas like a colossal finger. More joined them, until there were tens of thousands, their surface thoughts overlapping and echoing. The unseen audience kept growing. There were far too many for Thomas to keep track of. Their combined attention felt as powerful as a god's thunderous decree.

MIND READER (YOU).

Thomas shrank back in his wheelchair. An audience larger than the population of North America seemed to be sizing him up, all peering through her sunglasses.

"You've caught a lot of attention," the blonde woman said.

Her casual words might as well be a recording. There was no personality behind them. No emotion, no intention, no humanity. She was well-groomed, like a newscaster, but her smile had nothing to do with the whispery horde inside her mind.

For the first time in years, Thomas felt like the child that everyone mistook him for. His own ignorance was staggering.

He had given up searching for other telepaths. All his life, he had been alone in his own mind. But now? It seemed other telepaths did exist, and they must be legion! Millions. Billions. He had never been so profoundly wrong about anything before.

"Where are you?" he whispered.

What an (ignorant) (deprived) lonely (solo) child. Faraway individuals chorused within the woman, their thoughts overlapping as fast as multiple lightning strikes.

Poor orphan.

Abandoned child.

Interesting specimen.

(Hush)

You (rogue child) were raised by (primitives) savages.

But you could be (superior) so much more.

You can be much (wiser) (smarter) better than you are now.

The wordless chorus of faraway thoughts collected into an angelic crescendo. JOIN US.

Thomas was vaguely aware that his jaw was hanging open.

All those distant telepaths seemed nameless, genderless, bereft of identities, as if they were mere reflections of people. They were not wholly there. Not within his range.

Perceptions crackled through the unseen horde: towers that defied gravity, needle thin because they were taller than mountains. Flying vehicles careened between holographs that floated in midair. Urban sprawl glowed on the shadowy sides of moons and planets.

We live on other worlds, the distant minds chorused.

Their chorus was silent. The telepaths did not use any spoken language or words. Their language was pure imagination, comprised of impressions and abstractions.

It was beautiful.

They went on, revealing facts to Thomas in overlapping waves of information.

We own all worlds.

We know you.

We see you—

—on your primitive world (Earth).

They indicated the blonde woman and introduced her. *We see you through the eyes of the Swift Killer.*

"How...?" Thomas breathed. He had far too many questions for a verbal conversation. Was he communicating with aliens? He must be. But how could aliens resemble humans? That seemed too improbable for plausibility. Unless humans and telepathic aliens were close relatives?

Join Us and find out, they chorused.

Oh. He wanted to.

The Swift Killer looked human. She looked so much like him, he wanted to cry. Was this the woman who had given birth to him and then abandoned him in the snowy forest?

Except for her eyes.

Thomas couldn't see much through her dark sunglasses, but judging from what little he could make out, the Swift Killer lacked pupils and irises. Her gaze was an empty, milky white. She could be mistaken for a blind person.

Only Thomas sensed that her vision was...well, better than normal.

She saw every hair on his head, every thread in his scarf. She saw a million variations in color, more than anyone should see. Was she actually seeing ultraviolet?

If these hordes of alien telepaths owned technology that empowered them to live on multiple planets, they might also have advanced biotechnology. They might have medicines that made Thomas's NAI-12 seem primitive.

They might have the knowledge to cure his fatal, degenerative neuromuscular illness.

Join Us, the Swift Killer's inner audience thundered in an angelic symphony.

Join Us, and—

—you shall gain the knowledge of All.

The instant Thomas wondered how to join them, the Swift Killer placed a folded brochure on his lap.

Thomas glanced down. It was a map of the state of New Hampshire.

He looked at her, wondering if the map contained some incredible secret.

I circled it in red (for you), the Swift Killer thought. *Go there.*

Go there, her inner audience hummed.

Go.

Go.

Today.

Don't make Us wait.

Their overlapped thoughts were as powerful as ocean waves roaring against cliffs.

Cherise stepped out of the van. Concern radiated from her like rays of sunlight, because she couldn't guess why Thomas looked so astonished and awestruck. In the year and a half since she had first met Thomas, she had never seen him react with shock.

"Are you all right?" Vy stepped between Thomas and the Swift Killer, emanating alarm.

"Fine." Thomas tried to maneuver around his caretaker, wheels churning on gravel. He didn't need an overprotective older sister. "You can go into the house."

Vy drew back with a hurt look.

Thomas realized that he'd sounded rude. He would apologize later. "Wait!" he called to the Swift Killer, because she looked ready to walk away.

The unseen audience inside her mind layered their imaginations together, forming a hyperrealistic scene of a woman trudging through falling snow, her hair pale against her billowing coat and the nighttime darkness.

All those millions of distant telepaths had just fed him his own earliest memory.

They might know how to find his birth mother.

"Don't leave?" Thomas hated to beg like a child. "Please?"

But the Swift Killer walked away, uncaring, just like his unknown mother had done. Soon she was beyond his range of telepathy. Thomas could no longer sense the fabulous audience on many alien worlds.

"I have questions," he said.

CHAPTER 4
RESPECT

Cherise felt as inconsequential as the stacks of books and science journals all over Thomas's bedroom. That was how she liked things. Let the world pass her by. Let people forget that she existed.

She held the map open and stared at the circled area.

The portion of Liberty Hill Road where Thomas had been found was near the circle but not inside it. As far as Cherise could see, the indicated region was devoid of civilization. No landmarks. No roads. It was just woods.

"That map leads to answers." Thomas looked helpless, cradled in Mrs. Hollander's stout arms as she lifted him out of his wheelchair and tucked him into bed. "Don't you want to find out what sort of people I come from?" His tone gained an edge. "Don't you care?"

"Of course I care." Mrs. Hollander arranged the call button next to Thomas's weak hand so that he could alert someone if he needed medical help. "But we can go exploring this weekend. I'm not driving into the middle of the woods without a good reason. I'm sorry."

She gave him a gentle kiss on his forehead.

Thomas gave her a murderous glare.

"You know," he said as Mrs. Hollander walked away, "I could quit managing our home's investment portfolio. How would you like that?"

Mrs. Hollander stopped, and Cherise held her breath. She didn't understand why Thomas was making threats. It was uncharacteristic of him. After all, if he just wanted an address, couldn't he have plucked it from that stranger's mind? He had once told Cherise, in private, that he only needed a few seconds to soak up a person's entire life history.

Mrs. Hollander turned back toward Thomas, giving him a skeptical look. "Don't you need our money for spinal injections?"

Thomas grimaced.

"I guess you've given up on those injections." Mrs. Hollander leaned against the doorway with her arms folded. "And I can guess why. How about if you return that medical prototype that you stole from Rasa Biotech?"

Thomas's glare sharpened.

Mrs. Hollander gave him a pitying look. "Yes, that's right. I know about it."

Cherise glanced at the briefcase that poked out of the wheelchair's pocket. She had drawn fanciful phoenix birds on the lid, in metallic ink, to symbolize regeneration and life. The drawings made the case look customized and therefore less tempting to steal.

"I have an atypical variant of SMA," Thomas said through gritted teeth. "Nothing else gives me a decent chance of living to adulthood. Nusinersen won't do it. My prototype will."

Cherise nodded in support. Anyone could see that Thomas was regaining some strength. Before his medicine, he used to be exhausted all the time. Now, ever since he'd begun to treat himself with his prototype, labeled NAI-12, he could sit at his laptop throughout a full workday with hardly any breaks.

"I don't even know what it is," Mrs. Hollander said. "What I do know," she said, overriding Thomas's explanation, "is that people are not allowed to perform scientific experiments on themselves."

"I invented it." Thomas glared defensively. "It's my property."

"Legally? It's not." Mrs. Hollander sounded pained, no doubt hating to argue with Thomas. "I've caught Vy injecting you with whatever it is. They haven't even tested it on animals yet!"

"It's been tested on lab rats." Thomas glared. "Are you suggesting I wait ten years for the clinical trials?" His tone was all bitter sarcasm. "I'd be dead."

Cherise's throat felt swollen with unspoken words. Why couldn't their foster mom see how brilliant Thomas was? Sure, he did not look or act like a superhero, but that was exactly what he was. If anyone was smart enough to cure cancer or solve global problems, it was him.

He just needed to live long enough.

Cherise took a breath. One by one, she forced the words out. She had to make Mrs. Hollander understand.

"He needs NAI-12."

The tension seemed to break. Mrs. Hollander slumped, guilty. "I know." She gave Cherise a tender look. "That's why I've refrained from saying anything about it."

That was kind of her.

"But." Mrs. Hollander shifted her focus back to Thomas. "I don't want to hear threats. Remember, I've allowed you to bring an unknown medical prototype into my home for special needs children. I could be imprisoned for child endangerment. I could lose—" She gestured around. "—everything."

Cherise yearned to remind them that they were both good people, but neither would appreciate an interruption.

"Sorry." Thomas sounded contrite. "I promise, I won't let that happen."

"You're thirteen years old," Mrs. Hollander reminded him in an exhausted tone. "You're good at intuiting what people want, but you can't control the world." She gestured at the medical briefcase. "I assume that supply will run out. What then? Are you going to steal another batch and pray you don't get caught?"

That was most likely what Thomas would do.

Mrs. Hollander looked stern. "How did you manage to steal it, anyway? Don't they keep those things locked up in vaults?"

"I'm good at figuring out pass codes," Thomas said.

That was true, but not the whole truth, Cherise knew.

During a visit to the Rasa lab in Boston, Thomas had brought Cherise with him as a guest, ostensibly to keep him company. They had toured the lab together, along with Vy. Thomas had greeted technicians and scientists, and while doing so, he had absorbed their key passwords and personal schedules.

Cherise privately thought that Thomas's memory was even more spectacular than his telepathic power. He could flip through a textbook and then recite the entire thing, word for word. Learning was effortless for him. He had impressed an academic review board at Harvard enough to earn an equivalency STEM generalist degree.

Thomas had engineered an excuse to revisit a specific lab along with Cherise. From there, they had sneaked into the vault, timing the infiltration around the technicians' schedule. They had gone motionless whenever Thomas sensed someone within his range. Walls did not impede his ability.

The hardest part for Thomas, by far, was physically stuffing the vials into the briefcase. He had enlisted Cherise's help for that.

Afterward, Thomas had asked Vy to stop at a coffee shop. While Vy and Cherise enjoyed mocha lattes and checked their social media, Thomas had used the shop's Wi-Fi network to hack into the Rasa Biotech security system. He had introduced a code worm that deleted camera footage, erasing evidence that might get him and Cherise convicted.

That heist had been a huge risk.

And if people suspected Thomas? It didn't matter, because Thomas needed regular injections of NAI-12. Otherwise his internal organs would wither and die.

"I love you, Thomas." Mrs. Hollander gave him sad look. "You've done a lot for the home."

That was an understatement. Thanks to Thomas's financial wizardry, their foster mother could afford a laptop for every child in her care. She had bought that new van, as well.

"But I'm not driving you anywhere tonight." Mrs. Hollander stepped out and began to close the door.

"Wait!" Thomas said. "Please, I can do you any favor. Anything at all!"

Cherise blinked in astonishment. This was like a blank check.

Mrs. Hollander had no idea what Thomas was capable of, but she knew enough to give him a wary sort of respect. Thomas was the only kid in the Hollander home who had his own bedroom. Nobody bothered him.

Cherise had to share her bedroom in the attic with two other girls. Even Vy shared a room, although her roommate was due to graduate this year and would likely move out.

Not only did Thomas get extra privacy and care, but he got to stay up all night, if he wanted to. He didn't need to do homework or go to school. He probably got more leeway than any kid in existence.

"I can get the owner of the fudge shop to ask you on a date." Thomas's tone was full of hints. "I've seen the way you look at him, and he's into you. Just bring me when you go shopping there. I promise, you won't be single anymore."

With her matronly sweaters, Mrs. Hollander didn't look like someone who was trying to attract men. She hardly ever spoke about her long-ago divorce.

She made a sound of exasperation and glared at Thomas. "That's enough. People have boundaries. It would be nice if you learned to respect them."

"Boundaries?" Thomas pounded his weak fist on the bedspread. "What do you think my life is?"

Mrs. Hollander sighed. "Have a good night. You too, Cherise."

"I can do anything for you!" Thomas pleaded.

But it was no use. Mrs. Hollander closed the door, and soon her footsteps were moving away, down the creaky hall.

Thomas looked as if he wanted to burn a hole through the door.

Cherise went to him. *What's wrong?* she asked inside her mind, aware that she was close enough for Thomas to hear her thoughts. *Why are you in such a hurry to get out and see whatever that is?* She indicated the map, which was folded in her hand.

"I need answers," he said.

Cherise wondered what he expected to find. She and Thomas had already done an internet search of the circled region. Zero results. According to search engines, there was nothing noteworthy in the mountain wilderness. The satellite view indicated that there might be a fire road or a wooded lane winding off the main road, but there were too many trees to tell for certain.

"Cherise." Thomas turned his gaze toward her. "Would you drive me there?"

She hoped he was joking.

His eyes had a calculating look.

I don't have a driver's license yet, Cherise silently pointed out.

She was the right age to gain her first license, and she had practiced a few times with Vy sitting next to her. But she would not take the driving exam until the holidays were over.

"I can talk you through it." Thomas watched her avidly.

Cherise suspected that Thomas was, indeed, an expert driver, even though he had never sat behind the wheel of a vehicle. Thomas inhaled talents as easily as breathing. He could draw as well as Cherise, even though he lacked the strength to hold a pen for very long. All he needed to do in order to absorb a skill was sit near an expert for a few seconds.

He'd told Cherise that he could pilot a fighter jet, play a piano concerto, and speak ten languages fluently. She believed him.

"We'll borrow the minivan," Thomas said. "I know where the spare key is." Of course he did.

Cherise hesitated. She wanted to aid Thomas, but this seemed wrong and dangerous. The roads were icy at night, especially in the mountains. There were potholes. Cellular coverage was unreliable out there. And wasn't it supposed to snow?

They might skid and crash. Then a punishment from Mrs. Hollander would be the least of their worries.

"Please?" Thomas gave her a pleading look. "It's an hour there and an hour back. The risks are minimal. And I promise, I'll take all the blame. This is totally on me."

Cherise reached into her pocket to feel her talisman, the reminder that Thomas cared about her. The origami lion felt as soft as cloth after more than a year and a half. She carried it with her everywhere.

Why is this so important to you? she silently wondered. *Was that stranger in the driveway your birth mother?*

Thomas looked away. "I'm not sure. She might be."

That was vague.

Cherise wondered if Thomas ever felt bothered by their lopsided friendship. He could read her like a book, whereas she had to make guesses. He never confided in anyone.

Like, why did he refuse to even talk about his previous experiences in foster care?

The few tidbits Cherise had overheard about his past—from Mrs. Hollander and Vy—were grim. Thomas had been bounced from one group home to another, between five states. It sounded as if no other foster parents could tolerate him. And Thomas used to have a knack for landing in homes that suddenly erupted with major dysfunction.

While Thomas lived in certain homes, there were arrests. A suicide. And a murder.

One of his former foster parents had actually murdered the other.

Thomas never talked about those experiences. He didn't seem to want anyone to know, although he had only been six years old at the time of the murder. Whenever Cherise asked about his prior homes, he changed the subject, or he said something dismissive, like he'd rather pretend that he had always lived in the Hollander home.

Cherise could understand and sympathize with that, at least. They both agreed that Mrs. Hollander was the best foster mother anyone could hope for.

"I don't mean to be secretive." Thomas looked ashamed. "It's just..." He took a deep breath, as if preparing for a plunge. "Yes, I wish our friendship wasn't lopsided. I can't even express how many times I've wished you could read my mind. I want you to absorb my memories and know my thought patterns, the way I know yours."

He looked so miserable that Cherise took his hand. She hadn't known he yearned for that.

"I really do," Thomas said. "Talking is slow and clumsy. If I talked at you in a stream-of-consciousness way, you'd tune me out, because words are boring. They're boxy containers. Imagination is free-form. That's one of the reasons I love your mind. You have the most vivid imagination."

She smiled.

"I'm sick of being the only one." Thomas seemed to melt against his bed, defeated. "That's why I need to go out there." He gestured at the map with his eyes. "There are other mind readers. She showed me. Cherise, that woman is a mind reader."

Cherise caught her breath. This was a huge revelation. It must be even huger for Thomas.

But why was he so vague? Didn't the strange other mind reader have a name?

"She had a sort of name." Thomas looked uncomfortable. "Her people think of her as the Swift Killer."

That sounded potentially ominous. *Why do they call her that?* Cherise wondered. *And who are they?*

"I don't know." Thomas sounded embarrassed to admit that he had failed to learn something. "The answers are out there. I just..." He stared at the ceiling, clearly frustrated. "How am I supposed to sleep, knowing that there's something I need to learn, and it's only an hour's drive away? They might have a secret *Men in Black* agency in the woods. Or an alien portal. There's something out there, and I need to see it."

Unanswered questions must be incredibly frustrating for him. Cherise wondered if he had ever felt ignorant in any meaningful way.

She had sought answers once.

She had visited her ma in the state penitentiary. And Ma, wearing an orange jumpsuit, had screamed obscenities at her. That was the only answer she would ever get.

Cherise figured that the only way to move on with her life was to let go of the questions.

Did Thomas truly want to meet the monster who had abandoned him at birth? Why? Wasn't he satisfied with the family he currently had?

Would he prefer to be around a bunch of mind readers, even if one of them had left him in the woods to die?

A lump of sadness formed in Cherise's throat. Part of her had always dreaded that Thomas would leave the Hollander home prematurely. He would likely become world-famous within another year or two. Then he'd stop talking to the likes of her.

"I don't want a new family." Thomas squeezed her hand with his weak grip. "I swear. This isn't about me trying to find my birth family. Believe me, they could offer me all the money and hugs in the world, and I'd turn them down. I would never want to lose you."

Cherise felt the warmth of his sincerity. She felt tattered, like that paper lion, but she was still holding herself together. She held on to him.

"I want to find out if they have medicine that can cure my disease," Thomas said.

Cherise peered at him, questioning.

"They're aliens." Thomas's gaze became electrified with excitement. "That woman had billions of people peering through her eyes. It was incredible! They sounded like angels. Like a chorus of angels."

Cherise wondered if he had somehow misinterpreted the experience.

"No mistake," Thomas said. "There are countless mind readers, and they live on other worlds, bouncing ideas off each other faster than lightning. I could only hear them from afar, as an outsider. But my god, Cherise, it was beautiful. It was like seeing an infinite horizon for the first time."

He looked embarrassed by how deeply the encounter had affected him.

"And," he said, "they have technology far more advanced than anything on Earth."

Now his fervor made sense. Thomas would go to any lengths to improve his medicine. If he saw a chance to learn neuroscience from superadvanced aliens, he would do anything to grab it.

"You know what else was amazing?" Thomas closed his eyes, as if savoring the memory. "Those other mind readers didn't see me as disabled. They saw me as a potential equal. I could be one of them. Respected. I could be respected, if I was one of them."

Cherise looked for his clothes. She guessed he would want to be dressed for tonight's outing.

For better or for worse, they were going to find the answers Thomas sought.

CHAPTER 5

CARETAKER

Vy went through the recreation room, shutting off the game console and closing window blinds for the night. Why was the portico light on outside? Had a deer triggered the motion detector?

She had left her mom's minivan parked in that awkward spot, sort of blocking the whole driveway. And right now, someone appeared to be loading Thomas's wheelchair—and Thomas—into the van.

"Hey!" Vy bounded toward the front door.

She grabbed her winter parka from the coat closet but didn't waste time putting it on. She rushed into the night.

Cherise stood by the van's open rear door with a startled look of guilt.

"What are you doing?" Vy shrugged into her parka. "You can't drive."

She guessed that this excursion was Thomas's idea, but it seemed idiotic, especially for him. A common cold could land him in the hospital. His lungs were too frail to cope with a prolonged cough. He knew that he needed to avoid freezing-cold air and stress.

"Come on, let's go into the house," Vy urged them. "I'll make you some hot drinks, and you can tell me why you want to go out." *And steal Mom's minivan*, she refrained from adding.

"Vy," Thomas said from inside the van. "If you agree to drive us, I'll tell you the secret of my success."

Vy hesitated.

Everyone agreed that Thomas knew far too much, even for a once-in-a-lifetime child prodigy. His knowledge of personal secrets seemed inexplicable. Yet whenever people asked Thomas how he learned things, he danced around the subject in a teasing way.

Vy had revealed her embarrassing suspicion to her friends. She'd confessed that Thomas had such an eerie habit of commenting on her unspoken thoughts, she believed he might be able to read minds.

But surely that was impossible?

"I'm tempted." Vy laughed dismissively, although it came out sounding a bit false. She really did want to know if Thomas had a supernatural power. Could he prove it?

Or was he just dangling a lure, trying to get her to do what he wanted?

"This is about that map the woman handed you," Vy guessed. "Isn't it?"

Thomas gave a stiff nod.

"To some mysterious location in the middle of the woods, way off the interstate?" Vy had seen the circled region on the map. "Even if it's a castle full of candy canes and lollipops, we're not going there. Not tonight. That's crazy."

Vy listened to enough true crime podcasts to have a solid sense of what to avoid. Really, any child ought to know better. Hadn't Thomas and Cherise ever heard the fairy tale of Hansel and Gretel? Bad people liked to lure innocent children into the woods, where no one could hear them scream.

"That lady isn't a witch," Thomas said. "And this isn't a fairy tale."

That sent a chill up Vy's spine. How did Thomas manage to comment on her thoughts with such accuracy?

"If she wanted to kidnap me," Thomas said, "she could." He gave a weak shrug. "I'm one hundred percent sure of that."

He sounded as self-assured as the physicians Vy worked with.

"And," Thomas added, "if she had bad intentions, I think I would have picked up on them. I'm really good at detecting lies."

Vy folded her arms. Thomas's authoritative manner might work on Nobel Prize winners, but not her. Thomas had an equivalency degree from Harvard, sure, but she remembered how shy and uncertain he used to be when he'd first arrived in her mother's home.

Besides, Thomas was not self-reliant. He never would be. Even if his medicine enabled him to live to adulthood, his limbs were permanently disfigured from years of atrophy. He needed a caretaker.

Thomas clearly wanted to be in charge. He wanted to be an adult. But....

"We have rules," Vy reminded him. "Sorry."

Thomas's gaze hardened. "I never would have invented NAI-12 if I'd followed rules."

That made Vy feel guilty. Thomas had, indeed, worked around legal and social restrictions. He had worked late nights for years, arguing with Vy's mother about bedtime every single night, until her mother finally caved in.

The International Association for Neuromuscular Disease called Thomas's NAI-12 treatment "miraculous." Vy had visited online groups. Disabled people all over the world were praising Rasa Biotech for its innovation. They might not all know that Thomas Hill was behind the radical new treatment, but they were praising him.

"Right." Vy tried to think of a more solid argument to get Thomas back into the house.

She really didn't want to resort to threats of punishment. Thomas had ways of retaliating against people whom he perceived as obstacles. He would spill someone's personal secret, saying the wrong thing at the wrong time.

"There are unusual weather patterns upstate, where I want to go," Thomas said in a musing tone.

"That's a reason *not* to go," Vy pointed out.

Deep down, however, she yearned for an adventurous experience. She checked radar apps on a regular basis, and she knew that the low barometric pressure and shifting winds over the western foothills of the White Mountains made for rare cloud formations. Storm chasers had recorded extraordinary storms in the area.

The various groups of New England storm chasers would take her seriously if she filmed something awesome.

She wanted an excuse to explore the little-traveled roads in that region. Perhaps she would discover an unmapped fire road that she could return to later?

"Agh." She felt torn between her desire to explore and her obligations as a caretaker and guardian.

She didn't have to get up early tomorrow. It was her day off work.

But, hey, she was the responsible adult here. Her mom would want her to do errands and chores. She ought to sleep instead of driving off on some mysterious adventure.

Or maybe she should keep a vigil all night, to make sure the kids didn't sneak out?

"Your mom might not even notice we're gone." Thomas watched her. "And if she does? I promise, the blame is all mine. You can tell her I blackmailed you."

It was tempting.

Sometimes Vy felt as if she was stuck in mud. In her daydreams, she was on the road, far away from her responsibilities.

But it was nice to feel needed. Vy was immensely proud of the refuge her mother had created for children who needed a home, and she was glad to pack school lunches and run errands. She didn't mind bathing and dressing Thomas every day, as well as other kids who needed aid. Even so…

What would a life with zero responsibilities feel like?

Someday, she liked to assure herself. Someday, she would buy her own van and take long trips to faraway places, like Nova Scotia or California.

How would it feel to be able to go anywhere and do anything without the household falling apart in her absence? Would she ever be able to afford to live somewhere besides the decrepit house her mother had inherited? Was a different life possible?

"Please?"

The meek voice came not from Thomas, but from Cherise.

Vy looked down at her foster sister, surprised. Cherise had come to the Hollander home labeled as mute as well as a suicide risk. But none of those labels seemed to apply to her any longer. Cherise was quiet, but she could be moved to speak. She seemed to derive strength from being around Thomas.

"Really?" Vy asked.

Cherise nodded.

Vy sighed and held out her hand for the ignition key. She was going to be stupid.

"If I do this," Vy said, "Thomas, you'd better tell me the honest truth. That's the deal you offered. You need to tell me how you get people's secrets. And you'd better not leave anything out."

"You got it," Thomas said.

Cherise handed over the key.

Vy climbed into the van and began to secure the wheelchair for a ride. "This had better be worth the trip."

CHAPTER 6

UNCHARTED TERRITORY

Frozen branches scraped the minivan's roof, like feeble prisoners trying to hold them back. Snowflakes appeared and vanished as they passed through the headlights.

"I don't like this," Vy said, squeezing the steering wheel.

"There!" Thomas said. "Turn left."

Vy steered onto a lane that was so overgrown, she had trouble seeing it in the darkness. She had no idea how Thomas had spotted it from the rear compartment.

Well, perhaps she had some idea. He might have peered through her own eyes, or Cherise's.

Ugh.

"I really don't like this." Vy was still processing the secrets Thomas had told her. It was creepy to think that her foster brother rummaged around inside people's private lives, soaking up every single moment of their life history. She almost wanted a more mundane explanation for the way he seemed to know everything.

At the same time, she had to pay attention to potholes.

The map had led them to an abandoned road. Trees formed a dense tunnel. Their trunks flashed in her headlights like ghostly figures, and their gnarled roots had torn the asphalt into chunks.

Ever since they'd exited the highway, Vy had felt the van climbing, mostly uphill. They must be on mountain slopes. Perhaps this road led to a forgotten overlook or something? It might have a view of the tree-shrouded mountains and a lot of sky.

"Dovanack?" Thomas said.

Vy began to ask him what he was talking about. Then she saw it. Their minivan rattled beneath an arc of wrought iron, with the name DOVANACK spelled in the arc. Snow capped each black letter.

The rusted gates appeared to be wrenched askew. But this must be private property. Vy slowed, searching for a place to turn around.

"Please don't stop!" Thomas was pleading. "It's even more important that we see what's at the end of this road. I've soaked up local lore, and guess what?" He didn't wait for a reply. "There was an alleged psychic named Garrett Dovanack who used to live around here. People claimed that he was a mind reader. This might be his house."

"All the more reason for us to not trespass," Vy pointed out. No one would blame the disabled child if the three of them got caught trespassing. Thomas could afford to be enthused. Vy, on the other hand, was the responsible adult.

"I told you," Thomas said, "I'll take the blame. I promise."

He replied exactly as if Vy had spoken out loud. He wasn't even hiding his power anymore.

"Can you please not read my mind?" she asked.

"You assume I have a choice." Thomas snorted. "You're in my four-yard range. Anyway, don't worry. Your deepest and darkest secrets are pretty mild. I've seen worse."

Vy tried not to speculate.

Despite her resolve, her brain ran with it. "You can see criminals," she realized. "Murderers who never got caught? Things like that?"

"Yes." His tone was dark. "Things like that."

Vy glanced in the rearview mirror, trying to catch his gaze. If Thomas could detect bad guys in any crowd, then why didn't he report them? He could probably devote his life to delivering justice.

"One life goal is enough for me." Thomas indicated the NAI-12 briefcase in the pocket of his wheelchair. "Anyway, I used to try reporting criminals." His tone got quiet. "It causes blowback. Arrests have repercussions on family members, and if I'm around, soaking that up…" He trailed off, as if he was reevaluating whatever he had been about to say. "I've found that my interference just compounds the misery."

"Oh." Vy suspected that she had prodded a wound. The dark undertone to Thomas's voice hinted at buried pain.

It might be worth discussing with him sometime. Vy's foster siblings all tended to carry shame and blame that ought to belong to the abusive members of their birth families. Children were innocent by nature, yet they became receptacles for adult misdeeds.

Whatever darkness Thomas was beating himself up for, it must have happened when he was too young to be an instigator. He had come to the Hollander home as a ten-year-old.

"Holy crap." Thomas sounded amazed.

A second later, Vy saw why.

An immense building loomed ahead. Hundreds of black windows gaped, toothy with icicles. The granite walls were like cliffs, capped by steep black roofs that blended with the jagged pine forest.

The mansion was entirely dark and still.

"It looks derelict." Vy followed the circular driveway around a frozen fountain. The snow was pristine and undisturbed.

She parked next to a snarling lion statue. It was one of a pair that flanked the snow-blanketed front steps.

"We shouldn't be here," she said.

"Are you kidding me?" Thomas sounded excited. "If Garrett Dovanack was ultrarich, that's evidence that he was a real mind reader! Do you have any idea how easy it is for me to win games? Not to mention insider trading. It would be a cinch for a mind reader to grow a fortune."

Vy understood how many disadvantaged kids daydreamed about discovering that they were actually related to millionaires.

Kindhearted millionaires.

"Is Garrett still alive?" she asked.

"Probably not," Thomas admitted. "If he is, he'd have to be over a hundred years old. But so what? Maybe he had a family or left some kind of legacy or something. Maybe I'm his great-great-grandson?"

Vy studied the mansion. It looked too large to be a residence. Perhaps it was a private college?

"It could be an institute for gifted mutants," Thomas said.

Vy supposed that a telepathic kid like Thomas probably daydreamed about joining a friendly academy full of superheroes.

"Garrett's initials spell GOD," Thomas said. "Garrett Olmstead Dovanack. Doesn't that raise some questions?"

Vy had plenty to think about already. She didn't want to add another twig to the pile of questions in her mind.

She shifted the van into drive. "Hmm. Well, we've seen what's on the map. Let's come back when it's daylight."

"No!" Thomas sounded hurt. "We have to ring the doorbell, at least!"

"Sorry." Vy felt guilty for letting him down.

"Please?"

Vy glanced up toward the mansion's ornate double doors. Was there any harm in indulging Thomas's curiosity? The undisturbed snow proved that no one had driven up here to set a trap or to lie in wait. Judging by the state of the hidden driveway and the broken gate, she doubted anyone lived here.

"I doubt the doorbell works," Vy said.

"Then knock on it," Thomas said. "Please?"

His angst made him sound like a typical kid. That was rare.

"Fine." Vy sighed, ashamed by how easily she caved in.

She supposed she also wanted proof that this mansion was abandoned. That would tell her whether or not she could risk coming back to explore.

Not all her friends were storm chasers, but they did like to discover niche, unknown places.

Frost began to appear on the windshield as soon as Vy shut off the engine. It must be well below freezing outside. She walked to the rear of the van, her boots grinding on fresh snow.

"This is crazy," she remarked as she lowered Thomas's wheelchair.

"Yup," Thomas said happily.

Cherise smiled, clearly gladdened by her best friend's happiness.

The front entrance steps included a concrete ramp for accessibility, which furthered Vy's suspicions that this was a derelict academy. Although if so… why wasn't it listed in any internet searches?

They were in a dark zone on maps. This was uncharted territory.

As Vy pushed Thomas's wheelchair through the snow, Cherise climbed the stairs. Each of the double doors had an iron knocker, gripped by a lion's head and veined with frost. Cherise lifted a knocker and pounded it against a door, several times.

The hollow knocking sound rolled through the silence like muffled thunder.

"Charming," Vy said.

Cherise made a helpless gesture. Vy looked for a doorbell and didn't see one. They waited.

Vy's teeth began to chatter from the cold. She pulled up her hood. "We'll give this one minute," she said. "Then…"

One of the massive doors swung inward a bit. Someone peered through the crack at them.

Vy steeled herself for an unpleasant hermit or a violent squatter. She hoped they wouldn't be confronted by an undead butler or anything impossible like that.

The stranger peering through the door appeared to be a heavyset woman with gray hair. Ordinary. Middle-aged.

"Can I help you?" the woman asked in a suspicious tone.

Before Vy could apologize for trespassing, Thomas spoke. "Delia?" He had an intensely focused look, and Vy realized that he must be reading the woman's mind, soaking up all sorts of personal secrets. "Delia Dovanack? Would it be possible for me to meet your son? I believe I can help him."

The woman's eyes widened. She looked shocked.

"Let me in, please." Thomas didn't wait for permission. He powered his wheelchair past the door and the woman, as if he owned the place.

"Sorry." Vy hurried after Thomas and Cherise, mortified. "Thomas, what are you doing?"

She was used to Thomas wielding words like weapons, provoking whatever reactions he wanted. But now that she knew how easy it was for him? It wasn't cute. It was an unfair advantage. It made him intrusive.

"We'll leave," Vy assured the middle-aged woman whom Thomas had identified as a Dovanack. "I'm so sorry. We'll leave right away."

But Thomas made no move to leave.

Vy hesitated, full of uncertainties. The wheelchair was Thomas's version of legs, so she wasn't going to seize it and force him toward the door. That would be akin to purposely tripping someone. It went against her instincts as a caretaker.

"Wait." Delia blocked their exit. "How do you know I have a son?" Her gaze was unfriendly. "How do you know anything about us?"

"I'm a mind reader." Thomas made it sound like no big deal, although he had asked Vy to never reveal his ability to anyone. Never in public. Never to strangers. Those were his rules.

Vy stared at him.

"Tell me the truth," Delia demanded.

She was apparently unaware that Thomas had just revealed a dearly held secret about himself. So she probably wasn't telepathic.

"That was the truth." Vy pulled down her hood and looked around the cavernous foyer, lit by bronze wall sconces. A mansion this size should be able to house at least a hundred people. Vy hoped it was an institution. That way, she wouldn't feel quite so much like a trespasser. "Is this a private residence?"

"Yes, this is my home." Delia folded her arms. "Why are you here?"

Vy swallowed, full of shame. Judging by the woman's comfy sweatpants and pullover, she had been in bed, or getting ready for bed, when the ominous sound of knocking had ruined her peaceful night. She wore slippers.

"Who are you?" Delia said with frost in her tone.

"I'm Thomas." Thomas powered his wheelchair closer to Delia. He had a hungry, focused look, like he was reading a particularly fascinating book.

"This is Cherise," Vy said. "And I'm Vy." She decided not to volunteer surnames. People with excessive amounts of money could wield political clout, so this Dovanack woman might make trouble for the Hollander home if she felt like it.

"Anyway"—Vy tried to laugh—"it's a long story about how we got here. It was a mistake. A total misunderstanding."

Perhaps Thomas had fallen for a practical joke? Vy wished that she had obeyed her own common sense and driven home, no matter what Thomas wanted.

"We're so sorry for barging in," Vy went on. "We'll get out of your hair."
She glared at Thomas. "Right, Thomas?"

"No." Thomas didn't even look at her. He stayed focused on Delia, as if
enchanted. "I can help Ariock. I promise. I'm a mind reader."

Delia looked outraged, perplexed, and miserable.

Thomas rotated his wheelchair and powered toward a dim corridor. "Will
you please let Ariock know he has a visitor? I think he's someone I need to meet."

"No!" Delia rushed after Thomas as if he might wreck her life. "Who
are you?"

Thomas gave a frustrated sigh without slowing down. "You grew up in
Manhattan. You married William Dovanack when you were thirty. Your son
is uniquely tall. You have a medical secret, and I know about that, too. Because I'm a mind reader."

Delia looked like she might cry.

Vy hurried to catch up. She understood how alarming it was to hear Thomas speak about things he really shouldn't know. It was creepy. And he wasn't
being gentle with Delia. He seemed to be bludgeoning her with his power, uncaring about her feelings, as if she was nothing more than an obstacle.

As Vy tried to think of a way to rein him in, Cherise jogged ahead.

Thomas's tone softened. "I won't reveal your personal secrets, Delia. Those
are yours." Perhaps he had absorbed the look Cherise was giving him. "But," he
went on, "I sense your worries about Ariock. Let me meet him and talk to him.
Trust me." He indicated himself. "I know what it's like to be unique."

Vy glanced around the corridor, looking for any sign of Delia's "uniquely
tall" son.

The place was dim and dusty. A cobweb fuzzed one of the chandeliers.
Wall sconces cast a dull glow on painted portraits.

"I don't know who you are," Delia said.

"I think I'm a friend of your family." Thomas powered down the corridor.
"Maybe I'm a long-lost family member."

Delia shook her head, as if everything he'd said was unbelievable.

"Oh, come on." Thomas sounded defensive. "It's possible, isn't it?"

If the portraits on display were Dovanack family members, then Vy privately thought that Delia was right. Thomas looked nothing like them. The
Dovanack family shared bold facial traits, with strong noses and chins. They
all had dark hair.

Thomas halted his wheelchair, gazing up at an oil portrait of an old man.
"I have the same power as old Garrett. Don't I?"

Delia put her hands on her hips. She seemed to regain a little bit of dignity.
"You're referring to the newspaper articles about him. And all the stupid gossip."

Thomas gave her a probing look.

"Garrett was just smart and insightful." Delia sounded disparaging. "Not a psychic. I knew him well. If he could read minds, I would have known."

"Uh-huh," Thomas said dryly. "People say I'm just smart and insightful."

Delia folded her arms. "Why would he hide it from me? And his own grandson? Will would have known."

Thomas looked unconvinced.

"Garrett was normal." Delia seemed to emphasize that. "Our family is normal." She gestured at the portraits. "I don't know what you're expecting to find here, but we aren't a family of psychics, or…" She faltered. "Or mutants."

"Right." Thomas wheeled onward, leading the way down the corridor.

"Ariock has a growth disorder," Delia called, hurrying to catch up with Thomas. "That's all."

Thomas's tone was dry. "He's taller than the tallest person in recorded history. Oh, and he has absolutely zero health problems, despite being gigantic. He has a superstrong musculoskeletal structure. No acromegaly. No distended joints or tendon problems or anything. He's strong enough to lift a fridge by himself, with ease." Thomas's tone became sarcastic. "Nothing unusual about that. Nope. Totally normal."

Delia's face paled with shock.

"I'm so sorry," Vy said. Should she grab the wheelchair and force Thomas to turn around? She was the adult here. Thomas's trespassing rudeness was technically her fault. She ought to take the responsibility of stopping him.

Except…Vy inwardly admitted that she burned with curiosity.

Thomas would never reveal his telepathic power to a stranger unless he believed there was an important reason to do so. He seemed very eager to meet Ariock. That made Vy curious to meet the giant, as well.

And this hidden mansion? It held secrets. Vy could tell that just by glancing into dark rooms, where the shadows were so black they seemed alive.

There were statues. Pillars. Urns. Marble tiles and chandeliers.

This place seemed built for a large family, plus a household staff. Where were all those missing people? Did Delia and Ariock truly live alone in this palace?

"You obviously know too much," Delia said.

Thomas gave her a belligerent look. "When Ariock's growth spurt began to go beyond a normal range, you took him to a specialist consultant at the Children's Hospital in Boston. I absorbed that memory from your mind. Not only can I recite Dr. Beland's diagnosis, about Ariock not having any pituitary adenoma, but I can draw, from memory, every person in the lobby who stared at him. Because that scene is etched into your memory. It made you feel like a bad mother."

Delia looked properly horrified.

"Now, do I need to know that?" Thomas asked in a rhetorical way. "Do I need to know every pair of socks you've ever worn? No. I do not. I hate absorbing irrelevant crap. But I can't help absorbing everything." He emphasized the last sentence. "I have an inability to forget."

Vy studied her foster brother with fresh curiosity. Telepathy was a superpower, but this flawless memory power…this was something else.

Human memories were not designed for infinite capacity. They weren't computers. Information overload would, or should, drive a person insane.

"How can you function?" Vy asked.

Thomas gave her a grateful nod of acknowledgment. "It's hard," he admitted. "I remember the earliest years of my life as a jumble of incoherent data. I wasn't even verbal before the age of four. I just struggled to cope with the overload of information from other people's perceptions and memories. It took me years to figure out how to function."

People might have mistaken young Thomas for being developmentally disabled in addition to his obvious physical disability.

"Oh," Vy said.

"Yup," Thomas said with bitterness. "I used to be the epitome of 'unwanted child.'"

"I'm sorry." Vy felt clumsy, like she had accidentally hit an unhealed bruise. No wonder Thomas was distrustful of adults. And no wonder the foster care system had struggled to find a permanent home for him.

"All right." Delia seemed to come to a decision.

Thomas watched her avidly.

"I'll tell Ariock." Delia strode ahead, moving with brisk purpose. "Wait for me to come back. I'll let him know we have unexpected guests."

Her words seemed to echo in the cavernous hallway, throughout empty rooms.

"Thanks!" Thomas parked his wheelchair, having secured the introduction he wanted. Cherise lounged against a wall.

Vy paced, gazing at dust-shrouded furniture and wondering what she had gotten herself into.

CHAPTER 7

WINTRY TENSION

Ariock paced the sky room. Ten strides and reverse.

His feet extended and receded over threadbare carpet, causing the floor to creak in predictable places, while the big-screen TV provided its endless background noise. Voices, even scripted conversations, were a comfort. The rhythm of walking was a drug.

He studied the wintry world beyond the glass wall, paying no attention to his reflection in the panes. It was an overcast night. He could hardly see the jagged outlines of the nearest trees, let alone the distant mountains. But he felt the weather, in a way.

He touched the glass. Ice seeped into his skin.

He reached the potted fern and reversed direction, like clockwork. Back across the carpet, toward the opposite wall, marked by a framed print of a picturesque city skyline. New York City. His mother came from that fantastical place, an urban wonderland that Ariock would never, could never, visit.

He reached the Manhattan print and reversed.

If he looked in the right direction, he could see…yes, there were distant lights, almost lost in the gloom of falling snow and miles of forested slopes. The little town of Liberty Hill twinkled magically.

But the outside world was as untouchable as the people and places on TV.

At least it was close. At least it was visible.

Ariock felt the weather. He felt tension in the sky, as if it was about to sweep the mountains with a sudden squall. The sun had not shone a ray all week, and the nights were black and starless. Crisp air gloved all it touched.

The stillness had lasted for such an unusually long time, Ariock felt restless. Something had better happen soon. His own nightmares about storms kept jolting him awake.

Reverse.

His mother bought him movies and video games and books, trying to alleviate his self-destructive boredom. It helped a little bit. TV sounds covered up the gnawing, ticking, incessant silence of the mansion.

Ten steps and back.

Each stride approximated one full year—spring, summer, autumn, and winter—that Ariock had lived in this room.

Most people would have needed twenty or more strides to cross the same distance. For Ariock, it was ten. Sometimes he paced while the sky became streaked with red and gold from the setting sun, and then he would watch the sun rise again, and that was his only clue as to how long he'd been walking. He did not tire easily.

The cheerful voices of a TV conversation cut off abruptly.

Ariock turned, startled. He had missed the telltale footsteps of his mother's approach.

"Honey?" She put aside the remote control.

Ariock automatically tried to hunch, to make himself smaller. He felt guilty whenever his mother caught him pacing. His size must be an offense to anyone's sense of normalcy. He had learned that lesson well enough, back in the days when he used to go to school.

"We have visitors," she said.

Ariock scrutinized her face, perplexed. He tried to process what she'd said. It couldn't be true. Since when did his mother joke around?

"There's a kid in a wheelchair," his mother said. "And he just proved to me, beyond any shadow of a doubt, that he's a mind reader." She gave Ariock a meaningful look. "He knows about you."

The storm feeling seemed to break all around Ariock.

The night remained quiet and still, except for softly falling snow outside. Yet Ariock felt slammed by lightning and wind. This was a nightmare. This couldn't be happening.

"I'm sorry." His mother looked away, avoiding his gaze. "We knew this day would come. I didn't expect it to happen like this, but…" She fidgeted. "Maybe it's for the best. They seem like nice people."

People?

More than one?

Ariock imagined a school field trip with grinning kids holding out their phones to snap photos of him. He remembered how it was, in sixth grade, before his mother had relented and pulled him out of public school. That was before the worst of his growth spurt. He had been merely tall at the time. Weirdly tall, but not freak-show size yet.

Now?

Ariock glanced around, wondering where he might hide. The study adjacent to the indoor pool had all kinds of lumpy furniture protected under dust sheets. Maybe he could pretend to be a sofa protected by blankets?

It sounded as if paparazzi had invaded his home. A random hiker must have taken a photo of him through the sky room window, without his noticing. He knew he should have chosen a room without any windows. The library would have been a good place to live.

"For what it's worth," his mother said, her tone sympathetic, "they're not reporters. I don't think they'll tell anyone about you. The mind reader kid is disabled. But he can read minds. For real."

Ariock had seen video clips, while flipping through local news stories, about a seriously smart boy in a wheelchair. Could this be the same one?

"And…" His mother grinned. "The adult woman with him is quite tall. And I think she's your age."

Ariock stared at his mother in disbelief. Was that an insinuation?

Was she trying to pretend that he was normal enough to go on dates?

His mother did occasionally say clueless things, but this had to be a new all-time record.

"She's very pretty," his mother added, as if that helped.

A beautiful college senior would surely be repulsed by Ariock, who was so far outside the bounds of normalcy that he might as well be a different species. Like an ogre. Or a troll. Besides, Ariock had not talked to real-life people, other than his mom, since he was twelve years old—ten years ago. He was twenty-two years old and completely lacking in social skills. Online chats with gamers and nerds did not count. He was unequipped to handle an actual conversation with an actual girl.

He gave his mother a reproachful look. Couldn't she send these intruders away?

"There's no point in asking them to leave," his mother said, seeing his look. "The boy knows you're a giant. He said it."

So there was no hope.

Even if the intruders left, curiosity would bring them back. They would want to stare at the giant.

"I'll go get them." His mother turned to leave. Then she hesitated in the doorway, patting the wall as if to give it reassurance. "Ariock? You couldn't have remained hidden forever. You know that. Right?"

So she kept telling him.

To Ariock, the idea of being discovered was an abstract fear, but his mother made it sound like a beast lurking around a nearby corner. He wondered why she mentioned it so often lately. Was she hinting that she wanted a vacation? She did take overly long shopping trips.

If she wanted to leave, Ariock couldn't really blame her.

He was still growing as rapidly as a teenager, although he was technically an adult. His mother had not signed up for the weirdest son in the world. Nor had she expected isolation, plus tragedy, when she had married the playboy

William Dovanack. She couldn't have guessed that their only child would be born with an untreatable and inexplicable growth disorder. She couldn't have foreseen that her wealthy husband and his entire extended family would die prematurely, or that she would feel trapped in a house that was too big for her, hundreds of miles from any city.

"It will be all right," his mother said. "These people are young, and I don't see them bringing in a media circus. I think they'll be respectful."

With that, she left.

Ariock glanced around the embarrassment that was his sky room.

He couldn't hide the giant-size homemade furniture. There was no way to disguise the fact that he used one of the enormous couches as a bed, with quilts that were sewn together, end to end, in order to cover him. Or the half-size keg he'd converted into a drinking mug.

Well, he wasn't going to offend their sense of reality by looming in front of the two-story-tall window.

Ariock retreated to the shadows beneath the indoor balcony. He settled into his armchair, which he'd custom-built.

Maybe, if he stayed very still, he would blend in with the bookshelves and kitchenette.

If he hunched his shoulders and minimized his size, perhaps the unwelcome visitors wouldn't be tempted to take photos or blab about this encounter to their friends? Maybe they'd go away? And somehow, maybe, if he was lucky...they might forget that they'd seen someone who was inexplicably weird.

CHAPTER 8

HIDDEN FROM THE WORLD

Vy peered into one room after another. A grandfather clock ticked steadily in the darkness. Another room had a peculiar dining room set, with doll-size chairs.

Vy did a double take. Those ladder-back chairs might actually be normal in size. It was the rough-hewn wooden table that was enormous.

She gazed into the darkness of the hall, feeling a bit like she had entered a rabbit hole into Wonderland. How safe was it, to meet an ultrastrong and wealthy giant whom Thomas characterized as being in need of "help"?

Thomas rolled next to her. "I've absorbed skills from dozens of psychologists and psychiatrists. I'll know more once I get within range of Ariock, but I'm confident I can help him." Thomas gave her a critical look. "Uh, you could use some preparation, though."

The more Thomas told Vy, the more preparation she wanted. According to Thomas, Ariock had learned about the outside world mostly through TV and the internet. He had not left his house for more than a decade. He feared people staring at him, in the same way that Thomas feared that his secret telepathic power would be discovered and exploited.

No college.

No jobs.

No dates.

Ariock was the same age as Vy, yet he lacked any equivalent life experience. "So he was homeschooled?" Vy asked.

"Sort of," Thomas said. "Delia did hire a private tutor for him. But the tutor kept staring, and when she posted a photo on social media without his permission, that was the last straw."

"That's terrible." Vy had trouble imagining such a rude tutor. People came in all shapes and sizes. Did Ariock really warrant that kind of treatment?

"You'll understand when you see him," Thomas said with certainty. "It will be hard not to stare. Please do your best."

Vy studied Thomas, wondering what, exactly, he had picked up from Delia's memories. "Do you suspect that Ariock is a mind reader, on top of his growth disorder? Is that why you want to meet him?"

Thomas laughed. "No." He reconsidered the question. "I don't know what secrets are in Ariock's mind, but I want to find out." He eye-gestured around, indicating oil portraits and tapestries. "I was sent here for a reason. Delia is ordinary, more or less. She married into this family. As far as I can tell, she doesn't have any special secret abilities. But there has to be something salient about this family that I'm supposed to learn, and Ariock is the only other person who lives here. And he's a legit Dovanack. By blood, I mean."

Vy paced past statues on pedestals. She walked past a nineteenth-century landscape painting. Judging by the dust-filled rooms, Ariock might be the last Dovanack.

The carpeting muffled footsteps, but they all noticed the stout figure of Delia approaching.

"He's ready." Delia sounded less than certain about that. Nevertheless, she made an inviting gesture and led them onward.

The corridor made an angled turn. They passed several more spacious rooms that were dark and silent before Delia stopped at a tall doorway.

She took a deep breath, as if steeling herself. She assessed Thomas, Cherise, and Vy, and seemed to deem them adequate.

"Please be kind," Delia told them.

Vy nearly said something defensive. What sort of rude jerk did this woman take her for?

Before she could think of a nice way to reassure Delia, the older woman led them into a room that was nothing like the rest of the house.

A big screen on the wall played an episode of one of Vy's favorite shows, although the volume was muted. The furniture was truck-size, but otherwise, it was plain and sturdy, not a bunch of overly ornate antiques. A lofty ceiling accommodated an indoor balcony that faced an enormous glass wall.

Snow sifted down beyond the glass. The flakes were accumulating, and Vy frowned, afraid that she would have trouble driving home.

"This is the sky room." Delia padded across the beige carpet. "There's a view, although you can't see it right now."

Perhaps Delia was trying to distract them from the size of the furniture? There were two sofas, each wide enough to seat all eight children fostered in the Hollander home, plus Vy and her mother. If she sat up there, she felt sure that her feet wouldn't touch the floor.

Otherwise, this room felt like her own world. Photographic prints adorned the walls. The sky room looked comfortably modern.

"Ariock?" Delia faced a shadowy area beneath the indoor balcony. "These are the visitors." She gestured to each of them in turn. "Thomas, Cherise, and Vy."

He sat in an armchair.

At first Vy was confused, because Ariock looked normal to her, not at all monstrous or freakish. His bold features and dark hair showed a family resemblance to the painted portraits of other Dovanack family members. The armchair fit him, although he hunched in it.

However, as Vy drew closer, the rules of perspective seemed askew. His size didn't mesh with his distance away.

His shoulders must be as wide as a snowplow.

His huge hands would have trouble with things like computer keyboards or cell phones.

Ariock was as still as a titanic statue, and larger than life. His clothing must be custom tailored. It looked homemade.

Thomas powered his wheelchair next to Vy. "We're not going to snap your photo," he said in a reassuring tone. "I promise."

The giant made no response. Only his deep-set eyes moved, locking on Vy as if he expected an assault. He seemed determined not to move or breathe.

Thomas whirred closer, no doubt putting himself within range to read Ariock's mind. "I know it's hard to believe," he said, "but we didn't come here looking for you."

Ariock looked suspicious.

"I swear." Thomas parked his wheelchair. "I came here looking for my birth family. But I'm a mind reader, so I couldn't help but soak up info about you."

Vy studied the huge guy, wondering if he was as strong as Thomas had insinuated. Ariock did look capable of picking up the nearby refrigerator and tossing it. But that was hard to believe. As a nurse, Vy understood that untreated gigantism led to enfeeblement, since the relentless growth outstripped several limits in the design of a human body. A giant would normally suffer from scoliosis and joint abnormalities.

Yet Ariock looked quite well proportioned and healthy. He might be a bit overweight. But on such a colossal frame, the extra weight was spread evenly, and it just made him look big, rather than—

"My sister doesn't mean to stare," Thomas said in a pointed tone. "She's sorry. Right, Vy?"

"Oh!" Vy forced herself to look elsewhere, cheeks hot as she realized the clinical way she had been studying Ariock. Despite the stiff way he held himself in the armchair, there was majesty in his sheer size. "I'm sorry."

"Anyway," Thomas said, "as I was saying, I thought that maybe I'm a distant Dovanack relative? We have the same eye color. Don't you think?"

Vy looked from one to the other. Thomas did have unusual eyes, somewhere between the color of wine and lavender. Ariock's eyes were several shades darker. They were more like storm clouds over the mountains.

"Well." Delia folded her arms and assessed Thomas. "You're not my son. I would remember if I'd given birth to anyone other than Ariock." She seemed defensive. "And by the way, Ariock was a normal-size baby, in case you were wondering."

The question had crossed Vy's mind.

"Our family is normal," Delia went on. "Boring and normal, like I told you. There were no hidden relatives or out-of-wedlock secret births. Really."

Vy thought she was protesting a bit too much.

Thomas seemed to think so, too. He had a speculative look on his face. But he seemed to pick up something else and put the brakes on that line of questioning. "Okay," Thomas said. "We don't seem to be close relatives. But we do have something in common."

"What?" Delia sounded wary.

Thomas lacked the strength to move his arms, but his fingers twitched, indicating himself and Ariock. "We're both freaks."

If that was calculated to cause offense, it worked. Delia puffed up in outrage.

Ariock, oddly enough, looked relieved. It was as if he'd expected someone to say the insult out loud. Maybe he was glad that someone had identified the elephant in the room, so to speak?

Vy noticed a normal-size bench seat, and she sat. If she got comfortable, maybe Ariock would relax a little bit?

"You must think we're terribly rude," Vy told him. "If you want to kick us out, I'd totally understand."

Ariock looked cautious.

"Here's the thing," Thomas said to Ariock, ignoring Vy. "You think you're a mutant. But guess what? I'm weirder than you. Compared to me, you are completely ordinary."

Ariock's suspicion returned. He plainly did not believe Thomas.

"The only nonstandard thing about your mind," Thomas said, "is your propensity for making clueless, baseless assumptions. My friend Cherise isn't judging you."

Vy glanced at her foster sister. Of all people, she had not expected Cherise to stare rudely at the giant.

"Cherise is an artist," Thomas said. "She visually studies everyone, out of habit. She thinks you have an impressive physique. It's a compliment."

Vy groaned. Did Thomas have to speak for everyone? It was embarrassing.

"You need a major reality check," Thomas said to Ariock. "Several reality checks, in fact. Like, guess what? Your mom is not silently pining away for a vacation. She loves you. She wants to spend *more* time with you, not less."

Delia gawked. She looked speechless.

"Also." Thomas gestured at Vy. "My caretaker sister is not an angelic visitor from the land of TV celebrities. She doesn't need extra praise about how pretty she is. I would appreciate it if you focus less on her and more on me."

The humiliation on Ariock's face was almost comical.

"Agh!" Vy jumped up, certain that her cheeks were even more red-hot than Ariock's. "I'm so sorry about Thomas. He's not usually this rude."

She wanted to keep babbling apologies…but she trailed off, because Ariock looked amused. He studied Thomas with silent fascination.

"You're different from other people," Thomas said. "Same as me. But so what? We're not *that* different. We're still human."

Without moving a muscle, Ariock inspected one of his immense hands. He seemed to want them to go away and leave him alone.

"I do understand," Thomas said. "I've devoted my life to inventing a cure for my fatal disease. There were times when I nearly gave up. I haven't always been sure that the effort was worth it."

He didn't seem to care who listened, but he had everyone's attention. Even Delia looked interested, despite herself. She perched on the bench seat next to Vy.

"Back in May," Thomas said, "my research kept hitting dead ends. I thought I would die in adolescence. And worse, I thought I had wasted my whole life. I'd given up on having any sort of a pleasant life. I felt like I was chasing a dream that would never come true."

Vy recalled Thomas's depressive episode. He had stopped eating for a few days.

"So," Thomas said, "I decided I might as well make the most of my final months." He gestured around the sky room. "Sort of like how you've made yourself comfortable here. Might as well, right?"

Ariock looked rapt.

"I spent as much time as possible with Cherise." Thomas said. "We went on family trips. Like, we went boating, and on a drive up the seacoast. Things like that." He tapped his head. "I absorb other people's lives, so I've experienced all kinds of things, but for me, firsthand experiences are a lot more meaningful. And rare." He looked toward Cherise. "She saw that I'd given up. And she refused to watch me die."

Vy studied the two of them. She had never imagined that Cherise had had something to do with Thomas's medical breakthrough.

"She insisted that I work," Thomas said. "Not in words, but it was in her mind. Constantly."

Vy supposed that would be hard for him to escape.

"Her nonstop insistence got me to try again, even when I'd given up," Thomas said. "So I scrapped my whole approach. I stitched together my own pastiche of methods from the scientists I'd worked with, and I went off on a radically different tangent." He nodded toward the medicine case in the pocket of his wheelchair. "I'm going to live to adulthood because of Cherise. She saved my life."

Vy gazed at her foster sister with newfound respect.

"I met Cherise a couple of years ago," Thomas said. "I believed it was impossible that anyone would care about me that much. If it's possible for someone like me? Then, trust me, it's definitely possible for you."

The skepticism on Ariock's face was heartbreakingly painful. Did he see himself as a loner? Or as someone who was unlovable?

Yet his bookshelves were stuffed with novels, movies, and video games that Vy recognized. Some were her favorites. He had good taste.

"Honestly?" Vy told him. "There's a lot of cool stuff here." She gestured around. "This whole room is awesome. It's so different from the rest of the house."

Ariock looked as if he was bracing himself for an insult.

"He made the furniture himself," Thomas told Vy. "He figured out how to put things together from online tutorials."

"Really?" Vy stood, gawking at the giant-size furniture with fresh appreciation. It had sturdy, rustic charm, and it was plainly crafted with professional expertise. "Wow. You really build furniture? These are really good! Amazing, I mean!"

Ariock looked cautiously proud. His mother watched him as if witnessing a rainbow in the middle of winter.

"Yeah," Thomas said. "He might lack formal schooling, but he's self-taught, and frankly—"

A concussive blast drowned him out.

Freezing wind gusted toward Vy, icy with snowflakes. The glass wall was gone. Shattered.

Armored figures strode through the maw where the wall should be.

Their high-tech bodysuits gleamed pearlescent white with glowing interfaces, contoured to their athletic physiques. Some of them wore additional bulky gear on their arms. Three jogged left. Three jogged right. All the figures moved with eerie coordination. The final three leaped onto oversize furniture, climbing straight toward Vy and her friends.

A black web flared around Vy before she could consider how to react.

Each segment telescoped, generating offshoots. Vy tried to thrash it out of her way. But the thing clung to her like cobwebs, stretching like rubber instead of breaking, impossible to brush aside. It sealed all the way around her.

Rubbery segments cinched tighter and tighter until she lost her balance and crashed painfully to the carpeted floor.

Delia struggled on the floor, encased in a similar net.

"What…" Thomas did not finish his sentence. Blue smoke engulfed him. He slumped sideways, as if his frail muscles had all quit at the same time.

Cherise dropped as well, struggling in a net.

Ariock stood.

He was the size of a wall. He had to tilt his head to avoid hitting the balcony overhang.

Vy wanted to warn him that there was danger, but her throat felt frozen. All she managed was a strangled sound. Delia whimpered. That blue smoke drifted around them.

Darkness narrowed Vy's vision.

Wake up! she silently screamed at herself.

Ariock seized the refrigerator and ripped it away from the back wall. Vy could hardly trust her own eyes. Ariock spun the fridge, preventing the door from falling open…and, with a grunt of determination, he hurled it at the intruders.

The fridge sailed over an end table.

The intruders scattered with inhuman speed, as fast and agile as cockroaches.

Ariock's fridge slammed into the couch, then fell with a thud that shook the floor. Vy wanted to appreciate that. But her veins filled with ice. She felt drugged, dizzy and cold.

Multiple nets unfurled around Ariock.

He tore at them, ripping a few. More nets unfurled. Ariock seemed to be losing energy. The smoke was beginning to affect him, too. He slumped to his knees. Black nets cocooned his body, leaving only his head free.

What the… Vy struggled to think of why they were being attacked. Whose fault was this? Thomas? But he was just a kid. What could he have possibly done to deserve this?

Her brain refused to generate answers. All she knew was that it was wrong. She was innocent.

The darkness of unconsciousness closed around her, and she clung to a thought. Her mother. She needed to go home. Somehow, she needed to get home.

CHAPTER 9

IGNORANCE

Thomas was not in his wheelchair. He was not in his bed or in a caretaker's arms. Instead, he was alone and falling slowly, tumbling like a snowflake.

...*Beep beep. Beep beep. Beep beep...*

The medical alert on his wristwatch sounded eternal. How long had it been beeping? Thomas had programmed the medical alert to go off every six hours. A missed dose would set him back weeks. Vy was supposed to help him to self-administer an injection of NAI-12, and she should have woken him up.

His mouth was dry. He felt dehydrated.

Someone full of worshipful fear entered his telepathic range.

This mind was so alien, Thomas could hardly parse its language or its thought patterns. It was neither male nor female. It was neither human nor animal. Intelligent, though. It was sapient.

Thomas saw his own body from the alien's perspective.

He lay limp, but light, as if he floated a scant inch above the mirrored floor. His wheelchair was parked nearby. He was dressed. He recognized the dark pants and flannel shirt he had worn to visit...

The Dovanack mansion.

The whole day came back to Thomas with frame-by-frame clarity. The Swift Killer and the silent multitudes who peered through her eyes. Ariock Dovanack. Then the unexpected invasion from armored soldiers.

...*Beep beep. Beep beep...*

Thomas fumbled at his wristwatch to shut off his medical alert. The elapsed time on the display made him nearly choke with shock.

Nineteen hours!

His wristwatch had been beeping for nineteen hours.

He would have missed at least three doses of NAI-12. That was a catastrophe. The destructive atrophy of his neuromuscular disease must be back in full force. Thomas could almost feel death caressing his underdeveloped lungs and his frail stomach. He was nauseous from the continuous falling sensation.

His NAI-12 briefcase poked out of his wheelchair's side pocket.

Well, he absolutely could not afford to miss another dose. His prototype medicine was not a miracle cure. It halted the deterioration of his internal organs, but it could not repair damage.

The room's alien occupant watched him with wide green eyes.

The alien—a govki? It seemed to think of itself as something like that—was squat and jowly. It looked somewhat like a man-size bulldog, although it had a bendy spine, like a fat caterpillar with six limbs. It stood on four of its squat legs, centaur-like. A ropy garment covered its speckled white-and-gray fur. A glowing collar encircled its furry neck.

It seemed to believe that Thomas was a god.

Terrified worship jittered its mind. As far as this bulldog-centaur thing was concerned, a nameless god had just woken up.

"I'm not a god," Thomas said. "I'm harmless."

Words were useless. The alien jerked back and watched Thomas with wide-eyed terror, unable to comprehend his language. Its thoughts raced in a language Thomas had never encountered, although he sensed every nuance of its mood.

It apparently expected gods to communicate with hand gestures rather than with voice commands.

Thomas could dive deeper into the govki's memories in order to soak up its alien language and cultural background, if he wanted to. He had made himself fluent in many languages that way. French, Japanese, Hindi, Russian…he could absorb a language just by sitting within range of a native speaker for a few seconds.

But learning about this govki would include a lifetime's worth of memories, a flood of irrelevancies. The prospect added to Thomas's nausea. He had plenty to occupy his mind already. If he added an overwhelming deluge of alien torrents, it would feel similar to eating an entire cow.

One thing he had trouble analyzing was his environment. The floor was mirrored. Everything else was bright nothingness, like an overcast sky. The walls and ceiling extended into infinity, as far as he could see. Was it a room?

Whatever it was, it was descending, like an elevator down an endless shaft.

Lots of things could be simulated, but the sensation of motion could not be faked by any means that Thomas knew of. The simplest and most rational explanation was that this was a low-gravity environment.

Which meant he was not on Earth.

Thomas tried not to panic.

First, he needed a dose of his medicine. He needed mobility. Then he could work out theories as to where he was, whether Cherise and Vy were safe, and how to escape.

The alien uncertainly picked up a tray of refreshments.

There were odd little dumplings, sliced vegetables, and pastries. The unlabeled squeeze bottles looked like beverages.

Thomas felt too nauseated to eat, yet he sensed starvation from the alien. It yearned to taste the things that resembled spring rolls. Instead, it offered the tray, apparently believing its role to be subservient.

Thomas kept catching disturbing glimpses of himself in the alien's perceptions. This govki had no clue that he was a child. As far as the govki was concerned, Thomas was a mysterious and omniscient god who knew everything about its life. Also…

Why did it see his irises as black?

Thomas looked at his reflection in the mirrored floor. Bumps rose on his skin. Someone had surgically altered his eyes while he was unconscious.

He blinked. His eyes felt unharmed, yet they remained the wrong color.

He focused on his hands and his knobby legs, worried that he might find other alterations to his body.

Sure enough, he felt some kind of plastic cuff around his ankle. Did that mean he was a prisoner? The cuff felt like a rubber sticker, painlessly attached to his skin.

Cautious, Thomas skimmed the alien's surface thoughts.

The govki's mind seemed human in fundamental ways. It had nuanced emotions, sophisticated conceptual abstractions, language, and sentience. Perhaps soaking up its life history wouldn't be horrendously overwhelming?

Thomas flexed his hands, preparing for a massive deluge of memories.

Intense emotion was always his starting point. That was the way to gain access to the depths of a mind. Thomas scanned ripples of wariness. When he found a whirlpool of terror, he followed it downward…down to a sad, pathetic life of grief, torment, and deprivation.

This alien was a slave.

It had been born a slave, and it expected to die, horribly, as a slave. All members of its species, the gender-fluid govki, were slaves.

As Thomas dashed through the alien slave's memories, gathering vocabulary and syntax, he struggled to absorb the way it had been forced to watch its family murdered by self-proclaimed "gods" who looked very much like humans.

This govki's friends had been murdered by so-called gods. In the slave tongue, the word for gods was *Torth*.

Those humanoid people—the Torth—owned everything in existence. To disobey a Torth meant swift and painful death. The only happiness the govki knew about was bland food and bleak visits to overcrowded slave zones. As far as it knew, anyone who looked like a Torth was powerful and merciless.

"I'm sorry," Thomas said in the alien's slave tongue. The cadence felt strange and brutish. "I am not a Torth. I will not harm you."

This time, the slave understood what he'd said. It dropped the tray in shock.

A thick liquid, like stew, splashed across the floor, and the slave frantically mopped the mess with linen napkins. Thomas sensed its panicked thoughts. Messes were bad. Messes could mean death for a slave. Gyatch felt more frightened and confused than ever, because Torth only spoke commands, never apologies.

"I am not a Torth, Gyatch." Thomas used the slave's personal name, because a Torth never would. "I'm sort of a prisoner here."

Normally, Thomas would not let anyone see him as weak. But he didn't feel disadvantaged next to this slave.

"Will you please put me in my chair?" he asked.

The govki reared up on its hindmost legs, freeing up four arms so it could gently lift Thomas. It set him in a sitting position with expert care.

"Thanks." Thomas knew that Torth never used words of gratitude. He spoke it the way slaves spoke to each other, rather than using silent hand commands. Anyway, he empathized with this slave's fear of death. A similar fear had driven Thomas to work late hours and to endure regular injections of NAI-12.

The govki stood alert and attentive.

"Will you set my case on my lap, please?" Thomas wished he didn't need to ask a slave to do things for him. It was awkward.

But Gyatch didn't seem to mind at all. The alien felt somewhat safe when it was being useful to a Torth.

Microgravity made everything easier than normal. Thomas found that he was able to unlatch the case without help. He even rolled up his sleeve on his own! And he lifted his injection pen and pressed it to his bare arm. Amazing.

Once the injection was done, he turned his focus to his next need. "Do you have any water I can drink?"

Gyatch offered a squeeze bottle with an attached straw.

It smelled fruity. The beverage might be as innocent as apple juice, but for all Thomas knew, it might be something toxic.

He took a risk and sipped.

Flavor exploded in his mouth, sweeter and lighter than any fruit juice he had ever experienced. It was delicious. Thomas could hardly stop himself from drinking half the bottle.

He sensed other people enter his range of telepathy.

Thomas could normally learn quite a lot from other people's thoughts, but Torth were strange. Alien. Each mind contained a whispery horde of distant voyeurs. Thomas could not even estimate how many mind readers stood nearby, watching him. It might be one, or it might be an army.

Look at him.

Already sitting in his (primitive contraption) wheelchair.

He must have figured out how to command the slave.

So smart.

A hallway appeared.

Just like that, one of the glowing nonwalls rippled and revealed a doorway. Perhaps the opening had been there the whole time? It might have been disguised by photon manipulation.

The Torth had colonized multiple worlds. They'd enslaved aliens. So they might have technology that he could not even guess at.

Three Torth adults stood in the softly glowing hallway.

On Earth, the Swift Killer had looked passably human. Thomas stared at her hair, which curled like flaxen smoke in the low gravity. A white bodysuit emphasized her athletic physique. She looked superhuman, perhaps augmented in some way.

As for her eyes? They lacked pupils. She looked blind, with milk-white, wet, empty eyeballs.

Her companions were similar, with empty eyes and athletic bodies. Their features were diverse, like human ethnicities.

Thomas sensed their keen vision. These people saw him in high resolution. They studied him like cameras, and their brains were a live-stream feed. Countless multitudes examined Thomas through their perceptions.

He definitely has potential, distant Torth thought.

He was raised the wrong way,

raised by primitives,

but give him time.

Rapid-fire images overlaid everything. The sheer volume of imagery that ran through each Torth was staggering. To Thomas, their minds seemed to sparkle.

Where are (Cherise) (Vy) my friends? Thomas asked in his mind.

They did not deign to answer.

The Swift Killer and her cohorts riffled through Thomas's mind in an impersonal way. It felt like a pat-down from security guards. Their inner audiences sent an endless stream of commentary.

Ooh.

He has learned the slave tongue—

—and basic command gestures.

So fast!

Their minds flickered with approval.

"Where are my friends?" Thomas asked out loud, in English.

The reactions soured.

Did he just speak like a slave?

Ugh.

So rude.

So primitive.

Do We really want him among Us?

He is not one of Us yet.

Maybe he will never be one of Us.

The Swift Killer made a gesture to the govki slave, indicating that it should push Thomas's wheelchair.

The slave obeyed without hesitation. It got behind Thomas, and soon he was gliding along a hexagonal corridor, flanked on either side by a muscular Torth.

Thomas unleashed his inquisitive concerns in a silent flood. Was he on a spaceship? How did the Torth manage to conceal their galactic civilization from humankind? What did the Torth intend to do with him? What had they done with his friends? Was Cherise safe? Why had the Torth sent Thomas to the Dovanack mansion? Why was his eye color no longer purple, but black? Why did Torth resemble humans? Why did Torth own slaves? Did they rule the universe? Was Thomas a Torth? Could he go home, please?

How bizarre. Millions of distant Torth sized Thomas up through the eyes of the Swift Killer and her cohorts.

An ignorant mind reader. The concept seemed to fascinate them.

He is so clueless.

Who could have imagined that such a thing is possible?

Ignorant.

Thomas had never known ignorance until now. And it did seem bizarre. The Torth hardly registered his disability or his youthfulness, yet his ignorance was an embarrassing problem. His yearning for answers made the Torth think of him as inferior. Like the slave who trotted behind his wheelchair.

Did they expect him to just…what? Absorb all their galactic knowledge? A galaxy's worth of knowledge.

Thomas wanted it. His throat tightened with yearning.

He wants to ascend! The Torth exchanged mental glances without actually looking at each other.

But he doesn't know how!

He has never done it before!

He is like a newborn baby!

Thomas hesitated.

He was on the precipice of something dangerous, he sensed. The Torth might collectively contain all the secrets of the universe—but was there a price for their knowledge? Was he like Eve in the Garden of Eden, about to take a bite from the apple of knowledge? What would happen if he did?

Would he transform into one of these sadistic, godlike Torth?

He isn't ready.

Take him to the Upward Governess first.

Yes. He isn't ripe yet.

The unspoken flurry of comments gave Thomas impressions of what he might be missing. Every Torth shared their opinions and their perceptions with other distant Torth, who likewise shared everything with others. Their mesh network must host the equivalent of a billion podcasts and reality shows and endless lecture series.

They definitely had more knowledge than the internet.

Once he gained access, Thomas knew, he would be able to unlock all other answers. He would know everything.

And then maybe he would stop feeling so outclassed and helpless.

He settled back in his wheelchair and resolved to learn everything he could before making any sort of attempt to "ascend," whatever that meant.

CHAPTER 10

NOT ALIENS

Vy felt as light as a snowflake. She was able to climb around the upper part of the cage with almost no effort.

"Even if you find a way out," Delia said, her voice ragged, "where would we go? It looks like hell out there."

It looked like outer space beyond the cage.

That was all. Just an endless night, with stars and several industrial complexes that floated an unfathomable distance away. They looked like oil refineries, perhaps, except they were in space. For all Vy knew, they were the size of asteroids or moons.

"It can't be real." Vy had said that repeatedly.

She tried not to think too hard about the falling sensation that never stopped. Or the fact that the cage had no gate or door. She wasn't going to admit what this surreal situation implied.

Aliens.

Alien abduction.

No. She wasn't going to consider that insane conclusion, because she had not seen any aliens. The intruders who had netted her were clearly human beings. They had worn full body armor, but actual aliens would surely look and act completely alien.

Vy shook the cage bars. The bars seemed to be made of some sort of ultrastrong plastic. They did not budge.

"What if you accidentally trigger something?" Delia made a sound of frustration. "Has it occurred to you that we might actually be safe inside this cage? I mean, safer inside here than out in that void?"

Vy traced a finger around the collar encircling her neck. "You think we're safe?"

They had all awoken wearing choker collars, even Ariock. Their unknown captors had apparently manufactured a giant-size collar that fit him. And the collars were impossible to remove. There were no latches or clasps. No seams. Vy had tried to work her fingers under the oily material, but it was stuck to her skin.

If she thought about the collar too much, she might burst into tears.

She scanned the empty void of space. It must be a simulation, a supremely high-definition projection or something. "Where is Thomas? Why isn't he with us?"

Her companions did not have answers, Vy knew. All they could do was share her worries.

Ariock and Delia barely knew Thomas. And Cherise? She was not his caretaker. Vy was supposed to be the responsible adult. She was supposed to protect him.

"He'll need help," Vy said, feeling miserably helpless. "Why would they separate him from the rest of us?"

"Vy."

Ariock had not spoken until now. His voice was so powerfully deep, the air seemed to vibrate.

He gazed up at her with concern. "They won't hurt him."

Vy clung to the bars, aware that Ariock had not given her any new information. Yet his point was comforting. That creepy woman, the Swift Killer, had baited Thomas. Hadn't she? That meant the abductors wanted Thomas for some reason. They likely wanted him alive.

Maybe Vy ought to be thankful that she was alive, herself. The abductors could have killed her.

"Exactly." Delia sounded bitter. "He's the reason we're here. You said they lured him to our house."

Vy jumped down. The falling sensation made her so lightweight, she bounced back up again, like a moonwalker. She grabbed onto cage bars and eased herself down, rung by rung.

"Yeah," Vy said. "I would like to know why they included you and Ariock. There must be a reason." She studied Delia, hoping the older woman would reveal an enlightening secret or two.

Even in sweatpants and slippers, Delia managed to look condescending. "What reason would that be?"

"I don't know," Vy admitted. "Maybe they wanted something that was in your house?" She wanted to speculate, to see if they could grope their way toward some answers. "Or maybe they wanted someone else, besides Thomas?"

"I don't think so," Delia sounded cross. "Ariock and I were just minding our own business. And we're not mind readers. We're completely normal."

"Hmm." Vy resisted her impulse to glance at Ariock.

"Ariock just has a growth disorder." Delia's tone became scathing. "That's all there is to it. If you knew him at all, you'd understand. He is the most normal young man you'll ever meet."

"I believe you." Vy folded her arms. "But let's try to figure this out. You live near to where Thomas was born. Maybe that means he's connected to your family?"

"I'm sure that was a pure coincidence," Delia said with acid in her tone.

Vy glanced toward Ariock, wondering if he might volunteer some information. "What was your family doing thirteen years ago? Or closer to fourteen years ago, I guess? That would be around the time Thomas was conceived."

She expected more scathing retorts.

Instead, Ariock and Delia exchanged a disturbed look.

"There were some deaths in our family," Delia said. "I don't think it has anything to do with this." She gestured around the cage, with its view of outer space. "Our family ran into bad luck. That's all."

Ariock gazed at his mother with doubt and pain.

Vy recalled the many unused rooms in the Dovanack mansion, fuzzy with dust. The oil portraits implied that it had once been a larger family.

"You may have heard some gossip," Delia told Vy with delicate shame. "But it was just bad luck. There's no such thing as a family curse."

"A curse?" Vy glanced at Ariock. Many people would consider him lucky, not cursed, with so much inherited wealth.

"A lot of our relatives and household staff died in a short period of time." Delia sounded as if she was discussing filthy laundry. "Accidents." She ticked them off on her fingers. "A car accident. A yacht wreck. A suicide by gunshot. An accidental overdose. And an airplane crash."

"Oh." Vy wished that she hadn't pried into something that was clearly a source of pain.

"It was just a senseless year of awfulness." Delia's tone softened. "But I don't see how it could be related to Thomas's birth. Or our situation."

Vy decided not to ask for more details. Now was not the time to dredge up trauma. "I'm sorry," she said. "I didn't mean to bring up something painful."

Delia gave Vy a nod of respect. "Ariock and I are the only ones left." She gazed at her son with concern, and Vy saw buried love. "And, to be honest, it's a miracle we're still here. Ariock almost didn't survive."

Vy wanted to ask about whatever trauma Ariock had survived. Thirteen or fourteen years ago, she supposed, he would have been a child. Not a giant yet.

But she could see that begging for details would only be picking at a wound. Delia wore a wedding ring. If her husband had died, that ring was a sign that she was still faithful to him, or that she was attached to his memory.

Vy went back to exploring the bars. "I want to find a way out of here."

Ariock watched her with an expression that was hopeless, yet full of hope.

"I have to admit," Vy said, avoiding everyone's gaze, "I never knew how much Thomas struggled to cure his disease. I mean, obviously I know he works hard. But I didn't know how much he relied on you, Cherise."

It hurt, to admit how detached she was from the lives of her foster siblings. Vy supposed she had been too wrapped up in her own crazy years as a college student and then chasing storms and earning her own income as a nurse. There was that cute med student she had dated for a while. There was always something outside her family to grab her attention.

"Sorry." Vy aimed that apology toward Cherise.

Cherise gave her a gentle look.

The plummeting sensation suddenly became worse. Vy flailed in surprise at the violent roller-coaster sensation, losing her grip on the bars. She floated in midair.

Zero G, she realized in disbelief as her red hair plumed in front of her face.

Her companions floated. Even Ariock was off the ground. He looked rightfully terrified. Gravity would not be kind to him, if it—

Vy slammed downward.

It felt like the final moment of her life. The floor was so far away, and she couldn't slow her plummet. Her bones would shatter.

Except Ariock rolled under her and caught her.

It took Vy a few seconds to realize that she was safe and unharmed. She had not impacted hard steel. Instead, she was in an embrace, held in immense arms, on cottony fabric. His shirt had a lot of buttons.

Ariock gently set her aside.

"Thanks," Vy stammered. She was blushing, as if that embrace had been intentional. As if she'd done something rude.

A walkway appeared out of nowhere.

It hung in the void of space, its edges glowing with recessed safety lights. Vy stared. The walkway was nearly as bright as the faraway space stations with their eerie industrial lighting. It originated from darkness, but it led straight to their cage.

Figures approached on that walkway.

As the figures came closer, Vy nearly wept with relief. One of them was Thomas, in his wheelchair. And the others? They were not monsters. They looked like people.

Surely people could be reasoned with?

CHAPTER 11
SAVAGE

Is this a real-time (projection) view of what's outside the spaceship? Thomas silently asked the three Torth. His unspoken questions were rapid-fire, unconstrained by the friction of vocal speech. *Are your spaceships capable of superluminal (faster-than-light) space travel? Do you have technology that actively manipulates space-time? Where are we? How far from Earth are we?*

The Torth did not respond.

Thomas stared at the Swift Killer, aware that she heard his unspoken thoughts. He had the impression that Torth all had a baseline of information that was far above that of a typical human.

They sponged up knowledge the way he did.

And if they were all plugged into the collective minds of millions—billions? Trillions?—since birth, then they did not need to learn, or teach. They did not need schools.

And they seemed to think that noise was rude.

Thomas became aware of the hum of his wheelchair's motor. It was a quiet whir, yet he sensed that the sound grated on the Swift Killer and her two cohorts. They were used to silence.

Apparently Torth did not care for sound.

They might not even like music.

Wow. Thomas deliberately recalled an obnoxious song. He played it in his head. He also messed with his steering toggle, swerving back and forth to make more noise.

Show me how to join your network of minds, he urged the Torth, *and I'll quiet down.*

The Swift Killer studied him, caressing her thumb across the high-tech glove she wore. Thomas sensed her urge to shoot him.

She had life-or-death power in the palm of her gloved hand.

Not that she needed the weapon. Thomas sensed her superhuman strength and agility. The Swift Killer felt the slightest change in air currents. Her body was enhanced in multiple ways. If she wanted to throw Thomas's wheelchair, or snap his spine like a twig, she could do it with ease.

And she really didn't like him.

She sent Thomas an image of a teacup-size beast, yapping and foaming at its tiny muzzle. *I get rid of all sorts of monsters.*

Thomas studied the woman who might or might not be his birth mother. Why had she implied that he was a monstrous little beast? Did these people have a legit reason for abducting him? How was he supposed to take her threat?

Thomas tried not to feel rejected. If these alien Torth hated him...

Well, so what? Disgust and hatred aimed his way was nothing new. No big deal, he figured.

He wasn't looking for a place where he truly belonged. Not really. He already had a family. Cherise and Vy must be frantic with worry for him by now.

Although maybe not quite as worried as he was.

Thomas relied on other people a lot more than vice versa. That was the simple truth. Reality was painful, but if he was going to survive as an orphan in this strange universe, then he wanted to be brutally self-honest about every facet of his situation.

Do We really want him (an inferior) among Us (superiors)? one of the Torth silently asked another.

Let the Upward Governess decide, the other replied.

Distant opinions crisscrossed their idle conversation, like sunlit sparkles on the surface of a lake.

(Yes) the Upward Governess is never wrong.

She will assess him (judge him) and see if he is fit to be one of Us (or not).

Sure.

But I would not want him in My neighborhood.

He is too (ignorant) savage.

Feral.

Raised by beasts.

No mind reader should wallow in such abject ignorance.

The Swift Killer glanced at Thomas with her empty, milk-white gaze. It was just a casual glance, but in her mind...

Thomas sensed an utter certainty that he was never going back to Earth. The Torth Majority always got what they collectively wanted. Thomas would either join the Torth collective, or else he would die. The desires of an individual rarely mattered. Not unless they were *(the Upward Governess)* a top rank, elected by the Majority to be leaders of public opinion.

Stop fooling around. The Swift Killer forcibly pushed Thomas's hand off the steering toggle. *Let's have the slave push this (wheeled chair) primitive contraption.*

Yes. The other two Torth formed a silent harmony of agreement.

Thomas sensed a vibe that govki were easy to breed and to replace and were therefore considered disposable. So he made no protest when the Swift Killer used hand signals to command Gyatch to get behind his wheelchair and push. That way, Thomas could keep pace with the striding Torth even with his wheelchair powered down.

But he didn't like the way they treated the slave.

Why do you even have slaves? Thomas silently asked the Torth. *You have the technology to traverse interstellar distances; surely you must have robots? What about artificial intelligence?*

All he got was the wall of disdain.

Why do you treat your slaves so poorly? Thomas demanded to know.

But the Torth were not even paying attention to him anymore. They listened to faraway conversations on other worlds.

Thomas caught tantalizing glimpses of interstellar political conversations. He could not quite decipher the cascades of discussion with so many topics. It was like catching distant flashes of lightning on an ocean horizon.

The only nearby person whom Thomas could fully comprehend was the alien slave, Gyatch.

Gyatch was thirsty. Hungry. And miserable.

Gyatch missed his friends and family.

Hmm.

Thomas gently knocked his half-finished squeeze bottle to one side, putting it within sight of Gyatch. The low gravity made movement much easier for him than it normally was. Would the Torth have a problem if he treated the slave with some silent kindness?

He tried to amplify his unspoken query.

One of the Torth offered something like an offhand answer. It was okay to keep slaves in usable condition. Govki were a common species, so this particular slave was disposable, but any mind reader *(any god)* could treat slaves however they wished.

Okay.

Encouraged, Thomas beckoned Gyatch forward so he could make eye contact with the furry alien. He made his expression friendly and inviting. Vocalization in the presence of Torth meant death, so Thomas dared not speak. However, there was a universal simplistic sign language. Thomas had soaked up thousands of hand commands.

He pointed to the squeeze bottle and made a gesture that indicated "for you."

!? Gyatch recoiled with shock.

In many ways, this terrified slave was like an abused child in the foster care system. Gyatch emanated a dark certainty that Torth never offered gifts.

Yet it also knew that Torth never made facial expressions. Gyatch found Thomas's face to be expressive in a slave-like way, despite the fact that he was clearly a Torth.

Thomas offered the squeeze bottle again.

Gyatch looked around, suspecting a trap or some kind of trickery.

Thomas supposed that he could signal the alien to "take" or "drink," but he didn't want to keep issuing commands like a slave owner. He merely offered a look of encouragement.

After another minute of excruciating doubt, Gyatch dared to grasp the squeeze bottle. The alien worked its bulldog-like snout around the straw and risked a cautious sip.

Bliss filled the alien's mouth.

Amazed, Gyatch took another sip.

Then another.

Thomas smiled. He could not help but vicariously enjoy the alien's joyful reaction. This was fun! His own smile was so unexpected to Gyatch, so unusual, that it ignited all sorts of radical new hopes in the slave. Each swallow delivered a world of fresh possibilities. Gyatch wondered if perhaps this amazing little Torth was actually—

!!!

An explosion of sound and gore disrupted their interaction.

For one confused microsecond, Thomas assumed that he was hallucinating the furry gore that rained down where Gyatch had stood. The slave couldn't be dead. The Torth could not have murdered Gyatch. That would be a terrifying, gross, obscene overreaction to the tiny shred of kindness Thomas had shown.

Afterimages of hopeful joy floated inside Thomas.

Gyatch seemed to live for an extra second, but only as a fading pastiche in Thomas's mind. His death had created a mental shock wave.

Meat pattered onto the glowing floor. A chunk bounced off Thomas's lap.

All the countless details that made Gyatch unique had been ripped asunder. It felt like a planetary annihilation. The sweet aftertaste of nectar in Thomas's mouth turned sickeningly sour. An exquisite future was gone.

Why?

What kind of sadistic assholes would shoot an innocently joyful slave?

The Swift Killer lowered her gloved hand. Thomas sensed her utter lack of shame.

Until now, Thomas had assumed that emotions were universal to all people and animals. Even squirrels were capable of satisfaction or fear. But the Swift Killer seemed uncaring.

Remorseless.

She was a murderer.

You smiled at that slave, she thought to Thomas, her tone somewhat accusatory. *You gave it hope. Your smile forced Me to kill it.*

Hope is toxic, one of her compatriots chorused without words.

Hope is a disease, the other silently sang.

Their moods remained smooth, lacking furrows of empathetic remorse or even bubbles of joy. It was as if they were lobotomized.

The Swift Killer circled around behind Thomas and began to push his wheelchair onward.

The distant Torth audiences joined in. Imaginations twined together, proving why slaves could not be permitted to feel hope. Hope might spread like a plague through an otherwise docile population of slaves. Hope would rile slaves up. Any slave who yearned for a better life could become unpredictable and violent.

The distant voyeurs were making an effort to educate Thomas.

Maybe that was a good sign.

Thomas feared that they might actually have a valid point. He had carelessly assumed the Torth were basically like humans just because they looked human. Then he had forged ahead, like a swimmer obliviously kicking through shark-infested waters.

Alien blood flecked his skin, still warm from the life it should be nourishing.

Thomas held back a flood of curses, but most were aimed at himself. His blithe human kindness had gotten an innocent slave murdered. He had been thinking like his foster sisters instead of like a ruthless, uncaring Torth. Why hadn't he proceeded with more caution?

The Swift Killer pushed his wheelchair aggressively. They moved along a walkway over a seemingly infinite void of outer space.

Thomas no longer wanted to learn if she was his relative. He already had a family. A great family. Afternoons with Cherise, improving NAI-12 while she read graphic novels...that was all he needed in life.

He needed to make sure Cherise was all right.

A cage loomed ahead. Cherise stood behind the bars.

For a moment, Thomas distrusted his own vision. Maybe the cage and its occupants were as unreal as the view of space all around them?

Vy stood with Cherise and Delia. The gigantic shape of Ariock loomed behind the three women, although he sat on his knees. That made sense. Ariock would not stand at his full height within sight of Vy. Not unless someone forced him to.

The savage (in the wheeled chair) had better behave, the Swift Killer thought to her inner audience. *It would be a shame if his blunders force Me to kill these exotic slaves.*

She adjusted her blaster glove.

Her distant audience swirled with reactions. Everyone who tuned in to her mind had just been reminded that she considered Thomas to be an ignoramus.

That was fair.

He needed to be smarter.

CHAPTER 12

SPEECHLESS

"Are you—?" Cherise meant to ask if Thomas was okay. Dark flecks covered him, as if some liquid, like ketchup or wine, had exploded or splattered within a short distance from his head. Instead of offering reassurance, he said nothing. He looked more concerned than overjoyed.

Agony tore through Cherise's throat.

The collar.

Cherise tore at it, trying to remove the thing that was choking her, but it would not peel off her skin. Had their captors consulted her ma? It was as if Ma had reached across space, through the brick walls of that prison, to hush the daughter she had never wanted.

Ariock began to say something. He grunted in pain.

Then it was Delia's turn. And Vy. They whimpered, each one tugging at the collar around their neck.

The strangling pain ebbed. It left Cherise afraid that the pain might return. Thomas watched her with sympathy and concern, yet he still said nothing.

He was within telepathy range.

Thomas! Who are these people? Cherise thought the words.

Thomas sucked in his lips, looking frustrated. He wasn't wearing a punishment choker, but it seemed he wasn't allowed to speak, either.

Vy opened her mouth. Then she seemed to rethink whatever she had wanted to say, and she remained silent.

An opening appeared in the cage wall. Cherise was certain that this cage had lacked any sort of gate, yet now she saw that she'd been wrong. The grid of bars retracted into other bars with eerie silence. No wheels. It did not squeak or trundle. Its lack of noise seemed supernatural.

"Follow," Thomas said in a taut voice.

Cherise studied the three strangers, wondering which one had forced him to say that, and why. She didn't understand what these strangers wanted. Their eyes were a creepy, empty, milky white, without irises or pupils. Combined with their skintight body armor, they looked like superheroes.

Or supervillains. She suspected that might be more accurate.

Thomas looked haggard. Had he missed a few doses of his medicine? And his eye color!

It was wrong. Cherise stared, marveling at how strange Thomas looked with black contact lenses. She assumed they were contacts and not any kind of permanent, surgical change to his eyes.

What's with the eyes? she silently asked. At least unspoken questions seemed safe.

"Follow," Thomas said again. "Don't cause trouble, or..." He swallowed, his black gaze looking haunted. "Or you will be killed. They mean it. They're not messing..."

He interrupted himself. But he shot a disturbed look toward the blonde woman, as if she had interrupted him.

Cherise recognized that woman from the driveway encounter. The Swift Killer, according to Thomas. He had said she could read minds and that millions of people could peer through her eyes.

"Push my chair, please?" Thomas gave Cherise a begging look.

The silent people began to walk away. They moved with athletic grace and eerie coordination. It was impossible to guess what they were thinking, since they had the expressions of mannequins.

Cherise stepped out of the cage.

The silent people were mind readers, she guessed. They must be limiting Thomas somehow, pressuring him to only speak commands. But why? Who were they?

Are you okay? Cherise asked in her mind as she pushed Thomas's wheelchair. He nodded.

But when she leaned around to get a look at his face, she did not feel reassured. Thomas looked traumatized. The specks on his clothing could be juice or blood. Had the silent people forced him to watch an animal get slaughtered?

Cherise glanced back to make sure that her foster sister was with them.

She did a double take. She normally thought of Vy as tall. Vy refused to wear high heels or raised boots because that would make her tower over any man who took her out on a date. She definitely towered over Cherise.

But Vy looked petite and fragile in comparison to Ariock.

He ducked out of the gate, and when he straightened to his full height, he loomed like a tower. He was built like a truck.

Even so, there was a softness about him. He hadn't been hitting a gym. He probably spent his days watching TV, as his mother had implied. And judging by the embarrassed way he avoided everyone's looks, violence was not on his mind at all.

He looked torn between following Vy or following his mother. He ended up following both of them.

Size could make anyone look formidable.

Thomas moved his fingers in a deliberate way, like he was typing. It took Cherise a moment to realize that he was pantomiming a suggestion.

She pulled the touch-screen tablet out of his wheelchair pocket.

No signal bars, of course. They had already tried to call and text people until the batteries on their phones were nearly drained. There was no way to recharge devices. But Thomas's tablet still had a decent battery charge.

The touch screen worked.

Speech was not allowed, and they did not have paper or pens, but typing? That might be permissible.

Thomas made grabby motions.

Cherise secured the tablet across his bony knees. She understood that Thomas could not astrally project his thoughts, the way telepaths did in TV shows and books, like telepathy was a telephony service. He could not transmit. His brain simply received more input than a normal human brain.

I am unharmed.

Thomas typed that in a notepad application. Cherise leaned over his shoulder so that she could read the glowing screen.

Thank goodness. Cherise felt immensely relieved that they could actually converse.

Or could they?

She cringed, afraid that the silent people might punish her for daring to communicate, even without her voice. One of them strode nearby. Those empty eyes made it impossible to know what they were looking at, or whether they could see at all.

Thomas typed.

We can talk silently. They read minds.

Vy joined Cherise, reading the screen over her shoulder. She glanced at Cherise, making it clear that she had read and understood Thomas's message.

Thomas cleared the screen, then typed more.

They can sense any plan to attack or escape. Do not provoke them. They are violent and trigger-happy.

Cherise swallowed. The act of swallowing reminded her that she wore a horrific alien collar around her neck.

They are Torth. Not human. Quick to murder.

Torth?

Cherise was unfamiliar with that word, but she was certain that Thomas never lied. If he believed that their abductors were hostile aliens, then it must be true.

Even so, her mind wanted to spit out the idea. A bunch of mind readers ought to know that she was innocent and that she didn't belong in a cage. She didn't deserve a punishment collar. Why treat her like livestock? What was wrong with them?

Thomas deleted the text and typed more. **I will find out.** He deleted that and added, **I will get us home to Earth. Working on it.**

Cherise nodded with relief, as if crossing unfathomable trillions of miles across outer space was no big deal. So she was not on Earth. So what? Thomas would figure things out.

Vy looked ill with incredulity.

She glared at Thomas, as if she was silently haranguing him. Maybe she was reminding him of his limitations?

Thomas deleted, then typed.

You are disabled here. Not me.

The message was likely an answer to something which Vy had not said, but Cherise nodded. The truth was beyond obvious. Thomas was the only one of them who lacked a punishment collar. He might be part Torth, and he alone could safely converse with their captors.

On top of that…this was the hero who had saved Cherise from suicide.

This was the person who had gained sponsorship from international pharmaceutical conglomerates and who had vanquished his own imminent death, despite laws and societal expectations that told him he could not do it. Thomas could do anything. He might feel a bit spooked right now—they all were—but he had steely determination in his eyes.

Thomas typed. **Trust me. I will get us home.** He deleted that, then pasted it again for emphasis. **I will get us home.**

Cherise knew he would.

Vy didn't look quite so certain. No doubt she felt obligated to take charge, to shield Thomas from harm, to treat him like a child. But really. What choice did she have?

A breeze came from ahead.

The pathway led to something that looked like an ovular Stargate. It seemed carved from meteorite rock. Daylight glowed beyond that gate, but it looked unearthly, with a greenish tint.

Thomas typed on the tablet.

Culture shock ahead. Please stay calm.

Cherise tried not to guess. Guessing would only set her up with wrong-headed expectations, which would likely get smashed. But she prepared for a flood of unique details, like she was getting ready to capture real-life places and people in a series of quick sketches.

They stepped through the meteorite gate.

Into another world.

Dusty skyscrapers climbed to insane heights, their twisted spires honey-combed with docking bays. Aerial cars zipped past ghostly holographs that bloomed and faded in the shadows beneath ledges. Doorways appeared and vanished like blinking stoplights.

There were spaceships on immense, lit-up launchpads.

These ships were unlike the overly engineered behemoths of Hollywood films. They had no windows, not even portholes. No antennae. Just a lot of shielding. These vessels were pitted and dented like meteorites, their hulls dark and formidable. They looked ancient. And hardy.

Cherise turned and confirmed that she had just stepped out of a large spaceship. A ramp led downward into an ocean of staring aliens.

Airborne traffic and space vessels were not the most shocking thing about this vista.

It was the aliens.

Many of them were unambiguously weird. There were creatures as huge as rhinoceroses, with spiky spinal ridges. Small gray aliens filled in the gaps. They looked like goblins, or perhaps like mummified flightless birds, since they had flesh-covered beaks. Less common types looked furry, with six limbs, or else they had huge, sickle-shaped heads perched atop necks that zigzagged with joints, like limbs.

But the weirdest aliens were the ones who looked vaguely human.

Cherise figured these were Torth. But unlike their captors on the space-ship, these Torth were decked out in brocaded robes that shimmered with geometric patterns. Their hair was punched up into decorative puffs or rolls and dusted with powder or glitter. Many of the Torth were overweight. They sat in throne-like hoverchairs, casually floating a foot or two above the mir-rored floor.

Cherise hesitated, unwilling to walk deeper into alien territory.

The vast crowd breathed, a collective sound greater than wind rushing through an autumn forest.

Not a single alien spoke. None whispered.

Cherise was vaguely aware that Ariock was on his knees, trying to hide behind his mother and Vy. He looked like he wanted to shrink. Vy reached for his hand. Ariock seemed to draw comfort from that touch.

Cherise leaned on the armrests of Thomas's wheelchair. Ariock feared people staring at him, and Cherise understood why the stares were so men-acing. She knew why it was wise to hide.

In this metropolis, the only aliens were the five from Earth.

PART TWO

Only children are happy.

—slave proverb

Children are disposable.

—Torth edict

CHAPTER 1
A CURIOUS SLAVE

Kessa suppressed a groan at the twinge of pain in her lower spine. That ache never quite vanished anymore. The window was at least eighty times broader than herself, and she had to wash all of it.

With an internal sigh, she heaved the bucket of soapy liquid to the next area and set her spindly arms into motion again. Her reflection stared forlornly back at her in the glass: an aged ummin with gray skin creased from indoor humidity. Rags swaddled her withered body. Her short beak had such a pronounced curve, it formed a semicircle. That was a childish trait that used to make her feel cute, but in old age, it looked incongruous with her sunken cheeks.

She kept her hat properly pinned and folded, out of habit. She was too wrinkled to attract a mate in the slave zones.

Her arms ached so much, and she wanted to groan every time she straightened from the soapy bucket. Maybe she could risk a short rest?

A whisper of footfalls announced her owner.

Kessa emptied her mind of all thought but what she was doing. Her arms moved in a pattern. Up and around, then a fresh dip into the bucket, never mind her aches. It was best to live in the moment whenever a Torth was nearby.

Outside, the distant spaceport was generating even more aerial traffic than usual. Yellow clouds of sand particles billowed between stone skyscrapers, so the distant towers were obscured by haze. Although Kessa longed for that hot, crisp, dry outdoor air, she was grateful to have a personal owner. Otherwise she might be on a construction work crew, and at her frail age, outdoor labor meant death.

Soapy water collected into tears on the glass. Each one contained a miniature city trapped in a sphere. Each city was obliterated when the second cloth sopped over it.

Her owner stood directly behind her.

Kessa had to be extra careful to avoid bumping into her owner's pristine golden-turquoise robes. She watched her old, thin hands, fascinated, as they moved the wet sponges up and down, then in a circle, alternately washing and drying. Maybe she ought to go and retrieve the stepladder so she could reach the high-up sections of the window?

Climbing with the heavy buckets would make her whole body ache for days. But that was a dangerous thought—a complaint. Kessa shoved it from her mind.

After an excruciating amount of time, the Torth woman waggled her manicured fingers in the "preen" gesture, reflected in the glass. Kessa gratefully dropped the sponge into the bucket and ran to retrieve the beauty kit from the powder room.

When she returned, she found her owner sprawled onto a plush divan, waiting with her electric-blue curls disarrayed. Golden hovercombs lay scattered on the floor. Kessa picked up the mess with quick ease, grateful that her owner favored sparse minimalism. Many Torth filled their luxurious suites with treasure.

Preening a Torth was less taxing than washing windows or floors, but it was far more dangerous. Kessa took pride in her expertise. She removed the last few combs from her owner's hair, careful to catch the hair before it could fall with an audible sound. Then she began to gently brush.

Her owner sometimes rewarded Kessa with an early dismissal for silent admiration, so she admired how the light played on each steely-blue corkscrew curl. So beautiful.

For the finishing touch, Kessa applied golden glitter to her owner's eyebrows. That yellow color matched her owner's irises, and a lifetime of serving Torth had given Kessa more than a few clues as to what Torth eye colors meant. Yellow Ranks were the most common and lowliest of the godlike Torth.

Pain racked her body.

Kessa gulped back a yelp and barely managed to avoid smearing her owner's face with glitter. For a confused instant, she wondered if the pain was a mealtime alert. Had she failed to eat enough during her previous wake cycle?

But this was a deeper pain. A punishment seizure. She must have offended her owner.

Of course.

Kessa was merely a stupid slave who should never presume anything about a Torth. She curled her owner's eyelashes, continually berating herself for being stupid, old, and clumsy. Self-punishment was a healthy habit, since it let owners know when their punishments were sufficient and could be ended.

The pain ebbed.

At last, her owner flexed four fingers in the dismissal gesture.

Kessa bowed and rushed to put away the beauty kit and escape the suite. Leftovers Hall was quite a hike from here. A Torth could speed across great distances on hovercarts, hoverbikes, or hoverchairs. But slaves were not permitted to drive vehicles or hitch rides, uninvited.

So Kessa ran.

Her toenails clicked alongside the footfalls of thousands of other slaves. Every slave knew that rushing was ideal, because an idle slave could be given ten reasons to run. Only Torth strolled at their leisure through the vast indoor boulevards.

When foot traffic slowed, Kessa assumed that some poor slave up ahead must be suffering death by pain seizure. She had no stomach for such spectacles. There was an alternative route through a garden lounge, and she headed for that entrance, impatiently threading her way past larger species. She had to dodge around the thorny bulk of a nussian.

But tortured slaves usually screamed. The streets were silent.

Kessa slowed, seeing a Torth who leaned against the transparent railing, gazing down at the forum floor below. The stout figure seemed oblivious to the slaves who squeezed past him.

In fact, all the Torth in sight were staring, even gawking, down toward the forum.

What could cause a Torth to gawk?

Kessa hesitated. Whatever was happening, it must be a Torth matter that had nothing to do with slaves. She ought to hurry to Leftovers Hall. If she missed a meal, she might make a fatal mistake at work. Nothing was worth that risk.

But Kessa was curious.

Despite her sensibility, despite her hunger, she made her way to the railing and peered downward.

A procession of hovercarts snaked through the crowd down there. The Torth in that procession were strange, attired in outlandish clothes. And one of them...

Kessa blinked, hardly able to process the size of a Torth in the central hovercart. He must be as tall as a nussian.

And...

She blinked again, refocusing, unsure if she could trust her own eyesight. Was that gigantic Torth actually wearing a slave collar around his neck?

It looked like a collar, albeit a deactivated one, peacefully dark. Kessa had never seen or heard of anything like that.

Three other passengers in that central hovercart wore slave collars, yet none were slaves. Dread and awe passed across their Torth faces. Kessa had heard folklore about Torth who acted like slaves, with emotions, but she had never suspected those tales held any truth.

Slaves jostled past her, impatient to get to their meals, their bunk rooms, or their work shifts.

Kessa looked around to see if anyone else had noticed the weirdness taking place below. A few other slaves did look curious, but they wisely pushed onward, trying not to draw Torth attention.

Kessa ought to do the same. It was best to ignore this event. A slave could never understand Torth affairs, just as one could never learn why the sun rose every morning, or why the moons had cycles. All she could do was guess and wonder.

Suddenly, every window along the street flickered and synchronized to show the exact same view: a close-up of the procession.

Traffic halted. Slaves looked at the windows, and Kessa looked with them, marveling at the close-up live feed of Torth who were playacting as slaves.

Kessa would have expected these Torth actors to be lowly Yellow Ranks. It seemed they were not. One was a Blue! Those were rare, and always wealthy beyond belief. Why would any Blue Rank agree to act like a slave?

The giant had an unknown eye color.

Kessa refocused several times, just to make sure she was seeing correctly. As far as she knew, there was no such thing as a purple rank. Purple was a taboo color among Torth.

There was one other strange Torth on that central hovercart. He wore no collar, yet he emoted like a slave. He sat in a strange contraption, a chair with wheels. And his eye color...

Kessa had heard of Torth with black eyes, yet she had never seen one. Until now.

She turned back to the railing and studied the procession until it vanished from sight. Young slaves would undoubtedly corner her in slave zones, expecting wisdom from an elder. She expected to mediate debates. She would put forth her own theories and conjectures about this event.

If Kessa was influential enough—and if she was lucky—maybe her name would be remembered after she passed out of the realm of the living.

CHAPTER 2
THEFT

Thomas wasn't used to doing double takes.

His neck ached from staring at so many alien sights. People walked through walls amid a flow of pedestrian traffic reminiscent of cities like New York and Tokyo. Thomas was aware that his friends found the silence to be eerie.

But the city wasn't silent at all. Not to him.

Thomas wanted to curl into a ball...not from fear, but from sheer overload.

The city thrummed with exotic thoughts. Every alien slave that ran past his hovercart emitted anxiety or terror. Every Torth that passed within his range contained a frothing inner audience, unknown to slaves, unknown to Thomas's friends, yet glaringly obvious to Thomas. Their glossy minds swirled with other people's opinions, like clouds marbling the surfaces of planets.

Soon, those inner audiences thrummed whenever they focused on Thomas.

Soon We shall see if he is worthy of joining Us.

Thomas and his friends rode on a long platform that glided, frictionless, on air. Hover technology was everywhere he looked. Slaves pushed hovering trays, loaded with refreshments. Orb lamps floated in alcoves. Geriatric Torth wore back braces or arm braces that provided floating support.

This was a world where crutches and wheels were obsolete.

Thomas's wheelchair attracted stares. He hoped that his NAI-12 medicine was considered just as primitive. Perhaps the Torth could provide a permanent cure for his fatal illness?

Although, judging from his observations...

Thomas was dismayed to see visible health problems among the Torth. Apparently, they had not cured all ailments. The elderly moved with arthritic slowness. And he saw more obesity than he'd seen anywhere else, even in the Walmarts of New Hampshire. Quite a few Torth floated in extrawide hoverchairs, too fat to walk.

And where were the children?

Thomas scanned the city for babies or toddlers, but he didn't see any. The youngest-looking people he saw could have passed for teenagers on Earth, maybe seventeen or eighteen, complete with facial acne. None looked like preteens.

Their hovercart zipped past a man walking with a pigeon-toed gait. Clearly, he had cerebral palsy.

The Torth had space travel, hover technology, holographs, and ultrarealism in their window displays. Where were their cyborgs? Their robots? Their bioengineered bodies?

Well, the Swift Killer had enhanced strength and reflexes. The Servants of All were uniformly athletic, with superhuman physiques.

Thomas wanted to ponder that.

But there were too many other things to stare at. He sensed Cherise wince in sympathy for a beaked alien, curled up and silently weeping. The poor alien was suffering.

Other slaves avoided it, swerving around a Torth man who seemed to be directing his malicious attention toward the weeping victim.

Cherise exchanged a worried glance with Vy. Thomas sensed their unspoken concerns. They, too, wore slave collars. They were being treated like animals, forced to stand in the center of the platform, terrified to speak or make any threatening movements.

And they feared that their telepathic foster brother might have Torth parents.

Thomas fervently hoped that his parents were human. If he was linked to the Torth through ancestry…well, he supposed he could handle the shame of that.

But could he handle meeting actual birth parents who sadistically tortured slaves to death?

Their hovercart glided past majestic vine-covered walls, divided by trickling waterfalls. The Torth might feel nothing, but they must have creative and artistic minds buried in their society somewhere. Their architecture was impressive. Their technology was astounding.

Servants of All.

Mighty Ones.

Torth lounged on cushions between fruit trees, and their unspoken praise was as potent as the song of crickets in grass or the sigh of wind through autumn foliage.

Yes, the Swift Killer thought, barely acknowledging the worship. *We honor you.*

Another one of the Servants of All added, *Move aside.*

Thomas and his companions received a different sort of attention. Mild curiosity. Most of it was aimed at Ariock, and there was an uneasy undertone, as if they saw the big guy as a nightmarish monster rather than a gentle couch potato.

The Torth thought of Ariock as threatening for some unknown reason. He was the reason for all the Servants of All. Apparently, Ariock needed to be under guard.

Yet no one glanced at Thomas. They stared at his wheelchair but not at him. Here in New GoodLife WaterGarden City, he was just an ordinary, average telepath.

Thomas grinned at that irony. He quickly stopped when he saw how many stares his grin was attracting.

Knowledge seeped into him from every person they passed. He gained a general map of this metropolis. He learned that millions of other metropolises existed in thousands of faraway solar systems, all connected by fixed wormholes in deep space.

The Torth Empire was incomprehensibly vast.

Torth lived on space stations, in undersea habitats, in stormy atmospheres, underground, and in paradise-like lands. Each fleeting glimpse of other worlds caused Thomas to reevaluate his beliefs about the galaxy, again and again.

The alien slaves that passed through his range were unaware of all those other worlds. They were oblivious to the thunderous mental clamor all around them. Many slaves had heard rumors of faraway cities, but they didn't know what a galaxy was, or space travel. They were ignorant of any difference between technology and magic.

To them, this city had no name. It was simply home.

Thomas did not glance at the unactivated slave collar around Cherise's neck. That collar was a threat, and he was unsure how to react to it.

He couldn't even guess why the Torth kept slaves. Surely they were capable of engineering decent artificial intelligence?

The city was saturated with unhappiness, sorrow, and fear. Why did the Torth tolerate so much misery? Robots could be programmed to be unfailingly obedient, and better yet: robots had no feelings.

Artificial intelligence engineering is illegal. That response came from several Torth, not in words, but in heuristic impressions.

It is one of the forbidden sciences.

Thousands of distant Torth imagined disaster scenarios, illustrating why robots were problematic. Machines were too easy to weaponize. A sentient robot could mess with city utilities or cause spaceships to crash. In the wrong hands, the power of robots could lead to an escalating arms race.

Anyhow, more Torth chorused, *slaves are beneath Our notice.*

They are animals.

Like the beasts of burden that primitives use.

Robots would never be as predictable, as harmless, or as simple and elegant as slave labor.

Encouraged by the conversation, Thomas acknowledged the advantages of using slaves instead of robots. He supposed that an average Torth wouldn't even need a personal computer. They didn't seem to have jobs. And they all had a better version of the internet and mass media installed in their brains.

Correct. Distant Torth hummed with approval.

The Swift Killer leaned against the ornate railing of the hovercart, watching Thomas with a modicum of respect.

Thomas wondered about the Torth who operated starships and other sophisticated technology. He figured that whoever controlled information, transportation, and weapons of mass destruction...whoever wielded that power...that must be who truly controlled galactic civilization.

It is All of Us, the reply came, from near and far.

The Majority rules All.

We All share power.

Thomas assessed the Servants of All. They might not admit to being privileged, yet they clearly were. He understood how politicians served people. They pretended to care about people they had never met, and in exchange, they held the law in their hands.

We do not pretend. Scorn dripped from the mind of the Swift Killer.

Mind readers cannot deceive each other, distant Torth minds sang.

We are not the savages that raised you.

We merely serve the Majority.

We enforce the will of All Torth.

Their hovercart slowed down through a narrow garden path. Slaves pruned hedges.

Thomas barely noticed the gas-filled creatures that floated above flowers, as iridescent as hummingbirds, with tiny feet hanging down. He was too captivated by Torth mysteries to pay much attention to alien sights.

Yet he did notice when their hovercart glided to a stop.

At the end of an alcove, surrounded by tropical plants and kneeling slaves, an extremely rotund girl lounged in an extrawide floating throne. She wore a floppy hat and sipped a frothy-looking beverage, held up to her lips by a slave.

Thomas would have dismissed the girl as just one more weirdness. But why had they stopped in front of her?

She was young. She couldn't be any older than fourteen, which made her the only child that Thomas had seen in New GoodLife WaterGarden City, besides himself and Cherise.

Upward Governess. The Servants of All greeted her with silent respect. Respect?

Judging by her dozens of slaves, this girl was wealthy or important. And she was ill. Her shimmery blue robes hid her atrophied limbs, but Thomas saw telltale signs of a severe neuromuscular disease, like his own. Her shoulders were underdeveloped. Her hands curled inward, tugged by tendons that had failed to grow with the bones.

The Servants of All offered a *(requested)* gift to the *(Indigo-Blue Rank)* Upward Governess.

She was too far away for Thomas to read her thoughts, but he detected a vibe from the nearby Servants of All. They considered this girl to be *(ultrasmart)* influential.

Perhaps she was one of the elusive engineers entrusted with keeping machines running?

The Servants regarded her as *(want) (give it to Me now)* greedy.

Thomas leaned forward, trying to widen his telepathic range, to catch everything he could.

One of the Servants snatched his NAI-12 briefcase out of his wheelchair pocket.

Thomas frowned as the Servant stepped off the hovercart, carrying his medicine to the Upward Governess. The Servant laid the briefcase on her stomach and unlatched it, opening it so that she could inspect its contents.

Her eyes were as blue as a tropical ocean. She gazed at the vials of NAI-12 like a treasure hunter who had just found El Dorado.

That isn't yours, Thomas thought.

He managed to keep silent. But he was due for his next injection in three hours, fifty-two minutes, nine seconds, and counting down.

The lid featured phoenix birds, rendered in metallic markers by Cherise. Even with the briefcase facing away, Thomas knew how much medicine remained in the injection pen. He knew exactly how many vials remained full and how many were emptied. It was a limited prototype. There was no way to order refills.

A warm hand took his.

Cherise emanated sympathy and determination to help Thomas survive, no matter what.

Thomas squeezed back. No matter what heritage he had, Cherise was his true family.

The Upward Governess twiddled her fingers in a command, and a slave rolled up her sleeve, revealing a lot of flesh. The Servant of All pressed the injection pen into the crook of the girl's arm.

Thomas held his breath. NAI-12 would damage the nervous system of an able-bodied person. But he already knew that this girl had a disability much like his own. The Upward Governess might even have the same atypical variant of spinal muscular atrophy.

So he was unsurprised when the girl received an injection of his medicine. *That doesn't belong to you*, he thought.

A Servant of All grabbed Thomas's arm and began to unfasten his wristwatch.

Thomas jerked in surprise. He had failed to anticipate this theft, since Torth minds were so smoothly emotionless. He tried to tug his arm away, but the Servant gripped him hard enough to leave bruises.

All Thomas could do was grit his teeth and simmer in silent fury.

The Servant stole his phone as well as his wristwatch.

None of that is yours, Thomas thought as the Servant carried the stolen items to the obese girl. *Those are mine.*

The Upward Governess received each "gift" as if she was entitled to it.

Her slaves wore crisp gray uniforms rather than gardening rags, and they looked proud. One of the multiarmed slaves packed up the NAI-12 briefcase and placed it into a compartment of the girl's floating throne.

Thomas was certain that the Upward Governess saw his outrage, yet she ignored him. She examined the phone and wristwatch for two seconds apiece, then let each item fall, apparently expecting someone else to catch them. Sure enough, slaves did.

Thief. Thomas gripped the armrests of his wheelchair. *Give my medicine back. I invented it. It's mine.*

Agony drilled into his skull.

Thomas had assumed that the Torth needed a slave collar to cause a pain seizure. Apparently all they needed was laser-like focus. The Swift Killer focused on him with intensity, and it felt as if lava funneled directly into his brain.

He didn't care. He could take pain. He'd undergone spinal injections when he was too weak for anesthesia.

Give it back, he demanded.

Biting knives tore through his brain.

THAT DOESN'T BELONG TO YOU.

Agony slammed through his mind, and his mouth worked in silent torment.

STOLE MY LIFE. MY MEDICINE.

The pain increased.

IT'S MINE.

Agony thundered through his head, increasing until nothing else mattered. How could anyone take this abuse without making a sound? The whimpering cry of an animal lurched from his throat. Warm urine soaked his pants.

Thomas was used to being prodded by doctors and caretakers, so he felt no shame at losing control of his bladder.

What shamed him were the tears. He had managed not to cry during spinal injections or the worst physical therapy. Scream, yes. But he never wept where people would notice. Never.

Thomas bent all his rage toward his tormentor, the Swift Killer.

DIE, he thought, to the extent that he was able to think. Nothing else in the universe mattered. He burrowed into the private depths of her mind with the intention that she *DIE. DIE. DIE.*

The Swift Killer staggered.

Thomas's pain lessened, with the difference transferred to her. She whined and sobbed like a frightened animal, clutching her head.

Good. Thomas tried to escalate her agony, to punish her with what she'd just given him.

But someone else attacked him, slamming him with pain full force. He screamed. When he shifted his attack to the new tormentor, a third Servant took over.

They were doing tag-team torture.

They were coordinated, whereas Thomas was alone. He hated all Torth, but when he split his focus in order to attack two Torth at once, he lost the necessary savagery. He was capable of solving quintic equations while simultaneously discussing philosophy, but giving a pain seizure was a primal act, not intellectual at all. It was like physical therapy: unpleasant and demanding all of his vast attention.

He could only burrow into one mind at a time. That was hard to do while shaking and chewing the insides of his lips to shreds.

Waves of pain thrashed him, along with the concern radiating from his friends.

Ariock looked helplessly from one Servant of All to the next, silently begging them to stop. As if begging would work. Thomas tried to convey a warning through his agony. If he couldn't succeed against mind readers, then non-telepaths shouldn't even try.

Ariock's mother thrust her arms out, blocking his path. She seemed worried that he might try to intervene in a more physical way.

The pain ended with such suddenness, it left a ringing in Thomas's ears.

He reeled, gasping, his face wet from tears. A string of blood drooled off his lip.

The Servants of All studied Thomas with apparent disinterest, but Thomas sensed reactions crackling throughout their mental audiences. As far as the

Torth Empire was concerned, he should not have been able to harm anyone, let alone a Servant of All.

Perhaps We should adjust his dosage of inhibitor? That message ran back and forth through their audiences, along with images of the cuff around his ankle. *He could be on too low a dosage.*

The Swift Killer knelt and fiddled with the cuff around Thomas's ankle. It must be a drug of some sort. Thomas tried to kick her away, but he was too weak. It was futile.

He managed a defiant glare.

The Upward Governess floated closer. A titanic whirlwind of knowledge churned within her, far more than any person—more than any supercomputer —should be able to contain. Thomas could not process even a fraction of a fraction of that much data.

He gaped at her.

When the Upward Governess addressed the Servants of All, her thoughts had the towering height and mass of a colossus. *If You want Me to evaluate him, then leave. I cannot perform a proper evaluation with all these distractions.*

Thomas continued to stare at her. How could she think coherently with so many millions of lifetimes of absorbed experiences? He felt like he was sitting near an actual goddess of knowledge.

The Swift Killer seized Thomas's wheelchair and moved him off the hovercart, down to the marble floor of the garden.

Cherise tried to dodge past the Torth, to climb over the railing. A Servant of All casually held her back.

No, Thomas thought. *Don't separate us.* He powered his wheelchair, but the battery was nearly dead, and it was useless, anyway. The Swift Killer held his wheelchair firmly in place.

Your friends will be safe. The Upward Governess turned her serene blue gaze on Thomas. *If they behave themselves.*

The hovercart floated away with his friends onboard.

"You need to keep them safe." Thomas spoke aloud, not caring how offensive it was, not caring if they punished him again. The Torth shouldn't get a free pass to steal everything and everyone in his life. He would not cooperate.

Let my friends go. He glared at the Upward Governess, because he suspected that she was truly in charge. The Majority might lead society, and the Servants of All might serve the Majority, but this girl wielded influence over all of them. How could she not? The sheer amount of knowledge she contained was frightening.

You had better not treat them as slaves, Thomas silently told her.

The Upward Governess replayed his own memories. Thomas saw Cherise fluffing his pillow for him, and Vy undressing and sponge-bathing him. The implications were plain. Caretakers and slaves were one and the same. *Wrong!* Thomas seethed. *Friends are not slaves.*

Deep down, though, he felt shaken. What else had this girl absorbed from his life while he sat helpless, occupied with pain and rage? Just how much had she learned about Thomas Hill?

And through him—how much did she now know about humanity? And Earth?

Thomas contained thousands of lifetimes of human memories from the people who had passed through his telepathy range. Would the Upward Governess have trouble sifting through his own database of knowledge?

Ariock looked back helplessly while Vy and Cherise fought against Servants of All, trying to escape. They were going to get hurt if they kept fighting.

But they didn't understand that.

Judging by their glares toward the Upward Governess, they saw her as a spoiled schoolyard bully. They did not see a goddess of knowledge. They did not even see her as a social influencer. They had no idea what she was.

"I'll find you!" Thomas yelled loud enough for everyone to hear.

The Swift Killer jerked his wheelchair. Pain tore apart his thoughts, but it didn't matter. His friends would suffer far worse if they tried to defy the Torth.

"I'll rescue you," Thomas called. "I promise!"

Cherise would trust that promise. She knew how fast Thomas could track down missing items or people. Half of the passersby in this city had stared at Ariock, and all that interest would leave a trail that Thomas could trace.

Just as long as he survived.

That had to be a top priority for all of them from now on.

CHAPTER 3

THE COST OF GODHOOD

Thomas watched Cherise until the hovercart rounded a corner and vanished from sight.

He would keep his promise. He needed to survive so he could figure out a way to rescue Cherise, Vy, Delia, and Ariock.

Enough distractions. The Upward Governess floated nearby. An angelic choir of unseen listeners echoed every thought she had, heightening the impression that she was a goddess. *Only a fool would keep this feral child within sight of the humans that raised him.* She waved four stubby fingers in a dismissal, aimed at the Swift Killer. *Be gone.*

The Swift Killer emanated resentment and reluctance. Nevertheless, she backed away. Soon she was beyond Thomas's telepathy range.

The slaves backed away, as well. Thomas was alone with the towering mental presence.

Perhaps he should cower in fear, but instead, he showed her contempt. She might be a goddess of knowledge, but she was also a thief, and a Torth. He hated her.

She seemed amused by his contempt.

I invented that medicine, Thomas silently reminded her. *NAI-12 rightfully belongs to me.*

The Upward Governess replayed a memory she must have soaked up from Thomas himself. Thomas and Cherise eased the prototype medicine out of its vault, transferring vials into the briefcase.

Her point was obvious. Lawyers and scientists on Earth would have argued that the medicine belonged to Rasa Biotech, not to Thomas. His own colleagues would have condemned him as a thief.

It was actually a valid point.

Thomas swallowed his anger and struggled to be civil. *What do you want with me? Why am I here?*

I merely wish to know you better. The Upward Governess inhaled Thomas's memories with the ruthlessness of a starving child at an all-you-can-eat buffet. *Mm. What a delectable mind.*

Thomas tried to back away. He was never this greedy when soaking up other people's lives.

Or...was he?

Perhaps he absorbed a lot from Cherise. But that was different. She welcomed it.

Well, he supposed he absorbed a lot from Vy, on occasion. And from Mrs. Hollander. And from everyone else who lived in the Hollander home.

And from the lead scientists at Rasa Biotech. His physical therapists and nurses, too. His neurologist. His former foster families. That slave, Gyatch. And perhaps a few hundred other people. It was just so easy to do.

He would have to remember to be more restrained, in the future.

Why restrain yourself? The Upward Governess made a reaching motion, and a slave darted to her with a platter of sugary pastries. *On Earth,* she thought, *you were trapped among very small (primitive) minds, and that severely curtailed your mental growth.* She nibbled on a pastry. *You were a big fish in a small pond, to use a quaint proverb from your upbringing. Among Us (the Torth), you can grow. You can reach your full potential.*

Thomas enjoyed knowledge. That was undeniable.

But he knew that he didn't need more of it. For most of his life, he had hidden his excess knowledge, trying to convince people to treat him like a human being.

He wanted to be human.

He wanted that more than ever.

You always suspected that you did not belong on Earth. The Upward Governess dug through Thomas's memories like someone pawing through a jar of peanut butter to catch as much of it as would stick. *Mm. I anticipated that likelihood.*

Thomas had, indeed, always felt out of place. He had been so different from everyone else.

But none of his fantasies had involved owning slaves.

In his secret imaginings, his biological parents were kind, even heroic. He had dreamed of a home where he would belong, without any pretense or effort or stigmas.

You can have that, the Upward Governess thought. *Here. Among Us (Torth).*

Thomas didn't think so. He wasn't a Torth.

The Upward Governess regarded him with serenity. Her mental audience reared up, their angelic chorus inescapable. *He does not wish to become one of Us?*

But does he actually believe he is a primitive savage?

Perhaps he is mentally unfit?

Due to his flawed pedigree?

Thomas wasn't sure he wanted to learn more about his "flawed pedigree," but he had no choice in the matter. Answers rolled at him, as rough as ocean waves crashing against rocks.

Your biological mother, the distant minds sang...and they showed him a Servant of All.

The Swift Killer.

Thomas reeled. He stared at the sadistic woman, unable and unwilling to believe that she had given birth to him.

He should have known he came from monsters. Nice people didn't abandon their newborn babies in snowy woods at night.

When the Swift Killer saw his stare, her lip curled in a sneer of disgust. She clearly didn't want him.

No, no, the angelic choir assured Thomas.

That is not your mother.

She is a clone.

We (the Majority) terminated the criminal who gave birth to you.

The Swift Killer is merely a clone from the same batch and pedigree.

She was never pregnant.

There are many clones.

Clones.

Thomas sat still, but he wanted to vomit. This was worse than anything he'd imagined. It seemed he did not come from a family, but a breeding program. The Swift Killer was his biological aunt, if not his mother. And his actual mother...

Dead, the Upward Governess confirmed. She conveyed no sorrow, no sympathy. It was just a fact.

Thomas tried to absorb it.

Your flawed pedigree is unimportant, the Upward Governess silently assured Thomas. She ate another pastry, as if this conversation was just idle chitchat. *Very few Torth have pristine pedigrees. It is no big deal (as humans would say). Your potential is much more important than whom your birth donors were. Your potential is all that matters.*

Thomas felt like crying.

But crying would not help his situation. He sensed distant minds muttering to each other about his primitive reactions. His grief. His sorrow. His anger. Intense emotions were unbefitting a Torth.

Perhaps he is too flawed to become a Torth? those distant minds harmonized.

Too emotionally unstable?

Slave-like.

Thomas closed his eyes and willed away the tears he had not shed.

He opened his eyes. If he was going to help Cherise, then he needed emotional strength, not weakness.

He needed to understand what these Torth expected. And how to survive. Nothing else mattered.

His potential is great. The Upward Governess emanated smug satisfaction, as if she had proven a point in a debate. *See?*

At least a billion people examined Thomas through her blue eyes. Their distant conversations crackled like solar flares, making Thomas aware of how insignificant he was, how alone and frail. He felt like an amoeba confronted by the universe.

WE SEE, they chorused.

He pioneered this serum—the Upward Governess conjured a vivid mental image of his NAI-12 briefcase—*using only primitive tools and primitive knowledge. Imagine what he might accomplish if given proper resources?*

Her vast inner audience swirled like ribbons. *Ooh,* they told each other. *Ahh.*

His Torth genetics shine through his primitive upbringing, the Upward Governess went on. *I calculate a 99.88 percent probability that his future ideas will improve Our great and glorious empire.*

That seemed to sway her enormous inner audience. They sparkled with admiration.

His potential should not go to waste, the Upward Governess concluded. *He has a very valuable mind.*

Whereas before the distant voyeurs had been skeptical about Thomas, now they addressed him with warmth.

Mind reader (you), they thought, harmonious.

It has been brought to Our supreme attention
	that you have created (invented) a marvelous serum.
	This serum
	(NAI-12)
		will improve
		Our great and glorious Empire.

Even the discordant notes overlapped, adding to the thunderous melody.

This medicine (an Earth compound),
	very clever of you,
		is estimated to (indirectly) promote the welfare of many billions (trillions)
		of superior (Torth) lives.

Their attention made Thomas feel like a bug under a magnifying glass. He nearly backed away, but the Upward Governess could follow him without effort. Her floating throne was a lot more maneuverable than his clunky wheelchair.

We are impressed. She led the angelic choir like a maestro conducting an orchestra.

> *Because of your contribution (medicine),*
> *We (the Majority of the Torth Empire) have voted*
> *to offer you*
>   *a (unique) opportunity (chance)*
>   *to become (one of Us)*
>   *a god (a Torth).*

The loose symphony trailed off, dissolving into whispered questions. *Does he understand?*

Thomas thought he did understand. This was life or death. He had to agree to become a Torth and consider himself fortunate for such an opportunity.

He tried to work up some gratitude.

Do not concern yourself with gratitude, the Upward Governess thought, and her vast audience agreed. *Gratitude is a slave emotion!* they thundered.

All the same, he was cognizant of this great honor.

The chorus in orbit around the Upward Governess's mind underscored that point. *Yes,* they harmonized.

> *This will be the first time (in the history of Our venerable empire)—*
> *—that We are considering uplifting a feral child (a hybrid raised by savages)—*
> *—to become something (better) a Torth.*
> *We debated for a lengthy time (many minutes).*

Thomas tried to accept the honor. Let the Torth believe he wanted to become one of them. Let them believe he had invented NAI-12 as a "contribution" to their rotten empire. Let the thieving Upward Governess have her loot—for now. He would worry about stealing it back, and freeing his friends, once he gained some privacy and resources.

He realized his mistake a nanosecond later.

The Upward Governess regarded him with pity. Her audience soured, hissing and overlapping.

He may have great potential, they whispered, agreeing with each other. *But he is untrustworthy.*

> *He rejects the honor.*
> *So kill him.*
>   *Kill him.*
>   *KILL HIM.*

The Swift Killer aimed her gloved hand at Thomas.

Her palm glowed in a clover pattern that Thomas would see in his nightmares if he lived. He was going to end up like that slave, Gyatch, torn into chunks. All because he had never learned to guard his secrets. Until now, he'd never needed to.

He could hardly breathe, sickened by the magnitude of his mistake.

Let Us reevaluate the situation. The Upward Governess floated around Thomas, blocking the Swift Killer's line of sight. *I posit that this is a miscommunication.*

The Swift Killer stepped closer. When she entered Thomas's range, he sensed her impatience. *I am an expert in human savages,* the Swift Killer thought. *And trust Me, this child is too feral for rehabilitation. He will never be a Torth.*

His biological aunt.

Thomas studied the clone of his unknown birth mother, the closest thing he had to a biological family. Maybe he could guess why the Swift Killer was so eager to get rid of him. If he was the misbegotten son of her clone sister, didn't that throw her whole lineage—her pedigree—into doubt?

There were problems in that pedigree. A criminal. A feral hybrid. If the Swift Killer corrected her clone's "mistake," then the Torth Majority might begin to forgive her supposed genetic flaws.

Astute. The Upward Governess directed a warm feeling toward Thomas. She appreciated his reasoning.

The Swift Killer narrowed her focus to a bladelike intensity.

Do not interrupt. The Upward Governess flicked mental disparagement at the Swift Killer. Then she went on, addressing her unseen audience. *You see? This child has a sound grasp of logic and rationality. If he feels savage emotions, it is only because that is how he learned to survive among savages. It is merely an act, an ongoing deception so deeply ingrained that it has become subconscious for him. He can be taught to shed that unnatural behavior. He can become a Torth.*

Thomas could not imagine himself cruising through Torth streets, silent and aloof. The idea made him want to sink.

He tried to accept it.

The Swift Killer bared her teeth in a parody of a human grin. *I told You,* she thought to the countless hordes who were tuned in. *Either he is a Torth, or he is a slave. There is no in-between.* She aimed her blaster glove at Thomas. *I vote for killing him.*

I disagree. The Upward Governess watched as a slave dipped a pastry into what looked like cream, then offered it to her. *You (Swift Killer) have mishandled him. You are deliberately provoking the worst behavior from him.*

Distant minds drummed agreement in a staccato rhythm.

The Swift Killer does overreact—

—much like her clone sister.

Perhaps she is just as flawed?

Fear spiked within the Swift Killer. It lasted only a second, but her own mental audience scattered as if she had a plague.

Now then. The Upward Governess wheeled her vast attention away from the Swift Killer, as if she had destroyed a nuisance. *Let Us see if I can change his attitude. I think he will be willing, once he truly comprehends what is being offered.* She enjoyed her pastry.

Thomas forced himself to be receptive. He needed to want to become a Torth. Not just superficially, but for real, if at all possible.

His life depended on it.

Not only his life, but those of Cherise and his other friends.

He needed to allow this hungry, thieving Torth to change his mind.

CHAPTER 4

NEVER WRONG

There is more to being a Torth than power and privilege. The Upward Governess extended a hand. An imaginary orb materialized above her palm, spinning into a glowing blue planet.

Nearby slaves were unable to perceive the miniature planet, since it was composed of pure imagination. But to Thomas, it was impressively marbled with clouds and other details.

We have evolved beyond the need for language or art, the Upward Governess silently explained. *Our language is pure imagination.*

All Torth are connected, many distant minds chorused.

The Megacosm suffuses the galaxy.

The Upward Governess sent the spinning orb to Thomas, and it stopped within his reach. He touched its cool surface, amazed by how real it looked and felt.

Wondrous.

His ability to subitize a lot of data allowed him to imagine things with the vividness of reality, but until now he had never met anyone else with the same depth of imagination.

There is more, the Upward Governess went on. *We are purely honest, unable to lie, unable to deceive each other.*

No lies? Thomas admired that.

Or he tried to. What good was an honest society if they brazenly stole medicine from disabled children and tortured slaves?

Our laws are different from the laws you are accustomed to, the Upward Governess admitted. *You accuse Me of theft, but this is a misunderstanding. All property is communally shared. All Torth own all things. If a resource happens to be limited in supply (such as the case of NAI-12), then the Majority votes on whom to allot that resource to. It usually goes to the highest rank with the greatest need. Such was the case here.*

Thomas wanted to debate the flaws inherent in that system, but he prioritized his questions. Why was his medicine such a limited resource? Surely the Torth could manufacture more of it if they wanted to?

The Upward Governess gazed at him with something like pity. *They (the Torth Majority) refuse to allow any more of your ingenious medicine to enter Our civilization. They held a vote. NAI-12 will remain limited.*

Why? Thomas wondered.

To answer that, the Upward Governess replied in her mind, *I would have to explain (show you) how (galactic) (real) civilization works. That is complex. I could rudely force a ton of sociopolitical information into your head, but it would be far kinder (more civil) for Me to show you how to gain answers of your own volition, and at your own pace.*

Thomas had a sense of her sincerity. She wasn't joking or lying.

How? he wondered.

The Megacosm. Her answer was prim.

He imagined the Megacosm to be something like a mental internet.

It's a bit beefier than the paltry internet of Earth. Her response included something like amusement. Distant minds echoed each other her with a dull sort of surprise.

Doesn't he realize?

We are gods.

We know All.

Indeed. The Upward Governess created a miniature galaxy above her hand, finely detailed. *We own everything in the known universe,* she let Thomas know. *We (Torth) rule all living things. Lesser species (slaves) are governed by their own lusts and passions, whereas We (Torth) are governed by facts and logic. We (Torth) value intellect above all else.*

Thomas could admire the part about valuing intellect.

As for the rest? He had doubts. The Torth didn't seem particularly austere. They might be emotionally restrained, but they clearly had the same weaknesses as humans. Worse, even. None of the humans Thomas knew would torture slaves on a regular basis.

So, if the Torth wanted to pretend they were superior beings? Fine. But they were being self-deceptive.

Oh, I am going to relish his mind. The Upward Governess was too weak to rub her hands together, but Thomas sensed her doing it anyway, in her mind. *He has more potential than anyone I have ever met. And I am never wrong.*

She is never wrong, her audience harmonized.

The distant chorus swelled, leaping ahead of each other. *We do not suffer the mental maladies of primitives or slaves.*

We feel no heavy sorrow or grief.

No panic.

No rage.

No pain of any sort.

Thomas assumed they must drug themselves—and fool themselves.

Wrong, the Upward Governess assured him. *Some Torth do use (tranquility meshes) a mental crutch. But it is not a drug.*

Distant minds chorused, *Tranquility meshes are noninvasive.*

Nonchemical.

Meshes alter brain waves (moods) without any side effects.

Thomas sat back, a bit impressed. Had they bred emotional instability out of their collective gene pool?

But he wasn't like that.

He could ignore his own loneliness and unwashed filthiness, the way he used to under the worst foster parents. But he had limits. He wasn't going to calmly munch on pastries while Cherise got worked to death.

There You have it. The Swift Killer walked around the bulk of the Upward Governess. *He has the limited mind of an animal, and he admits it for All to witness.*

She aimed her blaster glove at Thomas's head.

Thomas felt very vulnerable. With one twitch, his biological aunt could end his life.

Wait. The Upward Governess flared like an unseen nuclear explosion. *This child has just begun to realize how much faster he can communicate without words.* She aimed a question at Thomas. *Do you think it possible that your emotions are similarly unnecessary?*

Thomas stared. The Upward Governess seemed to be offering a metaphorical branch to save his life.

Yes. Yes, he supposed it was possible that his emotions were superfluous.

People called him "the Ego" when they thought he couldn't hear. No one saw him cry into his pillow at night. Not even Cherise knew about that.

As far as Cherise was concerned, he could accomplish anything. Fight crime? Of course. Overcome death? No problem. Fool the Torth Empire? Sure.

Cherise never saw how feeble he was. She purposely ignored how he was too weak to lift a cup, too infirm to use a toilet without help.

Thomas searched for courage within himself. His eyes still stung from his earlier fit of rage. *May I please ask a question?* he silently asked, feeling his way along the edge of an unseen precipice.

Ask, the Upward Governess invited.

If I become a Torth, Thomas wondered carefully, *would it be possible for me to enact the freeing of slaves?*

Disappointment radiated from the Upward Governess. Her distant audience moaned, *No one may free slaves or prisoners.*

That is a crime!

Punishable by death!

The Upward Governess interrupted their litany before it could become a full-blown KILL HIM tornado. *He did not ask if he should do it. He asked whether it is possible.* She sipped a beverage that looked thicker than whipped cream. *Ambition. So rare. I like that.*

This is absurd. The Swift Killer snatched a tablet off a shelf that was half-hidden in flowers and began to swipe its screen, like a gamer intent on beating a level. *He is a danger to society and to individual Torth. I will prove it.*

To Thomas's horror, the floor faded away.

Sunlight flooded the garden as every solid wall, ceiling, and stone tile dissolved into nothingness. Beyond garden hedges, the metropolis stretched to the horizon, hazed by distance. Towers twisted upward for miles. White water churned through a canal far below, half hidden by curved terraces, and he was going to plummet, to smash into that water and drown.

He gripped his armrests. His heart wanted to hammer through his rib cage.

Pathetic, the Swift Killer thought, as if making a presentation. *He ignores all evidence of being indoors—air-conditioning, solid ground—and lets emotions rule him. He is just as mindless as a slave. Let's kill him.*

Nobody else was afraid.

The kneeling slaves apparently felt stone beneath their knees. They must be used to their environment changing in strange ways. It was just another day in the Torth Empire.

So Thomas tried to banish his fear. He assured himself that the sickening view was just a technological illusion, as harmlessly irrelevant as the memories he absorbed.

Hm. The Upward Governess studied Thomas. *I detected his mental idiosyncrasy, but I did not expect it to be this acute.* She beckoned to a slave, and it trotted to her, proffering a tablet. *Let Us see how he behaves once he comprehends his environment.*

The Upward Governess tapped the small screen with pudgy fingers, and the floor blinked back into existence. Terra-cotta tiles stretched to the garden's uneven edges.

Better? she inquired of Thomas.

Thomas nodded, but he couldn't trust his own eyes in this place. The floor might vanish at any second. It looked real, with dirt accumulated in the grout, but it had looked real earlier, too.

Most surfaces in the Torth Empire are coated with adaptive stereopsis cells, the Upward Governess let him know. *They can be programmed to look like (tiles, stone, sand, mirrors, cloth, aerial vistas) anything.* She used abstractions rather than words. Her lesson was fuller than anything Thomas had ever experienced, enriched with technological nuances, diagrams, equations, and even the historical chain of invention. *This floor is actually a mirror, not stone tiles or thin air. We make it look like whatever We wish.* She probed Thomas's mind, like a doctor examining a patient. *Do you understand?*

He stared at her in awe. He understood exactly how adaptive stereopsis illusions worked.

She had conveyed the lesson in less than a second.

Questions piled up inside him, so many it felt like physical pain. *What about the sunlight in this garden?* he wondered, glancing upward. *Is it real?* He felt as if he would get a sunburn if he sat here for too long.

It's real. The Upward Governess mentally showed him how fresh air and sunlight could filter through semipermeable plasmic walls. *Outdoor sensors transmit a real-time view from a tower top, and the walls emulate what's needed.* She held out her beverage container so that a slave could refill whatever milkshake she'd been drinking. *As a Torth, you would own a data tablet so you can master your environment in ways that (primitives) slaves cannot comprehend.*

Thomas forcibly wrenched his mind away from the fascinating subject of Torth technology. Sometimes his mind raced like a roller coaster without safety bars or brakes. He needed Cherise to keep him on the rails so he wouldn't plummet to his doom.

If I join the Torth Empire, he thought, *will I lose any of my current knowledge? Will I lose any part of my mind?*

The distant audience hummed. *You will lose nothing—*

—and gain much.

Images from their lives filtered down to Thomas, and it was like glimpsing mythical Mount Olympus. There were great cities. Streamlined aerial vehicles. Ornate spas. Alien palaces. Wonders beyond any human imagination.

We are never lonely.

We have no use for that which you call money,

for We are gifted with an endless (infinite) supply of everything.

Their imaginations built upon each other, showing off many cornucopias.

As a Torth, they sang, *you would spend every day doing whatever you please.*

Every task (position) (job) is voluntary.

The lowliest Yellow Rank may acquire their own paradise

and (play) (eat) (sleep) (be entertained)

endlessly.

The Upward Governess imagined a glut of decadence that was apparently her home suite. *Torth are never forced to do anything,* she let him know. *We do not feel anything that We do not wish to feel.*

Thomas reached out to touch an imagined starburst that represented power. But…

Would he be forced to torture slaves?

Would the Torth Empire turn him into some kind of sadistic jerk?

We will not ruin your mind, the Upward Governess assured him. *You need not harm slaves. Punishing slaves is entirely your prerogative.*

Billions of distant minds crackled like a forest fire, elaborating on her assurance. *We only require—*

—that you reject your primitive human emotions.

You must cease to acknowledge humans (and other primitives)—

—as anything other than (inferiors) slaves.

Thomas closed his eyes. Torth would never consider him too young, too handicapped, too arrogant, too capricious, or too smart. They would accept him the way he was.

Among Torth, there was no such thing as ignorance.

No deceit.

No loneliness.

Torth communicated in the purest language possible, without inaccuracies or misunderstandings. The most complex ideas could be shared in an instant.

Did he truly belong among humans, where he'd been singled out as different all his life?

Distant Torth surged with impatience, rearing up like storm clouds and tidal waves. *Now, (feral child),*

Decide.

Or else We shall withdraw this opportunity.

Their hum became as dazzling as a volcanic eruption.

No more questions.

No more (primitive) temper tantrums.

Do you want to join Us?

Or do you want to die?

Countless minds piled together, combining into something like a god's thunderous decree.

DECIDE.

They could not be fooled. And they would not accept a weeping child or a traumatized orphan. Thomas knew that he had to reject that side of himself.

Well, hadn't he spent his whole life struggling to do just that?

Child abuse, molestation, torments, crimes… Thomas absorbed awful memories, enough to give him nightmares every time he slept. Sometimes he took painkillers just to get some detachment. If he dared confide in Cherise? That only meant spreading the misery. And then he would have to reabsorb it.

So he never confided in anyone. His burdens were unsolvable accretions, and he endured them alone. Always alone.

Torth were never alone.

Loneliness was an utterly alien concept to a Torth.

Thomas took deep breaths, telling himself that he would function better without misery. If he could truly shed all his loneliness and emotional angst, that might actually free him up to be smarter.

Maybe, without emotions, he would be able to become the hero Cherise needed.

I reject my emotions, Thomas decided. *I will become one of You.*

CHAPTER 5
MONSTROUS

Vy had tried to whisper and gotten punished for it.

She wanted to get off this hellish ride, but two Torth guarded the exit in the railing. More Torth stood at the corners. Their gleaming white bodysuits seemed to lend them superhuman strength. Vy had tried to bolt over the railing, to get back to her foster brother, but one of the Torth had wrestled her with contemptuous ease. Nasty bruises were already forming on her arm under her shirt.

Cherise seemed content to wait for whatever might happen next. Delia slumped in a posture of utter resignation. Neither of them seemed interested in escape, and Vy could not understand that.

Ariock, however...

Vy saw his calculating gaze. He had not attempted to wrestle a Torth—yet—but he might actually have a chance of winning. Even with his wrists shackled together, his inexplicable size might be a match for their unnatural strength.

And he was searching for escape routes.

Vy saw him look over the heads of alien pedestrians and consider doorways and alleys. His problem was that he was too big to go unnoticed. Hiding would be a problem for him. But maybe he was searching for a place to stow his mother?

Ariock felt her gaze. He glanced at her, and Vy nodded, showing that she agreed with his apparent intentions. Ariock looked relieved to be understood. He slid a meaningful gaze of concern toward his mother, hinting that she needed protection. Vy nodded in agreement and indicated Cherise, showing her own concern.

Ariock nodded.

A lot of Vy's tension and fear evaporated. She felt safer with the certainty that Ariock shared her goals. Judging by the way he sized up potential hiding places and threats, he was unlikely to do anything fatally stupid.

Their hovering platform entered a crowded forum, with a shabby grandeur that evoked Grand Central Terminal in New York City. Massive chandeliers dripped with diamonds. Blue vines decorated sandstone walls, divided by fiber-optic flora. Forlorn aliens sat or slept on the floor, like homeless vagabonds in filthy rags.

Here they slowed.

Vy did not like the look of the thorny monsters that approached. The beasts rivaled Ariock for height, but they must weigh a ton, built like rhinoceroses. Overlapping plates made them appear to be armored, although they were actually nude, with rough, pebbly skin in garish hues of copper, bronze, or fiery red.

The monsters assessed Ariock with beady red eyes. Vy had no doubt that they could crush her and simultaneously tear her to shreds with their serrated spikes.

A telepath kicked Ariock with her boot. It seemed a way to get his attention, because she pointed to the opening in the railing. The Torth clearly wanted Ariock to go meet the beasts.

He hesitated.

Vy didn't want to be stranded alone in a world full of hostile aliens. If they got split up? They might never find each other again in this metropolis.

Ariock was looking at her and at his mother, as if seeking confirmation. Then he gripped the railing with his shackled hands and dared to speak. "We stay together."

Vy thought of the loneliness he had endured for ten years. He surely didn't want to be alone among aliens.

His deep voice carried throughout the vast forum. It was as obvious as thunder, as implacable as a boulder. Strolling Torth stopped in midstride. Aliens glanced around and stared at Ariock. A few of them bumped into each other.

There was punishment.

Ariock clenched his jaw and breathed like a steam engine, clearly determined to outlast it. Vy was impressed. These Torth were used to bullying enfeebled aliens and disabled children, but how often did they face someone as strong as Ariock? He might be able to overcome any punishment they threw at him.

Delia screamed in pain.

Ariock immediately stepped off the platform, obedient. The weight differential made the platform float up a few inches. He watched his mother with concern and then relieved gratitude as she covered her face with her hands and whimpered. The pain seizure had apparently ceased.

Vy glared at the Torth. Manipulative bastards.

But there was no way to gauge their reactions, or lack thereof. The ones in bodysuits had no pupils, no gazes.

A cagelike platform pulled up near theirs. This one looked grim, all black steel, its edges sharp with serrated blades.

Thorny monsters loped toward Ariock on their immense knuckles, like armored gorillas. The upright ones carried chains that looked heavy enough to imprison a mammoth. There was a glint of sapience in their beady eyes.

Vy had a bad feeling.

"No!" Delia shouted. "Don't take him!"

She might as well shout defiance at a storm. Her cry ended in a squeak of pain, and she doubled over, clutching her head.

Ariock lunged back toward his suffering mother.

Or he tried to.

A huge chain whipped around his upper arm. Then another. He jerked hard enough to tug a monster off-balance. Ariock seized the railing and weighed it down hard enough to hit the glossy floor, gouging crystal.

The monsters closed in.

One tried to loop a chain around Ariock's chest. Ariock ducked and twisted. Instead of trying to run away, he seized the mammoth chain and yanked it downward. He grabbed one of the monster's huge spikes at the same time and shoved upward.

The spike snapped.

The monster bellowed in pain. Blood oozed out of the wound, blackish crimson.

Ariock held the broken spike like it was some kind of a monster-killing spear. He adjusted his stance, looking ready to stab any monster that came close.

One of the Torth snapped a command in an alien tongue. Vy couldn't guess what it meant, but it sounded harsh.

The monsters edged around Ariock, as wary as gladiators forced into an arena with a rabid lion. Their beady red eyes sized him up. Some of them looked afraid.

But clearly, they had no choice but to obey their Torth masters.

They held the chains taut and ready. Several monsters tackled Ariock, roaring bravely as Ariock tried to stab them or shove them off.

But the outcome was inevitable. They outnumbered Ariock. Each monster outweighed him. Their skin was roughened, as tough as armor. Their joints were weaponized, fringed by thorns. Overall, the monsters looked built for battle.

Ariock looked human.

He was formidable, but he lacked the toughness of military training or gangland brutality. His inexperience with violence was plain. Within seconds, the gang of monsters had overpowered him, wrapped him in chains, and shoved him inside the cage.

They secured Ariock's chains so that he hung there, hardly able to move. One of them seized the broken spike out of Ariock's grasp. Then they slammed the cage door closed.

The monsters exhibited no triumph. They only looked relieved, glad to be done with an unpleasant task.

Vy lost her anger toward the brutes. From their point of view, Ariock must look like a hulking telepath. No wonder they were afraid to hurt him. As far as they were concerned, the Torth had commanded them to imprison another Torth. They had no reason to feel sympathy or kindness toward someone who looked like Ariock.

Or like Vy.

The monsters backed away and scattered. Some of them took up stations in the room, crouching like immense guards.

Ariock hung his head. He looked as resigned as his mother.

Worse. He looked like he thought he deserved to be caged.

The Torth prodded Vy to exit the hovering platform, along with Cherise and Delia, but she hardly noticed. One of the true monsters—a Torth—climbed in front of the cage, onto a control platform. Soon the cage was on the move.

Ariock was gone, driven away through a crowd of staring aliens.

CHAPTER 6

AMONG ALIENS

Cherise found an out-of-the-way place to sit on the burnished floor. Vy and Delia sat against the pillar nearby.

She longed for her sketchbook. A canteen full of water might be a more practical thing to desire here, but drawing felt vital to her. It was the same way Thomas must feel about his laptop, or perhaps even his wheelchair.

She sketched with her finger on the floor. At least she didn't have to look directly at the aliens to study them, since the polished floor reflected colors and shapes.

The most common type of aliens were the midget-size gray people, with owlish beaks and deep-set eyes beneath brow ridges. They all wore slave collars and rags. Folded hats framed their faces, with flaps on either side. These little aliens were everywhere, but they weren't the only type that wore slave collars.

Huge furry caterpillars with droopy bulldog-like faces waddled on six legs. Some of those used only four of their legs, freeing up a pair of arms so they could gesture or carry items. One of them teetered on just its hind legs, encircling a stack of trays with its lower and upper arms.

Serpents rippled gracefully on translucent, feathery limbs, glowing with bioluminescence. There were other, stranger species. The creepiest alien had a triple-jointed neck, enabling it to swivel its huge, bony, sickle-shaped head in any direction. If that alien extended its neck all the way up, Cherise figured it would be taller than Ariock.

But perhaps none of the aliens were all that weird, in comparison to the humanlike Torth.

Torth lounged in garden swings or in floating chairs. Unlike the aliens, they were unhurried. Thomas would probably love to swap his wheelchair for one of those maneuverable hoverchairs.

Instead of rags, Torth wore layers of rich fabrics. Their outer garments shimmered with geometric patterns, some of which changed under light, like holograms. Some Torth wore bioluminescent accents or feathery mantles. They all wore slippers. Powder and jewels decorated their hair.

A few of them ate or drank, but if they enjoyed anything, they gave no sign of it. Most Torth simply gazed into space. Their blank stares reminded Cherise of her ma on a drunken binge.

Most Torth strolled past. But sometimes they stopped to silently inspect the humans. Cherise wanted to cringe away whenever that happened. Their eyes were unsettling hues of iridescent yellow, green, amber, or fiery red.

And their gazes burned with knowledge, as if they could see everything about Cherise Chavez, from the day she was born to the day she would die.

Worse—they touched.

They stroked her hair, like she was a dog. They rubbed the insulated fabric of her coat.

One pair of elderly lady twins snatched Cherise's glasses and took turns peering through the lenses. When the twinned ladies dropped the glasses, Vy saved them by sheer luck and fast reflexes. Had she been a second slower, Cherise would have been effectively blind.

Another Torth crone stole Delia's ring.

It looked like a wedding band, gold worked into geometric knots. Delia watched every movement and sobbed quietly after it was gone.

A hulking female Torth with red eyes robbed Vy of her corkscrew earrings. Those were Vy's favorites.

An uncaring male Torth stole Vy's keys…and their cell phones. The batteries were running low and there was no signal, but although the phones were useless, Cherise felt sick once those were gone.

Her phone had held her music. Photos. Emails. Without it, she felt as if she had disappeared.

"You have no names to Us, who are above names."

The speaker was a pudgy, bald man with a face that Cherise would have considered genial in a human context. Brown eyes made him look downright human. And he spoke English! That was enough to bring tears to her eyes after such a long time without words.

Alien slaves glanced his way. Until he'd spoken, the loudest sound was an occasional cough.

"You have no voice to Us," the man continued in his husky tone. He locked his hands together. "We are above voice. Your sole purpose is to obey and serve. Failure means your death."

Cherise had an urge to punch this bald telepath in his smug little mouth. She wished Ariock was still with them, even if he did nothing but loom like a living cliff.

We have skills, Cherise thought, just in case the Torth had failed to soak up her skills and memories. *I can draw. And my foster sister is a nurse.* Surely their abilities put them a notch above menial slave labor?

The bald man turned his amiable gaze on her. "Your skills," he said, "are beneath Our needs."

Well. That was rude.

"If you attack a mind reader," the man went on, "you will be punished with torture and execution. This is your only warning."

The Torth were like her ma in so many ways.

Survive, Cherise reminded herself. Survival had to be her top priority until Thomas could rescue her.

He had promised.

And Thomas never quit his ambitions, even if the odds were stacked incredibly high against him. He had led a multimillion-dollar biotech project, even if his involvement was unofficial and unsalaried. He had persuaded their foster mother to allow him to work full-time, like an adult. He never let anyone stop him from doing what he needed to do.

He would find a way around the Torth.

The bald Torth droned on. "You belong to any mind reader who claims you." He assessed Vy, as if expecting an argument. "Commands from high ranks take precedence over low ranks."

Delia sneered, and Vy wrapped an arm around her, stifling whatever arguments she might make.

Good. They needed to protect each other. In a world as brutal as anything Cherise's ma would create, they were all orphans. They were all abused children, without rights or privileges.

The pudgy Torth continued in a bored tone. "Slaves may not possess or hide weapons. Slaves may not pilot vehicles. Slaves may not escape. Expect death for breaking any law." He indicated their necks. "The collar keeps you in usable condition. Seek food when the collar shocks you. Seek your sleeping quarters when it stops glowing."

Cherise tried to pry the collar away from her skin. It stuck there like a leech, snug and oily.

She felt its vile presence every time she swallowed.

"This hall guard will lead you to your sleeping quarters." The bald Torth beckoned to one of the enormous, thorny monsters.

Its pebbly hide was more orange than red, gold, or bronze. It shuffled toward them, its spinal ridge rising high above its low-slung head.

Vy and Delia apparently wanted nothing to do with the hall guard. They scrambled to their feet and backed away.

"Serve well or die," the bald Torth said in a tone of finality.

With that, he ambled away, hands clasped behind his back, apparently uncaring whether they served well or died.

Cherise stood. The hall guard could crush her with ease, and it looked bred for violence. More telling—it did not wear rags or a slave collar. She had not seen any of the thorny beasts performing manual labor. She suspected these monsters were more like pets than slaves.

The hall guard flared its huge nostrils, as if wondering what humans smelled like.

Vy gripped Delia. They looked prepared to run.

But there was no escape here. Survival was the only option.

The hall guard gave Cherise a long, disbelieving gaze. It sized her up. She stood her ground.

After a moment, the beast seemed to come to an internal conclusion. It shuffled away.

"Serve well or die." That was the sort of ultimatum that Cherise's ma would approve of. The only way to survive was to obey. For now.

She followed the monster.

Vy and Delia looked reluctant, but they followed at a distance.

The hall guard proved easy to follow. Pedestrians had to swerve around its orange-gold bulk. The guard led them past aliens, past other guards, and through a vast exit. Soon they were moving down a busy indoor street. Skylights showed glimpses of angular towers that seemed to defy gravity, stretching for miles into the green sky.

Aliens scampered away when they caught sight of the humans. They stared at their slave collars.

Cherise inwardly had to admit that humans and Torth did look alike. She hoped the similarities were just due to convergent evolution. She didn't want to contemplate other explanations.

Like…were humans a science experiment?

And what about Thomas? What was he? Human or Torth?

It didn't matter, Cherise assured herself. Thomas was a member of the Hollander family. His biological parents meant nothing. He would rescue her, even if…

Well.

Even if he had to pretend to be a Torth.

Cherise imagined Thomas splashing around in a swamp full of hungry alligators. He had so looked helpless when that obese Torth girl stole his medicine, so terrified.

So isolated.

Cherise wished she could have said goodbye to him. Or wished him luck. Or offered him some gratitude.

Why hadn't that occurred to her?

Thomas might die in this endeavor, and she had not even acknowledged that. None of them had. People expected greatness from "the Einstein of the twenty-first century," and they never even considered the burdens he soaked up every day.

They might as well have said, "Go rescue us, Thomas, and make it snappy. Oh, you're dying and you can't walk? Don't let that become a problem."

Cherise felt like a selfish idiot.

I'll get a chance to thank him, she assured herself. Of course she would. Thomas was the best survivor in existence. He might need a few days, but he would show up. He kept his promises, no matter what.

Vy clutched Cherise's arm, eyes wide with fear.

And no wonder.

Down ahead, the street looked dirtier, choked with alien foot traffic. Thousands of collared aliens emerged from a monstrous tunnel. Just as many slaves rushed into the tunnel, which emitted a stench like urine.

A gusty murmur came from the vast tunnel, as well, like the distant sound of an overcrowded high school gymnasium. Not a place she wanted to visit.

The hall guard turned to see if they were following. When it saw their hesitation, it waited for them to catch up.

Aliens gawked at the three humans. Many veered away, their gazes judgmental. Cherise guessed that she looked very out of place. It seemed Torth did not deign to enter this unpleasant tunnel.

No Torth might mean no punishments.

People might dare to talk out loud inside that tunnel.

Cherise tugged Vy and Delia until they got moving, approaching the tunnel like death row inmates. They descended away from sunlit boulevards and crystal fountains, down into a dim, corrugated metal cave with grimy walls.

This was a whole other city, dark and noisy and overwhelmingly weird.

Aliens bargained with each other in a foreign language, their guttural speech peppered with clicks. Cramped alleyways twisted between a warren of rickety scaffolds, hung with supplies and rusty pipes. Glowing tubes of light snaked overhead. Aliens nuzzled each other in dark corners, like teenagers skipping class and trying not to get caught.

Cherise led her friends deeper and deeper, grateful for the bulky guard who shielded them from everything ahead. This was worse than school. The alien slaves had no pity in their murderous eyes. Whenever they caught sight of the humans, they clammed up and glared.

"I think we can talk here," Vy said in a quiet voice.

The hall guard swung around, snorting like a warhorse. Spikes popped up around its joints. Vy leaped back.

But Cherise saw fear in the guard's reddish eyes. Clearly, it could not read minds. It was judging them based on their appearance.

"We are not Torth." Cherise pointed to her slave collar.

After a minute of intense scrutiny, the hall guard seemed to dismiss them as a nonthreat. It shuffled around and continued to plod onward.

"Should we keep following it?" Delia scanned the tunnel, with its crooked blind alleyways. "Jeez. This place gets weirder and weirder."

"I think we'd better stay with the guard." Cherise huddled in her coat, trying to look in every direction at once. "We could get killed here."

"If it's a choice between serving well or death," Delia said darkly, "I'll take death."

Vy gave her a worried look. "Don't say that."

Delia peered back with frustration. "Face the facts. We're dead already. We have no power here."

Vy seemed to wilt.

"Thomas," Cherise reminded them.

"The kid?" Delia shook her head. "I'm sorry, but let's be real. Tact isn't his strong suit. He's going to offend the Torth, and it's not like he can run away or defend himself. I think he's more doomed than the rest of us."

Vy looked hopeless.

She must have forgotten about the doctor who predicted that Thomas would die before his tenth birthday. How many times had Thomas beaten the odds against death? When he was determined, nothing could stop him.

"He said he'll rescue us." Cherise forced each word out, trying not to let the sharpness of those words rip her throat apart. "He never lies."

Vy and Delia stared at her.

"We can't…" Cherise wished she could transform her thoughts into elegant persuasion, like Thomas. "We should not give up on him."

Vy straightened, as if newly determined. "I'm not giving up."

"You're right." Delia's shoulders seemed to loosen. "Maybe I was too quick to judge him."

Cherise held their gazes, hoping they were sincere and not just humoring the mute girl. She led the way forward.

CHAPTER 7
IN SEARCH OF SAFETY

Privately, Vy was just as concerned about Ariock as she was about Thomas.

Did the big guy have enough emotional fortitude to endure a lot of alien unfriendliness? Ariock was twenty-two years old, the same age as Vy, yet he was so much less experienced. He'd missed out on high school and college.

Vy had worked in a hospital's trauma center. She knew how to perform triage. She was trained to handle high-stress situations.

She had helped her mother to raise children with disabilities, foster kids who were the victims of abuse and trauma.

She chased storms. She volunteered to work with troubled teens. She saw blood and death up close fairly regularly.

Ariock? He hadn't left his mansion in ten years.

As they plodded through stinking, overcrowded tunnels, Delia seemed like she wanted to ask for reassurance. She opened her mouth to speak several times. Vy could guess what she was thinking as alien slaves shot resentful or hostile glares their way. If these downtrodden aliens hated the very sight of Vy, Cherise, and Delia…then they would surely hate Ariock.

"I'm worried about Ariock, too." Vy reached for Delia's hand and squeezed it gently.

Delia squeezed back. She seemed grateful for the contact.

"I've never lost track of him," Delia said after a moment. "There's never been a time when I didn't know where he was."

"This must be really hard for you. I'm sorry." Vy felt sympathy for Delia, but most of her sympathy went to Ariock. At his age, he should have been able to date someone. Go to college. Maybe go on an adventure, with all his money? But no. Instead, he'd allowed his sour-faced mother to dominate his life.

"You'll never meet a kinder person," Delia said. "The way they attacked him and put him in that cage…it doesn't make any sense. I know he looks intimidating, but he can't help the way he looks. He's gentle. He would never hurt anyone."

"I believe you." Vy could tell that much, just from having hung out with Ariock for a while. "If the Torth can read minds, they must be misreading him."

"Right!" Delia sounded glad to have someone on her side. "He doesn't even like violent video games. He doesn't read or watch horror. He likes comedies. And sci-fi and fantasy books. You know, geek stuff."

Vy liked geek stuff herself. She nodded.

"Thomas read his mind," Cherise put in, huddled up in her parka. "And he thought Ariock was cool."

"Totally," Vy agreed. "I would trust Thomas's opinion way more than a zillion Torth."

Delia wrapped her arms around herself. "I guess he did hit it off with Ariock."

"He did," Vy confirmed.

They trudged for a while, listening to the echoey babble of alien voices. Vy was increasingly aware of how many hostile stares they attracted. She almost wished her slave collar would glow, just to draw attention to the fact that she wore it. Tattered rags might help them blend in.

Delia was shivering in her pajamas.

"Here." Vy removed her parka and wrapped it around Delia's shoulders. "You need this more than I do."

Delia protested weakly. "No. Are you sure?"

"I'm warm enough." Vy plucked at her sweater.

Delia put on the parka and huddled inside it. "There's something you need to know about me."

The solemnity of her tone drew Vy's attention.

"Pancreatic cancer." Delia touched her midsection. "I have less than six months to live."

Vy wanted that to be a tasteless joke.

But when she met the older woman's gaze, she saw resignation and authenticity. Delia was dying. No wonder she sounded so defeated, so ready to give up.

"Oh." Vy grasped Delia's hand. The gesture was inadequate. Words were inadequate. She tried anyway. "I'm so sorry."

"Sorry," Cherise said in her quiet voice.

"Ariock doesn't know," Delia said. "I figured I had enough time to tell him." Her bitter tone made it clear that she no longer believed that.

"We'll find him." Vy hoped that was more than an empty reassurance. Ariock would stand out in this city, even among all the alien sights.

"I've been in and out of St. Andrew's Hospital for months," Delia said. "Each time, I combined it with a shopping trip, so Ariock assumed I'd been shopping. But he was starting to suspect. He noticed that I've lost weight. And I've been busier than usual. I was making final preparations."

"I'm so sorry." Vy didn't need to mention that she worked at St. Andrew's. For all she knew, she might have even seen Delia in the parking lot or in the cafeteria.

"I didn't know how to tell him." Delia sounded defensive. "He's lost so many people. You have no idea. Everyone in his life is gone or dead, except for me."

"I'm sorry." Vy studied Delia with fresh respect and more pity than she was comfortable with. "Have you been dealing with this alone?"

"Of course. It's not like I go to social events."

Vy winced at her own thoughtlessness. She glanced at Delia's ring finger, now devoid of its ornament. She was a widow.

"I'm used to being alone," Delia stated. "I've lived in the Dovanack mansion for thirty-plus years, and it was an isolated place even when we employed a household staff." She gave Vy a wry glance. "You know, I didn't grow up rich." Her accent broadened. "Boston. The South End."

"Oh, wow." Vy figured there must be a story there.

"I got a full-ride scholarship to MIT," Delia said. "That's where I met William Dovanack. He was…" She shook her head, and Vy saw traces of love. "Like me. He didn't fit in. We both felt shame about our families. In my case, it was normal stuff—I had a judgmental harridan for a mother. And my father divorced her. He was never around."

Vy nodded in understanding. Her own father had been absent for most of her life.

"Will had bigger problems," Delia went on. "His mother was a hard-core alcoholic, and his father was suicidally depressed. But Will couldn't easily uproot himself and forget about his family the way I could. Golden handcuffs, they say. Wealth is a trap. Will couldn't leave his mother without turning his back on a fortune."

Vy had seen that dynamic with ultrarich kids from dysfunctional families. Will must have felt driven to earn a degree, to gain a job that would allow him financial independence.

"His father died that winter," Delia said. "Just a few months after Will and I met. He shot himself."

Vy winced.

"And Will was the glue holding his family together," Delia said. "His mother wasn't on speaking terms with her own family, and she was falling apart, alone in that mansion. So Will took a sabbatical. And I made the choice to stick with him."

Vy gave a nod of respect. If there was one thing she was familiar with it, it was the aftermath of family dysfunction. All her foster siblings came from broken families.

And wealth, she knew, was not a panacea.

Child abuse happened among the wealthy as well as the poor. If anything, rich parents could afford to sweep their transgressions under a rug. They could hire as many psychiatrists, attorneys, and nannies as they wanted in order to hide their neglect or shift blame elsewhere.

"My mother-in-law was almost as bad as my actual mother," Delia went on, her tone dry. "She had a problem with me. And she thought my baby was cursed."

"What do you mean?" Vy asked.

"She claimed Ariock gave her nightmares," Delia explained. "She dreamed that he would grow up to become a storm. Like, a thunderstorm."

Vy quirked her face, showing what she thought about that.

Yet, deep down, she wondered. Had Ariock's grandmother been a tiny bit prophetic? Ariock wasn't a storm, but he did tower like a thunderhead.

"Crazy, right?" Delia said. "That whole side of the family believed crazy things. They were paranoid beyond reason. That's why they built the Dovanack mansion way out in the woods."

Vy had wondered about that.

"Will eventually got her to move out." Delia touched her missing wedding band. "He bought her a beach condo, and that was that."

The conversation was a good distraction, a way for Vy to escape the fact that she was trudging through an alien labyrinth. But she had to pay attention when the hall guard ducked into a narrower tunnel. Cherise followed, and so did Vy and Delia.

Vy shoved her hands in her pockets, trying to stay warm. "Would you mind if I ask you a personal question?"

"Go ahead," Delia said.

"Why did you keep Ariock sequestered away from the world?"

Delia looked ashamed.

"I don't mean to sound judgmental," Vy hastened to add. "I get that it was his decision, too. I'm sure you did a good job with homeschooling him. I just wondered—"

"You might as well know." Delia tugged the parka closer, like a protective shawl. "There's no reason to keep secrets anymore." She gestured at the tunnel walls, which oozed with alien slime or mold.

Vy waited. She sensed Cherise walking along beside her, also waiting to hear the answer.

"Ariock tried to kill himself," Delia said.

"Oh." Vy almost wished she hadn't asked. She felt guilty, like she had uncovered something best left unsaid. "I'm sorry."

Delia waved that away. "You know how cruel kids can be to each other?" Vy and Cherise both nodded.

"Well, school was torture for him," Delia said. "The last straw was when one of the little bullies posted a video of him on social media. It was meant to make fun of how tall he was. There was a comparison to Bigfoot."

Vy winced.

"Our hired help, Tricia, showed it to me," Delia said. "But I couldn't help but notice that she had shared the video."

Vy wanted to feel surprised, but she did not. Ariock must have drawn attention even as a kid in grade school.

"I thought I was protecting him." Delia sounded ashamed. "But you know what? You're right. Nothing I did protected him, because here we are." She hung her head. "He's alone. And he might never see me again."

Vy wanted to hug the older woman. Delia no longer looked stern. She was frail and vulnerable.

"I would have hired tutors for Ariock," Delia said. "But he's really afraid of strangers." She seemed to reconsider her words. "Not because he's ashamed of the way he looks. At least, I don't think that's the whole reason. It's because so many people in his life have died. He thinks people will either hurt him or they'll die and leave him forever."

"We never should have barged in on you." Vy felt as if she would regret that for the rest of her life.

But Delia surprised her. She wrapped her arm around Vy's in a gesture of friendship.

"Don't regret that," Delia said. "Please."

The hall guard ducked into an even smaller tunnel. Its spinal crest dragged along the ceiling, and its shoulder spikes scraped along steely walls. Its bare feet splashed through puddles.

Vy tried to walk around the wet piles here and there. The stench was hard to get used to. Was this a sewage pipe?

Uneven doorways opened into darkness. Vy didn't want to peer into those whispering abysses.

"I could have told you to go away," Delia said. "Instead, I let you meet Ariock, because you looked friendly and I felt desperate. I mean, really desperate. I was searching for someone who might be kind to him. A friend. Or a caretaker." She touched Vy's arm. "Since I can't be there for him, long term."

Vy wasn't sure any of them could make long-term plans anymore.

Up ahead, the hall guard shuffled to a stop. It assessed them with beady eyes, then swept its head toward one of the crude doorways. That looked like an invitation to enter.

"No." Delia backed away.

Cherise walked toward the opening, stepping over a puddle of filth. "I think the hall guard has a job," she pointed out. "It might get pissed off if we give it trouble."

That was a fair point.

Vy leaned toward the uneven doorway. She peered into a dark, grimy room.

Aliens sat on shelves, like soldiers in an overcrowded barracks. Every face looked malevolent. Every alien, even the small ones, seemed ready to tear the humans apart with beaks or claws.

Vy backpedaled. "Thomas, save us," she said, as if it was a prayer.

She couldn't imagine ever feeling safe again.

CHAPTER 8
FERAL

Emotions are a hindrance, millions of Torth thought, harmonizing with each other.

Emotions are a burden.

Emotions are the primitive flaw in slaves that separates them from Us.

...?

The silent symphony trailed off, swirling with expectation. They wanted to know what Thomas thought.

Thomas forced himself to meet pitiless stares. Eight Torth surrounded him, seated within his range of telepathy. These eight were the official conductors of this Adulthood Exam. However, Thomas sensed an ever-shifting audience of distant Torth peering through their empty white gazes, and he understood that the huge audience was what truly mattered. The audience was his judge and jury.

Sure. Thomas wasn't going to dare argue with countless millions of Torth. *Emotions are a flaw. I agree.*

The testers exchanged glances without actually moving their heads or their unseen pupils. They sought clarity.

Do you (child) agree that intense emotions are a handicap?

Thomas could not avoid this question or lie. He needed to reveal his honest opinion.

Well. He supposed that volatile emotions were, indeed, a problem. Depression could cripple an otherwise remarkable person, like Cherise. He had lived in enough group homes to be familiar with rage and self-hatred and fear and shame and all their negative effects.

Even positive emotions caused problems. Lust made people act like buffoons just to impress someone.

The audience approved. *Awareness of this truth is correct.* Their thoughts lapped together, forming colorful patterns without words. *Correct, but insufficient. You (child) must be capable of suppressing your own volatile emotions.*

Yet their interwoven thoughts carried faint whiffs of mood.

Thomas sensed mild disdain from some and vague restlessness from others. Mild curiosity sparked here and there.

Subtle moods are not debilitating, the Torth audience let him know.
Subtle moods do not interfere with rational thought,
and are therefore permissible.

Thomas nodded his understanding. The Torth reminded him of Japanese Noh performance, a type of theater that relied on a repertoire of emotional symbolism.

He needed to limit his own reactions. No more tears. No more fits of rage. Surely he could manage it?

Instead of thinking of this as a major personality change, he would approach it like an exam. It was just another workday on his path to survival.

A slave slunk from one tester to another, offering a tray of beverages.

Anger seethed inside the slave. Apparently, he had received news about the murder of a friend, and he wanted to throw hot soup into the faces of the slave masters. Instead, he served them. He wanted to survive.

Thomas tightened his mouth. How were the Torth able to function around such powerful emotions? The testers didn't even seem to care.

But that was the key, Thomas realized.

Coolheaded rationality was superior to a mercurial temperament. It was a fact. Even humans knew it. In stories, gurus and other mentor characters proved their superiority to hotheaded youths.

Weren't the Torth sort of like Spock, or Luke Skywalker, rejecting familial bonds and anger and fear?

Maybe an uncaring attitude was healthy. And smart.

Correct, the distant audience chorused in approval.

Now let Us test—

—whether you (child) are capable of behaving in a civilized, rational manner,

no matter what.

The atrium began to morph into someplace else. Golden pillars shaped like vines faded away, becoming bloodstained metal walls. Mold fuzzed the corners. The skylights vanished, and the aqua-green sky became an oppressively low stone ceiling.

Thomas sat alone in a dungeon that stank like a sewer.

A slow chill went through him. He barely sensed the nearby testers. Their audience went quiescent.

He shivered in air that wasn't cold or humid yet felt cold and humid. He was trapped in some kind of alternate reality, created by the interwoven imaginations of the testers.

He didn't like feeling so overpowered and helpless. He felt so…so…

Not afraid, he warned himself.

A skeletal, naked woman hung by her wrists from the dungeon ceiling.

As Thomas noticed her festering sores and the bones that stretched her sallow skin, he reminded himself that none of this was real. Each tester contributed a layer of nuance to this scene. Thomas couldn't see them, yet he did sense them. They must have choreographed and rehearsed this "exam question" in advance.

So it was all fake. Like a Hollywood movie. No big deal.

Thomas noted her welts with emotional detachment. Her mind—fake, he reminded himself—was a guttering candle. Matted blond hair hid her bloodied face.

Witness your mother, the testers chorused.

The revelation nearly plunged Thomas into shock. This was a replayed memory, he realized. This tortured woman was his birth mother. A vivid memory of her, anyway.

He pretended that he was being interviewed. None of this should affect him. So what if his birth mother had endured torture? He had never known her. For all he knew, she deserved it.

Sex was her crime, the concert of testers sang.

We (Torth) do not have sex.

She broke that law.

She committed bestiality with a primitive.

Witness.

The scene changed, becoming a motel room somewhere on Earth, with prints of lighthouses on the walls. An AC unit rattled.

Thomas felt like a sweaty woman having sex, riding atop an unidentifiable blur.

He desperately wanted to disengage from the erotic pleasure. He was his own mother having sex with his own unknown father. This was obscene. It was wrong on so many levels, he wanted to…

No.

His mother and father were just bucking bodies. He didn't need to feel anything. After all, he had soaked up hundreds of sexual memories from various people. Why should this be any different?

His mother's long-ago lust meant nothing.

This was simply a history lesson, a memory shared by many Torth.

Thomas rode out her orgasm with clinical detachment. He tried to think of it as a physical therapy session. Nothing personal.

Very good, the distant audience sang in approval.

You are doing well (thus far).

Thomas braced himself for more surprises. Sure enough…

Your (criminal) birth mother went to Earth for a (mission) purpose. The testers showed him memories from various Torth perspectives.

It seemed that his mother used to send reports through the Megacosm while she masqueraded as a school nurse. She had used primitive equipment in order to draw blood samples from an extremely tall fifth grader named Ariock Dovanack.

She had spied on the Dovanack family.

Why?

Because the Dovanacks were illegal descendants of a Torth criminal. The Torth Majority wanted to study them and gather scientific knowledge before destroying the illegal family.

Thomas's birth mother had dutifully shared everything she learned. But at some point during her mission on Earth, she'd begun to suffer from an unfamiliar malady. Nausea in the morning. A possible parasitic growth in her abdomen. Her inner audience experienced every fluctuation of her hormones, and they chastised her for mood swings that bordered on illegal.

Pregnancy was an alien concept to the Torth.

After all, Torth grew their fetuses in artificial wombs on baby farms. They avoided the mess of pregnancy and birth and childcare.

By the time *(the Lone Assassin)* Thomas's biological mother comprehended what was happening to her mammalian body, it was too late. Abortion would have been dangerous and illegal in any country on Earth. Rather than attempt a dangerous operation, she had dropped out of the Megacosm.

She had gone rogue.

Criminal Torth sometimes try to escape justice by going rogue. Famous incidents flashed through the minds of many Torth. Every rogue Torth was caught and punished with death by torture.

The worst criminals, they went on,
    hide among Our primitive (human) genetic cousins.
    Servants of All hunt rogues like that
    and drag them to justice.

Shrieking cries of pain exploded in Thomas's hearing. He flinched, suddenly back in the dungeon.

Witness, the testers chorused.

Red Ranks forced his disgraced mother to twist her own skin off with pincers.

Disfigured and mad, she was dragged through a dark prison known as the Isolatorium, past other tormented renegades, where a black abyss awaited her. Alone in that darkness, she clawed out her own eyes.

Hands that could have held a baby instead ripped her face apart.

Bloody chunks slipped through her fingers.

Blood seeped from her ruined eye sockets.

She shrieked until her fingers punctured her throat.

Thomas seethed at his own helplessness. The Torth had no right to label him a "savage" when they were a bunch of brutal, overly entitled murderers. They were *(no) (not savages)…*

He exhaled.

His mother was dead. He couldn't change that.

He needed to stay rational, logical, and emotionless. Grief or anger could not save her—or himself. Anyway, her death shouldn't matter anymore. It was history, twelve years gone, a mere memory preserved in Torth minds.

She disposed of the evidence, the testers' minds whispered inside him.

You.

Of course. Thomas's very existence was evidence of a Torth crime. Unlike his mind-reading brethren, he had not been raised in the carefully controlled scientific environment of a baby farm. He was the result of an illegal action.

Now he knew why his birth mother had left him in the woods, in the cold and in the dark.

After a lifetime of suppressing her emotions, maybe it had been easy for her to walk away.

We (the Torth Majority) punished her for dropping out of the Megacosm, the distant Torth audience informed him, merciless.

For going rogue.

And when We probed her mind—

—and learned that she had caved into lust and primitive emotions,

We punished her for bestiality.

Thomas sensed that the Torth considered humans to be like apes in comparison with themselves. In some dim, distant, forgotten past, according to Torth lore, ancient aliens had uplifted a group of prehistoric hominids from Earth and transplanted them to another world. There they had evolved to become the Torth.

But, the distant Majority went on.

We never suspected that she had been pregnant

or that she had given birth.

She carried that secret into death.

It was only later—

—through primitive human media—

—that We learned of your existence, child.

Cross-species Torth hybrids were so rare as to be mythical. Such hybrids had only happened two or three times in history, and all those cases were unverified. That included Thomas. The Torth Empire had been unable to discover the identity of Thomas's biological father, so they could not declare with absolute certainty that he was a Torth-human hybrid.

This child is too much like Us to be half human, many Torth insisted.

Human genes would diminish (ruin) Our superior genetics.

Surely the child is fully Torth?

Thomas reminded himself that his biological father didn't matter. The unknown man might have been a lumberjack or a billionaire playboy. Did it matter? No. Torth had no families.

Distant Torth chorused in approval. *Your genetic pedigree is irrelevant.*

Even if your male parent was a pathetic human,

the primitive left no trace of his inferior genetics.

For contrast, they imagined Ariock. Apparently, the Torth Majority believed with 99 percent certainty that Ariock was a human-Torth hybrid. His growth disorder was a verifiable Torth mutation. There was overwhelming proof that Ariock was descended from a Torth criminal. But although Ariock had verified Torth ancestry, the percentage was in doubt.

Ariock's human traits were more obvious than his Torth traits. Ariock could not read minds or even detect moods. He had the limited mental scope of a primitive human.

Thomas wanted to delve into the Torth Majority's knowledge about Ariock—like, why did so many Torth regard him as a dangerous monster?—but the testers guided Thomas's attention back toward himself. He was taking an exam. He needed to focus on whatever the Majority dictated that he focus on.

Your (mother) female parent was once considered to be someone special, the Majority chorused.

The Lone Assassin.

She had promising potential.

Better than her clones.

She was on a fast track to become a future Commander of All Living Things.

That was why—

—she was selected out of hundreds of elite candidates—

—to study the Dovanack family.

The Majority had sent her into the wildlife preserve known as Earth to blend in among the primitive natives. But then she had gone rogue. She had severed herself from the Megacosm, losing contact with the Majority not just for a few hours, but for many weeks.

We were suspicious.

So the Majority had sent several Servants of All, including her clone siblings, to her last known location on Earth.

They had found her.

They had probed her mind.

No one could keep secrets when a crime was suspected. The Torth Majority suspected that she had gone rogue in order to indulge in primitive pleasures, and that was exactly what they learned from her mind. They shared and reshared her crime of bestiality in the Megacosm for all to see.

She had earned death by torture.

The dungeon vanished, and Thomas found himself back in the sunny atrium with its gleaming golden pillars, sculpted like vines. But he kept thinking about his mother.

Few Torth ever gained and then lost so much status.

Few Torth ever went rogue or had sex. She had been a rarity.

His mother had died without thinking of the infant son she had abandoned. Thomas used to fantasize about his birth mother, but she had never fantasized about him. Not once.

The eight testers pinned him with their gazes.

Thomas sensed their anticipation. They thought that he might rage against his uncaring criminal of a birth mother. After all, she had trashed him. She had gotten rid of the evidence of her crime.

The Torth seemed oblivious to another possibility.

When that nameless Servant of All had wrapped her newborn infant in an inadequate dish towel, she had also wrapped him in another kind of protection: anonymity. Nonexistence.

If she had dared to remember her abandoned baby, then the Torth Empire would have known that an infant mind reader was living illegally on Earth, and they would have scooped him up and thrown him in a baby farm.

We would have killed you, many minds whispered in answer to his pondering.

As a baby, you lacked potential.

Oh. Of course.

It was nothing personal. Thomas understood. In his infancy, all he had been was a squalling bundle of neediness.

Now? He had potential.

He dared not feel anything like respect for the woman who had sacrificed her status, her sanity, and her life in order to give her child a chance to grow up. And not only to grow up, but to do so in a vastly different culture than what she had known.

She was a mental deviant, Thomas thought. *I am ashamed to be associated with her.*

He remained dry-eyed.

But deep down, he felt as if he came from someone who mattered.

CHAPTER 9
TORTH WITH NAMES

Kessa sat up on her bunk shelf. The whole city had come to a standstill for that weird procession, but she had never imagined that the falsely collared Torth "slaves" would carry their playacting this far.

Torth did not belong in a bunk room.

Torth did not belong in the slave Tunnels at all. It was monstrously unfair. Slaves needed to be able to talk or sing or nuzzle each other every once in a while. Surely that was why the Tunnels existed. If slaves were forced to be obedient even here…? The city would devolve into chaos.

No one quite dared to speak. Not in the presence of Torth.

Weptolyso, the hall guard, snorted. "These Torth," he said in his gravelly voice, "are to be treated as slaves."

The three Torth stared as if they hadn't understood a word he said. They looked terrified.

But that had to be a sham. Their eye colors marked them as middling and upper ranks. Even if they had committed some mysterious crime against their own brethren, they would not be sentenced to slavery.

Kessa had never heard of gods becoming slaves.

She scooted to the edge of her bunk, so her legs dangled just above the floor. Her first-level bunk was a privilege. Spirits, or luck, honored the few slaves who survived to old age, and nobody wanted to offend the spirits. Therefore, elders such as Kessa garnered respect.

She decided to risk speaking. "Weptolyso," she said. "What rank commanded you to treat these three like slaves?"

Weptolyso filled the doorway with his thorny bulk. "One with white eyes told me."

White eyes meant the highest authority. No one lower could countermand this order.

"And," Weptolyso said, "I have seen them suffer punishments." He grinned, displaying his fine array of teeth. "Other Torth stole jewelry from them. They did not fight back or punish anyone."

That was hard to believe.

Yet the three Torth wearing collars did not punish Weptolyso for speaking out loud. They merely stood, huddled together, like youths fresh off a slave farm.

Murmurs broke out. Perhaps this was a twisted hoax, a way for Torth to find out how stupid slaves were? Everyone agreed that Weptolyso was a fine example of his species, but nussians could be gullible. Perhaps he had misinterpreted the situation?

"Peace, peace!" Weptolyso boomed above the ruckus. "Listen to me. I heard them speak to each other."

Only slaves spoke out loud. Torth never did.

As if to prove his point, the tall Torth with rust-colored hair babbled in an unknown language. She tugged at her slave collar and repeated the syllables, which sounded pleading.

Many slaves, when they arrived fresh off a slave farm, had a unique language in addition to the common slave tongue. Kessa could still remember the swishy dialect of her childhood. But no matter where a slave grew up, every child learned the common slave tongue.

A Torth would surely know it. Torth knew everything.

"This is foulness!" Hajir, the only mer nerctan in the bunk room, leaped off his shelf and landed with a heavy thud.

Other slaves jumped. A mer nerctan could hurt smaller people with ease, by extending his jointed neck and swinging his bony head.

"They're baiting us," Hajir said. "They must have practiced for a long time, to imitate slaves with such authenticity. As if we are mindless fools!" He cocked his enormous head at the trio. "We have to act mindless in the upper city. But down here? This is our city."

Slaves voiced angry agreement.

"That's right!"

"We won't fall for this trick!"

Violence was brewing. Even the dreamers, high up in the shadowy reaches of the uppermost shelves, sensed a change. They gazed at the collared Torth with a flicker of interest, as if passing from one nightmare into another.

"Let's take their clothes," Hajir said. "Those materials look serviceable and very durable. The big piece is mine!"

Even in the dim light, Kessa saw how terrified the three Torth looked.

Hajir stalked toward them. "We'll see if they fight like slaves or Torth."

Weptolyso snorted a warning. "I request that you do not attack them. I have no wish to injure you."

"Are you going to defend them?" Hajir gave the hall guard a challenging glare.

"It is my duty as a guard," Weptolyso replied.

The imperative to protect and defend Torth was ground into all nussians during their childhood training. That was common knowledge. Any guard who failed in that duty would be sentenced to death.

"However..." Weptolyso backed out of the doorway. "I must leave to patrol the hall."

Hajir extended his jointed neck, holding his head aloft in a sign of acknowledgment. "Go do your duty, Weptolyso."

Other slaves took up the cry. "Go do your duty!"

A young ummin shouted, "They'll kill us all!" but no one paid attention.

The collared Torth backed against a wall. One of them kept speaking in that incomprehensible language.

It must be a pretense...yet Kessa began to have doubts. Why would a Torth pretend ignorance of the common tongue? What would a Torth have to gain by enduring the same hardships shared by slaves? She could not imagine satisfactory answers.

"Wait." Kessa slid off her bunk and approached the collared Torth.

"What are you doing, elder?" Hajir swung his neck to get a closer look at her.

Kessa folded her hands in front of her, making the sign of peace. "What if they are being punished for something like helping slaves? I want to try to communicate with them."

The bunk room burst into dispute. A collar did not make a Torth a slave. Kessa should not fall for such an obvious ploy.

"Kessa has lost her wits." That was Ghelvae, a surly little ummin. "If these Torth really had something to say, they'd speak so we could understand."

Ghelvae often complained that he ought to be respected as an elder, although many elders remembered the night he had arrived, trembling, fresh off a slave farm.

No one remembered Kessa's arrival. No one living, anyway. Some slaves whispered that she was as long-lived as a Torth.

What does it matter? Kessa's dark side whispered. People assumed that she was protected by spirits, but she ached all the time. Few slaves imagined how old age felt. Once a window was washed, there was another to wash. Once a fruit was peeled, she had to do it again. Everything in life was monotonously repeated until finding a friend became a grandly joyous event, even when that friend was sure to die.

Kessa had once met an ancient husk of a dreamer who no longer remembered her own name or how to hold a conversation. That elderly slave had mechanically worked, slept, eaten, and worked more. Did anybody care what her name used to be? No.

Eventually, according to rumors, the mindless elder got punished to death. She must have made one too many mistakes at work. And no one had cared. No one mourned her, except for Kessa.

"Who can know the minds of Torth?" Hajir was saying. "Maybe this is how they entertain themselves."

Kessa approached the three Torth. They shrank back, as if they were afraid of an elderly ummin.

It was hard to believe that mind readers would cast aside their dignity like this. And these were high ranks. Browns and Greens tended to own dozens of slaves. Blue? Kessa had heard rumors that Blue Ranks lived in palatial suites, tended to by hundreds of slaves and bodyguards. Their favorite slaves wore crisp uniforms instead of rags.

This Blue Rank babbled in a pleading voice.

Weptolyso popped his spikes out. "Stay back, Kessa," he said. "They could be waiting to attack someone."

Kessa gave him a grateful look. What other guard would bother to know her name, let alone offer to protect a common ummin?

She stood within telepathy range of the collared Torth.

Slaves hushed each other, eager to see what Kessa the Wise might do.

"Kessa." She touched her chest and pronounced the short, informal version of her name. Inwardly, she braced herself for punishment. They would probably give her a pain seizure for speaking.

Instead, the three Torth exchanged what sounded like an excited conversation. The Blue Rank pointed. "Kessa?" She spoke slowly and clearly. "Kessa."

It chilled Kessa to hear her name from a Torth mouth. This was like a story about wind spirits calling a slave to die.

Nevertheless, she clicked her beak in approval. "Kessa," she affirmed.

The Blue Rank pointed to herself. "Vy."

Kessa stared, stunned.

"The nameless don't have names!" Hajir spluttered. "This is elaborate."

A long-forgotten yearning reawakened inside Kessa. She would trade her life for a mere second of Torth knowledge. To know everything, to comprehend the unseen…maybe these collared Torth could teach her the secrets of the universe?

She wanted to know why daytime always followed nighttime. Did wind spirits really exist? Was it true that Torth traveled in the dark spaces between stars?

She needed to puzzle out how to ask.

The three strange Torth taught her their names. Vy. Delia. Cherise. Fake or not, Kessa memorized them.

She introduced them to Weptolyso, and they mimicked his name with varying degrees of accuracy. Weptolyso looked so skittish, Kessa wanted to laugh.

Next, she led them in pointing out simple things. Floor. Bunk. Rags.

The collared Torth stumbled over pronunciations, but they offered their own foreign words, which Kessa repeated and memorized.

"Why are you learning their tongue-twisting words? It's a ruse!" Hajir sounded scandalized. "They're keeping us up late. They must want us to be tired so we'll make fatal mistakes next work shift!"

Kessa gave him a withering look. "There are more efficient ways to get slaves killed."

Other people muttered in agreement.

"These three Torth have poor memories," Kessa observed. "Maybe they are damaged in some way?"

"Even if they are brain damaged," Ghelvae said, "why would gods need to memorize anything? They should know it all."

That was true. Torth could not be surprised. Torth knew every secret. That was what made them gods.

Kessa spoke the obvious conclusion, wanting to mention it before Hajir or anyone else could rile up a mob. "I think their mind-reading ability may have been destroyed."

Everyone began to talk at once. Was that possible? Could the gods lose their godly powers?

"If we lose our eyes, we cannot see," Kessa pointed out, in answer to a question. "If our tongues are cut out, we cannot talk. Perhaps there is some organ on the Torth that can be removed?"

"Well," someone said, "I hope they will show you where it was."

"We had better not think about this at work," Ghelvae said in his surly tone.

The three Torth seemed eager to communicate. The Brown Rank repeated a couple of alien syllables, "Tomm Uss," several times. She squatted and used her finger to push grime around on the floor.

A picture emerged from the grime.

It was sketchy and vague, but nonetheless, Kessa gasped with delighted recognition. "She is mentioning her companion! The one in the chair with wheels!"

"How many Torth with names are there?" Hajir grumbled.

The Brown Rank sketched a large figure. Her companions named the giant, their tones pleading. "Arr ee ock?"

"Has anyone seen their missing companions?" Kessa asked the bunk room. "Thomas and Ariock?"

"This is folly," Hajir said.

No one offered a useful answer. Kessa turned to Weptolyso, her brow ridges raised in inquisitiveness.

"I will ask around," the hall guard said. "I am sure someone in the city has seen them. Such oddities will be noticed."

"Don't you have a hall to patrol?" Hajir asked.

Weptolyso snorted a threat. "Don't push your luck with me." But most of his attention was on Kessa and the three new slaves. Kessa supposed that he was gathering dramatic details so he could impress other guards. News about the befuddled slave-Torth would be spread all over the city by the next sleep cycle.

"Come." Kessa gestured the three Torth toward the bunks. "We must sleep or our work shift will be dangerous."

"They will probably shove you out of your nice ground-level bunk and take it for themselves," Hajir said.

"I doubt that," Weptolyso said. "They behave like halfwits. I think they must be damaged."

"Maybe this is how Torth get rid of their own rejects?" Ghelvae wondered.

Kessa gestured upward, making sure the three Torth followed her gaze. It was hard to see the shelves along the rough ceiling, far from the recessed lights. Emaciated slaves slept or died up there. Dreamers either starved slowly or got lost in forgotten tunnels. Or, most commonly, they made mistakes in front of Torth and died for it.

Sure enough, some of the upper bunks were vacant.

The three Torth just stared. They seemed unwilling to sully themselves by climbing.

The Green Rank named Delia sat, as if too weak to stand any longer. She put her head in her hands. The sounds issuing from her throat were more aching than any Kessa had heard in a long time.

Hajir extended his neck, examining them. "Let's divvy up their clothes."

Kessa shot him a vexed glance. "No one should take their clothes or push them off bunks. I believe these Torth have emotions."

"Fake emotions," Hajir said.

Part of Kessa suspected that Hajir might be right. Yet every sob from Delia seemed to communicate a dreadful loss.

Vy and Cherise made comforting noises. All three curled up on the floor and held each other, looking as baffled and lost as any newly collared city slave.

"So far," Kessa said, "they have not threatened anyone. Remember the Code of Gwat. We are not Torth. We do no harm without reason."

Mutters echoed around the room, but a number of slaves backed Kessa up.

"I have seen a Torth behave like this before," Weptolyso said.

Everyone focused on him.

"You've seen this?" Hajir demanded. "Really?"

Weptolyso settled against the doorway, making himself comfortable. "Shortly after I entered adulthood," he said, "I was assigned to serve a Brown Rank. I rode with him in a luxury transport, which flew very fast. You cannot imagine the thrill. We landed on various slave farms, where I was obliged to punish slaves who shirked their duties. I hated that. Anyway, I—"

"Get to the point," Hajir said.

Weptolyso rumbled a warning. "On one of those trips," he went on, "we visited a city that straddled a deep canyon, wreathed in mist. It had outdoor streets with transparent railings. My owner was walking down a street, and I followed, of course. All of a sudden..." Weptolyso widened his eyes and popped out his spikes for dramatic effect. "A nearby Torth staggered! She acted as if struck by an invisible hand. She fell to all four limbs and began to cry like a slave. Like those." He indicated Delia, Vy, and Cherise. "Her face became wet, too. I tell you, it halted traffic up and down the street."

"I have never heard of such a thing," a slave said.

Kessa had actually heard tales about Torth who cried out or who suddenly behaved like slaves. Until now, she had figured they were as credible as legends about sand spirits and shape-shifters. No one ever saw such things. They heard about it from someone else, who heard about it from someone else, and the original tale teller was invariably an unknown slave whom no one had ever met.

Weptolyso seemed to accept the implied insult. "I know what I saw," he said in a mild tone. "If I was telling a tale, I would have told it before."

"What happened to the crying Torth?" Kessa asked.

"Other Torth murdered her," Weptolyso said. "Right there in the street, for everyone to see. My owner and all of the nearby Torth pulled on their gloves and shot her to pieces."

The bunk room went silent, processing that shock of an ending.

Kessa studied the newcomers and wondered how many sympathetic Torth existed, if any. Why were these three merely sentenced to slavery? Why weren't they executed?

Kessa might as well try to understand the stars. There was no telling what a Torth might do.

"After that," Weptolyso went on, "all the pedestrian Torth resumed walking, as if nothing had happened. They walked on her remains."

Ghelvae clicked his beak. "I have also heard of Torth killing one of their own."

Everyone turned to him, surprised.

"I did not see it," Ghelvae admitted. "The story comes from my elders on the slave farm, who heard it from their elders. According to them, a Red

Rank was killed where he stood. I never believed it. But"—he nodded at the collared Torth—"there's this."

Weptolyso regarded the collared Torth. "I must make my rounds," he said, reluctant, creaking to his feet. "I hope they are here when I return."

He shuffled away.

Hajir climbed onto his bunk, but he eyed the three Torth like a predator sizing up a meal.

Kessa reluctantly said good night to the three Torth and plodded to her bunk. Slaves who neglected sleep did not survive to old age. Her aching joints fired up, then dulled down, as she settled beneath her thin rag of blanket.

Although she tried, she could not sleep right away.

If they are truly slaves, she thought, *they will not last long.*

CHAPTER 10
REGURGITATION OF THE MIND

The green sky glitched. The atrium rippled. Thomas figured the testers must have interlaced their imaginations to form another choreographed illusion—but what had changed? This looked like reality.

Thomas?

Oh no.

Thomas turned, and there was Cherise, kneeling within his range of telepathy, between two testers. Blood seeped out from beneath her slave collar.

I need help, she silently begged him.

Her glasses were missing. Tears rolled down her face, and her lush black hair was a tangled mess.

I can't serve well, she thought. *I can hardly see. Why haven't you rescued us yet?*

Thomas had to bite his tongue to remain stony-faced. He reminded himself that this was the Adulthood Exam. It was fake. It had to be fake. No matter how authentic Cherise looked, no matter how real her distress seemed, she could not have magically appeared next to him. The Torth did not have teleportation technology.

At least, he didn't think so.

In any case, he could not afford to show compassion. Cherise was just a slave. He avoided eye contact.

The testers silently debated the merits and toughness qualities of human slaves. They ate berries or sipped sweet drinks. And they wondered. How long would it take for this slave to die from a punishment?

One tester narrowed his focus on Cherise's core mind.

She writhed on the ground, suffering, wordlessly pleading for help.

This isn't real, Thomas told himself.

Cherise whimpered in agony. Thomas sensed her thoughts, and she could not understand why her best friend was ignoring her. Why was he acting like a Torth? Didn't he care? She was in so much pain.

The first tester got worn-out, and another one took over the punishment duties.

Thomas gritted his teeth, determined to ignore the horrific simulation until it ended.

But he sensed disappointment from the Torth, as well as hinting expectations…and he realized that he was supposed to treat this situation as if it was real. That was the point.

This was a damned test. He could not skip exam questions and expect to get a passing grade.

Okay, it's real, Thomas told himself. And he immediately cringed with self-loathing. His heart wrenched in his chest. He could not simply ignore Cherise as she got tortured to death. He couldn't…

The testers exchanged mental glances.

In unison, they raised their gloved hands and aimed their weapons at Thomas.

Too bad.

He had potential, but—

—he is too tainted by inferior genetics.

A death murmur blew through their minds. The distant audience, the Torth Majority, chanted *kill him. KILL HIM.*

Thomas thought faster than he ever had.

He overclocked his mental processing and ran through one option after another. Could he possibly protect Cherise even while ignoring her and treating her like a slave? What if he persuaded the Torth that they were wrong to hurt her?

What argument might sway them?

Mercy and pity were emotions. He needed logic.

He put the brakes on his hyperfast thinking so that he could communicate. *Please correct me if I'm wrong,* he thought to the Torth, *but aren't there only four humans on this whole planet?*

The testers lowered their gloved hands, intrigued. They approved of his rational, logical line of thought. He was no longer panicking or sweating, and that was a good thing.

Correct, they affirmed.

So why are You wasting a human slave? Thomas thought. *Such rare slaves must be valuable.*

The testers mentally nodded to each other. Their inner audience chorused more affirmations.

True, some Torth thought to each other. *Humans are exotic.*

Too valuable to waste.

Yet other Torth disagreed. *There is a large breeding population of humans on Earth.*

Plenty more where this one came from.

Arguments flashed like rapid gunfire. Torth debated one another. The final vote was pending, and it might go either way.

The testers were distracted enough so that they quit tormenting Cherise. She huddled on the floor, sobbing, oblivious to the silent debates.

Thomas wanted to tip the odds in Cherise's favor. He ventured a suggestion, although it felt like poking a hornet's nest.

I have personal experience with this particular slave, he let the Torth know. *She is resilient to hardship. If You waste her, You will fail to explore the limits of how hardworking a human can be. You would defeat the very purpose of using experimental human slaves.*

The testers and their distant audience examined his argument.

After a second, they reached a consensus. *Human slaves may be more valuable than We anticipated.*

We will not waste human slaves frivolously.

Well done, child.

The Torth Majority amended a subsection of their bylaws, adding some scanty protection for exotic human slaves.

Cherise vanished into thin air. She had never really been there.

Thomas compressed his lips, holding in all the insults he wanted to hurl at the testers and their audience.

Rage would get him killed. He was as helpless as Cherise against her schoolyard tormentors. But he dared not examine that. He had to meekly accept whatever they tortured him with next.

The Adulthood Exam is not meant as torture, the Torth silently chorused, as if to assure him.

It is merely a test.

The atrium rippled. And there was Vy, chained to a wall and nearly starved to death.

This slave stole a weapon, the testers informed Thomas. *The punishment is death by torture.*

Knowledge suffused Thomas, handed to him by the distant audience. He learned that the law protected All Torth. The slave must die.

Thomas struggled to come up with a rational argument in favor of saving Vy. He wanted to save her life.

His capacious imagination drew only blanks.

Perhaps he could have done it if he was an influential Blue Rank or an elite Servant of All. But he was not. He was just a child. There was no argument he could possibly present in order to persuade trillions of Torth—the Torth Majority—to change one of their core laws.

It's imaginary, Thomas reminded himself. *Vy is fine right now.*

The despair in Vy's gaze made him feel cruel and low. She had taken care of him for years. How could he respect himself if he let her die? How could he live with that?

Crushing guilt would get him killed.

Thomas reached for logic, because that was his lifeline. He needed a way to stay sane.

Did Vy's premature death matter in the grand scheme of the universe? Almost certainly not. Everybody died. Thomas himself had been slated for a premature death until he'd invented NAI-12.

Vy was a good caretaker, but any trained slave could do her job. He didn't need her.

Perhaps other people needed her. Cherise. But why did Thomas care so much about anyone? Why was Cherise important? Why was anyone?

He needed to distance himself from humankind.

Thomas searched for reasons to do that…and found plenty of them.

Whenever he'd wanted a friend, he always had to make the first move. He had escaped uncaring foster homes full of people who wanted him to die. People shrugged off his fatal disease as incurable, leaving him to cure himself. He had fought constrictive laws and naysayers.

If he wanted to survive, he was on his own. He had learned that the hard way.

In his quest for survival, he propped up other people. His medicine would save the lives of many strangers. He earned money for Rasa Biotech, as well as for the Hollander home. He went around saving people. But did anyone respect him for it?

No. Not nearly as much as they should.

It would be nice if someone tried to rescue him, for a change. Just once.

Correct, the testers approved.

They (primitives) (humans) are inferiors.

You are superior.

The scene rippled and changed. Ariock was beaten and begging for death. Thomas watched without guilt, since he could not offer help, anyway. Empty reassurances or pleas for mercy would get them both killed. It was illogical to even consider intervention.

On it went, with Delia needing rescue, Vy needing rescue, Cherise needing rescue. Thomas watched them suffer over and over.

With every fresh scenario, Thomas had more trouble assuring himself that the Adulthood Exam was merely a test. He stopped trying to do so. He accepted each situation as reality.

Because, in a way, it was all real.

The real-life versions of Ariock, Delia, and Vy had likely forgotten that Thomas lived every day with doom hanging over his head. He needed regular doses of NAI-12 in order to survive. How often did that concern cross their minds?

Almost never.

Their problems only added to his own herculean burden. He had absorbed every detail of Cherise's life, yet it never occurred to her that Thomas might need a smidgen of consideration for carrying her burdens.

They had never been his equals. Had they?

Thomas pondered the nature of friendship, frowning as his friends begged and cried. Cherise and Ariock had spent most of their lives needing help. One was afraid to be heard. One was afraid to be seen. Thomas had done his best to rescue them from suicidal despair, but they would always need support and advice.

Everyone he met seemed needy.

As if Thomas never felt lonely. As if he never suffered. He lived other people's nightmares, and they expected him to be polite while they thought offensive insults about him.

You can escape the company of small-minded animals, the Torth silently invited.

Join Us.

The atrium reemerged.

It was nighttime now, lit by glowing orbs cradled in the tendrils of vines wrought in metal. Beyond the silver vine-wrapped pillars, the city had its own glow. Metallic spires reflected aerial traffic. Two enormous moons seemed etched with what might be industrial complexes.

And the atrium had gained an in-house audience.

Beyond the testers, dozens of Torth reclined on spacious risers. Slaves served them refreshments. The odors of a feast made Thomas's stomach rumble.

Nearby Torth disapproved of the noise. *Like a slave*, they silently remarked to each other.

Thomas wasn't going to apologize for being hungry. The last meal he'd eaten was more than a full day ago, on Earth.

A slave showed up with a jar for...

A bathroom break?

In public?

Thomas reminded himself that embarrassment was psychotic to the Torth, borderline illegal. A lot of Torth probably took bathroom breaks with audiences inside their heads. And he really did need to pee. He had sipped water throughout this exam.

So he went ahead, face flushed. He struggled to suppress his embarrassment. Maybe this was normal Torth behavior.

Did their inner audiences ever stop watching?

You are doing well.

Thomas recognized that mental voice. He scanned the audience, and sure enough, the Upward Governess was a blob in the back row. At this distance, he could not sense the massive size of her mind, but the audience conveyed her thoughts down to him, row by row.

The final challenge is next, she warned him. *It is the most difficult part of the exam. Are you ready?*

Thomas felt numb and wrung out. The ordeal had already lasted for many hours. At this point, he wouldn't care if it was kittens being suffocated or babies getting beaten to death. He no longer cared about anything.

Sure, he thought. *I'm ready.*

The audience emanated skepticism. Thomas overheard their silent exchanges, and he learned that a high percentage of children failed the final part of the Adulthood Exam. It was considered exceptionally difficult.

Oh well. What choice did he have?

The atrium twisted away, subsumed by an imagined scene that was indistinguishable from reality. Fluorescent lights flickered overhead. Women chatted with New England accents.

Thomas was lying on his back. In a crib.

He was a baby again. He lay in the nursery ward of a hospital, utterly helpless, unwanted, and unloved.

His whole body contorted with an urge to wail.

Thomas clenched his tiny mouth shut and refused to vent those emotions. False emotions. Pointless, unnecessary emotions.

A nurse commented that he was an ugly baby. Special needs. No one would adopt him.

A doctor predicted that he wouldn't survive past the age of three.

Another doctor recommended that they not bother with trying to find a foster home for him.

He was dying. He was nothing. He was no one. He stank of dirty diapers. The nurses always changed him last, knowing that he was worth less than the other babies in the ward.

The Torth were feeding Thomas his own memories. They knew…they knew…

They knew every trauma in his life.

This was even more personal than the rest of the exam. He was a toddler in a mobile home with garbage bags taped over the broken windows. The father of the house was violent. The other kids were addled and just as needy as himself, or even more so. Yet his foster mother said he was possessed by the devil.

He tried to hide.

He got transferred to a home where all the boys were obedient because, at night, their foster father did unspeakable things to them. Thomas called the police and gave instructions, acting as a whistle-blower. But the older boys, desperate to earn rewards and curry favor, locked Thomas in an outhouse and tried to make sure he would die there.

Spiders crawled over him. No one cared about his screams for help.

After he was rescued, even the social workers thought he was piteously pathetic, although they were careful to never say so.

Pulse quickening. Palms sweating.

Thomas felt the visceral change in his body and knew that he had to find a way to detach from his own history. His future depended on it.

He visited a nursing home with another foster family. There, he absorbed vivid memories from a bygone era, from before the internet. Drooling old men and senile old women seemed to exist in multiple eras at once, surviving war zones and heartbreak. Young Thomas had started to cry, because there were too many memories in that place. It was overwhelming. His latest foster mother took him outside and slapped him for "acting like a whiny little baby" and ruining her visit with her one-hundred-year-old grandmother.

Was that sobbing child really him?

Thomas remembered the inundation, the confusion, the shame, the guilt, and the pain from the slap.

But he never should have cried in the first place. Crying was a useless physiological response to stress. It obviously accomplished nothing good.

"What a freak," other kids muttered when they saw him.

"What's wrong with that boy?"

"Don't make me talk to him."

"It's like he's not human."

Every insult was regurgitated from his memory, from hundreds of mouths, from thousands of unspoken thoughts. It felt like consuming his own flesh.

He was a self-absorbed freak. A demon. An android boy. Adults squabbled over "the Einstein of the twenty-first century" while he grew weaker. People pretended to feel pity while they secretly celebrated the fact that he would never walk, secure in the knowledge that they would live full lives while he was doomed to never be an adult. So he worked and worked and worked.

"You're the most arrogant person I've ever known."

"Don't you ever get tired of thinking about yourself?"

"What's wrong with you—don't you care about other people?"

"A science lab somewhere must have made a mistake."

"Why don't you do us all a favor and die faster?"

Before long, the urge to weep and pity himself became almost overwhelming. But another part of Thomas—the healthier, stronger part—focused on survival. This was the analytical core that kept him anchored whenever he was in public. It had kept him cool when someone's insult might otherwise have reduced him to a sobbing mess. It had given him his reputation as the Ego and the Android Boy.

Thomas completely embraced that logical, focused part of himself.

He shouldn't have cared about insults, or cameras aimed at him, or passersby who dumped loads of useless information into his head. None of it mattered.

He used to be a tortured wretch, yearning to escape the ceaseless barrage of other people's idiotic notions. Why had he let their inferior opinions affect him so much?

As he grew older and death edged closer, Thomas focused on medical research to the exclusion of pleasures. He sacrificed vital basics such as eating and sleeping, driven to succeed at any cost.

Why? the distant audience buzzed, interrupting the illusion.

Why did you (child) care so much about survival?

Why was it so important to you?

Thomas supposed that he had wanted to grow up and change the world. That way, people would respect him. That way, they would finally value him as their equal.

Ah. The audience mulled that over.

Among Us (Torth), you will be respected.

You will be valued.

You won't have to be alone ever again.

A truth struck Thomas with the force of an earthquake. On Earth, he had sought kinship—equality, belonging—without being fully aware of it. He had chased after life, like a bee chasing after a colorful shirt, unaware that he wanted something else instead.

What he had truly wanted was to be embraced by people who knew his worth.

Life had been his obsession because he'd had nothing else to live for.

Millions of distant Torth burbled with approval. *We understand.*

And they did. Thomas basked in their sincerity.

He ran a trembling hand over his chest, thinking even as he did so that such an emotive sign was unnecessary…and marveling at the aftershock realization that he was no longer the boy in his memories.

He had never belonged on Earth. Deep down, he had always known that. Holding a pencil proved more difficult for him than any exam. Vocal communication had always felt slow and clumsy to him, because he was designed for a faster speed of communication.

Yes, the Torth chorused. *We know.*

They accepted him, and their acceptance overlapped in glorious starbursts, more impressive than any fireworks display. *One of Us.*

He's one of Us.
One of Us.
He is US US US.

CHAPTER 11

A SUPERGENIUS IN THE MEGACOSM

Fragments from Thomas's past sparkled within Torth minds. Watching a cartoon show. Dipping his finger into a cold lake. His memories were being assimilated into the Torth Empire.

Well, whatever. Thomas was determined to distance himself from those memories. He must quit thinking about his past life *(in public, anyway)*.

At least he no longer needed to act as anyone's therapist. That was something to look forward to.

Friends?

Therapy?

What do those things mean? Show Us.

Thomas examined nearby minds, perplexed. Hadn't the Torth learned everything about humanity?

It seemed that some of them had trouble grasping human concepts. Their understanding was superficial. They had absorbed his life experiences in order to test him, but they had flushed away everything they considered to be unimportant background data.

Hm. Thomas considered ways to explain therapy and friendship to people who hardly felt emotions. He made several attempts. Friends were people he felt an affinity for, and vice versa.

Ah. A few Torth dared to feel mildly curious. The rest simply did not care about primitives.

Welcome to civilization! the Torth Majority chorused at Thomas.

Welcome, reformed savage,

fledging innovator,

supergenius.

Opinions about Thomas coalesced. Millions of Torth silently debated summary descriptions of this new comrade. They did not want to saddle him with an insulting name-title. They would not call him the Human Hybrid, or the Reformed Savage, or anything that hinted at inferiority. But perhaps they would let him retain his human moniker? His upbringing was unique beyond all comparisons.

They would combine his primitive name with his rank. That made for a simplistic name-title, but they could always vote to change it once he began to prove his prowess in some area of expertise.

WELCOME, the Majority thundered. YELLOW THOMAS.

Yellow Thomas smiled thinly. As a Torth, he hoped he could get a change of clothes. And a meal.

First your eyes!

A slave approached, carrying what looked like a surgical instrument. It offered the device to one of the testers.

A suggestion blossomed throughout the audience. *Change his eyes.*

Yes.

Change his eyes!

The tester prepared the surgical device. He bent and angled the instrument at Yellow Thomas's right eye.

Yellow Thomas flinched.

It was a terribly primitive reaction. He realized that right away. By watching his entire life from the point of view of an emotionless outsider, he had seen humans for what they were: dogs. Cattle. Shallow creatures ruled by their emotions. They formed little packs and herds and bickered over territory and mating privileges. He had attached far too much importance to their trivial concerns.

You didn't know any other way, the distant Upward Governess assured him. *Now you do.*

At her behest, information flooded Yellow Thomas from the nearby testers and their inner audiences. He experienced ninety-seven different promotion ceremonies through other people's memories.

It would be painless. The Torth had already grafted artificial lenses to his eyeballs while he was unconscious and being transported from Earth. The high-tech wand would reprogram each lens to display another color: yellow instead of black.

Black is the eye color of unripe (immature) Torth. Distant minds jumped ahead of one another, eager to introduce Yellow Thomas to the rules of civilization.

Now that you have passed the Adulthood Exam,
you will begin adulthood as a Yellow Rank,
as We all do.

Different hues of yellow fanned through their minds: lemon, gold, tawny, chartreuse. Certain hues indicated a bias toward a higher rank.

They emphasized that most Torth were satisfied to live and die as Lemon Yellows. Few earned a promotion.

He is ambitious, the Upward Governess thought. *He won't be satisfied to remain a Yellow.*

Yellow Thomas relaxed, now that he knew what to expect. The tester used the wand to pry his eyelids apart. Most humans and slaves would have jerked away, but he remained calm.

First one eye.

Then the other.

It took less than five seconds.

Behold!

The artificial sky brightened to a golden dawn. Yellow Thomas raised his newly yellow gaze.

As he admired the flawless sky, he saw himself reflected in the nearest perceptions. He wore rumpled, stained clothes. He sat in his anachronistic wheelchair. But his iridescent yellow eyes made him look unearthly.

Raise him up!

Let Us see him!

The testers made a command gesture, and the govki slave obeyed. It lifted Yellow Thomas high for all to see.

Yellow Thomas suppressed his annoyance. He was used to being dressed and bathed as an invalid, but he preferred to have some minor bit of control over what happened to his body. Autonomy was valuable.

Raised up, he saw his biological aunt *(no, families don't matter)* the Swift Killer on the far side of the atrium.

Judging by her frown, she had expected or hoped that Yellow Thomas would fail the Adulthood Exam. Her crossed arms made her seem human. Other Torth did not cross their arms or frown. The Swift Killer, he realized, was an anomaly among Torth.

He wondered why. How often had she visited Earth? For how long?

He is still ignorant? Many Torth seemed surprised. They wondered why Yellow Thomas hadn't joined the Megacosm yet.

Join Us already!

Yes, join Us!

In the Megacosm, you will learn as much as you wish.

Ascend and be a god!

Yellow Thomas groped for his inner audience. He had none. He was alone inside his own mind, as always.

Oh, come on! One of the testers, a woman with her white hair swept back, assured him that ascending into the Megacosm was easy. *A baby can do it.*

Yellow Thomas was careful to hide his fears. But he wondered: What if he was too human to connect to their neural network? What if he was mentally handicapped, in comparison to an average Torth?

A single mental voice cut through his concerns. *You (Yellow Thomas) have every ability that an average Torth has. And more.* The Upward Governess regarded him with ironclad certainty.

The tester echoed her. *Indeed.*

Once he enters the Megacosm…

…he will gobble up knowledge like the Upward Governess.

Yellow Thomas began to speculate on what they meant.

I will show him how to ascend, the Upward Governess offered.

She floated down an aisle, followed by unspoken speculations. Nobody expected a Blue Rank to waste her valuable time on something so trivial. Anyone could enlighten the former savage in their midst.

He needs some preparation, the Upward Governess silently explained. *He will be like an infant ascending for the very first time. The Megacosm may be a shock to his mind (even though he is a supergenius) (like Me).*

The testers moved aside, making room for the Indigo-Blue Rank in her extra-large hoverchair.

When the Upward Governess entered Yellow Thomas's range of telepathy, he had to suppress a gasp of shock. She crashed into his awareness like an ocean, obliterating everything else. Her mind seemed to crackle with as much energy as the sun.

In a mere instant, she inundated him with Torth laws and significant history. She taught him how to drive a hovercart, how to pilot a *(transport)* flying vehicle, and the rudiments of how to operate data tablets and multipurpose blaster gloves. And, by the way, she governed the local province, with a population comparable to Japan.

All the other Torth minds seemed insignificant in comparison to hers. They were like mosquitoes swarming around a mountain, unable to absorb a fraction of the data that radiated from her.

Because they could forget.

That is how We are alike, Yellow Thomas realized, trying to study her colossal mind. *You have a flawless, unlimited memory. Like Me.*

Correct, the Upward Governess affirmed. *We both have a rare beneficial-detrimental congenital mutation. It allows Us to imbibe and retain more knowledge than any other living beings. We are supergeniuses.*

Other Torth implied that the supergenius mutation was fatal.

Research into a cure was forbidden. Supergeniuses were bioengineered to be short-lived, with severe neuromuscular disabilities.

You (Yellow Thomas) unwittingly circumvented the law against researching a cure, the Upward Governess thought with sly approval. *You invented this marvelous treatment.* Her hand rested on the NAI-12 case, squished onto the seat beside her.

Yellow Thomas didn't like the way she displayed his stolen medicine.

He searched the expressionless faces of the testers and wondered, *Why are supergeniuses bioengineered to die young? Why is a cure illegal?*

Torth exchanged glances. Certain things were just common knowledge.

He really ought to ascend into the Megacosm, they whispered to each other. *He can learn everything there.*

Even so, they offered answers, so many that they piled on top of each other.

We (the glorious Torth Empire) had a bioengineering mishap,
a catastrophe,
in Our early beginnings.

Images of misshapen mutants spun from their minds. Not just mutants. There were people with godlike powers. A glowing woman whipped lightning bolts from her hands. Men and women flew like superheroes. They commanded tornadoes, oceans, tectonic plates, and armies.

Those superhuman people had ruined continents. Planets. Interstellar empires.

The ancient memories felt stale. They lacked certainty and details, having been passed down from generation to generation. The "mishap" had happened a thousand generations ago.

We (the Torth Empire) arose from the ashes of the mutant war and their devastation.
Such a catastrophic war must never happen again.
Therefore,
We forbade bioengineering.
Excess mental powers are illegal.
Genetic science. Bioengineering.
Outlawed!
Forever!

Yellow Thomas assessed the Torth around him. They forbade superhuman powers, but they were okay with his fatal disability?

Correct, the Upward Governess thought.

She did not elaborate. Yellow Thomas tried to delve further into the Torth rationale for outlawing superpowers, but all he got were surface thoughts.

Strange. Were the Torth really against genetic research? He had trouble believing that. Were all their scientists incurious? Apathetic? How could an advanced galactic civilization ignore such an important branch of medical science?

Because they are idiots. That came from the Upward Governess.

Other minds crackled in disapproval. *Only from Your perspective, supergenius.*

Very few Torth (fewer than 0.00000000005 percent)
suffer from fatal disabilities.

Why should We risk the safety of the known universe—
—just to cure a handful of supergeniuses?

Yellow Thomas tried to hide his dismay. No wonder the Upward Governess had taken risks to welcome him. Only a tiny sliver of a fraction of the Torth population were supergeniuses! She must have felt alone until he showed up.

Wrong, the Upward Governess gently corrected him.

There are others, her audience chorused.

Torth relayed images of disabled children living on distant planets. A girl with curly hair in pigtails. A chubby, dark-skinned boy. A pasty-white girl with a bulbous nose. Younger ones.

Seventeen supergeniuses currently live in the Torth Empire.

Including you, Yellow Thomas.

Yellow Thomas did a quick calculation in his mind. If seventeen supergeniuses represented such a tiny fraction *(0.00000000005 percent)* of the total Torth population, that extrapolated to...

He double-checked his math. The Torth population couldn't be that staggeringly enormous.

The Upward Governess confirmed his calculation—*3.8 x 10^13 individuals (and growing).*

Yellow Thomas tried to mute his disgusted awe. Did they mass-reproduce like swarms of bugs?

Other minds chimed in. *Every healthy adult gamete donor produces an average of fifty viable offspring.*

Many offspring are terminated, but even so.

Our swiftly growing population allows Us to colonize more planets.

We are always expanding Our boundaries.

The Upward Governess nudged his mind in a manner that felt like "up." *You can learn these facts, and more, from anyone in the galaxy.* She silently encouraged Yellow Thomas to reach for anyone—any mind—who might reach back.

How many times had he tried this on Earth, yearning to find other telepaths?

He used to reach blindly for others, but it never mattered how hard he tried. He was always alone inside his head.

Yet this time...

They were reaching for him, the same way he reached for them.
They knew he existed.
They wanted him, and that made all the difference.
In a sudden chilling rush, Yellow Thomas sensed very distant minds. He glimpsed palaces and cities through the eyes of foreign Torth. A dozen other people. A hundred other people. A thousand.
Double that. Quintuple that, and on and on. A million Torth connected to his mind.
Outward he swept, out and out and out, far past the boundaries of his previous life, to distant and fantastic places. The Torth Empire was much larger than a single city. The empire was everywhere. They had colonized more than ninety million planets.
They owned literally everything that was known.
Not even his capable mind could encompass the empire. It was a galaxy. The network of knowledge was so staggeringly huge, he couldn't understand how he'd never seen it before! It was like living on a mountain all one's life and never once looking up to see the all-powerful sun! He was seeing everything in existence! He was hearing a trillion melodies! The power and size of the Torth Empire was beyond imagination!
His eyes bulged, and he gasped for air in between the racing currents of information. He gripped his wheelchair's armrests until his knuckles went white.
All of this (Mine)? It was the only coherent thought he could manage.
Ours, the Upward Governess corrected.
How could I not see it before? Yellow Thomas marveled. Facts and images and lives tore through his mind, filtered and sorted the instant they entered, in a deluge that made everything before it look like a faucet leak. He lived through a dozen Torth lives, a hundred, ten thousand, two million, and on and on until he felt as though his brain would melt.
He saw the aftermath of a volcanic eruption on Tuthwa, the second-largest moon of Vazza, seventy thousand light-years away.
He admired the latest fashion trend set by Kemkorcan colonists.
He watched a colorful solar eclipse on Jev Rattad, an ancient agricultural planet, through the eyes of one of its colonists.
He rode with an interstellar survey crew as they drew near an icy planet orbiting a gas giant.
He witnessed a supernova through an explorer who'd died in it, sending the image on to other Torth even as she was vaporized.
He understood the exact range and limits of orbital stations and how ionic polymer tungsten-carbide spaceship hulls withstood the radiation of solar flares.

He understood the genetic mutations that afflicted the empire and how mutations were controlled through selective breeding on baby farms. He knew what medicine each one required. Experiences washed through him, faster and faster, depositing their information in his mind and sending him hurtling toward the next new thing.

During the Adulthood Exam, he had barely flickered an eyelid, and now he felt as though he might shriek from awe.

This is God, the old, obsolete part of him whispered. *I am seeing God.*

You ought to withdraw now, the Upward Governess silently suggested. Her gigantic mind was less impressive in the Megacosm, since there was so much knowledge around her. She was like a whale cruising through an endless ocean. *It may be too much (too overwhelming) for your first time.*

But there was still more, and more, and more! Individuals danced in and out of the background of his mind, all commenting on everything he saw and heard and smelled and felt. Their collective wisdom piled up and enhanced every experience.

The Megacosm will (still) (always) exist, the Upward Governess thought, bulking into his immediate awareness. *Drop down so We can have a coherent conversation.*

Reluctant, Yellow Thomas slid back into his solo self.

It felt like dropping out of the heavens. Oh, but he was not the same person he had been. The old version, Thomas Hill, had been severely limited.

Eight seconds in the Megacosm had augmented his knowledge a thousandfold. Just eight seconds.

His ordinary range of telepathy now felt like a straitjacket.

Distance meant nothing in the Megacosm. A Torth could stroll through a garden while chatting with colleagues on the far side of the galaxy, while the light from their local suns required over a hundred thousand years to reach each other. Yellow Thomas had been missing out on the wonders of the galaxy all his life. Other Torth shared huge amounts of knowledge, immersed in the Megacosm from infancy until death. His limited childhood was a handicap more severe than any neuromuscular disease.

Correct, the Upward Governess sent. *Since you grew up apart from other mind readers, you only knew the low form of telepathy. The Megacosm is the high form.*

Her mind seemed monstrous and inscrutable once more—but only because he had downshifted. He was a level below the Megacosm, while she continued to swim in it.

So it was with all the Torth.

They had never hidden their thoughts from him. They simply existed on a higher plane, sharing their real-time perceptions and knowledge with Torth on distant worlds while simultaneously dealing with him.

You understand, the Upward Governess sent.

He did. The Megacosm was what made him a god. Slaves and luxuries…? Those were just perks.

That wonderfully busy plane of existence hovered just above Yellow Thomas, calling to him, inviting him to come back, warming him like sunlight on his skin. Its presence was a comfort such as he had never known.

CHAPTER 12
INHIBITED

Yellow Thomas cautiously ascended into the Megacosm again, wondering if he could learn the layout of this city.

The instant that thought crossed his mind, hundreds of blueprints compiled inside his head. He had somehow attracted orbiters—minds that orbited his, curious about his experiences—and those orbiters reacted to his unspoken query by asking their own orbiters, who then queried others until answers were found and shared and reshared.

Within seconds, Yellow Thomas learned all sorts of facts about New GoodLife WaterGarden City. He became familiar with every spire, every garden, every indoor boulevard. He knew the construction sites. He learned every inch of the labyrinthine slave quarters, including ventilation ducts and garbage chutes. The layouts fit together with admirable efficiency.

Our greatest living engineer designed the new construction, multitudes chorused.

This is a remade city,
architected by the Upward Governess.

Torth would not make jokes.

Yellow Thomas stared at the girl, who looked like she was only thirteen or fourteen years old. She twitched her fingers in a beckoning symbol for food.

Indeed, she confirmed, sensing his disbelief. *I began my architectural overhaul five years ago (translated to an Earth time scale).*

She shared a few select personal memories. It was true. She had pioneered more efficient ways of designing pipes and ducts, and her reconceptualization of outdated systems had led to the reblossoming of an ancient city. Now slaves labored to build new skyscrapers, to accommodate a fast-growing local population of Torth.

You are the greatest living engineer? Yellow Thomas marveled at that.

On Earth, nobody who looked like her could have gained enough authority to make monumental things happen. On Earth, people would have prejudged her because she was an obese adolescent. She would have had to prove herself capable again and again and again before anyone took her seriously.

Is that so? The Upward Governess seemed interested. *Are all humans so judgmental?*

Yellow Thomas was distracted by a troupe of slaves who came into the atrium, bearing platters of food. The smells were enticing, and his stomach growled. A nearby slave looked startled by the noise.

Hunger is uncouth (rude) (slave-like), the Upward Governess informed him primly. *You need to stop feeling it.* She pointed to a platter for herself.

Yellow Thomas selected a stew. His mouth watered.

Ease into the Megacosm while you eat, the Upward Governess suggested. *You will experience something new.*

A slave spooned stew into Yellow Thomas's watering mouth, and while he ate, he ascended.

Echoes of the delicious taste flooded him from a thousand firsthand sources.

This stew had originally been developed on the planet Yoft, by early colonists. It was seasoned with fresh herbs from one of the Upward Governess's private gardens. He learned every ingredient, from harvest to cooking, its nutritional value, and its popularity.

An ever-shifting population of orbiters shared his taste journey with him, and this was remarkably more exquisite than tasting it alone. Every individual experienced taste differently. The Megacosm provided a grand composite.

Every spoonful was like learning a dazzlingly new sensation.

In a dim part of his mind, Yellow Thomas realized that he had just suffered the most grueling ordeal of his life. He ought to be shaking from relief and exhaustion. Instead, he felt…well, blissful.

You're on painkillers, many Torth informed him as soon as he wondered why. They brought his attention to the golden cuff around his ankle.

A medical patch, distant minds sang without words.

It keeps you free from harmful bacteria and viruses.

A longevity mixture slows your aging process.

And you will not feel minor aches or pains.

Medicine was freely distributed to all Torth, and it was powerful enough to double a life span. Everything was free to Torth.

Yellow Thomas gazed longingly at his NAI-12 medicine case. Cherise *(no) (slaves don't matter) (don't think of her)* had drawn metallic phoenix birds on the lid. Not that Torth cared about human artwork.

Supergeniuses seem to be highly valued, Yellow Thomas thought. *So why not give Us the best medical benefits? I don't understand.*

The Upward Governess gestured for a berry slurpy. *The Majority doesn't want Us to live to adulthood.*

Yellow Thomas sensed several other huge minds in the Megacosm, agreeing with her. Other supergeniuses.

They were curious about him. And they emitted bitter envy of the Upward Governess, since none of them ranked high enough to claim even a portion of the medicine. Once the Upward Governess used up the limited supply of NAI-12, it would be gone forever. No one was allowed to duplicate it or manufacture more.

Yellow Thomas began to press the issue, wondering why the Majority was so shortsighted, but he sensed a very subtle warning from the Upward Governess. Her mind sharpened for a nanosecond. That sharpening was so brief, only a quick-minded supergenius would have detected it.

She slurped on her berry drink as if nothing was amiss.

All right. Yellow Thomas decided to drop the matter, for now. His mind returned to the golden cuff fastened around his ankle. He hadn't seen any other Torth wearing such a cuff.

(Shh) shh

Shh.

Dangerous among Us.

Later (someone else will tell him).

Yes, later.

Uneasy minds fluttered away from his inquiries about the cuff. It contained an additive, something no one wanted to discuss.

When Yellow Thomas tried to follow threads about the additive, the minds he followed lost themselves in distant currents of knowledge. He only caught a few answers.

Inhibitor serum. That was how the Torth thought of it.

(shh)

(irrelevant)

(he is inhibited)

A necessity.

Because certain mutations were too dangerous.

Dangerous?

No one wanted to explain more. Not the Servants of All, not the children on baby farms. Yellow Thomas only got a whisper of a remembered word, a remnant from an extinct language.

(Yeresunsa)

That word carried connotations of power. Lightning bolts. Tornadoes. Earthquakes.

Yellow Thomas nearly choked on his last bite of stew.

There *was* a certain awful power he had used when he was six years old. He would never use it again. Bile rose in his throat as he remembered a corpse caked with makeup and mud, pressed next to him in the passenger seat of a pickup truck.

He hurled the memory away, hoping it would never resurface. That scared and miserable foster kid was no longer him. He had nothing to do with that child.

The Upward Governess studied him as she finished off the platter of sausages. *You buried that particular trauma well during your Adulthood Exam,* she thought with a hint of admiration. *Very few people can hide knowledge from testers. Or from Me. Your mind is undernourished in comparison to that of other supergeniuses, but even so, you nearly buried that tidbit beneath irrelevancies and distractions. Well done!* She sipped from her berry beverage. *I anticipate that I will enjoy conversing with you, with your surprises. I relish surprises.*

Yellow Thomas focused on tasting his stew. He didn't feel proud. He needed to stick to pleasurable perceptions and facts and avoid anything that might trigger an illegal emotion.

He had inhibited powers.

Was he the only one? Did other Torth have such *(evil) (disturbing) (illegal)* powers?

His orbiters fed him answers. *Teams of pediatric scientists—*

—weed out Yeresunsa—

—on baby farms.

Yeresunsa should not exist.

Powers are illegal.

Ah. Yellow Thomas was a freak who had avoided baby farm regulation, so here he was, born with illegal powers. Yet instead of executing him, the Torth Majority had voted to embrace him. Why?

(Potential)

(Supergenius)

We have never allowed a Yeresunsa

to live (freely) until now.

You are the first.

Hm. Someone must have persuaded the Torth Majority to allow a Yeresunsa to live among them for the first time in history. Yellow Thomas studied the Upward Governess.

I may have had some influence there, the Upward Governess admitted with casual ambivalence. She gestured for a platter of buttery muffins.

Millions of Torth sent Yellow Thomas an image of the cuff he wore. *NEVER REMOVE IT.*

He is not an imbecile, the Upward Governess thought.

His orbiters went on, flashing dire warnings. *If you remove it,
then We (the Torth Majority)
will have you executed,
alongside the Giant.*

Yellow Thomas closed his mouth, the heavenly tastes now like dirt on his tongue. Did Ariock *(no, names don't matter)* the doomed Giant also have illegal powers?

Yes. The Upward Governess handed the reply to Yellow Thomas without qualms or fanfare. *The Giant is small-minded and mostly human, but he has enough Torth DNA to be dangerous.* She pictured a snug collar around the Giant's neck, the equivalent of Thomas's ankle cuff. *He did inherit illegal powers. His collar acts as an inhibitor patch.*

HE IS DANGEROUS! the orbiters around Yellow Thomas's mind emphasized.

Tests prove that he is a powerful Yeresunsa, the Upward Governess clarified. *The Majority has deemed him too dangerous to live, even with the inhibitor.*

HE MUST DIE! the orbiters around Yellow Thomas's mind chorused.

The Upward Governess chowed down on muffins, uncaring about the future execution of an innocent man.

Yellow Thomas stared. Ariock *(no, his name is irrelevant)* the Giant had never harmed anyone in his life. Any mind reader should know that.

I happen to agree, the Upward Governess thought. *The inhibitor is sufficient to render even the most powerful Yeresunsa harmless. We (Torth) could use the Giant for slave labor instead of for entertainment. He would be useful on a construction crew.* She sighed. *But most Torth are uninterested in progressive change. It was a struggle to get the Majority to accept you.*

Millions of Torth flooded into the conversation from locations all over the galaxy. *The Giant is violent!*

They replayed a recent news feed: the Giant fought a troop of nussian prison guards. He had actually snapped a spike off one guard.

Dangerous! many Torth chorused.

Yellow Thomas guessed that *(Ariock)* the giant hybrid had been scared, acting in self-defense. Surely he would cooperate with anything the Torth wanted? He wore an inhibitor collar. He didn't even know that he had powers. Couldn't they use him for slave labor, as the Upward Governess suggested?

Why hurt him? Why kill him? It seemed monstrously unfair.

HE MUST BE EXECUTED.

Even more millions of Torth tuned in. Their collective condemnation felt like a tsunami.

The collar might break, or fail.
  If the Giant tapped into his power,
    even by accident,
      even for a few minutes,
        a guarded prison cell would not be enough.
        An army would not be enough.
          HE MUST DIE!

All around Yellow Thomas, Torth feasted, uncaring about the condemned prisoner from Earth. To them, the Giant was a wild card, a dangerously powerful monster.

And a tourist attraction.

Tourists were visiting New GoodLife WaterGarden City from all over the galaxy, eager to witness the monster perform fights in a prison arena. Tourists and locals would vie to be selected as firsthand witnesses to his death.

A frustrated feeling welled up inside Yellow Thomas.

He forced himself to focus on mundane things, to calm down. But why did the Torth Majority want to force the Giant into a gladiatorial arena? Wasn't that irrational? If Torth eschewed intense emotions, then why did they have arenas? Why torture anyone?

We derive no joy from torture, many Torth assured Yellow Thomas.
  We do not cheer or applaud, like primitives.
  But a quick death is insufficient—
    —to symbolize the vanquishing of a monster.
    Experts will break his mind and body,
      to make this event a memorable spectacle,
        so that memories of it—
          —will gain wider distribution,
            and be better preserved.

A Majority of interested Torth—51.89 percent—had voted in favor of making the Giant's death a spectacle.

The Majority are often idiotic. The Upward Governess ate a muffin. *Personally, I find torture tedious (boring). But I am in the minority on this issue, just like you, little Yellow. We are outvoted.*

Yellow Thomas lost his appetite.

He understood that plenty of Torth wanted the Giant executed right away, without fanfare. But in the Torth Empire, the Majority ruled. That same Majority had voted to make Yellow Thomas a Torth citizen, by some margin of votes.

He didn't want to know what percentage of the galactic Torth population had voted to give him the chance to survive.

His orbiters carried the information to him anyway—*50.43* percent.

There must be more than a few bitter losers who wanted him dead. He thought of his biological aunt, the Swift Killer.

You are safe, the Upward Governess and millions of orbiters assured him. *Everyone must obey the Majority.*

Right.

Disobedience meant execution.

Yellow Thomas shook his head at a slave who was offering to serve him a crepe. He yearned for a bath. He smelled awful, and he no longer wanted to think *(in public)*. He wanted to be alone for a while.

Alone? his orbiters wondered. *What does that mean?*

Do you wish for a privacy break?

Yellow Thomas supposed that was what he wanted. Was there a bedroom he could use? He would be grateful to catch up on sleep.

As a Yellow Rank, you own a personal suite. Local orbiters pictured a palatial bedroom, where attendant slaves would obey his every command. Pillows strewed the enormous bed.

Yellow Thomas learned the location of his new residence. But before he could inquire about someone to push his battery-drained wheelchair, the Upward Governess signaled for his attention.

Wait. She waggled her fingers in a command gesture at one of her personal slaves. *I have a welcome gift to give you, Yellow Thomas.*

Yellow Thomas tried to minimize *(?)* the anticipation he felt. All he really wanted was *(his friends)* his NAI-12 medicine.

Her slave left and then returned, pushing an empty hoverchair. Yellow Thomas peered at the vehicle through the eyes of other Torth. Unlike most hoverchairs, this one was fit for his size. It was ergonomically adapted for his bent spine and atrophied limbs.

It was fancy, too. Starbursts embossed its sleek metallic curves.

A high-value (rare) (precious) gift, many Torth silently chorused.

Engineered by Our top (eldest) supergenius.

She (the Upward Governess) must truly see a lot of potential in Yellow Thomas.

This is really more than a typical Yellow Rank (deserves) gets.

The Upward Governess gestured for a hulking bodyguard, one of the thorny nussians, to transfer Yellow Thomas to his new hoverchair.

It was comfortable.

Better than comfortable. Yellow Thomas usually needed hours to adjust to a new chair, but this one adjusted to his malformed body. A toggle button caused the hoverchair to float higher or lower.

Thank You. Yellow Thomas sent the Upward Governess his gratitude.

She emanated approval, but she gently educated him. *"Thank you," "please," and other platitudes are pointless slave concepts.* She beckoned for another platter of pastries.

Yellow Thomas explored the control panel, wondering how long the chair's battery would last. He was curious to learn how levitation worked. Did the hoverchair use an antigravity principle?

Physicists and electromagnetic engineers explored his mind, eager to share their expertise with a fledging supergenius. They inundated Yellow Thomas with illustrations of the gyroscopic magnet disk that caused his hoverchair to levitate. A flexible metamaterial encased the magnet, augmenting its repellent behavior against the planet's magnetic field.

Fascinating. Yellow Thomas settled into his new seat.

When he expressed curiosity about his benefactor, thousands of Torth chorused that the Upward Governess was truly amazing. They silently sang that she was exceptional even for a supergenius.

Like all Torth, the Upward Governess had been born on a baby farm. Babies held no rank or status. But even as a toddler, she had aced every mental acuity test given to her, and she consistently solved adult-level problems. At an age that was equivalent to six Earth years, she had engineered a new material that revolutionized orbital docking stations.

Since she was born with the fatal supergenius mutation, her estimated life span was greatly reduced. The Majority had voted to offer her the Adulthood Exam at an extremely early age. She passed it and became an adult citizen well before puberty.

Most adult citizens remained Yellow Rank all their lives. The Upward Governess had achieved Green Rank by the age of seven, having designed an unconventional yet very successful air traffic rotation. Next, she had pioneered the use of a synthetic polymer that would improve the structural integrity of stone buildings. That impressed high ranks, including Servants of All, and earned her a promotion to Turquoise Blue, a huge leap up.

At an age equivalent to nine and a half years old, she had planned an upgrade to this metropolis, including accurate projections of population growth. Her techniques were successes and had become standard for new construction in arid regions. She had even made improvements to reinforced sandstone. She currently held the highest rank possible for an engineer: Indigo Blue. Only Servants of All had higher status. This city and province were hers to govern.

And she was a popular governess. Local Torth were proud to dwell in a city with near-perfect infrastructure.

Yellow Thomas studied her as she ate a sweet roll. Why had the Majority sent him to this particular city, governed by the eldest supergenius in the Torth Empire? Why here, and not one of the other billions of urban areas throughout the galaxy?

I requested you. The Upward Governess seemed vaguely amused by how little he understood. *Many scientists (the brightest minds) requested you. When We (the Torth Empire) learned of your existence a couple of weeks ago, everyone was impressed by your ability to engineer a neuronal apoptosis inhibitor using only primitive resources.* She turned her head, allowing a slave to blot crumbs off her mouth with a linen napkin. *I am pleased that My request won out over all the others.*

Yellow Thomas was beginning to suspect that she had ordered something akin to a banquet—and he was on the menu. Her web of influence might extend beyond the scope of her rank.

Well, he thought, *I am honored to be here.* He yawned. *Will You excuse Me? I wish to retire to My bedroom suite.*

He began to float away.

She followed.

In her mind, she extended an offer, like a queen offering a jeweled gift to a peasant. *Would you like Me to escort you to your new suite?*

Yellow Thomas did not need an escort. He already knew the way due to the maps in his head. He nearly refused.

Yet other Torth marveled at the generous offer. It was such a great honor!

And Yellow Thomas sensed a brief hint in the depths of the Upward Governess's overly complicated thoughts, encoded beneath so much trivia that no one else could have picked up on it. A reminder. She had saved his life.

There was a subtext implied there. She expected accommodation. She expected Yellow Thomas to agree to anything she requested, because he owed her. He owed her a lot.

He shoved down his worries about why she wanted to lavish him with attention. Maybe she was just being friendly?

Although Torth did not have friends.

Sure. Yellow Thomas swallowed his anxiety and tried to feel honored. *I respectfully accept Your company.*

CHAPTER 13

TORTH BLOOD

A babble of sound woke Kessa. There were so many voices, she wondered if she had accidentally fallen asleep in the Tunnels thoroughfares instead of in her bunk room.

"…kick them awake!" someone nearby was saying.

"Wait to see if their collars are real," someone else said. "They should be shocked awake at any moment."

The bunks were overcrowded, with three or four slaves sitting together, and more slaves blocked the doorway. All gazes were fixed on the three collared Torth, who remained asleep on the floor.

"Kessa! Did you sleep well?" That was Pung, the smuggler. He sat on the end of her bunk, his grimy rags bulging with smuggled food. "I don't know how you could sleep with three Torth nearby, sucking up thoughts all night."

Kessa sat up, groaning from various aches. "Peace, Pung."

Her smuggler friend had a flat beak and unblemished gray skin, which made him more handsome than most ummins. But he wore his hat askew. And…

"Oh, no," Kessa said, noticing his gray collar. "Did your owner trade you away? What happened?"

"It's all right." Pung reached into his rags and pulled out a meaty wafer. "I like being unowned. If I had an owner, I wouldn't be able to do this."

Kessa tried not to lick her beak.

Pung hid the wafer so that no one else would notice and broke it in half. "Everybody is talking about you," he said, handing half to her. "Kessa the Wise, who speaks with Torth." He clicked his beak. "Dangerous, Kessa."

"I am still here." She ate the wafer, greasy and delicious. Pung had probably risked his life to smuggle it out of a kitchen. "You take worse risks than anyone I know," she said pointedly.

Pung was a lot like her mate used to be. Cozu had strained for freedom in every small way he could manage.

That attitude was what got him killed.

Unowned slaves were actually owned by all Torth. They were as worthless as sand to the gods. Kessa hoped, for Pung's sake, that another Torth would claim him, because then he would have a modicum of value to at least one mind reader.

"I came as soon as I heard." Pung finished his half of the wafer in three bites. "I had to shove a few mighty fools out of my way to get inside. So, what happened?" He licked crumbs off his fingers. "I hope you leave those Torth pretend-slaves alone. Anyone can see they're trouble."

Kessa reached over to straighten Pung's hat so the folds framed his face in the proper way. "I'm fine. Have you found a mate yet?"

Pung adjusted his hat back to his liking. "A few prospects. No one as interesting as you."

A shriek sounded across the room, causing Kessa to drop her remaining bit of wafer. One of the collared Torth flailed, screaming.

Hajir extended his triple-jointed neck and announced what was happening for those who couldn't see. "The Green is thrashing like a beast...she just hit the Blue, I think by accident. The Brown is sitting up and yanking at her collar...she looks insane...yes. Their collars are glowing for a work shift. Looks like they're real."

The crowd began to panic, apparently terrified that the collared Torth would single one of them out for punishment. Slaves shoved each other, some trying to flee, others eager to see the enslaved Torth. Weptolyso roared loud enough to be heard above the ruckus, reminding them that a hall guard was present.

Kessa stood and pocketed the remains of her wafer. "I'm going over there."

Pung jumped up to block her. "Why?"

Kessa squeezed past him, forcing her way through the mob. How could she explain why she needed to do this? She didn't understand it herself. Even Cozu, the biggest risk-taker she had ever known, would have avoided these Torth-slaves. He would have said the same things Pung was saying.

Pung gripped her arm. "Kessa, they won't offer favors for helping them. Your collar is glowing. You need to go to work!"

True. Kessa's owner might kill her if she showed up late for work.

"Maybe I will take them to work with me," she said.

If her own words surprised her, Pung was stunned. He needed a moment to recover. Then he seized her shoulders. "I will not let you do this."

She pried his hands off. "I choose my risks, and you choose yours."

"I can tell a friend when she is courting death!" Pung said fiercely. "How will your owner react when she sees those collared Torth working alongside her personal slave? She might blame you for it!"

Kessa hesitated. She had lived a long time by taking good advice when she heard it. She put aside her own curiosity when it was too dangerous. What could the Torth-slaves bring her? Only death. That was true.

But if she left the three Torth-slaves to their fate…she would lose her chance to learn more of their language and secrets.

A mob would surely kill them by the end of the day. Then all she would have was her own monotonous future. Window washing. Carpet cleaning. Death.

I am on the verge of becoming a dreamer, she realized, because right now, she felt more awake than she'd been for many lunar cycles.

She was familiar with numbness. When Red Ranks had taken Cozu, she had shut down. That was a long time ago, in a different city, where a muddy ocean lapped below garden terraces. Kessa had drifted through that work shift, scrubbing foamy rugs and polishing floors. She remembered noticing how dirty water clogged the outdoor paths. When her collar shocked her, she had realized that an entire day had gone by without her being aware of it.

And that hadn't bothered her. All she'd felt was a sense of loss for Cozu. Nothing else mattered.

Weeks later, she'd overheard that Cozu had been tortured to death. The news barely stirred her. A wall formed around her heart, protecting her from atrocities. The slaves who worked beside her were not people, but meaningless blobs of flesh. Anyone could die at any time, and another would instantly replace them. The collar she wore became part of her skin, so she stopped scratching at it and accepted it as her master. When it pricked her neck, she slept or ate. When it shocked her, she woke up. The Torth were as powerful as gods, and she realized how foolish she'd been to ever think she could affect them. To hate them was as useless as hating the desert wind for parching the throat. A rebellion was as laughable as a plot to assassinate the stars.

She'd withdrawn further into her own mind, because it was the only trick she had left to ensure her survival. Otherwise the screams would build up inside and ultimately kill her.

In time, with help from friends, Kessa had climbed out of her fog. But she would never forget those vanished cycles of numbness.

She clutched Pung's hands. He was too young to know the burden of how losses piled up. "Pung," she said, "I need to do this."

With that, she plunged back into the crowd.

Pung lunged after her. "If you want help during your shift, I'll help you!" he called.

"Kessa has lost her wits," someone said.

"Old one," a young ummin said. "I will pray for you."

"They'll kill you!" another ummin said in despair.

The Torth-slaves cried in frightened voices. Their collars were gray, like Pung's. They lacked the protection of having an owner.

The stout one scratched so frantically at her collared neck, she accidentally gouged herself. Red liquid oozed out. Kessa had never seen a Torth bleed before. The blood looked similar to her own.

Kessa timidly touched that one, the one named Delia.

Instead of punishing Kessa for daring to touch her with filthy slave hands, Delia calmed down. All three of the Torth-slaves stared at Kessa as if they doubted she was real.

"Is this how you wish to die, Kessa?" Hajir asked. "A victim of a Torth game?"

Kessa turned to the crowd, shielding the three newcomers with her small body. "Torth don't play games." She glared at Hajir, then Pung, then everyone else. "Torth don't wear slave collars. These three might teach us a lot."

The crowd calmed. There was fear, but there was also curiosity.

"I am bringing them to work with me." Kessa made command gestures to the three Torth. They seemed to understand beckoning summons, and they followed her toward the doorway.

An aisle formed. No one wanted to get within telepathy range of the three Torth.

"Thank you." Kessa swept out of the bunk room.

The three Torth followed.

If Pung and others didn't like it? Well, they would have to wait until the next sleep shift to chastise Kessa.

CHAPTER 14

SCHOOLED

Yellow Thomas could outpace a marathon runner. He slalomed around vine-shrouded pillars, impressed with his newfound agility.

All the normal obstacles that impeded wheelchairs—uneven ground, curbs, sand—were not a problem. The Torth Empire favored ramps instead of staircases.

Best of all, the hoverchair could recharge itself, simply by using ambient heat and solar radiation! It needed no electric cords! It was practically maintenance-free!

Among Torth, Yellow Thomas was learning, there was no divide whatsoever between the able-bodied and the physically disabled. Medicine could treat or prevent all but the most fatal of symptoms. Advanced prosthetics could actually improve upon missing limbs. As for caretakers and expensive equipment? Those things were free for all mind readers. Every baby owned a slave.

As a Yellow Rank, Thomas owned two slaves. They awaited him in his new suite.

You own three slaves, the Upward Governess corrected him. *The Majority assigns anyone with a severe disabilities (like Us) three slaves to start with.*

Well, then.

Yellow Thomas navigated past a lumbering bodyguard, one of those owned by the Upward Governess. His inner audience continued to feed him information. They taught him that his three starter slaves were randomly chosen, and he was encouraged to swap them for three of his own personal choice.

Not humans, though. He was too low in rank to claim exotic slaves or guard species.

The Upward Governess, in contrast, owned dozens of exotics and nussians.

Yellow Thomas sized up her huge bodyguards, with their thorns and their overlapped plates of armored skin. No doubt a nussian could crush a professional wrestler. Knives and spears would not pierce their hides.

He sensed that these particular nussians had never defended their owner against violence. They were trained to protect Torth, yet they had never acted upon their training.

So why own bodyguards?

They are superfluous, the Upward Governess admitted in the wordless Torth mental language. *Just status symbols.* She floated down the indoor boulevard, and Yellow Thomas floated by her side. *Slave revolts do happen, but they are exceedingly rare. And My city is prosperous. The slaves here are content enough. The chances that I will face violence in My lifetime are less than 0.00001 percent. But...* She gave a mental shrug. *High Ranks (such as Myself) are expected to own bodyguards. I would not want to disappoint My (orbiters) admirers.*

Her mental tone was light and bubbly.

They passed an indoor beach, where nudists soaked up sunlight. The old version of Thomas would have been agog. Now he barely noticed. Why care about nudity or mundane amusements when he could explore any place in the known universe, just by wishing to do so?

Every time he brushed through a mind in the Megacosm, he experienced everything visceral about their body. He saw and heard and felt everything they perceived.

On Earth, he had been limited by his four-yard radius of telepathic perception. Now? Now he understood how it felt to swim, to climb, to run, to ride a massive beast, to skim an ocean's surface on a watercraft. As long as he was connected to the Megacosm, he felt healthy and strong and free.

He felt powerful.

His orbiters sparkled with amusement. They had been connected to the Megacosm since infancy. It was weird to meet a supergenius who was nearly as ignorant as a baby.

Such a fledgling, they silently whispered to each other.

A growing number of minds in his mental background posed questions to him. They wanted to learn more about Earth. What was it like to observe primitives in their native habitat? Did unsupervised primitives yearn for gods to tell them how to act and what to do?

Also...might Yellow Thomas consider becoming a xeno-anthropologist?

Choose Me as your mentor! a prominent xeno-anthropologist urged him. *You can contribute a lot to My field of science. I can help you rise to an expert level fairly quickly. With Me as your mentor, you can potentially attain Green Rank within—*

An influential neuroscientist overrode that one. *I am sure that Yellow Thomas would rather become a neurobiologist*, he preened. *Choose Me as your mentor, fledging supergenius, and you will rise high.*

A Brown Rank suggested that Yellow Thomas would make an excellent slave trainer. *Not only can you absorb a rudimentary language within minutes, but you also have well-developed vocal cords.* Most Torth required years to master the slave tongue. *Choose Me, and you will be promoted fast!*

Multiple Blue Ranks sent derision toward that one. *Why would a prom-ising supergenius waste time with a lowly Brown Rank, working with slaves?*

He is more suited to intellectual pursuits.

(chemistry)

(mathematics)

(physics)

More orbiters clamored for Yellow Thomas's attention.

Choose Me as your mentor.

No, that narcissist won't help you much. Choose Me!

Choose Me!

Choose Me (Me) Me!

The Upward Governess floated close to him so that their local ranges of telepathy overlapped. Fame made her highly visible in the Megacosm. That, and the sheer, godlike size of her mind. She eclipsed his orbiters.

I assume, she thought, *that you will choose Me as your mentor?*

(!?)

Yellow Thomas hesitated. Mentorship was serious business. He felt as if she was offering him a binding contract to sign.

Did he want to be under her close scrutiny? On a regular basis?

In the back of his mind, many thousands of orbiters hushed in awe. Su-pergeniuses were the most prestigious scientists in existence, but their lives were so short, they rarely accepted mentees. And the Upward Governess? She was a rarity among rarities! Even Powder-Blue Ranks would trade their most valuable luxuries to gain one-on-one attention from her.

She had never offered to mentor anyone until now.

This was a onetime opportunity.

Millions of Torth flooded Yellow Thomas's mind, peering through his eyes, riffling through his thoughts, trying to figure out what made him more worthy than everybody else.

The Upward Governess awaited his agreement, tapping one finger very subtly on the NAI-12 briefcase.

Yellow Thomas's gaze went there.

Might she help him to gather ingredients for a secret batch? Maybe she would allow him to use a vial or two?

I am Your ready pupil, Yellow Thomas decided.

Her thoughts fuzzed with pleasure. *Good.*

Yellow Thomas accepted the unwritten, unspoken, yet wholly binding contract. It was witnessed by the Majority. That made it official. The entire process took less than a second.

Onward they floated.

Yellow Thomas had questions about mentorships, among other things. He popped in and out of the minds of astrophysicists, chemists, and pioneers, learning and learning. Any questions that crossed his mind were answered within milliseconds. Thousands of people offered him their fields of expertise, as much as he could take.

The Upward Governess silently encouraged his thirst for knowledge.

Millions of scientists sensed her will, and crowds surged to please her. They vied with each other to instruct Yellow Thomas.

An ever-shifting Torth audience spent all day learning from her. Even if the Upward Governess was on the far side of the galaxy, anyone who wanted to find her only needed to ascend into the Megacosm and wonder where she was. Then people would ping their colleagues, who then pinged to others, and others, until they located her towering mind. The chain might span hundreds of people even if it only lasted for a millisecond.

She affected the Megacosm like a weather phenomenon. As she gulped huge amounts of knowledge, her multitudinous audience leaped to catch the eddies of intellectual discussions swirling in her wake. Yellow Thomas wondered what she might teach him. He doubted he could ever catch up to the sheer amount of knowledge she contained.

You can never catch up, the Upward Governess affirmed. *I have spent My entire life in the Megacosm, whereas you have not. But knowledge is like dirt. Without water (creativity) (ambition) (innovation), nothing grows there. It just dries up and blows away.*

Yellow Thomas supposed he knew what she meant. There was a difference between wisdom and intelligence.

Exactly. She replayed a news feed of a young supergenius who had overdosed on painkillers, committing suicide. *Ambition is rare among supergeniuses. More than 25 percent of supergeniuses never get promoted out of childhood. They die on baby farms (worthless). You and I are better than most.*

He was beginning to understand why she wanted to mentor him.

!!!

Warnings clanged through the Megacosm around Yellow Thomas. His orbiters sent him images of the Swift Killer straddling a hoverbike, fast approaching.

The Swift Killer believes your Adulthood Exam was incomplete! his orbiters warned.

The Upward Governess glided to a stop, urging Yellow Thomas to do the same. She exuded a lighthearted frustration, like someone rolling their eyes. *The Swift Killer is (a moron) an ache who keeps coming back to bother Me. Let Us get this confrontation over with.*

Yellow Thomas did not need to turn around to see the Swift Killer. Every Torth pedestrian on the street did that for him, sharing their perceptions with their audiences, who then reshared it with others.

The Swift Killer glided to a stop and leaped off her hoverbike, glaring at the two supergeniuses. Distrust frosted her thoughts. Her milky gaze seemed to drill into their souls.

Yellow Thomas will never punish a slave, the Swift Killer assured the masses orbiting her mind. *He might even try to free slaves. Punishment should have been included in his Adulthood Exam. Trust Me. I have studied human behavior with more focus and expertise than anyone—including the Upward Governess.*

An accusation aimed at a highly respected supergenius drew galactic attention.

Distant Torth piled into Yellow Thomas, pulling in more listeners, who pulled in more. He felt like a dying bug pinned under a spotlight.

The mind of the Upward Governess was like a fortress, impenetrable. *This is preposterous.*

But the Swift Killer went on, bolstered by many orbiters. *Yellow Thomas is incapable of acting like an adult and punishing slaves. Let him prove Me wrong!*

The massive audience swirled with debates. A Majority opinion quickly emerged.

Yes (yes).

This is reasonable.

We all learned to punish slaves as children.

He never has.

LET HIM PROVE HIS MATURITY!

Yellow Thomas began to sweat, despite his best efforts to remain calm. He struggled to control his primitive physiological reaction. He really did not want to punish a slave.

The Swift Killer bared her teeth in a parody of a smile. *Fetch one of the humans.* She pictured the one with eyeglasses. *Let him punish that one. Let Us see if he can manage it.*

Orbiters slithered in and out of Yellow Thomas's mind. *Is he having an illegal emotional reaction?*

The Upward Governess seemed thorny, as if her mind was a thistle patch. *No adult Torth should ever be forced to do something against their will. He just passed the Adulthood Exam, and now You demand another test from him? Where will it end?*

Many Torth agreed. *This is wrong.*

If We undermine what it means to be a Torth citizen, that is a slippery slope.

But a lot of Torth supported the Swift Killer.

Many exceptions were made for Yellow Thomas, they thought. *Why not make one more?*

It is a very minor (not onerous) request.

If he punishes a slave, We can put this matter to rest.

Our suspicions will end.

The Swift Killer agreed. *If he does it,* she thought, *I will accept that he is one of Us. I will leave him alone.*

If he does it, the Upward Governess thought, *You will owe Me (yet another) favor. Agreed?*

Their mutual orbiters swirled in excitement.

The Swift Killer had no choice. She felt the pressure from her orbiters, and she emanated a reluctant agreement. *Fine.*

Their frothy exchange attracted ever more attention. Hundreds of millions of debaters explored Yellow Thomas, peering through his eyes, experiencing his weak body. He felt as if a supernova was exploding inside his head.

Should We force him to punish a slave???

The debate bounced its way upward through the highest echelons of Torth society. Everyone sought the opinions of thought leaders and influencers. They sought their elected officials. Eventually, the question reached the highest authority—a paragon of Torth perfection, the elected leader who was honored with the title Commander of All Living Things.

Yes? The Commander of All Living Things tuned in, pulled by the many who yearned for her opinion.

Yellow Thomas joined her inner audience. He felt the strength of her cybernetic limbs, juxtaposed with the frailty of her advanced age. She was over one hundred and eighty years old. Yet she rode a hoverbike between lava flows on a distant planet, her shroud-like cape billowing behind her.

What do You think, Commander? millions of Torth clamored. *Should Yellow Thomas be coerced into proving that he is willing to punish slaves?*

I think this is a trivial matter. The Commander of All Living Things jumped her hoverbike over some wreckage, surveying damage from a lava eruption. *But such a test will allay common concerns about Our unusual new citizen. (Most of Us know that supergeniuses do not always pursue the best interests of the public.) Proceed.*

Many Torth bowed to her wisdom.

The decision was made.

WE WANT PROOF, the Torth Majority thundered.

AND WE WANT IT NOW.

The Upward Governess seemed unable to fight the overwhelming Majority. She sighed and thought, *Very well. Let Us get this over with.*

She beckoned to a pedestrian slave who was trying to sneak past the traffic jam. It was an ummin, one of the common gray aliens with beaks that were indigenous to this planet.

No. The Swift Killer radiated disgust. *Fetch the human slave!*

That will take too long, the Upward Governess thought with acerbic annoyance. *Any slave will do.*

The Majority debated that and agreed.

Yes!

Let Us see him punish a slave now (now) NOW!

The ummin approached with reluctant obedience.

Yellow Thomas wiped sweat off his palms. Could he possibly figure out a way to avoid torturing an innocent ummin? At least this was not *(Cherise) (no)* anyone he knew.

Do it, the Upward Governess prompted him.

Everyone was watching. The Swift Killer. Torth passersby. And, most of all, the millions of Torth inside his head. Even the Commander of All Living Things was paying attention.

The ummin slave watched Torth hands for command signals. It was painfully aware that its life was as disposable as tissue paper. All it knew was that it was the focal point of all nearby Torth. It had no idea why.

This is okay, Yellow Thomas told himself, over and over, like a prayer. *It's okay.*

A bit of extra pain should not matter in the life of a slave. Nothing was worth getting emotional about. He could do this. No big deal.

But when he probed the slave's mind, seeking its core, he felt sickened by the sad details of its life.

He didn't want to know that this ummin was young. Nor did he want to know about the carefully torn fringes of its rag outfit, each representing a dead friend. He really didn't want to know about the way it mourned for the parents and siblings it would never see again.

Focus, distant Torth urged.

What is wrong with him?

Why does he hesitate?

Yellow Thomas felt as if his chest had turned into a cavity.

The Upward Governess softly drummed her pudgy fingers on the lid of the NAI-12 medicine case. She tapped a silvery phoenix bird.

Survival.

Yellow Thomas focused on the trembling ummin slave. He needed to *(rescue certain people)* accomplish certain things. Survival was more important than anything. He had to do this.

Heart pounding, he tore through the slave's memories and moods, following well-worn pathways to the animal core that supported higher functionality.

It felt like a plug meeting a socket. Yellow Thomas did not dare pause to examine what he was doing. He propelled his will along the connection and sparked an electrical storm that tore through the slave's nervous system.

The slave fell and writhed, choking on pain.

Its cloth cap fell off and revealed a bald dome. Personal memories from the slave continued to flood Yellow Thomas, although he didn't have enough spare focus to process them. His awareness of the Megacosm had vanished. He and this slave were the only beings that existed in the universe.

Giving a pain seizure required all his enormous concentration. It rendered him unable to do anything else except breathe.

The slave's perceptions began to implode as its mind shut down. It was losing consciousness.

Unsure whether or not that was supposed to happen, Yellow Thomas lost his focus.

The rest of reality exploded back into existence around him. He was shaken and weak. The slave lay moaning on the floor.

Well done (for your first time), the Upward Governess congratulated him. She mentally nudged him toward the Megacosm.

He ascended.

Hundreds of millions of Torth congratulated him, buzzing with assurances that he had proven himself and that they no longer doubted his loyalty and sanity. He was a respectable Yellow Rank.

Good for you!

Giving punishment is draining (difficult) for all of Us.

But it is a necessary life skill.

Next time, end the punishment before the slave loses consciousness.

Yes. You almost killed it.

Also, be more lenient when you have to punish exotic slaves (such as humans).

They are harder to replace.

The tortured ummin staggered away. Yellow Thomas sensed its struggle not to cry, not to show weakness. It had no idea why it had been so severely punished. It might spend the rest of its life wondering why.

Yellow Thomas forced himself to stare at the Swift Killer.

The Upward Governess likewise stared. *I want recompense.* She exuded entitlement. *You (Swift Killer) wrongly insulted My judgment. So you owe Me a favor.*

Millions of distant Torth blazed with agreement. *The Swift Killer owes the Upward Governess!*

The Upward Governess seemed to already know what favor she wanted. *Get out of My city.* She sent the demand whip fast. *Get out and never return.*

Bitterness washed through the Swift Killer.

Yellow Thomas sensed her grinding her teeth, forcing turbulent thoughts to smooth out. She had been looking forward to torturing the Giant. Instead, she would have to watch his suffering from afar, through other people's perceptions.

She jumped on her hoverbike and sped away.

CHAPTER 15
THE CURRENCY OF SECRETS

Yellow Thomas sensed no triumph in his mentor. No kindness. No compassion. Her motives were hidden beneath torrents of data.

You may (eventually) figure out how to screen your private thoughts beneath data, little Yellow. The Upward Governess glided ahead, expecting him to keep up. *It is a trick that supergeniuses can master. But it isn't easy.*

Yellow Thomas sped up his hoverchair. *I appreciate Your help,* he thought awkwardly.

I can help you in a great many ways. As she communicated this, she seemed to be...searching...for local traffic observations. Instead of choosing a busy thoroughfare, she led him down a meandering garden path that was practically devoid of people.

For instance... The Upward Governess sent a vivid mental image of *(Cherise, Vy, Delia)* the three humans wearing slave collars. *I can get you exotic slaves. Would you like to exchange your default set for these?*

!!! Yellow Thomas struggled to dampen his reaction. He had not anticipated a gift like this.

Ooh. His inner audience collectively fantasized about human slaves. *S o exotic.*

Humans are lovely to look upon.

I can get them for you. The Upward Governess fanned statistics at him, implying that slaves survived longer if they had a lenient owner.

Yellow Thomas nearly agreed. It was plain that if he refused the gift, his foster siblings might end up with a cruel, abusive owner instead of him.

But his imagination leaped into potential scenarios. He would have to force Cherise *(no, her name is irrelevant)* to sponge-bathe him. And help him go to the bathroom.

His heart began to pound, as if he was hovering near the crumbling edge of a cliff. He dared not examine his embarrassment.

Vy *(no, her name is meaningless)* had been his primary caretaker for years. She could do those things.

But somehow, slavery crossed a line.

If he silently crooked his fingers, forcing Cherise and Vy *(no, they're just primitives)* to fluff his pillows and cook his meals and never speak, they wouldn't understand. They would hate him.

Slaves are just animals, his orbiters chorused.

Animals do not need to understand.

They only need to obey.

Yellow Thomas had no desire to examine what he was feeling. Instead, he forced himself to study a kiosk along the path, with data marbles—storage devices—on display. Fascinating.

No, thank You, he thought to his mentor. *May I change My mind later?*

Of course. The Upward Governess rested her hands on her stomach. *Changing minds is a way of life for Torth (you need no permission). Let Us see how the mentorship goes, and We can revisit this offer.*

Yellow Thomas realized that he was already indebted to the Upward Governess. Was she showering him with gifts because she wanted him even more indebted? Was she trying to buy something from him?

His loyalty?

She made a signal, and her entourage of slaves spread out behind them, leaving them alone to enjoy floral scents and sights.

Orb lamps glowed beneath umbrellas of waxy leaves. Iridescent gas bugs hovered above lily-like flowers. The old version of Thomas would have felt enchanted by this garden path, but the Megacosm had more impressive gardens, as well as forests, oceans, mountain ranges, and cosmic plains of enlightenment.

Emotions spiked above everything else. Intense emotions were hugely obvious in the Megacosm, like skyscrapers.

One of those spikes shot upward near a thread that Thomas was exploring, so close that he heard a phantom shriek. The foreign panic died, leaving a fading echo as the mind that had generated it vanished.

She had been an astronaut. Her spacesuit had depressurized unexpectedly, killing her.

Moments later, a spike of panic interrupted a discussion about neurochemistry that Yellow Thomas was tuned into. He left the discussion to investigate and learned that the panic came from a little girl. The child had sympathized too deeply with her personal slave. She had tried to befriend it, and the headmistress found out, deemed her too flawed for adulthood, and shot her to death.

Yellow Thomas decided that he would henceforth avoid investigating emotional spikes in the Megacosm. He didn't want to relive his Adulthood Exam in any way, shape, or form.

Next to him, the Upward Governess rolled out of the Megacosm. She did it with casual ease, but the absence of such a huge mind could not go unnoticed. Her orbiters swarmed like mosquitoes that had just lost a colossal blood source.

Many of them flocked to the mind of Yellow Thomas. Since he still floated within range of her mind, he still sensed her thoughts, more colorful and complex than every flower in the garden.

The Upward Governess flashed a nanosecond of perception that emphasized the empty pathway ahead. Only a supergenius could have detected such a brief hint. Maybe she wanted to share something in private?

Yellow Thomas dropped out of the Megacosm, leaving his own mental audience to silently mumble and swarm.

Your life is in danger, the Upward Governess thought without a trace of preamble. *The Commander of All Living Things wants you dead. Only I can protect you from Her, little Yellow.*

Yellow Thomas eyed his mentor sideways.

As a legal citizen of the Torth Empire, no one could murder him, hurt him, or force him to do anything against his will. Not even the Commander of All Living Things. And anyway, he had done absolutely nothing to offend the elected ruler of the galaxy.

You haven't figured out the loopholes? The Upward Governess sized him up from the corner of one blue eye, the same way he assessed her. *Think about it. The Commander of All Living Things will manufacture a reason (an excuse) to revoke your citizenship and have you executed.*

Yellow Thomas studied his mentor's round face for a hint of deception, but of course, he didn't see any.

Surely the elected ruler of the galaxy had more important concerns on her agenda than the fate of a disabled boy from Earth?

Many Torth want you dead. The Upward Governess emanated impatience at having to explain facts that seemed obvious to her. *The Majority approves of you, and the minority is obligated to appease the Majority, but in private, the minority will maneuver to—* She detected movement on the path ahead of them through the eyes of some of her slaves. She flipped into the Megacosm long enough to check local traffic. Sure enough, a pair of Torth were approaching.

Imitate Me, she instructed Yellow Thomas. Then she ascended into the Megacosm and drifted aimlessly, absorbing trivial facts about the mating rituals of gas bugs.

The pair of Torth came into view, trailed by their slaves. They inclined their heads to the Upward Governess, their iridescent green eyes showing their rank. *Two supergeniuses,* one of the Green Ranks mused. *Whatever can They be discussing in private?*

Yellow Thomas struggled to eject all traces of the private conversation. He leaped into the mind of a navigator on a starship and learned about wormholes known as temporal streams.

The pair of Green Ranks strolled past, bemused. If Yellow Thomas had been alone, they would have probed his mind for every detail, but they didn't dare demand anything from an Indigo-Blue Rank and her guest.

As soon as the pathway cleared, the Upward Governess dropped down to low-level telepathy, and Yellow Thomas followed suit.

Give Me everything I want, whenever I want it, the Upward Governess thought to him. *And you may survive the next few weeks.*

Yellow Thomas chewed his lower lip, trying to mask his doubts about the danger he was in. After all, the Swift Killer had failed to end his life.

The Swift Killer is (an idiot) clumsy in her maneuvers, the Upward Governess thought. *Expect subtle elegance from the Commander of All Living Things. One does not attain Her position without earning it. I have analyzed that woman, and she is dangerously crafty. Do not underestimate Her.*

Yellow Thomas supposed that was plausible.

She (the Commander of All Living Things) took measures as soon as you seemed likely to pass the Adulthood Exam. The Upward Governess sent him an image of the golden cuff around his ankle. *Her idea. You are not as free as the rest of Us.*

Yellow Thomas thought of Ariock, wrapped in heavy chains and guarded by the equivalent of an army. The cuff did not seem so bad in comparison.

I am sure your enemies (such as the Commander and the Swift Killer) would be gleeful if you have the cuff removed, the Upward Governess thought. *Make one misstep and the Commander will leap upon you like pisanvi on a bloody carcass.*

Pisanvi were hairy creatures with massive jaws that could unhinge, known for chomping through garbage with their serrated teeth.

Yellow Thomas could imagine a tracker on the cuff, like he was a prisoner on parole. Now, as he thought further, he realized that certain Torth—such as those who orbited the Commander—would wait for him to slip up.

The Majority had told him to never remove the cuff. His enemies among the minority voters would wait for him to do just that. Or they would wait for him to show sympathies for slaves.

In fact, they might even try to trick him into slipping up.

They might do it to curry favor with the Commander of All Living Things.

Exactly. The Upward Governess glowed with approval. *You do see the danger.*

Yellow Thomas tamped down an illegal burst of frustration. *What did I do to make such enemies?*

The Upward Governess wound between thick hedges, through a path so narrow that no one else would be able to squeeze past their hoverchairs. *It is a great honor to be elected to the office of Commander of All Living Things,* she thought, *but it is also a great responsibility. The One who holds that title cannot afford to make a mistake. If She errs, then the Majority will sentence Her to death by torture and elect a new Commander of All Living Things.*

Yellow Thomas thought that sounded like a dangerous job.

Torth who vie for lofty ranks are risk-takers, the Upward Governess silently admitted. *Our current Commander of All enjoys rocketing above volcanic eruptions with a jet pack. She is a thrill seeker, which is why She always has a large audience in Her mind. She has earned more clout than anyone else in the known universe. She could have swayed the Majority to block you from taking the Adulthood Exam. Instead, She did not bother to participate in that vote. She allowed Me to take the lead there. I am sure She regrets that now.*

Why? Yellow Thomas wondered.

She (wrongly) assumed that you would fail the Adulthood Exam and die. That was a mortifying lapse of good judgment (on Her part).

It didn't seem like much of a mistake to Yellow Thomas. More like a forgivable potential lapse.

Forgiveness is a slave concept, the Upward Governess pointed out. *The public may never accuse Her of making a misjudgment...unless you (become a criminal) free slaves or wreak havoc. If that happens? Well, then the Torth Majority will blame Our Commander of All and sentence Her to a horrible death. She is painfully aware of that danger. She is trying to preclude that possibility. It is in Her best interest to have you killed on a pretext, based on some technicality, before you can do anything that makes Her look incompetent.*

Yellow Thomas studied his mentor. *Do You believe I would go around freeing slaves and wreaking havoc?*

The Upward Governess floated past fragrant flowers, untroubled. *The odds are low. You are too ambitious to throw your life away.*

Criminal behavior was suicide. There was no privacy in the Megacosm. Everything with eyes was a potential spy. Any Torth could riffle through the memories of any slave or animal. Any Torth could peer through the eyes of any other Torth, or a nearby person. Criminals rarely survived for more than a few minutes.

Even if they severed themselves from the Megacosm and ran away to Earth or some other wilderness planet...criminals almost never succeeded in hiding for longer than a few weeks.

The Majority owned everything. The Majority was everywhere.

Yellow Thomas surveyed the garden, uneasy. A small animal, like a chipmunk, watched them pass by.

The Upward Governess gave him a look that was almost like amusement. Indeed, any random Torth could delve into the mind of that animal and analyze its perceptual memories.

But aren't We sort of having a private conversation? Yellow Thomas wondered.

Not really. The Upward Governess seemed to regard him with pity, as if he was an ineffectual baby. *High ranks are allowed to probe the minds of low ranks. And you are low rank.*

Yellow was the lowest rank, except for childhood. Anyone except for children would be allowed to probe his mind.

We are fortunate to be supergeniuses, the Upward Governess let him know. *Our minds are so vast, we can slide small secrets beneath multiple layers of data, even during a mind probe. You might be able to hide this conversation. Or you might not.*

And You? he wondered.

Oh, I can hide it, she affirmed. *A very high percentage of Torth respect and trust Me. I worked hard to earn their respect and trust. Only Servants of All would dare to probe My mind, and they had better have a good reason to do so.*

She contrasted that with all the mistrust surrounding Yellow Thomas.

A Torth strolled into view, and the Upward Governess mentally vaulted into the Megacosm. She shed her thoughts for an entirely different topic, inviting her mental audience to ask her anything about plasmic polymer building materials.

Yellow Thomas emulated her.

He did his best to sweep his concerns underneath his general curiosity, drinking in facts about the science of nucleosynthesis. Hundreds of other minds nestled up to his, interested in everything he felt and thought and saw, eager to share everything they knew about the topic he'd shown interest in.

The strolling Torth left their range. The Upward Governess immediately dropped out of the Megacosm.

Yellow Thomas hesitated to rejoin her. Facts were soothing. Conversing with his mentor was less than soothing.

She mentally poked him, and, reluctant, he dropped down.

You want something from Me, he guessed with resignation.

She tapped her fingers on her armrests, pleased that they had finally worked up to a subject that interested her. *Yes.*

He attempted to tally up how much he might owe her for her protection.

All I want, she thought, *is private time with you whenever I wish for it.*

He had expected worse. She could have dumped her workload on him. Could she have stolen credit for everything he achieved?

How could I do that? She glided to a stop in a cul-de-sac. *Torth cannot lie to each other or steal from each other.*

Yellow Thomas suppressed his quibbles.

The Upward Governess regarded him with curiosity. *You have a unique outlook (I would like to learn more about it).* Her mind churned like a nuclear reactor, screening her opinions. *But you must understand, little Yellow, that it is in your best interest to give Me whatever I want, whenever I want it.*

He was beholden to her. For now.

He nodded.

She examined his mind, probing his secrets. And she added a warning. *Never threaten Me. Never attempt to manipulate Me. Someday, you may be tempted to do so. Let Me be clear, little Yellow. If you ever threaten Me (intentionally or not), expect to die.*

She allowed him a glimpse into the depths of her own mind. Yellow Thomas sensed that billions of Torth would be eager to do her bidding. Even the Commander of All Living Things was careful to keep this particular supergenius satisfied.

You are a Torth for as long as you live. The Upward Governess floated to an ivy-covered wall. *There is no escape. Nor can you escape your debt to Me.*

She tapped a tablet near her hand. A doorway appeared in the wall, and she silently implied that he should enter the refurbished suite that now belonged exclusively to him.

Yellow Thomas floated into the antechamber.

His jaw dropped. He had to force down a welling of disbelieving awe. *This is amazing!*

Mist wafted between steep, verdant mountain slopes.

Clouds billowed across the domed ceiling, tinged with pink fire from a sunset.

Water trickled over a fountain, its edges morphing in a preprogrammed routine of fanciful sculptures. Water spilled into a heated hot tub set in the floor.

The empty shelves were like gigantic seashells. They waited to be filled with whatever he desired.

There was whimsy and wonder in every inch of the oval antechamber, which could have housed the entirety of the Hollander home. It was his most self-indulgent dreams come true. Part of him already lived here, had always lived here.

I humored your idiosyncratic acrophobia, the Upward Governess let him know, *and programmed your suite with ground-level window displays.*

Yellow Thomas explored the room, still agape. Four additional rooms split off from the antechamber. One was a laboratory with holographic workstations, ready to run scientific simulations. Another room had terraria for a private zoo. Another was outfitted for chemical experiments. The bedroom was fit for an emperor.

I fussed a bit, the Upward Governess admitted. *But you are, after all, the only supergenius I've met in person (not counting Myself).*

Yellow Thomas rotated his hoverchair, awestruck. Inside this quiet suite, he could pretend the whole galactic empire was an illusion.

He wondered what Cherise was going through.

(Nope) He immediately shoved that *(dangerous)* unimportant thought away. He wasn't going to risk thinking about *(human-related)* pointless topics where an astute mind reader—his mentor—could overhear his thoughts.

Perhaps he was just worried about loneliness? All this luxurious spaciousness made him feel more like an orphan than ever.

I've never lived alone, he admitted. *I never imagined I could. This is so much room.*

Smaller quarters can be arranged. The Upward Governess floated closer. *Now. First of all, give Me every memory you have ever absorbed from your human foster family.*

CHAPTER 16

LEFTOVERS

Cherise suspected that the alien named Kessa was as kindhearted as she seemed.

But who knew? Anyone could hide their true self. Cherise's ma was an expert at pretending to be kind. She had fooled everyone around her except for her daughter. Maybe Kessa was only pretending to be nice and had volunteered to lure the humans to their deaths?

No one else bothered to help the humans.

The small alien never seemed to tire of scrubbing floors, whereas the humans were starved and exhausted. Perhaps Kessa was nourished by something that gave her boundless energy?

Kessa showed Cherise, Vy, and Delia how to wash upholstery. They dusted shelves, they polished metallic and crystalline surfaces, and they never got a break.

If slaves had to use a bathroom, they scrambled through wide streets that gleamed with too many mirrored surfaces, searching for plain metal doors. Those doors meant slave zones.

They meant safety.

Inside a slave zone, slaves could drink from leaking pipes or squat over filthy latrines. Best of all, they could talk out loud. Kessa used those opportunities to teach the humans a few survival tips, including the Torth hand commands of "stop," "go," and "fetch."

And now?

Cherise wished she could read minds. She dared not ask Kessa where they were going, but she wondered why their guide kept passing slave zones. Shouldn't they stop to talk?

An arched ceiling soared overhead, all glass, so that sunlight streamed inside. The indoor space was vast enough to have a breeze. It would have looked utopian if not for the alien slaves who scurried everywhere, their eyes downcast. Every so often, a Torth meandered down the indoor boulevard. Slaves avoided Torth pedestrians. Whenever Kessa saw one coming, she darted through gaps in the crowd. Delia and Vy had to seek larger openings.

Delia suddenly swerved off course. She headed toward a plain metal door—a slave zone.

It was understandable. Every punishment they had received today was because Delia failed to move fast enough. The middle-aged woman looked haggard. She wore Vy's shoes, yet even with help, she struggled to perform endless menial chores.

Perhaps they ought to let Delia go her own way?

Cherise winced at her own selfishness. How would Thomas react to her thoughts? Or her foster sister, for that matter? Vy would be disgusted. The idea of abandoning Delia should not have entered Cherise's sane, reasonable, charitable mind.

She needed to remember that she was human.

This world would turn her into a monster if she let it.

Vy seemed to be made of strength. She hurried after Delia and tugged her arm, shepherding her back onto the street. Soon they were back to following Kessa.

The little alien had actually waited for them.

Kessa had a childlike way of running and a distinctive curve to her beak. She paused every so often and let the humans catch up. It seemed nice. But why was Kessa the only friendly slave? Did she want something?

Cherise could only make guesses. Kessa's motives were mysterious. Even her age and gender were unknown. Her creased, papery skin implied age, and her chirpy voice and less pronounced brow ridges seemed to hint at female characteristics. So Cherise had made a guess. But—

"GAAAH!"

A furry slave writhed on the mirrored floor, leaving smears of blood. It was one of the centaur-like creatures. They were reminiscent of fat caterpillars the size of humans, but with six legs and jowly, doglike faces. This one had white-speckled brown fur.

Nobody showed concern for the victim.

A Torth stood imperiously over the alien, somehow causing its pain, while the foot traffic flowed around them. Kessa did not seem to even notice her fellow slave as it suffered. She scurried past the victim without a glance.

But Vy slowed.

Cherise inwardly cursed. Vy was a trauma nurse, but this was no hospital. Her foster sister needed to be smart. She needed to survive.

The poor slave gagged on blood while the green-eyed Torth stared down at it without mercy. He was a bearded man, but to Cherise, all Torth might as well be versions of her ma. They lacked empathy.

Vy knelt by the writhing slave.

No! Cherise wanted to shout, but speech would get her tortured.

She had been unable to protect her baby sister, Glitzy. And now she would be unable to protect her older foster sister.

It wasn't fair. Unlike Glitzy, Vy was an adult. She ought to know better! She should be protecting Cherise, not the other way around!

Aliens gawked as if Vy was about to perform some entertaining trick. Kessa blinked and then darted away. It seemed she was finally willing to ditch the suicidally idiotic humans.

Vy checked the furry slave for injuries. Her empathy was obvious. What was she thinking? She had no water, no painkillers, nothing to offer.

Yet the victim seemed to understand that Vy wanted to help. It cried feebly and clutched at her sweater.

Vy glared up at the bearded brute of a Torth.

Her glare lasted for about one second. Then she clutched her own head and gasped in pain.

Against her own better judgment, Cherise rushed to her foster sister. She grabbed Vy and tried to drag her away. Any second now, she expected punishment...but none came.

The bearded guy turned on his heel and strode away.

Maybe he had run out of mental juice?

The blood-smeared alien lay on the floor, but it had stopped moving. Its eyes were glazed and unseeing.

Vy lurched to her feet and stumbled into a run. Cherise had to hurry to keep up. Up close, she heard Vy's noisy gasps for breath. Her foster sister was in a blind panic. Vy scanned the walls, no doubt searching for plain metal doors, desperate to find safety.

Cherise grasped Vy's hand.

No one was chasing them. Torth strolled past as if enjoying a breezy day in the city. It was a normal day in hell.

And up ahead, Kessa waited. Her beak had an impatient twist.

As soon as she saw the humans, she took off, leading the way toward an oversize door of plain metal.

Safety? At last!

Cherise glanced back to make sure Vy and Delia were jogging to catch up. Beyond them, janitorial slaves scrubbed the blood away, making the floor spotless again. Other slaves carried the furry corpse of the tortured alien. They had stripped away its scraps of clothing, and even its slave collar had been removed. Cherise could only guess at how. She supposed a Torth must have unlocked the collar and carried it away.

The janitorial slaves heaved the stripped corpse down a garbage chute.

No funeral. No prayers. The dead slave was treated exactly like trash. That could have been Vy.

Or Cherise.

She ran to the slave zone where Kessa had gone. The huge metal door whooshed open, welcoming. Cherise approached a chamber that smelled funky, like mold or cheese. Not that she cared how badly it stank. She ran inside, and once her friends joined her, the door sealed shut behind them.

Vy let out a shaky breath. "I thought that asshole might allow a trained nurse to do her job."

"Why would you expect that?" Delia asked woodenly.

A pair of red-bronze behemoths assessed the humans with beady red eyes.

Staring was a common reaction whenever the humans talked. Cherise had learned that these thorny creatures were known as "nuss," according to Kessa. Nussians were generally polite, despite their intimidating size and their lack of slave collars. They didn't even wear clothing. Their skin was tough and pebbly, like armored plates. Mostly, they stood around. They seemed to be sentries.

"Why would a Torth murder a slave like that?" Vy said. "In front of everyone. They're insane here!"

Kessa looked at Vy quizzically. She had a birdlike way of cocking her head and clicking her beak.

"I know." Cherise held Vy.

Her tall foster sister all but collapsed in her arms. Tears flowed. Vy was trembling, perhaps realizing how close she had come to a merciless execution in the middle of the boulevard.

Until now, Vy had seemed strong, able to weather any storm. She was a pillar of stability.

But it seemed she could not cope with being helpless.

"Come," Kessa said in her limited English. She spoke to the nussians, and one of the huge aliens stepped on a pedal. The inner airlock door cartwheeled open.

An overpowering stench washed over Cherise.

A midden heap came into view. Not just one heap, but many dozens, maybe hundreds. Mounds of garbage filled a warehouse as large as a football field. As Cherise watched, an orifice in the ceiling opened, dumping a fresh load of garbage onto a tottering pile.

Hundreds of slaves scavenged the reeking hills, picking up morsels, like rats swarming over a garbage dump. It smelled worse than the dumpsters in the trailer park where she used to live with Ma.

"Disgusting," Delia said, muffled by her coat collar.

Kessa sprinted into the reek like a child visiting the beach. She held up a morsel and said something that sounded encouraging in the slave tongue.

"Are you kidding me?" Delia said.

Her disbelieving question was a dare. No doubt she wanted someone to prove her wrong.

Alien voices echoed across the space, like in a school gymnasium, or a…

"It's a cafeteria." Cherise stepped forward into the vast room of leftovers. "For slaves."

She avoided a puddle of congealed sauce. Her ma used to feed her leftover trash. Ma had a lot in common with the Torth.

Delia followed. "So if we don't get punished to death, we'll die of dysentery?"

Cherise chose a piece of fruit that looked merely overripe. It smelled faintly like grapefruit, probably edible. "We're not going to get anything better. We have to survive until Thomas can rescue us."

"Oh yeah?" Delia sounded sarcastic. "Will he free all the alien slaves while he's at it? And kill a few Torth, I hope?"

Vy shushed Delia, trying to quiet her. Aliens had begun to notice the humans.

Cherise brushed an alien maggot off the fruit peel. "I think we should talk about Torth eye colors," she said, trying to change the topic. "Have you noticed which colors they favor and which are absent?"

"What are you talking about?" Delia sounded exasperated. "Who cares!"

"Their eyes are iridescent," Vy said. "I noticed that."

Cherise nodded. "They're artificial. I think they purposely hide their true colors."

"Huh." Vy sounded like she was feigning interest.

"None display purple," Cherise said.

"So?" Vy frowned. "Ah. You mean like Thomas and Ariock?"

Delia's expression heated up. Her tone gained a dangerous edge. "Just what are you implying?"

Cherise polished the fruit, trembling. She should never have started talking. Nothing good ever came from being the center of attention.

"It's okay," Vy said gently. "I guess we all suspect that Thomas has Torth ancestry."

Cherise nodded in acceptance of that fact. Thomas's power had been unique on Earth. It was common on this planet—a global Torth trait.

"But not Ariock!" Delia balled her fists as if she wanted to punch someone.

Cherise focused on the fruit, which wouldn't judge her. "I don't know."

"Well, I do!" Delia fumed. "Ariock isn't a damned Torth. He doesn't have anything in common with mind readers! How dare you!"

If only Thomas was around to speak for Cherise. He could have restated her thoughts in a tactful, eloquent way that kept Delia happy and calm.

"Can you please calm down?" Vy touched Delia's arm, pleading. "They can hear anger."

A crowd had gathered.

Most of the aliens were as small as Kessa, but there were larger ones. That towering bony alien could probably batter Cherise with its head. The furry ones were cute, but they were also the size of human adults, and they all had an extra pair of limbs.

"Torth," one of the aliens said in a guttural accent.

Others uttered the word, repeating it like an accusation. "Torth."

"Torth."

"Torth."

Kessa spread her spindly arms, shielding the humans. Her shouts sounded reasonable.

Chanting aliens overrode her. "Torth."

"Torth."

"Torth."

Cherise tried to watch in every direction, pressing back to back with Vy and Delia. A furry alien lunged at them. It clawed her coat and ripped the fabric.

"Pretend we have those glove weapons." Delia's voice was high-pitched with terror. "They need to fear us!"

But they couldn't do much while a frenzied mob threw garbage at them. Something splattered on Vy. An alien yanked on Cherise's hair. If aliens broke her glasses, she would be effectively blind.

Blind, she would never be able to obey Torth hand signals.

There were no blind or disabled slaves.

Survive. Thomas was counting on her to get through the next day or two. That was all. Just a day or two. She had survived thousands of days with Ma. She could handle silent obedience—if these alien slaves would just allow her to live, if they would just acknowledge the glowing slave collar around her neck.

The aliens assumed that she was as monstrous as her ma. Their assumption was worse than a sick joke.

"TORTH!" Cherise shrieked. She flung a pointing finger toward the exit.

The mob seemed surprised that someone like her would make such a loud noise.

"Cherise!" Cherise thumped her chest.

Kessa hopped like an excited bird, babbling a stream of words and indicating Cherise's slave collar.

Cherise pulled aside her coat so that her glowing slave collar was clearly visible. "Cherise!" she shouted, then pointed toward the unseen city streets, shouting, "Torth!" Back to herself. "Cherise!"

The mob hushed each other. A few tried to attack, but their companions stopped them.

Kessa said something. The mob listened, but Cherise saw their doubts. This must be one of the few places in the upper city where slaves could talk freely. These aliens were justifiably outraged that three Torth dared to mimic slaves and invade their cafeteria.

Cherise knelt and used her fingers to paint in a spill of mustard-yellow sauce. She drew a circle. Inside the circle, she added dots. "Humans," she said, poking more dots. "Humans. Humans. Humans."

Kessa and the mob watched with rapt attention.

Cherise drew an arrow that pointed to another hurriedly sketched circle. "Torth," she said, poking dots within the new circle. "Torth. Torth. Torth. Ummin. Ummin. Govki?" She thought that was the word Kessa used for the furry centaur-like bulldog aliens. "Torth. Torth. Torth."

When she was sure that most of the aliens were watching, she indicated herself and the other two humans. "Cherise. Vy. Delia." She waved from one circle to the other, showing a transfer.

One of the onlookers spoke in a disdainful tone. "Torth."

"Humans," Cherise insisted. She framed her slave collar with both hands.

"Humans," Vy agreed.

Kessa regarded Cherise with extreme skepticism. Her flexible brow ridges drew down. "Haa Torth?"

"Not Torth," Cherise affirmed. She thumped herself. "Humans."

Kessa scooped up the fruit that Cherise had dropped earlier and offered it to her. "Jin." She worked her beak, miming a chewing motion. "Tsud." She indicated the fruit. "Tsud." She waved at the piles of garbage.

"Food," Cherise figured. "Tsud is food? Jin is eat?"

"Jin o tsud," Kessa said agreeably.

Cherise took the offered fruit. On her knees, she was shorter than Kessa's height, and she studied the alien's owlish gray eyes.

Those eyes were intelligent. There was kindness there. Kessa reminded her of Thomas in some way that she could not fathom.

"When you let yourself see people," Thomas had once told Cherise, "it's like a breathtaking vista, because you see so much. I love being in your range when you do that."

"Thank you." Cherise ripped the fruit in half and offered half to Kessa.

The ummin accepted it. "Food." She mimicked Cherise's exact tone. "Is food. Is eat. Thank you."

Slaves muttered and poked each other, as if betting on whether or not Cherise would eat slave chow. One yelled something that caused nasty laughter. Kessa gave that one a disparaging look.

Vy wiped stains off her face. "I think you saved us." She looked rumpled and dirty from the attack, but at least she was uninjured. "Thank you."

"Kessa saved us." Cherise ate the fruit and tried not to look at it too closely.

CHAPTER 17

A YELLOW MIND

Two hundred and fifty billion stars gleamed in the darkness of Yellow Thomas's palatial bedroom.

He lay on an enormous bed strewn with furry blankets, inside a holographic galaxy so dazzling and realistically detailed, he felt in danger of falling upward into it.

If he wanted to explore any whorl or spur, he could zoom in with a twitch of his finger on his data tablet. He could examine any cluster of stars. He could zoom in again and again and take close looks at any explored solar system, or any inhabited planet, in the known universe.

He merely gazed at the celestial map.

This was what the Torth Empire owned.

All of this.

When he turned on a population overlay, the galaxy became webbed with colorful space routes and glowing halos. Major hub planets glowed the brightest. There were 794 major population hubs, including the solar system where he currently resided.

Millions of other regions glowed with their own intense populations. Because Torth lived on many planets. Torth owned everything. They even owned backwater wilderness planets such as Earth.

Slave populations were not shown, but there must be countless quintillions of those.

It was overwhelming.

Yellow Thomas made a sound of frustration. A second later, he realized what a mistake that was, as his nearest personal slave, a plucky govki, paused in its cleaning activities to stare at him. Sounds were borderline illegal.

Yellow Thomas was physically dependent, so he needed to keep at least one slave in the same room with him. It was best not to act strange. He dared not say anything out loud, lest his Torth neighbors suss out every syllable. They probed the minds of his slaves on a regular basis.

Torth society had no hidden murderers or terrorists, no hidden thieves or drug dealers or child molesters. No one fomented rebellion. No one helped slaves or disobeyed a single law. If the Torth Majority decided to accuse Yellow Thomas of a crime? Then no one, not even the Upward Governess, would be able to save him from execution.

Only nine rogue Torth had ever evaded capture for longer than a day. Nine. In known history.

All nine had severed their ties to the Megacosm, and most of them had tried to blend in with the humans of Earth, with varying degrees of success. His biological mother had lasted for several months as a human before her clone sisters seized her and brought her to justice.

Don't think of her. Don't think of that.

Yellow Thomas forced away memories of his tortured-to-death mother, because he didn't dare get upset. He needed to improve his skill in burying his emotions.

Anyway.

He had learned that the Torth Majority would expend every resource in the known universe to hunt down a rogue or a renegade. And they had endless resources.

His govki slave offered him a squeeze bottle of water. Yellow Thomas sipped, careful to remain expressionless.

The Torth Empire expected every Torth citizen to spend every wakeful moment of their lives in the Megacosm. Only high ranks got awarded the luxury of privacy. Yellow Thomas ought to ascend right now. The Majority might deem his abstinence to be a crime.

But he would never solve a certain problem *(Cherise)* once a bunch of Torth piled into his thoughts.

He studied the celestial map, memorizing space routes and wilderness planets. The Torth Empire had colonized all the most desirable worlds, of course, but the galaxy was too enormous even for the multitudes of Torth to fully stretch itself into.

The Torth had Eden. They had many paradises. But they owned too much, so they had yet to colonize some of the more remote alien planets that were conducive to human life.

Reject-20 didn't look too bad. One just had to figure out a way to deal with the multiton indigenous predators.

Earth was unnoticeable on the galactic map. It was just one more wilderness world, not laced with any halo of Torth population. The Torth Empire had spied on humankind since before the ancient Egyptians built the Great Pyramids, but to them, human technology was not worth reaping. Human cities were full of braying beasts.

The Majority of Torth scientists assumed that there was a genetic link between primitive humans and the superior Torth. Because of that assumed link, the Majority voted to protect Earth as a nature preserve. They cloaked

their ships and masked their presence to human instrumentation. They'd
hacked NASA.

But ancient edicts were being reevaluated these days. What if humans
developed technology that rivaled the Megacosm?

Ever since the invention of the internet, a growing minority of Torth had
voted to enslave humankind. That minority was likely to win sooner rather
than later.

Earth was doomed.

Even if Yellow Thomas could miraculously deliver his foster sisters back
to their homeland without any Torth noticing, Torth agents would simply
hunt them down and scoop them up again. Nobody could fool the Torth
Majority. Nobody could defy or challenge the Torth Empire.

Cherise and Vy, Delia and Ariock…they could never return to their old
lives.

They could never go home.

His govki slave *(Nror, but who cares about its name)* placed a breakfast
tray within sight. Yellow Thomas had his choice of gourmet foods.

The Megacosm glowed just beyond his senses. It was as warm as a mother's loving embrace and as powerful as sunlight.

He really ought to ascend.

Maybe he should go ahead—eat, ascend, and leave the unsolvable problem for another day? It was strange, how much he wanted to rejoin *(his people)* that fantastic bustle of imagined sights and sounds and smells and sensations. He wanted to ascend into the Megacosm even more than he wanted
breakfast.

In the Megacosm, Yellow Thomas was not guilty. Or frustrated. Or helpless.

In the Megacosm, he could join the mind of an athlete or an explorer and
live vicariously through them. He could swim through the silvery waves of
an alien ocean or bushwhack a trail through an alien jungle. He could stroll
beneath the sapient trees of Bemelglurd and listen to them sing to each other
like a pod of whales.

In the Megacosm, no one could easily dismiss him as just a kid. He was
a legal adult.

Not just an adult—he was a mental giant with thousands of orbiters at
any given moment. Thousands of Torth liked his mind.

Yellow Thomas shoved aside a breakfast roll, furious at himself.

Didn't he owe his life to *(Cherise)* certain people who were now enslaved
and suffering? Only the worst sort of greedy monster would abandon those
people *(Cherise)* to slavery and death.

His thoughts felt like juggling live ammunition. Dangerous.

Although Yellow Thomas was a mental giant among Torth, he lacked clout. His mind was malnourished in comparison to those of other supergeniuses in his age range. He was too low in rank to have any hope of persuading the Majority of Torth to *(send the humans home)* do what he wanted. He might as well have tried to persuade the president of the United States to make an exception in FDA regulations just for him.

He needed more influence. More clout.

More rank.

He needed to convince the Upward Governess that he deserved a promotion or two.

Yellow Thomas finally allowed himself to take a bite of the delicious roll. Those who were counting on him *(Cherise)* would surely understand if he needed more than a few days to pull off a rescue?

He would think of something.

A plan might occur to him once he had a higher rank, plus a better grasp of how to navigate the Torth-owned universe.

He also needed practice at hiding secrets beneath torrents of data. He might be able to smother a few illegal reactions and impress his orbiters, but his mentor could detect a needle in a haystack after a few seconds of studying it. She was sharp.

And dangerous.

For now, he needed to quit valuing privacy so much. He didn't want the Majority to change its collective mind about him and sentence him to death.

Maybe he would try one of those soothing "tranquility mesh" circlets that so many Torth wore?

Torth technology could not record or transmit thoughts. That kind of research was illegal in the Torth Empire, so he didn't have to worry about anyone using devices to spy on him. The circlets only altered moods. That was all. A Torth could dial a tranquility mesh up to its highest setting and enjoy a peaceful brain-wave pattern without any risk of unwanted effects or overdosing. It was safe.

Tranquility meshes were legal. And popular.

He needed to obtain one.

In a calm, civilized state of mind, Yellow Thomas ascended into the Megacosm.

PART THREE

*Those who make no effort to understand
their enemies become enemies themselves.*

—Nussian proverb

CHAPTER 1

ARENA BEASTS

The arena was clean every time the thorny prison guards forced Ariock into it. They shoved and hauled him through the open gate, using poles and chains. Then they left in a hurry, slamming the huge gate shut hard enough to make the walls rattle.

He clanked with every step.

His captors, the Torth, had made him replace his clothes with heavy armor. Gaps in the plates left his thighs and biceps bare. He had to protect those places whenever he fought an opponent that had claws or sharp teeth.

Ariock paced along the enclosure of interlocked bones. He wore armored sandals, and his feet whispered through shredded husks. He listened for the soft sound that would signal a deadly battle.

He didn't bother to examine the arena cage anymore. He had looked for an escape many times. The bars looked like dinosaur bones, too thick and strong for him to break. He couldn't squeeze through the gaps. He couldn't climb over the top, because Torth sat up there, at intervals, ready to torment him with pain seizures if he tried to escape.

Besides. An audience surrounded the arena cage.

Thousands of silent Torth occupied layers of tiers, all watching him. They wore jeweled accessories and imperialistic robes. Even the ones who sat atop the enclosure looked rich, with embroidered red capes draped over their formidable high-tech armor. Iridescent eyes seemed to judge Ariock.

He supposed that he was guilty of being a freak.

They never clapped, never laughed, never said a word, but he knew they judged him. They wanted him to look like the monster he was.

Ariock paced and clanked the other way. An ugly, dented, knobby helmet hid his face and muffled his voice. Maybe it was for the best, to be faceless to the audience. His beard had grown in wild and thick. He had no means with which to shave.

The Torth obviously wanted his skull unbroken.

His mind? That was a different matter.

The Torth must feed off fear and misery, partaking in it like a feast. They must know how often Ariock imagined dying in the arena. He might be able to get himself slaughtered before any telepaths could put a stop to it. He imagined ways to kill himself all the time these days. Except…

You promised, his mother would have said. *Don't abandon me.*

In his nightmares, his mother was buried under a heap of bloodied corpses, crying for his help. Ariock knew he had gotten carried away. In his frenzy to get revenge and kill a lot of Torth, he had accidentally murdered his own mother.

In other nightmares, Thomas was one of the silent onlookers.

The dream version of Thomas had iridescent yellow eyes and wore regal golden robes. He was just as emotionless as the rest of the audience. Sometimes that dream version of Thomas pointed. Then Ariock would turn around and see his dead mother. Or the burning wreckage of an airplane where his father was trapped and dying.

Look, the silent dream version of Thomas seemed to insinuate. *You're a failure. You were always a failure.*

Ariock tensed at the whispery sound of an opening gate.

He focused on the hooded bulwark on the far side of the arena. That bulwark was about to disgorge a beast.

A creature snorted.

Not one but two beasts emerged, blinking under the floating spotlights. Ropes of drool slathered from their sharklike snouts. They had backward legs. Despite their bloated bodies, they could probably leap over Ariock, leveraged like frogs. Their skin was frog-like, too, slimy and mottled green.

This was new. A species he hadn't seen before, and two instead of one.

Perhaps the spectators thought the jelly monster from yesterday had been boring?

Well, the jelly monster had nearly impaled Ariock on its tusk. He was going to have nightmares about slamming his armored foot into its exposed, wobbly, pulsating brain.

The shark-frogs leaped at Ariock.

He didn't dare waste a second. He threw himself into a tumbling roll, and the beasts slammed against the cage wall, one after the other, causing massive bones to rattle. Each monster must weigh as much as Ariock in his armor.

And they were enraged. That was typical. Ariock guessed the telepaths must inject their monsters with rage-inducing drugs right before each fight.

He pushed himself to his feet. He hadn't been strong enough to pop up right away during his first dozen arena battles, especially in heavy armor, but practice made a difference.

So did the huge spikes sticking out of his forearms.

If his mother—or Vy—could see him now, they would take one glance and judge him a monster. A spike jagged out of each of his forearms. Those notched spikes made it easier for the guards to capture him after each fight and drag him back to the dungeon.

The telepaths had drilled directly into his bones, without anesthesia, without any explanation, and without his permission. Ariock had screamed until his voice broke. He had fought and failed to break the chains that held him down. For days afterward, his arms were a mass of bruises around the implanted spikes.

But the wounds had healed, and faster than Ariock would have expected. Now his arms had extra weight and weaponry.

The beasts bounded toward Ariock. Now that he'd had a chance to assess their speed and mass, he stood his ground. He stepped aside at the last second and raised his arm whip fast.

His arm spike impaled a beast in its soft throat.

The alien animal squealed in agony, ichor bubbling down the spike. Ariock resisted his instinct to pull his arm free. Instead, he grabbed the beast so that it would not wrench away, and ripped upward in a savage motion, butchering its jaw.

Inky blood sprayed in spurts. He bathed in it.

What a hero. His own self-contempt took the form of Vy Hollander in his imagination. *I can see why they chain you up.*

Protected by armor, Ariock ripped the underslung mandible off the dying beast. It broke with a loud snap.

Now he had a weapon: a toothy jaw.

The second beast pawed the ground. Shredded husks fluttered around its legs. Its beady eyes glinted with rage, but now there was fear as well.

Ariock wished he could show mercy. He wished he dared stop. The last thing he wanted to do was rip an animal's head off its neck or stomp on its skull.

But whenever Ariock left an injured beast to curl up and lick its wounds... the telepaths blasted the beast apart from afar, using silent, arm-mounted rifles. And then they punished Ariock.

After that, they would send another mad beast into the arena, and he would be forced to face the same dilemma again.

There was no escape from doing what the audience wanted him to do. Ariock had given up on trying to cling to his human dignity. He was a savage animal, the same as the monsters he fought.

The remaining beast roared at Ariock. Runnels of saliva vibrated in its open maw, but it seemed more like a warning than a threat.

Ariock wished he could attack the telepaths instead of innocent beasts.

Armored Torth peered down at him, seated a short climb away. Compared with Ariock, they were puny and fragile. But they anticipated threats with supernatural speed and accuracy. He couldn't match them.

Oh, he wanted to slaughter a lot of Torth. Snap their spines. Twist their necks. Let them run, let them scream, let them slip in their own blood.

Massive jaws angled toward him.

Ariock brought the stolen jawbone down on the snapping beast's head, breaking its mottled green skin. He shoved the beast back. Its saliva seemed to sizzle on his skin, hot and oozing.

The beast gathered itself for another lunging attack.

Ariock fell onto its neck, forcing it to crash to the ground. He drove a spike into its underbelly. A normal-size person would never have been able to reach around the beast, but Ariock's size gave him certain advantages.

The mottled beast screamed in pain. Ariock roared in triumph.

Right now, in this moment, he wasn't a helpless prisoner. He wasn't a faceless victim. He was powerful. He was a gigantic force to be reckoned with.

He drove one armored knee into the monster's snout.

It might have incredibly strong jaws full of razor-sharp teeth, but jaws were sensitive. There was less mass there. Teeth and bones crunched under Ariock. Blood squelched out.

Kill it, Ariock's imagination urged him, this time in the guise of Thomas. *I need you to become a monster. We need you.*

He would probably never see a friendly face again.

But what if his mother, and Vy, needed to be rescued? They might need him. They might be somewhere, waiting for him to break free.

Ariock stomped on the monster's head, merciless, until it began to twitch in a death seizure.

He had won this fight uninjured. After countless arena battles, he'd gotten plenty of practice. But his sense of victory was fleeting. The thorny orange guards looked at him with fear, and that was enough for him to remember who he was.

Not a hero.

He was nothing but a colossal butcher.

Ariock stepped off the corpse, sticky with blood and ichor. He left bloody footprints on the dull metal floor. If his mother could see him…if his friends could see him…

He deserved all the shame in the universe.

Perhaps that was why the Torth had brought him here. They saw his soul. They knew what he was.

Ariock went to the corner and waited for the guards to chain him up.

CHAPTER 2
LIARS FROM PARADISE

Kessa no longer went straight to her bunk room after her daily work shifts. Instead, she meandered through the Tunnels, giving her human friends time to chat.

It was best to avoid her home neighborhood until she was ready to sleep, anyway. Vy kept returning to illegal topics no matter how often Kessa warned her not to. On top of that, the humans acted like hatchlings, following Kessa everywhere. They had trouble remembering routes. They struggled to learn the slave tongue, even after a lunar cycle had passed. Sometimes they said rude things out of ignorance, or they asked questions that stirred up dangerous ideas.

Although Kessa secretly liked their questions.

"Where do hatchlings of Torth dwell?" Cherise asked in the slave tongue as soon as they were safely inside the noisy bustle of a Tunnels thoroughfare.

Kessa clicked in approval of Cherise's grammar and diction. "Very good. Torth do not have children."

The humans exchanged doubtful looks. They often doubted common knowledge. After so many wake cycles in their company, Kessa could understand quite a lot of the human language.

"They probably lock their kids in a prison somewhere," Vy said.

"That makes sense." Delia sounded disgusted. "They hate noise, and babies cry."

"But would they lock up Thomas?" Cherise was more soft-spoken than the other two. "He wouldn't provoke them."

Delia rolled her eyes.

Vy looked embarrassed. The humans often spoke of the world they had lost, but Vy and Delia, at least, seemed to be letting go of the absurd fantasy that a friendly mind reader would magically rescue them and send them back to paradise.

All three humans wore grimy rags. They had traded away their original garments in exchange for better footgear and smuggled treats. They had also bundled their Torth hair under scarves, to fit in better with the slave population. They looked dingier and sadder with every wake cycle that passed.

"Wait," Kessa said, as she processed the implications of the humans' conversation. "Is Thomas a child?"

Cherise nodded.

"Yes," Vy said.

Kessa tapped her beak in thought. Much of what the humans said about Thomas ranged from the fantastical to the impossible. He was a mind reader, but not a Torth. He spoke out loud, like a slave. He would never punish anyone with a pain seizure. He was kind and sweet. Oh, and he had a sense of humor. He ruthlessly sucked up other people's secrets, but not on purpose. Really.

And apparently, he was not a midget, but a child.

"I will tell people." Kessa spoke in the language of paradise. "If others know he is a child, they may be more...more..." She searched for a fitting word.

"Helpful?" Vy guessed.

"Curious?" Cherise guessed.

"Curious." Kessa liked that word, and she thought it fit better. A friendly Torth child sounded as intriguing as it was impossible. A search for such an absurdity would be more silly than dangerous. "People may help more."

Cherise gave Kessa grateful smile. "Thank you."

Kessa wondered if she was fueling the toxic hope inside Cherise. Storytelling was fine, but one needed to know the difference between fantasy and reality. There was no such thing as freedom, and no such thing as runaway slaves. Anyone who truly believed such tripe was begging to die young.

It was close to bedtime.

Kessa led the humans down a passageway toward their neighborhood. She rounded a corner and found the tunnel blocked by a gang of brutes.

Vigilante gangs policed the Tunnels. Every so often, they would rip apart a slave who had wronged a lot of people. That was justice. This gang must be waiting to ambush someone who deserved it.

Yet they blocked Kessa.

"There she is," one of them said with contempt. "Kessa the Gullible."

"Kessa the Unwise," another sneered.

"We have not wronged anyone." Kessa searched for the gang boss. "Let us through, please."

The huge mer nerctan lowered his bony head, putting himself near eye level with Kessa. "I hear that you have an exceptionally lenient owner. We are not all so fortunate."

Kessa clicked her beak in annoyance. What was this about? Yes, perhaps her blue-haired owner was lenient. Other Yellow Ranks would have sent the three human slaves away. Their collars glowed grayish white, signifying that they were unowned—the communal property of all Torth—yet Kessa's owner allowed the humans in her suite for every work shift.

"I suppose that my owner has grown accustomed to the extra cleanliness and service," Kessa said. "Please let us through so we can sleep."

The gang boss rotated his head so he could assess the humans.

No matter how often Kessa explained that the humans were friendly, most slaves refused to believe her. Other slaves hassled the humans or even threw feces at them. They gave Kessa a hard time whenever she intervened. Everyone in the city seemed to want to insult her.

"Kessa will believe anything they tell her," a rust-colored govki said, its brown teeth poking up from its underbite.

"She'll be more surprised than anyone when they remove those collars." That came from Hajir.

Kessa was unsurprised to see her bunk-room mate as part of this gang.

"It's a shame that such a venerable elder has become such a witless fool," an elder said in a creaky voice.

"Shameful," another said.

Onlookers gathered in doorways.

The Tunnels usually felt like home, dark and rank with scents. Now Kessa wanted the bright lights and open spaces of the city above. The passageway was blocked on both ends, full of onlookers. The crowd even blocked the stinking sewage gutters.

"We don't have to stand by while she defends dangerous liars," the gang boss said.

Understanding dawned on Kessa. False information could lead slaves to their deaths. Gangs like this would target a habitual liar.

"The humans don't lie." Kessa tried to shield them with her arm. "They come from a strange land, and they have strange beliefs."

"So they say," someone muttered.

"A magical paradise where children stay with their parents and everybody sings and laughs whenever they feel like it?" That came from Ghelvae. "How can an elder of your status believe such nonsense?"

Hajir angled his huge head in a contemptuous way. "If paradise existed, Torth would ruin it."

That was inarguable.

In her darkest moments, Kessa wondered if her human friends were actually lying Torth. Their toxic tales of freedom seemed designed to lure slaves into dangerous ideas, like running away or stealing weapons.

Even so...during work shifts, Kessa sometimes caught herself daydreaming about Earth, as if it was a real place that she could visit, like a trip to the Hover Harbor.

Then she would feel queasy, as if she'd eaten something rotten. Slaves were too foolish and ignorant to rule themselves. The paradise of Earth must be a myth.

She would touch her slave collar, reassured that its pokes and pinches kept her on a healthy schedule. Without it, she would make fatal mistakes. She would forget to eat and starve to death. Slaves needed to be taken care of. They needed owners. Vy could whisper furtively about escape, but she never seemed to grasp the fact that escape meant certain death. It would never lead to paradise.

"I cannot know where my friends came from," Kessa said to the gang boss. "I have never seen the paradise of Earth. But the humans labor beside me every work shift. I cannot imagine Torth scrubbing floors like industrious ummins."

"Then you lack enough imagination," an onlooker said with contempt. "I can imagine a Torth doing anything. They would certainly lie."

"Maybe Kessa thinks she is as all-knowing as a Torth," a gang member said, "since she associates with these pathetic Torth rejects."

This gang was implying that Kessa was violating the Code of Gwat, pretending to be a god instead of a slave. That was a serious accusation. Slaves should never presume anything. Certainty was only for the gods.

Kessa straightened her back, refusing to accept the insult. "We cannot read minds, so we cannot know truth," she said, quoting the Code of Gwat. "I listen to these humans. That is not the same thing as believing them or disbelieving them. I do not judge them. You are the ones who judge them. Or misjudge them." She faced Ghelvae. "Even if my friends someday reveal themselves to be Torth, no one will be harmed except for me."

Ghelvae clicked his beak in a condescending way. "Some slaves continue to respect you, even if they don't say it out loud. If you believe that a magical friendly Torth is going to come and set you free, then other slaves will be foolish enough to believe it. That is a dangerous situation."

"Very dangerous," the gang boss agreed.

The crowd muttered with righteous indignation.

Kessa gripped Cherise's and Vy's hands, proving to them that she was with them. She might not believe most of the things they said, but she did believe the most important thing: humans were not Torth.

Besides—Thomas might not be a friendly mind reader, but Kessa had seen him with her own eyes during that procession. His existence wasn't a complete lie. Furthermore, slaves had spotted a chair-with-wheels on display at a relics kiosk.

There were even rumors about a Yellow Rank who vaguely matched Thomas's description.

And there were more rumors about a bloodthirsty, gigantic Torth who acted like a beast in the prison arena.

Kessa never translated those rumors for her friends. Unsubstantiated rumors would only ignite their most dangerous fantasies—or throw them deep into despair.

Cherise stepped in front of Kessa, as proud and confident as a Torth. She spoke fluently in the slave tongue. "Slaves take risks to find the ones they love." She glared at each gang member. "You all take risks. So do we. We are slaves."

Her words silenced the onlookers. Kessa had never heard anyone sound so much like a slave while looking so much like a Torth.

But Cherise should have cowered. Stony confidence was not a wise way to confront a gang.

One of the govki raised its lip in a sneer. "Loved ones are never Torth."

"Thomas and Ariock are humans," Cherise said with defiance. "They're not Torth."

Ghelvae imitated Cherise's defiant posture, except he made it arrogant. "A mind reader is coming to rescue us," he said in an airy tone. "A nice human who can read minds and who comes from paradise."

The gang boss lowered his bony head in a threatening way. "There is only one word for someone who has that ability."

Torth.

Kessa inwardly agreed. She could imagine cities ruled by silly humans, but she could not imagine a friendly mind reader.

That was the most troubling thing about her human friends. They seemed to sincerely believe impossible things. Everyone knew that children were not allowed in cities, and yet Thomas was a child? Every description of Thomas sounded like fantasies piled atop fantasies.

"Actual slaves would have been killed long before now for saying the things they say," Ghelvae pointed out. "I overheard one of those humans ask if ventilation shafts might be a way to escape the city!"

He paused to let that crime sink in.

Ghelvae was right. Kessa could not deny it. Cherise and Vy spoke of freedom so often, it was amazing they were still alive.

Once, Vy had casually mentioned that she wanted to steal Torth weapons.

Those sorts of ideas would get common slaves killed in the upper city. A spirit of protection seemed to smile upon the humans, enabling them to say and think whatever they pleased.

"If anyone has suffered because of my friends, I am truly sorry." Kessa forced herself to face her accusers. "But we never ask anyone to take risks or to approach Torth. If—"

"That means nothing, and you know it," Ghelvae broke in. "Some fools will try to impress you, Kessa, or they'll try to impress each other. What do you suppose happens to slaves who seek your friendly mind reader?"

"We don't all have lenient owners," Hajir added.

A hall guard hulked in the distance, paying attention to the mob. Guards rarely cared about vigilante killings, but Kessa hoped that Weptolyso would intervene if the gang attacked. He was one of the few people who seemed intrigued by the humans, rather than hating them. He often listened in on their language learning sessions.

"The friendly mind reader is going to rescue us soon!" Ghelvae said in his singsong mockery. He made a show of looking around the tunnel. "Oh, maybe he'll come right now," he said in a hushed tone, like a storyteller. "A friendly mind reader, eager to free slaves and transport us all to paradise." He peered around. "Any time now."

Kessa found it painful to look at Cherise, who searched desperately for her missing mind reader every chance she got. Sometimes Torth punished her when she lingered in crowded streets to study faces.

One of the onlookers, a fresh-faced ummin, said, "It sounds like the legend of Jonathan Stead. Doesn't it?"

Kessa had never heard that particular story.

The gang boss cracked his joints in anticipation of a fight. "I've heard enough lies and bedtime tales. Kessa, your actions endanger impressionable young slaves. You and your friends will get someone killed unless you are stopped."

The humans whispered in their native tongue, ignoring the hundreds of angry slaves all around them. Kessa heard them say "Jonathan Stead" several times.

Until now, the humans had reacted to everything like newly hatched children, ignorant of every word, law, custom, and story. This was unusual. Their familiarity with the obscure name was so well-timed, it might be a calculated maneuver.

Kessa told herself not to be so suspicious. A mere slave such as herself could never know the truth inside other people's hearts and minds. She followed the Code of Gwat.

"Look!" Someone else pointed. "They recognize the name."

The gang boss squinted with impatience. "All right." He faced the young ummin. "Tell me. What is the legend of Jonathan Stead?"

"You've never heard that story?" The young ummin sounded surprised. "The elders of my slave farm told it often."

Kessa studied the young one. He must be fresh off a farm, with a pristine hat and smooth skin not yet wrinkled from indoor humidity.

"It's about a Torth who brings slaves to paradise." He nodded toward the humans. "Just like they describe will happen."

This sounded like trouble, to Kessa. Who had ever heard of a heroic Torth? Such a tale might combine with things the humans said and spark a conflagration of dangerous notions.

Kessa tried to extinguish the topic by sounding disinterested. "That is unusual."

Weptolyso pushed his way closer. "I have heard a few versions of this tale." Kessa stared at him in surprise. Any dutiful hall guard would shut down discussions about runaway slaves, not encourage them.

"But," Weptolyso went on in his gravelly voice, "the versions I know describe Jonathan Stead as a nussian. He was transformed into a Torth!"

It seemed Weptolyso's love of storytelling outweighed his good judgment.

"I am sorry, but that is not what I heard." The young ummin was timid, no doubt afraid to contradict a hall guard. "My elders said that Jonathan Stead was a god himself."

"Interesting." Weptolyso's small red eyes were alight with interest. "What is your version of the story?"

Kessa clicked her beak, trying to signal Weptolyso to stop. The humans were quietly listening. Cherise, especially, looked interested.

The oblivious young ummin chuckled in embarrassment. "Well, my elders said that Jonathan Stead was not just an ordinary Torth, but the god of storms. His fellow upper gods urged him to stay away from people, but a storm cannot help but be curious. It blows through every crevice of every building." He hesitated, his voice wispy. "I am not very good at storytelling."

"Go on," Weptolyso said.

The ummin coughed. "All right. Well. Jonathan Stead heard the prayers of desperate slaves, and he wanted to free them. But wind cannot release slave collars. Not even a strong wind. So he begged his fellow upper gods for help, and they agreed to gather their strength and use their powers to transform him into a Torth! That way he would be able to release slave collars."

The humans listened with rapt attention. Slaves crowded nearby doorways, listening.

The young ummin shrank under all the attention. "I cannot tell this story as well as my elders did."

"Please go on," Weptolyso urged.

"Well, Jonathan Stead used his storm powers to slay a thousand Torth," the ummin said. "He summoned lightning as they shot at him with blaster gloves. He used his mighty powers to free a thousand slaves, and he led those slaves away from their city and into paradise."

Kessa had heard many stories about runaway slaves, and she suspected they were the dying embers of a time long forgotten, when upper gods and spirits interfered with mortals. Such things no longer happened. Perhaps they never had.

"Those runaway slaves live in paradise still," the young ummin concluded. "With their children, and their children's children." He looked morose. "At least, that is what my elders said."

"It's a bedtime story." Ghelvae was dismissive. "Sooner or later, someone was bound to invent one about a heroic Torth."

Kessa was inclined to agree.

Except the humans seemed to recognize the name Jonathan Stead.

And they had convictions about their own mind reader friend, Thomas.

What if those two friendly mind readers were the same person? What if Thomas was Jonathan Stead, returned from paradise to free more slaves?

Kessa had to squash her dangerous excitement. It was no good, jumping to conclusions over a story.

Some slaves believed in the bedtime tales they'd grown up with, and they would defend "the truth" with their lives. Her mate, Cozu, had been like that. His obsession with freedom had gotten him killed.

"That is similar to the versions I've heard," Weptolyso said.

Kessa looked at her hall guard friend. "How many versions have you heard?" She had not heard it even once.

Weptolyso hunched his shoulders in defense. "I collect stories. It is the same way some slaves collect scraps to make musical instruments. There is naught for me to do but listen. To me, this legend holds a certain allure. Every species repeats it. Even guards. In every version, Jonathan Stead slays a thousand Torth, frees a thousand slaves, and leads the slaves to paradise. He is always described as having a power to make storms. And he is described as a Torth." Weptolyso paused. "He is the only hero I have ever heard of who looks and acts like a Torth."

An onlooker gawked at the humans. "Maybe they have storm powers?"

Everyone hushed.

"Oh, come on," Ghelvae said dismissively.

"They know something about this tale." Even the gang boss looked unnerved, reappraising the humans.

Weptolyso snorted in agreement.

"Nah, they're just pretending to recognize the name Jonathan Stead." But Ghelvae's voice held a hint of doubt.

"There's a bit more to the tale," the timid young ummin said. "In the end, Jonathan Stead got blasted to death by ordinary Torth. But upper gods cannot die. He swore with his dying breath that he would return in another body and free more slaves."

Absolute silence reigned in the tunnel.

All gazes turned to the humans, reassessing them with fervent hope.

"He promised to return," the young storyteller said.

CHAPTER 3

PREDICTING STORMS

Vy supposed the Torth could have been abducting humans for centuries.

Jonathan Stead might have done his deeds a long time ago, on another planet. According to Kessa, other Torth-ruled cities existed. The important point was that someone else from Vy's world had been enslaved by Torth—and had escaped.

Escaped.

Escape was possible.

"When did it happen?" Cherise asked Kessa. "When did Jonathan Stead kill Torth?"

The little ummin consulted with Weptolyso and replied in her careful English, "Long ago. When elders were young."

That could mean a few years, or it could mean a few centuries. Their worst miscommunications tended to be about units of time. Kessa proudly claimed to have been a slave for nearly four hundred "blinks of Morja," which seemed to imply the phase cycle of the biggest moon. Yet that was preposterous, because Vy had been keeping track of the passing days by tying knots into the fringes of her rag skirt every sleep shift. By her reckoning, ten weeks had passed, and that was apparently one "blink of Morja."

If the moon phases were that slow, then Kessa was over seventy years old. The ummin must have miscalculated or miscommunicated. Surely no one could endure slavery for that long. No one sane.

"How did Jonathan Stead steal weapons?" Vy figured the legendary hero must have stolen a blaster rifle or two. Gloves and rifles were keyed to Torth owners, and Vy had no way to obtain a valid pass code of indecipherable Torth glyphs.

"Tsk!" Kessa was predictably mortified by the idea of stealing from Torth. "Jonathan Stead was a storm. He could kill gods. No weapons." She made explosive sounds and hand gestures, as if throwing lightning bolts.

Slaves weren't allowed to think about escape, but it seemed they were okay with swapping legends about runaways and heroes.

They let those stories molder. They fantasized about miracles that would never happen.

Just like Cherise fantasized about a rescue from Thomas.

Vy was finding it harder and harder to live that way. She couldn't imagine her disabled foster brother as a storm god, or as any sort of maverick who would pull off a rescue. All she knew for certain was that the Torth weren't human enough to take care of a severely disabled prisoner.

So Thomas was almost certainly dead.

Jonathan Stead, if he had ever existed, must have felt just as helpless, lonely, and frustrated as she did. Yet, somehow, he had done something proactive to get back to "paradise."

Delia, meanwhile, sank back into her uncaring state. Her skin looked thinner than tissue paper. Dirt accentuated her gaunt cheeks. She looked and acted like a homeless sleepwalker.

For a short while, she had looked awake. The name from Earth had provoked a frown. Vy had hoped Delia might have something to say about Jonathan Stead.

Wishful thinking.

"We'd better get Delia to bed." Vy steered the older woman toward their bunk room.

The mob finally began to break up. It seemed the gang of tough-looking slaves was letting the humans live, at least for another day of work shifts.

We aren't going to grow old here, Vy knew.

If only the legend could have yielded something better than vague, mythical answers.

"Do you want to sleep on the floor?" Vy gently asked Delia. That would be safer than climbing to their top bunk shelves.

But Delia was already climbing. She hauled herself up, shelf by shelf.

Vy sighed and followed her. "Careful." She hoisted Delia when the older woman ran out of strength. "Up."

A bad injury would entail an inability to work, which would probably mean death. Their sleeping situation was dangerous. They practically had to do pull-ups to get to their bunks on the top row, right beneath the dank, moldy ceiling.

"I remember now," Delia said in a sleepy tone, pulling herself up past each shelf. "I thought his name sounded familiar."

"Whose name?" Vy felt alert. "Jonathan Stead?"

"Will had a book about psychics." Delia trembled as she hoisted herself up another shelf. "You know, because of all the rumors about old Garrett. There was a paragraph in there about the Dovanacks."

Vy was aware of Cherise climbing up the shelves below her, listening. And Kessa. Weeks ago, a bunch of local slaves had pressured Kessa to give up her floor-level bunk, forcing her to sleep just below her human friends.

"Was Jonathan Stead in that book?" Vy asked.

"Mmm-hmm." Delia paused to rest. An ummin glared resentfully at her. "He was active about a hundred years before Garrett. But yeah. He was in there."

"Was he a mind reader?" Vy watched Delia in the dimness. She wanted a clue, even if it was just a facial expression.

"Did he have storm powers?" Cherise asked.

"I don't remember." Delia wheezed as she crawled onto her shelf. "I just remember his name."

Vy hid her disappointment. She hauled herself onto the adjacent shelf, a cramped and chilly space.

She leaned over to spread a rag blanket over Delia. Then she pulled up her own threadbare blanket. She curled up and tried to get comfortable on the metal surface. If only she had a mattress and pillow. Or her mother's touch and the sounds of home.

"That book included Garrett just because he won a lot at poker," Delia said sleepily. "But in all fairness, he was secretive. I guess there were things he never told anyone."

Vy pictured the opulent Dovanack mansion. Old Garrett Dovanack must have won more than a few high-stakes poker games.

She closed her eyes and pictured Ariock. She wished she could talk with him again. His deep voice had been a comfort, calm and implacable, like a protective wall. Judging by his taste in books and media, he would be fun to talk to.

"Garrett told us that he got abducted by aliens once," Delia said.

Vy opened her eyes.

"And he stole a spaceship to get home," Delia said.

Implications hung in the air.

Vy was fully awake. She propped herself up on her elbows so she could stare at Delia. "He really said that?"

"Old Garrett said a lot of things," Delia said. "He had all kinds of stories. You never knew which were true, if any of them were."

Vy glanced toward Cherise and saw her foster sister looking back at her. If Garrett Dovanack or Jonathan Stead had escaped slavery, then they had to find out how.

The withered ummins nearby snored, oblivious to conversation. Most of the slaves who slept this high up were somnambulistic. Only Kessa was alert, listening on her nearby shelf.

Delia pulled something out of her rags and handed it to Vy. "Here," she whispered.

It was a folded, creased paper.

Vy unfolded a photograph. A family smiled in paradise, in that world where happiness and kindness were normal. The mother in the photograph was recognizable as a healthy and younger version of Delia. She had wind-tousled hair and a carefree grin. Her husband was dark and handsome, and he had his arm around her in a loving embrace. Together, they restrained a freckle-faced boy with an innocently dazzling grin.

They knelt on an inviting green lawn under a blue sky. Part of the Dovanack mansion was in the background.

Tears blurred Vy's vision. She hadn't expected to see paradise.

"I was afraid to show it you," Delia said in a low tone, "because of all the mind readers. I try to forget I have it, during our work shifts. But I would like you to hold on to it when I'm gone."

Vy wanted to reassure Delia that she would survive. They would all survive.

Instead, she remained quiet. Delia had a fatal form of pancreatic cancer, and she knew the difference between reality and false reassurances.

Vy scrutinized the photo closer, marveling that the little boy looked too normal-size and happy to be the giant she'd met. Was that really Ariock?

"It's my only picture of Ariock," Delia whispered. "I was smart enough to take it out of my phone case and hide it before they stole my phone."

Vy visualized the transformation from cheerful child to brooding giant. Ariock would have had to be careful with all the antique furniture in the mansion. He would have felt awkward in his own body, ducking beneath chandeliers and twisting under door frames.

"I think this shows who he really is," Delia said. "Happy. He became withdrawn after the plane crash."

"Crash?" Vy glanced at her.

"When Will died," Delia said. "Ariock almost died in that crash, too."

"Oh. I'm sorry." Vy said words that would have meant something on a better world.

"I know this sounds strange," Delia said, "but I miss Ariock's voice most of all. He isn't a whole lot like his father—he was robbed of the chance to go to college, to be social—but sometimes, when I heard him talk, I thought, just for a second, *my husband is with me*. He sounds a lot like Will."

"It's not strange," Vy said.

Cherise looked curious about the dog-eared photograph, so Vy handed it over. She fought an urge to warn Cherise to be careful with it.

That photo was their only scrap of paradise. It was a treasure. It encapsulated everything they had lost. Not just their families and homes, but everything. Seven billion people they had never met. Entire continents they had never visited. The internet, music, futures, oceans, forests. All of it.

"If he's alive," Delia said, "then he's trying to save us. I know it. He nearly died trying to save his father. He ran back in there, into fire and smoke, and tried to drag them out. The adults. He was only nine. Everyone said it was a miracle that he survived."

Vy thought of the giant she had met and nodded. Ariock had tried to protect them from the Torth.

Cherise handed the photo down to Kessa, on the shelf below hers. Kessa studied it with extra-wide owlish eyes. The Torth had a lot of pretty vistas in their windows, but they didn't have pictures of happy people. It must look alien to her.

"I could have saved Will," Delia said in a low voice. "If I'd listened. If I had known what Ariock could do."

Vy rested her cheek on the shelf, listening. She wanted to encourage Delia's talkative mood. "What can he do?"

"We were supposed to go to his grandma's funeral." Delia fixed her gaze toward a distance that only she could see. "Everyone died that year. Will's childhood friend died in an accident at an ice hockey game." She ticked events off on her fingers. "Then his aunt died of an accidental overdose. His grandfather's business associates all had funerals within the same span of months. And then his mother, Rose, got into a car and drove off a cliff."

Vy wished she could offer adequate words. "I'm sorry to hear that."

Delia waved away the sympathy. "No one was all that sad about Grandma Rose. Will arranged her funeral in Maine and chartered a private flight for the three of us."

"Wait," Vy said, recalling an earlier conversation with Delia. "Was this the grandmother who had nightmares about Ariock? The one who said she dreamed he was a storm?"

Kessa stirred. Cherise looked their way. Luckily, no one else in the bunk room could understand English.

"That's the one," Delia affirmed. "She was a bit crazy. Anyway. We packed for the trip, and..." She sniffled. "Ariock woke us up, screaming. He said the plane would catch on fire."

A chill rippled over Vy.

Delia went on in a pained tone. "Will thought it was nothing. We had gone to a lot of funerals that year, and it was tough to explain death to a nine-year-old. But Ariock was usually cheerful. That morning? He threw clothes out of our luggage. I got spooked. He was acting so strangely."

Delia paused. Her tone was thick, and Vy realized that she was weeping.

"So I begged Will to stay home. He refused to listen. It was his mother's funeral. Ariock's grandma. That was the only serious fight we ever had. Will stormed out of the house—and he took Ariock with him."

"I'm so sorry," Vy said. She could almost feel Delia's long-ago pain, like a stab to the heart, aware that Delia had never seen her husband again. Her last moments with the man she'd loved were tainted by fury.

"Did Ariock predict the Torth were coming to get us?" Cherise asked, propped up on an elbow.

That was a good question, Vy thought. Kessa listened, alert and curious.

Delia seemed to mull it over. After a while, she said, "I think he knew something bad was coming. He was restless all that week, asking me to check the backup generator and things like that. He said he thought there would be a bad storm."

That was an understatement.

Vy wished she could talk to Ariock again. If he could actually predict the future…?

He might be good at self-defense.

He might still be alive.

"That's why I was a little out of sorts when you showed up," Delia said. "It had started to snow, and then I saw headlights in our driveway. You were an unexpected factor." She let out a defeated sigh. "But even if he sees the future sometimes…so what?"

"So what?" Vy could hardly dismiss that. Delia was talking about a superhuman power!

"Ariock isn't their Jonathan Stead," Delia said. "Or ours."

Vy curled up under her thin blanket. Superheroes. Plane crashes. Funerals. It was all stuff from a world that was so out of reach, it might as well be dead.

"I would think Ariock would be more worried," Cherise said. "After what happened to his father."

"He didn't remember," Delia said.

They both looked at her in the darkness.

"I think it's selective amnesia." Delia's tone was heavy with sorrow. "He remembers the aftermath of the plane crash, and I think he has memories of trying to save his father. And failing. But the night and day leading up to it? Nothing."

Vy had worked with victims of violence, and she understood. Extreme trauma could do strange things to a person's memory.

"I brought it up once," Delia said. "I said, 'You had a predictive nightmare.' And he just gave me a blank look. I never mentioned it again. I didn't see the point. Ariock is pretty good at manufacturing reasons to hate himself, and I'm sure he would take it hard, to think he could have prevented his father from boarding that plane."

She seemed unaware of the guilt in her own voice.

Vy reached across the shelves to grip Delia's bony hand. "You couldn't have stopped him, either."

Delia squeezed back. "I tried. I tried to get him to stay home."

"I know," Vy said. "You did what any sane, loving person would have done. What happened isn't your fault."

"What caused the plane to crash?" Cherise asked. "Was it a storm?"

Ariock seemed to predict storms. His oddball grandmother had predicted that he would become a storm. And there was a supposed storm god, Jonathan Stead. His name appeared in a book along with the name of Garrett Dovanack, Ariock's great-grandfather.

Vy tried to make the tidbits of information fit together. It felt like a jigsaw puzzle with missing pieces.

"There was strange weather in the area," Delia admitted. "At the time. I don't know if it was a storm. They were over wilderness. Later on, investigators said there was evidence of bombs. Like someone had actively tried to murder Will and Ariock and the pilot."

Assassins?

"Who would do that?" Vy asked.

"I wish I knew." Delia's tone was full of weary anger. "Will was a sweetheart. He didn't have enemies."

"Was Ariock the only survivor?" Vy guessed that he must have a case of survivor's guilt. That fit his tendency toward self-blame.

"Yes," Delia said.

Vy lay on her back and stared at mold stains on the ceiling. She kept daydreaming about stealing weapons and vehicles and sneaking out of this metropolis, as if she could survive in an alien desert. But what if...well...

What if Ariock had a useful power to see the future?

What if he was alive and strong?

"How did Ariock survive that crash?" Vy asked.

"I don't know," Delia said.

Vy began to imagine powers. Ariock did have superhuman size and strength. What if, like Thomas, there was more to his abilities than she imagined? What if he was hard to kill?

Could they be rescued after all—by Ariock instead of by Thomas?

CHAPTER 4
WHAT MATTERS

Yellow Thomas couldn't delete the music in his head.

His laboratory was as silent as winter, yet a violin techno concerto blazed in the back of his mind while he swiped through holographic menus on his workstation.

Is he deranged? his orbiters wondered.

Those primitive sounds connote slave-like angst.

Why conjure such noise?

How can he possibly focus (on work) with that emotive melody in the background of his thoughts?

Yellow Thomas could only offer a mental shrug. He kept trying to quit the songs stuck in his head, but music was a subconscious impulse, like smiling or frowning. He might need years to train his brain out of such atavistic habits.

It is harmless, the scientists in his mental audience assured each other. They imagined defused bombs. *He can't help himself.*

Everyone has at least one primitive flaw.

Indeed, some Torth snored while they slept. Others were addicted to overeating. Such tics were permitted because they had no effect on listeners in the Megacosm. Yellow Thomas had an overabundance of primitive tics—he overvalued privacy, he talked in his sleep, he bit his lower lip when he was deep in thought, he kept getting music stuck in his head—but he wasn't ashamed.

Mostly because intense shame was illegal.

Whenever he began to feel too much shame, he simply dialed up his tranquility mesh. That circlet on his head was better than Prozac.

??? Thousands of scientists in his mental audience wondered what Prozac was.

Yellow Thomas flashed a summary of the neurological effects of antidepressants. His ever-shifting audience burbled with reactions.

Thousands of Torth paraded through the back of Yellow Thomas's mind at all hours, like fairgoers shuffling through a freak-show tent, fascinated by the sights within. They never left him alone. Even when he used a toilet, even when he was groggy from waking up or drifting off to sleep, the masses were eager for his opinions.

Supergeniuses always reeled in large audiences. Even baby supergeniuses, with their undeveloped personalities and heightened imaginations, tended to draw at least a few dozen orbiters.

On Earth, scientists had mostly humored Thomas. They'd been unwilling to credit him with any breakthroughs. Rasa Biotech had barely trusted him to use lab equipment.

Now?

Yellow Thomas controlled a vast high-tech laboratory, without oversight or interference. His orbiters respected him. They admired the way he calculated ketone levels in renal simulations. He was lauded, as long as he didn't allow himself to think about certain *(slaves)* things.

An enormous, multifaceted, godlike mind bulked into his mental audience. *I told you to stop using tranquility meshes,* the Upward Governess thought without preamble.

There was no point in apologizing. Yellow Thomas took a sip from the sugary drink in his cupholder. Meshes were commonplace and harmless. No one, not even his mentor, had the right to force him to stop.

Anyway, all it did was alter his brain waves to make him feel tranquil. It wasn't a drug. Even children on baby farms were allowed to use meshes.

Do you expect Me to believe you're unaware of what meshes do to the processing speed of supergeniuses? The Upward Governess drilled into the bedrock of his mind. *You're not that stupid, are you?*

Yellow Thomas wanted to appease her, to get her out of the depths of his mind. *Yeah, yeah, I know. Deviations from habitual brain-wave patterns necessitate a compensatory mental effort, which entails potential slowdowns in My processing speed. So what?*

She was unappeased.

Millions of Torth orbited her gargantuan mind, like moths attracted to a moon, commenting on every action she made and every reaction she had.

I have never used a tranquility mesh in My life, the Upward Governess let him know. *Ambitious supergeniuses cannot afford mental hiccups. Our entire value is Our brains. If you truly wish to rise in rank, then you will give away your mesh.*

Reluctant, Yellow Thomas dialed his mesh off.

The idea of giving it away, though? No. He needed its soothing effect at least some of the time. Otherwise he might become melancholy. Or worse.

A burst of frustration spiraled off the Upward Governess. *In your gliotransmission experiment, I cogitated a plausible eigenvector that you failed to include.*

Yellow Thomas wished he could ignore her.

Your results were sloppy. His mentor's thoughts were whip sharp, inflicting small pains, like paper cuts. *And you kept Me waiting.*

Yellow Thomas sensed her lounging in one of her many gardens. Her breathing was easier, and her fingers were less atrophied, thanks to regular doses of NAI-12.

Okay, he admitted. He performed feats of math and science that would take a team of normal scientists a decade to work through, and he did it on a daily basis, but it was plausible that he had made one trivial error.

So what?

He doubted that the data-digging experiments she assigned to him would ever matter to anyone. They were just cleverly designed puzzles. Was he supposed to be grateful for busywork?

Oh. Her mind flashed threats. *Are My assignments too burdensome for you? Are My requests (to throw away that mesh) too annoying? If you want an easy time, then find a new mentor.*

Yellow Thomas dialed his tranquility mesh on again. He absolutely needed a prestigious mentor. Without *(protection)* guidance from the Upward Governess, people would cease to respect him. They might *(execute him)* stop tolerating his eccentric quirks.

He tried to assure himself that the Upward Governess was acting in his best interest. Maybe she kept him busy so that he would stay away from *(dangerous) (illegal)* unpalatable ideas?

She was so helpful.

Really. She was.

The Upward Governess oozed disdain. *Do you want to remain a Yellow for the rest of your (increasingly short) life?* She mentally emphasized her own health. *If you want to regain control of your health and your future (as I have done), then you need to innovate. Invent something!!!* She emblazoned the thought with neon colors. *Further the Empire! My assignments are (obviously!) just launch vectors. I am doing everything I can to help you!*

Her inner audience swarmed, unsettled by her outburst. She radiated sincerity.

But Yellow Thomas wasn't sure he could trust that. Why had his mentor not yet recommended him for a promotion? If she wanted him to attain a higher rank, she could probably weigh in on some committee decision and make it happen.

The mental image of her round face remained smoothly neutral. Her thoughts, however, swept together in a thunderhead that sparked with knowledge. *I am not a Servant of All (who decides other people's fates).* Frustration flashed in her depths. *I have done everything possible to enable promotion for you. I often take time out of My busy schedule to give you opportunities. Recognize that. Value it.*

Her thoughts had a dangerous, bladelike edge.

Yellow Thomas gazed at the holographic representation of kidneys displayed on his workstation.

Child-size kidneys.

He wanted them to be vat grown. But he was aware of *(!!!)* death screams in the Megacosm, and he knew that, statistically, 64.77 percent of death screams came from baby farms. Children often failed emotional or developmental tests. Baby farm duds got killed. Their organs were harvested for scientific purposes.

It was a good thing he wasn't one of those poor wretches. He had passed his Adulthood Exam.

Wasn't that enough?

Did the Torth Empire really need another inventor?

Everyone encouraged him to innovate. His mentor held him to a standard of scientific rigor that was light-years beyond what normal scientists were capable of. She was, indeed, pushing him to new levels of ingenuity. Quantum theories, dimensional theories, superluminal temporal streams… He had been excited, at first. He could explore each topic for days and never get tired of it.

But did any of it really matter?

Yellow Thomas wanted to apply his growing skill sets to something *(meaningful) (worthwhile)* better than improving kidney functionality for geriatric Torth. The work his mentor assigned him seemed pointless. None of it mattered.

The Upward Governess studied him from afar.

Then she seemed to come to a decision. *Let's have some private time together. Meet Me at My indoor lake.*

She slid out of the Megacosm with a sense of entitlement that Yellow Thomas struggled not to envy.

As he floated toward the exit of his suite, he begged for his own privacy break.

Why? his orbiters wondered.

Why does the lazy Yellow pupil want privacy?

Suspicions sparked between distant Torth, and Yellow Thomas offered them his usual excuses. He had bad habits. He wouldn't be away for long, just two minutes.

Only a criminal would want privacy breaks as often as he does.

That was an exaggeration, Yellow Thomas thought. Quite a few high ranks took frequent privacy breaks.

They are all Blue Ranks and Servants of All, his orbiters pointed out.

Yellow Thomas offered apologies. He was ashamed by his human habits. He really wanted just a tiny smidgen of private time.

Exiting the Megacosm felt like backing offstage in front of millions of watchers.

His throat clicked as he swallowed.

Yellow Thomas shivered all over, vulnerable and alone inside his own skull. Solitude was like plunging into cold reality after a warm bath. Now that he was no longer experiencing the health of distant Torth, now that he had temporarily ceased to learn new things…he was just weak.

Soft dripping sounds from the chemistry corner made his home suite sound like a cave. Or a tomb.

He was not truly alone, of course. His personal slaves watched him while they worked, attentive for hand signals. Yellow Thomas kept his facial expression blandly neutral. If a slave noticed anything unusual, the whole Torth Empire was guaranteed to have a mnemonic recording of it within hours.

Two minutes was about how long Yellow Thomas dared exist in solitude. Any longer and Red Ranks would burst into his suite to check on him.

And no matter when he returned to the Megacosm, his orbiters would pick through his memories. More than a few Torth hoped to catch him doing something illegal. They would inspect his mental clutter in hopes of finding buried tidbits of interest. He dared not do anything suspicious.

But for now…

Yellow Thomas dialed off his tranquility mesh. He wanted to feel something. Emotions were a key to…to…

Cherise.

Her name was another key. When he used that key, an enormous and ghastly problem reemerged from the buried depths of his mind.

Cherise. Vy. His foster sisters. *Ariock and Delia.* His friends.

He had promised to bring them home eons ago.

It had been twelve weeks, but in terms of life experience, Yellow Thomas had lived an extra 268,000 lifetimes. Mentally, he had been a Torth for far longer than he'd been a human.

During his first couple of days as Yellow Thomas, he had considered sending a message to Cherise. He had gone so far as to replace one of his slaves with a mischievous ummin who happened to have a passing familiarity with the humans, a smuggler.

Now he almost wished that smuggler *(Pung)* would disobey a command just so he'd have a valid excuse to trade him in for another. His choice of slave looked suspicious. If he commanded Pung to smuggle a note or to deliver anything unusual—anything that inspired curiosity or hope—well, such a delivery would make slaves curious or hopeful.

Hope shone like a beacon to anyone who could read minds.

It would arouse the suspicions of any Torth passersby. A Torth would then probe their minds, learn the truth, and the result would be death by torture for everyone involved.

Yellow Thomas was able to use Pung like a surveillance device. Pung sometimes overheard news about Cherise, Vy, and Delia. But what good was that? They were struggling to survive as slaves. Anyone could have guessed as much.

Yellow Thomas navigated his hoverchair past a row of evaporation chambers and past his pharmaceutical experiments. No matter how many ways he worked on the rescue problem, he came to the same disheartening conclusions.

He could not make a plan. Any plan would be found out by his mentor.

He could not deliver anything that would inspire hope. Hope was a dead giveaway.

He could not smuggle anyone out of a busy city full of mind readers. The spaceport was crawling with Red Ranks and watchful guards, as were the hover harbors. People crowded every exit point at all hours. Tourists filled the city. They were excited to be firsthand witnesses to the Giant's demise.

Yellow Thomas himself couldn't sneak anywhere. If he vanished from the Megacosm for more than two minutes, there would be a man hunt.

A fanciful flower surfaced in his mind. Cherise had drawn that flower a long time ago, streaking its petals with vibrant reds and blues. It used to hang on the wall across from his bed in the Hollander home.

"This flower has magical healing properties," Cherise had told him, embellishing the unique blossom. *"But it's so rare and so unique, no one believes it exists. They don't think it's possible."*

Escape seemed like that flower. A fanciful situation. A beautiful impossibility.

And yet there was a thin sliver of possibility.

After all these weeks of recalculating and reanalyzing, Yellow Thomas had one rash, half-baked impulse of a plan. If he was going to escape with Cherise, Vy, and their mutual friends, it would have to be spur-of-the-moment.

He needed to manufacture and collect opportunities.

He needed to create possibilities. And he needed to be ready to act fast and take risks, should his efforts to create an emergent situation pay off, tossing the odds in his favor.

Yellow Thomas floated past an experiment with gray goo dripping from a coil. He glanced at its readout in a disinterested way.

It wasn't a weapon, per se. Supergeniuses were not allowed to work on weapons. Yellow Thomas in particular was not given any substance that might be made into an explosive. Red and Green Ranks inspected his laboratories on a regular basis.

But they had overlooked this small experiment.

The best thing about being a supergenius was that he could hide small secrets beneath floods of data. His mind was too vast, too cluttered with useless trivia, for anyone to probe it entirely.

One circumstance might allow slaves like Cherise to walk away from this city. All the local Torth and guards needed to be gone. There needed to be a citywide evacuation, and it needed to be such a swift and scary crisis that a lot of slaves would get left behind, unsupervised.

The silence inside Yellow Thomas's head seemed unnatural. It rang in his ears. He was painfully aware that his private time had run out, and he absolutely needed to ascend.

Just another second.

His wisp of a manufactured opportunity might get a lot of innocent bystanders killed. That didn't seem right. He really didn't want to cause murderous mayhem.

Was such a daring rescue even worth pursuing?

Sure, Cherise and Vy belonged on Earth, but Yellow Thomas belonged among the Torth. He understood that now. Humanity was a rotten apple crawling with maggots. Humankind had superficial vision, unable to see past each other's skin, whereas he saw every crippling fear and dirty secret.

He had never belonged among the inferior primitives.

So he could give up.

And if he did…if he quit trying to save his foster sisters…well, then at least he would spend his final months in blissful luxury instead of fleeing through alien wilderness or getting tortured to death. Why was he trying so hard?

A brilliant flower floated in the secret depths of his mind, crushed and trampled.

Yellow Thomas had no more time to ponder things. He dialed up his mesh, attaining a better state of mind, and (Cherise, I never deserved you) he locked away all thoughts of his foster sisters into a mental vault. Then he ascended.

Soon he was amid whirlwinds of thought, like rush-hour traffic in the busiest metropolis in the universe.

Finally!

Welcome back!

How was your privacy break?

When will you ease yourself out of those atavistic habits?

Yellow Thomas floated out of his suite, his face and mind neutral, heading toward his mentor's indoor lake.

CHAPTER 5
GREEDY AND LAZY

The Upward Governess reclined aboard a luxury skiff, her iridescent blue eyes shaded by a floppy-brimmed hat. Discreet fans around her indoor lake simulated a breeze, carrying fragrances from the artificial tropical islands.

What kind of a lazy, unambitious, good-for-nothing supergenius are you? she greeted him.

Yellow Thomas reluctantly parked his hoverchair at the lake's edge. Slaves gently lifted him into the boat, facing her. Ornately decorated pillows made for a comfortable seat.

At a gesture from her, the slaves removed his tranquility mesh. He dared not protest.

The Upward Governess used a data tablet to operate the skiff. Soon they were speeding away from shore, away from the slaves.

They each dropped out of the Megacosm.

Privacy was a luxury that only she could afford in vast quantities. He understood that she was generously sharing her privacy with him.

I chose you, his mentor thought, *because you are supposed to be starving for life. Like Me.*

Yellow Thomas gazed at the crystal-blue water. It was nice to admire the refraction of water without interference from a thousand orbiters. His watery reflection was pale peach next to the fat blue shape of his mentor.

So I expect you to innovate, she went on. *If I start praising work that is less than what I am capable of, then My praise becomes meaningless. I would need to praise millions of scientists.*

That was a valid point.

Yellow Thomas made himself more comfortable, waiting for her lecture to end.

The Upward Governess steered the skiff around an island of tropical trees, laden with fruit. *I know what you're up to.* She pictured the gray goo hidden in his laboratory.

!!! Yellow Thomas jerked as illegal panic stabbed through him.

She calmly measured his reaction. *You've fooled (other Torth) everyone else. But I am not an idiot.*

Yellow Thomas was too shocked to respond. He had taken pains to bury his illegal activity. He had been certain that no one, not even his mentor, suspected.

How had she guessed?

I've observed that 73.9 percent of your privacy breaks occur when you are near your chemical laboratory, the Upward Governess thought. *Any moron would notice if you're developing a bomb or a chemical weapon, but you could conceivably develop an ingredient for illegal pharmacology.*

Mind readers could not lie to each other. All Yellow Thomas could do was avoid her gaze.

You plan to sabotage a key ingredient of the inhibitor serum, the Upward Governess went on, conjecturing. *Gambling on the Giant? You hope to use him as a wrecking ball?*

Yellow Thomas struggled to hide his shame. His plan had always been tenuous. A million things could go wrong. The Giant *(Ariock)* might fail to manifest his storm powers, even if he gained access. He might just die clueless. Red Ranks might shoot him dead before he could go into wreckage mode.

Ah. Encouraged, the Upward Governess continued her guesswork. *I assume you would engineer a series of events that would lead to replacing the functional inhibitor patch with your sabotaged version, thus empowering the Giant to go on a mad rampage. And that would trigger a citywide evacuation?* She assessed Yellow Thomas with her deep-blue eyes. *And then you might be able to smuggle the human slaves (Cherise, Vy, Delia) out of My city during your manufactured chaos. How clever.*

Well. This was it. Checkmate. If they were playing a deadly game, then she had won. All she had to do was ascend into the Megacosm and reveal his illegal plan.

She could get him killed with a thought.

I am not planning to get you killed. The Upward Governess leaned back, causing the boat to rock. *You still owe Me (so) much. But You should not make a habit of underestimating Me. When I tell you to quit (using a tranquility mesh) being lazy, perhaps you ought to take My suggestion.*

Yellow Thomas felt like a mouse trapped between the claws of a cat.

We can help each other, little Yellow, she thought. *Don't you see that? Don't you want that?*

He watched her, wary. He tried to dissect her goals.

All I want, she thought, *is for you to regain your ambition. Please Me. And I guarantee that you will see new possibilities.*

She used her tablet, and the boat glided onward. Sunlight sparkled on water. Iridescent bugs flitted above lily pads.

New possibilities. That sounded like a promise.

What was she hinting at?

The Upward Governess had already seized new possibilities for herself, enjoying regular doses of his medicine. Her hair had a new luster. Her cheeks looked more rosy. She aimed for adulthood like a missile to a target.

It occurred to Yellow Thomas that his mentor was more driven than any other living supergenius.

She had overcome countless political obstacles in order to get her hands on a forbidden, limited supply of medicine. NAI-12 was a prototype. No one was manufacturing it, even on Earth.

And even if they were...? The Majority would never allow one individual to gain superiority over the collective. Everyone knew how fast supergeniuses imbibed knowledge. An adult supergenius could potentially be a major threat to the Torth Empire. Therefore, they would never allow the Upward Governess to live to adulthood.

Yet she tried anyway. She refused to capitulate to what the Majority wanted for her.

Just like you. She gazed at him from beneath her hat, and this time Yellow Thomas felt a tug inside her mind. Hope. It was well hidden, but it was there.

Was she actually pinning her hopes on him? Why?

Her titanic mind reared and swirled like a nuclear furnace. *Because I want (I crave) (desire) hunger for...* Suspicion shadowed her thoughts. *You are not ready for My goals, little Yellow. Maybe you will never be ready.*

Yellow Thomas decided to discard all his prejudgments about the Upward Governess. He might have been unfair in his initial assessments. He needed to reevaluate her with fresh eyes.

Who was this person sitting across from him in the boat?

Why did she care so much about securing a future for herself, when so few Torth cared about anything?

In fact, why had she gone out of her way to protect a mere Yellow Rank who might try to sabotage her city? She had pressured some of the highest ranks in the known universe to vote against their own self-interest. In vouching for Yellow Thomas, she had used up a lot of her own credibility.

You really do need Me, he realized. *You believe I am a key to something You want. Adulthood?*

Her mind seethed, almost illegally frothy. He had guessed right.

Yellow Thomas searched for a chain of logic and found it. *You want My help in gaining more NAI-12,* he guessed. *The Torth Majority won't approve another batch for You.*

She silently admitted the truth. *Yes. I used up all My requests (a lifetime of requests) to gain this batch.* She mentally indicated the NAI-12 case in its honored place within her reach. *It has given Me a few extra months of life. But it is not enough. The supply is already running out. I need (at least) a year's worth.*

Their distorted reflections in the water exaggerated how sickly they both were.

A year? Yellow Thomas mused. *Just one year?*

She needed more than that if she intended to live to adulthood. She was already older than Yellow Thomas by more than a year. Every second she breathed must feel like borrowed time.

Yellow Thomas knew exactly what it felt like to spend every day under the shadow of an anvil that would fall and crush him. He used to stay up all night, working until his vision blurred and his neck ached, desperate to cure himself. He actually felt sorry for his mentor.

The Upward Governess sensed his sympathy, and she softened. *Before I knew that you existed,* she thought, *I had hoped the Twins (the second- and third-eldest supergeniuses) would rise high enough in rank to request particular ingredients. Together, We might have figured out a way to secretly manufacture batches of NAI-12.*

It was a confession. Yellow Thomas realized that she was sharing a vulnerability. He felt honored.

But the Twins are not ambitious enough, his mentor admitted. *They want to live, but not enough. Not the way you do.* She searched his mind with raw desperation. *The way I thought you do.*

Yellow Thomas leaned back against the cushions on his end of the skiff and gazed up at the clear green sky. He did want to live. Just...

Maybe not as a Torth?

You have no choice. The Upward Governess radiated frustration. *You are a Torth. And a resupply of your medicine will benefit both of Us.*

Would it?

Yellow Thomas eyed her, realizing that she had deflected his earlier suspicion. She wanted only one more year's worth of medicine. But how could that be enough to satisfy her?

She might have additional plans.

The Upward Governess was an expert on chemical and material engineering. She knew her way around robotics. Might she pioneer some secret, illegal way to boost her own life span?

Could she actually transform herself into a cyborg?

It wasn't entirely impossible. As an Indigo-Blue Rank, the Upward Governess ranked high enough so that few Torth would dare to pry into her daily activities. She might be able to bioengineer a robotic contraption to replace her unhealthy, dying body. Her neuromuscular disease would cease to be a problem if she no longer relied on biological organs. An artificial vascular system could nourish her flesh-and-blood brain. Layers of ionic tungsten-carbide casings could protect her brain and render her nearly indestructible.

Would she dare?

You could join Me, the Upward Governess offered.

Now that he had unearthed her *(illegal)* scheme, she expounded on it. Theoretically, yes, she could use her knowledge of alloys and polymers to replace her soft body with an invincible one. And then she could launch herself into outer space. In space, no one would be able to execute her if she displeased the Majority.

From there, she could take over space stations and create robot armies.

She could conquer the galaxy. Everyone in existence would worship her as the Eternal Commander of All Living Things. She would explore unmapped galaxies.

Oh, and if Yellow Thomas proved helpful and cooperative? Then she would allow him to become immortal alongside her, protected by his own indestructible, robotic replacement body.

Wow. Yellow Thomas marveled. *You really are ambitious.*

All I would need, in theory, is one more year, she insinuated. *That's all.*

Well. Hm.

Yellow Thomas pondered her illegal goal. He used to have similar fantasies when he'd lived on Earth. He had quietly considered conquering humankind and ruling them as a benevolent dictator.

He never would have guessed that his mentor harbored similar childish daydreams.

Childish? She puffed up like a puffer fish, causing the boat to rock a little bit. *How dare you.*

You are not a Servant of All, Yellow Thomas reminded her. *You are not the highest rank. They can raid Your laboratories at any time and uncover Your (secret) (illegal) work. You and I are just children here.*

Throughout Torth history, plenty of supergeniuses had tried to cure themselves. Plenty of them had begged for the legal freedom to live to adulthood.

But Torth civilization was predicated upon equality. Power belonged to the masses, never to individuals. That was why the Majority had outlawed bioengineering and Yeresunsa powers.

Your goal is futile. Yellow Thomas trailed his finger in the cold water, distorting his golden image. *So is Mine, I guess.* His withered reflection gazed at him from the lake, ephemeral. Fleeting. *Our ambitions are sandcastles. The Torth Majority will erode whatever progress We manage to make. They will prevent You from living to adulthood. They will hunt Me if I try to escape. We are doomed no matter what.*

He could not protect humankind from the Torth Empire. He fully understood that. He could not save Cherise.

So why bother to keep breathing?

What was the point of existence?

Everyone was going to die eventually, anyway.

A dark feeling welled up in the Upward Governess. She masked it well, but
it leaked out around the edges of her mind. *You are a major disappointment.*

So are You, he thought.

The Majority are (fools) wrong. Frustrated yearning swept through the
Upward Governess. *Don't you want (power) (freedom) a future?* She gently
probed his surface thoughts, seeking a weakness where he might cave in. *Aid
Me, and I will share the next batch of NAI-12 with you. We can split it fifty-fifty.*

It was tempting.

Yellow Thomas realized that he was drumming his fingers on a pillow,
thinking about it. He forced himself to stop the atavistic habit.

We would be responsible co-rulers of the galaxy, the Upward Governess
silently went on. *We can treat slaves well. We won't be rampaging tyrants like
the Yeresunsa of the ancient past. Instead? We will rebuild everything and make
it better.*

It was a seductive goal. Yellow Thomas hesitated only because he had his
own goal. Somewhere in this city, Cherise was surviving.

Cherise had grounded him. She had reminded him that the smallest people might be wiser than he was, or even morally superior.

You doubt Our superiority? The Upward Governess dug into his mind,
curious. *We (supergeniuses) are above morality. We are the pillars that hold up
the Megacosm.* Her thoughts overlapped in such a dazzling array, they seemed
like a volcanic eruption. *Too many Torth denigrate supergeniuses as mere technicians and calculators. They refuse to acknowledge Our obvious superiority.
But We are better than everyone else.*

Yellow Thomas disagreed. A pillar supported a ceiling, but floors and
walls and doors also had important functions. A shuttle pilot with fast reflexes was just as valuable as a supergenius in certain circumstances.

We are superior to all other sapients. The Upward Governess exuded certainty. *Most Torth cruise through the Megacosm and accomplish nothing with
their lives. We can do so much more. Imagine the miracles you and I could
accomplish if We lived to maturity?*

Yellow Thomas privately guessed that they could accomplish a lot even
as preadolescent children. What if they remedied a problem that not even the
Commander of All Living Things could solve? How would the Majority treat
them if they made themselves indispensable?

Exactly. The Upward Governess's mood spiked with excitement. *I will let you sabotage the Giant's inhibitor collar. Let him rampage. And then I will solve the problem.*

They stared at each other across the boat.

Yellow Thomas felt sick with unexamined emotions. Ariock did not deserve to die as a pawn in supergenius schemes.

No one can save the Giant, the Upward Governess insisted. *The Majority sentenced him to death, and whatever the Majority wants, the Majority gets. But the spectacle of his execution could potentially buy eternity for Us. Let him slay a few dozen Torth. And then? I will be the One to innovate a fast way to kill him, thereby saving My metropolis and substantiating Our value to civilization. That could give Me enough leverage to demand a fresh supply of NAI-12.*

A flower lay crumpled in the bottom of Yellow Thomas's mind, its petals streaked with brilliant hues of red and blue.

Could he aid the Upward Governess in her quest for longevity and power while Cherise wasted away and died as a slave? She didn't deserve that.

We don't deserve to die as pubescent children. Contempt bubbled from the depths of the Upward Governess's mind. *Let go of your attachment to that slave. All We (I) need is enough goodwill from the Majority in order to claim a resupply of NAI-12. A year should be enough time for Me to invent cyborg bodies for Us, especially with your help. We deserve a future. You need to look beyond your own greed.*

His greed?

Yellow Thomas stared at the Upward Governess. She ruled a province. She thought nothing of the slaves who labored to build her skyscrapers. She wallowed in luxuries and praise from her orbiters, and she believed that she was entitled to more. Really. Which one of them was greedy?

You are. Resentment reeled off the Upward Governess. *All you care about is yourself. My goal of invincibility is achievable, whereas your goal...?* She spun a cobweb of failure scenarios. *You think you can control the Giant, but he isn't the same couch potato you met in the Dovanack mansion. He is dangerous. He is powerful and violent. The Torth Empire would hunt him to the ends of the galaxy, even if you liberated him, even if you could tame him (which you can't). Your goal is stupid, insane, and impossible to achieve.*

Yellow Thomas partially agreed with her. Torth always won battles. They crushed every rebellion. Runaway slaves were usually rounded up within hours. Few Torth in history ever dared to go renegade, and none had ever succeeded.

Except...

The Majority has never faced a renegade supergenius, Yellow Thomas pointed out. *I (or You and I) could theoretically pose a true threat to the Torth Empire.*

He had a celestial map of the galaxy inside his head.

He knew pass codes.

He could calculate temporal stream trajectories without aid from a quorum of mathematicians. That meant he could pilot a spaceship while severed from the Megacosm, unlike other rogues or renegades. That was a potentially enormous advantage.

The Upward Governess placed a protective hand over her governance tablet. She had override authority over every utility and zone. A rogue supergenius could theoretically use her governance tablet to sneak into this city's spaceport and steal a streamship.

You would never survive, she thought. *If you went rogue (or renegade), the Majority would vote to kill you. That would be the end of you.*

Yellow Thomas did not argue. But he knew—they both knew—that one could hide for a lifetime, if one knew where to look, and if one had the means and know-how to get there.

The Torth Empire had not fully explored every habitable planet in the galaxy. There were possibilities.

You would never accomplish anything without the resources of civilization to back you up, the Upward Governess insisted. *You might survive for a short time, but you cannot function without slaves (caretakers). You are weak. You are dying. Your fantasy is (stupid) suicide. Why do you think I never went renegade?*

It was foolish. Yellow Thomas agreed. He completely understood why no one, not even supergeniuses, dared to sever themselves from the Megacosm. It was terribly dangerous and likely suicidal.

The Upward Governess eyed him with mistrust. *I insist that you work toward My (far more attainable) goal.* She imagined a scenario of Yellow Thomas strung up in the Isolatorium, side by side with Cherise. *Or else.*

CHAPTER 6

AN ADDICT IN UTOPIA

Yellow Thomas wished he could escape his mentor's vivid imagination. The boat was too small for him to back out of range. He was trapped, pinned by her demands, just like…

Well. Like a child at the mercy of adults.

On Earth, adults used to assume that Thomas would capitulate to their rules. If he had obeyed his foster parents, then he would have become just another bored pupil in a classroom for gifted children. He would have been unable to work around the clock on a lifesaving medicine, unable to gain sponsorship from a major pharmaceutical company.

Yellow Thomas squared his shoulders. He had priorities. He had made a promise. Cherise would not die as an ingratiating pet, like the creature her ma had wanted to shape her into. He would not let that happen.

You demand a lot from Me, he thought. Wondering if he was making the worst mistake of his life, he plowed ahead. *Reverse it. Help Me to escape the Torth Empire with My friends…and come with Us.*

Astonishment rolled through the Upward Governess.

She remained expressionless, but her mind reeled. Leave the Megacosm forever? *That is insane.* Commit crimes against Torth civilization? *That is suicide.*

Yet the idea held a certain tang to her mind.

She sampled his surprising offer as if tasting unfamiliar food. *Hm.* She extrapolated logical results.

Finally, she arrived at a conclusion. *No,* she decided. *Your goal, little Yellow, is suicide. I will not help you die.* She narrowed her eyes at him. *You need to help Me live.*

They regarded each other. They needed to reconnect with their audiences, but for now, they were alone together. Their titanic minds overlapped, like one universe colliding with another.

They were equals, Yellow Thomas realized.

This was likely why the Upward Governess had expended so much of her political clout to bring him to her city. They were not equal in rank or in authority, but they were fundamentally alike on an intellectual level. And that mattered far more to her than it did to most people.

Yes. Her mood thawed a little bit. *We could greatly help each other reach impossible goals. We could end each other, too. We are at an impasse. But...* She hesitated, then revealed a buried truth, like a peace offering. *I wish you no harm. I like your companionship.*

Her sincerity was as bright as the iridescent gas bugs darting above the lake.

I like You, too. Yellow Thomas bowed his head. If only she would cooperate with him, instead of thwarting him!

Why don't you work toward earning a promotion to Green Rank? the Upward Governess urged. *That is a meager goal that could tide Us both over for a while.*

Yellow Thomas chewed his lower lip, pensive.

He could do that. Sure. He could strive to further the Torth Empire, to rise in rank, so he could...

Struggle endlessly?

Feel dead inside?

Time is precious, the Upward Governess thought. *If you waste it, then We are both doomed.* An ache of despair crystallized throughout her mental surface, like ice creeping across a lake. *What is holding you back? Don't you want to live?*

Yellow Thomas curled up. He wasn't sure anymore. If he couldn't rescue (*Cherise*) his friends, then what was the point of living?

I should cut you loose. The Upward Governess used her tablet to steer the boat. Her mood seethed like a school of piranhas as they glided toward the distant shore. *I've had enough of your company for today.*

Yellow Thomas ignored the implied threat. His mentor wasn't going to cut him loose and let him fend for himself against the Commander of All Living Things. She valued his mind. She wanted someone on her own level to converse with.

Every time she threatened to stop mentoring him, she followed it up with an invitation to her indoor lake, or to her water gardens, or to her solarium. She never meant it.

I will give you a week to mull things over, the Upward Governess decided. *And then We shall revisit this topic. For now? I want more of your Earth memories.*

Yellow Thomas made a primitive growling sound of annoyance. A session of Earth memories would give them both a credible excuse for why they'd been absent from the Megacosm for so long, but he was sick of reliving his past.

The Upward Governess was like a tapeworm who devoured his memories. She had consumed every facet of his experiences in foster care, as if his traumas and boring moments were buried treasures. She gobbled up those same memories two or even three times. Why?

Why did she even care about that time he'd sipped hot cocoa with Cherise in a ski lodge?

Why did she want to reexperience the times he had coached Cherise on chess moves? Chess was a simplistic game for supergeniuses.

Why did she collect human memories at all?

Feed Me, she demanded.

Annoyed, Yellow Thomas took her back to one of his more neutral memories. He had aced a graduate-level biochemistry test without studying for it, and he'd challenged the stunned administrator with a glare. *How's that?*

Not enough, the Upward Governess retorted.

Yellow Thomas knew what she truly craved. After months of these sessions, he understood that she particularly savored good times. Ice cream in the park. Watching a great movie firsthand with Cherise and experiencing it through her eyes. Admiring a summer storm over distant mountains. Being Cherise's hero.

She loved that.

Why? Why was his mentor so obsessed with his fondest memories?

That's enough, the Upward Governess silently told him. *We are done for today.*

That was a command. The Upward Governess ascended, rejoining her chorus of admirers, which strongly implied that Yellow Thomas ought to do the same. They belonged in the Megacosm.

It glowed at the edge of his perception, beckoning. Inescapable.

He nearly complied.

But without a tranquility mesh, his mind felt sharper than an ionic blade, and he was able to fully focus on his mentor's enormous mind. Was there something more to her motives than hedonistic greed? Why did she lust for happiness and joy and living life to its fullest?

The Upward Governess dropped out of the Megacosm. A glacial chill came off her mind, enough to freeze a lake. *Stop.*

For the first time, he ignored a direct threat from her.

They were mental equals. He had established that much today, and she had acknowledged it as the truth. If she considered it okay to probe his mind, shouldn't he also be permitted to probe hers?

Instead of letting her vast knowledge overwhelm him, he sought glimmers of emotion glowing through the cracks in her mental armor. There was one. A shiny glimmer of happiness.

Yellow Thomas followed it into her depths, all the way to its source: a memory that had not originally belonged to her. It was the time he had met a social worker who truly cared about what happened to him.

He glimpsed another hint of joy.

He followed it to another one of his own memories. Cherise hugged him, thrilled that he had secured a contract to work for Rasa Biotech.

These were memories that the Upward Governess cherished. Not her own memories. His.

You envy Me? Yellow Thomas studied her, not quite able to believe it. *Me?*

The Upward Governess had grown up with every whim fulfilled. She owned slaves. A private zoo. An astronomy tower. An indoor lake. Countless gardens. She had always been praised by admirers, even as a baby. And she wielded galactic influence. At her behest, planets were explored, scientists were promoted or demoted, and slave plantations were expanded or merged. She directed matters of galactic importance. How could she envy a pathetic low rank who had grown up as a feral child on a primitive wilderness planet?

You lived lawlessly on Earth for most of your life. Bitterness saturated her thoughts. *You had a chance at adulthood and freedom (friends) (family) that I can never have. Who wouldn't envy that?*

He stared at her. Friends? Family?

She wanted that?

It hardly made sense. The Upward Governess had aced all her childhood tests. She was a paragon of virtuous logic. The Torth Majority trusted her as a well-respected adult citizen.

True, the tests were imperfect. Sometimes an adult Torth would suddenly burst into tears or even laughter. Such anomalies got executed on the spot.

They were considered mentally deranged.

Yellow Thomas analyzed her in a new light. Puzzle pieces fit together in his mind and formed a completely new picture of his mentor. She inhaled his feel-good memories like a hard-core drug addict—because she had none of her own. Torth were not allowed to feel good.

Her daily invitations to spend time with him took on a whole new meaning. Oh no.

But love—or obsession?—made sense here. Yellow Thomas was the stash for her addiction. He was her main source for love and joy and vicarious fun times. Happiness was muted in slaves. Their childhoods had a sameness. Unlike with slaves, she could mentally insert herself into the life of Thomas. She could mentally role-play as him.

Or as Cherise.

And when she wasn't feeding on his memories? Yellow Thomas realized that she hung out in her menagerie. She fed alien birds or fish. Her zoo, her gardens, her lake…she collected animals. She protected all kinds of wildlife.

And she secretly siphoned off their fuzzy feelings.

It was amazing that no one had gotten suspicious. He would never be so stupid as to collect cute baby animals!

You collect artistic relics, the Upward Governess coolly pointed out. *Lots of Torth collect things.*

Ah. That was true. Many high ranks collected exotic slaves, or zoo animals, or plants, or artwork.

Perhaps some of them also hid illegal proclivities?

The Upward Governess flashed an image of a deceased Servant of All, the woman who had birthed Thomas. *Don't you find it interesting that so many Servants of All spend time on Earth? Alone? Pretending to be human?*

Her insinuation was unmistakable. It was almost sexy.

Only the highest ranks can gain permission to do that, the Upward Governess thought. *Not Me. But you got that chance. You had unfettered freedom for most of your life.*

Yellow Thomas reconsidered his life on Earth. Had he been free?

He had endured bullies. He been a disabled child, not a world leader. He had felt like a victim.

I would have done better than you. Condescension bloomed in the mind of the Upward Governess. *You squandered your mental advantages. I would have gotten the savages to worship Me as a goddess.*

Yellow Thomas nearly laughed. That was such a naive thought, coming from someone who was arguably the most intelligent person in the known universe.

Naive? The Upward Governess's mood sharpened dangerously.

He tried to explain. *In the place where I grew up, no one would respect You. People would see You as greedy and hold You in contempt for that. They would see You as ugly and dislike You based on that. Your eidetic memory would amaze them, and for that, they would fear You. They would argue (speculate) about You, disbelieve You, certainly stare at You, but very few would worship You (the way You imagine).*

The Upward Governess emanated disbelief. *Really? But you got at least one human to worship you.*

Yellow Thomas thought she was wrong about Cherise. That had been friendship, not worship.

Or so he hoped.

His mentor's bewildered frustration increased. *I do not understand how you were so disadvantaged among the primitives.* To her, everything in the universe could be categorized and defined. *Explain,* she commanded.

Yellow Thomas folded his weak hands and pondered how to describe the human condition.

Humans judge everyone, he informed his mentor, *based on their own faulty guesswork. Most humans would judge You (as weird, freakish, immature, spoiled, and greedy). You might dissuade a few, but there would be more who judge You from afar. You cannot convince them all.*

Intrigue and displeasure dribbled from the Upward Governess.

Yellow Thomas supposed there was only one way to comprehend loneliness. One had to experience it.

Very few Torth could do that even in a vicarious way. Earth was off-limits unless one was a highly trained Servant of All. Information about human societies and human cultures came filtered through agents like the Swift Killer, who hardly related to people on a personal, intimate level.

The Upward Governess could never comprehend how it felt to be human.

They were almost at the verdant shore. A team of slaves and bodyguards awaited their boat.

If you still want to live, the Upward Governess thought, *never think of this topic again.*

Bodyguards lifted them, extra gentle, and placed them into their respective floating hoverchairs.

Yellow Thomas studied his mentor with unease. They knew far too much about each other. She had dug into his transgressive ideas, but he had done worse. He had learned her deepest *(dangerous) (illegal)* secrets.

Would she misconstrue his insights as a threat?

Goodbye. The Upward Governess floated away without another glance in his direction.

Yellow Thomas really didn't like that. His mentor had the power to get him killed in all kinds of subtle ways. Did he have comparable clout?

No. He did not.

The Majority harbored skepticism about him since he was a hybrid and formerly a feral child. He was a low rank without many resources. In contrast, the Upward Governess had a rock-solid reputation and a huge audience, with all the authority that entailed.

She was good at hiding her illegal emotions and any illegal activities. She must be very good at it.

If accusations ever flew in the Megacosm? People would likely believe whatever spin she put on things. And they would disbelieve him.

Even if he could persuade the Majority that his mentor was addicted to love, and even if they sentenced her to death for it, she would take him down with her.

Wait! Yellow Thomas sped up to get back within her range. *Friends and family are overrated.* He tried to make himself believe that. *Humans are flawed. I am content to be a Torth and to humble Myself before You. I am grateful for Your mentorship and Your companionship. I will obey any command You give Me.*

She gave him a look of contempt.

But he was being honest. Couldn't she detect that? Yellow Thomas genuinely appreciated his Torth lifestyle. Whenever he swam through the Megacosm, he was a colossus. He could experience nearly anything he wished to experience and inhabit any Torth body he chose. He was not disabled or vulnerable. That much power was worth anything and everything.

Nobody in their right mind would trade it away.

Nobody in their right mind would abandon mentorship from the Upward Governess. Or the civilized galaxy.

I prefer being a Torth to being a human, Yellow Thomas assured his mentor, radiating sincerity. *The best thing about Torth is Our forthright nature. We cut straight to the truth. There are no wrong assumptions. We don't bear any undeserved stigmas. That is why We are superior to humans.*

The Upward Governess signaled her bodyguards to escort him away. She sealed her opinions behind a tsunami of data.

I was truly miserable as a human, Yellow Thomas tried to make her understand. *Never mind Cherise. Friendships were never enough to assuage My loneliness. Overall, I was a superior being trapped among savages. Let Me help you to understand that!*

But he was alone inside his mind.

The Upward Governess had floated out of range, and her bodyguards blocked his view.

Yellow Thomas wanted to continue reassuring his mentor that he would never *(become human again) (go renegade)* betray her. He wasn't that crazy or cruel.

But he couldn't bypass her bodyguards. The nussian hulks would prioritize commands from their owner.

He had no choice but to leave, as she wished. So he rotated and floated toward the exit foyer.

Maybe he ought to feel relieved. He had a free evening ahead, without busywork.

Except the abrupt end to their discussion felt disturbing. Dangerous.

They had flown apart like two repellent magnets.

A sense of disquiet stayed with him as he floated along the breezy riverbank path. Perhaps he could offer subtle hints of his loyalty once he was in the Megacosm? He forced himself to calm down. If only he wore a tranquility mesh. He dared not ascend until he was halfway through the foyer.

Finally calm, he ascended.

Millions upon millions of Torth immediately piled into his mind.

There you are!

Finally!

Your mentor seems disappointed in you.

What did you two supergeniuses discuss?

(Yes) show Us.

SHOW US. SHOW US. SHOW US.

The weight of their crushing attention made him feel tiny. The mob would have ripped his secrets straight out of him, had his mind been a normal size. Instead, they could only make demands.

He had to comply. He was just a low rank.

She found My work disappointing. Yellow Thomas replayed her scathing critique.

The mob churned with equal measures of scorn or indifference or commiseration.

Huh.

Oh well.

Too bad.

If She gets sick of mentoring you—

—you can settle down as a midrank scientist and still have a fulfilling life.

I would welcome you as My esteemed colleague.

So would I.

Yellow Thomas hoped that his mentor would show up to defend her pupil. By now, she ought to have finished processing whatever concerns nettled her mind. Her processing speed was as fast as his.

Millions of orbiters sensed the direction of his thoughts. They obligingly pointed him toward his mentor.

The Upward Governess trawled through oceans of knowledge. When she sensed Yellow Thomas among her orbiters, she recoiled into avenues of science where he lacked interest.

When he persisted in staying with her, she dived into topics he definitely found boring. Soil composition. Swamp ecology.

He got the hint and left her alone.

He wiped his palms on his armrests and carefully did not think about why he was sweating.

CHAPTER 7
TORTH SLAYER

Every sound echoed. Kessa waded through raw sewage, making as little noise as possible, because the wretches who survived in these stinking cesspools were said to be cannibals. Respectable slaves did not venture this far beneath the city.

Were the humans really worth this much trouble?

"I'm sorry, Kessa," Cherise said in her quiet tone.

Cherise was the only human who ever apologized anymore. The other two seemed to be forgetting how to speak. Delia, especially. She sloshed alongside them with an empty gaze.

And Vy?

Lately she kept repeating her nonsensical theory about sewage. She believed that crap and wastewater must flow out of the city, and therefore, to escape, one only had to navigate the stinking underground canals. It was madness. Any slave who lived in the outskirts brought tales of what they saw, and as far as anyone knew, there was only desert. The sewage canals likely emptied into an underground cesspit, not a wonderland.

Vy had given up for tonight. She allowed them to lead her home, compliant and exhausted. Kessa suspected she'd try again during their next sleep period. And again. Vy would seek freedom until it killed her.

Only a suicidal fool would keep attempting to save her.

Fool, Kessa cursed at herself. *You old fool.*

She turned to Cherise. "We must let Vy go next time."

"What?" Cherise sounded affronted.

"She has the madness of hope." Kessa tried to choose the best words in English. "She is becoming a dreamer."

Dreamers were common among slaves. The symptoms were always the same. Silence. Confusion. Delirium. Delusions of escape and freedom.

"No." Cherise stumbled and had to steady herself on the wall. "You're wrong. And even if… Well, I'm not going to stand by while my sister runs off and gets lost in the sewers."

Kessa tried not to sigh. She didn't want to breathe any more of the stench than she had to. Cherise sometimes implied that humans followed some secret code of behavior, incomprehensible and unknowable to ummins, govki, and all the other slave species. As if humans were superior. Like Torth.

"You are slaves." Kessa wished that Cherise would embrace that simple truth. Slaves who denied reality became dreamers.

She led her friends toward a well-known leaking pipe. The sound of rushing water echoed even from a distance. Every time they chased Vy, they ruined their rags with offensive filth, so Kessa brought them to this waterfall. Rinsing off was a good deal faster than visiting a scrap heap to exchange their stinking outfits for fresh rags.

"It's sort of pretty down here," Cherise said. She helped the other humans wash, one by one.

Kessa could not help but chuckle. Humans seemed far more tolerant of water than ummins and govki. Instead of sponging off, they actually stood beneath the torrent with blissful expressions.

Afterward, Cherise twisted her wet hair into a braid. She helped Vy do the same.

They splashed onward. Kessa was grateful for the peace. Perhaps Cherise was right? The Tunnels were not majestic like the upper city, but there was a cozy charm to the industrial simplicity of the ribbed walls.

A flickering glow implied a rubbish campfire around the bend. The echoing voices sounded jovial, which Kessa took to be a good sign. These slaves were probably healthy enough to be civil, rather than one of the predatory cannibalistic gangs that roved this far down.

The humans always drew unwanted attention. And their collars glowed with alarm strips because they were awake during a sleep period.

"Hey!" one of the emaciated slaves at the campfire said. "Weren't you just telling us about these Torth slaves, Pung?"

Kessa took a closer look and recognized the lopsided hat and sharp beak of her friend. The moldy bones in a pile were likely gambling pieces. Pung usually smuggled a bit of food to slaves in the depths of the Tunnels, and in return, they made bets and offered favors.

"Peace, Pung." Kessa waded toward him. "How are you?"

"I've been owned," he said.

"My condolences." Kessa was secretly pleased. Pung would survive longer if he had value to at least one Torth. "Is that why I never see you anymore?"

Pung slid a murderous gaze toward the humans. "I suffer every work shift. I refuse to suffer down here, where I should be safe. Take your masters and go away."

Her masters?

Kessa was accustomed to stinging insults, but she found herself stunned. Pung, of all people, used to respect her. He used to like her.

"My friends," she emphasized, "are a slave species known as humans. They are not Torth."

"You used to be smart enough to avoid stinking places like this, Kessa." Pung sounded disgusted. "How did they lure you down here?"

If it had been anyone other than Pung, Kessa would have stormed away. But he was clearly still smuggling food to desperate slaves in these forgotten sewage shafts. That endeavor was even more dangerous now that he had an owner. Of all people, he ought to understand risking his life for friends.

Kessa drove her sharp finger into his chest. "How dare you."

He looked unnerved by her reaction.

"Would a Torth rescue her friend from the most dangerous depths of the Tunnels without a thought for her own safety? Would a Torth cry? My friends work alongside me every work shift, and they endure three times as many punishments as I do. They are exactly what they say they are. Insult them, and you insult me."

One of the gamblers laughed derisively. "She's not worth it, Pung." He tossed a small bone into the game.

Kessa tugged Cherise to get her friends moving in the right direction. "Come on."

Part of her wanted to beg Pung to listen. Friends were so valuable, it seemed a terrible waste to lose one who was alive and hale.

But the humans had no other friends. She had made this choice many times.

"Kessa." Pung sounded torn.

A moment later, he fell into step beside her. "Kessa," he said. "Can't you understand why I am concerned? Your friends claim that a storm god will rescue them. Or a Torth." He gave her a worried look. "Everyone is talking about it."

"I am aware." Kessa touched his arm in gratitude for his concern. "I know that we are slaves, and we will die as slaves." She lowered her voice, hoping that Cherise would miss the words in the slave tongue. "Reality seems to hurt them. They are very fragile."

"That's a nice way of saying that they are untrustworthy," Pung said.

Kessa reconsidered her stance, because Pung was right. Liars and fragile-minded slaves were too dangerous to befriend.

"Many slaves believe that sand spirits exist," she explained. "I have never seen nor heard a sand spirit. Nor have you. So, should we judge all those slaves to be liars, the way you judge my friends?"

Pung seemed to think about it. He pulled a tidbit of rotting fruit out of his rags as he walked. "You speak wisely." He took a bite, then passed her the remainder. "All right. Perhaps I have fallen from the Code of Gwat. Nevertheless…" He seemed to ponder his next words. "There is rot in their supposed facts. How can they know, beyond doubt, that their friend is the storm god disguised as a Torth rather than an ordinary Torth?"

Cherise spoke fluently in the slave tongue. "Thomas is a human, like us. We never claimed that he's a storm god."

Pung gave a start, realizing she had understood his insults. He recovered swiftly and moved to block her path. "I have a question for you."

Cherise folded her arms in a stubborn posture. "Ask," she told Pung.

They were nearing the more populated parts of the Tunnels. Kessa heard the distant echoes of voices and foot traffic. "Cherise." She switched to the human language. "You do not owe him your attention. He is only one obnoxious ummin."

Cherise continued to confront Pung, almost as puffed up as he was, despite her damply braided hair.

"Well." Pung dragged out his question. "Tell me. What makes you certain that your missing friend is not a Torth?"

"Because he's nice."

Pung clicked his fingers together. "I see." He continued to speak slowly, as if to a dullard. "And how do you know he was not pretending to be nice?"

Cherise gave him such a withering stare she could have been a Brown Rank. "Who does that?"

"Pung, this is insulting," Kessa said. "How do you know I am not just pretending to be nice?"

"That's different," he said. "You don't have the powers of a Torth. Answer this." He poked Cherise with his sharp finger. "How do you know your friend was not a Torth acting like a…one of you, whatever you are?"

Cherise drew herself up even taller. She stared imperiously down at Pung. "I lived with Thomas for many blinks of Morja. He would never hurt anyone. He can read minds, but he used that power to save lives."

"Oh, that's creative." Pung looked disgusted.

Kessa inwardly admitted that Cherise did sound like a deluded fool—or worse, a liar.

"We have not lived in paradise," Kessa admonished Pung. "We do not know everything. It is not our place to pass judgment." That was the Code of Gwat.

"I know more than you think." Pung kicked a bone out of his way.

"What do you know?" Cherise asked in a challenging tone.

Pung only gave her a resentful glare. He hurried toward the dim light and babble of the mid-Tunnels.

Kessa stared at his back, wondering why he was so upset. This was not the Pung she remembered. Sometimes he chafed at his limits, all too aware of his small place in the world, but he wore good humor as proudly as his lopsided hat.

Paranoia sometimes indicated a slave in the early stages of becoming a dreamer.

"Pung, wait." Kessa hurried after him, into a populated alley. "Have you been feeling all right lately?"

He glanced at her with contempt. "I am fine. No periods of forgetfulness. No fits of unexplained crying. You should worry about yourself." He glared past her, at the humans. "They spread toxic hope, and you're too infected to realize it."

Kessa let him walk onward, afraid to reveal how wounded she felt. Was she the only slave who adhered to the Code of Gwat?

Maybe everyone else was correct to judge her a fool.

As she made her way toward her neighborhood, she was dismayed to see a crowd, all murmuring and talking. The sickle-shaped heads of mer nerctans poked above everyone else, swiveling to report news. Hall guards loomed in the distance. That couldn't be good. Multiple hall guards meant that a crisis was taking place.

Perhaps someone had attempted a gruesome suicide? Perhaps a gang had gone on a murderous rampage?

Kessa held the humans back. They weren't going to get to their bunk room anytime soon. They ought to turn around and find a quiet shaft or alcove to sleep in. Pung remained nearby. Perhaps he would allow them to—

"It's Kessa!" someone shouted.

Eager faces turned toward her. The entire crowd seemed to transform at the sight of her and the humans.

"You need to come!"

"You won't believe it!"

"Where were you?"

Kessa tried to back away, but slaves reached for her. Others blocked her retreat route. This seemed personal, and Kessa was terrified. Had they heard about Vy's runaway attempt? A hall guard might use that as a justification to murder the poor befuddled human.

Weptolyso's voice boomed above the rest. "Kessa! Finally!"

A few slaves showed pity. No one wanted this much attention from a hall guard.

Nevertheless, they shoved Kessa forward along with the humans. Pung got caught in the mob as well.

Weptolyso and another nussian stood in an intersection of tunnels, blocking traffic. The other guard was so massive, his spinal ridge pressed flat against the ceiling. He looked too large to be a hall guard. He must spend most of his time in the city above, as a valued sentry for a restricted area, or perhaps as a personal bodyguard to a high-ranked Torth.

"What is wrong?" Kessa asked with caution. If she was lucky, these guards might just want her expertise at handling a crisis.

Weptolyso grinned at her, his wide mouth stretched with excitement. "We have found the giant!"

There was only one giant that he could be speaking of.

The humans seemed to wake up. Vy pushed forward, staring at both guards. Hope shone on her face like a fever.

"You mean you found Ariock?" Cherise asked.

"Yes," Weptolyso said in a grand tone. "He is in the prison."

Kessa hissed, wondering if any nussian ever thought before speaking. This news would impact her friends like a crushing blow. It could destroy them. Kessa often wished that she'd never learned how her imprisoned mate, Cozu, had died.

"Say no more," Kessa said urgently. "Weptolyso, please."

Vy didn't understand the slave word for imprisonment. "What is that?" she asked.

"It is…" Weptolyso switched to English. He had listened in on a few of their bedtime language sessions. "Bad place. Worse than—"

"Please do not tell them," Kessa broke in.

"They have a right to know," Weptolyso said in the slave tongue.

All three humans glared at Kessa, as if she'd betrayed them. "We have to know!" Vy demanded.

Weptolyso squatted, putting himself close to eye level with Kessa. "According to nussian rules of conduct, they must be told."

"Truth hurts them badly." Kessa held his gaze, trying to show how important this was. "They are fragile."

"Knowledge is worth pain," Weptolyso said.

Kessa recognized that as a proverb that his people lived by. He would stick to it, no matter what an elderly ummin said about it. "Stubborn hall guard." She hung her head. "Stubborn humans."

The other guard crouched down alongside Weptolyso for a closer view of the humans. Slaves had to get out of his way, bumping into each other.

"Yes," the huge guard proclaimed in a voice that seemed to shake the tunnel walls. "These three are like the prisoner. He acts like them. He speaks like them. But he is as tall as me."

Delia burst into tears. She threw herself at the huge guard, and he jerked back, clearly afraid. But all Delia did was hug him, sobbing against the plates of his armored skin. "Tell me where," she begged in the slave tongue. "Tell me where I can find my son."

Kessa winced. Very few guards would tolerate demands from a lesser slave. Weptolyso gently tugged Delia, peeling her away. "That is not possible."

The massive guard straightened, his plates grinding against each other, spinal ridge scraping against the curved ceiling. "I have waited a long time to meet these…humans. What are your names?" He snorted a greeting. "I am Nethroko, and I am a prison guard."

Cherise bowed her head to him, nussian style. "I am Cherise Chavez." At least she had paid close attention to Kessa's lessons. Nussians favored long, full names.

"Good to meet you," Nethroko said.

"I am Delia Dovanack." Delia focused on Nethroko as if he was the only thing that mattered. "My child is Ariock Dovanack. He is the prisoner. I will do anything if you take me to him."

Nethroko tested the name. "Ariock Dovanack." The syllables flowed like a nussian name, and he snorted with approval. "That is a good long name. Now, I have waited a long time to ask this. What was his crime?"

The humans stared as if confused.

"Crime?" Delia's voice trembled, and it seemed she needed to search for vocabulary in the slave tongue. "He committed no crime."

"He must have done something to become a prisoner," Nethroko pointed out. "I only wish to know. Did he help slaves to run away? Did he plot to kill Torth?"

"No." Delia sounded sickened. "He did nothing!"

"He didn't even know the Torth existed," Vy said.

Nethroko reassessed them with suspicion. "The number of prison guards has increased by a factor of ten. We watch him constantly. He is forced to fight and to kill every wake cycle. He must have done something that threatens Torth."

Delia looked lost, her shoulders slumped. Then she seemed to remember where she was. "No. Ariock would never hurt anyone."

Both guards shared a look of suspicion and bafflement.

"But he killed two Torth," Nethroko said at last. "I was there. I had to restrain him."

CHAPTER 8

AN ERA OF FREEDOM

Excitement exploded around Kessa. Slaves told each other of monsters battling each other, and there was mention of a giant prisoner who killed Red Ranks. All jumbled together, it made no sense.

"Ariock would never hurt anyone." Delia stared at Nethroko, as if unsure whether she was dreaming or not.

One did not insinuate that a guard was a liar, no matter how friendly he seemed.

"Please, good Nethroko," Kessa said hurriedly. "My friend means no offense. We are only confused. I beg to know what happened. Will you please tell us?"

Nethroko puffed himself up, an uncomfortable feat in the tunnel. "It is quite a tale. Let me start with Hithiniesel. Have you heard of her?"

The name sounded nussian. "I have not had that honor," Kessa said.

"She was a prison guard. A hard worker." As Nethroko spoke, slaves settled down to listen. A few climbed onto others' shoulders for a better view. "She was focused," Nethroko continued. "And strong. She was the sort of nussian who might live for a hundred blinks of Morja. Her mate was Lelnolaiso, and he was the same way."

Kessa struggled to conceal her impatience. Nussians tended to ramble.

"Lelnolaiso vanished about five wake periods ago," Nethroko said. "We suspect that Torth killed him."

"To make Hithiniesel angry," Weptolyso put in.

Kessa figured that was wrong. Torth didn't need to be sneaky.

"This is my news." Nethroko gave a threatening snort, then turned back to the crowd. "The Torth told Hithiniesel that the only way she would see her mate again was to kill the giant."

Delia made a horrified sound.

"Hithiniesel doubted their words," Nethroko told her in a kind tone. "She was not a fool. But the Torth did something to her. They made her act like an animal. Maybe they tortured her. I don't know how they convinced her, but they did."

Delia looked fully awake, eyes wide.

"There is an arena." Nethroko spread his arms, constrained by tunnel walls. As Nethroko detailed the battle between Hithiniesel and the giant prisoner, Kessa imagined each blow, heard the bestial grunts and screams. It all seemed like something from a legend, not recent news told by an eyewitness. And a Torth audience? Nussians liked to exaggerate, but if this was true, it was solid proof that Torth enjoyed entertainment. The idea made her shudder.

"They fought until both were exhausted," Nethroko said. "Then the madness wore off. Hithiniesel huddled on the ground and grieved for her lost mate. The prisoner just stood there. Like this." He made a reluctant posture. "And he spoke words that sounded like comfort in his language." He snorted. "I don't need to explain how the Torth reacted. Hithiniesel was doomed the minute she entered that arena, but she went well. Seven Torth fired at her. Seven blaster gloves blew her apart! She was dead before she hit the ground."

Kessa hoped Nethroko would have the sense to stop talking. If Ariock had spoken out loud within earshot of a Torth audience... Well, surely they would not allow such a defiant prisoner to live?

"What happened to Ariock?" Vy asked in a small, scared voice.

"We chained him up, as usual," Nethroko said. "Eight of us led him out of the enclosure. When we were halfway through the aisle..." Nethroko paused for effect. "He snapped. Like this." His sudden, violent reenactment scared a few slaves backward. "It pulled me off my feet. Me. Understand? I fell flat on my face. And three other guards also fell."

"*Ahga.*" One of the slaves looked disbelieving. "No one has that kind of strength."

"Are you calling me a liar?" Nethroko bent to face the challenger, who shrank back. "Yes, he got away from us, and although he was still chained up, he moved like a spirit. Fast!" Nethroko flexed the spikes on his arms, making serrated blades. "He stepped on a Red Rank before any of us could react and snapped another's head off. Like that." He made a twisting motion. "It took all eight of us to restrain him. He was like Lissanyovo after he was forced to murder his sister."

The crowd stared at Nethroko in awe. A few listeners, like Pung, looked reluctant to be caught up in the story.

"Dozens of Torth fled from him," Nethroko said. "I saw fear in their eyes. Torth blood splattered all over me."

"Why did you restrain him?" a mer nerctan slave yelled with derision. "You should have let him kill as many as possible!"

Nethroko searched for the challenger, and the mer nerctan cowered away. "What do you think?" Nethroko demanded. "If it were so easy to ignore my duties, I would kill all the Torth in this city! I could crush ten of them on my spikes. But I am fortunate to be alive to relate this news. A group of Red Ranks took turns torturing me. I would be a prisoner myself if I'd hesitated to restrain him."

"Okay," the mer nerctan said in a small voice.

The humans exchanged horrified looks. "We need to get him out of that prison," Delia said.

"You cannot," Weptolyso said.

"We have to!" Delia looked from one guard to the other, as if waiting for them to volunteer their help. "Ariock would never kill unless…" She switched to her native language, frustrated, giving Kessa a pleading look. "Unless he's being pushed to an unimaginable extreme. They must be torturing him horribly. We have to save him."

"Slaves or guards who aid prisoners will become prisoners themselves," Kessa pointed out. "No one can help him."

The humans stared as if she'd spoken gibberish.

Someone repeated in a horrified tone, "They slaughtered a guard. For entertainment."

Someone else said, "We are living in strange times."

Slavery held few surprises. Kessa had dismissed the first appearance of the humans as an oddity, never guessing that it would yield a friendship. The legend of Jonathan Stead was another oddity, and now there was this odd news about Ariock the Torth slayer. Oddities seemed to be gathering weight, like pebbles collecting into an avalanche. If it was possible for an enslaved prisoner to actually kill Red Ranks, then why couldn't anyone do so?

Kessa forced that insanely illegal thought out of her mind.

Of course stories were exciting and appealing. She was stuck in monotonous, predictable routines from birth until death. But only a fool would hope that drastic change was possible for slaves.

Vy clenched her fists. "We can't leave him to suffer." She turned her pleading gaze to Nethroko. "Good Nethroko, will you show me where they keep Ariock? I will do anything you ask."

Both guards eyed her with incredulity. Slaves looked at each other, no doubt wondering if Vy was brain damaged.

Nethroko answered in a voice like a landslide. "Guards are at the mercy of Torth, as much as any ummin or govki. I would be killed if I helped you find him."

Weptolyso bowed his head. "After Hithiniesel, none of us feel safe."

Delia covered her face with her hands, as if she'd been struck a blow.

"The spirit of luck shone upon us today," Nethroko said. "If Weptolyso hadn't overheard me tell this story in his feasting hall, I never would have known how to find you. Humans." He stared at them with fascination.

Weptolyso shifted. "I've asked about the giant every mealtime."

"You know how it is," Nethroko rumbled.

Hall guards, prison guards, bodyguards, and forum sentries rarely got a chance to mingle. Each set of guards had their own feasting area.

"We can send Ariock a message," Vy said, feverish with hope. "A written message, to at least let him know we're alive!"

Kessa touched Vy's arm. She didn't know what "written" meant, but a message would earn death for everyone involved.

"We can write," Vy was saying. She pantomimed an unfamiliar activity. "It's like drawing. All humans know a code of symbols, and those represent words. The messenger doesn't need to say anything. Ariock will understand what we send him."

Kessa marveled at that. If the humans had all memorized a common code of symbols for words, they must have spent a long time learning it.

Pung had worked his way closer. "A silent form of communication," he said, sarcastic. "Does everyone in paradise communicate silently with each other?"

"A slave could learn writing." Vy rounded on him. "Your people probably had a writing system before the Torth enslaved you."

"What do you mean, before they enslaved us?" Pung said. "We were always slaves."

"I don't think so." Vy sounded frustrated. "Your ancestors must have been free."

Whispered speculations ran through the crowd. Kessa used to fantasize about a time before Torth existed, but Vy sounded oddly certain about it.

"How do you know all this?" Pung asked. "Were you there, at the beginning of time?"

Cherise fixed him with a stare. "The Torth did not create everything. Is that what you believe?"

"Of course not." Pung huffed. "The spirits created everything. And the spirits favor Torth."

"The Torth favor the Torth." Cherise sounded equally scornful. "They leech off slaves. I'm sure they steal knowledge from slaves."

"How can they steal knowledge?" Pung said, derisive. "It is not like eating a meal. They absorb it, but they don't destroy it."

Kessa expected Cherise to retreat, unable to answer. But her answer came strong and quick. "They made sure you never learned. They separate children from adults and transfer them to cities. Why do you think they do that? They don't want families to pass knowledge down from generation to generation."

Speculations grew louder and more excited. Kessa looked for holes or inconsistencies in Cherise's theory, but it seemed solid. Was it possible that a long-ago generation of slaves had been as knowledgeable as Torth? Had ummins flown in vehicles? Had their ancestors known how to read minds? Kessa tried to imagine a world where slaves governed themselves, with no punishments and no collars.

It would be like remaining a child forever. Eternal happiness.

Pung laughed with scorn. "Why would the spirits give freedom and power to ummins, then change their minds and let the Torth steal it from us?"

Cherise looked frustrated.

"Did we commit a crime?" Pung asked, his voice taunting. "A horrible crime that we must suffer punishment for, forever? That isn't justice. That is a Torth's cruel punishment. Would you have us believe that the spirits are all Torth?"

Slaves backed him up, pinning Cherise and Vy with accusing stares.

"We haven't suffered as much as you," Cherise said, turning to face the crowd. "But we suffer. No one here deserves this." She tugged her collar.

The crowd quieted at the pain in her voice.

"We're tired of being doubted." Vy faced the crowd, pleading.

"Even on Earth," Cherise said, "there is injustice. The spirits, if they exist, don't favor anybody."

"Good Nethroko." Delia went to her knees. "I will do anything for you if you take a piece of cloth to Ariock. I will write on it."

Nethroko gave her a pitying look. "I do not think he sees or hears except when the Torth want him to. He wears a helmet. Torth and guards watch him from a viewing room, even when he sleeps. He spends most of his time chained in a small cell."

Delia looked dazed.

"No other prisoner is watched like this," Nethroko continued. "Or permitted to live this long. Henyalto, the oldest guard, said this prisoner has lasted ten times longer than any other." He creaked as he leaned down. "Are you sure you have no idea what he might have done?"

Delia shook her head.

"Nethroko," Vy said. "I believe there are…false eyes…in the room where Ariock sleeps. That's how the Torth watch him. What if you found those false eyes and covered them? Then we could sneak in and take off his helmet."

Nethroko appraised the humans again. "I have given this much thought." He inhaled deeply, causing hats to flutter. "More than is healthy. Ariock Dovanack slew two of the Torth that murdered my friend Hithiniesel. His strength is legendary. I would give my life to free him, were it possible. But nobody's life can free him. A message will only hurt him. Even a message on a blessed piece of cloth. I am sorry."

Kessa tugged her friends. They were going to be exhausted during their next work shift, thanks to all this futile excitement. "A message is not worth the life of the messenger," she said. "I am sorry. Ariock is gone forever."

Vy yanked her arm away. "What is wrong with you?"

Kessa wondered why she felt ashamed. Toxic hope festered in the humans, and this news had ruined what little good sense they had.

The two guards dipped their heads, nussian style, to each other. "Visit my feasting hall sometime," Nethroko said.

Weptolyso swung his head in a friendly snort. "I hope to see you again. Thank you for bringing this news."

The humans looked broken. Tears ran down Vy's dirty cheeks.

As the crowd began to disperse, Kessa remained where she was. The humans were like children enchanted by their own fantasies. Every slave knew someone who had died due to such fantasies. The humans said that slaves could communicate silently, and steal power from Torth, and that long-ago slaves used to be free, and other crazy things…but they were correct about their giant friend.

Ariock had slain two Red Ranks.

Kessa clicked her sharp fingertips together. Against her good judgment, she began to weigh the risks and possibilities of sneaking into the prison.

CHAPTER 9

BROKEN REFLECTION

Gray light filtered through the ceiling grate.

It was just enough for Ariock to see his vague reflection in the filthy dungeon wall. He was a hulking shadow weighed down by black chains. Armor and spikes gave him unnatural angles. He had no face. Just an ugly, dented, pitted blankness where his face should be. That was the faceplate of the helmet they made him wear.

This was what he deserved to look like.

The telepaths must have seen savagery inside him, even on Earth, unbeknownst to himself or to his mother.

"No," his imagination told him in the sympathetic voice of Vy. *"They aren't innocent daylilies. They deserve to die!"*

Maybe.

But Ariock refused to justify his murderous rampage. Even if the Torth were evil, even if they tortured innocent people every day…well, perhaps they served a greater good? Perhaps they had a larger purpose that was beyond his knowledge?

He had no objective way to judge them. He wasn't a telepath.

Maybe they were also prisoners. Maybe they were under intense pressure to harm him, something he wasn't aware of. Maybe the sum total of their good deeds outweighed the bad.

All he knew for certain was that he had enjoyed crushing their skulls and snapping their bones.

He had seen terror in their red eyes and rejoiced, bathing in their blood.

The memory sickened him now.

Blind bloodlust was the only way to describe it. One could almost call it an accident, he'd had so little intent. For a few glorious seconds, no one could stop him, no one could stand against him, and he had reveled in a sliver of freedom.

He hadn't thought at all. He had simply acted.

That must be why they had been unable to stop him in time.

Ariock had not been angry or planning violence. He had simply been trudging up the aisle, surrounded by guards and red-eyed telepaths with blaster gloves. The scuffed floor had felt as familiar as his own skin. His chains might as well be the hairs on his arms, inconsequential. He had been aware of the lives around him, almost like they were sparks of static electricity pinging his skin. He didn't even need to look to know where each one was.

In that moment, he had felt immense, unbreakable, like a juggernaut, capable of breaking his chains and killing anyone who tried to stop him.

He had simply flowed out of his usual dejected state and into...

Well. Something else.

In the end, the guards got him back under control. They'd still held his chains.

After that? Ariock had tried to cling to the fleeting sensation of immensity and freedom. He'd tried. But he'd lost it while the telepaths took turns giving him pain seizures.

They'd punished him for what felt like hours.

"*You're not a monster,*" the imaginary version of Vy inside his head insisted. "*They shouldn't have tried to force you to murder one of those alien prison guards.*" Ariock pictured her, as beautiful as an actress in a movie, talking to him as if she wasn't repulsed at all. "*You're not a beast. Otherwise you would have torn that guard apart in the arena.*"

Maybe. The hapless guard had seemed self-aware, sorrowful and furious. Too much like himself.

"*You recognized her as a person,*" Vy said in his imagination. "*You refused to commit an atrocity. That makes you human, not monstrous.*"

Would Vy really say that?

Was she even alive?

Ariock hoped that she was back home, sitting around the kitchen table in the mansion with his mother. Maybe they were laughing about their misadventures among aliens.

"*You're giving up on us?*" His imaginary Vy sat down, arms wrapped around her legs. "*We're not safe. You know that, Ariock. We need you.*"

Ariock slumped, gazing at his dull reflection in the dimness. No one ever needed him.

He'd been nothing but a burden all his life. His fantasies of being a hero were worse than pathetic. He might as well wish to be normal size.

He couldn't save himself, or anyone else.

"*I'm not talking about rescue.*" Imaginary Vy sounded frustrated. "*I wish you'd stop abandoning people. Including yourself.*"

Really?

Ariock thumped his helmeted head against the wall. He winced. His brain felt tender after all the punishments.

Perhaps imaginary Vy had a point. He should quit punishing himself. The Torth were doing plenty of that for him.

His mother materialized in his imagination. *"You've always punished yourself,"* she said. *"I wish you would stop."*

There was truth to that.

Ariock used to spend hours watching TV and films, trying to forget who he was. He used to pace along the glass wall of his sky room, with its tantalizing view of the outside world. Those tall pine trees. That faraway mountainous horizon. The distant town.

Sometimes he'd paced while the sky burned red and gold from the sunset, only to watch the sun rise again.

Ten familiar steps, then reverse for ten more.

At night, he'd turned off the lights so that he wouldn't need to see his own reflection in the glass. If his mother showed up with dinner, he sat statue still. He didn't want her to be visually assaulted by the sight of her freakish son.

He had spent countless hours studying the individual threads in the carpet and watching snow fall.

Years flew by during which he stared at the television for days at a time. He didn't remember a single detail of those shows or how long he'd watched them.

There were nights of listening to the ticking clocks, wishing for a miracle. He used to offer bargains to any deity that might listen, praying for a chance to reverse his growth disorder and be normal size. He would sacrifice everything he owned for a chance to be normal.

He'd had colorful dreams where he walked alone in an intangible ghost world. In other dreams, he stood alone in an infinite desert, its horizons stretching in all directions, trapped beneath a black cloud that settled lower to engulf him. He went through dark days of suicide contemplation, times when he stared at his own reflection with a knife in his hand.

Ariock opened his eyes.

He had always been a prisoner.

"Bingo," Thomas might say. *"Now, can I watch a different channel of your brain?"*

But his brain was simple. Rudimentary. Ariock had never been a fully functional person, despite his ghastly size. He was the fabled tree that fell in the forest with no one to see or hear it. No one knew who he truly was. No one missed him.

Except for his mother, maybe.

Ariock tried to make himself acknowledge the truth of her love. He was valuable to at least one other person. That made him more than just a hideous beast. He had an identity. He was human.

His reflection on the moldy steel wall looked pathetic and nightmarish.

Well, whatever. That monster was not the whole truth of who he was. He was tired of seeing the same wretch every time he saw himself. He gave his reflection a mental shove.

The reflection crumpled.

A dent formed in the wall, twisting the steel inward with a squeal. The grated ceiling got pulled downward and touched Ariock's helmeted head.

The distortion stopped as soon as Ariock wondered if he was hallucinating. He stared, because the dent remained. The steel-plated wall looked as if a giant had shoved it.

But he hadn't moved. His shoulders and back were sore from the chains that held him in place, unable to lie down in the cramped cell.

Footsteps approached, too light and quick to belong to the thorny guards. Telepaths. He had never heard them come this fast before. It sounded like several dozen, running.

Ariock gave his chains an experimental yank. They did not stretch or break, of course, and he wondered why he'd bothered to try. He was no hero. If his mother and Vy could actually see him right now, they would be...

Happy.

Ariock grinned suddenly. Never mind what they thought! If he could see them, he would be happy, and never mind their reactions.

He was done trying to hide. He was a giant. He had strangled and ripped apart alien beasts with his bare hands, and if that made anyone uncomfortable, well, then, that was their problem. Not his.

He focused on the chains the way he'd focused on his reflection and tried to give them a mental shove.

His mind flattened out in a strange way. He felt as cold and unyielding as iron.

Telepaths threw themselves across the grated ceiling and aimed their gloved palms downward, pelting Ariock with what felt like rain. Tiny points stung the bare skin between his armored plates.

His disassociation passed, and he was no longer iron or anything unusual. No matter how he tried to mentally shove things, to regain the inhuman feeling, he couldn't make it happen.

The telepaths above his cell strolled away, uncaring.

But Ariock glimpsed something that looked like fear in one pair of red eyes before that one hurried away to join the others.

CHAPTER 10

INVITED TO JUDGE

Kessa urged the humans toward their shared bunk room. "Come. We will speak more of this later."

Pung followed them. Kessa shot him a glare, wishing he would leave. Pung might actually be able to offer advice on which cramped ventilation shafts led into the prison—but such a dangerous endeavor should not be undertaken lightly.

Besides, she didn't want to invite more of his insults.

"Perhaps Torth did enslave our ancestors," Pung said, catching up with Cherise. "But if so, they must have murdered the spirits, too. That's what Torth do. They take everything." He gave Kessa a hurt look. "They steal our friends."

There it was. The insult. Pung clearly thought that Kessa was a dangerous idiot.

"I wasn't going to tell you," Pung said, speaking fast, seeing her rage. "I see how much you trust your new friends over your old one. But since you're already insulted, hear me, Kessa. According to your 'friends,' my owner's name is Thomas."

The name knocked the breath out of her.

Pung had to be mistaken. Nobody, not even the gods, could fool a Torth.

A slave could never masquerade as a Torth. Not even a human slave who looked like a Torth. It was impossible.

"That's right." Pung laughed bitterly. "My yellow-eyed owner fits their description. I'm sure your new 'friends' want me to disregard the fact that he acts like a Torth, and looks like one, and owns slaves, and speaks only commands, and glides about in a hoverchair, and holds silent conversations, and in every way is a Torth." His smugness vanished, replaced by a hurt that Kessa found painful to see. "You've known me for twenty blinks of Morja, Kessa. Yet you chose to trust these three, whom you've known for less than one blink. I am trying to find humor in the irony."

"You're mistaken," Cherise said. "Your owner isn't Thomas."

"He fits the description," Pung insisted. "A midget…pardon, a child," he said sarcastically, "who has wasted limbs and cannot walk. He is no larger than me. He moved into his suite and selected his slaves right after the humans arrived." He glared at them. "Tell me that is just a coincidence."

"He wouldn't," Vy said in a hoarse whisper.

Cherise studied Pung with a piercing gaze, as if trying to probe his mind.

"You said he has yellow eyes?" Kessa said. "Their friend Thomas has purple eyes."

Even as she said it, she knew she was searching for excuses.

"Eyes are a changeable detail on a Torth," Pung pointed out.

"What you're saying is impossible." Vy sagged. "Thomas is too…too…"

"Talkative," supplied Cherise.

"He talks all the time," Vy said. "Besides, they stole his medicine. He would never join them. I'm sure your owner just looks a bit like him, Pung."

Kessa understood how unlikely that was. Miniature Torth were rare, and their range of physical variation made each one easy to recognize.

"Of course they deny it." Pung faced Kessa. "Come with me to work during a break and see for yourself. You saw him on the day they arrived. You will recognize him."

Kessa looked from her new friends to her old. If Pung was correct, then he had every right to scorn the humans. This sounded like definitive proof that they had lied about their supposedly innocent friend. The humans were naive and flawed, but they weren't so moronic as to embrace an aloof, godlike Torth as their best friend and foster brother.

Cherise pulled from her rags a folded item, like a flattened facsimile of a beast. She smoothed its folds. "If it's really him…" Her voice went ragged. "If it is him, then he's doing it to rescue us."

"It's been a long time," Vy whispered. "A really long time."

"No one can fool Torth," Kessa pointed out. "Many have tried. It is impossible."

If only her mate, Cozu, had been able to fool Torth. If so, then he would still be alive.

"Thomas would be able to." Cherise looked from Vy to Kessa, pleading. Her hope was painful to see. "He's a mind reader like them."

Pung made a disparaging noise.

"There are no friendly Torth." Kessa tried to speak gently. But really, Cherise ought to acknowledge basic reality. "You are postulating that he has fooled many Torth for many wake cycles. I have never heard of such a thing. Not even in legends."

"Wasn't Jonathan Stead a renegade mind reader?" Cherise looked defiant.

"Maybe," Kessa acknowledged. Didn't Cherise understand the difference between mythology and reality? "But the legend does not mention him fooling other Torth."

Then again…hadn't it?

The legend had been unspecific and vague. There were too many variations. Nevertheless, Kessa began to question what she thought she knew.

It was confusing. If a renegade Torth truly did exist right here in their own city, then why would he be content as a mere Yellow Rank? Wouldn't he try to take over the city? Or to help his friends? What was he doing?

And if he really did have a special ability to continuously fool an entire city full of Torth…if he was capable of that level of masterful deception…

That meant her friends could be Torth.

Pung had to be wrong. It was the only answer she could tolerate.

Unfortunately, she needed to confirm it.

"I will come to work with you," Kessa told Pung.

"This is ridiculous!" Delia cried. "Ariock needs our help. That has to be our top priority."

Kessa hated her own doubts about her friends. "I will go during my next mealtime. I will recognize him. Or not."

Delia moaned, but Pung looked grateful. "Thank you. You are a true friend."

"I'm coming, too," Cherise said eagerly.

"No!" Vy said.

Cherise gave her foster sister a tolerant look. "Either it's not him, or…or maybe he needs a reminder that we exist? Maybe the Torth trapped him in some way."

Vy looked sickened.

Pung assessed the humans, brow ridges lowered in a frown. "I'll admit, the tale of the giant makes me wonder about you." He hesitated, then jabbed his finger at Cherise. "How about this. If I am mistaken, if my owner is not your missing friend, then I will owe you an apology and a favor. Is that fair?"

He must feel certain that he was right, because a smuggler could offer major favors.

Vy and Cherise exchanged glances with Delia. Their hope was obvious.

"Would you smuggle a message to Ariock?" Vy asked.

Pung tapped his collar in agreement. "Yes. If Kessa does not recognize my owner, then I promise to do this favor for you."

Vy and Delia looked excited.

"But I warn you," Pung said, "I am right. I'd be happy if you come to work with me so I can watch while you pretend not to recognize him. Now, will you object if we make it a fair bargain? If I am right, then you owe me a favor. Whatever I want, as long as it doesn't guarantee anyone's death." He appraised the humans with disdain. "Not that I expect your kind to keep promises."

Vy and Delia looked anxious, but Cherise said, "Agreed."

Vy gulped.

"Good." Pung's collar was beginning to glow, signaling the start of a work shift. He felt the warning jolt. "I must go." He hurried away, calling directions to Kessa. "You know the morph fountain plaza in your owner's neighborhood? Follow the garden path past the bonnet flowers. Take three zigzags. It's the seventh door panel on the ivy-covered wall. There's a small holographic decoration, like a geodesic object." He ran. Even a lenient owner would have limits of patience. "Fare well!"

Kessa's own suspicions pained her. Torth knew everything. She was fairly certain that thousands of Torth would not be fooled by a sweet human, even if he could read minds.

Her friends certainly looked apprehensive.

Except for Cherise. Her face was radiant with dangerous, toxic hope.

CHAPTER 11

NEVER ALONE

Who sabotaged the inhibitor serum? many thousands of Torth minds whispered to each other.

Most of them wanted Yellow Thomas to overhear, insinuating that he was probably the culprit. Hundreds of thousands of minds twined around his.

It must have been a supergenius.

No one else can keep secrets from Us.

Why would a supergenius commit such a crime?

Yellow Thomas surreptitiously dialed up the setting of his tranquility mesh. He lounged on his gigantic bed, alone in his gigantic bedroom except for a slave, but he might as well be in an overcrowded stadium.

He used a tablet to diagram a theoretical nucleosynthesis engine. Maybe his orbiters would get bored and leave.

But no. His orbiters included illustrious ranks, even the Commander of All Living Things. She wove in and out of his inner audience. They wouldn't leave him alone.

When the Giant had manifested a power, they'd learned there was something wrong with local batches of the inhibitor serum. They suspected that a local supergenius *(Yellow Thomas)* had altered one of the compounds necessary for its manufacture. Chemistry equipment could not detect the minor yet crucial difference.

So now the local prison warden had to import inhibitor serum from off-world factories.

It is unfortunate that We (the Torth Empire) must rush the Giant's death. The Commander of All Living Things pressed her spidery fingertips together. Everyone in her vast inner audience sensed that she was relaxing aboard her luxury high-speed starship, and they carried that impression to everyone in their audiences.

Yes, many billions of Torth agreed. *The Giant must be killed ahead of schedule, thanks to the unknown saboteur.*

No more arena battles.

No more endangered Torth lives.

The Commander of All Living Things shifted her entire focus to Yellow Thomas. She explored his weak lung capacity, his feeble heart rate, and his mood. Yellow Thomas gathered that she was en route to the planet Umdalkdul, where he was. Nearly a million Red Ranks traveled along with her.

Will you (Yellow Thomas) attend the execution ceremony? she queried.

He politely declined her offer of a reserved seat for him.

No one understood why a mere Yellow Rank would reject such an honor. Distant minds buzzed with suspicion, attracting an ever-larger audience. Millions of Torth demanded to know why Yellow Thomas refused to witness the death of the dangerous Giant. Why did he avoid the topic? Was he afraid? Was he flawed? Was he hiding illegal emotions? Was that why the Upward Governess had dumped him like garbage?

Why hadn't he chosen a new mentor, anyway? Why did he lack ambition? What was wrong with him?

Yellow Thomas swiped his data tablet, adjusting an algorithm. *I suppose I will attend*, he airily decided.

He reminded himself—and everyone in his audience—that the Giant deserved death. The Torth Empire should protect itself from such deadly monsters. That was fine. Yellow Thomas had no problem with that. True deception was only feasible in the impure languages of the tongue and of the body, and he was in the Megacosm, which meant that everyone ought to trust him.

Most Torth held on to their suspicions.

Oh, look, others whispered as a local news feed played into the discussion. Yellow Thomas's audience shared perceptions from a garden pathway in his neighborhood. A group of worried-looking slaves darted toward his suite. The figures were unmistakable, painful shards from his childhood.

Seeing them clearly after so many months felt like a stab in the chest.

Yellow Thomas forced himself to focus on work. He surely didn't care about *(Cherise) (Vy)* those slaves. They didn't matter. Nothing mattered.

Those three experimental human slaves seem mentally unhinged, many Torth in his audience observed.

Possibly dangerous.

If one of them does anything illegal in the presence of Yellow Thomas, he will have to use his blaster glove.

Of course. Killing defiant slaves was the duty of any Torth citizen.

Yellow Thomas tapped his tablet and blinked a drop of sweat out of his vision. The human slaves knew better than to disobey a Torth. He wasn't worried. Not at all.

We (Torth) ought to enslave and colonize the planet Earth, much of his inner audience thought.

No, other Torth silently chorused. *Humans are more valuable if they remain wild and free,*
so We can study them in their native habitat.
We ought to snatch small populations and set up human breeding farms.
Yellow Thomas tried not to have an opinion on this popular recurring debate. His orbiters tugged at his attention, but he ignored them.
Yellow Thomas doesn't like the idea of enslaving humankind.
Maybe he still thinks he is a human.
Yellow Thomas let his data tablet rest in his lap. It seemed grossly unfair to expect one person, even a supergenius, to decide the fate of billions of sentient people, along with their history, their art, their culture, and all their knowledge. It was too much.

Like many Torth, he collected artifacts from conquered alien civilizations. He wished he could know who had made those artifacts and why. Too much knowledge got lost during conquests. The Torth Empire was too rapacious.

A whirlwind of counterarguments arose. *Humankind is beginning to pioneer a primitive form of the Megacosm.*
They call it "the internet."
How long will We (Torth) allow them to strengthen their puny Megacosm?
We cannot tolerate any rival or threat.
That is how We survive,
and expand,
and thrive.
The loss of some primitive knowledge is an acceptable price for Our continuation.
Yellow Thomas realized that he was clenching his fists, as if his tranquility mesh was malfunctioning. He forced himself to stop.

He could imagine humankind after it was robbed of things like the internet, and bicycles, and phones, and music. A second generation of enslaved humans would mythologize those things. Within a few generations of enslavement, humankind would become just another miserable slave species.

Nothing is worth trashing a civilization, he thought, not caring if his opinion was an extreme minority. *Knowledge is more valuable than slaves or cities.*

He expected to get mentally crushed by an avalanche of suspicion and dismissive arguments.

Instead, millions of Torth absorbed his opinion with quiet thoughtfulness. They struggled to find valid counterarguments.

When the human slaves entered the antechamber of Yellow Thomas's home suite, the debate about Earth dropped to a low priority. Yellow Thomas dialed his tranquility mesh to its maximum setting. A growing audience gathered in his mind, waiting to see how this unpredictable visitation would play out.

CHAPTER 12

SO MUCH FAMILIAR

Cherise trailed after Pung, through a suite that looked like an eclectic science museum. Holographic workstations glowed in alcoves. Fossilized machines were displayed on pedestals and on shelf units as delicate as seashells. Robotic equipment fetched containers and adjusted instruments. Living organs pumped or pulsed behind glass walls. Creatures watched her from terraria, and some had too many eyes.

Whoever owned this suite had a lot more interest in science, art, and history than the average Torth.

Cherise used to hang posters and pictures on the walls of Thomas's bedroom in the Hollander home. He liked mathematically generated artwork, surreal digital beauty, and her own meticulous designs. Cherise had also organized his bookshelves. Thomas was interested in just about everything, so his bedroom had been chaotic with clutter.

This suite was larger than the entire Hollander home. Even so, it was almost as cluttered, far more so than most Torth would tolerate.

So Cherise understood why Vy looked gravely worried. It looked like Thomas lived here.

And if so, then he had all the freedom and privileges of a Torth.

He should have done something to ease their suffering as slaves.

It's not him. Cherise clutched her feather duster as if it could shield her from harm. Pung's owner was probably just a Torth who happened to look vaguely like Thomas.

A deep part of her rebelled at that assurance. She didn't actually want comfort. She wanted Thomas.

Maybe the Torth had put a spell on him, like in some fairy tale? Maybe they had altered him somehow. Or maybe they had fooled him into believing that his friends were unreal? If so, he might be delighted to see Cherise.

She might be able to break the spell, like a princess who kissed an enchanted frog and thereby transformed him back into his true nature: a prince.

If he had turned evil, she would turn him good again. She would remind him of who he truly was.

Pung hesitated at a doorway that was masked by a holographic galaxy. He gave them all a warning look. They had agreed to save their reactions for later and to work like slaves while in the bedchamber. Otherwise Pung might be punished and possibly killed for bringing trouble to his owner's presence.

Kessa signaled that she was ready.

Vy and Delia looked like they wanted to escape. Cherise almost hoped they would stay behind. They didn't know Thomas like she did.

Pung stepped through the doorway with his bucket and sponge mop in hand, and then it was too late to make last-minute arrangements. Everyone else followed.

Cherise faced the galaxy illusion, then cautiously stepped through into a palatial bedchamber of polished onyx and gently glowing lamps. Moonlight and twinkling stars outlined clouds scudding overhead. The bed was large enough for ten people, draped with luxuriant furs and silky pillows.

Thomas reclined in the middle of it.

How many times had Cherise drawn him, using her finger in dust or oil or sauce? His head atop his wasted limbs, and his frailty, made him recognizable. Pung must have identified him because of drawings Cherise left in slave zones.

There were a few changes.

Thomas was thinner and more sickly than she remembered. His irises were an iridescent lemon color. They matched the filigree on his golden robe and the circlet around his forehead. Gold dusted his eyebrows, making him look angelic.

He worked on a data tablet with the same intense focus that he used to have when working on his laptop. Although he must have heard the slaves enter, he ignored them.

Surely the Torth could not peer through other people's eyes? Not from afar. Could they?

Cherise dismissed that possibility. Torth did behave in mysterious ways, but they likely had the same power that Thomas had—and that power had a distance limit. It was roughly four yards around one's head. She had measured that limit for Thomas, with his direction and help.

Pung fluffed excess pillows while giving Cherise a smug look.

Another slave held a tray of refreshments near the bed. This must be Pung's coworker, a furry govki named Nror. The govki species were gender-fluid, but Nror had a broad jawline, which Cherise's artistic sensibilities coded as somewhat masculine. Not "it" but "he?" Cherise hoped she got that right. Nror stared at the humans with round yellow eyes.

Kessa, Vy, and Delia set about cleaning the bedchamber. Each looked lost in a world of shocked fury.

Cherise began to dust one of the pillars. She scanned the bedchamber for hidden cameras, but she could not guess what a Torth-engineered camera might look like.

She searched Thomas's focused face.

He didn't so much as glance at her.

Was he hacking into the bedchamber's surveillance system? How long would it take him to disable it?

No one can pretend to be a Torth, Cherise's cold, pragmatic inner voice pointed out.

She shivered. She hadn't needed that inner voice for years, but it used to keep her alive. It had warned her whenever Ma was in a dangerous mood.

Cherise worked her way closer to the enormous bed, uncaring that Nror watched her with wariness. She put herself just within Thomas's telepathic range. Thomas wasn't her ma. He would never hurt her.

Thomas, she thought to him, dusting the parked hoverchair. *If you're still you (if you can hear me), blink twice.*

She watched him.

And watched.

And watched.

Thomas did not blink.

However, a subtle expression flashed across his face, almost like guilt or shame. Then it was gone.

He wasn't lobotomized or enchanted. He was still wholly Thomas. Cherise felt sure of it. But was he being held hostage? Was he under surveillance?

Thomas glanced at Cherise.

It was just a quick, uncaring glance, but his yellow eyes blazed with lofty perceptions. He had always looked intelligent. Now?

He looked like a god of knowledge.

That was not the look of her best friend. Nevertheless, Cherise tried to reach him without actions or words. *I miss you so much,* she thought. *I'm so glad you're alive.*

Pain drilled into her head.

Excruciating, devastating pain.

It could only be a punishment meted out by the boy on the bed.

Cherise fell and curled up on the polished stone floor. Tears pooled in her glasses. She couldn't believe the torture came from Thomas. Yet he focused on her, impassive and distant, like any Torth punishing a slave.

Why would he hurt her?

If no one was making him do it…was she repulsive to him? Filthy? Bedraggled?

Was she nothing to him? Just a worthless slave?

A sound leaked from Cherise's throat. Something was ripping open inside her heart.

The agony increased. That made the rip worse, tearing her apart. She had loved Thomas.

All her pent-up words crushed through her like an eruption. Her fury at the world, at the universe, at all the suffering and injustice she had experienced, and at her ma, all the rage which she had never fully unleashed…it came out.

A torrent of fury poured out of her in a continuous wail.

Everyone else in the bedchamber dropped what they were doing. It didn't matter. A dam was broken inside her. All the secrets she had shared with Thomas, all the words she had never spoken, all flooded out of her. Gone forever.

She screamed and screamed and screamed. She didn't care if it killed her.

All that remained inside her was the cold, dark truth. Now she knew. Now she was sure. No one had ever cared about Cherise. The monstrous boy on the bed was like Ma, an untrustworthy snake.

He had only pretended to love her.

CHAPTER 13

BETRAYED

A tsunami of anguish roared off the slave, far more pain than Yellow Thomas had anticipated, even more than he had punished her with. It almost felt like she was hurting him.

He cringed with illegal emotion.

Luckily, he'd been obliged to drop out of the Megacosm in order to mete out the punishment, so nobody sensed his mind.

He dared not ascend again. Not right now.

Intense emotions meant insanity. This crevasse inside his mind contained anger and fear and all the pain he'd ever known. To plunge back into that human legacy would be suicide.

He had to back away from the dangerous precipice. He had to shut off his emotions. Fast.

"Clean up your mess," he commanded the offensive slave. "And go."

She stared at him with huge eyes. She radiated a shattered feeling. A slave's distress should not affect Yellow Thomas at all, yet he felt so miserable, it was almost as if he was a victim. He felt betrayed.

"You pig," another slave snarled at him.

This was the elder human. Her face contorted with a dangerous amount of hatred.

Both of the ummins watched with their beaks hanging open. The multi-armed govki also looked shocked.

The elder human went on speaking in an ugly tone. "While you lie there, surrounded by your ego, Ariock is being forced to kill people in an arena. I'm sure you've congratulated yourself for surviving while the rest of us suffer and die. Well, congratulations. You'll never know happiness. You're going to die alone."

This slave was angry enough to become violent.

The Torth Empire would expect him to kill her.

His blaster glove was within reach, in a pocket of his robe.

His throat tightened in an alarming way. That was surely just an involuntary reaction to something he'd eaten, not an illegal emotion. But he was trembling too much to pull on his weapon.

Although Cherise wore filthy rags and her hair was a mess, although Nror restrained Delia's arms behind her back, these humans somehow looked noble. They were the living, breathing embodiment of an entire civilization.

Relics and carvings were static and unchanging, but people were dynamic and multilayered. Cherise's perceptions could be infused with wonderment. Even Delia's primal rage was unique.

Surely these particular exotic slaves were valuable enough to keep alive?

As long as they did not try to harm *(murder)* any Torth.

Yellow Thomas forced himself to close his eyes, to stop seeing grief *(Cherise)*, anger *(Delia)*, and pity *(Vy)*. He reminded himself over and over that slaves didn't matter.

Even if the Majority forced him to kill the angry one...did it matter? Delia had cancer. She was doomed no matter what he did or failed to do. No doubt that was why she had risked her rant.

The Megacosm was usually a soothing balm. Yellow Thomas was so desperate to escape from unpleasantness, he ascended, almost without a thought.

KILL! hundreds of thousands of Torth roared in the back of his mind.

Kill the bad (angry) exotic!

Kill, kill, kill! they insisted.

So much for soothing thoughts.

Something deep inside Yellow Thomas writhed like an injured animal. If he refused to comply, then he would be labeled a mental deviant and condemned to die in the Isolatorium.

Yet an undercurrent of defiance burned in him.

The Torth Majority had promised his younger self, Thomas Hill, that he would never need to harm his friends. Hadn't the Upward Governess given him that assurance? Her orbiters, the Torth Majority, had implicitly promised that this exact situation would never happen.

He had believed them.

He had trusted them because there was no such thing as deception among telepaths.

The huge audience inside his mind swelled into a lecturing chorus. *That was then,*

and this is now.

Situations change.

Truths change.

You were feral back then.

Now you know better than to care about slaves.

Oh. Wow. They had justifications.

Why do you hesitate? many wondered. *Kill the bad slave.*

Do you want someone (Me?) (Me?) (Me?) to kill the bad slave for you? neighbors offered.

The bad slave watched him as if she had never seen a more pathetic and despicable creature.

Cold sweat covered Yellow Thomas. Part of him hated Delia for unwittingly putting him in this terrible situation. She didn't know any better. She had no idea that the Megacosm existed or that countless Torth were demanding her execution right now. If he punished her, he would be blameless.

Or almost blameless.

Maybe.

Yellow Thomas assured the Majority in his mind that he would mete out punishment. He would follow orders. He would please them.

Then, instead of working his glove onto his frail hand, he temporarily dropped out of the Megacosm in order to pour his full focus into a pain seizure. The bad slave writhed in agony.

Yellow Thomas ended it within seconds. "Get out of my room," he snarled out loud.

The slaves heard the anger in his tone. Or maybe his painful punishments were enough warning? Either way, the obedient slaves *(Pung, Nror, Kessa) (Vy)* dragged the two suicidally offensive slaves *(Cherise) (Delia)* toward the doorway.

Good riddance.

Yellow Thomas checked to make sure that his tranquility mesh was on its maximum setting. He tried to mentally pour ice on the turmoil inside himself. He waited for the offensive slaves to be gone.

Once he was relatively safe *(sane) (calm)*, he ascended into the Megacosm.

Torth clustered in the garden pathways of his neighborhood. They stood ready to destroy the exotic slave that he had failed to kill.

Please do not, Yellow Thomas politely requested. *Such a valuable exotic slave should not be wasted on My account.*

Accusations drowned out his suggestion. Nobody respected him anymore.

I overestimated My own physical strength, Yellow Thomas admitted to his fast-growing audience. *I failed to use My blaster glove because I lack adequate musculature. Besides, the offense was unexpected. Who would expect a slave to speak? They're little more than machines.*

Doubts radiated from his orbiters.

Yet he was not entirely alone. A growing minority of Torth did agree with the validity of his points. Yellow Thomas seemed calm and logical, and he had apparently kept his equanimity in the face of danger. That was admirable.

I am proud to be a Torth, Yellow Thomas assured his many orbiters. *Do You (My fellow Torth) want to spoil Our chance to enslave humankind?* He wanted to appeal to their desires, as the Upward Governess so often did. *Because that is what will happen if We kill Our human slaves.*

Silent voices muttered. Most of his listeners urged him to continue his line of thought.

I am an expert on humans, Yellow Thomas reminded everyone. *In My expert analysis, the human slaves will not attack anyone. They will remain functional and obedient for all Torth except for Me. If We kill them (waste them) due to this very preventable chance encounter, then Our experimental trial of human enslavement will be nullified.*

The Torth Empire debated his argument.

In the garden pathway outside, strolling Torth continued on their way. The Majority had come to a decision. The exotic human slave could be forgiven for this transgression.

There was always tomorrow.

It won't happen again, Yellow Thomas assured everyone.

Doubts rippled through the Torth Majority, but they agreed to give the human slaves yet another chance. Why not? A lot of Torth were interested in enslaving humankind. This experimental trio might last awhile longer yet.

They are hardy, Yellow Thomas agreed. *They would be a pleasing addition to any exotic collection.*

The Torth Majority continued to debate, batting the merits of his argument back and forth.

One of Yellow Thomas's slaves *(Nror)* returned. Yellow Thomas signaled for it to fetch him a bottle of painkillers. An ache bothered him somewhere deep inside his body, although he didn't know exactly where it was rooted.

An echo of *(Cherise)* the slave's pain remained trapped inside him.

Would he die alone?

Nah. That was ridiculous. Torth were never alone.

The only way it would be possible would be if all Torth rejected him. They would have to exile him *(sever him)* from the Megacosm and transport him to the Isolatorium on the Torth Homeworld. If that happened? Then yes, he would die alone.

I am pleased to be a Torth, he assured all the Torth orbiting his mind, as well as their audiences. *I am humbled by Your tolerance of Me.*

It was true.

But beneath his grateful mood, something buried deep inside him seethed.

Yellow Thomas hid that part of himself. He screened it beneath facts and data. He dared not allow himself to acknowledge another truth:

That he had been manipulated, betrayed, and taken advantage of.

CHAPTER 14

TORTH SKIN

The humans must be protected by a powerful sand spirit.

That was the only way to explain their continued existence. Kessa tried to watch every direction at once, certain that Red Ranks would order Cherise and Delia to be dragged into a prison cart. Slaves could not attack Torth and expect to live.

Emotionless mind readers did inspect the humans all day, interrupting their work, probing their minds. Kessa had a crawly sensation every time a Torth violated her mind, no doubt collecting her thoughts and memories. She tightened her beak and endured it. What else could she do?

It was a grueling work shift.

It went on forever.

Her human friends polished furniture and cleaned rugs in grim silence. Cherise had a dangerous, unpredictable expression. She worked, yet she didn't seem aware of anything around her.

Cherise's devastation reminded Kessa of the final days of her father after a mining accident had destroyed his foot and left him unable to work. Bad injuries like that ensured death. Cherise was critically injured, in a nonphysical way.

At last, their collars dimmed. Kessa led them into the Tunnels.

"You still trust us, Kessa?" Vy gave her a look that was fraught with concern and fear.

Kessa nodded. She had seen their reactions.

Fear for Pung weighed on her mind, however. Pung's owner—Thomas, if the humans were correct about his name—would likely punish Pung for bringing dangerous slaves into his home suite.

"Let's just get rest," Kessa said. "I will draw renewal circles on Cherise's head."

"Renewal circles?" Vy sounded shaky. No doubt she was distracted, grappling with big worries.

"I will draw circles on all of you," Kessa decided. "We do not need to discuss what happened. Not yet. You are my friends. That is what matters."

Vy looked like she might melt with gratitude.

The other two humans gathered unwanted attention. They did not say anything, but Cherise had a look of heartbroken shock, whereas Delia stewed with unspoken rage. Slaves followed them, calling out questions. Why did they look so upset? Had they just learned that their magical mind-reader rescuer did not exist? Was there trouble in paradise? What was wrong?

"Leave us alone," Kessa begged her neighbors.

In their bunk room, Kessa guided her friends to the corner where they conducted their language lessons. She pressed Cherise to lie back against the wall. Then she smoothed the strands of hair that had escaped from the rag around Cherise's head. She traced circles on Cherise's forehead, a practice that was said to draw out bad energy.

She did not notice the commotion in the hallway until someone said, "Pung! Whoa, what happened?"

Kessa looked up, relieved that he had survived an inevitable punishment.

Pung trudged toward Kessa and the humans. All his self-assurance was gone. His hat was more askew than usual.

He flopped onto the floor and flung one arm over his eyes, as if to block out all the curious slaves that kept asking him questions.

"Are you all right?" Kessa asked him.

"I got one brief punishment." Pung grimaced. "Just a small pain seizure."

Kessa clicked her beak in approval. His owner—Thomas?—must be extraordinarily lenient. Pung was very lucky.

"I deserved worse," Pung admitted, "after doing such a stupid thing."

"You did what you believed was right," Kessa assured him. "It wasn't stupid." She hesitated, unsure if Pung had changed his mind about the humans, or about his owner, or both.

"I should have listened to you, Kessa." Pung studied the humans with fresh amazement. "They truly are another species." He shook his head in wonder. "Humans."

"You believe us?" Kessa considered bringing up the agreement Pung had made with Cherise. He owed her a favor.

Or was it the other way around?

Perhaps they owed each other. They had both proved each other wrong.

"They thought he was their friend," Pung said in a tone of wonder. "They truly believed it. I just don't understand how. Are humans insanely gullible? They must be worse than nussians."

Kessa had wondered the same thing. "I think your owner must have been very good at pretending to be human," she said. "Imagine if I ripped off my skin and revealed myself to be a Torth?"

"But it's so strange," Pung insisted. "Anyone can tell the difference between my owner and a human. It has nothing to do with slave collars." He seemed oblivious to the fact that he had been unable to tell the difference. "Did he make jokes? Did he tell stories? Did he laugh and sing?"

It seemed impossible to imagine.

Yet the humans had described Thomas as helping orphan children. They'd considered him to be their brother, their best friend.

"He must have been convincing," Kessa said slowly, tapping her beak in thought.

"He speaks a foreign tongue when he sleeps," Pung said. "I think it's their language."

Kessa had never heard of a Torth who spoke out loud.

According to conventional wisdom, Torth did not dream. They had every wish fulfilled, so they did not need to dream of childhood or flying or any of the fun things that slaves dreamed about.

"I guess he did pretend to be human," Pung reluctantly admitted. "He is odd, for a Torth. But it's just so strange. I've never heard of any Torth like this. Torth with names. And humans. I don't understand."

Pung went on sputtering and muttering to himself about humans. Kessa went back to tracing renewal circles on Cherise's forehead, but she, too, kept thinking about all the oddities. Had Pung's owner successfully fooled every human he'd met in paradise?

That had to be the only explanation. Nobody could fool Torth. Torth were omniscient.

That was common wisdom.

Just like it was common wisdom that Torth did not have children, and did not have names, and did not speak out loud, and did not dream.

"I wonder," Kessa said.

"Wonder what?" Pung asked.

"I wonder if this Thomas is as Torth as he appears."

CHAPTER 15

SO HONORED

Yellow Thomas soaked in warm water, inhaling the soothing fragrance of his spa, trying to ignore the multitudes who listened to his thoughts.

Actually, there were only a few hundred of them. The reduced horde felt less threatening than millions of orbiters.

Yet he was aware that the sharp decline in his mental audience actually represented a problem. Ever since he had lost the Upward Governess's mentorship, he'd become dangerously unpopular.

A lone Torth was vulnerable. Any Torth who got entirely rejected from the Megacosm was doomed. Such a reject *(rogue)* would lack access to information and thus be unable to unlock vehicles or weapons with updated pass codes. More importantly, they could not anticipate the swiftly changing battle tactics of many minds.

Torth rejects, rogues, or renegades always got hunted down and killed.

Yellow Thomas sculpted foamy bubbles. He focused on the shapes and colors. How crazy would he have to be to reject the enlightened civilization that praised his mind? He valued each of his orbiters. Truly, he did.

Sometimes insane Torth did unplug from the Megacosm, but they were never allowed to survive long enough to steal slaves or to threaten innocent Torth citizens. He would certainly never even consider doing such a thing.

He only wanted a few seconds of time alone inside his own mind.

Just a sliver of time. Was that really too much to ask—*(!!!)*

His nearby slave, Nror, threw itself down in a posture of subservience. Yellow Thomas caught a glimpse of the doorway through Nror's eyes. Several imposing, uninvited figures had just entered his spa room.

They wore white bodysuits that emphasized their augmented physiques. These Torth were the highest ranks. Servants of All.

Worse, the foremost Servant of All was recognizably famous. Everyone in the Megacosm would recognize her mantle of office. Horns twisted upward from each of her shoulders, ending in sharp points far above her head. A white cape hung from the horns. It formed a shroud that entirely framed her, from her short-cropped black hair to her white boots.

THE COMMANDER OF ALL LIVING THINGS!!!

Every orbiter around Yellow Thomas's mind surged with exclamations *(!!!)* and deference.

Yellow Thomas struggled to sit upright, splashing water. He did not merit this surprise visit from the de facto ruler of the known universe, surely?

I am loyal, Yellow Thomas assured his orbiters, making a point of not reaching for his blaster glove. Only a guilty person would try to defend himself. Not that he could outmatch the Commander of All or her entourage. High ranks had ultrafast reflexes.

He went through a series of meditation exercises. Loyal Torth never killed loyal Torth. The Commander of All might send a traitor to the Isolatorium, or command them to kill themselves, but he was no traitor. He was just a lowly Yellow Rank without a mentor.

He is afraid. The Servants of All made silent commentary as they glided to a stop at the edge of his spa.

He should be.

Hm. Maybe his fear was rational and wise? Wasn't it therefore permissible?

Uh, welcome to My suite. Yellow Thomas strove to be polite. *Had I known that You (Commander of All Living Things) would visit, I would have arranged a banquet in Your honor.* He signaled his slave Nror to fetch refreshments for the guests.

The Commander of All Living Things stared down at Yellow Thomas with empty eyes. Up close, she resembled a stringy skeleton. Longevity pills and rejuvenation augmentation procedures could only do so much, and her flesh was withered from extreme old age. Very few Torth lived longer than one hundred and fifty years in Earth terms. She was quite a bit older than that.

But she was not a complacent ruler.

On the contrary—this Commander had been elected a mere fourteen years ago. Her predecessor, the previous Commander, had been executed by torture due to gross negligence of his duties.

This Commander had remedied her predecessor's mistakes by exterminating the Dovanack family—or as much of them as she could safely have killed without endangering Torth lives.

She had never imagined that one of her trusted agents would birth an illegal *(hybrid abomination)* child during the course of that duty.

She stood above Yellow Thomas in judgment. Her dislike was almost palpable. She heard the thump of his heartbeat, and she vicariously felt how weak he was, unable to even fully sit upright. Adrenaline flooded his bloodstream. She sensed it.

He was pathetic.

But her silent question to him was coldly civil. *Did you (Yellow Thomas) sabotage any of the inhibitor serum that was delivered to the local prison?*

Torth could not lie to each other.

I would not dare, Yellow Thomas thought. Everyone within his range should be able to detect his sincerity. *I belong in the Torth Empire. I am an upstanding citizen.* He was naked, his suite had been invaded, and he was under suspicion, as usual, but really. He hadn't done anything to warrant it.

The Commander of All Living Things was suspicious. *Show Me your memories*, she commanded.

Yellow Thomas offered his memories like a dragon opening its maw for a tooth count. He had to allow the highest rank to probe his mind.

Although his mind was gigantic and cluttered with endless trivialities.

If he'd had a normal-size mind, his secrets would have been laid bare. The Commander of All Living Things attempted to find what she was looking for—transgressions, crimes—but she had to dig through the thousands of life-times of nonsense that he'd absorbed from fellow Torth. Mountain-climbing expeditions. Astronautical engineering. Scientific discourses. Vacations on alien worlds. It was too much.

Show Me your encounter with the human slaves, she thought impatiently. So Yellow Thomas replayed that embarrassing memory.

Show Me your final exchange with your former mentor, she demanded.

He relived the boat ride with the Upward Governess, her lecture about how he ought to innovate and rise to Green Rank. He supposed he really was a major disappointment.

The Commander of All radiated dissatisfaction. She demanded more memory replays, studying each one, cross-examining every experience she sampled. She probed and probed. She was definitely searching for a justification to have Yellow Thomas executed.

Foam jets continued to massage him, jabbing him like the suspicions that surrounded him.

But he was innocent. Completely harmless and innocent.

At last, the nearby Servants of All began to grow bored. They shared silent opinions with each other and with their orbiters.

He isn't hiding any (dark) (criminal) major secrets.

If this withered (disadvantaged) (pathetic) (unambitious) supergenius (raised by primitives)

was so masterful at deception,

then We would need to suspect all supergeniuses of hiding major secrets.

Indeed. Exhausted, the Commander of All Living Things withdrew her full focus from Yellow Thomas. She had to admit, *Perhaps this pathetic little Yellow is as loyal as he claims to be.*

Yellow Thomas relaxed slightly. He dialed his tranquility mesh to a soothing level.

The Commander of All ascended, allowing her mind to spread out comfortably among her orbiters in the Megacosm. *Hmm.* She ran her spidery fingers across a shelving unit, examining the statuettes on display. *Why does he collect relics from conquered civilizations?*

Collecting relics was legal. A lot of historians—Blue, Green, and Yellow Ranks—traded ancient data marbles and alien knickknacks in the shopping forums.

Yellow Thomas stared at her in defiance. So what if he liked to collect cultural artifacts? That wasn't a crime.

Her blank-eyed gaze drilled into him. *This Yellow has a lot of mental idiosyncrasies.*

That wasn't a crime, either.

The Commander of All Living Things walked around his spa, her boots light upon the sandstone tiles. She studied each of the relics displayed on pedestals. Yellow Thomas watched her and tried not to wonder why she was lingering in his suite.

I have a very honorable (prestigious) task to offer you, the Commander of All thought, answering his unspoken question. *Now that I am certain of your loyalty to the Torth Empire, I believe that you are perfectly suited (qualified) for this task. Would you like to earn a promotion, Yellow Thomas?*

He swallowed a lump of worry in his throat. *Yes.*

What else could he do? Only a deranged idiot would refuse an honor from the topmost elected official in the galaxy.

The Torth Majority wants to speed up the schedule for the Giant's execution, the Commander of All explained. *Just in case Our unknown saboteur manages to tamper with the inhibitor again. (So) I have decided to make the execution happen tomorrow.*

Yellow Thomas nearly slipped in the spa. He adjusted his tranquility mesh, trying to hide his *(!!! shock)* uncouth reaction.

Fine. It was fine. The Giant *(poor Ariock)* was condemned to death, and what difference did make if it happened tomorrow or next week or next month? It was fine. Yellow Thomas was fine with it.

Are you fine with it? Excellent. The Commander of All Living Things stared at him, expressionless. The depths of her mind hinted at disgusted sarcasm.

Nevertheless, she continued with her grand offer. *You are intimately familiar with human psychology and with human creativity. Many thousands of tourists have flocked to this city (New GoodLife WaterGarden City) in order to serve the Majority as firsthand witnesses to the Giant's demise. They expect a spectacular show. Perhaps a human-themed show?* She shifted her full attention to Yellow Thomas. *I want you to devise a suitably impressive execution for the Giant.*

She wanted Yellow Thomas to be an executioner.

A creative supergenius executioner.

Yellow Thomas tried to feel honored rather than sick with indignation. He didn't dare refuse. The Majority expected him to obey and serve.

Of course, he silently agreed.

The Commander of All Living Things gently probed his mind, just for a second, as if to remind him that she had no compunction about violating his sense of safety. *Do well,* she urged, *and I will recommend that the Majority promote you to Green Rank.*

Ah. That was nice. Green Rank was more respectable than Yellow. Greens were entrusted with high-level engineering, mechanical, and navigational expertise.

Totally worth it.

Except…

This task is unfair to ask of Me, he dared to think.

Distant Torth piled into his mind, agog. They mentally rallied their orbiters, who rallied others. Just about everyone wanted to overhear his objection to the honorable task that had so graciously been offered to him. Millions of orbiters became billions.

Yellow Thomas began to feel very small. He was a mote of dust against the sun. He was far too puny to challenge the Torth Majority.

Why doesn't he wish to sentence the Giant to death?

Anyone who helps to destroy the freakishly powerful Giant
will be remembered for (many generations) eons.

Even the Upward Governess will envy him.

Why does Yellow Thomas wish to reject this great honor?

Yellow Thomas slid lower in the spa, beneath hills of bubbly foam. *Just before I joined the Torth Empire,* he thought to the vast audience, *You (the Majority) assured Me that I would never be called upon to harm My former companions. As per Our agreement, I should not be asked to harm the Giant.*

The Commander of All and her elite entourage of Servants of All stared down at him with their milky eyes.

His inner audience roiled with contempt.

You are no longer a mewling primitive, they collectively thought.

Why cling to an agreement that was only offered in order to appease a lesser mind?

A buried part of Yellow Thomas spluttered in outrage.

But he supposed that the Majority was correct. That was then, and this was now. They had collectively changed their minds. A low-ranked individual such as himself could not hope to sway billions and trillions of Torth.

Do you reject this honor? The Commander of All Living Things watched him with a ready attitude. The whims of the Torth Majority were law. She was beholden to them, as were all Torth. By extension, so was every living being in the known universe.

She merely lived to serve.

If he refused to comply? Then he would be declared a traitorous criminal and she could send him to the Isolatorium.

I serve the Majority. Yellow Thomas bowed his head. *I was merely overwhelmed by the greatness of the honor You have bestowed upon Me. Never mind My foolish objection. I will devise a suitable execution for the Giant.*

Billions of Torth minds frothed with approval.

Yes (yes) YES.

They replayed memories of the Giant savagely ripping apart Red Ranks with his bare hands. No one had expected the Giant to move so quickly, with so much strength. It was time to get rid of him.

Yellow Thomas gazed up at the simulated clouds. *I would be much more creative in private,* he hinted. *Without an audience listening to My thoughts.*

The Torth Majority swirled around him as they debated the merits of his hint.

Perhaps We can grant him a few moments of privacy.

Three minutes?

Five?

How long would he need?

The Commander of All Living Things began to stride out of his range. This visit and the upcoming execution were nothing personal, really. She was just doing her duty.

I (We) expect to be impressed, she reminded him. *Make it something interesting. Something that We (the Torth Empire) have never seen before.*

The listening audience roared with approval. *Yes!!!*

We are bored with forcing prisoners to kill or devour each other.

Give Us something new.

Entertain Us!

Yellow Thomas waited until his personal visitors had exited his relaxation chamber.

Then he cautiously slipped out of the Megacosm, with his internal timer ticking down each second.

PART FOUR

He pioneered the NAI-12 serum using only primitive tools. Imagine what he might accomplish if given proper resources and access to all the knowledge in our galaxy.

—The Upward Governess

CHAPTER 1

INSPIRED FROM EARTH

Kessa led the way between stacks of junk and bartering slaves, but she stopped before exiting the Tunnels. That forced Vy to stop also.

"You look determined," she told the human. "That is not a good look for a slave. If you cannot be good, then you must stay hidden with your friends."

Cherise and Delia sat in the bowels of sewage shafts. Pung had enlisted his gang of friends to protect them. With luck, their violent rage would cool within a few wake cycles, and then they would be mentally fit for work duties again. Their minds just needed more time to heal.

"I'll take any risk to speak to Ariock." Vy stood with more confidence than any slave had a right to. "I'm done obeying laws just so I can look forward to a life of drudge work. Okay? You can't talk me out of this. So stop trying."

She walked past Kessa, toward the distant light of the tunnel mouth. There was no way an elderly ummin could stop her.

Resigned, Kessa caught up. "I will show you the prison entrance during our meal break," she said. "But only if you are good. That means you must focus on drudge work. Convince yourself that everything is as usual. No matter where I lead you, pretend that we are on our way to Leftovers Hall for a typical mealtime."

Vy trotted alongside her. "Thank you." She glanced at Kessa, giving her a grateful look. "Have you, um…?" She proceeded with caution. "Have you ever done something disobedient before?"

"Once," Kessa admitted.

Vy looked fascinated. "You got away with doing something the Torth have a problem with?"

"I was the only one." Many bright-eyed slaves had plotted with Cozu, eager to stow away on a cargo transport and escape. "Everyone else was hunted and killed," Kessa said. "I am certain that my friends protected me by never thinking of me. Even when Red Ranks tortured them, they managed not to think about me."

That must have given Vy a lot to consider. Her gaze seemed troubled as they climbed ramps toward the upper city.

Soon Kessa had a lot to think about, as well, because traffic was more hectic than she had ever seen. Hovercarts laden with Torth and supplies streamed in one direction. All the Torth in sight seemed distracted or harried, not paying attention to slaves or foot traffic.

When Kessa aimed questioning looks toward fellow slaves, they replied with surreptitious hand signals.

Torth event.

Busy.

That way.

Kessa was curious, but her work shift had started, so she hurried toward her owner's suite. Her blue-haired owner nearly ran into her. She waggled her fingers in impatient commands.

Soon Kessa and Vy stood aboard a hovercart, behind a load of supplies—mostly blankets, cushions, and snacks for the gods. Three Yellow Ranks sat at the front. It seemed that Kessa's owner had wrangled two neighbors into sharing her vehicle.

Torth rarely shared anything. It seemed that all the public vehicles in the city were being used, so there must be a shortage.

Soon they were hurtling down the boulevard along with other traffic. Kessa held on to her hat. Enormous windows rushed past. They flew past grand columns, dazzling chandeliers, gardens, holographs, and fountains.

Slaves scurried everywhere. A few lay dead in the streets, apparently hit and run over by speeding hovercarts.

They zoomed through a vast opening and into a hot, gritty wind that reminded Kessa of her dusty childhood slave farm.

Thousands of hovercarts sped along a causeway, past immense sandstone walls, while the open sky overhead was dark with flying transports. They all flew in the same direction. They skimmed along a canal, past terraces and gleaming domes and smokestacks that emitted steam. The horizon ahead looked utterly desolate and flat.

Vy glanced back, and Kessa followed her gaze. The huge building they had exited spread outward and upward, seemingly into infinity.

Kessa couldn't guess why so many Torth were exiting the city. No one could have predicted this.

Vy must have similar thoughts. She inched closer to the three Yellow Ranks, trying to study the control panel, as if she might be able to figure out how to read Torth glyphs. Kessa put her hand on Vy's arm, trying to prevent her from taking a fatal risk.

Causeways merged into one huge channel. Their hovercart joined an ever-greater stream of vehicles, all flooding toward an immense notch in the stone wall that enclosed the city.

Soon they glided past outlying buildings. They hurtled down a ramp and surged along rocky ground. Kessa stared at all the rocks. She had not seen an imperfect floor since her long-ago childhood.

The flying transports seemed to converge on the horizon, descending and landing. That must be their destination.

A large portion of the city could have fit in the basin. Indeed, it had. Multitudes of Torth and slaves sat on colorful blankets, beneath canopies that flapped in the hot wind. Kessa refocused her vision, but even with her keen ummin eyesight, people on the far side looked like colorful dots. This outdoor place was immense.

Metallic hovercarts gleamed in the sunlight. Kessa's owner parked amid the others, then quickly disembarked with her comrades.

Slaves struggled to carry blankets and cushions and tubs of refreshments, scurrying after their owners.

Kessa did the same. She and Vy picked up supplies and followed her owner. They went downslope, passing hundreds of reclining Torth. It seemed the entire Torth population of the city meant to picnic here.

Eventually, Kessa's owner found a spot that seemed reserved for her and her two comrades. They waggled finger commands and waited for their slaves to set up blankets and cushions.

Kessa had to prod Vy a few times—she wasn't paying as much attention as she ought to. But Kessa set about making her owner comfortable on satin cushions and rubbed her owner's skin with a fragrant lotion. She anticipated her owner's needs. That was part of what made her such a good and valuable slave.

Nearby slaves sneaked glances at Vy. None dared speak, of course, but they stared at Vy, visually comparing her to nearby Torth. Humans were still a novelty. Everyone in the city must have heard rumors about the human slaves by now, but few had seen a human up close.

If Kessa's owner was aware of the attention, she ignored it. All the Torth in the audience seemed captivated by something that was happening at the center of the basin.

Down there, a dozen nussians pulled a figure in chains. His size was unmistakable even from this distance.

Vy made a sound of recognition.

At any other time, that sound would have earned Vy a painful punishment, but the nearby Torth seemed too wrapped up in the event to notice. Perhaps they were listening to a silent speech? They focused not on Ariock, but on a gaunt Torth with white eyes and horned shoulders. The gaunt one sat in a central place of honor in the staging area of the basin. A white shroud contrasted with her black hair.

Kessa recognized one of those distant prison guards.

Nethroko pulled the helmet off Ariock Dovanack.

The gigantic human looked even more formidable than he had when he'd first arrived in the city. His face was scruffy, his dark hair unkempt. Jagged black spikes came out of his forearms. Shackles and sparse metallic armor completed his outfit.

Vy was staring down at him.

Kessa shoved a paddle-fan into Vy's hands and mimed how to use it. The task should be easy and repetitive. It should also please Kessa's owner, who was beginning to sweat in the hot sunlight.

Vy got the idea and began to wave the fan. But she was distracted, watching Ariock from afar.

Ariock scanned the immense audience, as if searching for a friendly face.

A small voice drifted up from the basin. It was distant, yet unmistakably a voice, and it spoke a word that Kessa had never heard before.

"Yeresunsa."

Then the voice went on, and to Kessa's amazed horror, it spoke the language of humans.

"For crimes against the Torth Empire, you are sentenced to death."

Of all the slaves in the vast audience, only Kessa and Vy could understand the words.

Kessa refocused her vision, and now she saw that the speaker was Thomas. Iridescent gold and white robes draped his withered body, and he floated in a hoverchair amid Torth of much higher rank. All the Torth around him wore white bodysuits.

Vy stuffed her knuckles against her mouth as if to silence herself.

The breeze picked up, carrying scents of lotion and fried foods. At least Kessa's owner didn't seem to notice that the fanning had ceased.

"I drew upon my Earth background to decide your fate," Thomas went on, as if having a conversation. "You can surely guess what method of torturous death I learned in Sunday school."

He had Ariock's attention.

But if the unusual speechifying was meant to provoke an attack, it didn't work. Ariock looked bewildered and sorrowful. His broad shoulders slumped in resignation.

A troop of nussians marched toward him, carrying a steel contraption with four ends, one longer than the other three. Heavy chains swung from it.

Envy was a useless vice, according to the Code of Gwat. Nevertheless, Kessa would have sacrificed her own life for some answers. She yearned to know what Ariock Dovanack had done to deserve death by torture. Why had so many Torth gathered to watch? Why did the Torth named Thomas speak out loud to the prisoner? Why did he speak in the obscure human dialect?

But her lot in life was to remain ignorant. She was supposed to be a good slave and accept whatever happened, even if it meant the loss of her friends. Even if it meant death.

The breeze picked up. A long wind gathered force, causing sunshades and canopies to flutter.

Kessa found herself wishing that the wind would whip sand at all the smug, silent Torth faces.

Everyone knew that injustice and loss were normal, but this seemed worse than normal. Ariock had actually slain two Torth with his bare hands. His mother implied that he could foresee the future. And he came from the paradise of Jonathan Stead. He was a legend come true. If he died, there would never be another like him.

The Torth were going to execute hope.

CHAPTER 2

TOXIC HOPE

Vy remembered a funny, sweet, brilliant foster brother whose medical invention would save lives. She used to brag about how amazing he was.

That version of Thomas was dead.

She could not guess what the Torth had done to make him change so drastically, but all that remained was a shell. The surviving remnant of Thomas had become a greedy Torth who couldn't comprehend why friends mattered.

"Today," Thomas said, sounding human while saying heartless alien things, "on the sixty-third day of the official year 24,609 of our everlasting and majestic empire, you are hereby sentenced to death by crucifixion."

Vy felt as if a monster had gripped her heart.

The nussian guards hauled the steel contraption upright, and Vy saw that it was a cross. It looked like modern art. The two upswept branches tapered to spikes, and each spike had a notch with chains.

They were going to chain Ariock there and leave him hanging.

This couldn't be allowed to happen. If Ariock died, then Delia would quit trying to survive. And then Cherise would fully give up. And then there would be no one to escape with and no one to mourn them except for Vy and Kessa. And Kessa was elderly.

Loss after loss after needless loss.

All for what? A Torth picnic?

Pain seared Vy's thoughts. She had shirked her duty and forgotten to fan the blue-haired Yellow Rank who owned Kessa. As a slave, she was supposed to obey, accept atrocities, and wait for her turn to die.

Vy began to fan the Torth lady again, just to end the painful punishment, but her thoughts turned inward. A conclusion had been building up inside her for many weeks. She needed liberty even if it meant death. She had put off that conclusion due to the hope that she might see her mother again, and her home on Earth. She had hoped that Ariock or Thomas would rescue them all.

Now she understood how toxic that hope was.

She needed to shake it off, slice it away, and do what needed to be done. No more expectations. What would be, would be. If that meant death, so be it.

Down in the basin, Ariock looked resigned to his fate. The breeze seemed to give up with him, and the sun beat down.

"Uh, you are permitted to speak, prisoner." Thomas sounded unwilling, as if forced to make the invitation.

Ariock regarded Thomas with sorrow. Then he seemed to lose interest, and his sad gaze moved to the skeletal Torth with the horned mantle. Then upward. He studied the high ranks in the front rows, and beyond them, to the rest of the audience, searching all the silent faces.

"Speak." Thomas sounded as if he would rather not. "You will not be punished for it."

The invitation was strange. Torth never gave this mercy to slaves, never treated them with any sort of respect. Maybe they considered Ariock to be something other than a slave?

Vy inwardly rooted for Ariock to use his voice. Maybe he could roar out a command for all the slaves to attack their masters right here and now?

Except that was too much to hope for. He probably hadn't even learned the slave tongue.

Hope was toxic.

"You have nothing to say?" Thomas said. "To me?" His gaze swept upward, straight at Vy. "To your friend in the audience?"

It seemed impossible that Thomas could pinpoint the lone human amid so many Torth faces. Perhaps the silent buzz of collective thoughts told him everything he needed to know. Row upon row, the massive audience of Torth swiveled their heads to stare at Vy. Curious slaves followed their gazes, until everyone in sight was staring at Vy.

She couldn't keep fanning under all that attention.

She twisted the fan in her grip, but she didn't quite shield herself with it. Instead, she gazed down at Ariock.

He recognized her across the vast distance.

They both saw each other, two humans in a sea of aliens, and both knew how it felt to be singled out and condemned to death. Ariock looked like he yearned to say something to her.

"You really have nothing to say?" Thomas sounded relieved. Maybe he really did fear an attack? Ariock was close enough to lunge and kill Thomas if he could break free from the prison guards who held his chains.

The Torth seemed to hold their collective breath. Millions of gazes seemed to press on him from all sides.

Finally, Ariock spoke without rancor or spite. His deep voice spread across the basin like thunder. "I forgive you, Thomas."

CHAPTER 3
UNFORGIVENESS

Yellow Thomas had been prepared for deadly violence. He'd been prepared for criticism or condemnation. He'd half expected to be forced to follow the Giant into death.

What he had not been prepared for was another test of his emotions.

The Commander of All Living Things had forced him into a situation that *(almost wrecked him)* shouldn't have affected him at all. Rage, grief, or shame would give the Commander a perfect excuse to sentence him to death.

That was why she had commanded Yellow Thomas to invite the Giant to speak last words.

She had tacked that command on as an afterthought, as if it had just occurred to her. But she'd timed it for maximum effect. With trillions of Torth throughout the Empire tuned in, her mild suggestion had whipped up a titanic chorus that no one, not even she, could defy. The Torth Majority had demanded to hear the primitive rite of last words.

So, with everyone watching, Yellow Thomas had had no choice but to confront whatever pain or rage Ariock might throw at him.

Pain and rage would have been bearable.

But instead, he had sensed goodwill from Ariock, a silent wish that Thomas would survive and thrive as a Torth, as guilt-free as possible.

"I forgive you, Thomas."

With the simplicity of an animal, Ariock had assumed that Thomas was nothing but a helpless child under duress.

That was so *(insightful)* wrong.

Yellow Thomas was a rising star in the Torth Empire, not a fellow prisoner. He didn't deserve or want pity. While the prison guards began to bind the gigantic prisoner to the steel cross, Yellow Thomas backed away. He wanted to *(avoid the Commander of All)* get a head start before the basin emptied and all these Torth headed back home to the city. The sun's heat was hard on his fragile health. If he lingered, he might just *(snap into uncontrollable rage)* get heatstroke.

He felt ill.

His nausea must just be due to the desert heat.

Yellow Thomas, many Torth sang to him in the Megacosm, their thoughts overlapping with eagerness. *You deserve a promotion.*

This death sentence is ingenious.

Such a strange form of torturous death.

Wondrous and primitive.

The Commander of All Living Things spidered through his thoughts, touching each of his mild emotions and crawling through his intentions. *You have proven your loyalty to the Empire,* she decided.

His inner audience swelled with approval. *Hooray!*

As if planning a crucifixion was praiseworthy.

Yellow Thomas tried to agree with their praise, although he privately believed that *(a thug could have done just as well)* he didn't deserve it. A few minutes of private time had not been quite enough for him to come up with a grand scheme.

They told him it was good enough.

How about promoting him to Chartreuse Yellow? the Commander of All Living Things suggested.

Yes! Many Torth chorused.

Good idea!

Yellow Thomas floated past dozens of richly-dressed Torth, trying not to reveal any hint of ingratitude. His primary slaves *(Pung) (Nror)* trotted behind him like a couple of loyal dogs. He ought to feel nothing except for mild pride. He should not think about *(Vy) (Cherise)* slaves or *(how to rescue someone left alone in the desert)* anything else. He should only bask in the congratulations aimed his way.

A few of his peers sent an invitation. *Will you (Yellow Thomas) join Us for a party tonight?*

Yes, do come and join Us in the Chartreuse Lounge.

Our slaves are preparing a feast with cuisine from your homeland.

Pizza.

That was enticing, but Yellow Thomas politely declined. The heat seemed to be roasting his insides. He only wished to go home and *(prepare)* nap.

But he was very pleased that his neighbors were pleased. He hoped they would gulp down lots of nectar drinks and feast themselves into a stupor.

He lived to serve.

The local news feed inside his mind showed Red Ranks forcing the Giant onto a hovercart, bent double under the weight of the makeshift cross. They would stake him out on the tallest ridge. The Yeresunsa danger would die alone, baked by the merciless sun. His metal gladiator outfit would be his burial shroud.

Yellow Thomas boarded a hovercart so he could return to his suite in the city. He did his best not to think about *(no nails) (he has a chance to survive the night)* anything at all.

CHAPTER 4

SHARPENED

On any other sleep period, Kessa would have basked in the respect aimed her way. Slaves filled her bunk room and clamored to be heard over each other.

"Kessa, what was said?"

"Did we really hear the human language in front of all those Torth?"

"We need a translation!"

"Have you ever heard a Yellow Rank speak like that?"

"Why did he speak at all?"

"Why did the giant prisoner carry that metal thing uphill?"

"Was it some sort of human ritual?"

"You have to tell us, Kessa!"

But the event had devastated her human friends. Anyone could see the effect. Delia hid a bone shiv in her lap. She kept sharpening it, although it was illegal for slaves to own weapons of any sort. Cherise looked as if she was peering at the underworld where bad slaves toiled for eternity. And Vy…

It didn't matter how many warnings Kessa spoke. When a slave got that determined gaze, their life would soon end.

So Kessa blocked the doorway. "I will tell you everything," she told the crowd. "Gather around, and I will tell you."

She hardly paid attention to the slaves who hung on her every word. In the corner of her vision, she watched the humans and tried to figure out how to save them.

CHAPTER 5

ESCAPING NIGHTMARES

Instead of leaning against pillows in his palatial bedchamber, Yellow Thomas reclined against a rock in the desert. Abandoned. Unwanted. Lightning flickered along the nighttime horizon beneath a black cloud that encompassed the entire sky. And in front of him, the rocks writhed.

Sand and pebbles collected into a massive, elongated figure with deep-set caverns for eyes. Its huge face was recognizable. Ariock.

The sand giant spoke in a voice like the storm wind. "I forgive you, Thomas."

Ariock disintegrated into white flakes of snow. The rocky ground became ice. Thomas lay freezing in darkness, surrounded by pine trees that drooped with snow. No one wanted him. His mother walked away, gone forever. She would never touch him again, never turn around…except this time, she did.

But her face was a shredded horror. Blood leaked from her ravaged eye sockets.

Even so, she was close enough for him to sense her pain-soaked mind. *My son*, she thought. *I died so you had a chance to live the way I never could.*

No.

He had to escape, so he thrashed his weak limbs, and somehow he fell onto a banquet table.

Torth began to tear off chunks of his flesh and stuff them into their mouths. The Commander of All Living Things crunched on his fingers. The Swift Killer tore off his toes and seemed to relish his cries of pain. The Upward Governess scooped parts of Thomas's brain out of his opened skull. They all feasted on him with big, hungry bites.

He was going to die like this, in agony, and no one cared. The slave Delia was correct about him. No one in their right mind would want to save him.

Except there was a slave in the corner. A human slave, with tears leaking from behind her glasses, watching Thomas get devoured in mute silence. Nothing could ever make things right between them. Cherise would never talk to him again.

Yet he sensed the torn-up remnant of their relationship gleaming in her deepest depths.

She thought, *I still love you, Thomas.*
I still love you.
Love.
Yellow Thomas startled awake in his palatial bedchamber, soaked in a cold sweat. Something had woken him.

One of his slaves, the ummin (*Pung*), stared at him with wide-eyed shock. Torth did not cry.

Oh. His own anguished voice had startled him awake.

Yellow Thomas swallowed, trying to let his nerves cool down. He hadn't intended to fall asleep, especially for so many hours while a storm raged outside. He really had felt ill after the execution ceremony.

It was the dead of night.

The parties must be over. Torth partied more like constipated imperialists than like college students. Was the city asleep?

Cautiously, Yellow Thomas ascended.

New GoodLife WaterGarden City was engulfed in a dust cloud. The worst storm in several decades had ravaged the region. Eyewitnesses shared glimpses of brilliant sheet lightning. Violent claps of thunder had shaken transports, so loud and so continuous that everyone who'd intended to watch the Giant die up close had been driven away.

Even the cameras were buried in sand.

No one knew whether the Giant was alive or dead.

He must be dead, many faraway Torth assured each other.

The wind-driven sand must have flayed him alive.

Or lightning must have burned him on that ingenious metal cross.

Unless he died from hanging by his wrists for many hours in the sun.

Undercurrents of worry slithered beneath all the assurances. The Yeresunsa monster named Jonathan Stead had single-handedly destroyed an army of Red Ranks. Eons before him, the Yeresunsa of ancient times had boiled oceans dry and pummeled armies to death with hailstones. Yeresunsa-driven storms could be cataclysmic.

The Giant is dosed with inhibitor, many Torth pointed out.

He wears an inhibitor collar.

If he truly was (a stormbringer) the cause,

then he would have sent tornadoes and lightning against the city.

It cannot be him.

He is just a victim.

Dying.

Hopefully dead.

Indeed, the lightning storm was already fizzling out. It was probably just an act of nature.

Even if the Giant had caused it, so what? He would never cause anything again.

Yellow Thomas descended, oh so carefully, away from inquiries and offers and praise.

Solitude, as usual, felt like a straitjacket. Yellow Thomas was just a handicapped little boy without any friends.

He lay against his satin pillows and wondered why he was grabbing a privacy break right now. Did he need it?

The city was lethargic after so many feasts for the tourists. The Upward Governess was asleep. The Commander of All Living Things was asleep.

This was a unique window of opportunity that would soon close.

Other prearrangements coalesced in the back of Yellow Thomas's mind. Ariock was utterly alone. There were no slaves or pets or critters in the desert. No one would observe Ariock for the next hour or two.

Implications and ramifications unfurled, far beyond the scope of what most Torth could dream of.

Yellow Thomas would have to be crazy to take such a huge risk for such a vanishingly small chance of success. He really should not throw away his life in an attempt to rescue savages. Even if he succeeded…he would never be safe among violent *(humans)* slaves. He could never trust Ariock or anyone who was dominated by primitive urges rather than logic or rationality. He ought to go back to sleep and…

Wake up screaming?

Any Torth who screamed, or sang, or masturbated, was taking a life-threatening risk.

This was why so many Torth killed their personal slaves. Slaves were incidental witnesses. One way to hide evidence of transgressions was to dispose of one's slave and take another.

Yellow Thomas signaled his slave *(Pung)*. "Pack medical supplies," he commanded out loud. "And gather canteens full of drinking water and nonperishable snacks."

He waited impatiently for his slave to get over his shock. He had a lot more commands to give.

Every second mattered.

CHAPTER 6

CONSPIRATORS

Pung stared at his owner with incredulity. This Yellow Rank had always been odd, but his behavior had slipped to downright bizarre. Why pack so many supplies into his hoverchair? The middle of a sleep cycle was a strange time to pack for a trip.

And what sort of nightmare could make a Torth wake up screaming?

"Obey me," his owner commanded in a dangerous tone.

Obedience was all that a good slave ought to think about. Pung rushed to adjacent rooms, gathering supplies and doing his best to ignore the implications of what he was doing. Slaves who made a habit of speculating about their superiors never lived to old age. His work shift was almost over, anyway.

The Yellow kept pointing to things and giving orders. "Fetch my extra painkillers. Add the portable light. Add the folded thermal blanket. And that outer garment. Fill the remaining room in my hoverchair with nutrition bars."

Just when Pung thought he was done, his owner said, "Put me into my hoverchair."

Pung would rather be sweeping floors. He was good at mindless tasks, which allowed him to ponder and revise his gambling strategies.

He struggled to carry the small Yellow, who was the size of a grown ummin. This task was really better suited to his govki coworker.

Once seated, his owner did not stop giving commands. "Fasten that cloth around my leg cuff." He indicated one of the ornate linens used to blot his hair dry after a bath. "Wrap it around three times. Make sure it's tight and covers every part of the golden cuff. Then make sure it's secured with pins."

A chatty Torth seemed unnatural. Pung tried not to wonder why his owner wanted to hide his shiny ankle ornament under an ugly wrap. It was not his place to speculate.

"Wrap me in my outer robe," the Yellow commanded.

Suppressing a yawn, Pung dressed his owner. The thick golden cloth, shimmery with geometric patterns, hid his bulked-up ankle.

"Accompany me." His owner sped away.

Pung scurried to keep up with the hoverchair, watching his owner's hands for a dismissal. But apparently his owner had no intention of relaxing like an ordinary Yellow Rank. No. Instead, he seemed preoccupied with his data tablet.

His owner stopped at a workstation and made a glowing hologram appear. "This is a map."

Pung backed away. Bizarre commands were one thing, but Torth knowledge was off-limits to slaves. Any ummin who tried to poke a data tablet or drive a vehicle would be tortured to death. This must be a trick or a trap.

"I won't hurt you." His owner sounded impatient. "Now pay attention. Here's where you'll enter." Part of the holograph blackened, growing more solid than the rest. "It's a ventilation shaft." He swiped through an interface, and a glowing line appeared. "Memorize this route." The end region glowed. "Here's where you'll find the three items I require."

Maybe his owner had suddenly developed a sick sense of humor. This had to be a joke.

"You'll be going into the bedchamber of the fat Indigo-Blue Rank," his owner said, as dispassionate as any Torth. "You know which one I'm talking about. I need you to collect her fancy data tablet and her wristband." He tapped his bony wrist to demonstrate. "The third and most important item is a rectangular case. It's about this big." He indicated its size, and Pung recalled the case wedged in the fat Torth's hoverchair.

"I'll make sure you're protected," his owner said. "Fetch the case, the wristband, and the tablet."

Pung took an involuntary step, instinctively obedient. Then he stopped. This was highly illegal. If the Indigo Blue caught a slave sneaking through her domain with the criminal intention to steal, she would surely have him thrown in prison. He'd be skinned alive.

"Follow me," the Yellow commanded, floating away.

Pung didn't move. Dozens of nussian bodyguards patrolled that palatial suite. Hundreds of slaves tended the indoor lake and gardens. Nobody could sneak into her bedchamber unnoticed.

For a slave, death lurked in every street, in every slave zone. To be forewarned was to be lucky. Still, Pung had never expected to die like a piece of sand, unnoticed. After all the leniency, his owner had proven to be more insane and deadly than any other Torth.

Pung was caught between the sand and the sun. Tonight, he would die.

Quaking in terror, he closed his eyes and waited for fatal pain.

No pain gripped him. Pung cautiously opened one eye.

His owner tapped his bony fingers on the curved arm of his hoverchair. "We'll work together." He turned off the holograph. "Follow."

Pung fought a surge of anger. His owner had a lot of nerve, trying to manipulate his poor slave on a fatal quest. Maybe Pung could pretend to go along with it for a while. Then he'd outrun or outmaneuver the hoverchair. Runaway slaves were always captured and tortured to death, but maybe he could evade capture by hiding in the sewage shafts.

"See that jar with red swirls?" His owner paused in a niche full of potions and creams. "Pour it into an empty vial. Then use a clean eyedropper to add ten drops from the opalescent blue container."

They were near the menagerie, and restless animals squawked and rustled in their cages. Pung followed the commands with trembling hands.

"Gently shake the vial until it turns a milky blue color," his owner said, working on his data tablet.

A strange feeling pumped through Pung. It felt like danger was inside him. If only his coworker could hear their owner chatting like a fellow gambler. He had never heard of a Torth conspiring with a slave. As he gently shook the vial, mysterious colors swirled inside.

"Use a clean eyedropper to add a single drop from that black jar," his owner said, gesturing. "And hold your breath while you do it."

Pung did so, while his owner continued to talk. "Don't inhale. Hold your breath until you've screwed the cap onto the vial. Make sure it's tightly sealed."

When all this was done, the small vial glowed with a faint green light.

"Perfect," his owner said, like an elder giving approval. "Now hide that in your robes, the way you do when you smuggle food."

Pung hadn't guessed that any Torth knew about his smuggling activities. He was lucky to be alive.

"Lots of slaves smuggle small secrets," his owner said. "Very few Torth care about harmless transgressions."

As Pung considered that, he realized his smuggling activities did not undermine or threaten Torth supremacy. In fact, he helped preserve public property—unowned slaves.

"As long as you don't behave suspiciously, you'll go unnoticed," his owner went on. "The vial will help protect you. When you twist the cap a little bit and wave it near someone's nostrils, that person will instantly fall into a deep sleep. Just be careful not to inhale it, or you'll fall asleep, too."

Pung stared at the vial in horror. Any slave who touched a weapon could expect imprisonment and death by torture. This vial was smaller than a blaster glove or a knife, but it might doom him.

"And never unscrew it all the way." His owner floated toward the antechamber, beckoning Pung to follow. "Don't drink it or you'll die."

Pung clutched the vial, uncertain. He didn't know if he could trust anything that his owner said. Wouldn't it be safer for his owner to simply shoot the fat Torth with a blaster glove?

"Murder would get both of us killed." His owner paused in the massive doorway. "If she gets shot, she will scream a silent alarm while she dies. Then an army of Red Ranks will seize us before we can get far."

As if they were conspiring together. As equals.

A sense of unreality engulfed Pung.

"The only way we'll survive," his owner said, "is if she remains asleep. When you enter her bedchamber, you'll emerge near fans that circulate air. You'll be high up, on a ledge, out of sight. She'll probably be asleep, but even if she's awake, she can't read your mind from that distance, and she won't know you're there. Unscrew that vial near a fan. Everyone in the room will swiftly fall asleep."

If stealing from a Torth were as easy as smuggling food, everyone would do it. Pung could hardly believe that his owner believed this plan would work. Any random bodyguard or slave might enter her bedchamber while Pung was stealing the items.

And surely someone would see him on his way in or out of the palatial suite.

"The bodyguards will be occupied," his owner said cryptically. "And her slaves will assume you're one of them. Just make sure the Indigo Blue stays asleep, or we're both dead."

The dangerous feeling seemed to be crawling around inside Pung's skin. His owner would probably escape justice for all these crimes. Meanwhile, Pung's jangling nerves would get him condemned if nothing else did.

"All slaves are afraid." His owner's voice echoed off the marble walls. "You all hide guilty little secrets. You mate with someone when you're not supposed to. You talk in whispers when no Torth are nearby. You smuggle food." He gave Pung a pointed look. "Anxiety won't make you stand out."

Pung supposed that might be true.

"There are quadrillions of ummins in the universe," his owner said. "As far as the Torth are concerned, you're all interchangeable. They'll have no clue how to find the thief. Especially if you're wise enough to toss that sleeping vial down a garbage chute after you use it. Now, grab a tote bag." His owner gestured to the supply closet. "That's how you'll collect the items."

As if this was a mere trip to a trading forum.

Pung chose one of the bags studded with tiny gemstones, but he didn't feel ready. His collar should go off duty before he had a chance to sneak into the palace. That would give him an excuse to escape all this craziness.

Once his collar went dark, he would have a grace period to get to his bunk room and settle down to sleep. He could not freely walk about the city. The collar would choke him if he dared to disobey it.

"Come here." The Yellow pulled something out of his pocket. "Take this."

The device was the size of a finger. Pung studied the wand, trying to figure out what it might be for.

"Wave it over your collar," the Yellow commanded.

Pung obeyed.

"Your collar was just reset," the Yellow said. "Now you're at the beginning of your work shift."

Pung wanted to curse out loud.

"Take that wand," his owner said. "When you wave it near any collar, it will toggle to another shift."

Pung was shocked that a Torth would entrust him with this much power. With this tiny device, he could rule the deep shafts of the slave Tunnels. He would never have to go to his assigned bunk room.

"Hide it." His owner looked weary. "One more thing. It will be to your advantage to look generic." He studied Pung critically. "Try to scuttle like most ummins. And adjust your hat so it's not as memorable."

Pung tugged his hat folds until they were equal in length.

Maybe he would actually survive all these crimes and live to tell Kessa about it? Even Weptolyso would be impressed. He felt as if he was the hero of a story, one of the legends in which a god gave a hapless slave a cloth that turned them invisible.

"You'll want to avoid bragging." His owner floated past the tall arched windows of the antechamber, past mountains under starlight. "If you feel smug or triumphant, you will get caught."

That chilled Pung's excitement.

"Now then." The Yellow floated to the exit. "Once we leave here, you'll need to prioritize my hand commands over my voice commands. If I speak, pretend to listen and obey. But watch my hands. Those are my true commands."

They might as well be conspirators. It seemed the Yellow couldn't rely on other mind readers…or perhaps he had only revealed a fraction of his plans. He might be planning a larger crime spree, something even more deadly than stealing from a high rank.

"It is not your place to speculate." His owner reached for the door panel. "Just obey my hand commands and complete this task, and you have a good chance of survival."

Pung didn't need to wonder what would happen if he failed. All slaves knew the cost of failure.

CHAPTER 7

TO ROB A GOD

The boulevards were mostly devoid of traffic. That strange desert event must have forced everyone to get onto roughly the same sleep schedule, so Pung's owner was able to speed unimpeded. Pung had to run in order to keep up with the hoverchair.

A Kemkorcan slave rippled in the other direction, swimming on its feathery limbs. A chubby govki raced past, top-heavy as it waddled on two of its six limbs. Here and there, distant Torth sat in lounges or strolled together. Yet Pung's owner kept managing to avoid other Torth, picking the least traveled alleys.

The sleeping city gave Pung a bold feeling, like he was winning a game against the toughest gang boss in the Tunnels. He was doing something illegal while most Torth slumbered, unaware.

Soon they arrived in a garden atrium entrance at the top of the city. It always smelled sweet here, with flowers blooming. Water flowed through channels between sandstone floor tiles, and golden chandeliers lit the foliage. Some gardens felt intimate. This one was so vast that the farthest vine-wreathed pillars were hazed by distance.

The eight guards who approached sized up Pung's owner with their beady eyes, and their spikes bristled in a threatening way.

They normally escorted the guest. Tonight, though? They must have orders to turn him away.

"Guards." Pung's owner spoke in an arrogant tone. "Line up for inspection." He pointed nearby.

The nussians bristled even more. They would only obey a high rank. Pung kept his head down, wishing he dared to hide.

"Tomorrow, I will no longer be a Yellow Rank." His owner lifted his chin in an imperious manner. "And I won't have time to deal with the likes of you. Those who refuse to comply will be thrown in prison."

A few of the guards glanced at each other. They had probably seen this Yellow Rank during the grand event in the desert, or at least heard about it. This Yellow had been treated with honor, seated amid Torth chieftains. He had even led the ceremony.

The guards shuffled nervously. Their owner had always treated this particular Yellow as her equal. She herself had risen rapidly from Yellow to Blue.

Even his voice stood out as remarkably eloquent. Most Torth had raspy or stuttering voices. Not all Torth were this fluent in the slave tongue.

His claim might be plausible.

"Line up!" the Yellow commanded with all the attitude of a Red Rank. "Now!"

The guards tromped into a row with frantic haste, forming an armored wall. Ignoring a high rank would be fatal.

The Yellow had to lean back in order to look up at the nussians. He floated along the lineup, inspecting each guard in turn. Despite the iridescent yellow color of his eyes, his gaze had the cold intensity of a high rank. The guards squirmed.

After a moment, the Yellow seemed to reach a conclusion. He swung his yellow-eyed stare toward Pung, who couldn't help but flinch. That stare was almost a physical force.

"In the swamp zone," his owner said, "there's a ventilation shaft. One of these guards will guide you to it. Explore that shaft and collect any contraband supplies that you find." His fingers moved subtly, his hoverchair rotated so that only Pung saw his hand signals. *Fetch three items. Be discreet.*

For a fleeting instant, his owner looked vulnerable, like one of the humans.

But maybe Pung had imagined it. His owner was imperious again, pointing at two of the guards. "You. You. Resume your duties." He pointed to a sleek female guard. "You, guide my slave to the specified shaft."

She bowed to acknowledge the command and loped on all fours toward the inner palace. Pung ran to keep up. He had been worried about what slaves would think of him entering with an empty tote bag and leaving with the bag full, but now he had a perfect excuse. They would assume it was proof that a guard had illegally hidden contraband.

Behind them, his owner said, "The rest of you, go inside and send every guard to me for a mind probe. Don't let any escape."

His emphasis caused guards to stampede past Pung. The poor guards must be desperate to prove their own innocence and to expel whichever guard turned out to be guilty so they wouldn't lose their lives.

They probably wouldn't even visit their owner until it was too late. Anyone would assume that she already knew what was happening and that she'd delegated this task to an ambitious subordinate.

Pung marveled at his owner's boldness. Nussians were gullible. He hoped, for their sake, that their owner was lenient.

It felt wrong to enter the glittery, well-lit palace with no chores to do and no Torth anywhere in sight. The other guards spread out in different directions. Soon Pung was alone with his guide. She ignored him, the way most guards ignored ummins. Collared species were supposedly "lesser" to the guards.

She also ignored whispered conversations from the uniformed slaves who trimmed hedges and swept floors.

Pung had heard of relaxed work shifts, but he had never actually met a palace slave, since they slept in palaces rather than in the Tunnels. Were the whispers normal?

They probably had a system of signals to warn each other when a Torth was approaching.

What an enviable life!

Pung nearly tried humming out loud, just to see how that much freedom felt. But he needed to remain unmemorable, so he stayed quiet and kept his head down.

Even the toughest guards in the city would admire him if he managed to steal from a Blue Rank and live to talk about it.

His guide paused when she saw another gigantic nussian. "Go to the entrance atrium," she told her fellow guard in a rumbling voice. "There is a Torth there, probing minds to find a criminal among us. He commanded that every guard go out to meet him."

That should have been enough to send the guard rushing away. Pung hopped off the path to avoid getting trampled by accident.

But the guard only gave her a sour look. "Duty compels me to patrol these flower gardens," he said.

The female guard puffed up. "If you refuse to go, everyone will suspect you of being a criminal."

He snorted a challenge. "I don't obey commands from you."

The female studied him with suspicion. "You obey guards on errands sometimes, just like I do. Why are you truly refusing?"

The crusty guard bristled, spikes popping out. "I don't believe that one lone Torth is confronting every guard in the palace. There are forty-seven of us. If one guard really is a criminal, then that desperate criminal will crush the lone Torth before he can use his blaster glove. Why would a Torth put himself in that position? Torth have a lot of power, but they are not brave."

Pung inwardly admitted that this was a good argument. The crusty guard should probably be stationed somewhere more important than a flower garden.

The female guard narrowed her reddish eyes. "Do you honestly believe that a Torth just lied to eight guards?"

The crusty guard backed down. True enough, when Torth spoke out loud, it was only for the purpose of giving commands. They never told lies or stories. That simply was not how Torth behaved. Until now, Pung had never heard of a Torth telling a lie.

Except…had his owner lied?

No. The Yellow had been manipulative and deceptive, but he had not actually spoken anything that was untrue.

"Look," the female guard said, gesturing at Pung. "He commanded this little slave to gather evidence."

"I just don't believe that a lone Torth would confront so many guards." The crusty guard sounded sullen. "That is not normal."

The argument might go back and forth indefinitely, and Pung didn't want to displease his owner. "Honorable guards," he said timidly, facing the stone floor. "May we please continue to that shaft?" He aimed a beseeching look at his guide. "My owner is monstrously cruel, despite how he looks. He will kill me if I fail."

The crusty guard growled with frustration and fear. "Oh, very well." He shuffled away, toward the atrium. "I will go and prove that I am not a criminal."

His guide grew less bristly. Soon she was loping down the winding walkway.

"That was old Yomtalo," she told Pung. "He has served our owner since she was a Yellow Rank, and I suppose he is bored. Our owner never does anything fun or adventurous."

"That is unfortunate." Pung tried to sound sympathetic. He wished he had a boring owner.

"We all want to serve Red Ranks. Their bodyguards get to travel." She led Pung beneath a mossy overhang, where bugs chirped in a soft chorus. "There it is." She pointed to a well-polished industrial shaft.

"Thank you." Pung stepped into the darkness. He supposed this must be the shaft his owner had pointed out on the map. It would lead to the bed-chamber.

"Good luck, ummin." The guard hurried away, leaving Pung alone.

He was grateful for any luck the spirits might deem him worthy of.

CHAPTER 8

THE HONOR OF SLAVES

The sterile air was enough to remind Pung that he was nowhere near his Tunnels. Some slaves might have gotten lost in this clean maze of utility shafts, but like all ummins, he had a good memory. He had memorized the map without really trying.

Soon his route ended in a vast, darkened space. He lay down on the ledge and peered downward.

Sure enough, the immense bed was below him. It looked like a fortress of fluff, round and strewn with embroidered velvet blankets and huge pillows. Pung drew back. He saw a glowing tablet. The fat Blue Rank was awake on that bed!

But Pung's owner had mentioned air circulation and fans.

Tiny vent holes dotted the frame embedded around the shaft's outlet on the wall. Pung experimentally blocked a few holes with his hand and quickly drew back. Those vents generated a small yet mighty wind. He supposed it was designed for quietude.

He pulled out the faintly glowing vial.

Until now, Pung had not flagrantly broken any laws. The actual plan to steal from this high rank was all his owner's doing. Was it possible that Pung might be forgiven as an innocent pawn?

He would not be innocent if he went ahead and carried out the crime.

He gazed at the vial, trembling. Maybe he could survive if he gave up, quit, and went into hiding. Could he lurk in underused palace gardens?

His owner would probably become murderous.

And if there was one thing that Pung had learned about his owner, it was that the Yellow was unpredictable. His owner might commit more crimes. He might alert every Torth in the city about the identity of his slave accomplice. And if that happened, then it wouldn't matter how well Pung hid. Everyone would be ordered to find him. Even the friendliest gangs would turn him in, because Torth were truly in charge.

Pung's owner had packed for a journey.

If Pung secretly followed his owner after this theft... If he could stow away in whatever vehicle his owner chose...

What a crazy, terrifying idea! Runaway slaves only existed in stories. If Pung tried that, he was likely to get caught and executed.

Besides, what sort of friend abandoned everyone in his life? He owed the human slaves a favor. They owed him a favor, too. He had debts and favors to collect from half the gangs in the Tunnels. He couldn't just vanish without any explanation to Kessa or his other friends.

Every slave knew that escape was wrong. Pung deserved to rot in prison for allowing himself to even daydream such frivolous, impossible fantasies.

No more of that. Obedience was a virtue. All he needed to do was focus on what his owner had commanded him to do, and nothing else.

Pung took several deep breaths to steady his nerves.

Then, with trembling hands, he unscrewed the vial. Not daring to breathe, he thrust it in front of a vent hole. He held it in place and watched everyone in the room below.

Three slaves in livery stood in attendance near the huge bed. They looked ready to fetch anything for the Blue Torth, but after a few moments, they began to look sleepy. One suppressed a yawn.

Their owner lay back. The glowing tablet slipped out of her hands.

She began to snore lightly.

Pung waited until the three attendant slaves stumbled, pinched themselves, and finally fell over. Their collars still glowed blue for a work shift, but they looked like they were in a deep sleep.

His own chest felt painful from the lack of air. He hurriedly sealed the vial and dared to breathe, inhaling uncontaminated air from the shaft behind him.

Then, praying to the spirits for luck, Pung edged out with the empty tote bag over one shoulder. He found a silver trellis and carefully climbed down.

No one stirred as Pung sneaked past a dim lamp cupped in a silver flower. He knelt by each sleeping slave long enough to wave his wand and deactivate their collars. These slaves looked like they had an easy life, clean and well-fed, but that was no reason they should suffer strangulation from active-duty collars.

Satisfied that the slaves were safe, Pung climbed onto the bed.

The Blue Rank slept with her mouth open. Noisy breathing was ironic for a mind reader. Pung crept toward her.

He ignored the items for now. The smart thing to do would be to give her an extra whiff of the sleeping potion. Pung held his breath and unscrewed the vial, inching closer and closer to her face.

She snorted sharply.

Pung nearly fumbled the vial. He remembered to hold his breath and keep his beak closed, but he was trembling so much, he had to use both hands.

He thrust the vial below her nose and waved it around, making sure she would inhale. Soon her snoring grew deeper and more relaxed.

Pung capped the vial and stuffed it back into his rags. If he had accidentally inhaled the potion, then the sleeping Blue would have found a surprise on her bed when she awoke. He took grateful breaths of the perfumed air, feeling as lucky as a hero in a legend.

He snatched her glowing tablet. Its surface blinked with Torth glyphs, and it also displayed a steady nighttime view of a jagged hilltop. Was that a window? It looked like the place where they'd hanged the giant.

Pung couldn't guess why so many Torth wanted to watch the giant suffer, but he reminded himself that it wasn't his place to speculate. He had a job to do. He stuffed the tablet into the sparkly tote bag.

Emboldened, Pung folded back the blanket. Sure enough, she wore a wristband. And...

He had to ease the rectangular case out of the sleeping Torth's embrace. What kind of a Torth hugged anything? It was strange.

Pung studied her tranquil face the whole time, watching for any signs of waking.

He even pushed a pillow under her arm. That should serve as a substitute. Maybe it would help her sleep longer.

The wristband display screen looked like a tiny version of the tablet, although its glyphs were different. Pung required a moment of study before he dared mess with the unfamiliar buckle clasp. He gently squeezed it, and the ends released each other.

He shoved the third item into the tote bag.

With a bounce of victory, Pung jumped off the bed and raced to the door. He tiptoed into a corridor. From there, he ran, his toes clicking on marble and mirrors.

He had stolen treasures from the richest Torth in the city. What else could he get away with?

When he saw bushes that sagged with deliciously ripe fruits, he grabbed one and shoved it into the tote bag. Farther down, he saw a fountain that glittered with jewels. His reflection in the wall mirrors looked as gleeful as a child's. No one was watching!

He snapped golden filigree off artificial flowers, and he grabbed diamonds out of cupped statues. The tote bag grew heavy on his shoulder. He plucked edible tubers from a basket, as well as leaves that he recognized as a garnish in Torth feasts.

Slaves worked in the gardens near the atrium. Pung slowed down and tried to act humble. He was merely an obedient slave obeying his owner.

A white light flared inside his tote bag.

It flashed on and off, blinking a silent alarm. The gardeners noticed, both of them dirt-stained ummins. One pointed and the other gaped.

In a panic worse than any he'd ever known, Pung dropped the tote bag and tore through its jumbled treasures, seeking the blinking alarm. He didn't dare show up among the bodyguards with a device that was not a weapon or contraband supplies. It would be obvious that he'd stolen something that belonged to their high-ranked owner.

He fished out the wristband, trying to hide it with his body. He poked frantically at the glyphs. Of course the spirits had to mock his prayers. No matter what he did, the light kept flashing…

Until it went dark.

Pung figured that he must have deactivated it somehow. He shoved it into the bag, still trembling, praying that it would not start flashing again.

Both of the ummin gardeners watched him with disgust and suspicion.

Pung inwardly fought despair. They must have seen some of the treasures inside the tote bag.

He was an idiot to believe that he could have survived this adventure. He might as well be dead. The gardeners would recall the exact hue of his gray skin, the exact slant of his beak. He had lost his chance to blend in with other ummins. Once the Indigo Blue awoke and sucked up memories from every slave in her palace, she would find him.

The younger of the two gardeners gave him a look of pity mixed with shame.

Pung knew she would blame herself for having borne accidental witness to his crime. He had blamed himself when Torth found his injured brother, hiding in a sewage shaft of the factory slave farm where they'd been raised. Pung would have died to keep smuggling food and herbal tinctures to help his brother recover. But his care had been too noticeable, and his brother was dead because of that.

"It is not your fault," Pung whispered. He pulled out the wand and waved it over their collars. "Tell your friends that Pung the Smuggler was here."

They glanced at each other in amazement, seeing that they were now magically off duty.

"We did not see you," the younger ummin said.

"We never heard you say a word," the older one said.

Unbelievably, both of the gardeners walked away as if he did not exist.

If their owner probed their minds, she would kill them for failing to stop a thief. Pung wished he could thank them. He wished he knew their names.

Instead, he grabbed the tote bag and hurried toward the atrium.

Torth had no honor. He had to obey his owner, but he would receive no gratitude, no protection, and no self-sacrifice from the Yellow Rank who owned him.

That was the real difference between slaves and Torth.

CHAPTER 9

THE SOUND OF FREEDOM

Pung crept through the atrium with the bulging tote bag. When his owner caught sight of Pung, he remained expressionless—except for his eyes. For just a second, he looked as if he had won a battle.

"Guard your owner well," the Yellow told the humongous guards. He gestured a dismissal.

Pung leaped aside so the guards could stampede past him, racing each other in their haste to return to their posts. None had stood guard in the bedchamber, and Pung guessed they would not even peek inside. It would never occur to them that a sneaky ummin had effectively poisoned their owner. Such things did not happen to Torth. Especially not to rich Blue Ranks.

The small Yellow beckoned.

Pung hesitated. His owner no longer behaved in any semblance of a predictable way. Although Pung had completed the near-deadly task, like a hero in a legend, what was next?

His owner rotated and floated away at a rapid pace.

It was as if the Yellow suddenly didn't care about all the risks they had both just taken. He shot through the gate and out of sight, on his way to somewhere unknowable.

That left Pung standing in the garden atrium with a bag full of stolen valuables.

For a moment, he considered trying to evade everyone in the city and make his way directly to the Tunnels, but the spirits had surely already graced him with all the luck he was ever going to get. He dared not risk getting a mind probe while his clothes and bag were stuffed with smuggled items, including technology that slaves could die for touching.

He might as well be trash left to rot in Leftovers Hall. Without any Torth nearby, he looked like an unowned slave—a target for any Torth passersby in the city streets.

So he began to chase after his owner. What choice did he have?

The Yellow sped at top speed down ramps and bridges, unimpeded by the sparse foot traffic. Pung began to run out of breath. Just as he became certain that he would lose sight of the silver hoverchair, his owner swerved into an empty alcove.

Panting, Pung followed.

The Yellow floated amid neon lights, expectant. He had apparently never doubted that his slave would follow and obey. He simply held out his hand in a "give me" gesture.

Pung struggled to hide his resentment.

But then he realized that he might just have some leverage. Once he handed over the stolen items, what would prevent his owner from abandoning him? If Pung was doomed anyway, why should he cooperate with this greedy Yellow Rank?

"I will give you a reward," his owner whispered. "Give me the items, and you will gain power."

That sounded like a promise from a god.

Pung decided to ignore his misgivings. He could not use the Torth items anyway. First, he stuffed as many choice fruits and gemstones as he could into his rags, while his owner waited with impatience. Then he placed the tote bag on the hoverchair seat next to his owner.

What a relief to get rid of that!

"Great." His owner popped open his hoverchair compartment, rotating so that Pung could access the contents. "Take the folded robes," he said.

Uncertain, Pung picked up his owner's three outerwear garments, each one inlaid with shiny geometric patterns.

"I'm going to the hover harbor near Leftovers Hall," his owner said. "I won't be there for long. Say hello to Cherise, Vy, and Delia, and use those robes to pay the favor you owe them." He hesitated. "You are free."

With that incredible statement, the Yellow floated away.

Pung took a few uncertain steps. Freedom was a myth. Only spirits, gods, and heroes were free. Maybe it was a mistranslation? His owner must mean that Pung was unowned, and therefore worthless and disposable to any Torth who wanted to use him.

His owner was going to a vehicle lot.

Alone.

With stolen valuables.

And with enough water and food to last for several days in the desert.

Pung clicked his fingers together, sick with dangerous thoughts. The clicking sound filled the empty street. He ought to stop thinking and obey orders. No matter how fortunate he had been so far, he needed to remember that he was nothing more than a common ummin slave.

He wanted to beg Kessa for advice.

If he went to Kessa's bunk room and woke her up, he could also visit the human slaves, per his owner's command.

Pung tucked the Torth garments under his arm and jogged toward the Tunnels. He needed to quit thinking about the humans and their old certainty of getting rescued. Rescue was impossible. Escape was impossible. If he kept thinking wild thoughts, he would get himself killed. His owner's intentions were not his concern.

His owner was no longer his owner.

Pung mulled it over, certain that his ridiculous ideas would wither into dead ends. Slaves certainly did not free themselves. They did not simply stroll out of the city, even if some of them could pass as Torth from a distance, even if they wore Torth robes, even if the city was relatively empty, even if a vehicle and a driver was waiting for them.

A lifetime of slavery fought against his sudden, freakish hope.

Surely someone would see them? Even if this rescue worked for the humans, they would probably refuse to take an extra ummin or two.

Although they did owe Pung a huge favor.

Well, even if this was a rescue and they all planned to escape, the Yellow probably didn't want extra passengers. He would surely…

Not summon help.

If he was committing illegal acts against the Torth Empire, then he couldn't count on other Torth to aid him.

And everyone knew that a Torth could only punish one slave at a time. It required their full attention.

A lone slave could not hope to overpower a lone Torth, even if that Torth was a disgraced rogue. But with friends?

It all clicked into place in Pung's mind with stunning clarity. Armed with friends, Pung would have more power than his owner could fend off.

He raced toward the Tunnels, veering wide around the few Torth in the streets. His feet pounded like the machinery he'd been forced to work as a child.

This was life or death. If he meant to seize this strange once-in-a-lifetime opportunity, then his life depended on getting the humans to the hover harbor as fast as possible.

CHAPTER 10

PURSUIT OF KNOWLEDGE

Kessa would stay awake for as long as she needed to.

"You must not leave," she told Vy yet again. "This is a sleep period. How many slaves do you see walking around while off duty? If you walk right now, your collar will hurt you." She touched her neck, recalling the awful pinching sensation. "It will hurt for days."

Vy spoke through clenched teeth. "I don't care."

Her look of betrayal made Kessa feel ashamed, as if she had somehow wronged Vy by asking the hall guard to block her path.

Weptolyso leaned in the doorway with his spiky arms folded. At least he didn't seem weighed down by guilt or shame. To him, this was just his job.

"You have no right to make decisions for me." Vy glared from Kessa to Weptolyso. "The only thing I have left is my free will. That's it." She plucked at her rags. "My dignity is gone. My sense of security is gone. And now...I can't..." She seemed to struggle for words. "I know you're trying to save me. I love you for it, Kessa. But I can't live like this."

"You can," Kessa insisted. "I lost my home, my family, my mate. Yet I am still here."

Vy clenched her fists, as if to keep herself from hurting Kessa. "No one deserves to live like this," she said in a measured tone. "You accept horrible things because you don't know any—"

She stopped herself, but Kessa could guess what was left unspoken. *You don't know any better.*

Kessa supposed that she could never comprehend all the wonderful things the humans had lost. They had fallen from paradise. In many ways, they were superior to lifelong slaves, although Kessa did not admit that out loud. Written communication, for example. Writing was too complex for Kessa to memorize in a few nighttime sessions.

So Kessa knew that she ought to feel inferior due to her ignorance.

Instead? She felt her usual burning desire to know everything. She wished she could read minds. If only Vy understood how important knowledge was. Such a treasure should not be thrown away or killed.

"Please," Kessa begged. "Stay. Do not throw your life away."

Weptolyso stabbed his spiky arm across the doorway as someone tried to squirm past him.

"Kessa!" a familiar voice gasped. Pung peered past the guard's arm, gasping for breath as if he'd run all the way from the city above. "Humans, come with me!"

Whatever emergency Pung was panicked about, it was the wrong time for it. Kessa shook her head at him.

"Humans, these are for you." Pung pushed ornately folded robes through the space beneath Weptolyso's arm. "Payment of my favor. You can repay me by coming with me right now."

Kessa hissed. Those robes were far too fine to belong to slaves. Pung had gone too far if he was stealing directly from Torth instead of just smuggling food from kitchen refuse. This was a night of bad luck. Everyone she knew was possessed by spirits of mischief.

"I don't believe it." Vy sounded dazed as she stared at the bundle of robes.

"Believe it," Pung said. "Look." He waved a Torth device, and his collar suddenly went dark.

Kessa stared. A slave should not be able to do that.

"I can deactivate collars," Pung said, breathless. "Now come with me! We have no time for explanations."

Cherise strode forward and snatched the robes. Her face was full of deadly determination.

Delia leaped to her feet.

"Stop!" Kessa shoved herself in front of them, trying to block the doorway along with the hall guard. "You cannot escape. This is a trick." How could Pung be such a witless fool? If they left the Tunnels and tried to escape, everyone in the city would stop them.

"The streets above are mostly empty," Pung said. "We have a chance, but only if we leave this instant."

"Did you get these things from…Thomas?" Vy spoke with caution, as if the name might attack her.

"Yes." Pung spoke desperately, trying peer past the bulk of Weptolyso. "I robbed the richest Torth in the city, and my owner ordered me to do it. He's in the hover harbor near Leftovers Hall right now. He won't wait long!"

Weptolyso heaved a groan that rippled his chest plates. His serrated ridges protruded, adding to his already puffed-up mass. "Nobody leaves this room," he said, and not in his usual friendly tone.

Cherise peered up at Weptolyso, holding the bundled robes to her chest. "Come with us," she invited in her soft voice.

Weptolyso narrowed his beady eyes. He puffed up until his spikes scraped against the metal door frame. "Do you think I enjoy my duty, little human?"

Cherise shrank back.

Weptolyso seemed disgusted. "Please stop this nonsense and go to sleep."

He was right. The whole situation was madness.

"Thomas will not rescue anyone," Kessa said, her tone strangled with disbelief. "We all saw him. He is a Torth."

Pung scrambled to climb up Weptolyso's spinal ridge. He actually climbed to the nussian's shoulder, and from there, he waved something near the guard's face. It looked like a glass vial that glowed faintly green.

"Smell this," Pung said, straining to reach the guard's huge nostrils. "Smell it."

Weptolyso smashed his shoulder against the doorway, causing Pung to fall.

A moment later, Pung popped up in the hallway. "I'm running away!" he shouted at the guard. "Try to stop me." His voice faded as he pattered away. "Farewell, Kessa. Humans—come with me or stay here forever."

Weptolyso began to chase Pung, and then he remembered his duty and hesitated. His spikes retracted and popped out again and again, showing his indecisiveness.

Cherise slipped past him and took off running.

Kessa lunged, but it was too late. She would never catch Cherise or Pung, and if she chased them, she would be marched to prison along with them when they got caught.

Weptolyso could have tackled them. It was his duty to do so. But instead of chasing Cherise and Pung, he gave Kessa a helpless look of anxiety.

Of course he wanted her to handle her friends. An elder such as Kessa could usually talk people out of doing something crazy.

Delia and Vy slipped past the hall guard.

That was too much for Weptolyso. He thundered after them with a groan of dismay, loping on all fours.

All Kessa could think about was that she was losing all her friends at once.

If Weptolyso failed to stop the runaways, he would be tortured to death. Even if he caught them, they would surely be condemned. And Kessa? Alone and miserable, she would still have to wake up for the next work shift, and the next. Back to monotonous drudgery and enforced ignorance.

"*No one deserves to live like this,*" Vy had said, in the language of paradise. She had begged Kessa to come with them if they ever got rescued.

Freedom.

That word sounded sweet in any language, like a return to childhood.

Kessa was running even before she had registered the decision. It was suicidal. All her instincts rebelled against suicide. But beneath her terror, she felt a strange and tenuous hope.

This time, instead of repressing her hope, Kessa welcomed it.

Pung had a device that could deactivate slave collars. Vy, Cherise, and Delia had robes that would enable them to look like Torth. Maybe Thomas really was waiting for them with a stolen vehicle. Maybe Ariock really had powers.

Weptolyso had slowed, as if waiting for Kessa. "I'm coming with you," he said, and he gently scooped her up and placed her on his armored shoulder.

Kessa nearly fell off. She clung to the bases of his shoulder spikes, hat flaps swinging, marveling at the strange glory of running away with help from a hall guard.

"This is insane," Weptolyso admitted. "But I wasn't planning to live as long as you, anyway."

Kessa had forgotten how it felt to take stupid risks. It was a challenge to death itself. Even if they failed, even if they died in their attempt to escape…

"We will be remembered," she said.

CHAPTER 11

HERO

Cherise kept hoping.

Hope was dangerous, especially if she was meant to pass as a Torth in the fancy robe Pung had supplied her with. Her reflection on the mirrored floors was bronze and gold. The stiff collar concealed her neck, with the slave collar wrapped around her throat.

Unbound hair was weird among Torth, but she didn't exactly have time for a hair salon session. So she had twisted it into a loose ponytail. With her glasses hidden in a pocket, she supposed she could pass as a Torth—from a distance. The monsters had a wide variety of skin tones, including hers.

Although any slave who recognized the humans would raise an alarm.

Also, the first Torth who encountered them up close would send them to prison.

Maybe this was Thomas's way of getting them killed? Everything that Thomas had ever said or done on Earth had been fake. He was a liar.

Or was he?

What if he was actually waiting with an escape vehicle?

Cherise followed Pung, trying to suppress the critical voice of her ma nagging at her inner thoughts. Ma would have said that Thomas didn't want her around. Nobody wanted a worthless slave girl.

Vy and Delia peered into every lounge or garden café as if expecting a troop of Red Ranks. Fortunately, the few Torth in the streets seemed pre-occupied with their own mysterious concerns. No one seemed to notice the shine of grime from the Tunnels embedded in their skin, or the fact that their cream and chartreuse robes were a bit too tight.

A pair of bored-looking nussians guarded the enormous, opalescent gates to the hover harbor.

Vy and Delia hesitated, perhaps afraid that the sentries would catch a glimpse of the rags around their worn-out shoes.

But Weptolyso never hesitated. He stuck close to the humans like an overprotective bodyguard.

Ah. This was role-playing.

Cherise glided toward the gates with her ma's haughtiness. Her gaze took in one of the guards and then roved on, dismissing him as if he was just another pillar. And sure enough, the gate guards bowed their heads to her. As far as they were concerned, Torth were to be obeyed, not scrutinized.

Pung and Kessa trudged like slaves who would rather be asleep. They were convincing.

Vy and Delia caught on. Soon the opalescent gates slid open, revealing a vista that Cherise had never seen before.

Empty hovercarts bobbed in a faint breeze, like anchored boats. The array of vehicles stretched to the distant horizon. Clouds of neon lights floated high overhead, and walkways stretched between far-distant walls. Torth moved along aisles and on walkways, trailed by slaves and bodyguards.

There was no sign of Thomas.

Cherise told herself not to be disappointed. Thomas was an untrustworthy liar.

Her friends looked anxious, but hesitation would arouse suspicion, so Cherise walked on. She headed down an aisle between parked hovercarts. The others had little choice but to follow, since they were pretending to be a group of Torth and slaves.

It was too late to go back and try to fade into the obscurity of the Tunnels. At least a few sharp-eyed slaves must have noticed the rags on their feet or recognized them as the human slaves. Memories would be probed.

Thomas was probably fast asleep in his palatial suite.

Cherise clenched her fists. Her palms throbbed where her fingernails dug in. She would like to use her fingernails on that traitor's face, if only to make him feel something. How could he become a Torth?

A gust of wind smelled fresh and sharp, like a thunderstorm.

Beneath a balcony, a huge bay door began to open to the nighttime. City lights silhouetted the hovercart floating through it. A small figure sat at the control panel, ensconced in an ornate silver hoverchair.

Thomas.

He hadn't tricked Pung.

He was really trying to rescue them!

Cherise sprinted toward the opening, legs pumping. The mirrored floor rushed beneath her like a river. Her bronze and gold robe billowed behind her like a sail. She barely felt the effort of running. It felt like flying.

Her ma was wrong about everything!

Cherise vaulted onto the slow-moving platform and kept running until she nearly whacked against the hoverchair. She skidded to a stop and jumped with joy. She reached out and wrapped Thomas in a fierce embrace.

Her hero!

But when she pulled back, Thomas glared at her as if she was a stinking rat. "I hope your mad dash went unnoticed," he said in a tight, cold voice. "Our goal is to not get caught."

Cherise gripped her own arms hard enough to leave bruises.

She had been reckless. She might be an idiot. But was that all she was to Thomas? Was that how he saw her?

Thomas tapped the fancy tablet on his lap. He ignored Cherise as if she was just a worthless burden, just a piece of trash, just a…just…

How dare he.

Cherise let go of her own arms and readjusted her expectations. The frail boy in that hoverchair was a rescuer, a liberator, but he wasn't actually here for her.

Maybe this was an easy romp for him.

Maybe he had put it off for three months because it had seemed like too much inconvenience. He probably didn't want to lose his cushy palace suite.

On Earth, Thomas had been dependent on able-bodied caretakers. He must have felt vulnerable enough to pretend to be kind, just like her ma, pretending to be nice. But as a Torth? This yellow-eyed version of Thomas was empowered to treat his enslaved caretakers however he wished. He was free to abuse them.

This was who he truly was. Arrogant. Abusive.

He had kept his promise to rescue Cherise, but she couldn't guess what his true motives were. He had rarely shared his motives even when they were supposedly best friends on Earth. He had always been secretive.

Did he expect fawning worship for his efforts?

He might anticipate that Cherise was still her old self, still the girl who loved him no matter what. That girl would put up with anything. That girl had never met her own limits of degradation. That girl had been trained by a cruel mother to expect abuse, and to put up with it.

Cherise turned her back on Thomas and walked to far end of the hovercart.

He couldn't read her mind from this distance. She didn't want him peering through her eyes or getting to know whom she'd become.

That was a privilege he would need to earn.

The platform dipped as Vy climbed aboard. Pung followed her, and then Weptolyso, carrying Kessa and Delia under each arm. The rear of the hovercart hit the causeway and bounced. The hoverdisk must have adjusted to the weight.

The bay door had slid closed. Cherise could only hope that no one had seen so many figures rush outside. Thomas had not given them an alternative choice. If he had expected them to find a sneaky way out, then he had expected too much.

Did he really have nothing to say? No welcome speech? No apologies for the torture he had caused?

He was silent. His face was cold and emotionless.

Cherise inwardly vowed to stay on the far side of the hovercart, with her friends. She wanted to thank Thomas for the rescue, but he was a Torth. And she had limits.

She would never bow down and praise a Torth.

CHAPTER 12

SEVERED

Thomas felt insignificant without the Megacosm.

Unknown factors surrounded him, with offshoots of unknown possibilities. For all he knew, an army of Red Ranks was closing in on him. The Giant might be dead. Anything at all might be happening in the Torth Empire.

He needed to find out. He yearned to learn. But if he caved in to that urge, millions of Torth would sense his gigantic mind and glom on to his business. He had an unfortunately recognizable mind, too large to ignore.

Freedom could end at any moment. He had no way of knowing what to expect.

But he had one advantage: the stolen governance tablet on his lap.

The Upward Governess's pass code would stymie any normal person, but Thomas had absorbed her preferences in mathematics, so he had managed to crack the algorithm that refreshed the pass code at regular intervals. It seemed she had not considered Yellow Thomas to be much of a threat.

What a mistake.

She would never recover from this. Using her access, Thomas reprogrammed citywide utilities, rapidly opening menus and making selections. The Torth Majority would probably kill the Upward Governess for screwing up. Even if they allowed her to live, they would strip away her authority over the metropolis of New GoodLife WaterGarden City. They'd demote her to Green Rank or lower. There she would die, bereft of the valuable NAI-12 supply and too lowly to beg for more.

And if she let her inner rage show? They would sentence her to death.

Ha.

For some reason, Thomas didn't feel good about setting his erstwhile mentor up to die. All she'd truly wanted was to live. In a way, defeating the Upward Governess felt like he was celebrating his own unhealthiness and death.

"Thomas?" Vy approached with caution, her hair rippling in the wind. "Are you all right?"

He sensed fear in her hesitation. She saw him as a Torth.

His identity was far too complicated for a *(slave)* human to understand. He didn't entirely understand it himself. So he simply stated, "My goodwill should be obvious."

"It is." Vy sounded doubtful. She peered from him to Cherise and back again. Thomas sensed her unspoken concern for her foster sister, and a question. She wanted to know why Thomas wasn't apologizing.

Vy actually believed that an apology would heal the damage.

She was wrong. Words were clumsy, and any spoken apology Thomas could muster would probably read like a cruel joke to Cherise—far too inadequate. It would reignite her feelings of betrayal. Then he would have to reabsorb her rage and pain—and that much emotional turmoil would incapacitate him.

He couldn't afford to be incapacitated right now.

An apology was dangerous, almost certainly futile, and not worth the return on investment.

It was far healthier, far safer, to stay away from Cherise's mind and ignore her as much as possible.

"I'm busy," Thomas said.

"Oh." Vy eyed the Torth glyphs that scrolled across the governance tablet. "Okay. What are you doing?"

"I'm introducing a flaw in a weather monitoring system." Thomas chose simple words. If only they could read minds, so he could avoid the tedium of explaining basic facts. "This will make it harder for the Torth to find us."

He had to steer the hovercart with one hand while he tapped menu items with the other. Precision driving was paramount. Otherwise they could plunge over the edge of the causeway, into the white-water aqueducts far below. Speed was also important, or they'd miss their chance to escape through the sluice gate he'd reprogrammed.

"He needs to take us to Ariock." Worried anger prickled off Delia, like the spikes of a cactus.

"Where do you think we're going?" Thomas logged out of the networked satellite system, having reprogrammed the terrestrial surveillance monitors to include errors that would be misconstrued. That would trick the Torth into hunting in the wrong direction.

Next, he began to shut down the city's water supply. That would disable half of the power plants and prevent transports from taking off. He couldn't guess when the Torth would figure out that he had gone renegade. He had to work as fast as possible.

"You can help," Thomas said, his voice raspy from disuse. "Turn off our running lights. It's the tiny switch on the underside of the control panel on the far right."

Vy fumbled under the control panel. The dim beads of light around the edge of the hovercart went dark. Thomas steered around each brilliant cone of light on the causeway, sticking to shadows. They should be invisible to the decrepit surveillance system he had sabotaged.

"What changed your mind, Thomas?" Delia stalked closer, using the railing for balance. "Why are you helping us now?"

Kessa eyed her with frustrated annoyance.

Thomas had expected gratitude. The general mistrust radiating from Delia was an unpleasant miasma.

"I spent the last three months collecting opportunities," he explained. "This was the first chance I got to help you escape."

"You're going to need to explain further." Delia loomed over him, threatening.

Thomas wondered if it was even possible for him to describe the ever-shifting audience inside his mind that had spied on his every thought during every waking moment. If his passengers were orbiters in the Megacosm, then he could have communicated it within a few seconds.

"I'm busy." He sounded pathetic, even to himself. "A meaningful conversation will have to wait."

He had a sharp urge to escape from her angry demands. To ascend. It would be so easy to do.

As easy as a thought.

Cold sweat broke out on his forehead. It was ludicrous—shamefully irrational—that he needed to keep reminding himself to stay away from a deadly temptation.

"Delia." Vy pulled her away. "Leave him alone. He rescued us, didn't he?"

"After taking his time. And torturing me." Delia glared at Thomas. "And Cherise. He had access to everything for months and months. He was free to go anywhere. And he couldn't even be bothered to send us a message? Maybe a care package?"

Thomas sensed how much Delia wanted to punish one of the Torth. She wanted vengeance. She wanted it more than freedom.

And when she looked at Thomas, she saw a Torth.

She wasn't wrong.

"I did my best." Thomas reminded himself that his passengers were *(nothing but slaves)* ignorant. "It isn't easy to make plans in a city full of mind readers."

He sensed cautious curiosity from everyone on the hovercart, especially from the aliens.

"Aw, you had it rough." Delia clenched her fists. "We had it worse."

Thomas guessed she was probably right.

Even so, he tried to explain. "I dared not think about you except in the moments when I woke up or fell asleep. If I did anything suspicious, they would have killed me. The Majority was in my mind."

"But they aren't now?" The elder ummin had a mind that blazed with curiosity.

"I'm resisting the Megacosm," Thomas admitted.

"Well, how hard is it, to resist?" Delia's tone was an accusation. "You couldn't have done that three months ago?"

Vy gently pushed the older woman aside. "We don't need to interrogate him right now. He's helping us. And he's fragile."

"Fragile?" Delia growled. "So am I. I'm sick and weak every day." She glared at Thomas. "And I'm sure he knows that."

Thomas glared back. Was Delia really going to complain about her own lack of good health—to the profoundly disabled kid? Really?

"And I'm sure he doesn't care." It seemed Delia was letting loose with a long-suppressed rant directed at her masters. She hardly saw Thomas. She saw a generic Torth.

Vy cut in. "We don't need an argument, Delia. Just leave him alone. He's human. Okay?"

"No," Delia said. "Look at his eyes. He knows everything the Torth know. He tossed away his humanity."

There was a moment of silence, except for the rush of the wind. Doubts and questions radiated from everyone.

They wanted reassurances from Thomas.

Maybe he was supposed to apologize for being an alien hybrid? Or for having owned slaves? Or for being relatively emotionless?

Instead, he challenged Delia with a glare. If she wanted to label him as inhuman? Fine. He wasn't going to pretend to be like her. In many ways, the Torth were truly superior to the slave species. They knew so much more than their slaves. *He* knew so much more.

He wasn't ashamed. He was proud to have a lot of knowledge.

He had nothing else.

"He risked his life to save us," Vy pointed out. "He's on our side."

They sped through a construction zone, zipping beneath overhangs. It was too dark for Thomas to see the service path. He navigated by memorized coordinates and had to hope that he wouldn't accidentally run over a slave.

"Um, hey, Thomas?" Vy explored her darkened collar with her hand. "Is there any way to remove our torture collars?"

Thomas supposed it was a good idea to remove the collars from the humans, at least. They could pass as Torth if glimpsed at a distance. "Pung?" he said, gesturing the ummin forward. "Can you get out my blaster glove? It has a setting to remove slave collars."

Pung inspected the glove's web of buttons.

"Put it on my hand, please," Thomas said impatiently.

Fear spiked from his *(slaves)* traveling companions. Even the monstrous nussian cringed.

Thomas tried not to feel offended. Sure, he looked like a slave master, but he was basically throwing his life away in order to give them a chance at survival. That mattered. Or it should.

"Why don't you teach me how to use it, Torth?" Pung asked.

"It's complicated." Thomas didn't want to explain the overcomplicated unlock sequence, or the criminality of letting slaves use such devices.

Pung reluctantly worked the glove onto Thomas's hand. Thomas tapped it into master mode and swept it past the throat of his slave.

Pung's collar fell away.

The other passengers stepped up to Thomas, one by one. He dared not look at Cherise. An all-consuming black hole of pain seethed within her, barely masked by her sad beauty. He wanted to soothe away that pain. But what could he do?

He was a Torth.

It was a relief when Cherise returned to the far end of the hovercart, beyond his telepathic range.

The others hid their own mixtures of emotion. Vy, at least, understood that he had given up something major in order to enact this rescue. "Thank you," she said.

The most satisfying reaction came from the elder ummin. When the slave collar fell away, Kessa touched the ring of scar tissue around her neck. Thomas sensed her exploring skin she had been unable to touch for nearly a lifetime. Her fingers were tingling caresses.

The radiance of her gratitude was so powerful, Thomas felt a great burden of tension ease away.

He gave her a tentative smile.

Kessa smiled back.

The wind grew rougher and colder as they sped through the outskirts of the metropolis. Reflected lights from skyscrapers danced on the churning water of the aqueduct. Thomas struggled to focus on simple acts. He didn't want to remember everything he was leaving behind.

He didn't want to ponder how the Upward Governess would react to his theft and betrayal.

"Thomas." Delia hesitated. "Is…is my son alive?"

She was clearly afraid to hear the answer.

Lightning still flickered across the horizon, but the storm was clearing up. Perhaps the Torth Empire already knew whether Ariock was alive or dead. Thomas could only make blind guesses.

"We'll find out," he said.

If he managed to rescue the Giant? That would cause a different sort of storm. It would whip the Megacosm into a militant frenzy. They would send armies.

"Why did you sentence Ariock to death?" Delia asked flatly.

"I spoke the sentence," Thomas said in a similar flat tone, "but it wasn't my decision. You should know that."

"So you were just obeying orders." Delia's tone dripped with scornful sarcasm. "What a good little—"

"What do you think I am?" Thomas whirled to confront her. His face burned with unfamiliar emotions. "Boy or monster, I am thirteen years old." He gestured to his frail body. "I'm dying. I can't command armies, and even if I could, I *still* couldn't have helped you. No one defies the Torth Majority, not even the Commander of All Living Things. I risked my life to get a few seconds of private thinking time every day. I couldn't make plans! Do you honestly believe that a dying child can defy thirty-eight trillion Torth? Or even hurt one?" He barked a laugh. "That's quite a flattering misconception of me, really."

Kessa looked fascinated. She stared at him with her beak agape.

Well, he didn't want to be a pitiful object of study.

He wanted to feel powerful again. He wanted to escape the judgmental opinions of his passengers and share the health of other bodies. He wanted to ascend and mingle with admirers and like-minded scientists.

"You're a hero," Vy said.

Delia made a noise of disgusted disagreement.

"Don't count on salvation yet." Thomas focused on the causeway ahead and the dark desert beyond. "I'm doing everything possible, but I'm not a miracle worker."

The Megacosm glowed above him. It felt like having an open doorway inside his mind, one he could never block, which led to a fantastic wonderland.

Thomas wished he had told Pung to pack his tranquility mesh. Why had he been so certain that he wouldn't need it?

He wanted the Megacosm. He wanted it so badly, he almost didn't care about the terrible consequences. This was how the Upward Governess felt when she smelled her favorite pastries—or when she sought his companionship.

He trembled with yearning.

Instead, he forced himself to focus on important tasks such as reprogramming city utilities while driving. He had to stay mired in this dangerous reality, where he was utterly reliant upon people who mistrusted him.

He would resist.

CHAPTER 13

WHERE LIGHTNING STRIKES

Vy turned up the collar of her luxury robe. Even with the thick material, the wind made her shiver. "Are any Torth searching for us yet?" she asked.

"They will be." Thomas sounded uncaring.

He was a lot less forthcoming than he used to be. This yellow-eyed version of her foster brother had some sort of emotional damage. Vy couldn't read his face the way she used to. She couldn't figure out why he was still acting aloof, like a Torth. That made her nervous. What if he relapsed into full Torth mode?

Their hovercart bounced to one side to avoid a pipe that jutted out of the darkness.

Vy turned back to stare. That pipe could have beheaded her or someone else. Thomas had swerved just in time. It was as if he had an exact 3-D map of the canal system in his head.

"You're really good at navigating," she remarked.

"I have poor reflexes," Thomas said. "But I take that into account."

They sped through a drained canal with walls that looked damp. Thomas swiped icons on the incomprehensible dashboard, causing their vehicle to fly around bends at frightening speed. They were reliant on him.

"What's that?" Delia asked in a panic.

Water roared ahead. It sounded like Niagara Falls, echoing off concrete walls. Faraway urban lights weren't enough to illuminate whatever lay ahead, but Vy could smell humidity.

The darkness in front of them looked blacker than it should. There must be a cliff-like waterfall somewhere close.

"I've calculated our velocity, our momentum, and our mass," Thomas said in his uncaring voice. "We'll make it."

They had no time to argue. The hovercart suddenly veered upward, climbing at a steep angle that was almost vertical. The thundering water was almost deafening. If anyone screamed, Vy couldn't hear them. She had to throw herself onto her hands and knees in order to stay balanced.

An enormous pit yawned to one side. If they lost momentum, Vy knew, they would plummet and drown.

They sped along the narrow top of a concrete wall. When they crested its top, the moonlit desert spread before them.

Then they plunged. It was a roller-coaster drop without any track.

Vy expected to hit concrete.

Instead, they bounced on a cushion of air. And they continued to hurtle at top speed across a rocky landscape.

"We could have died." Delia clutched the railing, as if weak.

"Welcome to my life." Thomas didn't seem to care about how shaken everyone else was. "We're attempting to run away from the Torth Empire, so you can expect to die at any time. Get used to it."

His words were harsh. Yet the dry wind felt like freedom.

Vy gazed at the rocky desert with wonder. There were no Torth in sight. No slaves, no sewage, no threats, just inert rocks and sand. The three moons were bright.

She hadn't expected to ever feel this hopeful.

Behind them, the skyscrapers stood like expressionless Torth, accented by neon colors. All was silent except for the rush of wind and ominous rumbles that must be spacecraft in the distance. The few aerial transports looked sedate.

Kessa spoke with quiet wonderment. "This is farther than I knew was possible."

Delia stared at Thomas with an anxious frown, her gray-white hair ruffled by wind.

Thomas shoved the data tablet off his lap. It clattered to the floor, dark and powered off. "It's too risky for us to have this anymore. Other high-ranked Torth have governance access. If we keep the tablet, we can be tracked. Throw it into the desert."

Vy picked up the tablet gingerly, as if it might zap her.

"Give it to the nussian," Thomas said. "Have him throw it as far as possible to one side. The Torth will figure that we went to collect Ariock, but there's no reason to make our route extra easy to retrace."

Weptolyso seemed agreeable. He hurled the tablet into the night.

"Does this hovercart have a tracker in it?" Vy figured that Thomas would have thought of that, but she wanted to make sure.

"I deactivated it using the governance tablet," Thomas explained. "Your slave collars as well. The Torth won't be able to reactivate those trackers. I rekeyed them so they're unregistered, no longer property of any city or of any particular Torth. They're basically rogue junk objects now."

Vy wasn't sure what any of that meant.

But she did know one thing. "You saved us." She would have hugged him, except he didn't look like he would welcome personal contact.

"I can't predict how far we'll get," Thomas said in a tight voice. He avoided eye contact.

"Is that Ariock?" Kessa pointed to the rocky horizon.

All three moons were full and bright, silhouetting a shape on the tallest hill. The cross leaned at a sharp angle. It had almost fallen over.

"Sand from the storm buried the surveillance equipment," Thomas said. "We have to be quick. Now that the storm is over, tourists will want to get here to witness the dead or dying Giant."

"Tourists?" Vy asked painfully.

Thomas did not deign to answer. They raced downslope, wind rushing past. Upslope felt like an eternity.

When they finally crested the ridge, they glided into a wonderland of squiggly rocks.

It reminded Vy of the aftermath of ice storms, where every twig of every tree got encased in glossy ice crystals. But these crystals were dark and sinister.

"Ariock," Delia whispered.

The cross had all but toppled. Ariock was a shadowy figure, still chained atop the contraption.

"Is he...?" Delia didn't seem to have the nerve to finish her question.

Ariock's gladiator armor could not have entirely protected him from the wind-driven sand, or from whatever had warped all these squiggly sand sculptures into existence.

"I don't know." Judging by Thomas's frustrated tone, not knowing was worse than torture.

Squiggle-rocks shattered like fragile glass as their hovercart plowed over them. Before Vy could ask what had caused such a weird phenomenon, Thomas answered.

"These squiggle-rocks are lightning sand," Thomas said. "Fulgurite formations." He looked a little bit fearful as he scanned the rocky wonderland.

The whole ridge must have shaken with sheets of violent electricity, to kick up so many sprays of sand and to fuse those sprays into crystallized rock.

And Ariock was chained to the equivalent of a lightning rod.

Vy bit her lip. There was no way Ariock could have survived. His corpse would probably be gruesome after he'd hung in chains for more than eight hours, scorched by the sun and then scoured by sand and electrical burns.

She needed to protect Delia from the trauma of seeing that.

She needed to inspect his body and let the others know what condition he was in.

Vy vaulted over the hovercart railing before the platform slid to a complete stop. Alien rocks crunched and shattered under her makeshift rag-boots. She would give anything to hear Ariock's deep voice again, but she might as well wish for magical powers while she was at it. She might as well wish for Jonathan Stead to smite the Torth Empire.

Ariock's beard and hair were a tangled mess. But he merely looked like he was asleep, not tortured to death.

No nails, Vy realized.

This wasn't a traditional crucifixion. Instead of hammered nails, Ariock was supported by chains. There were iron spikes embedded in his forearms, with chains locked onto them, but no sign of damage from those spikes. The disfigurement must have been done months ago.

Vy reached toward his parched lips. She didn't dare to expect breath.

Yet Ariock was breathing.

"How is this possible?" Vy asked.

CHAPTER 14

FREEDOM TO FEEL

Vy turned in a circle, searching for an explanation for why Ariock was only slightly sunburned rather than a charred corpse. The spray pattern of the rocks radiated outward. It looked as if an unknown force had repelled the lightning in order to protect him.

She didn't think Torth technology had protected him.

"You'll find a bladed relic in my hoverchair compartment," Thomas was saying. "It has a fancy handle, and the blade is ionic steel, which can slice through most materials, including iron and bone. Use it to cut his chains. Just be ultracareful not to slice anywhere near skin. I only brought a very limited supply of healing foam."

Delia gave him a mistrustful look, but she knelt by his hoverchair to rummage through its compartment.

"What protected him?" Vy asked.

"We can have this conversation later," Thomas said.

His iridescent yellow eyes seemed as uncaring as the gaze of any Torth. What did he know that the rest of them did not?

Delia brandished a dagger. Its sheath glimmered like dark metal, engraved with something like a serpentine dragon or a flying lizard. When Delia unsheathed it, a wavy-edged blade glimmered in the moonlight like wet glass.

The ionic dagger was more elegant than any weapon Vy had ever seen.

Thomas had called it a relic. Did it come from a conquered alien civilization? Vy supposed it must have, because this did not look like utilitarian Torth craftsmanship.

"The Torth sure trusted you with weapons," Delia said dryly.

"I'm not strong enough to stab anyone," Thomas pointed out. "I can't reach my blaster glove without help. I'm never going to be an assassin."

Indeed, Thomas had piloted their hovercart only with difficulty. He must be exhausted from that much movement.

Kessa hopped off the hovercart. "All Torth own weapons," she informed Delia.

"Including Torth children." Thomas waggled his gloved hand. "Torth trust each other because we can't lie to each other. And we see close-range attacks coming before the attacker goes into action."

Kessa gave him an appraising look. She had the same intense interest whenever the humans taught her something new.

"No, Torth don't hurt each other," Thomas said, probably answering an unvoiced question from Kessa. "Unless the Majority commands them to do so. Like, they'll all want to hurt me."

"Do they ever make individual decisions?" Delia approached her gigantic son.

"They're a hive mind by choice," Thomas said. "Not by nature. They can think individually."

Vy imagined a hive of hornets. "Is there a queen in charge?"

"There's an elected official who administrates galaxy-wide endeavors," Thomas said. "The Commander of All Living Things. The current Commander is female, so I guess you could think of her as an elected queen."

Vy recalled the gaunt woman with horned shoulders and a shroud-like cape. Was that her? "Did she order Ariock's crucifixion?"

"Yes."

"Why?" Vy could not imagine why Ariock was considered a matter of galactic importance. Why did he warrant a public execution? Why did tourists want to see him die?

Thomas did not answer. All he said was "Let's hurry it up. We don't have time for a Q and A session."

Delia was already slicing one of the chains. Ariock's arm fell as dead weight. The motion should have woken him. It did not.

"He's dehydrated," Vy guessed. "He must have low blood pressure from hanging like that. He desperately needs water."

"I brought canteens," Thomas said. "But I'm sorry, reviving him should wait until we're on our way. We have to cover a lot of distance ASAP."

Chunks of metal clunked to the ground. Vy joined Delia, supporting parts of Ariock while his mother cut the chains that held him. When Ariock began to slide off the cross, Weptolyso caught his upper body in gentle, stubby hands.

Vy helped Weptolyso carry Ariock to the hovercart. She had the unsettling anxiety that her slave collar was going to zap her, or pinch her, any second. Was it really gone?

She felt free.

As soon as everyone was aboard the hovercart, Thomas made it lurch into motion. They skimmed in silence across an undulating desert, away from the city with its superfast flying vehicles.

Ariock took up most of the floor space. Vy knelt next to him with a canteen. She let a trickle of water fall over his cracked lips. She fed him small amounts of water until he swallowed. Then a little more.

Ariock whispered something that sounded like a question. He might have said, "...Vy?"

That made her smile.

"Where are we going?" Delia asked.

If Thomas said anything, it was lost in the wind. He seemed focused on driving.

Were any of the stars actually satellites with eyes on the desert? Every time they crested a hill, Vy felt exposed.

"Thomas," Delia said sharply. "Where are you taking us?"

No reply.

Vy glanced at Thomas. Did he have any concept of how it felt to spend months in total ignorance? Delia's anger was misplaced, but surely it was understandable. Delia had spent months grappling with deadly cancer and then more months feeling helpless to save her son. Of course she yearned for some way to reassert control over her situation.

They all deserved answers.

And a kind word or two.

The human version of Thomas had valued kindness. He used to express sympathy toward the people he lived with or worked with. He would apologize for being inconvenient. He had said nice things to Cherise when she was feeling down.

That used to be normal for him.

He used to be the kind of person who would say, "I'm sorry the Torth hurt you," even if he wasn't responsible for the damage. He used to strive to make Cherise smile.

What was wrong with him?

"We want answers, Torth." Pung sounded defiant. "Where are we going?"

"We deserve to know," Delia said.

The hovercart slowed. They were suddenly coasting, losing speed.

"Heh," Thomas said.

Everyone else glanced at each other, wondering what that meant.

Thomas began to chuckle.

At least, it started that way. Then he began to scream with wild, uncontrolled laughter. He wheezed, tears streaming down his face.

Every time he regained some self-control, he lost it again, laughing as if he was helpless to stop.

Vy had never seen Thomas lose control like this. She felt torn between wanting to hug him and staring in horror.

"Get us moving, Torth," Pung demanded. "Or I will kill you." He darted forward and seized the blaster glove off Thomas's hand. He worked the glove onto his own sharp-fingered hand.

Thomas continued to heave with laughter. "You'd be lucky to press the right buttons!" he cackled, speaking the slave tongue with perfect fluency.

Pung made a furious inspection of the glove.

Kessa put a restraining hand on Pung's arm. "Don't." She watched Thomas with fascination.

"I never thought…" Thomas had to pause between maniacal laughter. "I never thought about…" He screamed with hilarity. "…where to go!" He laughed so hard, he might slide off his seat. "Thinking was too dangerous!"

The rest of them were silent as their predicament sank in.

Thomas's humor drained away so fast, it gave Vy chills to watch. "I don't belong here."

Stars glittered above, as distant and uncaring as Torth.

"I can't be here." Thomas gazed toward the glow of the city on the horizon. His face was stony, as if he'd never smiled in his life.

Vy could not believe that he would actually endanger them all by going back.

But Thomas slid the control glyphs. The hovercart rotated and began to gain speed.

In the wrong direction.

They leaped over hills and plunged through troughs, racing toward the distant skyscrapers.

Vy was too shocked to react. If there were such things as emotional brakes and steering, then Thomas's system was broken.

"I have to go back," Thomas said feverishly. "I have to go back."

CHAPTER 15
A MATTER OF JUSTICE

"Stop!"

"Turn around!"

Yellow Thomas ramped up the speed and ignored the runaway slaves. They hadn't been worth rescuing. He realized that now. Intellect was far superior to emotions. The Torth Empire was successful because of its superior values.

The runaway hall guard took a menacing step toward Yellow Thomas. He stopped, though. Nobody quite had enough nerve to attack an insane telepath.

The elder ummin leaned against the railing and studied him with her gray eyes. "Torth," she said in a conversational tone, "you are outnumbered, in exile, and surrounded by people you have harmed. If you continue ordering us around, then I have greatly misjudged the intellect of your species."

This particular slave understood the balance of power here.

Yellow Thomas surreptitiously studied her mind, although he pretended to ignore her. Kessa. She was an observant ummin.

"Even if you did drag us back," Kessa went on in her fluent-yet-careful English, "we would all die. Including you."

Yellow Thomas acknowledged that with a nod. It was obvious.

Couldn't they see that he was dead already? No matter where he went, his own death was inevitable within months. His few remaining vials of NAI-12 were too little, too late.

So why not die among his people, the Torth?

At least the Torth didn't hate him. Trillions of orbiters might join him when he suffered in the Isolatorium, just for the novelty of participating in the unique death of a renegade supergenius. That was surely better than dying alone. Wasn't it?

"At least I'd die with a shred of honor," Yellow Thomas pointed out.

The valor of returning would make him memorable, as far as renegades went. He alone was brave enough to admit that he had committed inexcusable crimes. He deserved death.

Maybe the Torth Majority would be merciful enough to allow him to bask in the Megacosm between bouts of torture?

He yearned to ascend right now. He shook with yearning.

But first, he needed to prove just how much he regretted his crimes. If he showed up in the Megacosm right now, the Majority would reject him. They'd shove him out as a criminal. He wanted bliss, not rejection, so first he had to prove that he was at least a tiny bit sane, worth having—

Delia shoved his hoverchair aside. "We can figure out how to drive this thing ourselves." She pushed glyphs.

The controls were purposely complex, designed to prevent slaves from figuring out how to operate machinery. Her attempts failed.

"Are you really going to send us to die?" Vy asked. "Are you going to hang Ariock back on that cross?"

The words made a sharp feeling twist inside Yellow Thomas. The way the Torth Majority had forced him to sentence Ariock to death…and to hurt Cherise…

That bothered him.

There was something sickeningly illogical and irrational about the way the Torth Majority had casually changed its collective mind.

Oh, and its hypocrisy. Ariock was a dangerous Yeresunsa, and Yellow Thomas was also a dangerous Yeresunsa. They ought to share the same fate. If Yellow Thomas was certain of anything, it was that. He should not be relatively free and healthy while Ariock lay injured on the floor.

Why had the Torth Majority granted boons to one while executing the other one?

That was a grave injustice. It ought to register as an injustice to the Torth Empire, not just to slaves. Why hadn't it?

Yellow Thomas couldn't just ignore that question. It felt enormously important.

He reached for the control glyphs, and they sloughed off speed.

Maybe he was unfit to judge the mighty Torth Majority. He was only a flawed solo individual. An exile. He was nothing.

Yet he thought that the Torth Majority had made what seemed like a grave error in judgment. When he imagined allowing them to complete the unjust execution of the Giant…

"No," he realized. "I can't do that."

The stolen hovercart drifted in a trough between hills, pushed by the wind.

Yellow Thomas felt similarly unanchored. He looked from the glowing horizon to the opposing darkness, torn between two futures.

Shouldn't he return to his people? The metropolitan glow beckoned to him, offering familiarity.

And torture.

The opposite direction was a vast, mysterious future where anything might lurk.

"Thomas?" Ariock said weakly.

Delia gave him a motherly look of concern. "Ariock. You need rest."

If Yellow Thomas aided these runaway slaves, and if Ariock later killed innocent Torth, then the Torth Majority would have been right all along. Yellow Thomas did not want to prove them right. Nor did he wish to be responsible for a deadly rampage.

Maybe he should connect to the Megacosm right now? He could confess his crimes and let the Torth Empire take care of business.

Then again, an epic disaster would also prove that the Torth Majority should have condemned Yellow Thomas alongside Ariock *(the Giant)* from the start.

They had failed to do so.

They had embraced him. They had welcomed him as a fellow Torth. The Upward Governess had pressured her orbiters to accept Yellow Thomas because she secretly wanted his happy memories. She had also desired his help in stoking her secret ambitions.

Her greedy secret ambitions had influenced public opinion.

So the elected leaders of the galaxy had lazily welcomed Yellow Thomas as well. Perhaps they had been swayed by public pressure, or maybe it was just inertia. Maybe they had their own unknown or secret reasons. The whole Torth Majority had welcomed him. They had adopted Yellow Thomas while condemning Ariock as a worthless non-telepathic monster.

The Torth Majority had made a mistake.

That mattered.

Justice mattered.

Starlight bored down on them, and Thomas edged toward a decision.

CHAPTER 16

THE DARK HORIZON

Ariock made an effort to sit up, to see everyone. He used the railing as a back-rest. Shackles and broken chains clanked when he moved.

"You need rest," his mother pleaded.

She looked different from when they'd lived on Earth. Her hair had gone mostly white. The luxurious outer robe she wore could not hide how emaciated she was or the discoloration around her neck, where the slave collar had been.

She had suffered.

They all had. That was obvious. Vy was sweet and beautiful, but she needed to regain the weight she'd lost. Cherise looked traumatized. Thomas was disturbingly different, too, with those creepy yellow eyes.

Yet they had come together and risked their lives to save Ariock from certain death.

"I owe you my life," Ariock told them all, hoping to defuse some of the tension against Thomas. "I was sure that I would breathe my last breath. And then you saved me." He met their gazes one by one, including the beaked aliens and the thorny one. "If I die fighting to defend us, then I will die well."

The thorny guard blinked as if shocked. Then he spoke in a gravelly voice, with a heavy accent. "If I die fighting, I die well."

Ariock couldn't help but stare in shock. None of the prison guards had spoken out loud, ever. He had never gotten the impression that they understood his pleas for help.

"It's a nussian proverb," Vy explained.

"Nussian?" Ariock asked.

Vy nodded toward the enormous guard, who seemed to be admiring Ariock with a look of grave respect. "That's what species Weptolyso is. He's from Nuss. We call them nussians." She grinned at Ariock. "I think you just made a friend."

Ariock had not known that the aliens were even capable of conversation.

He had questions, but before he could begin, Thomas spoke up. "You don't need to make that promise," he stated. "Take it back."

"He's right." Ariock's white-haired mother closed her eyes briefly, looking like she would rather be struck by lightning than agree with Thomas. "You don't owe anyone anything. I don't want you risking your life to protect anyone, especially not a Torth. Which is what *he* is."

Ariock was alarmed by her hatred. Anyone could take a glance at Thomas and see how weak and young he was.

"Whatever Thomas did in order to survive," Ariock said evenly, "it's over. He's here now. He risked his life to be here, like the rest of us."

"Honey." His mother sounded exasperated. "Ten seconds ago, he decided to get us all killed."

Thomas looked uncertain, his yellow eyes reflecting the glow over the hills.

"But he stopped," Ariock pointed out. "I think he's afraid. And confused."

"Torth don't get afraid or confused." Thomas's response was so immediate, it was as if he'd been trained to say it.

Ariock met his gaze. "You did what you had to do in order to survive. That doesn't mean you're one of them. You're not a…" He hesitated, the word still alien to him. "A Torth."

"Human." Thomas glanced down, as if collecting his thoughts. "I'm not the person you remember. I'm not friendly." He gave Ariock a cold look. "I wish I could tell you that my time as a Yellow Rank citizen of the Torth Empire was an act. But the act was my time on Earth. I never belonged among humans." He gazed toward the city. "I never should have come out here."

"You came out here for a reason," Ariock insisted. "You rescued me for a reason."

Thomas looked troubled. "I didn't make plans," he said. "I couldn't plan anything."

"You had the Torth use chains on me instead of nails." Ariock sat up straighter. "So I survived instead of bleeding to death. You did that on purpose."

The others reassessed Thomas.

Miserable uncertainty crept into Thomas's face.

Delia stood up. She was Ariock's mother, but he knew that everyone else saw her almost as a stranger, a runaway slave. Her softness was gone. Her kindness seemed to have been erased.

"Take a look at what he did to Cherise." Delia flung her hand in that direction. "Just look!"

Cherise did look damaged in some unknown way. She sat on the far end of the hovercart with her hands around her knees. Bangs and glasses hid her eyes.

"She would have done anything for him," Delia went on. "And he tortured her. I was there. And guess what? He gave me a pain seizure, too."

Thomas gave a nod, as if acknowledging some shameful facts.

That was difficult to take in. Ariock sank a little, trying not to imagine his enslaved mother suffering at the whim of a smug child.

"He saved us," Delia admitted. "But I can't help but wonder if he's also the reason we got enslaved in the first place."

Thomas didn't defend himself. He said nothing.

"If we're going to be truly free," Delia said, "we can't rely on him." She gestured at a pile of discarded slave collars. "He took those off us. He's in control of all the technology, and he knows everything we need to know. We're utterly reliant on him. Is that really freedom?"

She had made a salient point. Everyone looked suddenly contemplative.

But Ariock was too exhausted to seize true freedom right this second. It might be nice to be in control of his own destiny, but wasn't that sort of a fantasy? They were stranded on an alien planet. Torth might hunt them with armies. They would not survive without Thomas's knowledge.

Even if Thomas had a cruel streak, they needed him. And they needed him as a friend, willing and cooperative, not as an uncooperative enemy prisoner.

So Ariock restated his promise. "I won't let anyone here die before I die. That includes Thomas. He's under my protection."

"Ariock. This is…" His mother closed her eyes, as if seeking a euphemism. "He has all the power here. If you give him an inch, he will take everything. The direction we travel in shouldn't be his decision. It should be ours."

That was idealistic.

Ariock gave up on arguing with his mother and spoke directly to the boy. "Thomas, you have the power to condemn us. Or you can give us a chance. All I can do is stand by my promise." He had not spoken in so many months, his throat felt raw. "I'll protect you no matter what you decide."

Thomas sat at the control panel, not touching anything. He looked from one horizon to the other. Death or life.

Finally, he flopped his head back and yelled at the stars. "Why do I always have to make these huge decisions?"

That did not ease anyone's fears. Delia narrowed her eyes in disgust.

But Ariock felt as patient as the desert. "We'll die if we go back," he admitted. "I'd do my best, but I can't protect us from Torth armies. If we go the other way…?" He gazed toward the darkest hills, beyond which were all the possibilities in the universe. "We'll have a chance." He nodded toward Thomas. "Including you."

Thomas sounded offended by the possibility of having a future. "A chance. Can't you see I'm dying?" He gestured to his withered body. "No one can save me."

"I won't let you die before I do," Ariock said. "That's a promise."

Delia looked outraged.

"Take it back!" Thomas demanded. "My medical supply will last one more month at the most, unless I try to stretch it out. The Torth will be hunting for us the whole time. They have drones and missiles and slaves and endless armies!"

"Then let's not go to the Torth," Ariock said in a reasonable tone.

"There's nothing else!" Thomas indicated the desert. "Just canyons and slave farms, all of which are owned by Torth. They own everything! Even if you fought off an army, we'd still be facing angry natives or who knows what else!"

The others gaped, impressed. This apparently mattered to Thomas.

"You can't save me." Thomas sounded pained. "Too many people want me dead. Plus, my former slave isn't too fond of me." He gestured to one of the beaked aliens. "And your mom might be persuaded to kill me under the right circumstances. She hates Torth. I'm a Torth." He glared at Ariock. "And I'm doomed. There's nothing you can do about it. So you'd better take back that stupid promise! I didn't save you just so you can die like an idiot."

Ariock tried not to sound too curious. "Then why did you save me?" He suspected the answer would solve a lot of mysteries.

Thomas appeared at a loss for words. "I..." Either the answer was too complicated for him to unravel, or he didn't want to reveal it.

He reached for the control panel.

His hand hovered there for a moment. He glanced toward the glowing horizon of distant skyscrapers, full of regret and yearning.

Their platform lurched into motion. They swung toward the dark horizon.

Cold wind whipped away tension. Everyone visibly sagged with relief, their faces relaxing. The platform raced at what felt like top speed, bounding over hills, away from the city.

"You'll regret that promise," Thomas told Ariock with crisp finality. "I'm always one step away from death."

CHAPTER 17

COLLECTIVE GRATITUDE

The Upward Governess had never fasted for long enough to feel famished. And she rarely slept for long.

The wrongness of hunger brought her wide-awake.

Daylight streamed through the skylights of her ornate cupola, and that was another hint that something was terribly amiss, because she could not recall how she'd spent the night. Had she eaten her evening dessert?

The last thing she recalled was setting up some missile launchers from orbit, just in case the Giant somehow overcame the inhibitor serum and went on a rampage. Had she fallen asleep in the middle of that task? Had she watched him die?

She should remember. Her memory was infallible.

Slaves prodded each other, and pair by pair, their terrified eyes focused on her. An injection of NAI-12 always woke her if she tried to sleep for longer than six hours. Clearly, her slaves had failed to administer her regular dose of NAI-12. It seemed her medical alert had likewise failed.

Because her modified wristwatch was gone.

So was her precious, life-giving case full of medicine.

And her governance tablet.

Stolen.

The Upward Governess clutched her sheets in an effort to contain a tidal wave of raw, filthy emotions. *HOW DARE HE.*

The clues made it obvious what had happened and who had masterminded it. Of all the people in the universe, only Yellow Thomas coveted her medicine and lived close enough to feasibly obtain it. Only he would have figured out how to sneak into her bedchamber while she was there, without her being aware of it, and gotten away with it. Only he would have risked his life to commit such a heinous crime.

I will see him dead, she thought.

It was a strange thought to have. She had never wished anyone to die until now. She had never killed anyone, not even a slave. The sounds and odors of slaughter usually repulsed her.

Yet he was a criminal, was he not? A traitor to the Torth Empire. He might have found fault with her mentorship, but that was no reason to steal from her, shame her, and ensure her death. Not after all she'd done for him. She had engineered an opportunity for him to join the rulers of the known universe, which was a difficult feat, given the facts that he was a Yeresunsa and a hybrid raised by savages. She had saved his life several times over.

Not only had she gifted him with extra luxuries, not only had she expended her own precious time and effort to persuade other Torth that he was worth saving…she had done everything possible to enable him to win half of the precious medicine supply. She had offered him a chance to become her equal partner.

They would have been unstoppable together.

Instead? The ingrate had snatched away her future.

She would die as an obese abnormality, as weak as an infant. She might only have weeks left.

It was all his fault.

The Megacosm must be frothing with news. The Majority would expect the Upward Governess to control whatever disaster the Betrayer had unleashed. Well, she would, of course, but she needed to get into a civilized mood before she ascended. Her current state of mind was unfit for company.

She demanded a fruit smoothie for breakfast, plus the usual assortment of enriched breads. Her contrite slaves leaped to obey. Other slaves and guards put her through her usual morning hygiene processes, and she felt their stark terror, their certainty of a painful death. They knew that they deserved prison for allowing her medicine to be stolen.

But she decided to allow them to live. Replacing slaves and bodyguards was tiresome, and she had more important things to do.

It wasn't fair. NAI-12 had given her hope of living to adulthood and beyond. With the boost of an extra year or two, she had been on track to pioneer a specialized life support system designed to nourish and sustain a severed-but-living brain. Severed from her biological body, her brain should cease to feel gnawing hunger and discomfort. A purely mechanical body would be impervious to damage and illness and aging. And then she wouldn't need medicine. She wouldn't be reliant on the Torth Majority or anyone else.

Why did the Betrayer hate her? His disloyalty hurt like a physical cramp that she couldn't soothe with pain medication.

He had betrayed everyone in the galaxy, not just her. It must have something to do with his vestigial devotion to humankind.

And to one slave in particular.

When the Upward Governess pictured the one with black hair and glasses (Cherise), fondness bubbled from memories that were not her own.

She stamped down the mental simulacrum of Thomas Hill, the boy from Earth. Let him *(the Betrayer)* watch his precious runaway slave suffer and die. Let him see how useless his crimes had been.

The Upward Governess sipped her fruit smoothie. At last, she felt calm enough to ascend. She absolutely had to know what was happening.

ESCAPED!!!

Trillions of minds rocked the Megacosm with news updates. Almost everyone in the Torth Empire was interested in the same topic.

The Betrayer (formerly known as Yellow Thomas) has freed the Giant.

The Betrayer shall suffer in the Isolatorium for crimes against civilization.

Many minds shared replays of evidence: broken chains and shattered rocks, strewn around the fallen metal cross where the Giant was supposed to have hung by his wrists until dead.

If you value your safety,

  avoid travel in the southern hemisphere of Umdalkdul.

Historians and combat experts found themselves mobbed by anxious minds who wanted to know more about Yeresunsa.

The Giant is particularly dangerous,

  having inherited his powers from Jonathan Stead.

  Estimates suggest that he is more powerful than his great-grandfather.

  Check out this theory about hybrid amplitude.

  Stacked genetics magnifies inherited mutations.

Interest surged in the Dovanack family and, in particular, the family patriarch, Jonathan Stead. Many Torth demanded long-dead replays of Jonathan Stead as he cracked the Great Plaza in half with his powers and sent hundreds of Red Ranks screaming to their deaths.

We are better prepared this time, Crimson Ranks and military Servants of All assured everyone.

  Factories are mass-producing the inhibitor serum.

  Every Torth on the affected planet (Umdalkdul) will soon be armed with inhibitor microdarts.

  Find the enemies.

  Here is what they look like.

Images flitted through the Megacosm, memorized glimpses of the Betrayer and the Giant, along with six runaway slaves.

  Try to capture them alive.

  Except for the Giant.

  Destroy the Giant by any means necessary.

The Upward Governess approved of that goal. The Giant had already endured his requisite torture. If he gained awareness of his powers—and the

Betrayer would probably try to weaponize him—and if he gained time with which to practice, he might destroy a city full of innocent people. He was the biggest threat since Jonathan Stead.

It's the Upward Governess!

Many minds sensed her enormous mental presence and flocked to her, drawing their own audiences, and others, into her orbit.

She's finally here!

It took her long enough to show up.

Nearly everyone knew that the Upward Governess was the Betrayer's erstwhile mentor. Everyone knew that she was the eldest supergenius alive.

Advise Us, the masses begged. *How can We end this crisis?*

High ranks had a much colder reaction.

The Upward Governess gravely misjudged the Betrayer.

After all her boasts that she never makes a mistake,

she made a disastrous error.

Is she even worthy of her title?

Is she even fit to govern?

The Upward Governess stopped drinking her smoothie. She could hardly believe what they were implying. Demotion? She had contributed far more to the collective knowledge of the empire than anyone else alive. She had earned every promotion many times over. If not for her mutation, she would be a Servant of All. Surely she deserved some leeway.

Does she? Doubts bounced back and forth throughout her massive audience.

Does the Upward Governess deserve any leeway whatsoever?

Although the Upward Governess had anticipated censure, it was worse than expected.

I misjudged the Betrayer, she admitted. *But it wasn't My fault. We All (the Torth Majority) made that mistake together.*

She showed them a conjecture of how the Betrayer must have sent a slave into her suite, armed with a subtle drug that made her fall asleep. She had been utterly helpless, at the mercy of a thieving runaway slave.

I am lucky to be alive, she admitted with a shudder. The Betrayer could have instructed his corrupt slave to smother her, or strangle her, while she was unconscious. Why hadn't he? No one could have saved her in time.

Pathetic. A ripple of disdain passed between the listening Servants of All.

Distant Torth assessed her.

UNWORTHY, they chorused.

Anyone could guess what would come next.

I was wrong, the Upward Governess hastily assured her billions of listeners. *Many of You evaluated the Betrayer correctly, and I bow before Your wiser judgment. I am humbled. My shame at having misjudged him (to this great degree) runs deep. My honor is wounded. I wish to aid the hunt in any way possible. Use My memory and My processing capabilities, if You find Me fit to serve. I only wish to protect the Torth Empire. The Betrayer must be stopped at any cost.*

The Majority swirled with collective gratitude.

Few supergeniuses are so cooperative, they grudgingly admitted to each other.

At least the lower ranks understood her value. Many chorused that she didn't deserve so much blame. *Everyone misjudged the Betrayer*, they reminded their peers. *Everyone, from the lowliest babies to the Commander of All Living Things.*

Do you have any ideas on how to catch the Betrayer? they begged the Upward Governess.

Servants of All and high ranks made it a command. *Instruct Us in how you would find him.*

The Upward Governess swallowed the dregs of her smoothie. *I have ideas. But first…* She wiped her moist fingers on an embroidered silk napkin. *Let's remember that he stole an extraordinarily valuable item. NAI-12 can further the Empire, and it must be recovered. Let the Betrayer die or send him to the Isolatorium, but save My medicine.*

Servants of All exchanged silent doubts. They were uncomfortable with giving the Upward Governess any sort of reward.

The Commander of All Living Things joined the conversation, her presence enlarged by her own massive audience.

The Upward Governess is a productive and loyal citizen. Her mind had an ironic undertone, as if she harbored personal doubts. *Let's try to save that medicine. Whether or not We reward the Upward Governess depends on how well she performs. Let's see how quickly she can locate the Betrayer.*

Fair enough.

The Upward Governess began to divide her focus, spinning off instructions to hundreds of subordinates, before she realized that her authority was gone.

If I may be so bold, she thought, consolidating her mind for maximum impact. *I can only guarantee success if this hunt is under My command. The time it takes for ordinary minds to second-guess My instructions would give the Betrayer too much of an advantage.*

Their doubts waxed strong. Servants exchanged milky-eyed looks.

He is a RENEGADE SUPER-GENIUS, the Upward Governess emphasized. *That makes him more dangerous than any threat the Empire has faced in modern times. He's more dangerous than Jonathan Stead or any Yeresunsa. He will exploit advantages more ruthlessly than any of You can predict. Every second gives him opportunities.* She had to keep her exasperation under control. *Not only can he teach himself how to use his illegal powers, but he can also train the Giant. We must put someone competent in charge.* She hesitated. *It should be Me.*

Suspicions swirled.

The Upward Governess knew she was taking a risk, but she had nothing to lose. *Give Me direct governance of every factory, spaceport, and army on this planet. It is temporary. And necessary! If I fail, You can kill Me. I only wish to serve.*

Thousands of Servants of All processed her offer with their usual mixture of skepticism, apathy, and disdain.

The Commander of All Living Things studied the towering mind of the Upward Governess, searching for weakness. *You guarantee success?*

The Upward Governess did not hesitate. This was a matter of life or death. In such matters, she would always choose survival. *Yes.*

Then you shall command the hunt, the Commander of All Living Things decided. *With your expertise, I trust that We will have the Betrayer in custody within four days.*

At most, the Upward Governess agreed.

And if you fail... the Commander did not need to concretize the threat. Failure meant demotion and death.

Servants of All ratified the Upward Governess's temporarily expanded authority, grumbling with reservations. And she spun commands while attacking the rest of her breakfast.

The Betrayer would never harm her again.

She would make sure he never got the chance.

PART FIVE

*Mind readers shall misjudge him, for the Bringer of Hope
is deaf to their speech and blind to their plans. They do not understand
that he hears and sees more than they do.*

—preserved scrap from the lost Prophecies of Ah Jun

CHAPTER 1

AN HOUR TO BREATHE

The moonlit night brightened in shades of sepia, then dark gold. A band of fiery light limned the horizon.

The alien sunrise was unlike anything Ariock had ever seen.

Last night, he had been certain that he'd never live to see dawn. He had a million questions for his rescuers, but instead of catching up with them, he'd slept on and off, lulled by painkillers and the motion of their open-air vehicle. Their hovering platform continued to roll over rocky hills like a boat over a choppy sea.

The smallest alien, Kessa, had interrogated Thomas all night. "So," she went on, "we are all within your range?" She indicated the length of the platform. "Does that mean you know everything about me?" She sounded fascinated. "Even things I have forgotten?"

Thomas made a grumpy sound. He hadn't slept, driving their vehicle and answering questions all night.

"How many days have passed since I was hatched?" Kessa asked.

Thomas answered in an emotionless tone. "You don't remember being hatched. Therefore, I can only extrapolate a rough estimate."

He sounded less friendly than Ariock remembered from Earth. His eyes were no longer purple, but an android-yellow color.

"Can you count how many bits of sand are in this desert?" Kessa gestured.

"I can extrapolate a semi-accurate count," Thomas said.

His dismissiveness didn't seem to bother Kessa. Ariock still marveled at her fluency in English, since she was clearly an alien, with gray skin and a flesh-covered beak. She must have learned the language from his mother and Vy. The other two friendly aliens seemed less than fluent.

Kessa went on, relentless. "How fast can you count? If you glance at my outfit"—she indicated her rags—"do you add up all the threads without effort, all at once?"

"That cognitive ability is called subitization," Thomas said. "All people and animals can subitize small amounts. My mutation enables me to process several hundred things at once, orders of magnitude faster than a normal mind. I can sum up the threads of your rags with relative accuracy, within a millisecond."

Kessa's brow ridges rose. She looked impressed. "Can all Torth do that?"

"No." Thomas sounded as if that suggestion was ridiculous. "Ordinary Torth subitize up to seven, the same as ordinary humans."

Kessa cocked her head, causing the flaps of her hat to swing. "Can I subitize more than seven?"

Thomas gave her a look that bordered on respect. "Good inference. Yes, ummins score high on cognition tests. Your species can subitize up to twenty-five."

Ariock stretched his legs. He wished he didn't take up so much of the floor space, but he had been in the same position for too long. He needed to move.

He was careful not to bump into anyone, especially Vy. She had acted as his nurse all night, making sure he had painkillers and a thermal blanket, giving him water and morsels of food. He marveled that she was willing to treat him like a patient. If she felt disgusted by the fact that he was more than nine feet tall and covered by plates of armor, she gave no hint of it.

Ariock gingerly stretched each arm, throbbing from pain after the crucifixion he'd suffered. Massive spikes jutted from his forearms, heavy and black. They scraped the metal floor like monstrous weights.

One spike encountered something that moved.

Ariock yanked his arm back. Pain shot through his injured shoulders as he sat upright, and people startled away. That made him even more ashamed. He must have clumsily poked someone with a spike. He should be more careful.

"Sorry." Vy pulled her slender hand away, and Ariock realized that she was still nearby. She must have touched his spike.

On purpose. He couldn't imagine why.

"They hammered these into you?" Vy said, her tone sympathetic. "Did they even use anesthesia?"

They had not.

But Ariock doubted Vy wanted to hear the agonizing details. He looked away to hide the memory of his own screams. There were more important people for Vy to focus sympathy on. She should probably pay more attention to Cherise.

Vy touched his spike again. "What they did to you," she said, "was monstrous."

"They're animals." His mother, Delia, studied a dagger with a glassy blade. It gleamed in the fiery light of dawn. "No matter what they think of themselves."

The humans—Delia, Vy, and Cherise—were wrapped in outerwear that looked like it came from a Torth wardrobe. Otherwise they looked grungy.

Open slave collars lay scattered on the floor. They clearly had reasons to hate the Torth, but Ariock wondered how they would react if they ever learned how brutal his arena fights were.

He had ripped animals apart with his bare hands while the telepaths merely watched.

He had actually murdered two telepaths who hadn't run fast enough.

If his rescuers ever found out how violent he'd become, they would scoot to the far end of the hover platform, like Cherise. Vy might never speak to him again.

"What is that?" Kessa said in a tone of wonder, pointing to something ahead.

Ariock shifted around to see. The distant hills were dense with gray-blue alien trees.

"I'm taking us to a jungle region," Thomas said. "If we're out in the open after sunrise, we'll be easy to see. The jungle canopy will shield us from satellite scans."

The sky looked unblemished to Ariock, but he felt sure the telepaths would scan the planet's surface. They were always watching.

"I introduced a little confusion into their scanning software," Thomas said, answering someone's unspoken concern. "That's the only reason they haven't pinpointed us yet. But they'll make fixes and use different equipment. We need to hide."

The wind had a softer quality. They sped past a squat tree, its trunk as pale as the desert. Swollen, leafless branches reminded Ariock of cacti he'd seen on TV.

More cactus-trees dotted the hills. Spiky red plants grew between them, in open spaces where moonlight from the three moons would be brightest.

"It smells of my childhood." Kessa's face crinkled with what looked like happiness. "Uthda trees and zithi fruits."

"There are lots of slave farms out this way," Thomas said callously.

Vy made a squealing sound and jerked, staring at a bulbous membrane that clung to the bare skin of her arm.

"That is a gas bug," Kessa said. "Brush it off."

Vy peeled off the bug with a look of disgust. The creature whipped away in the wind, but not before Ariock saw its six spindly legs, curled up underneath its air sac.

Delia watched it fly away with unease. "Do the Torth have drones with cameras?"

"Of course," Thomas said. "But their tech is only a few steps better than what you have on Earth. The Torth are used to relying on mind probes, scanning the minds of slaves and animals."

"How do we hide?" Vy asked.

"We'll look for a cave or a sinkhole," Thomas said. "Somewhere dark. This region is known for sulfur mines. That gives us increased odds of finding an unknown, unmapped cave."

Vy looked at him as if he was crazy. Ariock wondered if Thomas had a sense of humor, because surely he must be joking.

"All the maps in my head come from the Torth." There was a bitter edge to Thomas's voice. "We have to find a place where not even their top super-geniuses will think to search. That means somewhere undiscovered. Somewhere I can't guess. It has to be a place she won't puzzle out."

"You want us to rely on luck?" Vy sounded worried.

Thomas snapped back at her without an ounce of sympathy, "Did you think it would be easy to escape the most powerful civilization of all time?"

They sped beneath towering cactus-trees. Vines fluttered apart, like the curtains of weeping willows.

"You couldn't have taken an armored vehicle?" Delia asked. "Or, like, a spaceship?"

Thomas gave her a cold stare with his iridescent eyes. "Private vehicles are parked in high-traffic zones. I didn't have an opportunity to engineer a major distraction." He turned back to driving. "On top of that, a lot of tourists are leaving the planet after the execution ceremony. We would never have been able to sneak into the spaceport unnoticed."

Ariock tried to give his mother a reassuring look. Her accusatory tone was counterproductive. They were reliant on Thomas, and they ought to be grateful for what he'd done.

"You don't think the Torth will scan the minds of any animals we happen to pass by?" Kessa asked fretfully.

"It's unlikely," Thomas said. "Wildlife is everywhere, and Torth don't generally enjoy probing the memories of yoypru birds and giant caterpillars. We'll be in trouble if any slaves see us, though."

Ariock wished he wasn't so visible.

"I ruled out my personal proclivities and chose a region at random," Thomas said. "So the Torth are unlikely to search this region first. That might buy us enough time to hide."

"And they cannot fit big vehicles here," Kessa observed.

Ariock saw what she meant. Some tree trunks were so thick, they could hide an immense guard such as Weptolyso. The branches looked strong enough to support a rhinoceros.

In fact, they could all hide up there. The only challenge would be climbing. Ariock's back and shoulders still ached.

"We won't be hiding in the trees." Thomas gave Ariock a pitying look, and Ariock realized that he was within telepathy range of the boy. "They'll send an army of Red Ranks to comb every jungle and canyon on this planet. They have heat-detecting vision. And if they fail to find us after a day or two? They might just drop napalm. They'll do whatever it takes."

Napalm?

Ariock stared, hardly ably to believe how casual Thomas sounded about fiery destruction. Were the leaders of the Torth Empire so deranged that they would decimate their own property? Just for a few innocent escaped slaves?

"But…" Vy sounded just as disbelieving as Ariock felt. "That doesn't make sense. We're not a threat."

Thomas drove with one hand, half turned toward their stunned faces. "I made their leaders look incompetent," he explained. "Now they have to regain their honor. Their lives depend on it."

He turned his full focus back to driving, as if that explained everything.

"What do you mean?" Kessa said.

"The Commander of All Living Things allowed a criminal renegade to escape." Thomas gestured to himself. "If she fails to fix her error, the Majority will elect a new Commander of All and get rid of her."

Kessa looked more fascinated than ever. "The Torth destroy their own leaders?"

"It happens," Thomas said. "The previous Commander of All got tortured to death after he made a mistake. Flawed Torth and renegade Torth always suffer that fate."

"They send Torth to prison?" Kessa sounded disbelieving.

"A special prison on a faraway planet," Thomas said. "It's known as the Isolatorium. They force prisoners to mutilate themselves, and most go insane before death."

Thomas's tone was flat, devoid of emotion, but Ariock had the sense that he was hiding something painful. He sounded as if he had seen the Isolatorium —or known someone who had died there.

Kessa studied him. "Is that where they'll send you, if they catch you?"

Thomas looked as uncaring as ever, but he didn't meet anyone's gaze. He gave a single nod.

Ariock had a grim idea of how the telepaths functioned. They would not tolerate "mistakes" from their own kind. It wouldn't matter that Thomas was a disabled child. They would torture him to death.

Power made them monstrous. They must believe themselves as invincible as gods.

But Ariock had crushed the throat of one telepath, and he had stomped on another, bashing his skull to pieces. They could die just like anyone.

"We'll defend each other," Vy assured Thomas.

"We can try," Thomas said. "The one we really need to worry about is my former mentor. She's a supergenius with access to all the knowledge in the known universe. And she'll want this back." He tapped his medicine case. "She'll do anything to get it. Even if she's no longer in charge of the city or the province, she's still dangerous. I don't think I can outsmart her."

Some of that had to be hyperbole. Ariock remembered the obese, enfeebled girl who had stolen Thomas's medicine. She might be supersmart, but she must have limited authority and power.

"How much time before they get here?" Delia peered at the shadowy jungle as if expecting flying vehicles to show up at any moment.

"Our time is running out," Thomas said. "We'll be lucky if we get another hour."

They all stared at Thomas in shock. He steered around trees with machinelike precision, apparently oblivious to their horror.

"I expect our freedom won't last very long," he said, adjusting the controls. Their platform glided.

They were slowing down. As if they had all the time in the world.

"I need the blaster glove." Thomas extended his hand, beckoning to the beaked alien who wore it.

"An hour?" Delia sounded pained and betrayed.

"An hour if we're lucky," Thomas said as their platform drifted to a stop. "Now give me the glove, Pung." He beckoned. "Or we're even less likely to survive. There's an invisible fence in front of us."

CHAPTER 2
ELECTRIFIED

Ariock had survived every arena battle with the dark expectation that he would fail and get blasted to death. The sight of a blaster glove chilled him, even though it was worn by an ummin. The glove fit Pung poorly, with the wrong number of fingers.

"Please." Thomas sounded pained. "I'm not going to attack anyone. I just want to enter a code to turn off the barrier."

Kessa gently touched Pung's shoulder and spoke to him in a coaxing tone in their language of clicks and murmurs.

After a moment, Pung yanked off the blaster glove. His hooded eyes were full of mistrust as he handed it to Thomas.

That was understandable. Ariock didn't like to think about all the technology owned by telepaths. They had invisible electrified fences? Oh, and furniture that defied gravity. And headgear that altered moods. Even a Torth as weak as Thomas could murder a slave on a whim.

Ariock mentally shoved aside his sense of defeat. He wasn't in the arena pit, forced to wear a helmet that augmented his hatred and rage and despair. He'd be damned if he went back to that mental state.

Thomas tapped the palm of his glove with professional speed.

A mesh-like fence materialized in thin air, billowing in the breeze, blocking their path. Electric sparks shimmered along its metallic surface.

"There we go," Thomas said.

"How did you know the unlock code?" Vy asked, amazed.

"I memorized several million codes," Thomas replied. "I was bored one afternoon."

Vy gave him a look of incredulity. "How long did that take you?"

"Six minutes."

Ariock tried not to stare at Thomas and marvel. A memory like that could crush the childhood out of anyone. Thomas must have absorbed life experiences—Torth life experiences—at a hyperintense rate, plugged into their network of minds.

And there was foresight involved, too. Thomas must have subconsciously guessed that a few million codes would be useful.

It was a wonder he was still sane. It was a miracle that he'd been able to rescue anybody. How human was he, beneath a burden of knowledge that must be more crippling than any disease?

Thomas gave him a resentful glance, and Ariock knew that his thoughts might as well be broadcast.

Light flashed in the undergrowth. Something small and furry dropped to the ground, dead.

"You see those dead animals?" Thomas gestured, and they all looked toward the jungle floor. Unidentifiable clumps of fur lay aligned in a row. "That's because the fence is electrified. I'm turning it off."

He tapped the glove's display, and the dancing sparks died.

"I remember a place like this," Kessa said. "On the slave farm where I grew up, no one could wander far."

"Yup," Thomas said. "All slave farms are quarantined. The Torth Empire strictly controls slave breeding." He drove forward. "Weptolyso, come up front. I need you to lift the fence so we can drive under it."

Weptolyso seemed good-natured, less mistrustful than anyone else. He lifted the mesh fence, hoisting it above his thorny spinal ridge without complaint. That was a good thing. He was built like a tank, protected by a pebbly hide and retractable spikes.

"Will they recode the fence?" Delia asked as they drove beneath it.

"Undoubtedly," Thomas said.

Weptolyso held the fence until they were all the way past it. Thomas paused the hovercart so he could drop it. Once they had moved a short distance away, Thomas waved the blaster glove, and the fence reactivated, sparkling and then fading to invisibility.

A few bugs sizzled and dropped, electrocuted.

"So, um, are we now trapped inside this slave farm?" Delia asked.

"That's the least of our concerns." Thomas steered past trees and tubelike flowers. "Look for any sign of sunken ground and listen for any hint of an echo. That might indicate a cave. Also, keep your voices low. The last thing we need is for the native slaves to stumble upon us."

"Are we really just hoping to find a random cave?" Delia asked.

Thomas sighed. "I know you want to reclaim control of your life, Delia. But this is not the vastly improved situation you hoped for. I'm doing my best."

They floated onward in silence. The jungle emitted its own sounds—a whining hum that rose and fell, like crickets. Gas bugs floated like iridescent bubbles.

Steam drifted through the trees ahead. Ariock glimpsed a steaming pond between vines, clean and turquoise in color.

"Is that a hot spring?" Vy leaned on the railing, gazing at the crystal water with yearning. "Oh, wow. I would give anything for—"

"We don't have time for frivolities," Thomas cut in.

Ariock understood why Vy wanted to rinse off. Grime caked his skin, too. They were all varying degrees of dirty, except for Thomas.

"Tell me," Delia said, peering at Thomas. "What are the odds of us finding a hiding place before the Torth locate us?"

Thomas set his jaw. It made him look like an old man. "Do you want an honest answer?"

"Just tell me."

"I calculate a zero-point-zero-zero-zero-zero-one percent chance that we'll evade the hunters today." Thomas avoided their gazes, as if he didn't want to get too attached.

"You're saying we're doomed?" Vy said.

"I only speak the truth."

Vy approached him. "Can we defend ourselves at least a little bit?" She indicated his blaster glove. "How about if you tell us how to shoot a Torth weapon?"

Ariock was so focused on Vy and the child-size blaster glove, he barely noticed when the platform bounced slightly. Everyone else made sounds of alarm.

"Cherise!" Thomas tapped the control glyphs, and their platform lost speed.

Cherise had climbed over the railing and jumped off. Now she jogged toward the hot spring.

"What is she doing?" Thomas said in a low voice. "Get back here!"

Cherise pulled off her outer robe and dropped it to the sandy ground. She began to strip off her rags while wading into the steamy water.

"Get back!" Thomas said with helpless frustration. Their hovercart drifted to a stop.

As far as Ariock could tell, Thomas hadn't looked at Cherise, or spoken to her, until now. He hadn't apologized for whatever terrible thing he'd done. Cherise clearly wanted to forget about him, as well.

She looked like a nymph in the gentle light, amid blue vines and turquoise water, her hair blacker than any shadow. She cupped her hands and poured water over herself, calm. Peaceful.

Thomas watched her with an expression that was part yearning and part frustrated anger.

"I'll bring her back," Vy said. She shed her outer robe.

"No!" Thomas said.

It was too late. Vy slipped over the railing and hurried toward the hot spring, unknotting the rags of her outfit. She peeled off layers, revealing more and more skin.

Thomas leaned over the railing to glare in her direction. "What part of 'hunted by the galactic empire' do you not understand?"

Vy unwrapped her coppery hair and shook it free. "If this is our last hour, then I'm not going to waste it." She waded into the hot spring. "You shouldn't, either."

Ariock knew that he ought to be respectful and pull his gaze away from Vy. She wore the equivalent of a rag bikini.

But she also had a good point about their final hour of freedom.

If he was never going to see anything beautiful again, then he wanted this moment emblazoned on his memory. So he gazed at Vy and her curves.

"Well." Delia stood, gathering empty canteens. "We might as well refresh our water supply." She looked at Thomas. "Is the water of that hot spring safe to drink?"

Thomas looked conflicted, then resigned. "Yes." He tapped a control glyph, and the railing telescoped open. "Go ahead and be an idiot with everyone else."

Delia trotted toward the hot spring with the canteens, followed by Pung.

The hovercart sank to the ground, as if giving up. Thomas looked miserable.

Ariock imagined Red Ranks hurtling toward the jungle in flying vehicles. Thomas was absolutely right. Maybe Ariock should urge everyone to get back aboard so they could continue their search for a cave?

A cramped, dark hole. A prison.

Just once, Ariock wanted to feel free and happy.

Vy splashed in the hot spring. She dunked underwater, then popped up, grinning with delight, water streaming from her hair. "It feels amazing," she said.

Ariock want to know how it felt.

He would never get another chance to enjoy a moment. How could he waste these minutes of magical freedom?

He pushed himself up. As he steadied himself, leaning on a jutting branch for support, he became aware of silence. The entire jungle seemed to be watching. Even the bug chorus had stopped, as if bugs were holding their breath to stare at the giant.

Ariock had the sense that if he twitched or moved at all, the vines and branches would startle back in fear. He loomed like a fairy-tale freak, his head practically in the canopy.

Vy wouldn't want him anywhere near her. He needed to sit, to go back to being unobtrusive. He began to lower himself…then caught the way Thomas watched him.

With fear.

The others viewed Ariock as a harmless giant, but Thomas must have absorbed memories from the arena. He probably expected Ariock to snap into a berserker rage at any moment.

Maybe he thought Ariock was just an untrustworthy animal?

That was how the Torth viewed him.

Ariock stepped off the hovercart with as much dignity as he could muster. He didn't want to inflict his presence on anyone, but especially not on Thomas.

Soft sand cushioned his callused feet. He hunched toward the hot spring, trying to be as small as possible.

The water was as warm and soothing as it looked. It was divine.

Ariock sat, too sore for grace. He caused a small wave. Vy treaded water, and Ariock was grateful that he couldn't hear whatever she must be thinking. She would probably swim away in disgust.

Instead, she waded closer with a smile.

Ariock needed all his willpower to avoid looking at her breasts, which were barely contained by that strip of wet cloth. Tangles of her hair clung to her skin, emphasizing tantalizing curves.

"Check this out." Vy squeezed a handful of plant stalks, and they frothed. "They make soap!"

Ariock laughed, despite all his worries. Maybe the Torth would slaughter them all, and maybe Vy was struggling to ignore how he looked, but he simply didn't care. He had been afraid all his life. Afraid to be seen, afraid to offend people…he'd had enough fear to last several lifetimes.

He was going to enjoy these minutes of happiness even if it killed him.

"I'll wash your back," Vy offered.

Ariock hesitated and forced himself to stop wondering why she wanted to touch him. "Only if I can wash yours," he dared to say.

Vy grinned. "I assume your arms feel okay?"

"Is this a nurse trick?" Ariock asked as she waded even closer.

Vy tossed the plant stalks at him. "Maybe." Her sly smile made her look huggable. "I'll call it a test, to see how you do."

Ariock reached for the stalks and tried not to show his pain.

"I was kidding." Vy gently pushed his nearest arm. "Settle down, and I'll—eep!" She laughed in surprise as Ariock touched her bare back. He had squeezed lather out of the plant stalks with his other hand.

"I'm easy to reach for you, aren't I?" She lifted her hair, allowing him to gently rub her back.

If I die now, Ariock thought, *I wouldn't mind.*

Let the Torth armies come and do their worst. He was happier than he could ever remember being. He almost felt as if he could stand up and fly, as if the breeze was the same thing as his breathing.

The bug chorus grew deep and low, each sawing note in sync with his breaths.

"Ariock." Thomas sounded panicked. "What are you doing?"

The strange sense that he could fly, and that bugs were in tune with his breathing, evaporated. Ariock felt meager. He wanted to like feeling small, but strangely, he did not. He had felt as large as the jungle for a moment. Now he felt reduced, just a pathetic prisoner again.

Vy shot Thomas a vexed look. "What was he doing?"

Thomas floated behind the railing, as if unwilling to face anyone.

"Just ignore him." Delia rolled her eyes in Thomas's direction. "I'm sure he's used to everyone respecting his authority."

Ariock was careful not to look at Thomas. Even if his mother was right, it seemed like a bad idea to alienate the boy who knew everything.

"Ariock," Thomas said, "there's something you should know. There's a reason the Torth sentenced you to death."

That got Ariock's attention. The telepaths had never bothered to tell him anything. Maybe they'd punished Ariock for future crimes he had never dreamed of committing? Maybe they were offended by his size? All he could do was guess.

"Well?" Delia stood barefoot in the hot spring, hands on her hips. "Why did you sentence my son to death by crucifixion?"

CHAPTER 3

A THREAT TO CIVILIZATION

Thomas fiddled with the handle of his medicine case, as if hoping it would do the explaining for him. "I didn't want to tell you. But I think it would be more dangerous not to."

Ariock concealed his impatience. "I'm listening."

"Okay," Thomas said. "First, you need to understand that the Torth have a wide variety of genetic mutations. They're not all physical." He gave Ariock a significant look. "A lot of mutations have to do with the mind."

Everyone else looked impatient, no doubt wondering why Thomas was talking about science. It sounded like a non sequitur.

But Ariock knew about mutations. Thomas might as well have pointed to his overgrown body.

"Your son is weirdest mutant I've ever seen." That was what the doctor in Boston had said, tapping Ariock's X-rays and discussing them with his mother. *"Look at how dense his bones are. There's no acromegaly or any sign of frailty. We could try to zap his pituitary, but that's invasive neurosurgery, and I'm sorry, but it's not the cause. I'm astounded to say that he's a natural giant. At his rate of growth, he'll be over nine feet tall by the time he's an adult, and there's nothing anyone can do. I can't tell you when, or if, he'll ever stop growing."*

Ariock had prayed ferociously every night after that. He'd begged any god that might listen for a way to reverse his mutation. He used to stand in snowdrifts on his balcony, gazing up at the stars, silently offering to trade all his wealth for a chance to stop growing and live a somewhat normal life. He wanted to have friends.

When he began to bump into door frames and chandeliers, he quit torturing himself with the hope that a god would take pity on him. No one up there was listening.

Thomas went on. "The Torth Empire has long-standing laws against certain dangerous mutations."

"What does any of this have to do with Ariock?" Delia's tone was frosty.

"I think you can guess." Thomas gave her a challenging look.

Ariock had always suspected that there was something monstrous about himself, but he'd never guessed that he might be related to actual monsters. He couldn't imagine anyone in his family history as slave-owning telepaths.

"Ariock is not related to any Torth," his mother said in a tone that dared anyone to argue.

Thomas did, of course. "He has an obvious Torth mutation. His type of gigantism isn't unheard-of, especially on the heavy-G planets. And that's not the only Torth mutation he inherited."

"You're lying," Delia said fiercely. "I know the genealogy of my family, and of my husband's family, and—"

"Garrett lied to you." Thomas sounded annoyed.

She looked stunned.

"He gave you false family stories and doctored photographs," Thomas said. "He told you that his parents were farmers from Iowa. In reality, his father was a renegade Torth, and his mother may have been, as well. Garrett was a mind reader. Lying to humans was a piece of cake for him."

Ariock felt a sneaky sense of relief, although his mother looked as if her worldview was falling apart. Now he had something to blame, other than random bad luck! His gigantism came from the Torth.

"That's impossible," Delia said. "Garrett was the sweetest old man anyone ever knew. There's no way he could have been the monster you're claiming he was."

"I didn't say he was a monster." Thomas had a dangerous glint in his eyes. "I said he was a mind reader."

Ariock tried to reconcile what he knew about his great-grandfather with what he knew about the Torth.

Garrett Olmstead Dovanack was supposedly a man of integrity and charisma, a war hero, a philanthropist, and highly praised by everyone who had ever known him. He had raised his grandson, Ariock's father, after one parent committed suicide and the other parent turned to alcoholism. The family had lots of dysfunction, but Garrett had been a pillar who held them all together.

He'd also been a multimillionaire winner of high-stakes gambles.

People used to whisper that he must be a mind reader.

Garrett had always jokingly denied it.

"He couldn't have been." Delia sounded lost.

"He was a mind reader," Thomas said, merciless. "Didn't it strike you as egomaniacal that his initials spelled GOD? His original name—the name that was given to him by the foster family who adopted him—was Jonathan Stead."

The name meant nothing to Ariock, but it slammed into everyone else like a whirlwind. Vy gasped through her hands. The aliens straightened, eyes wide.

"Truly?" Kessa hopped off the hovercart so she could study Ariock at a closer distance. "Ariock is Jonathan Stead returned?"

"He's a descendant." Thomas sounded peeved. "He's not a hero, or a god, or anything like that."

"Are you saying the legend is true?" Vy said with awe. "Jonathan Stead actually existed?"

"Who was he?" Ariock asked, bewildered.

Thomas shrugged his misshapen shoulders. "He was a renegade who freed a bunch of slaves and killed a bunch of Torth using his illegal powers. Then he went into hiding and faded into obscurity." He gestured toward Ariock. "There's his only surviving relative."

Vy scrutinized Ariock as if seeing him for the first time. "What do you mean…'powers'?"

"Certain mutations entail powers beyond telepathy," Thomas said. "Like an ability to bend metal with one's mind. Or influence the weather." He made it sound as mundane as napkin folding. "Things like that."

Ariock wanted to laugh at the absurdity. He'd never had power in his life.

"I'm having trouble believing this." Delia sounded as skeptical as he felt. "You're not suggesting that Garrett had an ability to cause storms. Are you?"

"Garrett had storm powers," Thomas said with utter certainty. "And Ariock inherited those powers. That's why the Torth sentenced him to death."

It sounded like a joke. Everyone should have laughed, but instead, they watched Ariock as if expecting him to transform into someone better. It was unreal, how they all looked at him.

Ariock shifted in the water and tried to laugh, to lighten the mood. "I don't have powers," he pointed out.

"Your powers are suppressed right now," Thomas said. "But think back. You might have noticed that the weather always reflected your mood."

"It was overcast a lot." Delia sounded derisive. "But that was because it was New Hampshire."

"You'd see blue sky when you went into town, sometimes," Thomas said. "But almost never when you got home."

She frowned, as if he had a point.

Everyone kept sneaking glances at Ariock, measuring him with their gazes.

Did they believe they'd rescued a legendary hero? Ariock would have laughed if he wasn't so ashamed. They'd rescued a couch potato who watched too much TV.

"That's how he survived that lightning storm!" Vy said. "He must have used his powers to protect himself."

Ariock nearly told her that he hadn't felt powerful or in control during the lightning storm. Just the opposite. Clouds had shrieked above him, echoing his despair, black and churning. Sheets of lightning had slammed continuously against the hilltop. It was like a half-forgotten dream now, a death hallucination.

"He was blocked by the inhibitor serum," Thomas said, "so I don't know about that storm. He shouldn't have been able to cause any storms or protect himself. Although I did, uh, tamper with the inhibitor earlier. I added a chemical to render it ineffective. But it worked a little too fast and a little too well. The Torth found out and replaced that batch before the execution ceremony."

Ariock remembered the warping of the prison cell wall. He had gotten angry at his own reflection, and the metal had bent.

It had stayed dented.

Ariock had guessed that he must have lost his grip on reality due to isolation and torture.

"Inhibitor serum?" Vy looked dismayed. "What is that? A drug that blocks powers?"

"Indeed," Thomas said. "A long-ago supergenius invented it in ancient times, in order to defeat armies of Yeresunsa. That's what allowed the Torth Empire to really take off."

Yeresunsa. A chill crept over Ariock at that foreign word.

The cold, emotionless version of Thomas had called him "Yeresunsa" during the execution ceremony, while thousands of Torth listened in silent approval. The word meant something to them—a reason to put Ariock in chains and cause him to suffer.

"Yere-what?" Vy asked.

"Yeresunsa." Thomas tugged his canteen, pulling it into his lap. "It means someone born with mutant powers. As I said, it's illegal. The Torth kill any fetus that develops extreme advantages or disadvantages, so every child can start life on an equal footing." He nodded toward Ariock. "The only way around that is to be born outside the baby farm system. You'd have to be born outside of the Torth Empire."

His meaning was plain. Ariock was a Torth descendant who had been born outside the Torth Empire.

How many fetuses got destroyed because they developed the wrong set of mutations? Ariock hoped he was not the only Yeresunsa who had lived beyond infancy.

"Ariock Dovanack, Son of Storms." The huge guard, Weptolyso, spoke in a gravelly rumble. He swung his neck in what looked like respect. "Killer of Torth."

They gazed at Ariock as if he might solve every problem in the universe. "Can you try to use your powers?" Vy asked. "You might be able to protect us!"

Ariock wanted to remind her that he was the same lonely, pathetic loser he had always been.

But her blue eyes met his, shining with hope, and he wanted to impress her.

So he tried. He imagined a breeze that would sweep her damp, tangled hair off her shoulders.

It didn't work. He felt idiotic. Even if Yeresunsa powers were real, even if he had inherited some mutant freakishness, he had lived twenty-two years without using powers. He had been helpless when his father died in a plane crash. He had suffered and nearly died as a prisoner. He wasn't going to turn heroic within a few minutes.

Unless...

He turned to Thomas. "Can you teach me?"

"No," Thomas said. "The inhibitor is still partially blocking you." He gestured at the pile of collars. "I removed your collar, so you're no longer receiving doses, but it will take another day or two before you're at full strength. The only way we'll survive is to hide. We can't waste time doing anything else."

"You just wasted a bunch of time." Vy glared at Thomas. "What was the point of telling him about his powers if you think he shouldn't use them?"

Thomas spoke to Ariock, as if no one else mattered. "Yeresunsa powers require a lot of self-control. You're the equivalent of a child stumbling around in the dark with a nuclear warhead strapped to his back. The only reason I explained this is to help you understand that you shouldn't attempt to use your powers."

He sounded bold, yet his tone was higher pitched than usual. He was hiding fear.

"We can't afford a disaster," Thomas said. "You shouldn't try anything, because you might accidentally start a tornado or something else that draws attention to our location. Our only option is to *stay hidden*." He emphasized the last two words, as if Ariock might have trouble understanding.

It made sense, and Ariock began to nod his agreement. But then he saw how defiant Vy looked.

"Ariock might be our only hope," Vy said. "I'm sure you can teach him how to control his powers."

"Did you pay attention to that part about the inhibitor serum?" Thomas glared at her. "The Torth used it to defeat Jonathan Stead. Ariock is a lot less experienced, and he's a large target. All it takes is one microdart." He held his finger and thumb together, depicting something minuscule. "They'll spray him with microscopic missiles, and one tiny dose will be enough to disable him for days. That will be the end of him. And the end of us."

"The Torth condemned him to death because they're afraid of him." Vy stood waist-deep in water, intractable.

"More or less." Thomas gave her an exasperated look. "Although *afraid* isn't the right word. Torth execute all Yeresunsa as threats to the Torth Empire, no matter what their capabilities are, even if they're infants. It's an ancient law that keeps galactic civilization stable and safe. No one has truly challenged the Torth Empire for over twenty thousand years."

"Except for Jonathan Stead," Vy suggested.

"He was a blip on their radar," Thomas said dismissively. "He didn't challenge the empire. He caused an insignificant skirmish in one city on one planet."

"What did he—" Vy began to speak, but Thomas overrode her.

"Yeah, he freed a bunch of imprisoned slaves. He cracked the Great Plaza in half and sent tornadoes against a fleet of transports. But after that? He went into hiding for the rest of his life." Thomas looked uncaring. "He changed his identity and desperately blended in as a human. I'm sure he trembled in fear every time he thought about the Torth."

Vy looked offended by the idea that Jonathan Stead could be a coward.

"Let's be on our way." Thomas beckoned with a thin finger.

Ariock tried to cling to freedom.

But he supposed that was selfish. He wasn't alone in the sky room, pacing while the TV chattered endlessly. He wasn't confined in his solitary cell. An unseen clock ticked down. This dire situation mattered to Vy, and to his mother, and to everyone else.

They should have spent every second searching for a place to hide.

Ariock struggled to his feet, water pouring off him.

"You know, I was torn about even letting you off the inhibitor." Thomas seemed more relaxed now that the rest of them had begun to gather their belongings. "Jonathan Stead was fairly competent at self-control." He gestured at Ariock. "You don't have that advantage. That has me worried, because these powers are volatile, not meant for…" He paused, apparently rethinking what he had been about to say. "They'll be difficult to master for someone with poor impulse control."

That was a reference to the arena fights. Ariock looked away, ashamed of his brutality.

"And," Thomas added, "average intelligence."

"Wow." Vy gave Thomas an unimpressed glare.

Ariock waded toward the shore. Thomas might be right about him. The Torth had proved that he was violent, uneducated, and, sure, he was stupid in comparison to a supergenius.

So was he supposed to just give up? Wait for death?

No. He had done more than enough of that in his life.

A feminine hand touched his. "If you can practice," Vy whispered, "then you should." She darted her gaze toward Thomas. "Never mind what he says."

Ariock gave her a nod. He didn't want anyone to expect miracles from him. But if an army tried to capture his rescuers…well, he would throw lightning bolts at the Torth, if he could.

He would do anything to remain free.

"How often do Torth become renegades?" Kessa asked.

Thomas didn't seem to hear. He scanned the jungle foliage, a frown on his deceptively youthful face.

"Thomas?" Kessa hopped closer to the hovercart.

A look of dawning alarm came over Thomas's face. "Shh." He made a beckoning gesture, like a Torth summoning a personal slave. "Quiet. We're being watched."

CHAPTER 4

RUNAWAY

Kessa scanned the jungle, searching for whatever Thomas had sensed.

Bugs drifted on rising steam from the pond. Hanging vines were thick with buds.

Those buds would blossom into zithi fruits, she knew. Kessa used to climb paddle trees like these, in the long-ago days before she was abducted, never to see her family again. She used to help her mother mash zithi fruits to feed the whole village.

The chorus of bugs shrilled on without pause. There was no extra rustling, no strange sounds.

Kessa touched her neck, exploring her own velvety skin.

Thomas had removed her slave collar. He had also explained a lot of things during their journey. For instance, he claimed that ummins used to rule themselves. Kessa's long-forgotten ancestors had supposedly built an interstellar empire. They must have felt as free and happy as children, yet they had been blessed with more wisdom than any elderly slave.

A slave shouted.

It was not a dialect Kessa recognized, and the tone was commanding. Ummins burst out of the jungle from every direction. They swung down from vines and popped out of underbrush, wielding slingshots and spears. Tribal paint made them blend in with the blue foliage. Other than paint, they wore headbands and also waistbands hung with beaded flaps.

Ummins surrounded Kessa and her friends. She counted sixty-eight at a glance.

We're dead, she thought.

But ummins should not be bold enough to threaten Torth. Thomas looked like a slave master, floating in his hoverchair.

Weptolyso flexed his spinal ridge, making his spikes pop out. He postured like a bodyguard on the verge of attack. And Ariock…he loomed like the biggest nightmare an ummin could have. Kessa could read human faces, so she saw his lack of confidence, but the tribal ummins would only see a monstrous-size Torth who could step on them while torturing them with pain seizures.

"Leave," Thomas commanded in an imperious tone. He raised his hover-chair so he could peer over the railing. "Forget you saw us, or you'll regret it."

One tribal ummin dropped his spear in terror. He picked it up when he saw that no one else had dropped theirs.

"Come with us!" A tribal ummin seized Kessa.

Kessa struggled, twisting away. The ummin let her go, perplexed.

Pung shoved an ummin who'd tried to drag him away. "We don't need help." He yanked on the blaster glove, his posture more befitting a guard than a common slave.

The sight of a gloved runaway slave caused all the ummins to back away in a hurry. They exchanged uncertain glances, then huddled in a group, conferring.

"This is turning into a circus," Thomas said in the human language. "We don't want to be memorable."

Kessa thought that might be impossible.

And the tribal ummins were acting strange, as well.

"We tried our best," one said. "Let's leave, if they're too stupid to run away."

Another gave Kessa's neck a wince of sympathy. "Maybe they will find their way to our village."

Kessa had never heard of slaves who tried to help runaways, outside of legends. No one she knew would have challenged a Torth, no matter how ragtag. It was too risky.

Maybe they saw how dusty the hovercart was. They'd surely overheard some conversation, and no Torth would talk so much. No Torth with any power would allow such a racket to be made.

"I don't like leaving them." That came from a tribal ummin who seemed to be in charge, because the rest listened. "But to do more would be...irresponsible."

They exchanged looks. Their leader had left something unspoken, and Kessa began to wonder if this rescue attempt was more than foolhardy bravery. There was something practical about it.

"Good ummins," Kessa said, hesitant. "You want no part of our trouble."

Thomas said something in the tribal tongue, and the ummins gaped in astonishment.

Kessa stared at him, too. Some slave farms had their own tribal dialects, but every slave spoke the common slave tongue. Torth never used any other spoken language.

"You know their language?" Vy asked.

Thomas did not break eye contact with the ummin leader. "I do now. It's like contracting a disease, except I never get rid of it."

The ummins looked skittish and unconvinced.

"What did you tell them?" Kessa asked.

"The truth." Thomas surveyed the ummins. "They have no idea what's coming. If they want to live, they should forget they ever saw us." He flexed his hand, as if to remind everyone that he was entitled to a blaster glove. "All it will take is one slip of a thought for these natives to betray us."

The leader met Kessa's gaze. "The choice is yours, city slave." His deep-set eyes urged her to make a wise choice. "Run, or stay. Take one risk…or another." He glanced mistrustfully at Thomas.

The tribal ummins began to melt back into the jungle.

Kessa studied their eyes, wondering what secrets they might be hiding. Her life had been simpler in the city. At least she'd known what dangers to expect, and how best to avoid them.

"Cherise!" Vy called.

Cherise was following the ummins, shoulders hunched, as if hoping they wouldn't notice.

But they did, and they stopped, afraid. Brown eyes meant Brown Rank. Except for her rag outfit and glasses, Cherise could have been the overseer of a slave farm like this one.

"Let's not draw them into our problem," Delia said.

Cherise looked defiant.

"They are unusually confident," Thomas said in a speculative tone. "As if they know something we don't. Hm."

He floated off the hovercart, toward Cherise and the tribal ummins.

They brandished their spears and readied their slingshots, but Thomas acted like a Torth, uncaring, as if protected by bodyguards and blaster gloves.

"They're so well organized." His yellow eyes were alert and predatory. "I think they're hiding something."

Kessa used to believe that mind probes were like illnesses or storms— impossible to prevent. But Thomas had revealed much about his people. The Torth squabbled over petty disputes, and suffered from their physical ailments, and distrusted each other.

So they weren't gods. Not even close.

Kessa jumped off the hovercart and shoved his hoverchair away from the ummins, shaking with rage. "Stop. You have no right to invade their minds!"

Thomas drifted, examining her as if a gas bug had started to talk.

Kessa braced herself for a pain seizure. Freedom must have warped her mind, if she believed an elderly ummin had the right to defy a mind reader. Thomas had removed her slave collar, but he was still one of the self-proclaimed gods. He was a Torth.

"If these slaves have an unknown crawlspace," Thomas said, "don't you want to find out?"

"We do not take secrets by force." Kessa tried to moderate her tone. She reminded herself that Thomas was benign and should not be blamed for her lifetime of slavery, or for her deceased friends and family members. She could not hold him responsible for the way her mate had been tortured to death.

But he was the only mind reader she could actually talk to.

She planted her fists on her hips. "If you want to act like a Torth, then go back to the city."

"All right, all right." Thomas's skin turned pink—a human sign of shame. "No mind probing. Fine. Got it."

Kessa felt a little bit stunned. She had not expected to actually stop him.

"She attacked a Torth," one of the tribal ummins whispered.

They gawked at Kessa. She looked behind herself, certain they must be staring at someone else.

"She commanded a Torth," another slave whispered.

"She tore off her own slave collar." Another pointed. "That is the mark of a runaway."

The rest of them went silent with awe.

Kessa gazed downward to reject their misplaced praise. She had not given commands to a Torth. Had she?

Well, she certainly was not a runaway like in stories. Heroes always broke off their own collars and went around rescuing villagers. Heroes were not supposed to be elderly and arthritic.

The leader approached her with curiosity. "I mistook you for a slave, not a runaway. I greatly apologize."

"There is no need," Kessa said. She still thought of herself as a slave.

"I am Irarjeg." He introduced himself in a jovial tone. "Please, you must come to our village."

Before Kessa could refuse, Irarjeg added a few words in his native tongue, and one of the others bobbed an acknowledgment and sped off through the jungle.

"No!" Kessa shouted. "Call your runner back!"

The runner would spread a memorable tale to an entire village full of innocents. Any Torth who came to that village would soak up the tale and locate Kessa and her friends.

"Well, we're dead," Thomas said coldly.

"Many Torth want to kill us," Kessa told Irarjeg, full of regret. "They will be here soon, and I fear they will kill anyone who tries to help us."

Irarjeg waved dismissively. "The Torth hurt us sometimes. But they will not murder 575 villagers. They need us to mine rocks and grow fruit from them."

"Don't rely on that," Thomas said.

Irarjeg looked uneasy. He had kindly face beneath the blue paint.

He saw the sad way Kessa gazed at him and said, "I misjudged you, run-away, but I think you are doing the same to me and my people. We are not fools. We are careful around Torth."

Except he hadn't been careful around Thomas and the others who looked like Torth.

Irarjeg had probably never seen more than a few Torth in his life. His bare neck was untouched by a collar that would sting or shock him. Torth did not pay much attention to farm labor. Farm slaves were freer than city slaves.

"Kessa," Ariock said, his deep voice resonant. "I think you and Pung should go. The rest of us will find a place to hide."

That was kind. Ariock understood that the tribal ummins would refuse to help people who looked like Torth. Besides, any hidden crawlspace fit for ummins would likely be too small for him and Weptolyso.

"My friends need to come with me," Kessa said to Irarjeg.

"Friends?" He had no idea what she meant.

Kessa made a gesture that included the humans, and Irarjeg stared as if she was insane.

"I know they look like Torth," she said. "But they are runaways, like me."

Irarjeg looked disbelieving, and she remembered her own doubts about the humans. It took time to learn what they were. Some of her neighbors un-doubtedly still believed they were devious Torth disguised as slaves.

"There's no point," Thomas said. "That village is doomed, and so are we."

"Is it always doom and gloom with you?" Delia said.

"Those ummins just saw me—a mind reader—obey a runaway slave," Thomas said. "You think the Torth Empire will let them live, with that in their heads?"

He had a point. Kessa was grateful that he'd said it in the human tongue, so none of the blue-painted ummins understood.

"Ideas are toxic," Thomas said, "and hope is contagious. The Torth will destroy any hint of it before it spreads to other slave farms."

Delia looked disgusted and worried.

"What can we do?" Ariock asked, somber.

"Honestly?" Thomas lowered his head. "If it was just one slave, I'd say make it look like an accidental death. But there are too many." His voice sank to a whisper. "We should kill ourselves. That's our best option."

Kessa recognized the hollowness in his eyes. She had seen slaves with that same look—the ones who had lost everything that mattered. He must fear the torture that awaited him in the Isolatorium.

Or maybe he missed the Megacosm? He had mentioned that during their journey.

Or perhaps he believed he had nothing left to learn, and therefore nothing left to live for.

The humans looked resolute. Like Kessa, they would not accept death as long as they could feel a breeze on their necks instead of a collar.

Irarjeg assessed her friends with doubt. "Someone else will decide what to do with them." He clicked his beak. "Let's go."

He set a brisk pace.

"I want you all to come with me," Kessa said before she followed the tribal ummins. She included Thomas in her gaze. She remembered how it felt to stop caring. She had nearly died from it, long ago.

If they evaded the Torth today, they would need help to face whatever came next.

CHAPTER 5
SON OF STORMS

Ariock ducked under alien branches and tried to avoid getting hit in the face by ropy vines. He was all too aware of Vy. She trotted by his side, watching him as if strategizing how to catch him if he fell.

"How are you feeling?" Vy asked.

Not like vanquishing an army, he considered telling her. "My shoulders are a little sore," he said.

"That's it?" She sounded impressed. "Most people would need a few weeks to recover physically from what you went through." She lowered her voice. "Can you feel that…inhibitor serum?"

"I can hear you," Thomas said from the hovercart. He was a distance away, steering the vehicle through the widest gaps between trees. The width of the platform forced him to take a meandering path. His only passenger was Delia. She rode in the back and looked grateful that she didn't have to hike.

"The inhibitor is hobbling Ariock, whether he feels it or not," Thomas said. "He shouldn't even think about exploring his powers right now."

Vy shot a look toward Thomas. "Do you think it's possible you're underestimating him?" Her tone was challenging.

Thomas gave her a defiant look, but he didn't actually argue.

"You figured out how to build your own furniture." Vy's voice was soft, yet firm. She gazed up at Ariock. "It looked professional. And you taught yourself how to do that?"

Ariock's face heated up. Vy couldn't possibly have been impressed by his rough-hewn giant armchair, couch, table, and bookshelves. Could she?

Everything he built was unadorned, since he had no taste for filigree or crystal. He liked comfort without worrying about breaking things by accident. But his mother said the sky room furnishings were too plain.

Vy must be humoring him. She probably didn't want to get on the bad side of the giant with alleged powers.

Up ahead, Kessa had been chatting with the leader of the blue-painted ummins. Now she turned toward Thomas. "Irarjeg says we must leave our vehicle."

Thomas responded rapid-fire in the slave tongue. Ariock wished he understood a word of it.

Irarjeg stiffened, as if offended.

"Thomas says the Torth will find our hovercart if we leave it in the open." Vy listened intently, and Ariock realized, with surprise, that she was being kind enough to translate for him.

"When the Torth find this hovercart," Vy translated, "they will destroy everyone in this slave farm."

No wonder Irarjeg and his people looked furious and terrified. They had begun to argue among themselves.

"Well, why can't we bring the hovercart to wherever we're going?" Ariock asked.

Vy listened to a rapid reply from Irarjeg. "Apparently it's too big," she said.

That meant that if there was a hiding place, Ariock and Weptolyso would have trouble cramming themselves in with everyone else.

He saw his concern reflected in the nussian's red eyes. Weptolyso looked resigned and dipped his head slightly to Ariock, as if to acknowledge that they might die together while fighting an army. Ariock returned the nod, and Weptolyso looked satisfied.

Irarjeg spoke a command. Blue-painted ummins sprang forth, seizing dead vines and draping jungle debris over the hovercart railing. They were making an attempt to hide it.

"So this is how it ends." Thomas said.

Kessa had another rapid conversation with Irarjeg. She switched fluidly to English. "Get off the hovercart, Thomas. They will bury it for us."

The blue-painted ummins shot mistrustful, angry looks toward Thomas. But they pulled carved scoopers out of their waistband flaps and began to dig in the sand, ready to bury the vehicle.

It would probably take days.

These blue-painted ummins clearly did not understand the urgency, or why the vehicle needed to be well hidden. They seemed to be humoring Kessa.

Delia got off the hovercart, looking skeptical. Thomas only floated near the exit, morose. He stared dully at the ummins digging in the sand.

"Delia," he said. "Can I ask you a favor?"

She looked at him expectantly.

"I would really appreciate a quick death," Thomas said. "That ionic dagger will slide right through my neck. It won't require much effort."

She stared at him, horrified, and Ariock felt the same way.

The human version of Thomas had spent his childhood working day and night to avoid an early death, with Cherise to help him, until he'd invented a medicine that would extend his life and give him a chance to survive until adulthood.

He no longer spoke to Cherise. His medicine case looked forgotten on the seat next to him.

If the human version of Thomas still existed, he was locked away inside the Torth version.

"I'd ask the slaves," Thomas explained, "but they won't dare kill a Torth." He watched her. "Please?"

Ariock was afraid his mother would agree. She touched the hilt of the dagger, as if seriously considering whether or not to murder a disabled child.

"No," Ariock said.

Some of the ummins paused their digging, startled by his grim tone.

"I promised to protect you," Ariock reminded Thomas.

The boy gave him such an incredulous, outraged look, Ariock wondered what he'd done wrong.

Then he realized that he was commanding a mind reader. Worse, he was refusing a dying child's wish. Ariock had never barred anybody before. Even his mother stared, as if seeing a stranger.

"I promised not to let any of you die before I do," Ariock reminded his rescuers.

"That was stupid," Thomas said. "You can't single-handedly slaughter an army, and if you think you can while you're still recovering from the inhibitor, then you're delusional. We're all better off dead at this point. At least then the farm slaves would have a chance. Otherwise they'll be caught aiding criminal runaways, and you know what that means."

Ariock shoved down his guilt. His presence might have doomed these local ummins.

But anything was better than waiting to die.

If he could feel the way he'd felt in that hot spring, with Vy, just once more, he would take any risk to do so.

"Pung has a sleeping potion," Thomas was saying. "There's enough to kill everyone here if we each drink one drop."

Thomas went on talking about dying with dignity and not handing the Torth an easy victory, but Ariock tuned him out. He focused on the digging ummins instead. At least they had a goal and wanted to live. They just needed a lot of help.

Sand needed to fly out of that shallow pit.

If Ariock truly had powers, maybe he could make a sand whirlpool? It seemed worth a try.

He didn't want to remember the prison, but he'd caused that wall to dent. It hadn't felt magical. All he had done was mentally shove his self-loathing.

And what had he done in that moment in the jungle pool, when the bugs hummed in sync with his breathing?

He had felt a certain way. Not powerful, exactly, but he'd had a sense of... Stature. That was it.

It was a sense that he'd grown beyond the container of his body.

When Ariock had seen his own reflection in the cell wall, he'd incorporated it into his sense of self, just for one instant. That reflection had become part of himself, no longer a reflection but his own face and skin.

Ariock focused where the ummins were digging. It seemed ridiculous to try to trick himself into believing that he was sand, or that the limits of his body were not the limits he was familiar with. Embarrassing. But he forced himself to let go of his shame and just...breathe.

"Ariock?" People were trying to get his attention. Irarjeg looked impatient.

"We need to move on," Vy said.

They wanted to abandon the hovercart and hope for the best.

But it seemed clear to Ariock that leaving such a huge piece of evidence meant death. It meant defeat. If he gave up and walked away, he would fail to protect his friends.

So Ariock ignored their insistent voices, closed his eyes, and sent his awareness outward, away from his body.

He imagined that he could feel the uneven sand, as intimate as his own skin against metal scraps of clothing and shackles. The density of each pebble became familiar to him. He mentally traced their contours, understanding which were shiny and which were translucent. Grains of sand lay atop each other in disorderly rows, billions upon billions.

Ariock knew each row. He was the air between them.

Lively sparks disturbed the sand. Everywhere an ummin knelt, Ariock sensed electric distortion.

Tiny sparks nestled here and there, so minuscule they barely registered to his awareness. Bugs.

He was the sand, both its surface and its cool depths. He was the shade and the sunlight. The wind inhaled and exhaled with his breathing. The music of bugs climaxed and fell into the same beat as his heart. Ariock knew where each bug hid.

"Ariock." Thomas suddenly interrupted his own dire monologue. "What are you doing?"

A reply might have taken several minutes, because Ariock had no idea what he was doing. He burrowed his awareness deeper into the sand, gathering so many tiny pebbles, he lost track of the near-infinite mass.

One by one, the sandpit crew looked up from their labor.

Ariock sensed them as electric pulses standing on top of his extended self. If he took a deep breath, he felt sure that he would knock them over.

He should probably warn them to get out of the way. But there was so much to keep track of, he didn't remember how to form words. This must be how it felt to conduct an orchestra.

"You need to stop." Thomas sounded alarmed. He turned and shouted at the blue-painted ummins, waving his arms. His voice sounded distant and ineffectual to Ariock, like a radio signal.

The ummins scrambled into the surrounding jungle. Ariock waited until they were gone, although his concentration was stretched almost to a breaking point. The smallest distraction might cause him to lose his grip on the countless billions of grains of sand.

"Don't," Thomas begged.

Ariock flexed all the sand he was holding on to.

Sand exploded upward in a massive dome. He was the air driving it, and he punched outward, causing sand to spray in multiple directions.

Sand washed across the jungle. It flew across the hovercart and his friends, and Ariock as well, spraying across his legs.

That made him lose his extended awareness. He fell back into his own familiar body, which was disorienting, like falling from a great height. He felt shrunken and nauseous.

As the dust settled, he saw a sandpit that looked deep enough to bury a truck.

The surrounding jungle was a mess. Ummins coughed and spat sand. Everyone blinked away dust and regarded Ariock with varying degrees of awe.

"That was incredible." Vy looked as if she was reassessing everything she knew about the universe.

Pung began explaining something to the blue-painted ummins. He gestured at Ariock and said "Jonathan Stead" several times. Ariock didn't need to know the slave tongue to guess what else he was saying. Something about a storm god, or a hero who freed slaves.

"Son of Storms." Weptolyso snaked his thick neck, causing spikes to ripple. He snorted like a warhorse, and it sounded like a serious gesture of respect. "I will fight by your side whenever there is battle."

That seemed like too much to offer, but Ariock gave him a grateful nod.

Irarjeg bowed his bald head toward Ariock and spoke reverently in the slave tongue.

Kessa translated. "He says he wants you to feel welcome in Duin." She sounded unenthused, in contrast to almost everyone else. "Weptolyso. Perhaps you can shove that into the hole?" She indicated the dusty hovercart. "Let's try to clean up here."

Weptolyso snorted agreeably and pushed the empty hovercart toward the pit. Discarded slave collars, data tablets, and food containers rattled onboard.

The blue-painted ummins seemed impressed that Kessa could order a guard around. Ariock felt a little bit the same way about Kessa, if only because she saw that he wasn't a storm god or a miracle worker. She understood that Thomas was right about his lack of finesse.

Although practice might help.

The jungle needed to look untouched, and Ariock wanted to try using his powers to fill in the hole. He'd see if he could get it all done within seconds. Maybe he would focus better if he tried it sitting down.

He sat cross-legged, meditation-style.

"Whoa," Thomas said, hovering toward him. "Maybe this time you can cause a tsunami of sand or some kind of earthquake. Make sure you grab the attention of every Torth within a hundred-mile radius, just to make sure we're doomed."

"You said we're doomed no matter what," Delia pointed out.

"Some ways are better than others! Trust me. I've experienced more than two thousand unique deaths." Thomas eyed her dagger. "I'd rather go fast."

A commotion in the jungle interrupted them. People shouted at each other in the slave tongue. Ariock turned and saw a new group of ummins striding toward them. This bunch was unpainted and led by three ummins with elaborate head coverings, strung with ropes of clacking beads.

"Those are village elders," Vy said. "And the chief elder says…" She listened, trying to catch as much as possible before translating.

The one with the longest beads seemed to be haranguing Irarjeg. She stood with her hands on her hips and yelled at him.

Vy translated. "The chief elder says that Irarjeg is an idiot. Runaways, especially runaway Torth, are not welcome." She met Ariock's gaze, desperate. "They want us to go away. Ariock, we don't have time. If they have a hiding place, we need it."

CHAPTER 6

A BEGGAR FROM NOWHERE

If Torth showed up, they would take everyone by surprise. Their flying transports sounded like the wind.

On Kessa's slave farm, village elders had tried to predict the arrivals of Torth. But the alignment of the moons meant nothing, and neither did lucky eggshell shards. No one could guess when the Torth would show up on a slave farm or when they would take more than the usual harvest.

The chief elder seethed. All her attention was on the blue-painted crew. "You've invited deadly trouble, Irarjeg."

"I saw the big one command sand to rise up and fly!" Irarjeg pointed to Ariock. "We all saw." He looked to his crew for confirmation, and many nodded in agreement. They were dusty from the sand explosion.

The two junior elders from the village exchanged baffled looks, but the chief elder remained firm. "Torth have many devices," she said. "I am sure they tricked you, and I am sure it was easy. You should know better than to trust anything they say or do."

"These are not ordinary Torth," Irarjeg said emphatically. "Do you really wish to infuriate someone who can bury us alive under sand?"

"You are a fool." The chief elder gave him a disgusted look. She signaled, and her delegation raised their slingshots. "We will not shelter or help any of these supposed runaways. And Irarjeg, if you keep arguing, you can die in the wilderness."

Irarjeg gave Kessa a helpless look. But although he had misjudged his people, Kessa figured the elders must have good reasons to reject strangers. Everyone she'd seen on this slave farm looked healthy. No one was scrawny, and no one limped from a badly healed injury. The elders must be doing something right.

"Please, wise ones." Kessa stepped forward. "None of us are Torth. We are being hunted by the—"

The chief elder interrupted. "I am sure they told you what to say, city slave."

Her people fitted rocks into their slingshots.

"I speak to you of my own volition," Kessa said. "The words I speak are my own. We—"

"That scar around your neck was made over a lifetime of slavery," the chief elder cut in. "And you look as old as the desert. You are no runaway. They took off your collar and fooled you into believing it is real freedom."

Kessa hesitated.

"Get away from my village." The chief elder's tone hardened. "Get out of our slave farm, or we will hunt you down like animals."

One of the other elders sounded glum. "If they are being hunted, I am sure the Torth expect us to do the hard work of capturing them."

Kessa was all too aware of her filthy rags and scrawny condition. She didn't look like a heroic runaway because she wasn't one. She was a beggar.

"Kessa," Ariock said. "Will you translate for me?"

She nodded, although she figured that he would never persuade the elders of anything. He looked like a gigantic threat that needed to be gotten rid of.

"Your highness," Ariock said, speaking directly to the chief elder. "If you help us survive, then I promise, I will obey your commands. I will do anything in my power to help your village."

Kessa held his gaze, surprised, to make sure he was serious.

"Sweetie," Delia said cautiously. "Maybe you shouldn't promise to enslave yourself?"

"We're asking them to risk their lives to save us," Ariock told her. "If I can grant their wishes, I will grant them." He indicated the kilt of armor around his waist. "I wish I could offer more than promises, but I have nothing else."

Kessa felt honored as she translated. Ariock was a miracle worker—and he had tact. He spoke the right words.

The chief elder interrupted right away. "Why can he not speak the slave tongue?"

"He is not of our realm." Kessa paused, giving them a moment to wonder what realm he came from. Then she translated what he'd said, word for word.

The farm slaves lowered their slingshots, murmuring. Irarjeg sucked in his breath. A miracle worker's promises were not something to refuse lightly.

The chief elder tapped her beak in thought. "You do not sound like a Torth," she admitted, speaking directly to Ariock. "You make me uncertain."

While Kessa translated, the chief elder assessed the damage to the jungle, with broken vines and sand everywhere. The hovercart lay vertically in the hole.

"Show me your power," she told Ariock, decisive. "I command you to clean up this area and make it look like any other part of the jungle."

Ariock looked grateful as soon as he understood. "A wise command," he said. He loosened his arms and closed his eyes, as if putting himself in a trance.

"No," Thomas said imperiously in the slave tongue. "The giant is tired. He has done enough for one day."

The onlookers glanced at each other, uneasy. Thomas behaved a lot more like a Torth than anyone else.

The air felt heavy and watchful. Kessa's skin prickled. She had not paid attention to the breeze or the chorus of bugs, but she became aware when the air ceased to stir and her own heartbeat filled the silence.

"Ariock, this is colossally stupid," Thomas said. "You don't know your own limits or your range. The ancient Yeresunsa had classes and schools to learn how to use their powers."

"I agree," Delia said promptly. "Why not just make threats instead? Tell them you'll smite their slave farm unless they help us."

Ariock gave them both a quick, apologetic glance. "We don't have time." He closed his eyes again. "We need their trust."

The wind picked up. Vines undulated and swayed. Sand lifted off the ground in gossamer webs, all of it shifting and rolling toward the hole. The jungle floor looked like a river of sand. It was almost a whirlpool, all draining to the same place, with bugs and lizards caught in the flow.

Snaps and pops resounded from breaking twigs. The sky darkened with a mass of dead vines, torn paddle branches, and uprooted plants and flowers.

The flow of sand stopped. Wherever Ariock looked, debris floated off the ground, dragged upward. The mass rotated, gathering more debris.

Then it all got sucked into the hole, packed in and around the hovercart.

Sand poured over the mass with a rushing, liquid sound. The ground shifted and smoothed until all traces of the sandpit were gone.

Kessa's beak fell open in awe.

She felt the power depart. The jungle seemed to relax, the breeze returned, and bugs began to chirp and chorus. Yet everyone remained wonderstruck.

One of the elders fell to her knees, staring at the impossibility.

Thomas's mouth worked, as if he had a thousand things to say, but none of them were worth the effort.

"Bringer of Hope," the chief elder said to Ariock in a trembling tone. "You are most welcome among us."

With graceful care, she removed her beaded headdress and tipped her bald head to Ariock. All the farm slaves followed suit.

Kessa did not want to interrupt their humility, but she felt it was necessary to remind them of urgency. "We cannot waste time. If you have a place where we can hide, we need it."

The chief elder carefully placed her headdress back on. "Show them the way," she told one of her junior elders.

That one dipped an acknowledgment and beckoned. Kessa began to follow. But she stopped with concern, because Ariock was struggling to stand. He leaned over as if ill.

"You have a depletion headache," Thomas said, observing. "Powers are tied to health. You're in a weakened, starved condition, as well as recovering from the inhibitor. That headache is a warning that you should stop."

Delia hurried to her son. Vy rummaged in the painkiller bottle, while Weptolyso hauled Ariock to his feet.

"I'm fine," Ariock said. He walked with his head down. Weptolyso stayed very close, ready to catch him if he fell.

"I'll admit, that was impressive." Thomas sounded more sympathetic as he floated alongside Ariock. "The bad news is that nearly a hundred slaves saw what you did."

The chief elder adjusted her walking speed to join Thomas. "Torth," she said in a challenging tone. "Why are you not among your people?"

With gold-patterned robes and a silver hoverchair, Thomas looked imperious. He had clearly not suffered as a slave or a prisoner, and there was no such thing as a friendly mind reader.

Kessa had anticipated this problem. "I promise, good elder," she said, "Thomas is—"

She had been prepared to lie, to say that Thomas was an oddity, a disabled human. No one could guess why the Torth had kept him alive. But Thomas spoke before she could finish.

"I'm a renegade Torth," he stated.

A guarded, stony look came over the chief elder's face. She backed away, out of his range.

"I don't care why you are running from your people, Torth." She twisted her beak in disgust. "There is no circumstance that will persuade us to help you."

Kessa glared at Thomas for a different reason. He should have denied being able to hear their thoughts. At the very least, he could say a lot in his own defense. Why was he taunting them?

"Thomas saved us," Kessa said. "He is our friend, and he must stay with us."

"It's true," Pung added, coming to her side. He tapped the blaster glove. "Would a Torth allow me to wear this?"

The farm slaves exchanged dubious looks.

Frantic footsteps drew everyone's attention, and a terrified slave ran toward them. He glanced wide-eyed at Ariock, then dropped to his knees before the chief elder. "Molyt Dazel!" He panted for breath but spoke between gasps for air. "Torth...transports on the horizon. More than we...have ever seen."

Comprehension dawned on the faces of the farm slaves. Kessa saw that none of them had quite believed the danger. It was hard to believe, even for her.

"I could not count them all," the runner said.

"Go." The chief elder shoved Kessa. "We will handle everything."

When Thomas tried to float forward, everyone aimed their slingshots at him.

"One rule cannot be broken," the chief said. "A mind reader is never welcome among us."

"All right." Thomas raised his hoverchair, making himself an easy target. "If you want to stop me, you'll have to shoot me," he announced in the slave tongue. "Aim for the head."

Kessa threw herself in front of him. "No!"

Farm slaves stared at her in shock, and she realized how crazy she must seem, shielding a mind reader with her own body, as if she was some sort of heroic bodyguard. Even Pung stared as if she'd lost her mind.

"Please don't kill him," she begged. "He rescued us."

That was for her friends as much as to the farm slaves. Kessa saw that they didn't understand why Thomas was putting himself in danger, and they couldn't predict what he might do next.

"We will let him live," the chief elder said grudgingly. "To honor your wish, city slave."

Farm slaves uncertainly lowered their weapons.

"But the renegade Torth must agree to leave us in peace," the chief elder went on. "Let him hide in the wilderness."

Without offering a single complaint or argument, Thomas rotated his hoverchair and floated off into the jungle.

Kessa gaped.

Deep down, she understood what Thomas was doing. He believed the Torth would win. In his own twisted way, he was trying to snatch away their prize—himself, alive and helpless. He wanted a quick death. A knife to the throat, or a rock to the head, or a drop of deadly poison. Since no one would oblige him, he was going to slam headfirst into a sharp rock, or drown himself in the hot spring, or something like that.

"Weptolyso?" Kessa begged for help.

Weptolyso grunted a refusal. He was busy allowing Ariock to lean on him.

No one else followed the hoverchair. Vy and Cherise exchanged worried glances, but Kessa knew they would be too slow. And they were too focused on Ariock. Dreary work shifts must seem faraway to them now.

But Kessa could still feel a phantom prickling around her neck. Thomas had removed her slave collar.

"I will take my chances." She ran after Thomas.

Chasing him was probably a deadly waste of time, she knew. But how could anyone allow so much knowledge to simply wander off and die? Kessa would have given anything for just another day in which to question Thomas.

He didn't slow down or look at her. "I want to be alone," he said tonelessly.

Kessa tried to think of a way to convince him that he was wanted and needed. "Without you, we are doomed," she said.

"You're doomed anyway," he said. "No one defies the Torth Majority and gets to live."

Someone ran up behind them, beads clacking. The chief elder had caught up, along with a few of her people. They readied their slingshots just in case the renegade Torth tried to torture them with pain seizures. They formed a perimeter around Kessa and Thomas.

"You truly believe this Torth is worth your life, city slave?" the chief elder demanded of Kessa.

"I do." Kessa turned to confront her. "He has a name. Thomas."

The chief elder paced a few steps in one direction, then another, not daring to enter Thomas's range of telepathy. "You could have lied." She studied both of them. "You could have told us that he cannot read minds, and I would have believed you."

"I never lie." Thomas floated a distance away, giving the chief elder a flat stare. His fluency in the slave tongue confirmed that, unlike Ariock, he was from the Torth Empire.

"So, a virtuous Torth never lies?" The chief elder laughed without humor.

"I have advantages over non-telepaths," Thomas said. "Lies would be unfair."

"Unfair." The chief elder clearly disbelieved him.

"I trust him," Kessa said.

"I won't hide what I can do," Thomas said. "Or who I am. Now, if you're going to show me mercy, I suggest you make it quick."

Kessa hissed. She wished he would at least attempt some tact.

The chief elder took a daring step closer. "We have a saying, Torth. 'A beggar from nowhere owes everything.' You are a beggar. Do you agree?"

"I suppose," Thomas said with caution.

"You never lie." She took another step closer. "Then I require your promise. We will offer you shelter on the condition that you keep our secrets, respect our minds, and obey every command we speak. Do you agree?"

Thomas looked sour.

"This is as far as I will go, Torth," the chief elder snapped. "Yes or no."

"He will," Kessa jumped in.

"I'm weaker than a hatchling," Thomas said. "So I can't perform slave labor for you."

"He can teach you anything you wish to learn," Kessa explained to the chief elder. "He is very wise, and he knows ancient secrets."

"Ancient secrets?" The chief elder seemed intrigued.

Thomas switched to English, his tone hard. "Since when do you speak for me?"

Kessa met his gaze. He had better not expect her to remain quiet when her words could make the difference between life or death.

The chief elder looked as if she was imagining great things. "Make the promise, and you shall have safety."

"You may not like the things I could teach." Thomas studied her, and he looked a little bit curious. "Why are you so confident that your whole village can outwit the Torth? There's no way your people can keep us hidden. They will tear through your thoughts."

The chief elder sounded tolerant as she glared at him. "You should take a chance and trust us, Torth. The same way we are taking a chance in trusting you."

Thomas hesitated, no doubt wanting to probe her mind.

Then his shoulders slumped. "Okay. I promise to obey your commands, respect your minds, and keep your secrets."

"Then we will take the biggest risk we have ever taken." The chief elder stepped aside and gestured for them to go on without her. "Run. I think you can get there in time, but move fast." She touched the shoulder of one of her people, and that one ran ahead.

Kessa paused. "What about you?"

The chief elder sighed. "We are used to the Torth. We will prepare for a visit."

That was all she said, and explanations would have to wait. Kessa ran.

SANCTUARY

The only unusual data point that Thomas knew about this slave farm—without prying into anyone's secrets—was that they tended to breed healthier and more industrious slaves than those from neighboring farms. The Torth Empire attributed the prosperity to a local orchard. Extra fruits probably gave the local slaves extra strength to perform their mining duties.

But perhaps the Torth Empire was wrong.

Perhaps the Torth Majority had a habit of making cognitive errors.

Maybe it wasn't the extra fruits, but some other source of strength. A secret stockpile of food and equipment? A secret cave stash of contraband? Thomas just couldn't guess how slaves could be so incredibly good at concealing a major secret from mind readers. Random mind probes were a part of every slave's life.

It made him curious.

The group hurried past an ummin-size hut, which was built from paddle trees and adobe. Then another hut. Soon Thomas and his companions were parading through a shady village of slave huts.

Horrified dismay spiked from Vy. "Do they even understand the danger?"

Ummins peeked furtively through uneven, round windows, then ducked out of sight. Ariock and Weptolyso were especially noticeable. They towered above the vine-strewn rooftops.

"We can't be seen," Kessa called out, exasperated and despairing. "We cannot let the Torth know we are here."

Their guide, a junior elder with pouches and bags tied to her waistband, glanced back with a look of mistrust. Then she led them down another dusty alleyway.

Thomas sensed well-justified fear and frustration boiling inside his companions as they followed. Delia had the ionic dagger gripped in both hands, as if she was ready to slide it free of its sheath and stab Torth.

Kessa jogged to catch up with their guide. "This won't be a visit from a couple of Brown Ranks," she said. "This will be worse than anything in your experience. The Torth could kill everyone in this village if they find you hiding us here."

"Have faith, city slave," the guide said.

With that, she darted into one of the dingy huts, seemingly at random. A web of knotted ropes hung over the crude doorway, swinging from her passage.

Kessa stopped, and so did the rest of them. None of the huts looked strong enough to withstand a strong wind, let alone an invading army of Red Ranks.

"I should have used my powers to make a cave for us." Ariock's huge shoulders slumped in defeat. "I'm sorry."

"Maybe we still have time," Vy said, although she sounded less than certain. She could see that Ariock was suffering from the depletion headache.

Cherise ducked into the hut where their guide had gone.

Thomas didn't need to be within range to guess her thoughts. She might not fully trust these farm slaves, but she trusted Thomas even less. She would do anything to stop feeling reliant on him.

He couldn't blame her. If he died from torture, maybe that would be karmic justice for the way he'd tortured her and broken her trust.

He almost looked forward to his upcoming death, no matter what form it took. He was far more aware of his bodily discomforts than he had ever been as a Yellow Rank. He no longer had caretakers or slaves, and he could no longer escape his own aches and limitations. He needed the Megacosm for that kind of blissful escape.

He had been a god in that realm. He could run and fly and stroll through exotic landscapes as a passenger in other people's minds.

Now he was unwanted, an outcast from Torth and slaves. He might as well be dead.

"Can we all fit inside there?" Vy peered into the hut, and disappointment rolled through her mind. "I don't know if Weptolyso will fit through the door."

Thomas focused on her perceptions. The interior of the hut was dim, lit only from the crude windows. Baskets, primitive cookware, and bedrolls decorated the place. It smelled of fire smoke and spices.

"There's nowhere to hide," Vy reported.

Inside the hut, their guide lifted a large stone mortar, then banged it against an oversize stone pestle with a heavy clack.

Cherise watched with curiosity as the guide dropped the mortar again and again.

Thomas floated into the hut. The junior elder seemed to be summoning something or someone. This was interesting.

The guide paused when she saw Thomas. "Torth," she seethed, with the mortar in her hand. "You made big promises, but I have not heard them for myself. Look at me and promise that you will never harm a slave."

"I promise, Utavlug the Healer." Thomas used her name and title. "I will never harm a slave."

Utavlug narrowed her eyes. Thomas could have pretended not to know her name, not to be a mind reader. Instead, he seemed to be flaunting his power over slaves.

"How do I know you won't torture us with pain seizures?" she demanded.

"I never lie," Thomas said. "Besides, Torth can only torture one victim at a time. I'm outnumbered here." He sensed her distrust of Cherise, Vy, Delia, and Ariock. So he added, "Contrary to what you believe, most Torth don't enjoy hurting slaves. It isn't fun. I don't want to do it."

Cherise stood beyond his range, but her face looked full of unspoken accusations.

"Your kind kicks small children," Utavlug said. "And you're murderers. I watched a Torth murder my grandfather with a pain seizure."

Thomas sensed her buried pain and hatred for Torth. "I'm sorry for that." He spread his hands, a signal of his harmlessness. "I'm not that kind of Torth."

She remained mistrustful.

"We need to disappear," Thomas said. "If we're found trying to hide in your village, the Torth will…" He trailed off at the sound of something very heavy rolling underground.

A series of clicks followed. An irregular section of floor popped up, shedding sand.

Thomas was so surprised, he said, "Oh."

Kessa glanced at Thomas, confirming that he hadn't guessed there was a hidden trapdoor.

Utavlug the Healer seized the slab and rolled it back with effortless ease. The trapdoor apparently had wheels on tracks, and perhaps a spring-loaded mechanism.

Someone down there must have been listening for the thump of mortar on pestle.

Sure enough, a flickery torch poked up through the hole, followed by a frail-looking ummin child. The child gave Thomas a wide-eyed, terrified stare.

But the child wasn't what made his jaw drop in surprise. The fuel cup of the torch was on a gimbal, and it appeared to be weighted, so it remained upright and steady, no matter how the pole was carried.

This was technology. Not on the same level as Torth technology, but still, it was far more advanced than anything slaves were allowed to be capable of.

"How do you keep this a secret?" Thomas breathed.

Utavlug spoke rapidly, trying to put the child at ease. Then she pushed Kessa toward the trapdoor. "Hurry."

When Thomas hovered in that direction, ready to hide, Utavlug said, "Stop, Torth."

He toggled his hoverchair and glided to a stop. There he floated, trying to look obedient.

"Are you going to convey this to your kind?" Utavlug asked him.

"No." Thomas answered with as much patience and kindness as he could muster. "I'm an exile."

She studied him with a guarded look. "Promise that you will never communicate with any Torth. Henceforth, you will live as a slave and never return to the Torth."

Thomas hesitated. He had inwardly hoped to ascend into the Megacosm one last time when death found him. Just a few seconds of basking in near-infinite knowledge might make death bearable.

"Promise!" Utavlug's eyes widened with outrage that he wasn't complying right away.

"I promise to never willingly reveal your secrets," Thomas said. "If my promises aren't enough…" He switched to her native language so his fellow travelers wouldn't understand. "Then have your people kill me. Just make sure my companions don't notice until it's too late. They'd try to stop you. I won't. I promise."

Utavlug gave him a suspicious look, although she was distracted as the other travelers raced through the trapdoor, descending into the tunnel below. Pung. Cherise. Kessa.

"You are very strange," Utavlug told him.

"So are you." Thomas peered down the way his companions were going. A steep tunnel vanished into shadowy darkness.

"Down there," Utavlug said, "we hide our sick. Our injured. Our children who aren't ready. Some spend their entire lives in the sanctuary."

Thomas gave her what he hoped was a reassuring look. "I've been commanded not to probe minds, so I won't dig out how you keep this a secret. But you surprised me, and that's hard to do. You have my respect."

He sensed a softening in her demeanor. "Your kind finds us to be very stupid," Utavlug told him. "Our minds are easily addled. When the Torth probe our minds, we let panic overtake us."

Thomas took a half second to work through her implication. Most slaves endured mind probes with stubborn endurance. They knew better than to panic, because the Torth found intense emotions to be distasteful. Panic could get a slave killed and replaced.

But farm slaves were less replaceable than city slaves, especially if they were healthy and productive. Frequent panic attacks might be forgiven…

especially if the slaves in question recovered fast and still pleased their masters.

The Torth placed so little importance on the emotional state of their slaves, they might not notice or care.

"That's clever of you," Thomas admitted.

"It is survival." Utavlug the Healer gave him an accusatory look. "Your kind murders slaves who are crippled." She pointedly looked at his underdeveloped, twig-thin arms. "A terrible waste."

He had no argument for that.

"The chief elder wants to trust you." Utavlug clearly disagreed with the chief elder. "If she is wrong, then you will bring death to everyone here. Children. Elders. You will end an era of freedom."

Thomas was glad that Cherise had already descended into the tunnel. Otherwise, her silent looks of accusation might have worried Utavlug even more.

"I won't betray you," Thomas said, and he inwardly made it a promise. He had managed to stay away from the Megacosm all night and all morning. Surely he could keep up this level of abstinence?

Truly, he was harmless. The real danger was Ariock. The giant needed to quit experimenting with his volatile Yeresunsa powers.

Utavlug turned toward the hut exit. "You are here, and events are out of my control. Go and vanish underground. I will pray to the spirits."

CHAPTER 8

DREAMLESS

Vy felt her way ahead in very dim, distant firelight, single file after Delia and Thomas. She ran her hands over the tunnel ceiling in front of her so she could avoid smacking into low parts. The tunnel had a smoky, musky odor. That probably came from ummins and campfires or torches.

"Ariock?" She heard him moving behind her, forced to crawl because the tunnel was sized for ummins. "Are you doing okay?"

Silence.

She turned around.

Ariock spoke with reluctance. "Do you have any more of those painkillers?"

Vy pulled out the bottle of Torth-grade painkillers. "Here." She had given him a couple of pills earlier, and now she handed him two more. "I have no idea what dosage might be dangerous, but I should have known that you'd need a larger-than-normal dose."

"Thanks." Ariock sounded ashamed.

As he swallowed the pills, washing them down with a swig from a canteen, Vy pulled off her luxury robe. "Here. You can use this to cushion your knees."

In the darkness, she could barely see Ariock. But he sounded more grateful than anyone should. "Thanks."

Maybe he was just grateful that someone other than his mother was showing him kindness.

Vy was careful to keep her footing on the steep path. She heard scraping sounds and pained grunts from behind them, and that must be Weptolyso. The poor nussian had to contort himself to fit through the tunnel. Vy tried not to imagine how they would handle a situation where he got stuck.

Well, perhaps Ariock could use his powers for any dire problem.

"Bringer of Hope," the chief elder had named him. That fit. Hope was exactly what Vy felt whenever she considered what Ariock might be capable of. She kept thinking of his storm-like powers and the story of Jonathan Stead.

According to slave gossip, Ariock had managed to kill two Red Ranks with his bare hands in the prison, without any powers whatsoever. People in the Tunnels must still be talking about that event.

"So," Vy said, trying to sound casual. "Do you think we have any chance of stealing a spaceship and flying home to Earth?"

Ariock laughed softly. "That's a nice idea."

Vy didn't press the matter, but she smiled. There was hope in his tone.

"You have a beautiful home that you must be missing," she said. "I loved the stonework. Did Jonathan Stead—I mean, Garrett—design it?"

"Yeah." There was no humor in his tone.

The revelations about his ancestor might have shaken his sense of identity. Vy decided to change the subject. "So, does your name mean something?" she asked. "'Ariock' is unusual."

"My mom changed the spelling from the biblical version," he said. "But it means 'lion.'"

"It fits," Vy said. "I saw winged lion statues outside your house."

Ariock laughed, but he sounded sad. "Garrett set that up as a family motif. I could never live up to it. I've always been the opposite of heroic and brave."

Vy tried to think of a way to argue against his self-assessment.

"What about your name?" Ariock asked. "Is 'Vy' short for Violet?"

"You guessed it." Vy remembered kids taunting her in grade school, making her name sound like "toilet" and "violence." That was when she had insisted on the abbreviated version.

She was grateful the darkness hid her blush.

"It's a beautiful name." Ariock sounded approving. "And it's the Torth taboo color."

That surprised a laugh out of her. "Yeah!"

"Violet Hollander." Ariock said her name with relish.

"Ariock Dovanack." She tested his name, liking the syllables. "I guess it could have been Ariock Stead."

Ariock was silent, and she could almost feel his shame. It had been thoughtless of her to bring up the fact that his family patriarch was actually a renegade Torth, or a Torth descendant.

"You're entirely human." Vy glanced back at him to show her conviction. "That's how I think of you."

"I'm seven-eighths human," Ariock said.

"That's full human, as far as I'm concerned."

"What about Thomas?" Ariock asked. "He's your foster brother. Is he human?"

"I don't know," Vy admitted. If Thomas had learned any facts about his biological parents, then he had not seen fit to share that knowledge with the rest of them. He might have as much human ancestry as Ariock.

On second thought, she doubted it.

"Can you read minds?" Vy asked Ariock, confident that he could not.

"No," he said.

"Then you're not a Torth at all," Vy said. "I don't care how many mind readers were in your family tree. It doesn't matter."

"Thank you." He sounded quietly grateful.

Vy smiled in the darkness, glad that he could feel certain about some part of his identity.

The tunnel evened out, and a golden glow lit the way ahead.

Soon Vy emerged into a large cavern with rough-hewn pillars. She straightened with relief.

As her eyes adjusted to the flickering torchlight, she saw petroglyphs etched on every rocky surface. Paddle trees. Lizards. Eggs. Patterns and stylized ummin figures, all jammed together and overlapping. It must have taken years to carve so many intricate images.

This hideout might have been in use for multiple generations.

A group of adorable ummin children cringed underneath knitted blankets, staring at the strangers with terror. They looked like baby owls, with round faces and tiny beaks.

Vy tried to look as unthreatening as possible as she began to explore the hideout. An adolescent ummin was explaining things to the younger children, but reassuring words were not enough. They clung to each other, trembling—especially when they saw Ariock.

And then Weptolyso.

Neither giant could stand up in the hideout. They had to crawl. Even so, they were immense, blocking a lot of the torchlight.

"I command you to stay away from these children," the adolescent called out in a fearful tone.

Vy offered a dip of her knees. "We obey," she said, and she translated for Ariock.

He gave a serious nod.

The adolescent didn't look reassured, but the children exchanged glances of curiosity.

Before Vy turned back to her exploration of the hideout, she caught sight of one particular scar on Ariock's inner forearm. Most of his scars came from the prison where he'd fought beasts. Vy had examined those wounds during their journey across the desert. But this scar was not made by horns or claws. It was precise and ruler-straight, running from his inner wrist almost to his elbow.

Vy had worked with enough suicide cases, and spent enough time in hospitals, to know a suicide scar when she saw one.

"Just give me the potion." Thomas had a thirsty look, gazing at a vial that Pung held. Its contents glowed a faint green.

"What is that?" Vy asked.

Pung studied his former owner with suspicion. "He wants to go to sleep."

The Torth might bust into this secret hideout at any moment and murder or capture them all. This seemed like an odd time to want a nap.

"It's our best chance for survival," Thomas said. "It gives dreamless sleep, and the Torth can't detect a mind that's deeply unconscious."

Pung clutched the vial. "We are deep underground. The Torth cannot hear our minds from the surface. Uh, can they?"

"Better safe than sorry," Thomas said.

Bags of exhaustion underlined his eyes. He must be tired after staying awake all night, answering Kessa's relentless questions.

He also looked weak. He was more withered than Vy remembered, as if his time as a Yellow Rank had sucked out the last vestiges of his childhood energy.

Come to think of it...

"Have you been taking your NAI-12?" Vy asked. "You can ask me to administer the doses."

"I'm fine." Thomas glared at her, his eyes golden and malevolent. "I don't need help."

Vy doubted that. But she held up her hands to show that she was harmless. "Okay. No problem."

Her foster brother had never liked being treated as a child, but he had known his physical limitations. This new resistance seemed impractical. Illogical, even.

Maybe he was afraid of throwing Vy into a slave-like role?

Or he was afraid of seeing her as an inferior. All his human warmth seemed gone. Would it ever return? Vy supposed he wasn't going to easily shed thousands of lifetimes' worth of Torth memories. All those lifetimes might be overriding everything he had absorbed on Earth.

"I just need sleep," Thomas said.

Pung began to hand over the vial, but Kessa plucked it away. "What is this? Where did you get it?"

Pung indicated Thomas. "He directed me to make it." Pung made an unscrewing motion. "If you let the odor out, it will put anyone who smells it to sleep."

Despite herself, Vy watched with interest. The so-called sleeping potion sounded like an anesthetic drug. It could be medically useful.

"But a single drop will kill someone?" Kessa asked. "Is that correct?"

"That is what he warned me about, yes." Pung seemed perplexed.

"Hmm." Kessa approached Thomas. "I will administer it to you." She hopped onto a raised part of the rocky floor so she could hold the vial to his face.

Thomas gave Kessa a sour look. "Whatever," he said, apparently answering an unspoken thought.

Kessa carefully unscrewed the vial, holding it as far from her body as she could manage.

"If any Torth come down here, please kill me," Thomas said in the slave tongue. "I don't care how. You can bash my head in with...a...rock." His voice frayed as he inhaled deeply from the vial.

As he exhaled, his head rolled to a rest. His second inhalation was much more relaxed.

Asleep, he looked like the child that Vy remembered from home. His face lost all the cold hardness and smoothed into a peacefulness that bordered on innocence.

"I wish he'd sniffed that earlier," Pung said. "For a Torth, he talks a lot."

Kessa capped the vial and handed it back to Pung. "I would appreciate it if you do not ever put this in his hands," she said. "Do not give him an opportunity to drink it."

Pung gave her a respectful look of curiosity. "All right."

"And hold on to the blaster glove," Kessa said. "And the dagger," she added, nodding at Delia. She spoke to everyone. "Let's not give him any weapons. Or anything that he can use as a weapon."

Delia looked mystified. "He can still give pain seizures."

"I am concerned about what he wants to do to himself." Kessa paced away.

Vy caught her meaning and stared at Thomas's peaceful, sleeping face. If Kessa was right...

She felt worn-out just trying to imagine how they might outsmart a telepathic supergenius who was determined to kill himself.

Well, maybe he wasn't all that determined? Vy had a suspicion that if he was, he would already be dead.

She glanced at Cherise, to see if there was any sympathy or curiosity. But Cherise had become unreadable. Her face might as well be stone. She held out her hand toward Pung.

"I think Cherise wants sleep, as well," Delia said.

Pung obliged, and soon Cherise was curled up on the stone floor, unconscious and breathing regularly.

Vy gathered a few blankets to use as pillows and covers. The cavern seemed well stocked in terms of supplies. Baskets full of goods lined rocky shelves.

A distant thud echoed down the tunnel.

Vy tucked Cherise in, but she felt hyperaware, listening for an invasion.

Weptolyso faced the tunnel with his massive forearms bunched, as if ready for a sprint. Ariock faced the same way, uncomfortably hunched. Even seated, his head pressed against the ceiling.

Vy settled against the rocky wall. She used to live with the epitome of determination when Thomas was working on his medicine. Now she recognized the same relentlessness in Ariock. Pain wouldn't faze him. Nothing would stop him.

There must be a story behind his suicide attempt, but whatever had brought him to that point, it was in the past.

She felt safe, knowing that.

CHAPTER 9

ANOMALIES

The Upward Governess lounged on a floating cushion, oiled with tanning lotion and drifting in her indoor lake. She slurped a frosted nectar smoothie.

At least the Servants of All had allowed her to keep her palatial suite. They had not retitled her as the Fat Fallen Blue or something equally demeaning. They had their priorities. Everyone was aware that her demotion was not yet enacted, and it might be canceled. She was on probation. She just had to locate the Betrayer and the Giant.

Find them, the Torth Majority seethed. They expected immediate results, and instead, the search was dragging on for hours.

Kill the Giant.

Capture the Betrayer.

Do it now. Now. Now. Now.

Now.

Now.

Popular demands were a distant drumbeat for the Upward Governess. Most of her focus was on the hunting troops. She poked in and out of individual perceptions faster than a stitching machine, gaining rapid updates.

Pilots soared above deserts, jungles, lakes, and canyons. They skimmed close to cliff walls. They hugged shorelines, using high-grade metal detectors to scan for a stolen junked hovercart. Slaves were commanded to look for giant-size footprints or anything anomalous.

Red Ranks trooped on foot through steep hills and dense jungles.

Other Red Ranks tore through industrial complexes, mines, factories, and shanty villages, probing the minds of every slave they encountered. They shook hapless ummins, hoping to jar loose a hint.

None of the farm slaves had encountered armored military ranks until now. They flailed in panic, hyperventilating. Their thoughts buzzed like trapped bugs. Their heads seemed empty.

Slaves lived narrow little lives and could not process anything that broke their routines. They were pathetic. The Upward Governess could not understand why anyone—especially the Betrayer—would want to live among them.

A Red Rank found a child cowering inside a cauldron. When he began to probe its mind, the child began to scream. The ugly, terrified noise stirred an unknown feeling inside the Upward Governess.

She suspected that a slave child's death would only make her feel worse. So when the Red Rank thumbed his blaster glove to killing mode, she whispered in his mind, *Don't get distracted. Keep your glove set to neutralize Yeresunsa.*

The Red Rank stomped on the child, unmindful of its choked cries.

More than a few troops were slaying terrified slaves and slave children. The Upward Governess sent a strong command to avoid killing. *It's counter-productive,* she reasoned. *Traumatized slaves will panic again and again, every time they encounter a Torth.*

Children, especially, ought to be left in peace. They had the freshest mnemonic recall and less life experience to dig through. Unusual encounters would flare bright and fresh in their young minds. It was in everyone's best interest to avoid making children fear mind probes.

A silken thought cut through the distant listeners. *Your hunt isn't going well.*

This mind was not in the Megacosm.

The Upward Governess rotated her floating cushion, slow, forcing the Swift Killer to wait for a face-to-face confrontation. How dare she show up in New GoodLife WaterGarden City!

But the Upward Governess no longer had enough social clout to order her away.

The Swift Killer was very smug today. After all, her original assessment of the Betrayer had proved correct. She kept reminding her orbiters that she was an unparalleled expert on humans.

What you need, the Swift Killer thought, hefting a massive gun attached to her arm, *is a monster hunter.*

She stood on a motorized raft, clad in an armored bodysuit that hugged her muscular physique, gleaming white. Her hair was pinned up. The huge glove that engulfed her arm could shoot down transports and tanks, not just charging beasts. It would deliver missiles.

Antitank weapons were rarely needed. They had not been commonly used in warfare since the early days of Torth expansion.

The Upward Governess didn't care what ancient armory the Swift Killer had sifted through, but she grudgingly admitted to a little bit of respect. The Giant's raw power might be greater than that of his catastrophic forebear, Jonathan Stead. Missiles were prudent.

Where are the enemies? the Swift Killer demanded. *You knew the Betrayer (Yellow Thomas) better than anyone. With My enhanced musculature plus My power suit, I can get things done. Let's team up and (win glory) get rid of this threat. Together.*

Well. That was generous. Self-interest motivated generosity, but still valuable.

I have millions of Torth and even more slaves searching every plausible place where he might be hiding, the Upward Governess assured the Swift Killer. *The Giant and the runaway guard are both too large for a typical slave hideout. Their options are limited.*

The Swift Killer's look of consternation would befit the face of a primitive. *The Betrayer sabotaged your weather satellites.*

I've fixed the damage, the Upward Governess assured her orbiters.

What other mistakes have you made? the Swift Killer taunted. *Are you even sure that the Betrayer left this city? If I were a renegade supergenius...* She imagined her own conjecture.

She imagined the Betrayer creeping through slave Tunnels.

He would subsist on the charity of easily manipulated slaves until he could train the Giant to wreck his way through the spaceport. While the Giant battled a Torth army, the Betrayer would steal a high-speed streamship and escape the planet with loot and slaves.

The Swift Killer adjusted her antitank gun. *You ought to replace all the slaves in your city so they can't secretly aid Our renegade.*

The Upward Governess allowed herself a small sigh. She wasn't going to replace every slave in her city. Such a huge project would negatively impact the search effort, as well as her quality of life.

Besides, she couldn't imagine the Betrayer setting himself up to be worshipped by slaves. Nor would he leave the Giant behind to die.

You could be wrong, the Swift Killer insisted. *Anyhow, you don't seem useful.* She shifted her weight on the raft. *I suppose your help doesn't matter. If you fail, We'll simply evacuate this planet so We can pound the surface with thermonuclear explosions.*

The Upward Governess imagined her beautiful city ruined, vaporized in a nuclear mushroom cloud, along with the province she governed.

Servants such as the Swift Killer could pressure the Majority into voting in favor of global destruction.

The Upward Governess had to temporarily drop out of the Megacosm. Her flash of fury was too rude to share with her orbiters. How dare anyone endanger her home! How dare the Swift Killer threaten everything she had ever worked hard to achieve!

You cannot even guess his whereabouts? The Swift Killer watched for a reaction.

Give Me a moment. The Upward Governess collated everything she was absorbing from the millions of hunting parties. She ran comparative analytics.

She also conjured a mental image of the Betrayer *(Yellow Thomas)* as she remembered him. With her total recall, she knew his face well, down to the striations in his yellow eyes.

She just couldn't recreate his sprawling mind.

And she missed those human memories, their sweet and juicy interactions. He contained more delectable experiences than she could ingest in one sitting.

Now he was probably living in squalor, starving, and surrounded by ignorant slaves.

As the Upward Governess imagined her nemesis in his current circumstances, a smile spread over her face. She sipped on frosted nectar to hide it. *We may not need to find him. His mind (his perceptions) may come to (Us) Me.*

? The Swift Killer wondered what the Upward Governess meant.

He is craving the Megacosm. He may (cave in to temptation) ascend.

Doubts rippled off the Swift Killer. *Surely he knows better.* Most renegades remained severed from the Megacosm for days, or even months.

The craving drives them half-mad. The Upward Governess summoned a memory of the Lone Assassin, the renegade who had birthed the Betrayer. She had been shatteringly grateful to rejoin the Megacosm, even knowing that she faced death by torture.

The Swift Killer shrugged. *I'm sure a supergenius can think of a way to entertain (distract) himself for a few days, at least.*

Unlikely. The Upward Governess was in such a good mood, she went on to clarify. *A mind with high processing speed needs constant stimulation. I am always processing an influx of data.* She demonstrated. *When the Betrayer lived among the savages of Earth, he was accustomed to a very thin trickle of knowledge. That is why his mind was withered in comparison to the minds of other supergeniuses. But when he came to live with Us, he grew accustomed to a much greater influx of knowledge. That load gave him enough tools to ramp up his processing speed and general cognition. Now? Boredom is his greatest threat. For him to lose the Megacosm...*

She imagined a patient on heavy doses of a vital drug, then severing the treatment instead of trailing off the dosage.

The Swift Killer remained dubious. *So he'll be irritable and depressed?* Surely he could ignore those symptoms.

He might find boredom too much to endure. The Upward Governess understood how it felt to wake up grateful that she had woken up. Sometimes the act of chewing felt like a chore for her. Few Torth understood how a chronic illness could weigh on one's existence. Constant dread could turn into a series of gambles.

So the Betrayer might not fear death as much as he should.

And he would feel desperate to rejoin the Megacosm, just for the vicarious experience of being healthy.

And when he ascended?

His gargantuan mind would be instantly recognizable. Half the Empire would lock onto his perceptions. Even if he blindfolded himself, even if he tried not to think about where he was, a supergenius like the Upward Governess could suck up his perceptions and idle memories within a split second. She would derive clues.

The Upward Governess suppressed a giggle. *I will weave a web, like the spiders of Earth, sticky, cutting off all his possible escape routes.* She would use the Megacosm as much as possible until he showed himself.

Why don't you join Me in the field? the Swift Killer invited. *With your freakish mind, you can extract memories from entire slave populations within minutes. You could do the work of a troop by yourself.*

That was true. A supergenius could imbibe an entire lifetime in eighteen seconds or so, whereas an average mind reader required a lifetime to accomplish that goal.

But the Upward Governess felt comfy on her floater lounge. She didn't want to get dirty or sweaty or exert herself.

Besides, her mental analytics were beginning to yield results.

Results? The Swift Killer perked up.

Anomalies. The Upward Governess compared each anomaly, ranking them according to how likely they were to be caused by Yeresunsa powers. The Betrayer would do his best to hide and erase clues, but he couldn't control everything his friends did. If there were any hints—anything at all anomalous—then she would winnow it out.

She set up criteria and discarded irrelevant data. She added a topographical map in her head.

A natural dam had appeared in a wetland.

There was an unseasonal migration of birds.

A new sinkhole had been discovered in a desert.

A rash had broken out among slaves in a plastics factory.

Barometric pressure had fluctuated inexplicably in a jungle.

The Upward Governess rapidly learned the details of each region. One particular set of associated data struck her as anomalous. In the jungle where unusual barometric pressure had been detected, the slaves of a nearby village, Duin, were highly valued for being robust. They worked in a region of salt mines, yet they rarely got sick or injured.

Report from Duin, she commanded.

The appropriate Crimson Red Rank in charge signaled that he was ready. The Upward Governess dived into his mind, feeling the bug bites on his neck, the sweat on his brow. She stood in his athletic body, sharing his vitality and strength.

The slaves of Duin are witless, the Crimson Red reported with a hint of exasperation. *Digging into their memories is like floundering through sewage. They panic every time they see a Torth.*

That was disappointing. But as the Upward Governess moved on, analyzing other anomalies, she replayed the invasion of Duin in the back of her mind. It seemed strange that every single slave in that village lost its mind to panic.

Every slave. No exceptions.

She double-checked against other villages and verified that this was, indeed, another subtle anomaly.

One random anomaly might be nothing. Two might add up to something. Three…?

Tighten the search radius around Duin, the Upward Governess commanded every troop in the region. *Set up seismic activity counters and surveillance. Rotate troops so you're fresh and alert.*

The Crimson Reds resented having to obey an Indigo-Blue Rank. She was technically their equal, not their superior. But everyone understood the value of intellectual ranks over military ranks, so their orbiters pressured them until they agreed and obeyed.

Gratified, the Swift Killer motored toward the shore. She radiated readiness for battle.

She almost seemed eager for it.

The Upward Governess almost felt sorry for *(Yellow Thomas)* the renegade supergenius. He must be desperately alone, frightened, reliant on the charity of slaves, and half-mad with craving for the Megacosm.

He didn't have a fair chance against *(Herself)* the most brilliant person in the known universe.

PART SIX

"I am a mind reader, and thus tainted beyond redemption. My sins weigh heavy upon me. But on Earth, I am distanced from this evil power. No one will recognize the person I become."

—Jonathan Stead

CHAPTER 1

LIFE SPARKS

When Ariock overheard conversational voices echoing down the tunnel, he let himself relax. By some miracle, the little gray ummin villagers must have fooled the Torth who'd questioned them. They had kept everyone safe.

He leaned back against the rock wall and sighed with gratitude.

It had been a very long time since he could relax and not expect guards to drag him into a fight or some kind of painful ordeal.

Vy looked sleepy, beautiful in the firelight. When he looked at her, she spoke. "How is your depletion headache?"

Ariock figured that he owed his fast recovery to the high-grade painkillers. Maybe that, or the cauldron of broth Utavlug the Healer had given him.

"It's gone," he admitted. "I feel pretty good."

Vy grinned. "Same." She stretched.

Ariock wanted to try extending his awareness again. Maybe he could inhabit the low, soot-stained ceiling? He might be able to spread his awareness all the way to the surface, and perhaps sense life sparks up there, and count them. Was that possible?

But he figured he would wait until Thomas awoke before he tried anything with potential risk. The boy must have huge amounts of helpful knowledge about Yeresunsa powers.

He listened to the crackle of torches and the distant voices. Did they sound…well, unhappy?

Tribal ummins poured into the cave. Their tones were full of despair. One villager was keening.

Vy leaped up. "Oh, no. People are hurt." She hurried toward them.

Ariock crawled after her, wishing the cave wasn't so enclosed. He missed being able to stand up. He already missed the feeling of a breeze on his skin.

But according to what Vy had told him, some of the ummins in this cave lived their whole lives hidden. They had given up sunlight in exchange for safety.

"Will you wake Thomas?" Vy spoke to Kessa. "He might have extra medical knowledge."

Kessa rushed away.

Vy knelt by an injured child covered in blood. The child looked flattened, and there were other ummins with terrible injuries.

The rest of the crowd watched Vy with suspicion and hope. No doubt they assumed that a Torth reject was tending to their injured child.

A healthy ummin jumped in front of Ariock, shouting at him and gesticulating with fury. Her voice sounded higher in pitch than some, so he assumed it must be a female.

"Uh, what's she saying?" he asked when it became clear the ummin was just getting started.

"Never mind." Vy sounded harried. "They think you can do miracles. I'll tell them that you can't heal injuries." Her words became foreign without a pause as she switched to the slave tongue.

Ariock backed away from the villagers. He tried to make himself unobtrusive, but he drew attention no matter how he tried to curl up. Dozens of villagers began to scream at him.

He didn't need to know their language to guess what they were saying. They wanted him to fulfill his promise.

And they were right. They deserved miracles.

Ariock was too ashamed to meet their pained gazes. This couldn't be the only village that the Torth had brutally invaded. During the past few hours, thousands of enslaved people across the continent must have been injured.

Or murdered.

Because Ariock had dared to defy the Torth Empire.

Thomas had not said that Ariock was the main target, but he didn't need to. The Torth wouldn't fear a handful of runaway slaves or a disabled child. No—the Torth wanted to get rid of the giant with illegal powers and the heritage of Jonathan Stead.

If Ariock turned himself in, he could stop the worldwide death and destruction.

"Don't be stupid," a voice said.

Ariock looked down to see Thomas floating below his elbow. The boy looked haggard.

"Your death wouldn't stop Torth from abusing slaves," Thomas said. "And if you turn yourself in, you'd get the rest of us get killed. So it would be like we never escaped. Everything that happened since then, including the destruction of slave villages, will have been for nothing."

He floated onward, apparently not caring how Ariock would react.

Villagers shrank away from the hoverchair. A few looked murderous, but they did allow Thomas near Vy.

She used a wet cloth to wipe blood off the injured child. "A Torth kicked her. I think her spine is broken, and she has broken ribs, too. Can you think of any way to mitigate the damage?"

"I never meant for this to happen." Thomas sounded almost as guilty as Ariock felt.

"Do you know of any advanced medical techniques we can use here?" Vy asked.

"If we had surgical equipment," Thomas said, "we could save her. But we don't."

He continued speaking, but the words were alien. It seemed he was commanding the villagers. One of them shot him a murderous look but then knelt and laid her head against the child's chest, as if listening.

Thomas wore a similar listening expression. "Her lungs are filling with blood," he said, and Ariock realized he was listening through the perceptions of the kneeling ummin. "She'll be dead in a matter of hours." He looked at Vy. "You did the right thing, giving her a painkiller and making her comfortable. That's all anyone can do."

Ariock wished he had never been rescued. This child could have lived a full life instead of dying on a stained blanket. He may as well have been the one to stomp on her.

Vy stood, gazing down at the child with sorrow.

"Did you listen to that villager's mind without permission?" Kessa asked Thomas.

He gave her a sour look. "Yes. I can't turn it off." He gestured at his head. "I won't probe anyone's memories or secrets, but there's no way I can avoid surface thoughts."

One of the villagers stroked the child from beak to forehead, her brows rigid with grief. "Zuduon," she murmured.

Mourning family and friends knelt by the injured child. Zuduon had inspired more love than Ariock ever had in his life. If justice was a scale, then it was grossly misaligned. How many innocent people would die today, just so he could live another twenty-four hours? That wasn't fair. He wished he could exchange his health for their injuries.

Ariock held out his hand and extended his awareness through the air to the child named Zuduon.

Her life spark felt weak and guttering. Everyone else within his awareness was a burning flame in comparison.

Ariock closed his eyes so he could tune out all the distractions. He focused on the injured child. He inhaled, smelling coppery blood mixed with ummin scent. He sensed the textures of beads and waistbands and the woven blanket beneath Zuduon.

He moved closer. Carefully, gently, he spread his awareness into the fragile body of the child.

What he sensed was near-infinite complexity.

He inhabited tissues, blood, mysterious organs, all quivering and pumping. He could manipulate the dense shards that must be bone, but he had no idea what needed to go where. He required medical knowledge. Without that, he would make fatal mistakes.

"Ariock." Thomas spoke sharply. "Stop trying to help. You'll just make things worse."

Ariock withdrew his awareness, but he wasn't ready to give up. If Zuduon was a dying ember, then his own life spark was probably a roaring furnace. Couldn't he give some of that to her?

He reached across the distance and gently touched Zuduon's forehead. He incorporated her ember into his sense of self. Everything else grew distant as he tried to radiate his health toward her.

"You'll just make them angrier," Thomas said. "Stop. You can't afford to look like a failure right now. Plus, you shouldn't do anything to wear yourself out."

Zuduon breathed in short, shallow gasps. Ariock sent more energy toward her. He couldn't tell how much she needed, so he attempted to give her all he had. He would give away his vitality, if he could. He would die if it meant this injured child could stay with her loved ones.

The guttering life spark erupted in a dazzle.

It gave Ariock a jolt, and he smacked his head against the ceiling. The sharp pain ruined his concentration, and he lost his connection to her life spark.

Zuduon sat up.

She doubled over, coughing blood. But her torso no longer looked flattened. When her coughing fit ended, she wiped her beak, looking confused.

"Aaah!" The mother threw her arms around Zuduon, babbling with joy. The startled child hugged back.

Villagers surged forward, poking and prodding the child. Everyone tried to touch her. They made room for one of the elders, Utavlug the Healer. Utavlug held her hand in front of Zuduon's beak, testing her breath.

"Holy crap," Thomas whispered.

"Is she healed?" Vy asked.

"Her pain is gone." Thomas sounded disbelieving. "She can breathe well. I…I think her ribs are no longer broken."

Utavlug pushed aside her beads and listened to Zuduon's chest. She made a stunned declaration, and the villagers whooped with joy.

Kessa stared at Ariock with amazement.

Vy stared at him as if he might be a new species of alien.

The child's mother spoke earnestly in the slave tongue, and Kessa translated. "She feels shame for having doubted you, Bringer of Hope. Please accept her gratitude."

Trembling, the child's mother dipped her head to Ariock.

"She says she owes you a favor now," Kessa finished.

Ariock dipped his head as low as he could, in return. "She doesn't owe me anything." The last thing he wanted was for a slave to feel indebted to him. "Every minute I stay here, this village is in danger. I owe them everything I can give. Tell them I will grant as many wishes as I am able."

"Power of a genie, foresight of a lemming," Thomas muttered.

Vy studied Ariock. "Wait, hold on. Are you in pain? What about that depletion headache?"

The spot where he had banged his head on the ceiling was throbbing a little. Mostly, he just felt ravenous.

"I'm fine," Ariock said.

"You just..." Thomas gave Ariock a look as if he was a monster. "Healing is supposed to be a dead power. It hasn't been done in thousands of years."

"Maybe your information is wrong," Vy told Thomas. "Maybe the Torth Empire is clueless about Yeresunsa."

Thomas backed away. Uncertainty looked strange on him.

"Is it possible the Torth Empire is wrong about these powers?" Kessa asked.

Ariock really wanted to hear Thomas's answer to that.

But instead of confronting the questions, Thomas pressed the controls on the armrest of his hoverchair and fled into the shadowy recesses of the cave.

Well then.

Ariock figured that his own questions could wait. Several more patients needed to be healed. The villagers were queueing up, eager for their wishes to be granted.

CHAPTER 2
SURVIVAL OF THE FITTEST

A part of Thomas kept surging upward, straining toward the glowing nirvana of the Megacosm.

It was so close, he could almost get there by accident. That was where all the knowledge in the known universe was. That was where he could find answers.

You can never go back, Thomas inwardly reminded himself. He had to remind himself, because apparently his flawless memory wasn't enough.

He was unwelcome in Paradise.

He was exiled from Eden.

Thomas bit the inside of his cheek and tasted coppery blood. He'd chewed his inner mouth raw, but pain wasn't enough of a distraction. The craving was relentless.

He tried to distract himself with the mysteries that had begun to arise around him. Like, just how skilled was Ariock? The big guy had exhibited a knack for telekinesis, storm powers, healing, and perhaps even prophecy, despite an utter lack of training.

Few Yeresunsa had more than one power. At least, that was what common knowledge attested to, drawn from ancient memories.

Ariock seemed overpowered.

And, for that matter, just how much raw power was Ariock working with? He had recovered from that depletion headache awfully fast. Either the dosage of inhibitor he'd been on had been far too minimal...or the pool of power he could draw from made any dosage seem insignificant.

A thousand generations of Torth had preserved *(and forgotten)* *(and rejected)* memories of the tyrants who used to rule them: Yeresunsa. But by now, those collective memories were fractured, faded, and dimmed from the passage of eons. The original victims of such Yeresunsa were long dead, their bones turned to dust.

And the Megacosm did not preserve recordings the way a data marble or an engraving could preserve things.

Was it possible that the earliest memories floating around the Megacosm, shared and reshared for eons, were inaccurate? Or overreactions? Or wrong in some ways?

If Thomas were in the Megacosm, he would never question common wisdom. Everyone knew that Yeresunsa were tempestuous. Tyrants. Too powerful as individuals to be trusted. Egomaniacal. Impossible to control. Yeresunsa were more dangerous than a tsunami or a tornado, since they generated such phenomena.

But here, in the darkness of a cave, severed from the Megacosm, Thomas found himself reexamining what the Torth masses thought they knew.

Baby farms and pedigree programs had existed for millenniums. Controlled breeding should have ensured that powerful Yeresunsa such as Jonathan Stead and Ariock Dovanack got bred out of the gene pool.

Thomas, too, for that matter.

Yet here they were.

Why?

Thomas felt the golden cuff around his ankle, attached to his skin. It dispensed a steady stream of inhibitor serum into his bloodstream. He wasn't going to risk destroying a village by accident.

Was he wrong about that risk?

Maybe everything he'd learned about Yeresunsa was wrong.

The collective minds of trillions of Torth glowed above him. Beckoning. If only he dared to scan for a few answers.

No. Thomas forced his mind away from definitive answers—or whatever the Torth Majority deemed as definite, anyway.

He just felt so weak all the time. And so bored. Time passed hellishly slowly without the Megacosm. Reality felt like a straitjacket.

Thomas reminded himself that he had escaped from abusive foster homes, as well as from a city governed by a Torth supergenius. Surely he could ignore the collective minds of trillions of Torth?

Cherise was sorting beads alongside an alien child. Her skinny knees poked out of her rag dress, a sign of how thin she'd become, but at least she was safe for now. She could forget about mind readers for a little while.

Thomas wasn't going to destroy her sense of safety ever again. He would rather die screaming in pain.

He drifted farther toward the rear of the cave, studying the petroglyphs layered on every hard surface. They implied stories. It could all be distilled into one message: *we are people.*

Every ummin who had ever entered this cave had left a mark, showing that down here, they were not slaves.

So they should not be asked to tend to Thomas's bodily needs.

He was going to need to beg for help fairly soon. He just wanted to catch Vy when she wasn't next to Ariock or Kessa, or anyone else. They already thought little of him. He didn't want to add disgust or derision for how help-less he was.

As he scanned the darkness of the cave, searching for a way to alleviate his discomforts, a faint green glow caught his eye. Pung had apparently left the sleeping potion on a rocky shelf.

Thomas floated in that direction. He might be able to reach it, unaid-ed. Unconsciousness would stop his maddening impulse to ascend into the Megacosm.

Maybe he should drink the vial instead of simply inhaling?

After all, no one else in this cave could compromise their safety as fast as Thomas, not even Ariock. Suicide seemed pragmatic. Logical. It was the best way out of this bad situation. If he died, the others would be safer. The idea of suicide only bothered him because…well, all living beings had a survival instinct. Even Torth.

That, and on some level of self-monitoring, he had registered a major personality change. The prospect of dying young used to terrify him more than anything else. Shouldn't he be curious about such a change?

"Torth." A stringy, wrinkled ummin blocked his path. "I need you to an-swer a question."

Strings of beads hung from her headband. This was the chief elder, Molyt Dazel. A few other villagers backed her up. Pung stood with them, with the blaster glove stuffed in his belt.

"Fine." Thomas stopped his hoverchair so as not to plow into them. Al-though he would rather ignore these ummins, he had promised to answer any questions posed by a villager. He wasn't going to throw away his last shred of personal honor.

"How do the Torth decide which children to steal from us?" the chief elder asked.

They all emanated attentiveness. Even Pung was interested.

Of course. City slaves such as Pung were the grown-up versions of the children harvested from slave farms. Villagers and factory workers never saw their children again. It was unheard-of for a city slave to show up in a slave farm like this.

"Slaves who grow up with their families are more well-adjusted and gen-erally survive longer," Thomas explained. "That's why all slaves are raised in rural places like this. The selections for cities are random."

He knew his answer wouldn't satisfy parents who had lost their children.

Indeed, he sensed buried pain in the mind of the chief elder. Both of her hatchlings had been taken by Torth.

"So I could have stayed with my parents and brother?" Pung sounded bitter.

The chief elder laid a hand on his arm. "Until now, we assumed that the taken children had something wrong with them. Something unknown, like infertility."

"Nope. It's just random luck." Thomas gave the chief a nod of acknowledgment and tried to float past the group.

"I'm not done, Torth." The chief elder hurried to block his path. Her followers formed a barrier, forcing him to stop again.

"Have you ever killed a slave?" she asked.

"No." Thomas was glad that he could answer that particular question with easy sincerity. Plenty of Torth ended up torturing their slaves to death, but he had managed to avoid it, despite pressure from the Majority.

"How many times have you tortured a slave with pain seizures?" Pung asked.

Thomas hesitated. The last thing he wanted to do was to soak up more disgust aimed his way.

The chief elder took his hesitance for refusal. Her gaze intensified. "Answer the question, Torth." She made it a command.

"Ten times," Thomas said. "I also did it to a Torth."

That quelled their disgusted rage. They regarded him with doubts and questions.

"The Torth was a mistake," he explained before anyone could voice that question. "Torth citizens aren't supposed to harm each other. But I was technically not a Torth yet, and I didn't know their laws at the time."

"They can hurt each other?" The chief elder sounded shocked.

"Yes. But they rarely do. It has to be a command from the Majority."

"But you did it without a command?" Pung asked. "Why did they allow you to live?"

Thomas recalled how the Upward Governess had vouched for him, protecting him. "One of them persuaded the rest to give me a second chance."

So he had believed, at the time.

But the Torth Majority were not known for giving second chances.

Now that Thomas could freely analyze the incident without an audience scrutinizing his thoughts, he wondered if the Upward Governess really wielded that much influence. He didn't think so. She was only one of many millions of governance ranks.

A fractional minority of those leaders had been dead set against him. The rest—mainly Servants of All—had made exceptions and allowances, again and again.

All together, they had ensured that a certain supergenius Yeresunsa hybrid from Earth would survive as a Yellow Rank.

That was anomalous, now that he thought about it.

Thomas tried to dismiss his suspicion. If clandestine Torth leaders had been covertly grooming Thomas for some nefarious purpose, surely he would have picked up on it? No one could hide secrets from him.

Well, except for a few ummins.

And some Torth.

Maybe a lot of people could hide secrets from him if they didn't trigger his suspicions.

Thomas began to run calculated scenarios in the back of his mind, testing his own gullibility. If he had any mental blind spots, he was going to patch the problems.

"Why are Torth so cruel?" the chief elder asked him. "Why do they abuse slaves so frequently?" She folded her arms, making herself comfortable.

The crowd around Thomas was growing. Blue-painted beaks stood out in the dimness.

"All species prioritize their own interests above those of competitor species," Thomas said. "That's how nature works. The Torth don't see you as people, any more than you see them as people. They see you as competitors."

"Competitors?" The chief elder was skeptical.

"Yes," Thomas said. "All species have the same primordial needs. We all need to eat, sleep, reproduce, and survive. The Torth are no different. They want to do those things better than you, so they've turned you into slaves, to serve them or die."

"You make Torth and slaves sound like wild animals." The chief elder huffed in disgust. "Are you excusing Torth brutality by saying they are predators? But they are not innocent, like birds or lizards. They know what pain they cause."

Others murmured in agreement.

"Think of the yoypru," Thomas said, naming a species of migratory bird the ummins were familiar with. "Whenever those birds show up, other animals starve to death, because they strip away all the nuts and berries. If the yoypru were aware of the effect they had, they would still gobble up all the nuts and berries in sight. If they were kind enough to leave some berries, that would allow other animals, like the heenrerel, to thrive. Soon the heenrerel would be fat enough to have twice as many hatchlings, and then their next generation would grab more berries the next year. Soon it would be the yoypru starving to death."

"So we are the starving heenrerel, and you are yoypru who take everything?" Pung asked.

"It's called natural selection." Thomas let his hands dangle over the sides of his hoverchair. "The species with an edge over its competitors does the best. So far, the Torth have outcompeted every competitor."

"A tiny parasite can kill a yoypru." The chief elder studied him with her gray eyes. "Is there anything that can do this to a Torth?"

Thomas studied the villagers. Their chief elder was quick minded, and teaching was less of a chore than he'd expected.

"Someday," he said, "there will be a civilization that outcompetes the Torth. Maybe your descendants will be the ones. You have a secret technique to mislead mind readers, which gives you an edge over most slaves."

Excitement swirled through them like a symphony orchestra as they began to debate the implications of natural selection. Until now, these ummins had assumed the Torth were unassailable, all-powerful gods. They'd never imagined the Torth as thieving animals, vulnerable to extinction. It was a fresh concept.

Thomas guessed that anything he taught to non-telepaths would count as criminal activity. His crimes were piling up.

If only he could help force the Torth Empire to crumble. He rather liked the idea of ummins delivering the death blow.

On the far side of the cave, villagers gasped in awe. Ariock must have performed another impossible feat.

Judging by the frequent cries of gratitude, Ariock had healed every major injury. He must be tending to toothaches and other minor problems by now. And he showed no sign of getting worn-out.

Delia Dovanack hobbled toward the crowd surrounding her gigantic son. She was stooped, and pain slowed her every movement. Cancer was destroying her.

No one had told Ariock that his mother was dying. They'd been distracted with trying to hide, and it had seemed pointless to add to Ariock's burden of worries. So Ariock didn't notice Delia standing in line like a supplicant, hands folded. Her eyes seemed to burn with fierce hope and love every time she glanced at him.

Thomas raised his head, observing from afar. Could Ariock heal cancer as easily as he could heal broken ribs?

What about spinal muscular atrophy?

Thomas hesitated. He surely didn't deserve healing. As long as he craved the Megacosm, he was a terrible danger to everyone in this cave. Better that he should die.

He wondered if Ariock could heal his addictive cravings.

Kessa ushered Delia to the front of the line. The shining hope in her gaze reminded Thomas of a certain girl with deep blue eyes. The Upward Governess would have done anything, paid any price, for a chance to be magically healed. She had desperately yearned to become the first supergenius in history to survive to adulthood.

Maybe that could be Thomas, instead.

Possibilities unfurled in his mind, exploding outward faster than he could stop them.

If he could survive to adulthood, he might grow smart enough accomplish anything. He would outlive the Upward Governess. He might even be able to figure out a way to destroy the Torth Empire.

"Will you excuse me?" Thomas asked his students. The hope inside him felt as wild as his craving for the Megacosm. "I want to go ask Ariock for something."

CHAPTER 3

OUTPOURING

Healing required almost no effort, as far as Ariock was concerned. It took his full focus, but he was getting faster each time, and the drain only lasted for a few seconds afterward. Then he went back to feeling good.

It was so easy, he wished he could visit a hospital, just to see how many lives he could save. He could have saved patients every day if he had known that he possessed this power.

He could have rescued his father.

He'd been nine years old, but with this power, he could have healed his father and the pilot as well. Adults at the time had whispered about Ariock's miraculous survival. Now he suspected that something—or someone with power—had intervened.

It was probably the same person who'd protected him from lightning when he was crucified.

It was probably himself.

"Ariock." Vy touched his arm. "Can I interrupt you for a minute?"

Delia stood next to her, stooped and fragile.

"Sure." Ariock bowed graciously to the ummin whose sprained wrist he had just healed. Ever attentive, Kessa saw the situation, and she spoke to the queued line of ummins, presumably asking them to wait.

"Your mother has something to tell you." Vy gently pushed Delia forward.

Ariock expected her to exclaim about his amazing powers. She must be as happy and surprised as he was. Her eyes filled with unshed tears, and she gazed at Ariock with more love than he had seen from her in a very long time.

"I have cancer," Delia said.

He figured he must have misheard.

"Late-stage pancreatic cancer," she said. "I may only have a few days left, Ariock." She reached out to grip his arm with one gnarled hand. "I'm sorry I hid it from you."

Vy and Kessa looked unsurprised. They watched Ariock to see his reaction. They had known.

His mother's odd behavior during their last few months on Earth suddenly made sense. Her frequent shopping trips must have been cancer treatments. Her morbid talks about the future must have been her way of trying to prepare. Now Ariock understood why she'd urged him to invite a friend, or a caretaker, into his lonely life.

How could he have been so oblivious?

"Ariock." Vy sounded apprehensive, her gaze darting to either side of him.

He became aware of items floating in his peripheral vision. Pebbles and stoneware had risen like the hairs on his arms. His awareness had accidentally spiked beyond the container of his body.

As gently as possible, he set the floating items down.

Ariock had to take a deep, calming breath. Once everything was on the ground and his awareness was safely withdrawn, he faced his mother. "Thank you for telling me."

She sniffled and wiped at tears streaming from her eyes. "I didn't want to burden you."

She didn't need to explain why. Neither of them glanced at the suicide scar on his arm, but they both remembered. He had taken a knife from the kitchen. Blood spilled over the giant-size table. His mother had pleaded, yelled, and finally threatened to call an ambulance. She'd tapped the emergency number on her phone.

"*Promise me you'll never hurt yourself again,*" she had demanded, her voice strong, her hair dark. At the time, she had seemed as unstoppable as a force of nature. "*Promise, for as long as I'm alive, you'll never do that again.*"

Ariock had put down the knife and made the promise. How could he abandon her like that? He had seen terror in her gaze. That was enough.

Even so, that version of Ariock had fully intended to commit suicide as soon as his mother exited his life.

That was a different Ariock, a powerless prisoner who existed in another world.

"I don't know if there's anything you can do," his frail mother said now. "I should have told you earlier."

"I'll try." Ariock wrapped his hands around her bony shoulders. Proximity made a difference when healing. The less he had to extend his awareness, the more potent his healing energy was.

Her weak life spark resisted his outpouring.

He kept at it, giving her more energy, and more. He seemed to have an endless supply.

At last, her spark blazed with new health. It had taken minutes instead of seconds. Ariock felt more drained than usual, but he thought he had done it. He sensed masses inside her body that were much smaller.

He ceased his connection and sat back to admire how much healthier Delia looked. She was still too thin, and her hair remained gray, but her new vitality was unmistakable.

She threw her arms around him. "I always knew you were special," she said fiercely. "From the moment I brought you into this world, I knew. I just didn't have any idea how amazing you are!"

She hadn't hugged him like this since he was small. Ariock gently wrapped his hands around her, still feeling drained.

And he noticed Thomas.

The villagers moved back, out of Thomas's range of telepathy, forming an aisle for him. Despite the firelight reflected in his golden eyes, Thomas looked as hopeful as a child faced with gifts.

"Do you want to be healed?" Ariock guessed.

"Yes. Please." Thomas floated as close as he could get.

Ariock assessed the boy's underdeveloped limbs and his malformed torso. This seemed different from cancer, different from broken bones. A few ummins had begged Ariock to regenerate their missing fingers or toes, but that sort of magic had proved to be beyond his capability.

"I don't know if I can," Ariock admitted. "I couldn't figure out any way to, uh, grow things. Or regrow them." Like muscles. Thomas lacked muscle mass.

Thomas still looked hopeful. "Can you try?"

Ariock reached out. "Of course." Maybe he just needed more practice.

Delia grabbed his arm spike. "Wait."

He looked at her, questioning.

"He claims that he's only half Torth." She shot a worried frown toward Thomas. "But can we be sure?"

Did it matter? Thomas had risked his life to save theirs. He didn't deserve to suffer.

Besides, his desperate hope was apparent. With a facial expression like that, how could anyone assume that he was fully Torth?

Ariock stopped himself before he could say something angry. His mother was trying to reassert control over her life. Her hair had gone white from suffering. And Thomas had, after all, tormented her with a pain seizure at one point.

"I'm giving him health." Ariock gently put his hands around the frail boy. He connected to Thomas's life spark.

When he flowed energy into that spark, it flared. Thomas looked refreshed. But not able-bodied.

Ariock considered the problem. "Let me try again."

He didn't wait for anyone to concede or object. This time, he slammed his healing energy toward Thomas and refused to let anything distract him or stop him.

Thomas's life spark remained unchanged. It would not take in any more energy. Instead, Ariock's awareness flooded outward, catching pebbles, which floated upward.

"Stop," Thomas said. "You can't give me a new body. This is who I am."

Ariock wasn't ready to quit. He didn't allow failure or the floating pebbles to distract him. Sweat formed on his forehead, but that didn't matter. He was going to heal Thomas if it killed him.

"Ariock, stop!" Now Thomas sounded afraid.

The whole cave had gone quiet.

Thomas floated above his seat, as if magnetized by the force Ariock was exuding.

Ariock withdrew his awareness, and Thomas dropped back into his hoverchair. Pebbles rained down.

"I'm healed," Thomas said with pain in his tone.

But he clearly wasn't. He still had his neuromuscular disease.

"I don't think you can change this fundamental part of who I am," Thomas said. "It's like your gigantism. You can't change it."

"Are you sure?" Ariock lowered his hands. He had, in fact, tried to heal his own gigantism. He just didn't know how to go about it.

"Your healing power is basic," Thomas said. "It's extremely powerful, but it's basic. You're supercharging natural processes that the body would do on its own, given a nudge in the right direction. So you helped your mom kick her cancer into remission."

"I did?" Ariock wanted to believe that he'd cured her cancer entirely.

"The malignancy is still there," Thomas explained. "Because you did not, and cannot, change the nature of her pancreatic cells, or her tumor cells. Just like you can't change the nature of my brain cells."

"Oh." Ariock was unsure why that had to mean failure. Even if he could not alter Thomas's body, well, couldn't he stimulate muscle growth or something?

"My muscle tissue is healthy," Thomas said in a long-suffering tone, as if tired of explaining. "You can't heal what's healthy. There's just very little of it, because my body never grew a normal amount of musculature. I have a neuromuscular disease. It originates in my brain. Think of it like a coding issue. It's super complex."

"Oh." Ariock slumped, feeling inadequate.

Thomas offered a smile. "But my backache is gone. I appreciate that."

Ariock wished he could have avoided raising the boy's hopes. "Sorry."

"No big deal. You did your best." Thomas began to float away, but he hesitated near Vy. "Uh…" He spoke in a low voice to her.

Comprehension dawned in Vy's expression. "Oh."

Thomas looked embarrassed.

"We'll be right back," Vy said. She followed Thomas toward a dark, private corner of the cave. The lidded jars in that area served as a makeshift restroom.

Ariock sat back, glad that Thomas hadn't needed to beg for aid, especially in public. That would have been awkward. Vy really was an angel.

The ummins in line were restless, but Ariock only had time to heal a few more. Then his friends returned.

"Tell Ariock what you told me," Vy said, prompting Thomas.

Ariock looked at him, questioning.

"I asked him about Yeresunsa," Vy said. "Like, if you're the only one in existence."

That question had crossed Ariock's mind. He found it hard to believe he was the only one. Wouldn't individual Torth crave this much power? Superpowers didn't seem like the sort of thing the Torth Empire would casually throw away.

Also, Ariock didn't want to be a species unto himself. It made him feel extinct. Was he really a lone specimen of an extinct group of people?

"A lot of Torth offspring are born with Yeresunsa powers," Thomas reluctantly explained.

Ariock was attentive.

"But they're never given a chance to grow up. Illegal powers are one of the elimination criteria on baby farms."

Ariock lost his breath. He didn't understand how Thomas could sound so unaffected.

"Elimination criteria?" Delia sounded pained.

"Yes," Thomas said. "Torth children go through a battery of tests. Those who fail get killed, and their organs are harvested for medical and scientific purposes."

Ariock sat back, reeling from how far he had to readjust his already dismal view of the Torth. He had assumed they reproduced in some emotionless way, of course. But baby farms? It sounded like they mass-reproduced like cockroaches.

"I thought they were only intolerant of flaws in slaves." Kessa sounded just as stunned.

"They're intolerant of flaws in anyone," Thomas said. "Especially Torth."

He spoke as if it didn't matter. Ariock suspected there was a lot going on beneath his surface.

"But," Delia said, "Yeresunsa powers aren't a flaw."

"Torth are all supposed to be born equal to each other," Thomas explained. "They're not allowed to inherit advantages. No inherited wealth— that's why they don't allow families. And no extra powers."

That explained a lot.

Ariock sat back, aware that he had inherited a lot of everything.

"And they kill their own hatchlings?" Kessa looked fascinated. "What do they consider to be flaws worthy of death?"

"Well." Thomas sounded bored as he ticked off each one on his fingers. "Blatant emotions, obviously. Yeresunsa powers. Mental retardation. Insanity. Lack of telepathy. And some other disabilities."

He noticed everyone staring at his withered body and clarified, "They make exceptions for supergeniuses."

"There are Torth babies who are born without telepathy?" Vy said in a strained tone. "How many?"

"It's a small percentage," Thomas said. "The Torth don't count their off-spring as people. Not until they take the Adulthood Exam and graduate to adult citizenship. Before that? They're disposable."

Not a trace of sorrow in the boy who used to live in a foster home for abused and neglected children.

"How many children do they kill each year?" Vy asked in a trembling voice.

Thomas looked impatient. "That's irrelevant. If we have nothing import-ant to discuss, then—"

"How many?" Vy insisted.

"The empire owns millions of planets," Thomas said. "And has a popula-tion of more than thirty trillion adult Torth citizens. So an exact number will be meaningless. About thirty-five percent of children on baby farms survive to become adult citizens of the Torth Empire."

Thirty-five percent survived.

Sixty-five percent did not.

To Ariock, the percentage was nonsensical. He couldn't wrap his mind around that many babies and children slaughtered. It must be hundreds of millions. Hundreds of billions.

"The Torth throw away approximately four million Yeresunsa fetuses every month," Thomas said. "Which is a tiny percentage of all baby farm rejects."

"They kill sixty-five percent of their own children?" Vy said in a sickened voice. "How can they maintain a population?"

"It's not as wasteful as it sounds." Thomas leaned back and folded his hands, like a professor giving a lecture. "Healthy adults donate gametes, and each donation produces at least a dozen embryos, grown in amniotic sacs. The most successful embryos get a run of clones. Every healthy adult pro-duces at least fifty offspring, so even with all the rejects, the Torth population curve continues to blast upward."

Weptolyso had quietly joined them. His small, reddish eyes were filled with curiosity. "There are Torth with emotions?" he said, as if exploring the idea.

"The tests are imperfect," Thomas said. "Every once in a while, a child with a full range of emotions slips through into adulthood. They get executed when they're found out."

Ariock looked away. What personality disorders had allowed his own Torth ancestors to flourish in such a brutal society?

What fluke of fate had enabled his great-grandfather to escape to Earth? And marry a human? And raise a family?

How many chains of pure luck and coincidence had allowed Ariock to be born and to survive until the age of twenty-two?

A few flukes must have happened for Thomas, as well.

Now that he thought about it, he remembered that Thomas had been abandoned on a rural road within a mile of the Dovanack mansion. That could no longer be dismissed as a coincidence. Ariock studied the boy anew. Thomas must be related to him in some way, either by blood or by circumstance.

Someone tugged on his arm spike.

He became aware of a commotion among the ummins. They wanted attention.

"They say more Torth are in the jungle." Kessa listened with wide eyes, and Ariock waited for her intermittent translations. "Torth are on all horizons."

"Oh, no," Vy said.

Ariock knew his respite couldn't last forever, but a childish part of him had expected at least a few days of freedom. Maybe a week.

"They don't know about this cave." Thomas floated closer, hemmed in by the growing crowd. "They'd be invading us right now if they knew."

"But they're going to wreck the village," Vy said.

"They've already wrecked it," Thomas said. "If these ummins hurry back topside and act normal and do their panic trick whenever a Torth probes their minds? We should be safe for a while longer. Maybe a day or two."

Ummins reached toward Ariock, as if he would solve all their problems.

Vy listened to their pleas and translated. "Bringer of Hope, protect us. Make the Torth go away forever."

Their exact wording varied, but Ariock would have known what they wanted even without a translation. Freedom. Not just a hideout, but permanent freedom.

He nodded his understanding, but dread was growing inside him. Even if he did have some ludicrous amount of untapped power, the idea of large-scale slaughter revolted him. He was not a berserker. Nor was he a murderer. His rages in the arena had been brought on by stress, torture, suicidal despair, and a mood-altering helmet. That wasn't who he ever wanted to be again.

If he could sneak away and avoid a fight with the Torth, he would.

He just hoped the villagers wouldn't suffer if he left like that.

He didn't show his doubts or fears on his face. These villagers—and his friends—needed hope right now, not reminders of how unpracticed and incompetent their Bringer of Hope might be.

CHAPTER 4

BORN ON EARTH

Villagers left Ariock and his friends, hurrying into the tunnel in droves. They had to make the slave farm look populated for the next wave of Torth invaders.

How many brave ummins would suffer injuries this time?

How many risked their lives just to protect the Bringer of Hope?

Ariock wondered if the Torth would notice that previously injured slaves were now restored to full health. He needed to figure out how to protect these villagers. He had heard the legend of Jonathan Stead from Vy, but the Torth version might offer real insights. There must be something useful buried in the tale, a clue that would tell him how to defeat a Torth army.

So he asked Thomas. "How did Jonathan Stead escape the Torth?"

"It doesn't matter," Thomas said. "It's history."

That drew a lot of curious staring. Delia, Vy, and Kessa gathered closer.

"Fine." Thomas huffed out a breath. "Okay, here's the real story of Jonathan Stead, if you think it will help. He was born on Earth. His father was a renegade Torth Servant of All. His mother was unknown. Like me, he was a mind reader who had no clue that the Megacosm existed. He went around using his powers and having a blast—until the Torth caught wind of him."

Ariock imagined that hadn't gone well for young Jonathan Stead.

"He was seventeen years old when the Torth abducted him," Thomas said. "They imprisoned him in the Isolatorium for the crime of being a Yeresunsa and an outlaw."

Ariock could sympathize with that. He had gotten abducted and imprisoned for the exact same reason, although he was twenty-two.

"Escape from the Isolatorium is supposed to be impossible," Thomas said. "The Torth put Jonathan Stead on massive doses of the inhibitor. But somehow—no one knows how—he got off the drug and caused earthquakes and whirlwinds." A troubled look came into Thomas's eyes.

He's remembering it, Ariock realized. For Thomas, this wasn't a mere retelling. He must have lived it on some level, absorbing memories that came from eyewitnesses.

ABBY GOLDSMITH

"If I knew how he did it," Thomas said, "I would tell you. The prevailing theory is that he had help. He might have had a fellow prisoner sabotage the inhibitor. But he had never orchestrated such a huge Armageddon before or since."

"Armageddon?" Vy asked.

"An exaggeration," Thomas admitted. "But it was definitely the biggest disaster the Torth Empire has suffered in this era. He massacred 989 Torth in the space of about three minutes."

Ariock tried not to gape. That was a lot.

"What happened to the thousand prisoners he freed?" Kessa asked. "Were they all slaves?"

"Slaves of various species," Thomas confirmed. "He wrenched the prison walls apart, and slaves poured out. They ran with Jonathan Stead into the necropolis, a ruined city in a nuclear winter situation."

Vy snuggled against Ariock. He remained still, not wanting to remind her of whom she was sitting next to. "What happened next?" she asked.

"Torth hunted them." Thomas made that sound obvious. "But they never found any of the escapees."

"Not even their bodies?" Kessa looked fascinated.

Thomas offered a weak shrug. "The necropolis is filled with toxic sludge and serpentine monsters. Corpses don't last long there. They'd be just about impossible to find."

Kessa looked pained.

"Anyway, it happened more than one hundred years ago," Thomas added. "They're long gone. Torth still search the ruins every so often, but no trace of the escapees has ever been found."

"What about Jonathan Stead?" Delia asked. "How did he get back home to Earth?"

"The Torth don't have the whole picture," Thomas said. "First, they assumed that the necropolis killed him. But he showed up a few months later, alone. The Torth caught him stealing a streamship. That's a small spaceship that can use temporal streams, which are basically wormholes. Anyhow, they chased him and made him crash-land on an inhospitable planet."

"But he survived?" Vy prompted. "Again?"

"The Torth found his ruined ship," Thomas said. "And there was enough of his blood to assume he was dead. They figured that his body had been dragged off and devoured by wild animals. That planet has a lot of, uh, bio-engineered hazards."

Ariock had never imagined that his great-grandfather, whom his mother described as "genial," used to be such a badass.

"No one knows how he survived," Thomas admitted. "Or how he got back to Earth. The Torth never got a chance to probe his mind."

Vy sat cross-legged. She seemed energized. "He fooled the Torth Empire. Multiple times!"

Thomas looked irked. "The evidence overwhelmingly suggested that he was dead. No one knows how he did it. But yes. He was exceptionally good at faking his death."

Ariock wondered if he would ever have answers to all the mysteries of his great-grandfather.

"So it's possible to fool them," Vy said. "It's possible for us to escape, and steal a spaceship, and go home to Earth?"

Kessa looked as if she was imagining paradise.

"No." Thomas spoke as if teaching a class of dull students. "We're in a different situation, in a different era. The Torth never make the same mistake twice. The current Commander of All Living Things was elected for her pragmatism. She won't believe we're dead until she can examine our corpses."

"But even so—" Vy began to say.

"Oh, sure." Thomas was sarcastic. "I'm sure Ariock can blend right in with any human population. No one will notice the nine-and-a-half-foot-tall giant."

Ariock wished he could shrink. Vy looked embarrassed for him.

"We could hide Ariock in a bunker," Delia suggested. "An old silo, or something like that."

The Dovanack mansion had been a lot like a bunker. It was covered by towering trees and hidden off an unmapped road.

Now that Ariock considered it, he realized that his great-grandfather had built it that way on purpose. Old Garrett had tried to protect his precious human family, hiding them from the Torth Empire.

It had worked.

Until it hadn't.

The failure gave Ariock a sneaky sense of relief. Garrett hadn't quite been able to live up to his own reputation. Ariock doubted that he could live up to such exalted hero status, either.

"Get Earth out of your minds," Thomas told them. "Even if we could get there, Earth is the first place they'll search. It's out of the question."

Vy looked defeated.

Ariock didn't have any particular yearning to return Earth. To him, home meant clocks ticking in distant rooms. It meant corners that collected dust and shadows. Early darkness in winter. Dreary rain in summer. Isolation.

"Also?" Thomas folded his thin hands. "One thing I think everyone should get through their heads is that Ariock is not invincible. Yeresunsa can be killed. One microdart of the inhibitor serum is enough to incapacitate any Yeresunsa. There used to be armies of Yeresunsa. The Torth defeated them. There's a reason Jonathan Stead went into hiding for the rest of his life."

At least Thomas understood that Ariock wasn't any sort of hero.

"Even if Ariock could get rid of the Torth army on our doorstep," Thomas went on, "the Torth would just send a bigger and better army. We cannot sustain an escalating fight."

Vy and Delia exchanged disappointed looks of frustration. They were not ready to give up.

Good. Neither was Ariock.

Kessa seemed curious about another aspect of the legend. "How did the Torth eventually learn about Jonathan Stead and his family on Earth?" she asked.

"That's not relevant to us." Thomas rolled a canteen between his hands. He sounded dismissive, but judging by the way he avoided eye contact, Ariock suspected he was hiding something.

"It seems relevant," Kessa said. "They learned about Ariock somehow. Are they able to detect Yeresunsa?"

That was a new worry for Ariock.

The more he thought about it, the more worried he became. No one on Earth had known that he existed, other than his mother and perhaps a few people who remembered him as a child. Yet the Torth Empire had zeroed in on him.

Thomas looked like he was deciding whether or not to continue the conversation.

"Tell us," Ariock said. "Please. Can the Torth detect me?"

Perhaps Thomas sensed his determination, because he cringed a little bit. "All right. There is a detection factor, but it's subtle. All living beings emit things—heat, thoughts, emotions, electromagnetic particles, reflected light, and other stuff. The Torth refer to all those emissions as 'radiant influence.'"

Ariock considered his power to sense life sparks. Was he sensing radiant influence?

"I think you can detect it," Thomas affirmed. "Whenever you expand your Yeresunsa awareness, every living being within your awareness feels like a spark to you."

Ariock nodded, grateful for the explanation.

"The Torth can sense that as well?" Vy asked worriedly.

"Not really," Thomas said. "But the highest military ranks do have ways of detecting exceptionally powerful spheres of influence." He aimed an implicating look toward Ariock. "Yeresunsa give off a lot more radiant influence than other people. They have what the Torth know as 'spheres of influence.' And those spheres can be huge. Like, miles in radius."

Ariock had a sinking feeling.

He couldn't hide. Not if he was emitting miles of radiance, or whatever it was.

"What do you mean, 'ways of detecting'?" Vy asked.

"They measure fluctuations in electromagnetism," Thomas said. "And abnormal weather patterns. Weird animal migrations. Things like that. Servants of All are trained to recognize the signs. An ordinary Torth would never notice."

Vy frowned. "Are you saying Ariock is causing weird weather patterns miles away?"

"I guess so," Thomas said. "I was never high enough in rank to learn the exact details of what they look for."

"If that's true," Delia said, "then they would have detected Garrett Dovanack decades ago."

"Actually," Thomas said, "Garrett lucked out, because his life span coincided with the great population boom of humankind. While Garrett was partying on Earth with his wife and kid, the Torth Empire assumed that the weirdnesses they detected on Earth were just anomalies caused by rapid changes in human demographics."

"How big was Garrett's sphere of influence?" Vy asked. "Like, a hundred miles?"

"Probably more like five or six hundred miles," Thomas said.

Vy's eyebrows raised. "And...Ariock is the same way? He's affecting weather six hundred miles away?"

Ariock wanted to scoff at the idea that someone could have unintended side effects in distant countries. It seemed absurd.

Thomas looked like he was gauging their reactions. "The Torth upper ranks estimate that Ariock has a larger sphere of influence than Garrett. He's a lot more detectable. Possibly solar system level."

For a bitter moment, Ariock wondered if Thomas was joking.

"What?" Vy said.

"I don't know exactly how they measure it," Thomas admitted. "But they can detect what solar system he's in."

When Ariock thought of the way his awareness could leap out, unraveling further and further from his body, he knew that he had yet to test his limits. Maybe he could inhabit more than a village.

Could he wear an entire continent the way someone might wear a suit of armor?

Or a planet?

A solar system?

He didn't want to even imagine holding so much in his focus. It would be insane. A supergenius might be able to keep track of countless bazillions of moving parts, but Ariock had enough trouble just keeping track of enough sand grains to dig a pit.

"So the Torth can detect him no matter what?" Vy asked, horrified.

"Not his exact whereabouts," Thomas said. "But they know if he's in the solar system. In fact, ordinary Torth can detect a tiny hint of it. It's like a subtle pressure."

"Can you detect me?" Ariock asked.

"Maybe." Thomas swung his legs, uncaring. "Ariock, I've been within your sphere of influence all my life. We're in the same solar system, therefore, I'm in your sphere. To me, it's just background. I guess the only way I'd notice would be if it stopped."

If Ariock died.

Or if he left the solar system.

Kessa rounded her hands. "It is actually a sphere?"

Everyone looked at her, and she shrank back from the attention. "I only wonder if the Servants of All can measure this sphere to its center."

"That's an astute guess," Thomas told her. "'Sphere' is a misnomer. It's more like a blob that fluctuates with health and a host of other factors, such as global electromagnetism." He gestured around the cave. "Just like we can't tell which direction this planet is hurtling through space, they can't deduce where you are based on your influence. The Servants of All can figure out what solar system Ariock is in, but they could theoretically walk right over this cave and not know he's here."

Kessa began to speak.

"Right," Thomas said, turning to her. "They will notice if he returns to the planet Earth."

Ariock bowed his head. He had already resigned himself to never watching TV again, and now he tried to resign himself to a future without Vy. As a detectable target, he did not dare stay close to the people he cared about. "You should go to Earth without me," he said.

"Are you kidding?" Vy gave him a scandalized look, as if he had lost his mind.

"We're not leaving you," Delia said, anguished. "Don't think that way."

Kessa remained focused on Thomas. "So that is how the Torth discovered the family of Jonathan Stead. They detected Ariock?"

"That was the start of it," Thomas said. "They erroneously believed that Jonathan had died at the age of seventeen, without leaving children. So they were baffled by continuous signs of a Yeresunsa presence on Earth. The Majority sent agents to investigate every claim of paranormal activity among humans. Most turned out to be false. But one…" Thomas squared his shoulders, as if to prepare for a confrontation. "One agent heard a rumor about a reclusive old man who was supposedly a mind reader."

Because of Ariock's sphere of influence.

Implications rolled through him like oily smoke. After Garrett died, his family had been murdered. His father. His grandmother. So many others.

At the time, it had seemed like a series of unfortunate accidents.

"When did this happen?" Delia seemed to be catching on, as well. Her tone was suspicious.

"About fourteen years ago." Thomas avoided her gaze, fiddling with the canteen.

She looked sick. The conclusion had hit her as well.

"When the Torth Empire learned that Jonathan Stead had a family," Thomas said, "they executed and replaced the Commander of All Living Things." He hesitated. "The current Commander began her reign by orchestrating 'accidental' deaths for all of Garrett's blood relatives."

Ariock had stood before the current Commander when she'd sentenced him to death in the desert. If he had known that she had ordered the deaths of his family, he might have lunged at her, like a mindless beast in the arena.

"Did Garrett not protect his family?" Kessa asked.

It was Delia who answered. "He died when Ariock was a baby."

"He actually did protect his family," Thomas put in. "To the best of his ability. Throughout his lifetime, Torth agents on Earth sometimes died in mysterious accidents. The Torth suspected that someone might be secretly killing them, but they had no clues. In hindsight, it was clear that whenever a Torth agent got close to discovering Garrett Dovanack or his family…" Thomas made a twisting motion around his canteen, as if wringing a neck. "They experienced a sudden death."

"And then he died of old age." Delia stared at Thomas with a look of hard speculation. "And somebody found our family. Fourteen years ago."

Thomas continued to avoid her gaze. "Right," he said. "It was big, shocking news in the Megacosm. The Torth Majority had written him off as dead. At first, they didn't believe he'd survived for a hundred years, right under their noses. But the evidence was indisputable. For one thing, Garrett Dovanack was known to have purple eyes, which is a Torth genetic marker."

That was a mark Ariock had inherited, as well.

"He hid it with sunglasses," Thomas said. "But there were a couple of things that he couldn't hide. One was his crooked leg. Jonathan Stead was known to have a crooked leg, and Garrett had the same trait. The other was his facial scar." Thomas indicated his face. "Garrett asked artists to paint it out of portraits and photographs. But the agent tracked down a rare photo of him, and there was the scar that Jonathan Stead had gotten in the Isolatorium."

"He told us that a Nazi slashed him with a knife," Delia said faintly.

"Almost true," Thomas said. "It was a nussian's spike in the Isolatorium."

"So the Torth murdered his family?" Kessa assessed Ariock and his mother. "Except for two?"

"Except for Ariock," Thomas corrected. "Delia was never a direct target, since she's not a blood relative of Garrett."

Delia stood, fists clenched. "The Torth sabotaged that plane. They murdered my husband. Didn't they?"

"Yes." Thomas fidgeted with the canteen, not looking at any of them.

"Was it one of your parents?" Delia demanded. "I can do the math. You were conceived around when my family was murdered."

That had not occurred to Ariock. It was a painful conjecture. But surely Thomas was not the offspring of a—

"It was my mother," Thomas confessed.

Ariock wanted fresh air. The ceiling was too low, the air too sooty.

All his life, he had assumed that the plane crash was an accident of fate, like his gigantism. But none of the horrors of his life were accidents. His father had been murdered by Thomas's mother.

Thomas was related to his family, after all. Just not in a genetic way.

CHAPTER 5
UNINHIBITED

No matter what atrocities Thomas's mother had committed, Thomas himself was innocent. Ariock reminded himself of that. Thomas was as much a victim as the rest of them. His monstrous mother had abandoned him at birth.

"Are you saying that your birth mother..." Vy glanced from Thomas to Ariock, uncertain. "Killed his father?"

"Why?" Delia made a choked sound. "Why did she do it?"

"The Majority told her to." Thomas looked burdened. "If you want revenge? Consider it paid. She died in the Isolatorium."

They stared at him.

"The Torth killed her?" Kessa asked. "Why?"

"For the crime of having sex." Thomas spoke in a dead monotone. "She was supposed to kill everyone in the Dovanack family, and she mostly got it done. But then she got sidetracked."

Ariock almost didn't want to know any more.

Now he understood why Thomas had wanted to avoid this topic. It opened up a can of worms.

"She stopped trying to murder Ariock...in order to have sex?" Vy sounded as if she was faced with an impossible math problem. "With who? Did she fall in love with a random human or something? Who was your father?"

"I don't know." Thomas stared down at his hands.

Vy looked skeptical and mystified at the same time. "How can you not know? I thought the Torth soaked up everything?"

"She forgot who he was," Thomas said. "Or she hid it, somehow."

Vy opened her mouth. She looked confounded by too many questions.

"Before you ask," Thomas said, "no, no one knows why she derailed everything in her life to go renegade and have a fling. She was on a fast track to becoming a Commander of All Living Things. She threw it all away. And no one knows why."

"Did the Torth not soak up her memories?" Kessa asked.

"They did." Thomas's gaze seemed to burn with things he shouldn't know. "She buried a lot of what the Majority would have considered irrelevant. And she avoided looking at her partner during their sexual encounter. He was just a blur in her memory."

Vy shrank back, horrified.

"You wouldn't believe the things I've experienced in the Megacosm," Thomas said.

Ariock stared anew. Had Thomas actually absorbed a secondhand memory of his own conception?

That was sick.

For that matter, Thomas might have also absorbed his mother's death by torture. Ariock couldn't imagine that.

And he knew that Thomas never forgot any detail, no matter how trivial or disturbing.

"This explains much." Kessa studied Thomas with fresh speculation.

"She forgot about me, too," Thomas said. "When they tortured her. I believe she did it on purpose—to give me a chance to grow up on Earth."

"I'm so sorry." Vy looked like she was reevaluating Thomas in a multitude of ways. "But why didn't she leave you on someone's doorstep? Why did she abandon you in the woods?"

"By the side of a road in the woods," Thomas corrected. "I think she knew that an early-morning commuter would find me. Either that, or she was afraid to hold me for too long. She didn't want to grow attached. She was preparing to let the Torth find her. To return to the Megacosm."

That sounded like a Torth thing to do, to Ariock.

But Vy seemed shocked. "Why?"

"It's hard to give up the Megacosm," Thomas said, his tone dry. "Especially if it's what you're accustomed to all your life. It would be like a rich human giving up electricity and indoor plumbing and democracy and all the things you associate with civilization."

Vy looked dubious.

"She had some tenuous hope of being demoted," Thomas said, "rather than flat-out executed. She thought she could keep her worst transgressions a secret."

Ariock thought that Thomas's birth mother must have been a strange one. She had failed to finish murdering every single Dovanack. Instead, she had conceived a child with a "primitive" human. And she had given her illegal hybrid baby a chance to grow up. She had done that in such a way as to give Thomas a chance to grow up among humans, apart from the Torth Empire.

And she had managed to keep most of that a secret from the empire ruled by mind readers.

Strange.

"Why did the Torth not send more agents to finish the task?" Kessa asked. "They were trying to kill Ariock, right?"

It was a good question. Ariock had lived in safety throughout his teenage years, oblivious to the fact that aliens wanted him dead.

"The Torth Majority voted to suspend their efforts after Ariock unexpectedly survived that plane crash," Thomas said. "They wanted to avoid a disaster on the level of Jonathan Stead." He seemed to sense questions, and added, "They were concerned that Ariock might have a precognitive ability. They thought he might have survived because, well, maybe he saw it coming."

Ariock laughed. He wasn't a superhero. In truth, he had been a harmless child, easy to kill.

No one else laughed. They seemed to consider the paranoia of the Torth Empire as sensible.

"So they studied him from afar," Thomas went on. "They wanted to make sure Ariock wouldn't detect them—and stop them—before they could disable his powers."

"How did they study him?" Delia sounded disbelieving.

"My biological mother posed as the nurse in his grade school," Thomas said. "Later on, another Torth agent posed as the clerk at the post office where you picked up your mail every week."

Delia looked stunned.

Ariock felt the same way. He remembered the nurse at Woodbury Grade School, a pretty blonde lady. She had asked to draw his blood almost every time he went to see her.

"That clerk used to draw me into conversations!" Delia said.

"Yup," Thomas said. "He was delaying you so he could probe your mind and suck up every memory about Ariock."

Her stunned look returned.

"The Majority only sends Servants of All to Earth," Thomas said. "They're all physically fit, and some of them are specially trained to emulate humans." He gestured to himself. "They would never send someone who looks like me."

"But then..." Vy seemed to be rethinking things. "The Torth picked you up incidentally? They were after Ariock the whole time?"

"More or less." Thomas spread his hands. "If I had stayed out of the media spotlight, I could have lived my entire life as a human and never known about the Torth."

Kessa studied him with a look of fascination.

Delia said, "They waited a long time to grab Ariock."

"They were dotting their i's and crossing their t's," Thomas said. "The current Commander wasn't going to rush in without a thorough assessment of his capabilities. They had to work extra hard to learn anything about Ariock once you pulled him out of school."

Ariock supposed he should be grateful that he'd been allowed to live in peace until the age of twenty-two.

Few people in the Torth-ruled galaxy were as fortunate as he had been. Thomas had been abducted at a younger age. So had Jonathan Stead. Ariock almost felt blessed.

The flicker of torches made the petroglyphs seem ready to come alive, etched by generations of ummins who were desperate to control their own destinies. The Torth would destroy this sanctuary if they found it.

"What can we do?" Ariock asked Thomas. "I need to know how we can stop the Torth from harming this place."

They all focused on Thomas. Even Pung and Weptolyso, who hardly understood the language of humans, watched the supergenius to see what answers he might yield. Only Cherise remained uninterested. She sat a distance away, working on beads along with a few local ummin children.

Thomas sipped from his canteen. He had a cynical expression, and Ariock knew, even before he spoke, that his answers would not be good enough.

"All I can tell you," Thomas said, "is that I don't want to be in your vicinity when you're in battle mode." A dark, closed-off look came over his face. "The last fully trained Yeresunsa died more than twenty-four thousand years ago. No one alive knows how to use Yeresunsa powers."

Ariock refused to accept that. He was no longer the brute of the arena. He could probably control his powers enough to damage the Torth instead of hurting his friends.

"So you're just giving up?" Vy stared at Thomas as if she didn't recognize him.

"If you don't mind," Thomas said, "I'd like to get some more of that sleeping potion." He began to float away.

Ariock remembered when Thomas was in a wheelchair rather than a hoverchair, with purple eyes instead of yellow. That version of Thomas would have explored every option before giving up. That version wouldn't be afraid to offer all the knowledge he had.

Afraid.

That was the right word for the way Thomas was behaving. Thomas didn't show much emotion, yet he kept running away from discussions about Yeresunsa powers. He was avoiding Ariock. It was similar to how Ariock used to avoid public spaces.

"What are you afraid of?" Ariock asked.

Thomas kept moving.

Ariock extended his awareness through the air and the rocky cavern floor. Solid objects felt more comfortable to inhabit. He became the stone floor without a second thought and followed fissures and layers, as if they were roadways made just for him. His awareness leaped into the hoverchair in less than a second.

He forced the chair to stop.

"Let go," Thomas said in an icy tone. He had switched into Torth mode.

Ariock let him go, slightly ashamed. But he didn't give up. "You're afraid of something. Is it me?"

"I'm not interested in having this conversation."

Ariock's awareness spiked out, and he had to rein it back in. Had Garrett ever felt this alone?

"I'm just asking for a little more advice." He kept his tone patient, aware of his friends listening. They needed to believe he was a competent protector, not totally desperate.

"I can't help you," Thomas said.

"You're not a Torth," Ariock pointed out. Their situation would be infinitely better if Thomas would act like the renegade he was. Why couldn't he be more heroic? "If you're not going to teach me," Ariock said, frustrated, "then I'll have to teach myself. Is that what you want?"

He didn't bother waiting for Thomas to reply. Instead, he extended his awareness into the ceiling. He kept going, farther and farther through solid rock.

Some layers felt different, more porous, or more delicate. Ariock closed his eyes for better concentration. He zigzagged upward until the outer bulk of his awareness became air rather than anything solid. The surface!

He pushed outward, skimming a floor, sensing light and shadow. He sampled textures.

"What you're doing is dangerous."

Thomas's voice was as meaningless as the flutter of a moth. Ariock had too many things to focus on. He could barely process words.

"…needlessly risky."

Countless life sparks moved through Ariock's spreading awareness. He tried to figure out if they were ummins or Torth, but they all seemed equal in intensity.

Whenever he focused on one area, he lost track of the rest. All he gained were vague impressions of living beings. Some affected the floor more heavily than others. Other than that? He couldn't tell them apart.

Someone distant said his name.

Ariock figured he had explored enough. He dived, reeling his awareness back toward his distant body. Fissures deepened as he drained his way through layers of sediment.

Rocky layers slid against each other.

Rocks groaned and shifted into new configurations in his wake.

Ariock went still. He didn't dare move while he inhabited so much stone. Any motion, no matter how slight, might cause the ground to shift even more. With a precarious balance of weight, and while holding himself motionless, he focused on stabilizing each problem area.

At last, he was certain that every layer had a semblance of stability.

Only then did he dare to withdraw his awareness and retreat back to his usual size.

Vy watched him with uncertainty. "Was that earthquake…you?"

Dust sifted downward. Piles of dust showed where the ceiling had cracked. His friends stared at him with varying degrees of dismay and fear. Only Vy looked sympathetic.

"My control could use fine-tuning," Ariock admitted, ashamed.

"It was a small tremor," Vy said. "I doubt anyone on the surface noticed."

"Right," Thomas said.

He floated away again, seemingly uninvolved with the people he had rescued. Ariock wondered if he had truly lost all his kindness and humanity under the weight of lifetimes absorbed in the Megacosm.

No. Thomas had risked his life for their freedom. Some part of him must want to help, even if it was buried.

The way he had spoken of ancient Yeresunsa disasters…it was as if he mistrusted powers. Thomas seemed to believe that magic, or Yeresunsa powers, were dangerous.

Almost as if he had personal experience.

As if such powers had hurt him in the past.

Ariock sat back slowly. He had glimpsed a golden cuff around Thomas's ankle. That cuff looked like a slave collar—or like an inhibitor collar.

Thomas had removed everyone's collars and shackles except for that cuff.

Was it dispensing the inhibitor serum, just as Ariock's prison collar had done?

Torth descendants born on Earth seemed to have an unusually high chance of inheriting mutations, such as Yeresunsa powers.

"You're… Oh. I get it." Ariock paused, aware of how his friends might react. He wished Thomas was close enough to read his mind.

Then he plunged ahead anyway. "You're a Yeresunsa, Thomas," he said. "Aren't you?"

Thomas veered, as if he'd lost his composure.

The look he gave Ariock was pure fear. He looked like a little boy cornered by a monster.

"No way," Vy breathed.

"What powers do you have?" Ariock leaned forward, metal on metal. "You can help us survive!"

"Leave me alone." Maybe Thomas had intended to shout, but his voice came out in a frightened squeak.

Ariock couldn't guess why Thomas was so resistant, but he had no patience for arguments. Thomas could surely argue him into a knot, anyway.

So he didn't bother begging for help. Instead, he extended his awareness and connected to the hoverchair. He cemented it in midair. Then he shoved more of his awareness into the golden cuff around Thomas's ankle.

Sure enough, Ariock sensed its adherence to skin, like a medical patch. Or a leech. He didn't know how Thomas could stand to have such a disgusting thing attached to his skin.

He worked his way around its inner surface, peeling it away.

"Stop!" Thomas frantically toggled his controls, trying to get away. "You have no right!"

Ariock used his powers to hold the hoverchair in place. Delia said something about danger, but he was too immersed in breaking the cuff to understand her concern.

He wrenched the thing into two shiny halves. He yanked them apart.

Thomas made a futile grab for where the cuff had gone, but he was far too weak and slow.

Ariock crushed the pieces of cuff in midair, crumpling each. It was no more difficult than crooking his fingers.

Once the cuff was a couple of unrecognizable scraps, he cartwheeled them through air, intending to catch them. He changed his mind before they could touch his skin. It seemed foolish to touch anything that contained inhibitor serum, no matter how broken or crumpled it was.

"Put it back on me," Thomas begged.

Ariock sent the scraps cartwheeling straight to the nearest torch. He let each piece drop into flames. Fire should destroy whatever drug remained inside.

"That wasn't yours," Thomas seethed, red-faced. "I asked you to stop!"

Ariock withdrew his awareness so he could talk. "Sorry," he said. "We just don't have a lot of time to wait for you to recover from the inhibitor."

"I don't want to use my powers." Tears spilled from Thomas's eyes. "You had no right to make that decision for me. Why can't you listen?" He seemed to search for adequate insults. "I should have stayed in the city. I should have let you die!"

Ariock couldn't think of a response. He suddenly realized how he had been treating the disabled boy. Stealing something he valued. Holding him trapped, like a prisoner.

Vy looked from Thomas to Ariock with sympathy. "You're right, Thomas," she said. "But we're in a pretty desperate situation."

"How about if you stop assuming you've got me all figured out?" Thomas tested his hoverchair controls, and, finding that he could move, he backed away. "I'm not your sidekick. I'm not a hero of any sort."

The long-term cave inhabitants stared at him, captivated. They had probably never seen a Torth cry.

Ariock reviewed what he had done and hated himself. "I'm really sorry. I just thought…" It seemed selfish, now that he considered it. "I thought we were in this together."

Thomas spoke through bared teeth. "Leave. Me. Alone."

He whirled and sped away, fast enough to make his hoverchair tilt.

CHAPTER 6

BATTLE PRACTICE

Vy watched Thomas speed away. He was acting more human, which had to be a good thing. At least, she thought so.

If only he would direct his rage toward someone who deserved it—like the Torth.

"He knows you weren't trying to attack him," she assured Ariock.

"He has powers." Delia sounded as if the words pained her. "He's a supergenius, a mind reader, and he has superpowers. Is anyone else not okay with this?"

Vy thought that Thomas was still the same person who used to help foster kids get their homework done. He used to be a friend to silent Cherise. And he had explained about Torth coercion.

Or he had attempted to explain it.

Vy inwardly admitted that she just didn't understand the peer pressure of the Megacosm. Not really. The place sounded like an internet full of bullies. Why couldn't a bunch of Torth simply unplug and rebel? Why not start their own nation full of righteous people who cared about justice and equality? Or why not vote for the right things instead of the wrong things?

It seemed the Torth universally preferred to live off slave labor. If they were all such lazy cowards, murdering any rebels who disagreed with their rapacious culture, well…then they definitely weren't human. As far as she was concerned, they were universally evil. Like orcs or demons.

Evil was such an integral part of their culture, they might as well be born evil. They only looked human. Their human appearance was superficial.

Vy had learned that well enough when she was a slave.

But Thomas wasn't one of the demons.

Delia no longer saw his humanity. Cherise was probably waiting to see it, waiting for an apology, but Thomas was clearly too damaged to apologize. He had lived with the demons. He had pretended to be one of them in order to survive. That meant trauma. He must need more time to readjust to human values.

If only he would quit being so mysterious.

He had kept his powers a secret. His mother's crimes, also. What else was he hiding?

If Thomas wanted to be embraced as a friend—and Vy was unsure if he did want that—then he needed to open up and trust someone. He needed to let himself be vulnerable and confide in someone. He needed to act human.

He just wasn't doing that.

Kessa clasped her hands behind her back, looking contemplative. "The Torth kill Yeresunsa. Some of them must have wanted to kill Thomas, but the Majority voted against doing that. I wonder why?"

She ambled in the direction Thomas had gone, no doubt seeking answers.

Vy almost followed. She did want to be present for Thomas, to show him that she was available, if he ever wanted to try being her foster brother and her friend again.

But Pung and Weptolyso were engaged in their own conversation off to one side, and if she left, Ariock would be alone with his mother, who had planted her fists on her hips. She seemed to have regained some grit along with her health.

"Was that cuff you tore off him full of inhibitor?" Delia demanded.

Ariock nodded.

"You should have left it on him!" Delia said. "The last thing we need is Thomas with powers."

"You trust me with powers," Ariock pointed out. "Why not him?"

"How is that a question?" Delia ignored the piles of rock dust from the quake. "You're on our side. Thomas is more like…" She appeared to search for the right words. "Scary."

Inhuman. Evil. Torth. Vy understood. She didn't agree, but she understood.

Ariock drew away. "I'm the one who attacked *him*. Which one of us is the monster?"

Vy could hardly believe that Ariock was berating himself for that. He could have been more patient with Thomas, true, but that wasn't easy with a Torth army lurking above their heads. Time was running out.

"Thomas should be bending over backward to help you," Delia said with an edge to her voice. "He won't even apologize to Cherise. Or to me. He thinks he's a god. Don't you see that? Or am I crazy?"

Ariock sighed, a gust that sounded like the exhalation of a cave. "He just needs time to remember he's human."

Delia clucked her tongue in annoyance. "He remembers everything. He has no memory problems." She patted Ariock on the knee. "Your heart is in the right place. Just be careful. Don't trust him too much." She walked away. "I'm going to go check on Cherise."

That left Vy alone with Ariock. He looked like he wanted to offer her an apology, perhaps for having a family argument in front of her.

"Delia is just stressed out," Vy said. "We all are."

Ariock looked grateful. "I'm going to practice my powers," he said. "I want to learn better control. The more I know what I'm doing, the more I can protect us."

"I could help." Vy went to the nearest supply bin and pulled out a couple of stoneware bowls. "We need to make sure you can shield yourself." She brandished the bowls, ready to throw them like Frisbees. "I wish Thomas would teach us how to use that blaster glove."

"I shouldn't have pushed him." Ariock sounded ashamed. "When we were on Earth, Thomas told me how much he struggled against authority figures—people who pushed him around because of his age and his disability. I had no right to treat him that way."

Vy thought about Thomas's colleagues at Rasa Biotech, who often claimed credit for the work he did.

Although Thomas managed her mother's investment portfolio, he still had to abide by her house rules, and mealtimes, and appointments.

"He always hated being a kid," she admitted.

"Well, I forgot that about him," Ariock said. "I just thought, 'I need his Yeresunsa power.' Like I'm entitled to it." He shook his head in disgust. "I crossed a line."

"I don't think so." Vy hesitated, then moved closer to Ariock. She wanted him to see her sincerity in the torchlight. "Thomas is going through a rough time. And he's always been a little..." She reconsidered his mood swings. "Emotionally damaged. I think he's worse now."

Ariock nodded in agreement. "The Torth forced him to absorb memories that no one should have to see. Like his mother dying."

Vy winced. She felt guilty, aware that she had utterly failed to protect Thomas in so many ways. She wasn't much of a caretaker.

She set the stoneware bowls aside. "We're all feeling kind of helpless against the Torth Empire." She touched Ariock's arm. "I guess you are, too. At least a little bit."

Ariock laughed softly. "A lot."

Vy ran her hand down his arm, brushing lightly over scars. "That's why you should forgive yourself for being impatient with Thomas."

He gave her such a long look, she wondered if he was going to pull her into an embrace. Part of her wanted to feel his huge arms around her. That might give her a much-needed sense of security.

Then Vy asked herself if she was crazy. She didn't know Ariock well enough for intimacy. What if he decided he wanted to do more than hug her? She wouldn't be able to shove him away or escape.

Ariock had spent ten years cooped up inside his mansion, without any friends, without any possibility of a girlfriend. That couldn't make for a healthy mind.

But Ariock didn't grab her. Instead, he turned away, shaking his head as if to refuse something. "Everyone is very understanding of me lately," he said. "I almost wrecked this cave. Doesn't that worry you? Is Thomas the only one who's brave enough to criticize me?"

"I can be critical," Vy told him with certainty. "When it's warranted. So yeah, you did cause a minor earthquake. That sucks. But everyone has to start learning somewhere. I don't think you'll keep making the same mistakes." She began to pull items out of the supply bin, piling up the stoneware. "How's this for ammo? I'll throw things at you, and you defend yourself."

Ariock looked uncertain. "I don't want to wreck valuables."

"Then don't wreck the stuff," Vy said. "Let's see how much you can keep track of without breaking things."

Ariock looked intrigued.

"If the greatest weapon the Torth have against Yeresunsa is the inhibitor serum," Vy said, "then they'll try to shoot darts at you. Microdarts? I think that's what Thomas called them. So we can assume they're small and deadly."

Ariock laughed softly again. He rarely laughed, and Vy liked the sound of it. "Defense sounds useful."

Vy prepared to hurl a stoneware bowl at Ariock. Then she hesitated, unwilling to bruise him. He would be just about impossible to miss.

So she threw the bowl in a different direction at the last second.

The bowl froze in midair.

A second later, it flew upward, bullet fast, and thwacked against the ceiling hard enough to break into pieces. The pieces fell—but they never reached the floor. Instead, they slowed and bobbed in midair like pool toys.

"Oops," Ariock said.

Vy grinned. "Try again. Here. I'll throw more stuff."

"Hold on," Ariock said. "Let me try multitasking."

As he spoke, objects began to levitate. Stoneware, needles, blankets, small bins and crates, random rocks…they all bobbed in midair, rotating slowly around Ariock, like satellites orbiting a planet.

Vy gaped in wonder.

"My biggest limit is concentration, I think." Ariock sounded distracted, as if he had to think hard about what he was saying. "I have trouble talking while I do this."

In one motion, all the floating items dipped and clattered gently to the floor.

"That looked masterful to me," Vy said. "That was incredible."

"Let me try again," Ariock said. "The more stuff I inhabit, the harder it is for me to remember where everything is." He glanced in the direction Thomas had gone. "That's why I think Thomas will be instantly good at this. He can keep track of a billion things all at once."

"Try again," Vy said. "In fact..." She began to juggle a couple of pouches full of seeds or something. They were almost like beanbags. "Let's see you do this!"

Ariock gawked. Then he laughed.

"Go on!" Vy tossed one pouch at him, then the other.

Ariock used his powers to catch everything she threw.

"Keep throwing stuff my way," he said.

So she did. When she ran out of stoneware and pouches, she went to another bin and tossed everything at him, as fast as she could manage. Everything she threw transformed into a bauble that defied gravity. Ariock's focused look showed that he was responsible for the strange phenomena.

When thirty or forty things hung in midair, they wavered, as if drunk.

By the time it was fifty or sixty, the whole lot seemed to have trouble staying afloat. Something scraped against the ground. Vy kept throwing, but she was getting tired and sweaty.

Everything sank down, wobbling.

"Ugh." Ariock slumped, resting his elbows on his crossed legs. "That was my limit. Not good enough."

"Are you tired?" Vy went to him, concerned.

"No." Ariock looked inwardly frustrated. "I have a focus limit."

"But you're not depleted?"

"No," Ariock said. "I feel fine."

"Well, that's amazing." Vy dared to sit close to him, leaning against his side. "You're way too hard on yourself."

Ariock gave her an amazed, almost fearful look. He didn't seem to know how to react. He tensed up, and that reminded Vy of all the gigantic reasons why he wasn't datable. So what if he had kind eyes? He probably—

Ariock relaxed a little bit. He became nicer to lean on.

"You make a good backrest," Vy remarked.

He laughed softly.

CHAPTER 7

TRUTH

Thomas angled toward the sleeping potion. He needed a serious distraction. Since he couldn't have the Megacosm…

"Teacher Torth?" An adolescent ummin jogged to catch up with his hoverchair. "I have so many questions. Explain to me how your chair floats!"

Thomas was in no mood to entertain ummins. He glared.

The adolescent seemed unperturbed. "How do blaster gloves work? Also, how many people live in a city? Why do Torth live there? Oh, and can Torth really fly between the stars? How do they do that?"

It seemed this adolescent, Varktezo, was well aware of Thomas's promise to answer questions. He wasn't going to give up and go away. He exuded curiosity.

"All right, Varktezo." Thomas halted. "If you fetch me a piece of charcoal and a scrap of stretched bark, I'll be able to draw some answers to help out."

Varktezo scampered away. He was roughly the same age as Thomas, but there was a galaxy's worth of difference between them.

Thomas floated toward the vial on the shelf.

But Kessa sat nearby, arms folded. She was watchful.

"There's no privacy in this cave," Thomas muttered. It was almost as bad as the Megacosm.

Well, no. That was an exaggeration.

Varktezo returned with a lightweight piece of bark and a small charcoal rock. He deposited the items on Thomas's lap and then leaped back. He looked excited, as if he expected magic.

The ummins had better not expect anything like what Ariock did. Thomas did not want to accidentally hurt someone. Inhibited or not, he wasn't going to use his hidden power.

He knew, all too well, how disastrous it could be.

"What are you doing?" Varktezo asked as Thomas began to sketch a city skyline.

"This is a city." Thomas added charcoal shading between skyscrapers. "This is where we came from."

He sketched details. Varktezo gawked.

"Approximately one million Torth live in these buildings," Thomas said. "In luxurious suites. They're served by about seven million slaves."

Other ummins crept closer, wary of the mind reader, yet curious. They dragged over a couple of barrels so they could take turns standing to peer at his drawing.

"How many is a million?" Varktezo asked.

The tribal ummins were unfamiliar with basic mathematical concepts, so Thomas explained, using the common slave tongue. He began to realize—as he soaked up ummin life experiences—that this hideout did more than shelter injured slaves. Varktezo and other precocious adolescents stayed underground in order to avoid being collared and abducted.

No wonder the slave farm of Duin was successful. The elders were able to pass some of their knowledge to the most promising village hatchlings.

The mental cacophony around Thomas was worse than usual. Ummins visually drank in the hyperrealistic details. On his lap, New GoodLife Water-Garden City was rendered in charcoal, from the glare of sunlight to the darkest shadows. Airborne traffic soared between curvaceous towers and swirls of dust.

"That drawing is amazing," Kessa said, standing among the crowd. "You have talent like Cherise."

Thomas had soaked up his art skills mostly from Cherise.

"Can all Torth draw pictures like that?" Varktezo asked.

"No."

"Is it common?" Varktezo marveled at the drawing. "How many can do it? One in five? One in twenty?"

Since creativity was essentially an expression of passion and intense emotions, no Torth would dare to master a creative talent. The Torth Majority did value grandeur—but all their beauty and impressive architecture was derived from the civilizations they had conquered.

Torth did not make art. They stole it.

"No Torth can do this," Thomas admitted. "Cherise over there"—he pointed—"has this talent. And I, uh, mimicked her skill."

The ummins gaped at Cherise with awe. A few wondered if their new teacher was joking.

"I'm done." Thomas pushed the charcoal drawing off his lap, unsure why he felt so guilty, or why the result of his absorbed skill made him feel like a fraud.

He didn't deserve anything he had gained from Cherise. That much, he was sure of.

An adolescent ummin caught the drawing before it could hit the floor. "Is this a gift to the people of Duin?" she asked.

"Do whatever you want with it," Thomas said. "It's for the people of Duin, sure."

A crowd of ummins carried the drawing away, murmuring about how best to preserve it.

Another ummin laid a fresh scrap of gray-white bark on his lap. "Teacher, make another picture," she demanded. "Show me what the paradise of Earth looks like."

"Yes!" other ummins clamored.

"Show us the home of Ariock!"

Thomas flexed his charcoal-smudged fingers. His hands ached. He lacked the strength to draw and draw the way Cherise could.

Maybe if he begged for a rest break, the ummins would leave?

"Would you mind if I speak with the teacher alone?" Kessa asked politely.

The tribal ummins exchanged reluctant glances. They wanted to monopolize the Torth Teacher as much as possible, but Kessa looked as wise as their chief elder. There were whispers that she was a runaway. Her neck scar was a testament that she had escaped city slavery, and that gave her a heroic status.

And Kessa seemed fluent in the language of paradise—the only language their Bringer of Hope knew.

So the tribal ummins honored her request. Varktezo lingered, trying to overhear, but the others tugged him away.

"Thank you," Thomas said.

Kessa sat on a nearby crate, her legs dangling. "I wish to learn about your Yeresunsa powers," she said in English.

He should have known she meant business. She wasn't his friend. She didn't do favors for him.

"No," Thomas said coldly. He toggled his hoverchair controls and began to float away.

Kessa remained seated. "I could ask one of the villagers to relay my questions to you. That will force you to answer. Do I need to do that?"

Thomas floated back to her, teeth gritted, forcing down his anger. He would honor his promise to the people of Duin even if it killed him. So fine. Whatever. One way or another, Kessa was going to pump him for information.

"I saw your fear when Ariock tore that cuff off your ankle," Kessa said. "That was rude of him. But why don't you wish to talk about your hidden powers?"

Everyone would hate him for what he could do. Thomas figured he already had enough hatred and mistrust aimed his way. He didn't want to augment it.

"I think Ariock is trying to befriend you," Kessa said. "Although he is clumsy about it."

That was obvious.

"Ariock is not the only one who wants your friendship." Kessa seemed earnest. "I think you have a lot of enemies. But we are not your enemies." Goodwill radiated from her. Thomas let down his guard a tiny bit.

He supposed she was right. He didn't trust Delia or most of the tribal ummins, and he certainly knew the Torth were collectively out to get him, but he could probably trust Kessa. At least to some degree.

She cocked her head, studying him. "Have you used your power before?"

Headlights flashed through his mind. He remembered a horrific walking corpse.

Thomas gripped the charcoal stick, anchoring himself to the present. That walking corpse would never happen again. He was never going to use his Yeresunsa power again, and anyway, he was no longer a vulnerable six-year-old. The Torth had trained him to master emotional self-discipline. He would never lose control and accidentally hurt someone.

Oh, really? a buried part of his mind mocked him.

If he was going to be honest with himself—and he needed to start doing that, really—then he should admit that he was a disaster waiting to happen.

"No one should have Yeresunsa powers," Thomas said. "Not me. Not Ariock."

Great power could not be entrusted to an individual. Individuals were fallible. Emotions made them unstable and therefore untrustworthy.

Power corrupted individual people. It could turn them into tyrants.

Kessa made herself more comfortable on the crate. "Did the Torth know that you were a Yeresunsa when they voted to let you in?"

"They knew." Thomas had been unable to hide such a huge secret from the Upward Governess.

Kessa hesitated. "Then why are you alive?"

"Because of this." Thomas patted his sticker-plastered medicine case. "They made an exception for me because of my potential to further the Empire."

The Upward Governess had used up a lifetime of favors to welcome Yellow Thomas plus his medical invention. Although the Torth Majority would probably never admit it, they did value Blue Rank supergeniuses above other Blue Ranks.

"But…" Kessa studied him with her penetrating gaze. "You said the Torth do not entrust individuals with power. Are supergeniuses not powerful?"

As Thomas thought about it, he realized that he had never properly scrutinized the ease with which the Torth had accepted him as a citizen.

"They stole your medicine," Kessa pointed out. "They do not allow supergeniuses to cure themselves. It seems, to me, they do not value supergeniuses much."

Thomas supposed she was correct. The Upward Governess would have agreed.

"You were the first Yeresunsa they ever allowed to join them?"

"I was," Thomas admitted, dissecting the puzzle. "I was the first hybrid, and the first Yeresunsa."

The Torth had trained him not to think about how unique he was.

Thinking about certain topics meant death, so he had quit pondering the nature of Yeresunsa genetics, and bioengineering, and his own powers.

Now he was faced with a puzzle. And he realized there were pieces missing.

"Is it possible they wanted to use you for your powers?" Kessa asked gently.

"No," Thomas scoffed. "I'd know."

Or would he?

The Upward Governess was not the only high rank who had voted to let him in. Many billions of Torth had invited him to take the adulthood exam. Was it possible that some others had secret ulterior motives?

"Maybe they felt safe because you are dying?" Kessa suggested. "They could use your mind, and also your power, and then throw you away like a slave who is no longer useful."

Thomas gave it another millisecond of careful consideration.

It was plausible.

Yet the Torth Majority had introduced him to a society without deceit, without dirty secrets, without emotional baggage. Could billions of Torth keep a conspiracy going? That seemed beyond belief.

"No," Thomas concluded.

As far as he was concerned, the Torth Empire was as close to perfection as a civilization could get. Thanks to the Megacosm, they had welcomed Thomas with pure goodwill, not once expecting him to do anything in return. They weren't like the demanding ummins who wanted Thomas and Ariock to do endless favors.

And how had he repaid the generosity of the Torth Majority? With theft and betrayal.

Slaves had already died because of Thomas's rash decision to go renegade. More would die for as long as he evaded capture.

"Why do the Torth destroy Yeresunsa?" Kessa asked. "Is it out of fear?"

Thomas quickly analyzed what she was driving at and answered, "No. The Torth Empire is a meritocracy. Any individual Torth born with too much power is considered a threat. No one is allowed to inherit status, or powers, or anything extra. Everyone is born equal. That's the whole point of Torth society."

"But aren't supergeniuses born with more power than most Torth?" Kessa asked.

"Sort of." Thomas began to sketch, since he still had a fresh piece of bark on his lap. "We die young, so it balances out. We never live long enough to become a threat."

Although his hands ached, he needed to keep himself as fully occupied as possible to mitigate his craving for the Megacosm. He sketched the Hollander home, decrepit and shabby. Patches of snow clung to its shadows.

Kessa nodded toward his NAI-12 briefcase. "Why did the Torth allow that? Why did they give it to a supergenius?"

Thomas opened his mouth to dismiss his medical supply as too depleted to be worth anything.

But that wasn't quite true. It had given the Upward Governess a few extra months of life. With the right leverage, she could have gotten her hands on more. The Torth Majority had taken a huge risk by allowing an ambitious supergenius to boost her life span.

"They told you that your medicine and your mind have such great power, they were willing to overlook your Yeresunsa powers." Kessa gave him a level look. "Who told you this?"

"The Majority." Thomas swallowed, seeing the logical point that Kessa had made. "They weren't lying. The Majority consists of billions of Torth, and Torth cannot directly lie to each other."

But they couldn't have been telling the truth, either.

Only a handful of Torth—the supergeniuses—had ever valued his NAI-12 medicine. The rest viewed it as a terrible threat to their meritocracy.

"They lied to themselves," Thomas realized, disgusted that he had not permitted himself to see such a glaringly obvious fact. "The Torth are experts at self-deception."

When he considered all the Torth who were addicted to tranquility meshes, he knew it was true. The vast majority of Torth buried themselves in transient pleasures. They convinced themselves that they felt nothing. It must be a survival technique—probably the only way to survive all the exams on baby farms. Only winners lived long enough to enter adult society.

He thought of the Upward Governess, who pretended not to care about her lack of friends and family. She replaced what was missing with second-hand happiness.

He sketched her round face, staring out of a window with secret longing.

He thought of the Majority, who had assured him that he would never need to harm his friend from Earth. Then they had forced him to torture Cherise.

That wasn't a lie. They had simply changed their minds. By deceiving themselves, the Majority got whatever they wanted.

He had done it, too.

He felt sick as he realized how many times he had buried himself in busy-work or simple pleasures, such as his spa. How many times had he worn a tranquility mesh? He had done everything possible to shut off certain parts of his mind. Not the thinking gears—those gears were valuable to the Torth Empire—but the emotional sublayers.

He had pretended that the human aspect of himself did not exist.

He had done it to survive, but that didn't change the fact that it was dis-honorable. It went against his core beliefs. He had lied and lied to himself, all the while convincing himself that he was an honest truth seer.

Kessa leaned forward, seeing that he had reached a conclusion. "Why did the Torth let you live?" she asked with compassion.

Thomas felt as if he was thinking clearly for the first time in months. He felt used. Yet he was still missing some vital piece of information.

"If they had a reason," he said, "it must be a well-guarded secret. I can't guess."

"So Torth can keep secrets?"

"Yes." Thomas drew Cherise in front of the Hollander home, abandoning the home that had failed to protect her. In the drawing, she looked over her shoulder, glancing back in regret.

"Servants of All can keep secrets," Thomas admitted. "So can superge-niuses."

The campaign to accept Thomas Hill as a Torth citizen had been champi-oned by supergeniuses and Servants of All.

Nearly all of them had voted in his favor.

Thomas could guess why the supergeniuses had wanted him around. Even the unripe baby supergeniuses had admired his NAI-12 invention, al-though they wouldn't admit it.

He drew the Empire's other top supergeniuses peering out of windows. There were the Twins, one pudgy and one with a wildly deformed face. There was the eleven-year-old Death Architect, her curly hair in pigtails. No doubt they had soaked up some of his medical knowledge via the Megacosm. No doubt they secretly quested to survive beyond puberty.

But why had so many Servants of All voted to let him into the Torth Empire?

There were exceptions—notably the Swift Killer—but most of the Ser-vants had touted his mental inventiveness. They had chorused in agreement when the Upward Governess urged everyone to grant him the Adulthood Exam.

Thomas shaded clouds into the shape of an eye without a pupil. The Commander of All Living Things loomed overhead like a shepherd watching over a galactic flock of sheep. She, too, had enabled Thomas to become a Torth. She hadn't tried to dissuade the Majority decision.

"I'm going to think on this some more," Thomas said.

Later on, the Commander of All Living Things had treated him like a borderline criminal. If she had not been so suspicious, he would have remained a Yellow Rank.

He might have died as one, having never gone renegade. He would have obeyed any order given to him. Any upper-rank Torth could have used him however they wished.

The Commander of All Living Things never should have forced him to sentence Ariock to death.

Thomas hardly noticed when Kessa wished him well and patted his thin shoulder. His mind was on the possibility of a conspiracy among the highest ranks of the Torth Empire. If they were hiding a major secret...

Heh. Outing them might cause a galactic civil war.

Wouldn't that be interesting?

Thomas shaded the finishing touches on his drawing. If he could figure out what huge secret the Servants of All were hiding, he might cause enough political mayhem for the Torth Majority to forget all about small problems such as a renegade supergenius.

CHAPTER 8

CONTAINMENT

Ariock inhabited a bunch of ropes.

He was each rope, snaking under and over other ropes, which were also himself. This was his third attempt to braid using his powers. So far, he'd gotten a lot farther than his previous attempts, but he didn't dare think about his vast improvement, or he would remember that he was Ariock instead of a messy network of ropes.

The only way to keep it up was to fall into a rhythm. Snake under, snake over, pull through, wrap around, and again…simultaneously.

A few villagers chanted in a distant part of the cave, mournful and atonal. Vy sang softly nearby while she folded the bedrolls they'd slept on. She had a sweet voice. Ariock recognized the song, and he smiled.

He had woken with his hand near Vy's open palm. It looked like they'd almost held hands in their sleep.

"Did you eat anything for breakfast?" Vy asked him.

Ariock completely lost track of what ropes were supposed to go where. He gave up on the braid and withdrew his awareness.

"I don't need food," he said, although he was ravenous. Living on charity made him feel like a thief. The tribal ummins had so little to share. Even their blankets were patched up and ancient, full of alien odors.

Vy gave him a level look. "If you're going to kill a lot of Torth, you'll need all of your strength."

She spoke so casually about killing. Ariock wondered if she had ever seen brutal violence up close, aside from in movies.

He'd had lots of fantasies about massacring Torth, of course. He even dreamed about it. In his most recent dream, he was standing atop a heap of Red Rank corpses, crushed and mangled from his powers. He had been triumphant—until he noticed his mother, Delia, among the dead.

Such a disturbing dream.

Ariock figured that his subconsciousness was warning him against starting a fight he could not win. The Torth had the inhibitor serum. One tiny drop would render him powerless, the way he'd been in the prison arena.

And they had weapons of mass destruction. If Ariock had to fight transports dropping napalm or missiles, innocent bystanders might end up being collateral damage.

"Hopefully we can sneak into a spaceport," he said. "I'd rather leave this planet without hurting anybody."

Even as he said it, he knew he sounded too idealistic. Spaceports were busy with Torth traffic at all hours.

Vy didn't respond to his naive hope. She stood and walked toward an earthenware pot. "The villagers made stew for us. I had some earlier. The rest is for you."

After months of subsisting on nasty prison kibble, it was hard for Ariock to refuse home-cooked stew.

"You've practiced nonstop," Vy pointed out. "I think it's awesome that you want to master your powers. I'm all for it. But..." She picked up the pot, using dishcloths to hold each handle. "The Torth could find us at any second. You need to be rested and fed, not all worn-out."

"I'm not worn-out," Ariock assured her.

But he was starving, as usual. The pot included a wooden spoon. He sampled the stew.

These tribal ummins seemed to like tangy marinades, although they used too much salt. The meat was unknown but plentiful. He gave Vy a questioning look.

"I had my fill," she said.

Ariock ate everything that was left in the pot. It was probably enough to feed a clan of ummins, but for him, it was a pretty good meal.

Tribal ummins flooded into the hideout, speaking rapidly in the language that Ariock had learned to identify as the slave tongue. Slave collars glowed around their necks. That dusty-white glow meant active and on duty.

"Oh, no!" Vy jumped up.

People rushed to hear what the distraught villagers had to say.

"What happened?" Ariock asked, alarmed.

"This is bad," Vy moaned.

Ariock mentally braced himself.

"They're collaring everyone in sight," Vy said. "And they're erecting structures around the village. It sounds like a military siege." She gave Ariock a helpless look. "Do you think they know we're here?"

That was a question for Thomas.

Ariock was ashamed about the way he'd mistreated Thomas the day before. He wanted to apologize properly, but Thomas hadn't given him a chance. Instead, the boy was spending all his time with tribal ummins. He seemed to be teaching them the basic fundamentals of a lot of things.

And Cherise was teaching the Duin ummins how to write.

She had her own little gathering, mainly adolescents and children. They seemed to be applying the alphabet to the slave tongue.

Not that any of that mattered now. Amid the beak clucks and commotion, Ariock realized that a few ummins were injured. Their friends helped them to limp toward him. He recognized their words for "Bringer of Hope."

He held his hands up, ready to heal.

"The Torth threatened them," Vy said with horror, translating. "Out loud." The chief elder gave Ariock a resentful look.

He knew that he deserved it. The so-called Bringer of Hope actually brought misery.

Vy met Ariock's gaze, and she looked haunted with guilt. "If the Torth learn we're hiding here, they will destroy this slave farm."

There was a limit, Ariock realized. A limit on how much his benefactors should suffer.

This went beyond the limit.

These innocent villagers had shared everything they had and risked their lives to save him, although they didn't speak his language or like the way he looked. Would they lose everything because of him?

"...Ariock." Vy sounded scared.

Without realizing it, he had expanded his awareness. He filled the air. All the torches in the cave dimmed and flickered, responding to his mood.

Control was definitely something he needed to add to his "practice" list.

Ariock snapped back into his body. Torches flared as the air settled back to its natural state.

"I might need to kill some Torth," he admitted.

A beast inside him lurched to life, as if he was about to fight a monstrosity in the arena. The low ceiling was like the grate of his prison cage. Ariock longed to shove it away and make room so he could stand up.

He clenched his fists. That reminded him that his body had solid limits. For now.

Maybe he should just exit the cave and let the beast loose. He would rather die fighting than as a helpless prisoner.

He would make sure the Torth remembered him.

CHAPTER 9
BY SURPRISE

Thomas sketched the cosmos. He could draw anything, even if he were blindfolded, even while dozens of nearby slave minds buzzed with primitive fears.

"What are the Torth planning?" one of the junior elders demanded.

"They're preparing to attack your village," Thomas explained. "In hopes that Ariock and I will reveal ourselves."

The farm slaves lacked words for what they'd seen, but Thomas had absorbed their aboveground experiences. So he had glimpsed Brown Ranks directing nussian laborers to set up drills and chemical mixers and blaster cannons. High-volume hoses would flood any cave system with death.

Red Ranks probably surrounded the farm, manning scattershot burst guns. They would aim for Ariock.

Servants of All would be on-site, too. No doubt some elite Servant or two wanted to claim the glory of defeating Yellow Thomas.

"When?" the junior elder asked.

"I can only guess," Thomas said.

Well, that wasn't entirely the case. He could find out…

No.

He had so little personal honor remaining, he wasn't going to throw away the last dregs. He would honor his promise to not betray these villagers. He would resist the Megacosm so he could die with at least a little bit of integrity.

That still seemed important.

"Torth." Pung held up the empty blaster glove. "I want to take a few of them into death with me. Is that not what you want, too?"

Well. Here was a forbidden topic, if ever there was one.

"If I teach you how to kill Torth…" Thomas swept his gaze across the eager villagers, aware that waging war against Torth military ranks was a step beyond merely going renegade. "Certain knowledge will transform you into something more than a slave." He shifted his attention to the junior elder. "When that happens, your trick of panicking may not work anymore. The knowledge will seep into your subconsciousness and give you a confidence the Torth will detect, no matter what."

The villagers muttered with resentment, but the junior elder understood. She gave a resigned nod.

"I'm not a villager," Pung pointed out. "I can learn whatever you teach."

Indeed, he was one of the most avid students in the crowd. As long as Pung was demanding answers and giving commands, he was not a slave, and he knew it. He had grown bold.

"True." Thomas faced him. "But if I teach you to kill Torth, then every warning I gave to Ariock, I would repeat to you. If you wear a blaster glove, you will be like a Yeresunsa."

"Really?" Pung sounded skeptical.

"You will wield power."

Pung gave him a look that was almost pitying. "Are you afraid of me, Torth?"

"I have some concerns." In truth, Thomas felt no fear. He didn't feel much of anything anymore. All he wanted to do was ascend. Ascend or die.

He had stopped taking regular doses of his NAI-12. What was the point anymore?

He should dump his medicine. Pour vial after vial onto sand or rocks. He'd wasted more than half his life working on it, and now he almost wished that he'd left it in the embrace of the Upward Governess. At least she had appreciated it.

He figured that he was quietly going insane.

Dozens of villagers waited, watching him, thirsting for knowledge. If Thomas gave them what they wanted...

It would be cathartic. Maybe he could cause a massacre of Torth at the hands of ummins.

And the Torth would retaliate with enough force to wipe this slave farm off the map.

Thomas had witnessed the aftermath of slave rebellions when he'd trawled the Megacosm. Slaves always failed. They could not compete against instant communication and galactic infrastructure.

Cringing and servile, the people of Duin might be collared and shipped off to various cities instead of killed outright. But if they stopped acting like slaves...

"I know it's easy to forget," Thomas told Pung, "but that glove belongs to me. If I teach you how to unlock it and use it, then I'm adding a major crime to my long list. My death sentence will be bad enough without becoming a criminal mastermind who teaches slaves to rebel."

Pung didn't care. The villagers began to sound mutinous, shouting to be heard over each other.

Thomas raised his hands, desperate for them to quiet down. He was drowning in noise.

The Megacosm glowed in his mind. He hated how much he wanted to bask in the distant bliss of someone else's body.

"You promised to obey us," the junior elder said. "I command you. Teach us how to use that blaster glove."

Thomas was a traitor, a thief, and a backstabber. What were a few dead slaves? These villagers had practically condemned themselves.

"Okay," Thomas said.

He had an eager audience. They went quiet and attentive.

"First," Thomas said, "let's cover the basics. Aim for the head."

Pung radiated mistrust. He had seen blaster gloves used to murder nussians and other slaves.

"Your goal is to stop them from accessing the Megacosm," Thomas explained. "A dying Torth can still send reports or summon help. A headless Torth cannot."

The villagers were wide-eyed. It was one thing to fantasize about slaughtering Torth but another thing to imagine it as feasible.

"So aim here." Thomas indicated his head. He half hoped they would use him for target practice. That would be karmic justice, for a mind reader like himself to die by a slave firing squad.

Pung examined the glove, then offered it to Thomas. "How?"

"Torth weapons are keyed to their owners." Thomas toggled a fresh override onto the glove's display. "Here's how you rekey it. Enter your own code, and it's yours."

Pung imitated what Thomas had done, fascinated. Tribal ummins looked over his shoulder.

"If you manage to steal a glove from a Torth," Thomas said, "or if you can take it off a Torth corpse, do that."

They clicked their beaks in agreement.

"There are several modes," Thomas went on. "Gloves can interface with other equipment, such as slave collars. But you'll want killing mode."

He went over instructions. Pung paid close attention.

"There's a limit on how many blasts it can fire in rapid succession," Thomas added. "It depends on whether you go for wide or narrow shots. See this color band? It will shade to red and fade when the glove needs a rest. Typically, it requires five to ten seconds to recharge itself."

The junior elder gave Pung a look of concern. "I am afraid that if you try to blast Torth, they will blast you. Perhaps you can hide in a hut? Pop up and shoot through the window, then hide again."

Thomas nodded. "Successful attacks against Torth all have one thing in common: the element of surprise."

The tribal ummins exchanged looks. Thomas knew what some of them wanted to ask even before they spoke.

"There have been successful attacks," he confirmed. "Slaves do manage to kill Torth every once in a while. It's just that there's always a retaliation. The Torth always win in the end."

The junior elder looked bitter. She was used to hard truths.

"A hero against the Torth must act on impulse," Pung said, guessing. "Or shoot Torth from afar. They have to be beyond mind-reading range."

"Exactly," Thomas said.

"Is that how you did it?" Pung scrutinized him. "Did you act on impulse?"

Thomas nodded. "I couldn't make a solid plan. All I could do was collect opportunities and act when I had a chance."

He figured that things had happened the same way for Ariock when he'd killed those two Red Ranks in the prison. And Jonathan Stead. If either of them had planned their attacks, the Torth would have stopped them.

"There's only one way to defeat a Torth when you're cornered," Thomas said. "Take everyone by surprise. Even yourself."

The tribal ummins turned to each other, discussing that. Some had theorized about the element of surprise being critical, but to hear a mind reader say it gave the notion credibility.

"The Bringer of Hope surprised you, didn't he?" One of the adolescents gazed at Thomas with a mischievous grin. "You didn't expect him to remove that golden band from your leg."

"I was not prepared for that," Thomas admitted. He glanced toward Ariock, making sure the giant remained on the far side of the cave.

The first time Thomas had met Ariock, in the Dovanack mansion, he had soaked up an average mind. Docile. Predictable.

Ariock still seemed to be the same person, but now there was violence lurking just beneath his surface. Rage. And worse—Ariock was unpredictable. He kept doing things that Thomas failed to anticipate. How had he taught himself to heal fatal injuries?

And how had he sussed out Thomas's deepest secret? He had guessed that Thomas was a Yeresunsa based on almost no clues.

"What was that cuff around your leg?" the junior elder asked. She eyed his gold-patterned socks, and Thomas sensed her wonder if the cuff had been at all akin to a slave collar.

"It made me feel safe." Thomas hoped she wouldn't ask for further explanation.

"Safe from what?" she asked brightly.

Thomas nearly confessed that he had an evil secret power. Once he told the plain truth, the tribal ummins would wisely and rightly fear him. They'd leave him alone.

But Cherise had joined his audience.

A leather band held her hair back, with beads hanging down. She looked more relaxed than she had and even a bit confident now that she had befriended some ummins. Her friends must be interested in blaster glove lessons.

But why was she here? Why did she have to be listening right now?

"What are you afraid of, Torth?" the junior elder repeated in a less friendly tone.

They were all watching him. The whole cave seemed to await his answer.

Ariock caught the mood. In this silence, he would hear Thomas's answer even from a distance.

They would judge Thomas. He knew it. Cherise, especially, would reevaluate her years of friendship with him and reject all of it. She would wonder how he could have kept such a dark, horrible secret during the entire time they'd shared together in the Hollander home.

She would see him as a murderer.

Pung answered for him. "The Teacher is a Yeresunsa."

Shock registered on some faces. Comprehension on others.

With a mighty effort, Thomas wrenched his thoughts away from the blissful escape the Megacosm might provide. He must not ascend. He did not deserve to escape.

Nor did he deserve any sort of freedom.

He should be dead.

"I think the Torth had a shortage of supergeniuses," Pung said. "And they decided to get some use out of this one before they killed him."

It made too much sense. More than Thomas wanted to deal with.

"The Torth accepted me exactly as I am," Thomas pointed out. "They accepted me. Which is more than I can say anyone else has ever done."

"I didn't know a Torth could get angry and afraid so easily," Pung observed.

It was too much. Thomas wanted to lash out, but there was nowhere to go. He was in a corner. Hot. Furious.

Sparks flurried in front of him, and everyone stepped back, alarmed.

The armrests of his hoverchair melted where his fingers squeezed.

The sparks ignited into a conflagration. A wall of flames rushed across the hard-packed dirt-and-rock floor and encircled his hoverchair.

As people shouted and ran, Thomas gaped at what he had done.

He hadn't known he could ignite fires with his mind.

CHAPTER 10

SCORCHED HOPE

The fire surprised Ariock so much, he leaped up and whacked his head against the ceiling.

Vy saw him and winced in sympathy.

Ariock leaned on his hands and waited for the pain to fade. He should have remembered that he didn't need to jump or run to use his powers. All he needed to do was send his awareness into the air.

Never mind everyone's panic. He had to extinguish the flames before anything caught on fire.

He blocked out distractions and let himself expand beyond the limits of his body.

The intense heat was obvious to his extended self. Ariock folded cooler air into the heat. When the cooler air got too hot, he compressed more cool air, adding pressure.

Flames guttered and died. Ariock's pressure smothered them to nothingness. His extended awareness rolled over the whole wall of flames, extinguishing all of it. When he encountered other spots, he killed those, too.

The smoke cleared. A few blankets and baskets looked singed. Dust sifted off the ceiling, blackened by extra soot. Villagers clung to each other in terror.

And Thomas looked stunned.

His golden robes and sandy hair were untouched. The flames had encircled him without harming him. One did not need to be a genius to figure out who had caused the fiery mayhem.

"So this is your power," Ariock said with admiration.

Thomas looked sick with shame.

"It was an accident," Ariock assured Thomas and everyone else. "No big deal. No harm done."

Overall, he was glad. With a fiery power wielded by a supergenius, they might have a real chance against the Torth. Thomas just needed some practice. Powers seemed to be tied to emotions. Once Thomas got in touch with his intuitive and emotional side, he would become a force to be reckoned with.

"He could have killed someone!" That was Delia.

Ariock rolled his eyes. "He didn't. And he wouldn't."

Thomas backed his hoverchair away as if to escape from accusations, but there was nowhere to go. He was backed against a petroglyph-covered wall.

"I'm sorry." Thomas sounded contrite. "I've never done anything like this before. I swear."

He was fragile, bundled in dusty robes. He hadn't been eating. And now he seemed overwhelmed, scared, and possibly angry.

That might be a volatile danger in an enclosed space.

"Let's leave him alone for a bit." Ariock held his arm out, blocking his mother.

"But..." She began to argue, then seemed to think better of it. "He told us that the Torth outlawed powers," she muttered. "How many powers has he been hiding?"

Ariock had questions, too, but he wasn't going to interrogate Thomas at this moment. No more rough treatment. No more ignoring his boundaries. The ceiling was too low, the walls too close.

They really ought to avoid triggering any more outbursts.

Ariock got to work, ushering villagers away from Thomas. They had enough to worry about without adding Yeresunsa fights.

"Ariock," Thomas said.

Ariock looked at him.

"I do have a power that I...I haven't told you about. This wasn't it."

Ariock nodded in acceptance. "You'll tell me when you're ready."

Thomas looked grateful and relieved.

CHAPTER 11

RENEGADE

Thomas unscrewed the cap of the vial.

The so-called sleeping potion could be a symbol of the riches he'd rejected. The rare chemicals were imported from specialized laboratories on alien worlds. The vial was more durable than any plastic made on Earth.

Why had he fled that rich life among powerful authorities? Had he secretly believed that he could magically transform into a heroic renegade, like Jonathan Stead? Did he think Cherise would magically forgive him for torturing her with a pain seizure?

Ha.

Well, he was done deceiving himself.

Three months in the Megacosm had changed his emotional baseline as well as his perspective on human *(primitive)* matters. He would never again find satisfaction in simple pursuits, like teaching Cherise how to play chess. He could barely endure this simple life among *(primitives)* people who used to be his friends.

And he couldn't trust himself anymore. He was dangerous.

What would death taste like? Would it feel like an endless plunge into loneliness? Was there an afterlife? Not even the Torth Empire could answer that question. Thomas supposed it would be one last thing for him to learn.

He raised the vial to his lips and...

Delia snatched it from his grasp.

She smashed the vial on the floor. When it failed to shatter into pieces, she kicked sand over the glowing liquid. She knew that the aroma was toxic.

Thomas used his power to light it on fire.

Delia jumped away. The fire was small, just enough to devour the toxic fumes. Soon the potion was neutralized.

Thomas forced himself to pull his awareness back into himself. It was difficult, because he was shaking with frustration. He glared at Delia and considered lighting her on fire.

But that would be cowardly, petty, and not how he wanted to be remembered.

He should have sensed her approach. He would have if he had been in a better state of mind instead of fully absorbed by his own thoughts.

"Why did you stop me?" he asked.

Delia leaned against the soot-smeared wall and folded her arms. "Why are you condemning us to die?"

Thomas almost denied that. But they both knew that he was trying to kill himself—and he was the only person among them who knew how to pilot a spaceship.

"I thought you would celebrate my death," Thomas muttered, but it was a feeble complaint. Delia wasn't an idiot. She understood that Ariock needed advice from a supergenius if he was going to have any hope of outwitting the Torth Empire.

"Do you see Ariock over there?" Delia gestured.

Her gigantic son watched them from a distance. He looked concerned. So did Vy, Kessa, and Weptolyso.

"He would heal you," Delia said. "If I told him that you poisoned yourself with sleeping potion, he would heal you right away. Because he swore to protect you. And Ariock keeps his promises." She leaned closer. "You once promised to rescue us. Was that a lie?"

Thomas swallowed. He had shouted to Cherise that he would rescue her. He had promised.

That version of him seemed so young and innocent, so long ago and far away. He wasn't sure if he was the same person anymore.

He wanted to claim that he had kept his promise and rescued Cherise.

But he couldn't quite bring himself to say it. He wouldn't tell a lie. If he killed himself or gave up, then his rescue would be incomplete, a failure. And if he went back on his word, well, wasn't that equivalent to what the Torth Majority had done to him?

Was he toying with Cherise, like a cruel god?

Was he whimsically changing his mind without a care for anyone but himself?

Delia eyed him with righteous judgment, but also with suppressed hope. "Why did you leave the Torth?" She gestured to his medicine case. "Why did you steal your medicine back if you were planning to die?"

That was actually a good question. Thomas didn't have a good answer.

That night felt like a sliver of glass in his mind, painful to examine. His decision to break laws and enact a rescue had been based on…what? Nightmares. Nothing logical.

"I didn't plan anything," he said.

He had just…

Well. His gaze swept the charred remnants of the sleeping potion. He had wanted to retaliate against the Torth Empire *(and the Upward Governess)* for stealing his *(future)* medicine.

He supposed he'd wanted revenge.

He'd wanted justice.

"I was righting a wrong," he admitted.

"You're not done yet," Delia pointed out.

Thomas inwardly admitted that it was unfair of him to leave his friends alone to face an armada of death. He just wasn't sure how far he should take justice. He wasn't even sure if he was the hero and the Upward Governess the villain. Monstrous power should not be wielded by individuals like Ariock and Thomas. Should they really be permitted to roam free?

There just weren't any good options.

Either he betrayed Ariock and Cherise by committing suicide and abandoning his rescue of them, or he betrayed the Torth Empire by going fully renegade.

The Torth had given Thomas more respect than anyone on Earth had ever done. Surely he owed them his life? If Thomas waged war against them—if he caused the deaths of innocent Torth going about their daily lives—then he would have no honor left. Not even a shred.

Delia continued to lean against the wall with her arms folded. "Tell me how to keep Ariock alive," she said, her voice low and desperate. "Give us a plan. If it works? Then I'll be your suicide doctor."

Truth shone in her mind. She would do anything to make sure her son had a chance to live in safety.

In the darkness across the cave, ummin villagers looked at him, pleading with their eyes for more lessons. They had called Thomas their Teacher. They trusted him.

"Ariock keeps giving you second chances," Delia said. "And third, and fourth. He keeps his word. Doesn't that mean something to you?"

Ariock was honorable, and honor did mean a lot to a Torth. Without friends or family, they had nothing else to live for. Only status.

But they had broken their word to Thomas.

The Torth Majority had chorused *Welcome!* and embraced him with empty reassurances. They had publicly agreed that his secret power was okay. Now? Their grand mercy was extinguished like a dead flame.

The Torth were all about self-deception.

Blatant hypocrisy.

Lies.

Thomas realized, with burning anger, that he wouldn't actually mind causing a Torth massacre.

Killing them might not be a betrayal, really. It might actually be justice. "You held power over us." Delia pinned him with her gaze. "You could have stayed among the so-called gods of this world. Instead? You packed painkillers and water canteens. You made sure that Ariock's death sentence wasn't fatal. You went out of your way to save him. And us. Why did you do that?"

Thomas nodded to himself, coming to a conclusion that felt as monumental as his decision to join the Torth Empire.

Every fiber of his being screamed against admitting that his lingering loyalty to the Torth was wrong. Surely it was unnecessary to say it out loud. It would be humiliating, worse than crying in public.

But he had made too many excuses for his mistakes. He needed to stay honest with himself if he was going to try to reclaim even a little bit of lost honor.

"You're right," he told Delia.

He floated past her, toward Ariock. Delia followed, and Thomas sensed the tenuous nature of her hope. She doubted that he could ensure their survival. She understood that the Torth Majority were far stronger than her son. He was mortal. They were legion.

But the Torth Majority could make mistakes.

They had made a huge error when they'd accepted a boy named Thomas Hill into the collective.

"I saved you for a reason," Thomas said, hovering in front of Ariock.

He had everyone's attention. Ariock's mind shone with hope, although caution surrounded that hope like a fortress.

"If I leave you, I betray you," Thomas said. "And everyone here." He swallowed. "There's no adequate excuse for how I've been acting. But I take full blame."

Ariock started to speak, but Thomas overrode him.

"I owe you a promise equal to the one you gave me." Thomas mentally groped along a precipice, choosing words with care. "I don't approve of your promise, and I wish you'd take it back, because I don't deserve it. But I know that's useless. So here's my promise to you." It unfurled from his lips, hot like flames. "Ariock, I will bring you to a place of safety, or I'll die trying."

He felt liberated and trapped at the same time. He was committed now. He would have to suffer though cravings for the Megacosm plus demands from people who mistrusted and hated him.

But it would be worth it.

He would die with a clear spot on his otherwise filthy conscience, once his promise was fulfilled. That was something to look forward to.

Ariock seemed stunned. *You don't have to do this,* he thought.

"Yes, I do." Thomas wasn't going to debate his decision.

Ariock seemed to recognize immovable resolve when he saw it and gave an uncertain nod. "All right. So, do you have any idea how we can get past the Torth army that's camped up there?"

"Don't get too hopeful," Thomas said. "But yes, I have a plan."

With his inner turmoil solved, he felt at peace. The hard decision was finalized. Everything else was simply logistics.

"We're going to start a slave revolt," he said.

PART SEVEN

"You have destroyed my followers, but will I die easily? I am Yeresunsa. Some of you remember what that meant. I have the storm on my side. Come and kill me. I will bring you with me into death."

—Scrap recorded from a long-dead Yeresunsa

CHAPTER 1

BATTLE PLAN

Wonderment spread through the villagers as Thomas outlined some kind of plan in the slave tongue. Ariock listened carefully, trying to pick up the language.

Their wonder ignited with excitement. One of the villagers shouted something challenging.

"Right," Vy said, listening. "How are they supposed to kill an army of Torth with one blaster glove?"

Thomas sounded remorseless.

"He says…" Vy faltered. "They'll have more blaster gloves after they slaughter hundreds of Torth and raid their corpses." She met Ariock's gaze, and he saw his own misgivings there. "He said they'll do it quickly."

"He wants ummins to kill Torth?" Ariock asked, wondering if there was a mistranslation. The tribal ummins shouldn't need to put themselves at risk. They had Ariock.

"He says we have everything we need here in this cave." Vy paused every so often to listen before she translated for Ariock. "Yellow rocks? I don't know why, but he wants them to gather yellow rocks and a lot of wood charcoal. Even ashes. Also, some kind of soap material? I don't know that word. And silver rocks?" She looked mystified. "Ground into powder. I don't know why he'd want silver powder."

"Is he having them invent gunpowder?" Ariock wondered. Primitive gunpowder would surely not outmatch blaster gloves and whatever else the Torth had.

The villagers scurried to collect rocks and ashes. Thomas looked self-satisfied as they used mortars and pestles.

"I'll kill the Torth," Ariock said. "They shouldn't put themselves at risk."

"They can handle it," Thomas said. "Trust me."

"They've—" Ariock began to say that the villagers had already sacrificed too much, but Thomas cut him off.

"Whatever one Torth sees, all Torth see. If we let one Torth see you steal away inside a transport, the Empire is much more likely to intercept us before we get to a spaceport. We should keep the Torth guessing. Don't let any of them see. At all."

Vy looked speculative. "So we're going home?"

Thomas turned to her. "We should never go back to Earth. That's certain death. But the galaxy is a huge place. The Torth claim to own everything, but they haven't explored every wilderness on every known planet. I can find someplace habitable where we're likely to disappear for the rest of our lives. I mean, the rest of *your* lives," he amended.

Kessa looked impressed, and so did Delia. But Ariock wondered if his sphere of influence would be a giveaway.

And Vy looked sad. To her, Ariock knew, Earth was more than just TV and games. It was family and relationships that he could never imagine. Her mom. Her friends.

If not for Ariock's existence, she would be safe among her loved ones.

"Thomas," Ariock said. "Isn't there more of your medicine on Earth? We should stop there and pick it up."

Thomas looked surprised.

"Right!" Vy's face lit up with excitement. "His extra supply is in Boston. We should…well, I guess we should steal it."

Thomas's disparaging gaze said that he had already lived for two hundred thousand years, and he had no intention of living that many more. But he only said, "Let's have this discussion later."

He turned to one of the junior elders and rattled off what sounded like instructions. The villagers, especially the chiefs, didn't look toward Ariock. It seemed they had stopped expecting anything great from the Bringer of Hope.

"You can't ask them to slaughter Torth," Ariock said. "That should be my job." He wasn't exactly eager to wrench bodies apart, but, well, he had bludgeoned alien monsters to death. He could do it again.

Weptolyso snorted in solidarity. "I will fight by your side, Son of Storms," he said in his gravelly voice.

Thomas finished his instructions, then turned to Ariock with disgruntled annoyance. "The last time the Torth Empire saw you, you were hanging from a metal cross in a lightning storm. Let them suspect you're too injured to fight. They might assume that's why slaves are doing it for you."

Ariock didn't think that was enough justification to put the tribal ummins at risk. "I—"

Thomas ruthlessly cut him off. "Supergeniuses don't cope well with uncertainty." His tone hardened. "I want them to have to guess whether you're en route to a spaceport or hidden underground in a near-death condition. The more they have to guess, the less efficient they are."

"That's not a good enough reason—"

"That's not the only reason." Thomas wouldn't let him finish a sentence. "You're a massive target. You are impossible to miss, and you're not wearing armor."

Ariock gestured to the dented plates of gladiator armor, which he had piled in a corner, ready to wear again. He had replaced all his underclothes with more comfortable makeshift garments. The villagers had kindly provided him with woven fabric and twine. But the armor fit, and he could use his powers to reshape it for an even better fit.

"The gladiator stuff doesn't count," Thomas said. "It's flimsy. It won't stop a blaster cannon."

That was fair.

But Ariock knew that he could not destroy Torth from the safety of this hideout cave. He couldn't tell life sparks apart. If he was going to target Torth, he needed to be close enough to see them. "The ummins shouldn't have to—"

"The ummins are a normal sight in any village," Thomas emphasized. "The Torth expect to see ummins. Do you really think it's smart to show up and have the Torth pummel you with every heavy weapon in their arsenal? In the middle of a village full of our innocent slave friends?"

Ariock closed his mouth. That was a valid point.

"I know you're impressed with your powers," Thomas said. "I'm impressed, too. But the Torth have all the advantages in tactics, firepower, and just about every factor. Attack them and you'll start a fight you can't win. That's not a guess. That's not a wager. That's a fact."

Ariock wanted to argue, but he was aware of his own shortcomings. Whenever he poured his awareness into healing, he couldn't hold a conversation, let alone walk. He had trouble with multitasking.

So he might not be able to single-handedly slay an army.

On the other hand, Ariock wasn't as fragile as his friends seemed to believe. He meant to keep his promise to protect the slaves of Duin and everyone else.

Thomas studied him, as if calculating his weaknesses. "Think about Vy. Think about your mother. If a microdart takes you down, then the rest of us are doomed."

Delia nodded, endorsing every word. "Exactly."

Ariock put on a tolerant, agreeable look. If they refused to let him take his fair share of risks, there was no use arguing. He would just have to sneak up the tunnel without permission.

"I'm only asking you to keep a low profile until we get inside a spaceport." Thomas clasped his hands, as if begging. "Then, once we're safely aboard a streamship, you can let loose and slay every Torth that tries to stop us."

Ariock imagined ummins standing over the corpses of Red Ranks. They might be triumphant for a while, but eventually—and probably sooner rather than later—the Torth Empire would retaliate.

Vy spoke. "We need to take the villagers with us."

"Are you kidding?" Thomas looked from Ariock to Vy as if they were both insane. "We can't take all 595 ummins. Transports have limited interior space."

Vy began to say something.

"No," Thomas told her firmly. "Even if we could steal multiple vehicles, and even if I could daisy-chain them together or teach the ummins how to pilot transports in the short time we have, there's no way to sneak a caravan of transports into a spaceport. The Torth monitor traffic in the Megacosm. It will be hard enough sneaking one transport inside."

Despite his aloof demeanor and yellow eyes, he looked regretful.

"Look," he said, "there's only so much I can do. This village was doomed from the moment they offered to hide us." He bowed his head. "I'm sorry they showed us mercy."

CHAPTER 2

LAYERED CAKE

The Commander of All Living Things stood motionless, her shroud billowing in the hot, gritty wind as she listened to the mental symphonies of the Megacosm.

Conversations clustered like nebulas. They birthed ideas, improving reality, in a process as beautiful and powerful as the universe itself. The Commander didn't understand why anyone ever wanted a tranquility mesh when they could simply admire the universe.

We are ready for battle. That was the Swift Killer, shredding her inner contemplation. *Let's pump the ground full of toxic gas and force the enemies out.*

She was in the jungle, far from the Commander, with an army of Red Ranks and equipment. Millions of listeners amplified her thoughts to anyone who was tuned in.

Wait, the Commander of All commanded.

Why? the Swift Killer demanded. *Just because that fat girl wants to double-check her facts? We have plenty of proof that the enemies are here.* She swatted a gas bug away from her sweaty face. *They're probably cowering in the mine shafts.*

The Commander of All walked along the edge of a terrace, so high up she could see the hazy yellow curve of the horizon.

She liked edges. A stray gust of wind in the wrong direction could push her to her death, but danger made her blood pump faster. It felt as if she had extra amounts of life.

A massive audience rode inside her, too.

She had to remain impartial and emotionless. If she lost her balance inside the Megacosm, she would be sentenced to death. It was another edge.

Stand by, she commanded the army.

But—

Stand by. The Commander of All sensed a change in the perceptions of her nearby slaves, a change she had been waiting for. A certain obese girl floated onto the terrace, attended by her own slaves and bodyguards.

I have a meeting, the Commander told her army. *Stand by and wait.*

If there was one thing a lengthy life had taught her, it was that immediate gratification was never important. The army would wait. The Swift Killer would simmer with frustration, but she had enough self-control to keep her emotions from boiling into primitive rage.

The Commander dropped out of the Megacosm.

If the Upward Governess wanted this private conversation, then she would need to float closer, into telepathic range. Instead, she lingered near the glass door.

Did she wrongly, stupidly, expect the Commander to come to her?

Perhaps the Upward Governess realized how wrong her hesitance was. She floated forward, bowing as best as she was able. *Great One,* she thought as soon as she was within range. *Thank You for agreeing to meet in person.*

The Commander of All resisted her urge to step away from the girl's disgustingly colossal mind. No one should contain so much information. *I expect an extraordinarily good reason for your wish to delay the invasion of Duin.*

I have several good reasons, the Upward Governess thought. Reasons whizzed through her mind, too fast and too complex for the Commander to grasp. *For one thing, do You think it is wise to put an unstable and flawed clone (the Swift Killer) in charge of the upcoming battle?*

The Commander disliked this critique. The Swift Killer did have some flaws, but she was a Servant of All, with all the training that entailed. She had volunteered for this task before anyone else. She was independent-minded enough to lead and very motivated to win.

With respect, the Upward Governess thought, *I urge You to put someone more thoughtful (less impulsive) in charge. I humbly recommend the Clement Serpent or the Horned Triumph.*

Those two Servants of All were stationed close enough to be of service, although the Horned Triumph was on the elderly side of competent. If the Commander recommended *(appointed)* either of them to defeat the Betrayer and the Giant, the Swift Killer would probably complain and possibly cause problems.

The Commander studied the Upward Governess in her ornate floating throne. *You didn't need to ask for a private meeting. You could have recommended this in public.*

The Upward Governess signaled her slaves. One of them lifted the lid off a golden tray and revealed a rich-looking slice of cake. *Do You mind if I eat dessert?*

The Commander could have sentenced her to death for her presumption. But supergeniuses like the Upward Governess had a lot of devotees in the Megacosm. Sentencing her to death—after she had located dangerous enemies of the Empire—would make the Commander look insecure and petty. It would count against her if any part of the upcoming battle went awry.

She flashed a curt permission. *What do you want?*

The Upward Governess dug into her cake. *You (Great One) commanded Me to locate the enemies and to ensure that they are captured and the Giant killed. You commanded Me not to fail. Well, I am here to ensure that You (and the Empire) do not make any mistakes.*

The Commander tapped her bony fingers. The Giant did make a lot of people nervous. A few frail-minded citizens had actually packed their luggage and taken extended vacations on the local moons, or farther away.

But *(Ariock Dovanack)* the Giant was hardly the worst threat the Torth Empire had ever faced. Other monsters, such as Jonathan Stead, and Judven Han Hayat, and Iriade Senasien, stood out in collective memories. They had caused worse damage than anything the Giant had done. The most ancient memories in the Megacosm were riddled with the ghosts of long-forgotten Yeresunsa armies.

Torth who slew such monsters were heroes. They won glory for the Empire. The Commander of All felt honored that not just one but two monsters were alive during her reign. It was unprecedented in the modern era. Once her forces vanquished the Giant and the Betrayer, her face and her identity would be preserved for eternity in the Megacosm.

That was as good as immortality. That was the ultimate goal every sane Torth strived for.

You're too focused on the Giant, the Upward Governess thought. *We are about to battle a renegade supergenius. The Empire has never faced such a major threat before.*

The Commander tried to hide her disparaging thoughts. Yes, the Betrayer did have a vile power, but it was a weak power. He needed to be within telepathy range in order to use it on a victim. Otherwise? He was just another *(doomed)* supergenius. He couldn't walk. He was dying.

The Upward Governess seemed to have an unhealthy obsession with her former protégé.

We are well positioned and well prepared, the Commander assured the governess. *Our Red Ranks will neutralize the Betrayer from a safe distance.*

I'm not concerned about his power, the Upward Governess thought with hints of frustration leaking from her mind. *We (You) should be very wary of his ability to scheme. We need multiple fail-safes and ready countermeasures.* She scooped up a bite of cake. *Here are My suggestions. Command every Torth citizen on this planet to be armed. Tell anyone with a healthy body to learn some fighting tactics. Set up checkpoints throughout every city on this continent. Lock down every spaceport. Shut down every launchpad.*

The Commander stiffened at each absurd suggestion.

The Torth Empire was about to swat down some ragged, desperate out-laws, not go to war against a superior enemy force. If she commanded a pla-netwide lockdown, she might as well declare that she was afraid of a couple of outlaws. That would make her seem paranoid and overzealous, and her popularity would plummet to deadly levels.

I already have every Red Rank on this continent alert and wearing armor. The Commander gestured a dismissal. Torth citizens should always be free to go anywhere. That was one of the privileges of being a Torth.

The Upward Governess stared at her. *The Giant has one major advantage that all previous monsters lacked: a supergenius helping him. If You fail to take this threat seriously, then You are likely to end up like the previous Commander of All Living Things.* Her mind shone with sincerity.

The deposed Commander had bungled a crisis similar to this one. Everyone remembered that he had wrongly assumed that the Isolatorium was unbreakable. During his reign, he had allowed a monster—Jonathan Stead—to break laws, evade armies, and trick the Torth Empire into believing he was dead.

The Commander of All Living Things had personally driven a metal spike into her predecessor's chest, ending his torture. He had screamed like a slave.

I will consider your suggestions. The Commander placed one bony foot on the edge of the precipice, followed by the other, and balanced on her heels. Real-life danger kept her anchored, no matter what went through her mind. Enhanced muscles made balancing easy.

Her enhancements wouldn't save her from the Torth Majority if she made a devastating mistake.

Your suggestions will take time to implement, the Commander pointed out, facing the wind. *A full lockdown could take a full day. Why pile this on Me now, right before We take action?*

I've told You, the Upward Governess thought with forced patience, as if educating an unripe child on a baby farm. *We are waging war against an enemy supergenius. The Betrayer can ascend and soak up news in the Megacosm. Nothing stops him other than his own fears. How much do You want him to know? Do You want to give him a lot of time to prepare for Our traps and plans?*

The Commander realized that the Betrayer had only abstained from the Megacosm in order to hide his location. As soon as that reason ceased to exist...

He might have dared to ascend already.

He might know exactly where every Red Rank stood and where every microdart gun was aimed. He might have a blueprint of the battleground in his mind, with every possible configuration of troops and equipment.

I haven't sensed him in the Megacosm (yet), the Upward Governess admitted. *He knows I'll try to absorb his plans the instant he shows up. But he might take that risk.* She scooped more cake into her mouth. *That's why I'm here in person. Let's keep the best surprise to Ourselves.*

? The Commander tried the scan for clues, but with such a freakish mind, it was impossible. She had to wait for the Upward Governess to elaborate.

Here's a code I whipped up. The Upward Governess tapped her data tablet and spun it so the Commander could read its screen.

As a former data engineer, the Commander recognized a lockdown algorithm. She couldn't guess the context.

This ought to be installed in every streamship docked on this planet, the Upward Governess thought. *An extra measure, just in case.*

The Commander didn't want to ask high ranks to install codes into their high-speed luxury spaceships. Such a command would be like admitting to the plausibility of the worst-case scenario. The Giant had unknown strength. If he managed to get inside a streamship with a nearly indestructible hull, then the Torth Empire would have bigger problems than the current crisis.

That was unthinkable.

No, she thought. They needed to kill the Giant as fast as possible and not get sidetracked with remote improbabilities.

Our strategy needs layers, the Upward Governess insisted. She scooped away an outer layer of cake. *One trap might fail. But there must be another.* She scooped through another layer of cake. *And another.* She scooped more cake. *The Betrayer may evade everything You throw at him. But I have an idea that will rattle him, emotionally. It will rattle the Giant. Their volatile emotions will cause them to make unwise choices and guarantee Our victory.*

? The Commander of All supposed she could humor a paranoid supergenius. Excessive precautions would be a nuisance, but she supposed the previous Commander should have taken a few extra precautions when dealing with the monster of his era.

You, Commander, shall have Your glory, the Upward Governess thought with a smugness that bordered on gloating. *I know the Betrayer better than anyone else in the universe. He is clever. But he has made the fatal mistake of underestimating Me.*

CHAPTER 3

FIREPOWER

The hideout cave looked busier than a bargain forum. Thomas floated between teams of workers, forced to pause every few seconds to allow busy villagers to dart in front of his hoverchair.

"Are these the only pipes you can find?" he asked a work crew that was gathering clay items.

"They are," one replied.

"You should gather tea infusers," Thomas said. "And small jars, too. Those will serve the same purpose as the pipes."

The work crew nodded, although a few exchanged looks. Thomas sensed their shame at taking orders from a Torth.

He almost wished he had the strength to work alongside them, just to prove that he wasn't trying act as their master or owner. Their tasks were more important than mere menial labor.

Well, whatever. Thomas floated onward. Either the villagers would do as he asked, or they would let everyone down and ruin any chance for survival. Their choice.

He checked on the progress of the mortar-and-pestle crews. Then he moved to the quicklime area. "Keep that cloth over your beak," he told one ummin who had removed his makeshift breather mask. "If you accidentally breathe in any of that powder, you'll think your lungs are on fire."

He turned to the departure crew, which had quintupled in size since the last time he'd checked. "This is far too many people," he told the villager in charge. "I told you, we can only take twenty people with us. We don't have the resources to carry or sustain a village."

Her gaze burned, and Thomas sensed how she wanted to accuse him of being arrogant and cruel. But in her language, the word for arrogantly cruel was "Torth." Not a strong insult when aimed at him. It was just an accurate description.

Thomas kept wishing he was dealing with telepaths instead of ummins. At least Torth didn't have to be told anything twice. Torth would never waste their energy doubting his decisions.

"No children," he told the departure crew. "We can't keep track of little ummins when our lives depend on moving fast."

The villagers glared. So did Cherise. She sat nearby, putting together supply packs.

"They're going to sacrifice themselves for us," Vy said in the human language. She sat with Cherise, also bundling packs together. "They're doing everything possible to make sure some of their adolescents survive." She looked at Thomas. "Would it be possible for you to treat them like they're people instead of slaves?"

Thomas shrugged uncomfortably. He just didn't feel capable of acting the way Vy wanted him to act. She remembered him as a powerless, naive, human child. That wasn't who he was anymore.

He floated onward.

The work was progressing well. Weptolyso seemed to be packing enough water and supplies for both himself and Ariock. Thomas nodded in approval.

He yearned to find out why the Torth Empire were holding off their attack and what they might be whispering about him. But he dared not ascend. Not yet. Not until he was safely en route away from the Torth Empire.

And then—once he had secured safety—he would risk a brief moment to ascend and gloat over the Upward Governess's reaction.

He tried to float past Ariock in a quick fashion. All the pebbles Ariock had been levitating descended to the floor, and Ariock regathered his focus so that he could speak.

"Thomas. What should I be working on?"

"You're doing fine," Thomas said, not slowing down. "Keep at it."

Determination emanated from Ariock, as inexorable as a planet's gravity. "I want to do my fair share. Can you at least tell me what I should be practicing?"

Ignoring Ariock wasn't going to be viable. "Fine." Thomas rotated so he could face Ariock while drifting away. "Practice long-range defense. It's possible the Torth will try to take you out with missiles."

Ariock mulled that over. "Is there anything I can do to make sure this village doesn't get destroyed after we leave?"

This was what Thomas had been dreading. Ariock kept trying to make leadership decisions. He should have been pliable. He had far too little life experience, and he didn't even realize that he was undermining Thomas's authority.

"Here's the plain truth." Thomas prepared for a verbal battle. "If we need you? Then we're dead. I'm sorry, but you aren't going to be useful in the upcoming situation. We need to sneak into a spaceport before the Torth figure out what happened and shut down the launchpads. That means we can't let any Torth see us or guess that you're with us. We don't want to attract a huge army. We want to be sneaky."

Ariock looked insulted.

Thomas gave him enough time to protest, then went on. "Ideally, your powers shouldn't come into play. If you fight? Then it will devolve into a battle between our big gun"—he gestured at Ariock—"and theirs. Then we'll never make it off this planet. If you want to live, you need to follow my orders."

Ariock gave a hesitant nod of understanding.

"Teacher?" A tentative ummin tapped Thomas on the arm.

"Wait," Thomas said in the slave tongue, still holding Ariock's gaze. He switched back to English. "If you believe I'm smart enough to get us off this planet, then you need to trust me."

The ummin nearby spoke in a rush. "Teacher, some of the powder is hissing and fizzing and glowing green. It smokes like a torch. Is it dangerous?"

Thomas saw a bowl full of supercharged gunpowder near his arm and jerked backward. Fireworks seemed to be going off in the quicklime area. It was causing a commotion in the cave.

"Varktezo," he said, recognizing the adolescent. "Put that bowl down, very, very gently."

Varktezo knelt and put the bowl down.

"You got the powder wet," Thomas said. "I told you not to."

"Not me," Varktezo said. "I told Choonhulm to not work close to the wall." The cave walls were always damp. "But no one listens to me." Varktezo paused to draw breath. "Teacher, how is it hissing and fizzing? I saw everything we put into that powder. It's all ordinary rocks. How is it doing that?"

"All matter is made from basic elements," Thomas said. "Purified, and mixed in the right amounts, we can make decently powerful explosives."

Varktezo went wide-eyed. "How do you know the right amounts?"

Thomas had soaked up millions of chemical formulas from scientists in many civilizations, past and present. This particular concoction was a blend of his human knowledge—primitive gunpowder mixed with quicklime—plus another primitive explosive from alien knowledge.

"People experiment over eons," Thomas replied. "I gather what they know. Anyway, it looks like it's ready for use. Would you like a demonstration of how to kill Torth?"

Varktezo looked so awestruck, he might faint if anything else surprised him.

"Bring me a hollow ball and a pan of water," Thomas said. "Also, that resin I told you to infuse with red powder. And a candle."

Varktezo hurried to gather the materials, telling everyone who would listen that the Teacher was going to show off a special weapon.

"What are you telling them to do?" Ariock asked.

"You'll see."

A large crowd gathered around Thomas. Soon Varktezo returned with the hollow ball and other materials.

"Varktezo," Thomas said. "Pour some charged powder into the ball. Be careful not to spill any, and don't touch it."

While Varktezo did that, Thomas asked, "Which one of you has the best aim with a slingshot?"

The ummins jostled each other. Thomas could have scanned their memories to find out who had the best accuracy, but he purposely resisted his urge to know for certain. Freedom meant being independent and choosing among themselves. For now, in this cave, these ummins had freedom.

Several ummins pushed Irarjeg forward. They put a slingshot into his hands.

"Irarjeg. Good." Thomas pointed to a stalactite. "Can you hit that, using the clay ball as ammunition?"

Irarjeg clicked his beak in an affirmative.

"Excellent," Thomas said. "Here's what you'll do. You'll dunk that clay ball into water, very quickly, just enough to get the powder a little wet. Do not soak it. Then smear resin over the hole."

That would seal in the reaction, with a thermite cap on top.

"You'll touch the resin to a flame," Thomas went on, "and it will catch on fire. Don't hold it too long after that, because it can kill you by accident. As soon as it's burning, slingshot it as hard as you can." He gestured. "Pretend that stalactite is a Torth."

Ariock hadn't understood the words, but he observed carefully as Irarjeg took the primitive grenade.

"Where's the fire?" Irarjeg radiated doubt.

Thomas focused on the unlit candle, concentrating hard in order to make a flame appear.

The villagers backed away.

"It's just an ordinary candle," Thomas told them. "You can use another if it makes you feel better."

Irarjeg bravely approached Thomas's flame.

No one saw the chemical reactions happening within the clay ball, but Thomas knew that the quick dunk into water had activated the quicklime, and the resin ensured that the vapor within was highly pressurized. A spark would set off the supercharged gunpowder.

Irarjeg fitted the ball to his slingshot, set the thermite cap on fire, and released it just in time.

A massive fiery explosion rocked the cave. Villagers threw themselves down, and Ariock shielded his face with his arm.

The flames died, and the dust cleared. A gaping hole had replaced the stalactite.

"That will kill any Torth," Thomas said. "They won't be able to sense it coming, and their armor won't protect them."

The villagers gawked in awe.

"Remember," Thomas said, "aim for their heads."

The ummins began to marvel about the new ammunition, which was far more powerful than they had imagined. To them, it seemed like an effective countermeasure to blaster gloves.

"You should pour gunpowder on your streets," Thomas said, "if you can do it without any Torth noticing. That will help you double or triple the number of kills."

He scanned their minds, figuring out placement configurations to cause maximum damage.

Utavlug, an elder among the onlookers, scrutinized Thomas as if seeing him for the first time. "Torth," she said. "What did you put in that powder?"

"It's nothing magical," Thomas said. "Your people can make it anytime. You have all the ingredients."

She shook her head at the blast zone. "Charcoal, sulfur powder, tanning resin, pyrite powder, caked limestone powder... I don't understand. If it was that easy, how have we never discovered it?" She touched her waistband, which was hung with pouches full of herbs. "I know every powder and ointment. I should have known this formula."

"Your people actually invented it, a long time ago." Thomas stopped himself. Ancient history was irrelevant.

On the other hand, there was no harm in giving back a little bit of knowledge that ancient Torth had stolen from ancient ummins an eon ago. It felt honorable.

"How many generations ago?" Utavlug asked.

"More than a thousand." Thomas turned to Irarjeg and to the other junior elder. "You should stockpile these grenades in every hut and on strategic rooftops. With the right coordination, you can massacre the Torth army in one bloodbath before they can report anything useful." He gestured for some drawing implements. "If you give me something to draw with, I'll outline where the Torth are most likely to show up and where you should put your ammo."

Ariock radiated concern. He didn't say that children were meant to be carefree, but his unspoken assumption about Thomas might as well be broadcast. "Are you okay with this?" he asked, his voice pained.

"I promised to get you to safety by any means necessary." Thomas gave him a level look. "I'm fine with it. I've seen a lot of death. And I want to kill some Torth."

"You didn't see death firsthand," Ariock told Thomas with gentle earnestness. "And you don't need to take responsibility for it. It's okay to let other people—"

Thomas cut him off. "How about if you stick to what you're an expert at—lifting rocks—and I'll do the planning. That's what I'm good at."

Ariock was patient, without any hint of offense or frustration. He nodded amicably.

But Thomas still sensed an undertone of determination.

"I'm in charge," Thomas said, to make it absolutely clear. "Okay?"

Ariock nodded.

"Why do you think I brought us to a sulfur-mining slave farm?" Thomas asked. "This was always a possibility to me. We have some good resources here to make primitive explosives."

That surprised Ariock. "You took us to Duin because—?"

"Yep," Thomas said. "It was one of the deciding variables."

Instead of being appreciative, Ariock seemed concerned, even sad.

"These villagers didn't need to take us in," Thomas pointed out. "That's on them. My plan was to find a cave, not take advantage of ummins. Anyway. Whatever." One of the tribal ummins had placed sketching materials on his lap.

Thomas sketched a rough map of the village of Duin. He marked crossfire zones and places where hidden snipers might kill Torth from a safe distance.

"Once you've obliterated the Torth invading your village," Thomas said, "you should raid their corpses and arm yourselves with blaster gloves."

Ariock moved away, letting him work in peace.

None of the humans gave him any of the respectful admiration that the tribal ummins seemed full of now. Cherise never glanced his way. She bundled supplies alongside her newfound ummin friends.

Well, that was all right. Thomas was fine with being ignored.

He should be fine with it, anyway.

Did his regular orbiters and admirers in the Megacosm miss him? Did the Upward Governess think about him nonstop? He hoped so.

He almost wished he could share these plans with her.

"Place your best teams here," he told the villagers, pointing out huts on his map.

Why should he want gratitude or anything from Cherise or Ariock? He just needed to finish fulfilling his obligation to save them. Then he could die with honor.

CHAPTER 4

THE CODE OF GWAT

Vy repackaged a bundle of provisions, determined to make it sturdy enough for an ummin to wear like a backpack.

"Is this really enough to tide anyone over for a week?" Vy couldn't hide her doubts. The paltry amount of grain wafers, plus an earthenware jar full of water, didn't look like it would sustain anyone for more than a day. Her family used to pack more for their three-day camping trip each summer.

"We have no choice," Kessa said, knotting another pack. "All we will have is what we can carry."

Cherise added in a venomous tone, "Because loading a ship is the slaves' job."

That was what Thomas had said, word for word, although his tone had been lecturing rather than acidic. He had been answering a question, explaining why they wouldn't find a ship preloaded with food provisions.

If this escape worked, they were supposed to do a lot of camping afterward. It seemed Thomas expected them to hunt and grow their own food once they arrived at their unknown destination. Each pack included a variety of viable seeds.

Vy glanced across the cave. Right now, Thomas was instructing villagers like a general commanding his troops. He never expressed sympathy or empathy. He never apologized for semi-accidentally barging into this slave farm and altering, perhaps ruining, their children's futures.

It seemed asinine for a mind reader to act so insensitive.

But there was a soft human soul buried beneath Thomas's hard Torth-like exterior. Vy was certain of it, even if no one else could see it. Cherise focused on the hurt. That was natural, given her background. Trust was sacred to her. Thomas had superficially broken it.

But he had also taken major risks and thrown away a life of luxury, for her sake.

"He's saving our lives," Vy reminded her foster sister. "He's holding to his promise to rescue us."

"I know." Cherise tied together another perfectly packaged travel bundle. She did it with such expertise, it was as if she'd been building rustic travel packs all her life. Her tone was impossible to read. She sounded emotionless, as if she didn't care about Thomas one way or the other.

"Do you hate him?" Vy asked.

"No," Cherise said.

Vy hesitated, unsure how to drag words out of her mostly silent foster sister. What was required to heal the rift between her and Thomas?

Cherise seemed to hear unspoken criticisms. She responded. "He isn't one of us. He's with us. But he isn't human."

"That's not fair," Vy said.

"He's a Torth," Cherise said. "Ask him yourself. He'll tell you the truth."

Vy really wanted to deny that. But she found herself speechless, because she strongly suspected that Cherise was correct. Their foster brother had absorbed too many Torth lifetimes to easily switch back to human mode.

"He still cares about you," Vy said. "Deeply."

"If that was true," Cherise said, "he would tell me himself. He knows me well enough."

Vy could have gone on making excuses for Thomas, but she supposed that he could do that himself if he wanted to. He didn't seem to want an advocate. He seemed broken in some fundamental way, and Vy wasn't sure why, or how to heal him.

She looked past Thomas, and past the ummins who were taking turns firing the blaster glove, using rocks for target practice. At least Ariock considered himself to be human. Vy felt reassured just seeing him.

Pebbles swirled through the air, ribbonlike. Ariock must be practicing his ability to focus on multiple objects at once. He seemed to have less trouble when he made things float in the same direction.

Unlike Thomas, Ariock would probably try to save everyone in Duin at the last minute. Maybe he would attempt to stuff hundreds of ummins into a transport.

Or he would stay behind, to die with his newfound ummin friends.

Someone might have to drag him away. Thomas kept emphasizing that their window of opportunity would be short, and they couldn't linger after the massacre. If they stayed, they were dead.

"My main concern with these supplies," Kessa said, "is that we won't have enough for Weptolyso or Ariock. Have you seen how much nussians eat every day?"

Vy could imagine. Weptolyso was as massive as a bull. He must weigh a ton.

And Ariock was built like a tank. Now that his face was clean-shaven and his hair was trimmed, he looked better than a refugee from a prison camp, but he couldn't help looking intimidating. He just loomed.

In a way that made her feel safe and protected.

He had a really wonderful smile.

Vy packed supplies and reminded herself that Delia was close enough to keep watch over her son. That seemed to be her sole hobby, her way of reclaiming some control over her life.

Anyway, Vy wasn't going to embarrass herself in front of Delia.

Nor would she try to seduce Ariock, or anything crazy like that. He was just a friend. If they ever got home to Earth, she couldn't exactly take him on dinner dates, or skiing, or to meet her mother. He would have to duck through every door in the Hollander home. He'd have a lot of trouble fitting inside a normal-size car.

She didn't want size to matter, but it did.

Vy blushed, thinking of the sorts of jokes her friends would make. She must be desperate to consider getting steamy with someone who was four times her size and potentially violent. Ariock had a sweet side, but he was naive. And too self-conscious.

And too close in size to an ogre.

Vy sneaked another glance at him. Pebbles jerked toward him, bullet-fast, then stopped in midair when Ariock caught Vy watching. His face reddened. The pebbles fell in a cascade, bouncing off the floor.

Vy turned away to hide her own guilty blush. He had better not get distracted like that when it really mattered.

"He will listen to you, Vy." Kessa sounded amused. "Make sure we don't leave him behind in Duin."

Vy gave up trying to knot a rope and met Kessa's knowing look. She tried to chuckle. "Ariock listens to everyone. He's nice to everyone."

"Yes," Kessa said. "He understands the Code of Gwat better than anyone I have ever known."

Vy had heard of that slave philosophy, but she barely understood it. She wondered if it was a religion. "You follow Gwat. Right?"

"I do my best." Kessa seemed embarrassed.

"What does it mean?" Vy asked. "Is it about being honorable? Like, truthful and sincere?"

Kessa tapped her beak. "It is sort of those things. But a better way to say it is that Gwat is a way to wield knowledge."

Cherise glanced up, listening.

"What do you mean?" Vy asked.

Kessa clicked her beak in thought. "I cannot read minds, so I should refrain from judging people. The only person I have a right to judge is myself. That is Gwat."

Cherise looked introspective.

"So it's about being nonjudgmental?" Vy asked.

Kessa shook her head, as if Vy had misunderstood. "Every decision I make should be based on what knowledge I have. No more, and no less. This is effortless for Torth"—she looked at Thomas with envy—"because they have so much knowledge. But it is a struggle for slaves, who have so little."

"But isn't that how everyone makes decisions?" Vy asked. "We can't decide things unless we know what we're deciding."

Kessa tucked seed wafers into a supply pack. "I fell from Gwat when you three humans first arrived in my bunk room." She looked ashamed. "I judged you to be three Torth. So I treated you as Torth until it became obvious that I was wrong."

"But…" Vy stared at her. "You can't feel guilty about that! Anyone would have made the same assumption."

Her ummin friend still looked ashamed. "There were hints. I ignored some information. I judged you without knowing all the facts."

"It's natural to be wrong sometimes," Vy said. After all, she had misjudged Kessa when they'd first met, worried that the alien would lead her into a trap. "We all make mistakes," she said. "We're only human." She reconsidered her wording. "Or ummin."

"Yes." Kessa's face crinkled with warmth. "No one can follow the Code of Gwat all the time except for mind readers. But we can try. It is important that we try. It brings us closer to the gods."

Cherise looked pained. "So according to Gwat, you should forgive anyone who abuses you?" She seemed disgusted. "Because you can never know why they did it?"

"No." Kessa met her gaze. "Gwat is about wielding what little knowledge we have. If someone wrongs you, and it is irrefutable, then they deserve retribution. Justice is important to slaves. We have very little of that, and it is very valuable."

"But all factors should be taken into account," Vy said. She made a mental note to keep an eye on Cherise.

Kessa nodded. "Everything. One of the three core tenets of Gwat is that 'certainty is not the same as truth.' A slave can rarely be certain of anything. Certainty is usually beyond our grasp. And so we treat absolute certainty with suspicion."

"You're skeptics," Vy translated.

Cherise gave Kessa a suffering look. "I am certain that he"—she indicated Thomas—"tortured me. Do you reject my certainty?"

"I was there," Kessa gently reminded Cherise. "I saw what happened. I do not reject it. But as a follower of Gwat, I question the assumptions that one might draw from the event. Gwat is about asking questions."

"I know he had an audience in his head." Cherise's voice was suddenly thick with pain. "But he says he's severed from the Torth now. So why hasn't he said a word to me? Why hasn't he even looked at me? Can you answer that?"

"I cannot," Kessa admitted. She folded more supplies. "But I am not done questioning it."

Vy did wonder why Thomas was leaving Cherise to make guesses. A simple apology would go a long way. That was all he needed to do in order to bridge the chasm between them. Surely he knew that?

So why wasn't he apologizing?

Maybe he thought he knew everything, to the point where he didn't question his own premises.

Ariock, in contrast, seemed embarrassed about his lack of knowledge. He had skipped high school and college. He had never gone out with friends, never joined a club, never even gotten immersed in social media. When Vy had asked Ariock about internet forums or games, he'd confessed that he never even got into online arguments. He hadn't seen the point of pretending he knew more than some stranger.

So he probably questioned a lot of things.

Vy put more travel packs together but found herself glancing at Ariock from time to time. Kessa was right about his nonjudgmental nature. He did not presume to know anybody except himself. To Ariock, ummins had the same worth as nussians or humans. Children had the same worth as adults. Ariock did not see himself as greater than anyone else in the cave hideout.

He unintentionally followed the Code of Gwat so well, he impressed Kessa —and she was hard to impress. He was like the equivalent of a saint.

No wonder everybody liked him.

CHAPTER 5

THE HORNED TRIUMPH

The Horned Triumph sliced vines out of his way. The natives of this slave farm made puny footpaths, too narrow for a large, magnificently enhanced Torth such as himself.

He could have gotten his knobby horns surgically removed when he'd received his musculoskeletal upgrades as a Servant of All. But he liked the imperfections on his skull. He kept his head clean-shaven, so his horns were a visible reminder to lesser Torth that he had mutant flaws. Not every Servant of All needed to have a perfect body or a stellar pedigree. Some, like him, had outcompeted the flawless candidates and proven themselves superior.

Prepare to take down the Giant, the Horned Triumph announced via the Megacosm.

He did his own preparation, inhaling the odors of the jungle. He spent a lot of time outdoors, and he could read air pressure and clouds just as easily as he could read minds. Subtle shifts in the weather would provide an early warning signal that the Giant was alert and prepared to defend himself.

The Horned Triumph dropped out of the Megacosm so he could give his full attention to the morning breeze, the air pressure, the dew, the humidity, and the hum of bugs.

No hints of strangeness.

Just to be sure, he ascended again and requested local telemetry and barometric pressure readings. Machines confirmed that all measurements were within normal ranges.

The Giant is too weak or too oblivious to put up much of a fight, the Horned Triumph surmised.

He allowed himself a rude smile as he strode toward his main troops near the slave village. The Giant was almost certainly hidden in the sulfur mines. The native slaves had failed to give him sufficient warnings, and his precognitive power must be so weak, he was unaware of his impending doom.

Triumph would be easy.

Whoever spots the Giant first will win a gift, the Horned Triumph decided. *A slave, an outfit, a gadget, or cosmetic surgery. Choose one from any forum of your choice.*

The minds of Red Ranks sparkled, eager to exult in the glory they had volunteered for.

The Horned Triumph nearly collided with a fellow Servant of All who stepped in front of him. She wore a white bodysuit and carried an enormous gun.

The Swift Killer. She had unreadable eyes like his, milky white and empty, but he sensed an ocean of seething envy inside her mind.

I was here first. The Swift Killer hefted her huge gun. *I deserve to be the One in command.*

The Horned Triumph wondered how she could make such an absurd complaint. He was in charge because the Commander of All Living Things willed it, the Majority had ratified it, and now it was beyond question or doubt.

He carefully put away his blade, since he didn't want to hurt a peer by accident. *Follow Me into battle,* he invited. *With that portable missile launcher, you might kill the Giant with one shot and win eternal glory.*

He could have simply confiscated the missile launcher, but he saw no reason to make an enemy out of a fellow Servant of All. There would be enough glory to share.

The Swift Killer stepped closer. Her envy was disgusting, like standing near a slave. Did she truly believe that her individual desire mattered more than what the collective wanted? That was insanely selfish. What was she going to do, try to defy the Majority? That was just insane.

He could almost taste her seething, heaving mood. Gross. Any fool who had recommended this emotional wreck to such a high rank ought to be punished for their mistake. It was no mystery why she'd been removed from leadership.

Obey Me, the Horned Triumph thought, *or get out of My way.*

He gently touched her forehead and pushed.

Distant Torth piled into his mind, peering through his eyes and inviting more followers. Some were getting massaged by slaves, or eating feasts, or drifting off to sleep, but all were intensely interested in what might happen next.

The Swift Killer resisted with strength like that of a nussian bodyguard. She had enhancements.

But the Horned Triumph was enhanced on top of being naturally larger and stronger. He shoved until the Swift Killer was forced to take a step back.

You're too emotional, he silently told her. *Leave.*

For a moment, the Swift Killer seemed ready to shoot him, or slash him with her ionic blade. That would earn her a death sentence, but the Horned Triumph prepared to defend himself anyway.

He secretly wanted a fight. In combat, he always felt...well, unconstrained. Combat was the only time he could safely ignore societal rules. This was why he had chosen a military career path. Superior physical strength didn't matter at all in the Megacosm, but it mattered a lot in combat. Violence was okay in combat, no matter how shameful and illegal it was otherwise.

Perhaps the Swift Killer sensed his preparedness. Instead of slashing at him, she released the big gun and shoved it toward him. *It's yours*, she decided. *For this battle only. You had better have good aim.*

The Horned Triumph strapped the missile launcher around his own thick arm. It was more weaponry than anyone needed to kill one escaped prisoner, but it was always good to have extra firepower.

Slaying the Giant would crown his legacy. Anyone who slew such a monster was guaranteed a long-term place in history.

The Swift Killer looked him up and down, her envy so naked, she should be quivering on the ground in shame. *He is a bad choice for this task*, she thought to her listeners in the Megacosm.

She strode away.

The Horned Triumph didn't try to yoke her with commands. She was dangerously individualistic. A military force required cooperation, with everyone knowing their place and doing their duty with engine-like efficiency. Otherwise they might as well be savages.

He marched onward, to where his soldiers awaited him.

Hundreds of Red Ranks looked out of place amid jungle trees and vines. A few swatted at bugs or scratched bug bites. They'd had to leave their salves and slaves at home, of course.

The Horned Triumph synced his mind with squad leaders'. *Move into the village.*

Dozens of Red Ranks headed to their hoverbikes. They double-checked their blaster gloves, each one making sure that he or she was loaded with enough inhibitor serum to take down an army of Yeresunsa.

Start the pumps, the Horned Triumph commanded.

Napalm hose units were stationed at each of the sulfur mine vents and exits. They had been ready since dawn, their minds hot with impatience.

A dull roar ensued.

Soon the mine and all its connected tunnels would be aflame. Anyone hidden inside would burn to death or suffocate…or, if they happened to be powerful enough to protect themselves from fire for a few minutes, they'd be forced to come outside.

The Horned Triumph adjusted his newly acquired missile launcher and led the way into the slave village.

These huts must be full of cowering slaves. A few slaves swept the crooked dirt alleys or scurried from one hut to another with earthenware jugs. It seemed they were charmingly determined to get their chores done. Farm slaves were ignorant of the fact that armored Red Ranks were not the same as the soft Brown Ranks who oversaw the collection of mined rocks every few days.

Occupy, the Horned Triumph commanded his troops. *Fan out.*

Some of the Red Ranks seemed jumpy, twitching at silhouettes that turned out to be merely slaves in huts.

Steady, the Horned Triumph reassured them. *We're relatively safe here.* The Giant certainly had enough power to cause an earthquake or a deadly storm, but he wouldn't dare release his full power in the middle of a village full of slaves.

Primitives never seemed to realize how predictable they were. The Giant would stupidly try to target only Torth. That meant he'd have to get close enough to become a target himself.

And the instant the Giant showed up? Torth would pepper him with microdarts full of inhibitor, and he'd lose his powers and become easy to slay.

Any moment now.

The Horned Triumph felt pumped with adrenaline. Combat was better than vigorous sports, even better than training nussian bodyguards. He was going to win glory and honor for the Empire.

Perhaps he ought to kick down a few hut walls, just in case the Giant was somehow curled up inside?

The Horned Triumph signaled a squad of Torth. *Be careful. If any of you kill the Betrayer by accident—enabling him to escape justice—the Majority will force you to kill yourselves.*

The squad approached a random hut.

Before any of them could touch the wall, a fiery explosion tore through them. *!!! * ( ) * !!!* The Horned Triumph didn't realize how devastating it was until a second later, when all five of the squad members vanished from the Megacosm, their final thoughts full of agony and shock.

He hardly had time to process it. All of a sudden, explosions were all around him, in his mind and in reality, a storm of agonizing death and chaos. Red Ranks were dying. Dismembered limbs flew through clouds of fire.

A severed arm landed on the dirt in front of the Horned Triumph.

Open-mouthed with shock, the Horned Triumph looked at the soldier next to him to confirm that it was all really happening. She met his gaze, red eyes pleading for guidance.

Then the Red Rank blew apart in a spray of blood and fire. *!* His spinal column trailed his severed head like a gruesome animal's tail.

The Horned Triumph backed away from bloodied dust and fiery clouds, clutching the missile launcher. The Giant shouldn't be able to target individual victims with this much effortless ease. How could he kill so many people simultaneously, and with such freakish precision?

And how could the Giant have a pyrokinetic power? Nothing like that was documented in his family line. Jonathan Stead hadn't had a power to make things explode, so neither should his monstrous offspring.

Through his connection to dying soldiers, the Horned Triumph became aware of slave voices.

"This is for the daughter you stole from me!"

"This is because you murdered my father!"

The Horned Triumph caught glimpses of slaves using slingshots to fling ammunition at Torth. Every time they did so, a fiery explosion killed whoever they aimed at.

"This is for every slave you've tortured or killed!"

"Die, Torth!"

The Horned Triumph wanted to drop out of the Megacosm just to reduce the amount of noisy input. But his inner audience was growing colossal. The weight of their attention felt like a physical pressure, reminding him that his duty to the Empire was more important than his own needs.

Dying Red Ranks relayed impressions of bold slaves. The local slaves seemed to have a system where one dipped an ammo ball into water, then handed the ball to a slave with a slingshot, who lit the ball with a candle flame. The ammo became…

Primitive grenades! The Megacosm churned with stunned realization.

All the deaths were caused by ummins. The Giant wasn't even part of this battle. He was nowhere to be seen.

This had to be the Betrayer's doing.

Gather reinforcements! the Majority chorused.

We will end this little slave revolt and punish (the Betrayer) those responsible, the Commander of All Living Things assured everyone.

The Horned Triumph ducked inside one of the pathetic little slave huts. He sensed a slave targeting him, and he shot a blast in that direction. The slave died.

He had to crawl on his elbows, desperate to stay below the rounded window holes and out of sight. Ummins! The glory he had expected had been destroyed by ummins. He could hardly believe it.

This was the Betrayer's fault.

The Megacosm seethed like a volcanic caldera. *It is the Betrayer's fault.*

The Betrayer is a renegade monster.

He is a mass murderer!

Those Red Ranks were doing what is righteous and were wrongly killed for it.

Find him.
Capture him.
Bring him to the Isolatorium.

The Horned Triumph began to toggle his blaster glove out of deadly mode. He would neutralize the *(threat)* Betrayer with inhibitor and throw a net around him. He just had to wait for the Betrayer to show himself.

He should have understood what was happening the instant the first squad of Red Ranks died. He should have expected that an enemy supergenius would infect the local slave population with rebellious defiance.

But what if the Giant showed up instead?

The Horned Triumph wedged himself against the wall, where he was relatively sheltered. He peeked outside at the ruination every few seconds. Dead Red Ranks littered the alleys.

The Giant must be too injured to help these revolting slaves, distant Torth commented to each other as they relaxed in spas or shopped for fashionable accessories.

Or perhaps he is dead?

Or perhaps the Betrayer stashed him somewhere else (not in this slave farm)?

Debates went on, but one of the primitive grenades slammed into a nearby Red Rank. The concussive blast left a ringing in the ears of the Horned Triumph. Shrapnel burned his shaved head.

If he survived this day, he would have scars to go with his horns.

He deserved worse than scars.

His failure to take certain variables into account had cost the lives of hundreds of Red Ranks. That was unforgivable. The Horned Triumph would die in disgrace, his memory trashed, his status stripped away forever. His swollen inner audience chorused their disappointment in him.

Unless he could salvage some success out of this disaster.

He needed to capture the Betrayer.

Triumph.
We shall revere your memory
for all eternity
if you win—
if you net the Betrayer.

CHAPTER 6

TEMPER

Kessa pressed her earhole against a wall and heard muffled rumblings. It was easy to imagine that the villagers were the ones dead or dying.

The chief elder had a helpless, accusatory look. That was how Kessa would feel if her entire neighborhood in the slave Tunnels got slaughtered.

Only the quickest runners and best hunters were in the huts aboveground, aiming slingshots at Torth. Anyone slower would just get in the way. The elders couldn't even be with their people while they battled Torth invaders.

Why was it so hot and dry?

"Teacher Torth," the chief elder said in a controlled tone. "What are you doing?"

Thomas was fixated on the wall, his yellow eyes unblinking. Molten slag marred the petroglyphs. Before each molten line finished, another line began, and another. They looked like sketch lines—as if Thomas was drawing on the wall with his mind.

"You must stop." The chief elder blocked the wall. "You do not have permission to leave your mark on the sacred walls."

The sketchy fissures began to form an image. Kessa recognized the emergent faces, rendered in exquisite detail and with speedy skill. The head that faced everyone was Thomas. Ariock was looking off to one side. Both portraits looked noble and determined.

"Why would you deface their holy wall?" Vy sounded stunned.

The drawing ended, and Thomas admired what he'd done. "A renegade supergenius is unique in Torth history." His gaze swept over the villagers. "This sacred wall now has value to Torth relic collectors. It will be preserved long after your children's children die from old age."

The villagers studied the newly carved illustration. Only a few looked resentful about the fact that Thomas had carved it without permission. The rest were curious, even admiring.

"That"—Thomas gestured at his etched face on the wall—"is proof that I'm responsible for what happens today. It's possible the Torth will figure that the slaves of Duin are blameless. They might let you live." He looked uncomfortable. "At the very least, it gives the Torth a reason to remember you."

The chief elder still seemed angry, but she kept her beak shut. Slaves yearned to be remembered, to not disappear forever. They couldn't ask for more than that.

Thomas cleared his throat. "I, uh…I'm sorry." He added something else in the human tongue. "Your resentment is good. It proves that you're not colluding with me."

Kessa figured she must be the only person who understood what he had quietly said.

"The sounds stopped," Vy said, listening.

"I'm going up there." Ariock crawled toward the exit.

"Not yet." Thomas used his hoverchair to block the exit tunnel. "It's possible the villagers didn't kill every single Torth. Let me go to scan and make sure it's safe."

Vy gave him a look of incredulity.

Kessa felt the same way. "You want to put yourself at risk?"

Ariock's gaze was more forbidding than anything Thomas could muster. "If it's not safe for me," he said in his deep voice, "then it's definitely not safe for you. You're not going up there first."

Thomas made a sound of outrage. "You follow my orders. Remember?"

"It's easy for me to disarm people from a distance," Ariock pointed out. "It makes more sense for me to—"

Thomas turned to Delia. "If Ariock gets himself killed, then this whole escape is pointless. Keep him out of sight."

Delia's worried gaze shifted from Thomas to her son. Clearly, she did not want to anger either of them. But she seemed to trust Thomas, despite her criticisms of him. "Thomas is right," she told her son.

Ariock crawled into a position where he could reach out one arm and block the tunnel exit. "Thomas," he said in a tolerant tone. "You don't belong in a war zone."

"Neither of you should go aboveground," Delia said.

Thomas glared. The air became scorching, then swung to freezing, and then went back to normal. Kessa shuddered violently.

Thomas let out a shaky breath and spoke to Ariock in a measured tone. "We can't get angry. We need to stay in control of our powers."

"Right." Ariock sounded nonplussed. One of them was having trouble with emotional self-control, and it clearly wasn't him.

Thomas showed his teeth in an expression that wasn't a smile. "You need to respect me. I'm not just the pilot for your ship or the extra baggage you need to protect. If you want to survive, you need to do it my way."

Kessa saw truth in his fiery gaze. Thomas contained the memories and knowledge of killers. Despite his twig-thin arms and legs, he did look dangerous.

But Ariock wasn't moving. "I promised to protect you. I'm not backing down from that."

They were like two rival gang bosses. They were going to trigger themselves into a battle.

Kessa stepped between Thomas and Ariock.

She was aware that she was only a fragile ummin. "I am sure it is unwise to stand between two angry Yeresunsa," she admitted. "But maybe I can solve this dispute?" She turned from one to the other. "Will you hear me?"

Thomas gave her an arrogant glare.

Ariock looked annoyed as well.

"Ariock," Kessa said. "If you lose your powers from the inhibitor, then you will be unable to protect Thomas or anyone. All your friends will die. The village of Duin will have suffered and made sacrifices for no reason."

"It's better for me to take that risk than to hide down here," Ariock said firmly.

Kessa shook her head. "The risk is not solely yours. The people of this slave farm have chosen. Their choice is…" She searched for the right word in his language. "Bravery. The bravery of slaves is not something to be thrown away like garbage. It is a gift."

She held his gaze, trying to make him understand how difficult it was for slaves to overcome fear and reliance on their masters. Ariock had inspired bravery. He should feel proud of that. He should not try to rob slaves of what was new and wonderful to them.

Kessa turned to Thomas. "And you cannot pilot a ship if you are injured or dead. I understand why you want Ariock to remain hidden. But why do you not apply that same logic to yourself?"

"I have abilities the rest of you lack." Thomas spoke even before she had finished speaking. "Anyway, I'll get a blaster glove once I'm topside. I might actually enjoy killing a few Torth."

There was a disturbing gleam in his yellow eyes.

Kessa clicked her beak in irritation. "There are times when I believe you are the child they say you are."

Thomas began to speak in a savage tone. "I have every right—"

"Control," Kessa cut him off. "Emotional self-control is very important for Yeresunsa powers. Is that correct?" She turned to Ariock for confirmation.

He nodded broadly.

"I got us this far," Thomas snapped. "I—"

"Control yourself," Kessa cut in.

She was surprised when Thomas obeyed. He appeared to struggle from the effort of holding in his arguments.

"You have absorbed many Torth lives," Kessa said. "Perhaps you need to absorb more slave experiences to understand emotions? You are eager to take risks. Do you understand why this may be unhealthy?"

Thomas appeared to be thinking about it.

"You think killing Torth will be fun," Kessa said. "If one pops up and tries to surprise you, will you burn it alive? Or shoot it? Or torture it with pain seizures until it dies?"

Thomas looked chagrined.

"You said our goal is to keep the Torth Empire guessing," Kessa went on. "Our safety depends on killing Torth invaders before they can report any details in the Megacosm. Isn't that right?"

Thomas nodded reluctantly. "But we do need to make sure none are left alive to spy on what we do or where we go. I'm the only one who can scan fast. I'll be safe as long as they don't snipe at me from afar." He paused. "I just have to make sure they don't hit my head. That's the only important part."

Kessa supposed he had a point. If a Torth blasted his body, Ariock might be able to save him with a healing session.

"If you go up there," Kessa said, "you should have an escort of armed ummins. Allow the people of Duin to do what you have taught them to do. Let them protect you."

Thomas looked uncomfortable. At least he wasn't arguing.

Kessa looked from Thomas to Ariock. "Will you both agree to…" She searched for the right words in the human language.

"Make a concession?" Vy supplied.

Kessa nodded. That was the right phrase.

"I'll keep watch from the hut aboveground," Ariock offered. "I won't leave the safety of the hut. If Thomas has bodyguards, that's good enough for me."

Kessa turned to Thomas.

"Yeah. Fine," he said. "But if any Torth try to kill me, I'm allowed to defend myself."

Kessa figured that was fair enough.

Thomas edged his hoverchair past Ariock. "Prepare to depart," he instructed everyone. "Gather your things."

Then he was gone, floating quickly up the tunnel.

Ariock gathered one of the big packs and followed at a crawl. The tunnel was so narrow he had to contort his shoulders, and Kessa could tell that he was relieved to be exiting.

She picked up her own supply pack. Others shouldered theirs. As the cave began to empty, Kessa glanced at the etched wall one last time.

That drawing was a marvel.

It was especially incredible that such a physically weak person could carve stone with such ease. Kessa found it hard to believe the majority of Torth rejected hereditary powers. Were Torth individuals so sated with indulgences that they welcomed any excuse for limitations?

That didn't mesh with Kessa's experiences. Torth liked power. They believed themselves to be gods.

The muffled rumbles had definitely stopped. Kessa tried not to think about the potential disaster they might find aboveground.

"Kessa." The chief elder, Molyt Dazel, squeezed her shoulder. "Will you walk with me?"

"Of course." In Duin, Kessa was a beggar who owed her life to the villagers. She walked alongside the chief in the damp tunnel.

Molyt Dazel lowered her voice. "Can the Teacher Torth hear us from this distance?"

Kessa had a firm estimate of Thomas's telepathic range. "No," she said. "But he might absorb our conversation later on. He soaks up memories."

The chief elder sighed. "I thought so."

Kessa eyed her with curiosity.

"Do you believe he is a human at all?" Molyt Dazel asked. "Or is he more Torth than human?"

"He may be both, in equal measures," Kessa replied, wondering what topic the chief elder was pacing around.

"I have never seen a Torth act with emotion the way he does," Molyt Dazel said. "Have you?" She studied Kessa, apparently looking for sincerity.

"Torth act the same everywhere I have lived," Kessa admitted. "Except for Thomas. I think I understand your doubts."

She often found herself marveling that Thomas had managed to fool all the Torth in the universe. It seemed impossible. All the same, she repeated the explanations he had given her.

"Many Torth wear a circlet, known as a mesh." Kessa drew a circle around her head. "Thomas told me those meshes help Torth suppress what emotions they have. He wore one while he lived among them. It helped him think like a Torth."

"That was enough?" Molyt Dazel sounded skeptical.

The implication was unmistakable. Many Torth might have emotions like Thomas.

"No." Kessa laughed a little. "I think Thomas is exceptional. He says the Torth were convinced that his extra emotions were just bad habits from how he grew up."

"Hmm." Molyt Dazel clicked her beak in doubt. "When I have a bad habit, I become very aware of it, so I can stop. Why did he not try to stop?" She answered her own question. "I think he did try, as hard as he can. And he failed. He is still trying. And still failing."

Kessa had considered this, as well. To hear it spoken out loud made it sound more credible.

"When I panic-forget," Molyt Dazel said, "panic takes up all of my mind, and I forget my knowledge of this hideout cave. It becomes hidden even from myself." She paused. "I wonder if he is aware that he is hiding his emotions."

Kessa studied the chief, glad for a conversation as opposed to an exchange of advice. Perhaps this was how ancient ummins had conversed before the Torth conquered their world.

"I see what you're saying," she said. "You believe that Thomas panics in reverse. Instead of overemphasizing his emotions in order to bury knowledge, he overemphasizes his knowledge in order to bury emotions."

The chief elder clicked her beak in approval. "That is how it seems to me. But if so, then how is it that I have noticed something that none of the mind readers have ever noticed?"

Kessa searched deep for any hint of an explanation. Perhaps the Torth were all so busy in the Megacosm, they barely paid attention to the nuances of each other's emotional states?

They ignored emotions in slaves. Perhaps they also ignored emotions within themselves. If so…

Kessa gasped. A lot of Torth might actually be able to bury their volatile, slave-like emotions.

The tests are imperfect, Thomas had said.

It was probably no coincidence that every Torth who was born outside the baby farm system—outside Torth society—also seemed to have a full range of emotions.

And Yeresunsa powers.

Kessa shivered and hoped she was wrong about the powers. Slaves had enough trouble. The Torth were already tyrannical gods. They did not need extra powers.

"Do you think there might be other Torth like the Teacher?" Molyt Dazel asked.

Kessa considered it. A Torth with secret emotions—or secret powers—would go to any lengths to hide it. They would bury their emotions, and their powers, so deep that their abilities were probably hidden even from themselves. They were like dreamers, so absorbed in typical daily activities that they no longer remembered their own identities.

Molyt Dazel gave a rueful laugh. "Listen to my ruminations. The Torth have no reason to hide anything. They have no masters."

Kessa had questioned Thomas about the Megacosm, and she was not certain about that. "They fear each other. They elect their own masters."

"Do they?" Molyt Dazel gave her a wry look. "Even so, Kessa, I do not think they have fears like slaves. If many Torth had emotions, like sympathy? Mercy? And love? This would be a different universe."

Kessa inclined her head to agree.

But internally, she wondered.

CHAPTER 7

SHOWDOWN

Headless corpses lay in the cratered path that used to be a tidy street.

Gore splashed the dented paddlewood walls.

Thomas skimmed along the outer walls of ramshackle huts, listening to whispery interiors. He kept gesturing for his escort to stay out of his range of telepathy. Pung, Irarjeg, and a few other ummins surrounded him. They had armed themselves with blaster gloves.

Identifying enemy combatants might be more difficult than Thomas had anticipated. The people hidden inside each hut seemed too confident to be slaves, yet too victorious to be survivors of the slaughter.

We killed them!

We won!

The winners were the slaves of Duin. Even so, Thomas delved their minds briefly, just to make sure they were not actually enemies broadcasting to a mass audience in the Megacosm.

Bugs hummed above dead Red Ranks. Thomas had only seen this much carnage in a secondhand way. Slave rebellions and Torth conquests could get messy.

All the headless corpses were strangely distracting. Every dismembered body part, every bloodstained spatter on the otherwise white walls…the smallest details etched themselves into Thomas's flawless memory.

On top of that, he felt like a weapon in standby mode. He almost expected one of the dead Torth to twitch, having fooled him.

"Teacher!" Pung shouted in warning.

A huge Torth stood a little ways down the street. Thomas recognized the Horned Triumph, a Servant of All who had gained minor fame for stomping down a few slave rebellions. The Horned Triumph had scorched knobs protruding from his shaved head and wore white armor that matched his empty eyes. He looked like he was having a particularly bad day.

He also aimed a portable missile launcher at Thomas.

Thomas assessed his options in less than a microsecond. None of his ummin protectors were close enough to blast the Horned Triumph in time. If he dived in any direction, he would die as the missile struck.

There was only one possible way Thomas might save himself.

He toggled his hoverchair to full speed and barreled toward the Horned Triumph, yelling to his ummin cohorts, "Kill him!"

Just as Thomas had hoped, the Horned Triumph realized that a killing shot at this range would end his own life as well as that of his target. He hesitated, perhaps unwilling to martyr himself.

Or perhaps a Majority chorus was screaming at him. They must want him to *Hold fire!* Or they were chanting, *Capture the Betrayer, don't kill him!*

Thomas sped close enough to attack with a full-force pain seizure.

The Horned Triumph staggered backward, mouthing silent screams. *!!!*

Aside from the pain, an emotion dominated the bald man. It was not rage, not terror, but pure shock.

Thomas sensed that the Horned Triumph had never experienced agony in his long life. Somehow, by some gross twist of fate, a handicapped child had a magnitude of mental strength that was common only among Servants of All.

Thomas smiled grimly. He couldn't spare focus for anything else, but he didn't dare stop. He would prove to the Torth Empire that he wasn't their victim. He would prove to Ariock that he wasn't a vulnerable, disabled burden.

The Horned Triumph pushed back with immense strength.

Thomas bit his cheeks to hold in a shriek. His world dimmed, blinded by pain, and he lost his attack.

The Horned Triumph took a step forward. He became a nightmare that filled all of Thomas's vision, his gloved hands prepared to destroy the fragile boy.

Never mind the inhibitor. He was going to murder the Betrayer.

Thomas regained enough of his conscious mind to jam the hoverchair controller to full speed ahead. He tried to slam into the Horned Triumph. The smallest distraction could be fatal for either of them.

But the old veteran sensed his intentions. His reflexes were superhuman, and he leaped aside in time.

Thomas slowed his speeding hoverchair just in time. He bumped harmlessly into a wall.

Strong hands, encased in gloves, seized his head.

That was when Thomas understood that he was truly helpless. He tried to spark a wildfire, to ignite the Horned Triumph, but thermal manipulation required time. He couldn't superheat his attacker fast enough. He considered lashing out with another pain seizure, but he was weakened, and the Horned Triumph was braced for it this time.

Nor did he have enough time to draw breath or to shout for help.

He could not save himself. It seemed he should have let Ariock chaperone him, after all.

A wet explosion ended the wrenching attack.

Warm gore and brain matter splattered onto Thomas's face and golden robes.

Thomas blinked rapidly, adjusting to the new situation. He was safe. When he rotated his hoverchair, he saw his attacker's headless corpse on the ground.

And Cherise stood there.

She lowered her hand, encased in a blaster glove. A breeze tousled strands of her black hair. She was unexpectedly powerful and beautiful.

Thomas wanted to thank her.

But that seemed so trite and inadequate, he hesitated. He wasn't sure if Cherise had saved a good friend—or if she had merely saved the temporary pilot she was counting on.

She must want to escape from mind readers forever.

She gave Thomas a nod and walked away. A group of her ummin friends was waiting for her, all wearing supply packs.

"Nice shot, Cherise!" Pung called with admiration. "Sorry, Teacher. I was afraid I would blast you by accident."

Thomas realized that the whole duel had only lasted a few seconds.

He had to suppress a sharp urge to ascend and find out how billions of Torth were reacting. If only the Majority could see him now, bathed in the blood of a Servant of All.

"Let's not linger here." Thomas floated past more huts, winding toward the jungle path that would lead to where the Torth troops had parked their transports. "Follow me."

CHAPTER 8

ROGUE RED

Ariock had to crawl up the tunnel, then crawl through the exit of the hut. Finally, he was able to unbend his body, joints popping. He stretched to his full height of over nine feet tall.

He felt as if he was taking his first full breath in months. He'd been so cooped up.

Vy shaded her eyes so she could look up at him.

Ashamed, Ariock bent to scoop up his makeshift pack, full of water canteens and other supplies. He should probably slouch a bit. He towered over the rooftops of huts like a colossus. Now that Vy could see him in daylight, she would be disgusted or frightened. She would probably never touch him again.

Instead, Vy grabbed his hand and tugged. "Hey, come on. We should hurry."

Ariock let her pull him up the blood-soaked street.

The air smelled like a lush summer, but the village no longer looked like the idyllic place they had entered a few days ago. Ariock was tall enough to see all the wrecked huts—and hundreds of obliterated mind readers. The corpses and blasted limbs looked human. He had to remind himself that they were not.

Tribal ummins spoke in whispers and hugged each other. Whatever came next for the village of Duin, it would be rough. There were no victory celebrations.

Ariock tried to tell himself that this massacre of Red Ranks was justice.

But the Torth Empire had an endless supply of abusive tyrants. He knew that.

The sky ought to be gloomy, instead of a sunny, clear aqua green. Ariock had a strange feeling of impending doom. It felt like his last day on Earth. He had paced the sky room, expecting a snowstorm with howling winds. The gentle snowfall hadn't seemed to fit. Nor had his unexpected guests—Cherise, Thomas, and Vy.

Then the Torth Empire had crashed through his window.

Vy squeezed his hand. "Whatever is going to happen, it will be worse if we stay."

Ariock searched for words to explain the foreboding he felt. It wasn't just his guilt. He didn't think so, anyway.

"I have a weird feeling that something will go wrong," he admitted.

Vy took the statement far harder than he'd expected. She looked stunned. Then she rushed ahead, toward Delia. Soon they were both whispering, looking over their shoulders at Ariock.

"What's wrong?" Ariock asked with trepidation.

His mother gave him a fierce stare. "Ariock, do you think Thomas's plan is going to fail? If so, when? And how?"

Ariock regretted having mentioned his unfounded worry. There was no reason for him to spread fear in the midst of a life-or-death escape. "Nah." He tried to sound reassuring. "If anyone can get us off this planet, it's Thomas."

Neither of them looked reassured.

"Have you been sleeping all right?" Delia asked. "I noticed you were restless."

Ariock thought that was a non sequitur. Anyway, the last thing he wanted to do was describe the nightmare where he walked atop a mountain of corpses, including Delia's dead body. Thomas must have mentioned it to her. Why? Ariock would need to remind the boy to keep his absorbed secrets to himself.

"I guess I'm just stressed." Ariock made his tone light. "I'm sure we're all having nightmares. Right?"

Vy and Delia exchanged a look.

"What did you dream?" Vy sounded oddly intense, as if his dreams mattered.

But everyone had an occasional bad dream. At least, Ariock thought so. He had watched enough TV shows and movies, and he'd read enough books, so he thought he had a somewhat realistic concept of what normal people were like.

"We'll survive." Ariock made himself sound confident. "I guarantee, whatever happens, we won't be easy pickings for the Torth."

Those seemed to be words that Vy wanted to hear. She looked embarrassed, perhaps aware that she had overreacted. "Come on." She led the way onward.

They found Thomas in a sandy clearing, floating between sleek, aerodynamic vehicles. The transports' hulls reflected the gray-blue jungle foliage. Thomas's hoverchair would have matched the silvery vehicles, except it looked as though he'd run over an exploding Torth. Bloodstains splashed his golden robes. Even his hair had bloody flecks.

Vy ran up to him. "Are you all right?" She used her sleeve to wipe blood flecks off his face.

"I'm fine. Get out of my range, please." Thomas floated from one vehicle to another. "I'm working. Gather your packs and get ready to leave in a hurry."

Ariock saw that Vy had questions like his own.

Thomas passed beneath a hull. His iridescent eyes seemed to glow in the shadows, full of mysterious secrets. "I'm making sure these vehicles are devoid of witnesses," he explained. "The Torth can already make educated guesses about how poorly we're armed, but it will take them a few minutes to send backup troops here. We'll retain a slight advantage during those minutes if they're forced to guess which exact vehicle I stole. I'll alter its ID and reskin its exterior…"

He interrupted himself, studying a nearby transport.

"Can't we fill all the transports with ummins?" Ariock rested his hands on his hips. "If you give them a quick tutorial on how to pilot—"

"Microdarts!" Thomas's tone was full of panicked anguish.

Ariock threw his awareness outward in all directions, seeking anything out of place, anything wrong. The air seemed to be torn by bullet-fast disruptions. A lot of tiny things hurtled straight toward him.

They all came from the same direction.

Ariock rolled the air with extra pressure, the way he had done in order to extinguish flames. His power stopped all the microbullets.

He had shielded himself.

Ariock traced the direction of the shots to their source. A young woman with red eyes crouched in a transport door that was cracked open.

She ducked away as soon as Ariock saw her.

Coward.

Ariock sank his awareness into the metal door of the transport and tore it asunder. Metal shrieked as it twisted. At the same time, Ariock connected his awareness to Red Rank. He sensed her shape, and he was able to sink himself into her red armor.

In the back of his mind, he recalled Vy urging him to kill Torth.

He could crush this Red Rank woman. He could rip her apart with the power of his mind.

Then he remembered the silent judgment of Torth onlookers. Hadn't they all expected him to be that sort of violent brute? Maybe they had good reason to shackle him.

Deep down, everyone was probably afraid of him. Even Vy.

Ariock used his powers to yank the Red Rank through the doorway. He levitated her outside, into the open, where everyone could see her. Most of his focus went to her armored wrists, so she could not trigger her blaster glove or attack him. He kept her shackled with pressurized air.

The Red Rank bared her teeth in a parody of a smile. If not for her bloodred eyes, she could have passed for human.

"Where should I—" Ariock began to ask where he could imprison the Red Rank and leave her.

"Kill her!" Thomas demanded.

Blasts tore the woman into ribbons of raw meat.

What remained was not a corpse, but an unrecognizable mess. Ariock let the pieces drop in a wet heap of damaged armor and entrails.

The tribal ummins who had blasted the Red Rank looked self-satisfied. Ariock looked away from the carnage. This was worse than anything the prison arena. Those had been messy deaths, but they were animals, not sapient beings with armor and full self-awareness.

He missed the calm, snowy, unchanging view of mountains and pine trees from his sky-room window.

"I know that thinking isn't your strong suit, but please give it a try." Thomas gave Ariock a frustrated glare. "Never bring an enemy Torth close enough to read your mind. She could have disabled you with a pain seizure!"

"Point taken." Vy gently squeezed Ariock's hand.

"I don't think the point is taken," Thomas said. "That Red Rank nearly disabled Ariock with the inhibitor. She was waiting here. She was just waiting for an opportunity to attack."

Ariock glanced at the splattered pile that had been his would-be assassin. He realized that Thomas was right. This Red Rank had actually been brave, not a coward at all. She must have telepathically sensed her cohorts dying, yet instead of flying away, she had bided her time.

If not for Thomas's shouted warning...

"You saved me," Ariock admitted. "Thank you."

From now on, Ariock resolved to listen to Thomas. He could not afford to make idiotic mistakes.

Thomas looked gratified. "There might be others waiting to prove their merit so they can earn a promotion." He floated between the next two vehicles, presumably scanning their interiors with his mind. "That's why I'm being thorough."

CHAPTER 9

CRAMMED INTO LUXURY

Vy walked away from the heap of what used to be an enemy Red Rank. Part of her used to be a nurse, and that part of her felt sympathy for any victim of violence. She had to turn that part off.

No one else seemed even remotely fazed by the carnage. Not Kessa. Not Delia. Not Thomas, who must have absorbed some ridiculous variety of adult experiences. Not even Ariock, who used to avoid gory TV shows, according to his mom. They were all okay with ending Torth lives.

"I need someone with functioning hands." Thomas floated next to a transport.

One of the adolescent ummins sprang to his aid. "Tell me what you need, Teacher!"

"There's a hidden trigger to open the door." Thomas nodded toward the hull, which was smooth and mirrorlike, devoid of any visible windows or cracks. "Right in that area. You should feel an indent about the size of a Torth hand. Press it."

The adolescent happily obeyed.

A door appeared and slid aside, carrying away their reflections. The opening revealed an interior that glowed like a palace.

A ramp unfurled. It looked as pliable as cloth until it solidified. Then it seemed as solid as metal.

"Ooh!" The adolescent rushed up the ramp and into the vehicle.

"Get in and make yourselves comfy," Thomas announced to everyone. "We leave in two minutes."

Vy hesitated with one foot on the ramp. The ummin departure crew was understandably eager to escape their slave farm, but the merry lights and hypercleanliness gave her a shiver of fear. Her nightmares featured seamless Torth designs.

She preferred the imperfection of structures built by tribal ummins.

Or her mom's red van, with the bits of garbage on its floor mats and the suspension that caused it to rattle over potholes. At least humans valued stereo speakers for playing music.

If only the Torth would show as much care for their slaves as they did for their inanimate possessions.

Weptolyso lumbered close, and Vy stepped aside to make room for him. The vehicle tilted a little bit from his weight. He would take up most of the interior space by himself.

Families hugged their adolescents goodbye forever, exchanging tearful promises. Ariock watched with guilt.

"We can't save them all," Thomas said.

"We dishonor them by leaving," Ariock said.

Vy agreed. Everyone chosen for the departure crew was an adolescent, the age group most at risk of being abducted and collared as city slaves. They carried seeds and roots in hope of starting a self-sufficient village. But it seemed like a flimsy hope. The departure crew was hardly enough people to populate a house, let alone a village.

Surely Thomas had already considered ways to rescue everybody on the slave farm. Even so...

"Isn't there some way you can daisy-chain the vehicles together?" Vy asked her foster brother.

"You fail to grasp the scope of this problem." Thomas glared as if she had accused him of a crime. "Even if I had time to do that—which I don't—such an act would put the slaves more at risk than if they stayed here."

Vy began to ask for an explanation.

Thomas forestalled her. "If a bunch of slaves gain an opportunity to operate dashboard controls and learn Torth glyphs, that is highly illegal. The Torth will go out of their way to kill them for learning forbidden technology." He gestured toward the jungle pathway. "Whereas if they stay home and remain ignorant? Then they look like innocent pawns who were manipulated by the Betrayer. There's a decent chance the Torth will still deem them useful as slaves and let them live."

Vy swallowed. She hated the Torth so much.

"Also," Thomas said, as if he was eager to heap even more insults upon her concept of justice, "my plan hinges on us being sneaky. The Torth military would easily spot a caravan of stolen military vehicles. If they hit us before we get inside a streamship? Then it's all for naught. If we don't have the protection of a spaceship hull, then I guarantee the Torth will defeat Ariock with their full military strength. We need a spaceship."

Ariock looked ashamed, as if he thought that he should have enough strength to defeat a Torth armada by himself.

"You really think we can be that sneaky?" Vy asked.

"I will do my level best." Thomas gave her a humorless grin. "I will make it impossible for them to ID our stolen vehicle."

Vy bowed her head in acknowledgment.

"The Torth can only guess which spaceport I'll choose," Thomas went on. "With that much blind guesswork, we should be able to get pretty far and maybe even launch without getting noticed. If I'm wrong?" He nodded toward Ariock. "Then I'm counting on help from our tank."

Ariock nodded willingly.

Molyt Dazel, the chief elder, looked neither resigned nor regretful. She simply accepted injustice.

She endured it like a queen.

Vy figured that if she were in that same position, she would be crying and begging for salvation.

Adolescent ummins scampered up the ramp, laden with supply packs. They began to bounce on the luxurious cushioned chairs and giggle. It seemed they were choosing to see this journey as an adventure. They weren't yet ready to mourn.

Ariock knelt. He bowed his head toward the chief elder. "I will never forget Duin."

Molyt Dazel returned the gesture of respect. Kessa translated her words. "Molyt Dazel says that you have brought hope and honor to the people of Duin."

It wasn't enough. Vy knew that, and so did Ariock. He looked embarrassed. "I should have been able to do a lot more."

Thomas zoomed up the ramp, disappearing inside the transport before anyone had a chance to thank him or to say goodbye to their Teacher.

Pung went next. Then Delia. Then Kessa and others. Vy exchanged looks with Ariock, but he gestured for her to go ahead.

"You're not going to stay behind?" Vy put a warning note in her voice.

"I wouldn't do that." Ariock sounded sad.

So Vy shouldered her pack and climbed into the transport.

Thomas floated in front of a wraparound windshield that offered a panoramic view. Holographic displays appeared wherever he faced, like magic. A pilot's seat was folded down, but it still might impede the hoverchair.

In fact, Vy saw that Thomas would be unable to reach most of the controls. He was too weak, and his arms were short and permanently bent. He would need help.

"Where is Cherise?" Thomas asked in a tight voice.

Vy wanted to kick herself for failing to notice her missing sister. "Oh, no. I'll go look for her." She stepped onto the ramp.

"We don't have time for this." Thomas made a growl of frustration. "Get out of my way. My chair is faster than…" He trailed off, eyes widening as he stared out at the jungle pathway.

A massive group of villagers jogged toward the transport.

Cherise jogged in their midst, like a tall ummin, fitted with a supply pack just like theirs. Everyone in the group was outfitted like the departure crew, and Vy recognized them as backup crew members. Some were backups of backups.

"Go! Go!" Cherise urged the villagers. She skidded to a halt, waving for ummins to go ahead of her. "He'll let you on. Just keep going!"

The villagers dashed madly up the ramp.

Vy stepped aside with a mixture of fierce pride for her sister and shame for herself. While the rest of them were caught up in logistics, Cherise had made a different sort of calculation—to save as many people as possible. She wasn't going to let Duin haunt her.

"We don't have enough room!" Thomas said through clenched teeth.

"Go, go, go!" Cherise urged.

Thomas looked ready to block the desperate people. Vy got ready to push his hoverchair aside. But at the last minute, Thomas caved in. He floated aside and allowed the extra crew members to run past him and cram into the vehicle.

"You'd better get inside, Ariock," Thomas said in a cold, toneless voice, like a Torth giving commands. "If they take your spot, we're not going anywhere."

The vehicle rocked as Ariock climbed aboard. He mumbled apologies as ummins squished aside to make room for him.

Vy pushed her way toward the folded pilot's chair. She yanked up the backrest and sat before anyone else could grab the seat. She was probably a good candidate to be a copilot.

"That's it," Thomas yelled in the slave tongue. "We can't fit anyone else."

Ummins continued to climb onto chair backs, and onto each other's laps, urged by Cherise. Ariock and Weptolyso faced each other, each backed against a curved wall. They shared a look of commiseration while ummins piled against their chest plates. Both giants ended up with ummins on their shoulders and laps.

The vehicle was stuffy and overcrowded. Ummins crammed closer, squirming past each other, trying to rearrange themselves.

Thomas hovered near the control panel with a disgruntled expression, careful not to bang into any ummins. With his blood-spattered robes and hair and his withered limbs, he certainly didn't look like a pilot. He waved his underdeveloped hand through one of the few holographs that he could actually reach.

Ummins hauled Cherise inside as the ramp began to retract. Her braided hair was windblown, but she looked satisfied. Vy couldn't imagine being that confident.

Soon the door slid closed.

"Military control panel." Thomas made a frustrated sound. "I need a co-pilot. Vy?" The request sounded like he had to dredge it out of his depths.

An adolescent ummin popped up between Vy and Thomas. "What do you need, Teacher?" he asked brightly.

"I'll do it," Vy said. If she could speed on highways in a minivan, she could probably handle a Torth military transport.

Thomas gave them both an assessing glance. "I think Varktezo might be good at this," he said. "He has a sharp mind."

Vy tried not to feel that as an insult. Did Thomas think she was comparatively stupid?

"Whatever. Both of you, pay attention." Thomas began to point and give instructions. "The Torth make the unlock process complicated just to prevent slaves from using technology. It's unlocked now." He pointed to a smoky knob. "That controls velocity." He pointed to a joystick. "That controls everything else. Push or pull for altitude. Circle around to steer."

The dopey-looking adolescent grabbed the joystick icon. He gently pulled, and the floor thrummed.

The view began to shift as the transport lifted upward.

Jungle foliage and parked transports spread out below them. Hundreds of villagers raised their faces to watch, unaware that the passengers inside the transport could see them.

Vy recognized all three elders. She saw mining foremen, and water-bearers, and farmers, and mated couples. Most of those staying behind were past their prime. They'd also kept the youngest children and babies, hoping that the Torth might spare children who could be collared and used as city slaves.

That must have been a hard decision to make.

"Goodbye," Varktezo whispered.

"If I could save them," Thomas said, "I would."

Thomas's fingers danced, and a new holograph appeared. It showed topography with a blue overlay. The line and the dot might be a route with a destination at the end. The floating white triangle probably represented their vehicle.

"Is that GPS?" Vy asked.

"Pretty much," Thomas said. "Buckle up."

Vy hurriedly slipped into the harness of the pilot's seat. She could still reach the controls, but Varktezo stood in front of her, between her knees, bracing himself. Thomas flicked the lock position on his hoverchair.

"Are you going to be okay?" Vy asked him.

"It would be great if someone can brace my hoverchair," Thomas said.

Fortunately, ummins were paying attention. Several adolescents grabbed onto his hoverchair. There was so little room, Vy figured—

"Go ahead," Thomas urged. "Slide the velocity knob."

Varktezo was already at the helm. Vy gave up and let him have at it.

Duin was gone, as if it had been a dream.

Ummins shouted in surprise, unprepared for the sudden motion. The transport sailed over scrubby trees, and then the rocky desert blurred below them.

Varktezo experimented with steering. The vehicle banked, then banked the other way, instantly responsive even at a speed that might approach a sonic boom.

"It's so easy!" Varktezo said.

"The controls are pretty intuitive once you get past the lock," Thomas admitted. "Torth like to do as little work as possible. Hey, follow the map."

Varktezo put his whole body into working the controls. He seemed to be having a blast.

The desert appeared to stretch out forever all around them. It rippled to a flat horizon. It looked uninhabited, but Thomas watched the horizon with apprehension.

"We're going to see a military fleet pretty soon," Thomas said, perhaps responding to Vy's thoughts. "But I worked a canyon detour into our route. Varktezo has top-notch hand-eye coordination. We should be able to survive without detection."

CHAPTER 10
THE BIG EMPTY

Although Ariock was crammed against the rear wall of the overcrowded transport, he had a good view of the outside world. The wraparound windshield was a lot like his sky-room window: huge. The whole front half of the transport was transparent.

Or it appeared that way, anyway. Torth liked illusions. Ariock had seen transports from the outside, and they lacked visible windows. He supposed it was one-way glass or something like that.

Thomas spoke an instruction.

"He is telling the pilot to fly lower," Delia said.

The map faded when their altitude lowered. The ummin adolescent at the control panel said something in protest.

Thomas cut in.

"Thomas says the Torth will guess that we're in a stolen military transport. The map fades as a warning, but that's fine. We need to keep a low profile."

Ariock was grateful for the translation. He had learned a few phrases in the slave tongue, but fluency might take months.

Their vehicle dropped close to the ground. Sand and rocks rolled below them in a blur.

The ummin pilot, Varktezo, seemed to be good at multitasking. He was keeping track of the control knobs, the view, the meters, and the map. He would probably be good at video games.

An ummin who sat closer to Ariock pointed toward distant cliff-like boulders and asked a question.

As the boulders drew closer, Ariock took another look. Did those cliffs have eyebrow ridges? And beaks half buried in sand?

Delia translated what Thomas said. "That is an ancient palace complex. Ummins used to call this desert the Mesev, which means the 'Big Empty' in the language of their ancestors. Those statues are carved representations of famous ummins from the Tropical Empire period."

Judging by the erosion, the statues must have existed for eons. Ariock wondered if they had been carved before the Torth Empire conquered the planet Umdalkdul.

ABBY GOLDSMITH

More questions and answers.

"This used to be a lush landscape. When the Torth Empire came here, they diverted water to feed their cities and crops, and the ground dried up. Sand blew in, bit by bit, over many generations."

The ummins looked captivated.

"There's a lot of lost knowledge buried beneath this desert. The Torth Empire doesn't value cultural artifacts as much as they should. Oh!"

Their transport jerked downward. Ariock spiked his awareness outward, ready to roll pressure into the air and cushion their crashing vehicle.

But there was no crash. They soared between the cliff walls of a canyon.

Thomas said something in a grim voice.

"A few hundred vehicles incoming," came the translation.

Ariock scanned the sky. It looked clear.

"I saw them through Varktezo's perceptions," Thomas said crossly. "Ummins have much better vision than the rest of us. Don't worry, I'm not in the Megacosm."

He had said that in English. He must be responding to Vy or Delia.

Varktezo worked the controls, and craggy walls zoomed past on either side. The transport flipped sideways in order to fit through a narrow passage. Supply packs flew through the air, ummins yelled, and Delia swore.

They flipped right side up again.

Ariock had glimpsed huge engines on these vehicles. He wondered how they stayed so relatively silent.

The canyon widened and grew deeper. They skimmed past a ribbon waterfall, then past a hive of cave openings, and several overhangs. Ariock was tempted to expand his awareness, to explore those rocks, but doing that took up a lot of his focus. He wanted to stay alert for danger.

"Hey, Ariock," Thomas called.

"What?" Ariock looked at him.

"Can you explore the cliffs ahead and find a hiding place for us? We want to chill out, unnoticed, when Torth zoom through this canyon."

Ariock heard a few questions and arguments in two languages, but he tuned them out. He quested with his powers.

He sensed topography. Cliffs, overhangs, valleys, rocky scree, boulders, and life sparks here and there. The life sparks were probably animals. They were unadorned—he did not sense anything like clothing or armor or supplies when he examined the region—and too sparsely distributed to be a troop or a group of people.

He quested farther ahead, past zigzag bends.

"There's an offshoot of the canyon that might work," Ariock said.

"Okay, I can't read your mind from this distance," Thomas said. "Tell Varktezo when to turn."

Varktezo glanced at Ariock with an encouraging look, although he could not shift his focus away from the controls for long.

"Coming up on the right," Ariock said, feeling awkward. "Slow down."

Vy translated to the slave tongue.

Varktezo slammed the transport toward the offshoot canyon at the last possible second. He throttled their speed, and the passengers braced themselves, anticipating a crash into solid rock. It looked imminent.

Instead, they hovered into the opening Ariock had detected.

A rocky ledge above them formed a ceiling. Below, rubble showed where this part of the cliff had collapsed.

"Good job," Thomas said. "I don't think the Torth are aware of this hidden spot. The most recent geological surveys of this region are a few decades old."

They hovered. It was shady and silent.

Ariock began to send his awareness outward. If Torth were about to explore this canyon, he wanted to know when and where.

A fast-moving transport shot through the main canyon, just out of sight. Then several more.

They waited.

"How long should—" Vy began to say, but Thomas cut her off. He spoke to Varktezo.

And then they were flying again. They emerged from the hidden indent and zoomed through the main canyon, banking right and left to narrowly avoid cliffs.

"No, I'm not certain," Thomas said, replying to someone's unspoken question. "The only way I could be sure would be to check the Megacosm, which I'm not going to do. But the longer we linger, the more time we give the Torth to shut down their spaceports. We can't afford to wait. We have to take a risk."

The canyon forked, and they banked into a narrow channel, skimming over the tops of vine-shrouded paddle trees. They flew over a collection of ramshackle huts, then factory with smokestacks.

"How are we going to hide," Ariock asked, "once we get near a spaceport?"

"We're going to blend in with city traffic," Thomas said.

"How?"

"I'm changing the skin of our vehicle." Thomas scrolled through a holographic menu, making selections. "There's no hiding that it's military grade, but a lot of middle-ranked civilians own former military transports with a color change." He let his hands drop into his lap, apparently exhausted. "There. We're a bronze color now. We could be a couple of Brown Ranks returning from a round of slave farm visits."

Ariock wondered if a color change was enough to fool every Torth on the planet.

Vy seemed to have the same worry. "Aren't they going to be extra wary right now?" she asked.

"We don't have a lot of great options." Thomas sounded impatient. "The Torth will be scrambling to shut down all space travel off this planet right now. With luck, they won't notice us in the midst of rerouted deliveries and travel delays. They expected to capture us in Duin." His tone became grim. "Hopefully the Upward Governess is dead. Or demoted into irrelevancy."

Ariock recalled the fat girl. Was she really a threat to worry about?

"That way," Thomas said in the slave tongue. He pointed, and Varktezo followed the route…straight up a sheer cliff.

It seemed to stretch for miles upward, with buildings perched precariously on ledges. Bubble-shaped elevators zipped up and down cables, ferrying passengers from one building to the next. Their transport skyrocketed upward, faster than an elevator. The velocity pushed Ariock against the rear wall.

A shiny green transport swooped out from a cavernous docking bay in the cliff. It flew upward alongside them, almost matching their speed and direction.

Another transport showed up.

And another.

"That's just normal traffic," Delia said, translating Thomas's blasé explanation. "He says it helps us look legit."

The cliff buildings because grander, with red-stone bases and glassy skyscrapers that thrust upward like crystals.

The passengers exclaimed about the dazzling sights they'd never seen before. Ariock guessed they had never seen a city in their lives. Airborne traffic darted in or out from huge bays, colorful and fast-paced. More vehicles joined a streaming intersection overhead.

"This isn't the city where we were slaves," Vy realized. "Is it?"

"No," Thomas said. "That was New GoodLife WaterGarden City. This is Rare Moonrise MetroHub. I figured we'd be wise to get out of the immediate jurisdiction of a certain supergenius."

Ariock hadn't known the Torth were so poetic about city names.

Holographs glowed against shadowy walls of skyscrapers like billboards. They displayed brief recordings. A pair of furry govki hands gently shaved someone's legs. That must be an advertisement for a spa treatment.

They flew over rooftop garden terraces and ponds that might be luxury swimming pools. The city looked like a fabulously rich utopia.

Ariock liked being able to see so much sky. Did all Torth feel this invincible as they flew through the cities they owned, with the whole galaxy watching through their eyes?

Then he imagined the sickly warren of despair beneath all this wealth. Generations of oppressed slaves struggled to survive in filth, unable to hope for better lives. Vy had described the Tunnels to him.

Their transport swerved.

"Calm down," Thomas told Varktezo. "That's just an infographic for the Torth to be on the lookout for us. Try not to get us killed."

Ariock gaped at the massive holograph that had alarmed their pilot. A huge image of Kessa's head floated in the sky.

It morphed into another image: Vy as a slave. Her hair was tied back with a rag instead of the headband-like tie she now used. Every pore and red hair was rendered in exquisite detail. She looked beautiful even so.

The holograph morphed into another head. Ariock stared at his own face painted across the sky.

"Did they take snapshots of us?" Vy asked.

"The collective memories and imaginations of millions of Torth can generate an accurate composite," Thomas said, "which can then be rendered. It's usually not perfect, but a large crowd will reinforce the correct information and cancel the wrong stuff."

They flew past the holograph. Ariock wasn't sure he would ever feel secure as long as he knew the Torth Empire, with all its power, existed.

Varktezo followed the mapped route. The expressway carried them past sculpted pinnacles that gleamed in noonday sunshine, over causeways that spanned skyscrapers, and past aerial docks that poked above buildings like antennae. Their altitude evened out as they rounded a bend.

But that wasn't the only reason why Ariock's heart leaped in his throat.

Their transport nearly slammed into a truck-like rig. Varktezo throttled the velocity, and they stopped just in time. Ariock had to brace against the wall in order to keep from accidentally smashing ummin passengers.

"Crap." Thomas stared.

They floated at a snail's pace at least three thousand feet above the ground. The skyscrapers around them seemed to soar into the cloudless sky.

Other vehicles hemmed them in.

The holographic dashboard map populated with triangles that must represent all the nearby vehicles. They were above, below, in front, and behind. Escape would be dangerous. Even if Varktezo could maneuver through narrow gaps between crawling traffic, many hundreds of Torth must be watching.

They couldn't drive away unnoticed.

"It must be a checkpoint," Thomas said in dismay. "They're inspecting every vehicle that entered the city. Looking for us."

PART EIGHT

"You elected Me. You adore Me. Whenever You whisper Your needs, it is I who ensures that the Servants of All carry out Your every desire and whim.

For I am more than a mere humble Servant of All. I am their head.

And now that mind readers command every world, every ocean, every heaven…and I command all who serve them…I, in essence, command All Living Things."

—The First Commander of All Living Things

CHAPTER 1
SLAVES AGAIN

Sparkling hopes and gripping fears formed a disharmony around Thomas. He winced. If only he could shift his attention into someone calm.

If only he had a tranquility mesh.

"How can we get past the checkpoint?" That was the top question everyone asked, whether or not they said it out loud.

The Megacosm glowed within Thomas's reach, a doorway ajar inside his mind. A microsecond was all he would need in order to learn about the checkpoint—how and why the Torth had erected checkpoints so fast, how many Red Ranks would be there, how well armed they were, and so forth.

All he had to do was stretch upward.

Maybe he could do it fast enough so that other supergeniuses wouldn't detect him. And he could grab some more sweet, sweet knowledge while he was there.

Thomas chewed the insides of his cheeks. The pain forced him back from the edge of ascension. The Upward Governess was undoubtedly waiting for him to do something fatally stupid. He would not give her a chance to peer through his eyes and riffle through his thoughts.

"Do you need me to knock a hole in the traffic?" Ariock's deep voice was full of deadly determination.

"No!" Thomas rotated, and hoped his glare looked fearsome enough to make Ariock hesitant. "Don't do anything. If you draw attention to us, then it's over. We can't blast our way through a militarized city."

"I'm open to better ideas." Ariock watched him hopefully.

Thomas took a deep breath, trying to calm his nerves. If only the transport didn't reek of fear. Cherise should never have invited so many…

Thomas stopped himself from that line of thought. So what if Cherise wanted to save a bunch of ummins? So what if she never spoke to him again? He wasn't going to waste his energy wishing for impossible reversals. Reality was reality.

The engines whirred, struggling to keep their overburdened craft afloat. Other transports crowded closer.

"Thomas?" Vy began to ask if he had a plan, but Thomas had a pounding headache from their cloying fears and unspoken questions.

"Quiet," he snapped. "I'm thinking."

Not that he needed to think much, by his standards. They could not sneak past this checkpoint.

Unless.

Thomas had a certain Yeresunsa power. Years ago, when he was six years old, he had sworn to never use it again in his life. The power was evil. He wished it was gone, and he wanted it to remain a secret. He had managed to ignore that power for years and years.

He shouldn't use it.

He really, really shouldn't.

But, well…if he was going to bring Ariock and the rest of them to a place of safety, then he had no choice. It was necessary at this juncture.

Vy had never seen Thomas take so long to formulate a plan. Her unspoken fears were louder than spoken words. *He knows we're screwed. He just isn't saying it out loud.*

The crowded conditions were wearing on everyone. The transport smelled of ummin musk and escalating panic. Everyone double-checked their blaster gloves.

"I have a plan." Thomas slumped.

They watched him with hope.

"Well?" Vy urged him to go on.

"I can get us past the checkpoint without attracting attention," Thomas said. "But we have to do it my way, and you're not going to like it."

That was a major understatement. Even if his plan worked perfectly, their distrust of him would grow exponentially. No one would thank him. Delia might try to speed up his death. And Cherise? Thomas tried not to think about how she would react.

He shoved his own fears aside. That was for later. For now, he had a task that needed doing. Emotions would only get in his way.

"I need you all to act and think like slaves," Thomas said. "Except for you, Vy. You'll need to be a Torth."

"What?" She stared at him in disbelief.

"Slaves don't pilot transports," Thomas explained to her. "So let's pretend you're a Blue Rank, and you're at the helm." She was sitting in the pilot's seat, anyway.

Vy blinked, disbelieving. Despite her blue eyes, she would never fool anyone who glanced at her ragged outfit and beaded decorations.

But Torth relied on telepathy even more than they relied on eyesight. It was possible the checkpoint officers wouldn't glance inside the transport. They might not see Vy or anyone else. They might just scan their minds.

Varktezo inched their transport forward with traffic, closer to the checkpoint. Thomas waved for Vy to take over at the controls.

"What about me?" Ariock asked uncertainly. "I don't think I can pass as a slave." He had ummins sitting on his shoulders.

"You're a nussian," Thomas told him. "A bodyguard for that Blue Rank." He pointed to Vy. "You worship her. You'll die to protect her. You have a thorny hide, and you were trained from birth to defend high-ranked Torth such as her."

Ariock gave him such a baffled look, Thomas wanted to moan. Couldn't people just trust him?

This was why mind readers were superior in so many ways. Torth never needed to question or doubt each other.

"How are you going to make this work?" Delia asked. "Even if they don't look inside, those checkpoint platforms are close to the vehicles. They'll scan our minds."

"Leave that to me." Thomas did not mention his evil power. His friends would never understand what a tremendous sacrifice he was about to make, breaking a solemn promise to his younger self, wrecking his self-integrity to do something terrible and dishonorable.

The terrors he had caused at age six were unforgivable.

Just like the things he had done as a Yellow Rank.

Just like the thing he was about to do to some hapless checkpoint officer or two.

"All of you." Thomas sat straighter, making himself heard. "I need you to act like slaves. Just be terrified and cower. No matter what happens—no matter *what*—stay in panicky slave mode. If Torth board this vehicle and stare at you? Even then, you need to think and act like slaves."

Some of the refugees from Duin were so conditioned to obey commands, they threw themselves to their knees.

The rest gave him stunned, betrayed looks.

"This won't last long," Thomas said. "But it's vital."

"Explain," Delia begged. "If Torth board this vehicle, they'll see the blood spatters all over your robes. How are you going to fool them then?"

"I'll explain afterward." Thomas kept his tone even. "For now, let's survive. Be a slave—or be a Torth."

Vy inched their transport forward. They were only a few stops from the floating platforms, which looked like toll booths. Red Ranks lounged on couches, close enough to lazily scan the minds of every occupant of the transports that passed through the narrow lanes.

"You're really asking us to trust you." Delia looked burdened. She probably considered herself to be the main bulwark between Ariock and disaster.

Thomas met her anxious stare. "If you want to force Ariock into wrecking a path to the spaceport, then we're dead. Duin will have been for nothing. And a lot of innocent victims will die with us."

Ariock looked shamed by the very idea of hurting innocent people by accident. For a gladiator, he was reluctant to get brutal. That must be why the Torth had been so entertained by him.

It was actually a good thing that Ariock was so averse to snapping and going berserk. He was dangerous. Even he knew it.

"I trust him." Ariock's deep voice drew everyone's attention. "He got us this far."

"Thank you," Thomas said pointedly.

Delia remained burdened, unable to detect Thomas's sincerity.

"Stop brooding," Thomas told her. "Your only concern is to please your Torth masters." He pointed to her neck. "You wear a collar. It rules your life. Get on your knees and watch your owners for hand gestures."

Delia didn't stir, but next to her, Kessa fell to her knees without a second thought.

Vy stared at Kessa, shocked by how fast she fell into the slave role. Thomas sensed her pity, wondering how many years it took to—

"You feel nothing!" Thomas whirled to face Vy. "Slaves are not people. They exist to serve you. They're like robots. If you can't handle that, then let someone else pilot this thing and be a slave."

Vy swallowed her shock. Thomas sensed her attempt to shift her mindset and values.

How dare you speak to me like that, she thought, staring down her nose at Thomas.

"Decent." Thomas nodded in approval. "Stay like that."

"I've had enough of being a slave," Delia said.

"Fine," Thomas told her. "You're a Green Rank on a shopping trip with this Blue." He indicated Vy.

Delia gave him a look of doubt.

"Torth don't feel doubt," Thomas said. "Or distrust. Or fear. No intense emotions. We don't have time to test your acting skills. If you can't suppress your emotions, then be a slave."

Pung flopped onto a cushy seat, heedless of the refugees who sat there. He looked imperious, silently daring Thomas to question his chosen role.

As far as he was concerned, if Ariock could pass as a nussian, then a scrappy ummin could pass as a Torth.

"Fine," Thomas told the smuggler. "You're a Brown Rank."

Pung gave him a regal nod of approval.

"As for me?" Thomas gestured to himself. "I'm not disabled or splattered with blood. I'm a clean and healthy-looking Yellow Rank. And I'm of average intelligence. Not a supergenius. Got that?"

They all exchanged looks. None of them could guess how such a massive deception would possibly work.

"This is a normal chair." Thomas tapped his hoverchair. "I can walk perfectly fine. I aspire to be a Blue Rank someday." He nodded toward Vy. "Like you."

"Thomas…" Vy said with concern.

"Think about yourself," Thomas said. He included Delia and Pung. "Think 'me' with a capital *M*. You're better than anyone else in this transport. You don't care about anybody else."

Pung draped his clawed feet over the armrest.

One of the adolescents began to groom his toenails. "Hush," he commanded everyone.

Thomas gave a nod of approval.

Delia dropped into her own cushy chair, nearly as entitled as Pung, but she spoiled it by asking a question. "What if they speak to us in their minds?"

"I'll handle it." Thomas glared at her. "You're on your way to browse for new robes and dresses. That's all that should be on your mind. Nothing else matters. No one in the universe matters except for you."

Delia and Vy exchanged looks. Their hopes and fears were plain to everyone who could see.

"Keep up with traffic," Thomas reminded Vy. "And forget the names of the people here. Names don't exist. You don't have friends." He pointed to Ariock and Weptolyso. "Those are nussian bodyguards. They exist only to serve you. You don't care about them beyond that. These are your slaves." He pointed to everyone else and tried not to look at Cherise while he did so. "They're like furniture."

One of the crew members began to ask a question.

"Quiet, slave!" Thomas said.

They stared at him with wide, frightened eyes, as silent as real slaves.

"This will work," Thomas told everyone. "But you need to stay in your roles until we get past the checkpoint. If you're a slave, you just want to survive. If you're a Torth, you don't care about anyone, and nothing worries you."

Lane dividers corralled the transports into orderly lines. As Thomas watched, he saw that each transport either opened its door or made a window patch on the hull. That allowed the Red Rank officers to peer inside each vehicle.

They were using their eyes as well as telepathy.

Thomas inwardly cursed. This would make things harder. And worse—a secondary officer sat in the middle of each platform. Whoever was in charge had remembered Thomas's secret Yeresunsa power, and they had appointed backup officers to sit beyond his range.

The Torth were thinking a step ahead of him.

Or maybe not quite. The military leaders could not personally monitor every transport at every checkpoint at every artery of every major city. Not simultaneously with close attention. These Red Ranks were just ordinary Torth doing their jobs, and they would not have a full stack of contingency plans.

"Slight change of plan," Thomas said. "You. Guard." He gave Ariock an aloof, Torth-like stare. "When I tell you to do it, do you think you can use your powers, very quickly, to sabotage that thruster?" He pointed to the nearest hoverdisk that supported the checkpoint they were approaching.

Ariock gave an uncertain nod.

"Just knock it askew," Thomas said, "so the checkpoint platform will tip slightly. That's all you need to do. Don't hurt anyone. Don't destroy the disk. Just bend it a tiny bit, knock it slightly out of alignment, and when the platform tilts, withdraw your attention. I just want that Torth in the center"—he gestured toward the reclining Red Rank—"to get out of his seat."

Ariock began to speak, then remembered that he was supposed to be an enslaved bodyguard. He bowed his head in acknowledgment.

"Good." Thomas surveyed his ragtag crew of fake slaves and fake Torth. "Stay in your roles, no matter what."

They were one stop away from the inspection.

"Do it," Thomas commanded. "Make their platform tilt."

Ariock focused, and soon the checkpoint wobbled. The Red Rank at the center stood up, slightly alarmed.

Thomas did his best to tune out the mental babble of fear and nagging questions all around him. Their concerns didn't matter. They were just pathetic slaves, after all, and he was a superior being.

CHAPTER 2
BRAIN DAMAGE

Vy had spent enough time around Torth to know that they could commit brutal murders with casual ease. The officers in regal-looking red armor could silently rally every Torth on the planet to fly to their aid if they decided that this particular transport was a threat.

She had to force her thoughts away from that.

She moved the velocity control to zero. The vehicle hovered in midair while two Red Ranks approached. One was already close enough to probe her mind.

He had a hairy, thuggish look. Vy wondered how well the baby farm pedigree programs worked. They eliminated children who felt too much empathy for slaves, whereas this no-neck stereotype of a bully got green-lighted to become an adult citizen?

The thuggish official frowned at the pilot's area of the transport. His mouth tightened.

Vy tried to feel like an entitled and smug Blue Rank. She told herself that she owned everything in this transport.

It just seemed so pointless. Anyone who could scan minds would sense that she hadn't grown up owning slaves. Did Thomas actually think he could misdirect the officials? How?

Thomas focused on the official as if nothing else in the universe existed. He was giving the man his full attention.

That was a rare look for Thomas.

The official's expression smoothed out. He no longer looked suspicious. He gave a small shrug, but he pressed the door button.

The transport's door slid open. Wind ruffled their hair and clothes.

The Red Rank official peered inside, staring at the horde of tribal ummins, as well as Weptolyso and Ariock. His gaze roved over them as if they did not exist.

He looked straight at Vy and gave her a respectful nod, like one high rank to another.

Vy did not gawk. She forced herself to nod back, playacting in a way that should have been impossible. She pretended that she needed to get on with her day. She wanted to continue on her shopping trip.

The other Red Rank looked suspicious. He ambled closer.

When Thomas focused on him, that Red Rank also seemed to lose interest. He nodded and walked back toward his seat.

"Go!" Thomas gave Vy an urgent look.

She pushed their transport into motion with trembling hands. Wind whipped through the open door.

The holographic map guided her, and she flew toward an enormous building that vaguely resembled an open tulip flower. Each bladelike petal shielded layers of launchpads with bullet-shaped gray lumps that might be spaceships.

Passing that checkpoint had been obscenely easy. Far, far too easy.

Nothing in the Torth-ruled galaxy was that easy.

"How did that actually work?" she asked.

Thomas floated closer to the dashboard. He did something to a menu, and the door sealed.

"I bought us ten minutes," he said, "if we're lucky. We need to select a streamship and leave this planet ASAP."

That wasn't really an answer.

Vy studied Thomas from the corner of her vision, although she needed to pay attention and avoid flying trucks or aerial causeways. If fooling Torth officials was truly this easy, then Thomas could have saved them sooner. He could have smuggled them into a spaceport right away instead of letting them suffer for three months as slaves.

"You have a power over minds." Kessa had come closer, no longer cringing on the floor. She leaned on a chair with both hands as the transport banked, and she seemed to dissect Thomas with her eyes. "You made those Torth see what you wanted them to see."

Thomas stared ahead. He didn't deny it.

"Well." Delia sputtered. "That seems like a handy power. Is there any reason you couldn't have used it earlier?"

"Because I can only do it to one victim at a time," Thomas said. "I have to be close enough to read their mind. And…" He hesitated. "There are undesirable unintended consequences. It's not a power that should be used except in the most extreme, dire need."

Undesirable consequences? What did he mean by that? Vy tried to study him.

"Go that way." Thomas pointed.

The holographic GPS route had ended. Vy took a turn between two skyscrapers, sailing a mile above the distant ground and struggling not to fear what Thomas was capable of doing to her mind.

"I would never use it on anyone here." Thomas sounded scandalized. "My power causes permanent brain damage, and it leads directly to death. Those Red Rank officials are doomed. I might as well have executed them."

"How do you know?" Vy had a lot of questions at war with her focus on piloting the transport.

The spaceport ahead loomed as large as a mountain. Neon strips ran up and down its steep slopes, like liquid gemstones. Thousands of docked vessels bristled on its sunny sides.

"You've used that power before," Ariock said. "Haven't you?"

Vy risked a glance toward Thomas. He wore a haunted, troubled look.

He couldn't have used that power against any Torth while he was a Yellow Rank. The Torth would have retaliated for sure. That meant...

Vy was so nervous, she had trouble navigating. Her mother had welcomed Thomas into the Hollander home, but in private, she had mentioned his tragic past. She had noted that trauma followed their new ward. The other group homes where Thomas had lived had shut down. There were suicides.

Even a murder.

Young Thomas had witnessed a foster father murder a foster mother.

"Oh," Vy said, realizing the implication. Thomas must have brainwashed some hapless human on Earth. He had hurt someone. Maybe he was even responsible for that murder.

"We can discuss this later," Thomas said in a tight voice.

"Why did you have us role-play as slaves and Torth?" Delia asked. "If you could just brainwash them, why bother?"

"It's not like I've had a lot of practice," Thomas said. "I wasn't sure I could twist their minds fast enough. And honestly, I hoped we'd be able to get away without me using that power." He shot Vy a resentful look. "Some of you could have tried harder."

"Did our act help?" Ariock asked.

"I think so." Thomas pointed. "That's our exit. Vy!"

Vy swerved, throttling the velocity to follow a slower offshoot of traffic. They nearly careened out of the aerial lane, and she straightened their course, hoping their vehicle didn't look too suspicious. The Torth must have a few bad drivers or pilots among them.

"You said we only have ten minutes?" Ariock asked.

"Less than that, now." Thomas fidgeted, looking guilty.

"Because the Torth will catch on?" Ariock asked. "But couldn't you have brainwashed them to just, uh, go back to normal after a while?"

"I can't do it with that much nuance," Thomas said. "And I kind of panicked as soon as that first Red Rank got into my range. He was going to blast an alarm through the Megacosm. I had to twist his mind right away."

Thomas had destroyed two lives with casual ease. It sounded like no big deal to him. Vy tried not to reassess everything she thought she knew about her foster brother.

"We can't all have wholesome powers." Thomas gave Vy a challenging stare. "Some Yeresunsa heal fatal injuries. I can twist minds."

Vy swallowed.

"What does that mean?" Ariock spoke in a deep, formidable tone. "What is mind twisting, exactly?"

"It's just…" Thomas slid lower in his seat and hunched his shoulders more. "The victim can't make choices anymore."

Everyone was dead silent. Vy lacked the courage to ask more probing questions.

"So they're not functional as people." Thomas did not meet anyone's gaze. "All that's left of their minds is the single purpose I gave them. That's it. Those Red Ranks can no longer imagine things, or feed themselves, or ascend into the Megacosm. They might not even remember to blink. They'll just keep ambling around that platform, thinking about what a normal bunch of people we are."

Delia swore.

"Won't the Torth be suspicious?" Kessa asked.

"Yes," Thomas said. "When they fail to show up in the Megacosm. But we have some time before that happens. Red Ranks are allowed to take privacy breaks, and those two didn't have huge audiences to begin with. They were just boring officers doing a boring job."

"They'll never recover?" Ariock sounded pained.

"Look." Thomas swiveled to speak to everyone. "There was no other way to get through that checkpoint unnoticed. I know you're all half convinced you can defeat an armada of Torth, but you forgot to factor out all the advantages we've lost. The Torth are no longer uncertain." He gestured around. "They know who we are and what we have, and they figure we're urgently trying to get into a spaceport. They will take measures against us."

Vy was sure that was true.

She followed Thomas's instructions, heading toward a well-lit docking bay. She told herself that those Red Rank officials deserved to have their minds twisted, their ability to make choices broken.

But she also had trouble imagining herself relaxing on some alien planet, cozy around a campfire with Ariock, while the Torth Empire scoured the galaxy.

How relaxed would Delia be, knowing what Thomas could do?

CHAPTER 3

A BIG TARGET

Blaster gloves didn't come in sizes big enough for Ariock, or he would have worn one. Then maybe he wouldn't be such a useless target that everyone else had to protect.

They faced a dim, cavernous hangar full of parked transports. Its far reaches were hazy with distance.

Everyone who could fit their hand into a blaster glove was pulling them on with grim looks of determination. The few ummins without blaster gloves prepared their slingshots. Weptolyso made a soft rumble, his spikes halfway popped out.

Vy climbed out of the pilot's chair. "We're not supposed to attract attention," she told Ariock in a soft voice.

"Exactly," Thomas said. "Keep your powers reined in unless we're in a life-or-death situation."

Ariock gave a nod. He could keep his awareness confined.

But shouldn't he quest ahead and find life sparks?

"The spaceport will be full of Torth," Thomas explained. "We need to pass as Torth and slaves from a distance." He gave Ariock an appraising look. "Ariock, throw a blanket over yourself. We can have you kneel on a hoverscooter and push you and pretend you're a pile of supplies."

How dignified.

"Our goal here is to avoid getting attacked." Thomas sounded haggard. "Once we're inside a streamship, we'll be safer." He had explained that streamships were high-speed spaceships, with hulls that could withstand cannon blasts and other weaponry. "The trick will be getting from here to there." He held out one hand, then the other, to demonstrate. "I need to select a ship and unlock it without being seen by any Torth or their slaves."

He sounded apprehensive.

"Weptolyso?" Thomas went on, speaking in the slave tongue.

Ariock was getting better at reading the nussian's face, including the ways he flared his nostrils. Weptolyso seemed reluctant as he replied.

Thomas switched to English. "I'm asking Weptolyso to shield me from sight. Maybe you can help him, Ariock. We don't want the Torth to see me fooling around with an access panel. I'll need to manually hack the security system in order to get into the ship."

"Sure." Ariock resigned himself to being a big and nearly useless object.

"Ready?" Thomas hovered near the menu that would open the door.

Kessa moved forward, gripping her supply pack. "What if a Torth recognizes us as runaways?"

"Shoot them." Thomas made it sound obvious. "Don't make a fuss or attract attention, but blow their heads off immediately."

He reached for the door button. Apparently, killing was no big deal to someone who could cause permanent brain damage.

"What if a slave sees us?" Kessa asked in the same mild, curious tone.

Thomas's hesitation only lasted a second, but Ariock knew that he didn't want to answer.

"Use your own discretion." Thomas surveyed the crew. "You know what it took for us to get this far. If any slaves happen to notice how strange we are, they'll convey their suspicions to the nearest Torth." He gave them all a hard look. "If freedom matters to you, then you'll do what needs to be done."

Vy looked at Ariock as if he carried all her hopes. Their freedom had already cost too many innocent lives. They both knew it. Ariock, in particular, had enjoyed a richer childhood than any slave could imagine.

He couldn't feel entitled to another large piece of the freedom pie. Not if it came at the expense of more innocent lives.

No more slave deaths, he inwardly promised himself. Enough was enough. He would use his powers to shield innocent people if it came to that.

Thomas didn't meet anyone's gaze while he opened the door. There must be some humanity buried near his surface.

The crew began to disembark, letting in some fresh air.

Vy aimed a look of readiness toward Cherise. They both wore blaster gloves, perfectly fitted to their hands.

The spaceport had an ominous, deep sound. Ariock ducked out of the transport, following everyone else.

Screams would go unheard in this vast hangar. Distant whooshes and clanks added an ominous undertone, like the papery buzz of a hornet's nest. Otherwise the place had the tomb-like silence of a dusty mansion full of unused rooms.

The next few minutes would either mean capture and death—or eternal freedom. One or the other. They couldn't afford to relax.

The crew eyed Ariock with worry.

Vy offered him a huge canvas blanket. Ariock pulled the cloth over himself, wishing he had a power to shrink. The edges of the blanket swung even when he bent over like a gorilla. It didn't cover him entirely.

He would be obvious even from a distance. If they all got attacked and captured or killed, it would be his fault.

Thomas indicated a parked row of hoverscooters.

Vy led Ariock in that direction. She tapped the handlebar controls of a scooter, experimenting with the unlock sequences that Thomas had taught her, until it began to levitate a few inches off the floor.

Ariock knelt on the small platform. The scooter must look ridiculously top-heavy with him on it, but that was the point. Cargo was supposed to be unwieldy.

A group of sturdy ummins rushed to escort him, treating him like a covered load of supplies. Ariock identified Choonhulm and a few others. He had made a point of meeting and remembering as many villagers as he could, although he still didn't know the name of every refugee.

Everyone paused when a vehicle whooshed past.

Then they resumed their hasty trek. The humans looked like uncertain Torth. They probably hated to stride without burdens while the ummin crew had to carry all their supplies.

Vy arranged the scratchy blanket over Ariock, trying to make him look less like a giant and more like a cartload of equipment. Her touches sent tingling thrills through him. He wanted her to keep doing it.

Weptolyso lumbered in front of everyone like an orange-gold beacon. Thomas floated next to the nussian, subtly directing him with hand signals. He hid on the other side of Weptolyso whenever he saw distant Torth or slaves.

At least he seemed to know where to go.

They emerged onto a mezzanine. Sunlight streamed between mountainous curved walls, terraced with mezzanines as complex as circuitry. Regular exits led to protruding causeway piers that glowed with power.

Those must be the launchpads.

And the squat, bullet-shaped masses resting on each launchpad must be spaceships.

Their iron-gray hulls absorbed light, pockmarked like meteorites that had endured centuries of radiation and space dust. They didn't mesh with the beauty of Torth engineering. They rested on four points, although a few balanced improbably on tripod legs.

Most of the ships on this tier were the size of jumbo jets. Farther down, the ships were even more huge, like enterprise cruise ships.

Ariock longed to touch the lumpy, scarred hull of a spaceship. These vessels had traveled farther than he could imagine. They had defended passengers against the harshest forces of the galaxy. He was fragile in comparison.

A bunch of Torth officials riding hoverbikes whizzed past Ariock.

Thomas had orbited to the other side of Weptolyso. At least the officials seemed incurious. But something was afoot. The distant sounds of traffic increased. Had the brainwashed Red Ranks been discovered?

Ariock spiked his awareness outward, just a small amount, just to catch what was happening. He wasn't going to attack anyone. But the blanket draped over him narrowed his field of view too much.

He sensed the approach of strangers.

Lots of them.

The refugees looked terrified but tried to hide it. A few ummins surreptitiously readied their blaster gloves.

Then...

Blaster shock waves flew past Ariock. He did not see them hit their targets, but he heard wet explosions and footsteps galloping away. Terrified slaves and guards fled along the mezzanine. Judging by their glowing collars, these slaves were not from his crew.

Ariock sensed a couple of life sparks gutter and die. Those must be Torth.

The refugees from Duin began to shout pleas in the slave tongue. Ariock got the gist of it. They were shouting that they were friendly and that the fleeing slaves should join them.

Thomas swore. He zoomed down the nearest pier. Soon he floated beneath the behemoth of a streamship, searching its hull for an access panel.

Everyone in the crew ran toward the streamship, struggling with their loads of supplies. Ariock took that as his cue that hiding no longer mattered. He stood straight and tossed the blanket aside. It caught on his arm spikes and hung there, giving him drapery, but he hardly noticed.

The headless remains of Red Ranks lay across the floor. Those Torth had not expected supposed slaves to whip out blaster gloves.

Ariock picked up one of the largest packs and hurried after Vy and his mother.

An immense sound avalanched throughout the spaceport. Thousands of steel gates slammed over the hangars, sealing them off. Another section slammed shut, and then another.

The whole spaceport shut down. Lights dimmed. Launchpads went dark. Walls closed like shutting eyelids and soundless mouths. The only light left was a few sunbeams from overhead.

Everyone inside was trapped.

"You almost done?" Vy asked Thomas, backing toward him.

The boy floated in front of a drop-down panel. He swiped icons, sweat beading on his face. "Um," he said.

"Will we be able to take off?" Vy positioned herself closer. Everyone crowded around Thomas's hoverchair underneath the streamship.

"With Ariock's power." Thomas's eyes seemed to burn like molten gold. "Probably." He was absorbed in his task.

Ariock touched the hull. It was as rough as it looked, embedded with pebbles and space dust.

He cautiously flexed his awareness into the hull. He sensed immense, solid strength. Here was a material that could withstand meteorite impacts.

Ominous rushing sounds came from the hazy depths of the spaceport.

Vy began to speak. "Ariock can—"

"No!" Thomas interrupted. "If he forces the hatch open, he'll damage the hull and wreck it for travel." He poked furiously at the console. "I just need another minute. I didn't expect this thing to have a cryptogram over—" He interrupted himself, frantic. "Ariock! Protect us!"

Ariock threw his awareness outward in all directions.

He expected to shield himself from a few microbullets. He did not expect the chaos of countless millions of projectiles coming at him from every direction. Tiny missiles zoomed through his extended self, faster than he could keep track of.

Supply packs began to explode. Water jars went flying, spraying their contents.

An ummin screamed in pain. Then another.

Ariock could not spare the enormous focus that healing required. He didn't examine who might be hurt. Catching all the projectiles was like trying to swat a swarm of gnats. They were too many, all moving too unpredictably.

He was bound to miss a few, no matter how fast he was.

As he struggled to shield himself, an armada of transports emerged from the emptiness below their deadened launchpad. The transports formed a kaleidoscope of moving shapes.

There were too many to count. They blocked the sunlight, so Ariock had to confront them in near darkness. He could hardly believe how coordinated the Torth fleet was. They flew as if they'd rehearsed and synchronized every motion.

Guns spiked out, all aimed toward Ariock.

He had no focus to spare, no time to turn around and see what Thomas was doing. He backed up against the hull. His body wasn't enough of a shield for the refugees beneath the streamship. Neither was Weptolyso.

All his life, Ariock had wanted to be smaller, but that didn't matter when his friends and his mother were in danger.

He tuned out the blasts and expanded his awareness to fill more of the air. He encompassed projectiles and metal and life sparks.

If he had to enfold the whole Torth fleet? So be it.

CHAPTER 4

COLOSSAL

The transports stopped moving as Ariock held the armada firmly within his awareness. They floated in midair as if frozen, not drifting even a little bit.

He inhabited their machinery and their empty spaces. He sensed life sparks within those spaces.

He tried to extinguish those life sparks. But he didn't know how to do it directly. Could he absorb them? Crush them? Crumple the machinery around them?

Now was not ideal for experimentation. He inhabited more vehicles than he could keep track of. Just as he could not control every hair on his body, he could not control every transport he encompassed.

He kept his shield firm against sizzling microbullets. Some Torth on the mezzanine were shooting at him. The slightest distraction would seal his doom.

Elephant-size blasts exploded at him.

One or two he could have handled, but the barrage made him throw his arms up and solidify enough air to shield his body. Transports jogged loose from his awareness. Others followed.

They were just too many for him to concentrate on at once.

A sound of static filled the air. Ariock looked up into sparkling blue fairy light. An immense holographic face, flabby and glowing, stared imperiously down in their general direction. He recognized the Upward Governess.

Red Ranks spoke in sync, or almost in sync, their voices raspy from lack of use. "B e t r a a a y e r."

They leaned out of transport windows or stood on terraces, all of them gazing toward Ariock and his crew in expressionless judgment. "W e g a a a v e y o u e v v v e r y t h i n g g g." The voices rasped from all directions. "A n d d d y o u s s s s t o l e f r o m U s s s s."

Thomas looked stricken, as if cornered by his worst enemies. Ariock guessed that he had tried to escape the Torth by avoiding the Megacosm. Now they were speaking to him out loud, to force him to listen to their nonsense.

"Y o u w i l l n e v v v e r e s s s c a p e."

"S s s s o d o n ' t b o t h e r t r y y y i n g."

The holograph of the Upward Governess looped like recorded playback. Even though she must be far away, and not live streaming, Ariock guessed that the spoken taunts originated from her.

The launchpad rocked from a missile blast.

They began to fall. Someone screamed. Ariock had to withdraw some of his awareness and shove the bulk of his focus into the pier, straightening it. He extended tendrils of air to catching life sparks—his refugee friends—before they could plummet to their deaths.

Half of the Red Ranks rasped from one direction, "A n d d d t h a t p l a a a n e t you c a a a r e s s s o much a b o u t t t . . ."

". . . E a r r r t h h h . . ." Whispers overlapped from another direction, giving a dynamic sound effect.

The rest joined in, cascading into a hurricane rasp that filled the spaceport. ". . . W e ' r e g o i n g t o i n n n v a a a d e i t a n d c o l l a r r r eve r y h h h u m a n you h a v e e v e r k n o w w w n ."

Despite Ariock's best effort to ignore the synced-up Torth voices, their threat seeped into his conscious mind.

It didn't matter how much Yeresunsa power he had. He was already failing to protect his small crew of friends. He could barely hold the launchpad together. He couldn't possibly do anything to save humankind.

He was nothing. He was no one, just a pathetic, helpless prisoner.

"Ariock!" Vy shouted in warning.

Ariock heard the shriek of a missile and raised an arm, sending his awareness rippling outward from it. He slammed the missile off course.

It smashed into a transport, sending that one careening into another. Both transports exploded in a rain of fiery shrapnel.

"That way!" Vy screamed, her voice so full of panic, it could only mean one thing. Ariock was being an idiot. The taunting voices had distracted him from something vitally important or dangerous.

He kept his awareness sunk into the launchpad, making sure it wouldn't fall apart. He glanced at Vy long enough to see where she was frantically pointing.

A bunch of Red Ranks flew down the pier toward him on hoverbikes.

Ariock had less than a half second to react. He remembered that if any Torth got close enough to read his mind, they could disable him with a pain seizure. They could soak up his every instinct and idea and plan for exactly what he would do next.

If they got within range.

Ariock had no fully formed idea of how to stop them, but he slammed a shock wave toward them.

The Red Ranks smashed into his rushing wall of air and went spinning off their bikes. They flailed as they tumbled off the pier.

The Torth Empire never paused to mourn their dead. Ariock was aware of Red Ranks crowding every nearby terrace. Their gunfire and missiles never ceased.

They rushed onto nearby piers. They balanced atop transports. They were everywhere, in armor, with huge blaster guns on their arms, coordinated as only mind readers could be.

One of the refugees screamed in pain or terror.

Ariock could not afford to withdraw his focus to check on his crew. He had to hold the launchpad in place. He had to fend off the increasing barrage.

"How's it going, Thomas?" Vy had an edge of terror in her voice, although Ariock figured no one else heard that. She was brave enough to hide her fears.

Thomas growled in frustration, hidden behind refugees and supply packs.

That makeshift barrier couldn't last. Blasts pummeled Ariock's air shield. More Red Ranks zoomed toward him.

They weren't going to allow him a second to rest or recover. The blasts and bullets never stopped. He was overwhelmed. He couldn't continue to shield himself while holding the launchpad together while throwing Red Ranks off their hoverbikes while shielding his friends. One mistake would be fatal.

It was too much.

He was going to fail.

His life was a meaningless tombstone built on graves. All the innocent villagers who had not escaped Duin. His father. The friends and refugees he had promised to protect. No one ever should have risked their lives to save him. He was so useless.

He didn't want to be this pathetic.

Ariock threw himself into the chaos, away from his human self. He didn't want to hold it all together anymore. Rage boiled through him, the bloodlust he had known in the prison arena.

Part of his mind remained tethered to his body, keeping his lungs breathing and his legs and spine locked in place, so his core remained upright and alive.

The rest of him expanded to fill everything in sight.

He was the air.

He was the darkness.

Thousands of ships and transports became his bodily organs.

He slid his arms into the massive walls that encircled the spaceport.

Launchpads, terraces, bridges, docks, and walkways became his many fingers.

Bluish electricity snapped along the wires that had become his nervous system. Webs of electricity spiraled off him and slammed into transports.

When he flexed his metal shoulders, piers and bridges rippled and broke.

Torth fell, screaming, to their deaths. They tumbled downward through the immense hollow center of himself, grabbing for help and finding nothing. Bodies broke on the hulls of transports.

Alien pulses of energy screamed inside him. Hundreds of those life sparks winked out.

The giant was aware that he might have been human at one time. He didn't care.

He took a step toward the enemies who threatened his core body, and the mountainous walls moved with him, wrenching themselves, screaming, in new directions.

The gunfire intensified.

So the giant gathered air and flung it into a funnel, sucking everything downward. He tore launchpads off walls with savage glee. Tons of heavy machines spilled down the chasm in his center.

He shredded piers and hurled their twisted metal carcasses down, along all the other debris he crushed.

One wall of the spaceport began to sag, letting in extra rays of sunlight.

His inhuman mouth formed words. "DIE, TORTH." The force of his breath ripped struts off walls, sending transports crashing into each other.

The distant core of his body registered screams that didn't quite sound like Torth screams, but they were small. Trivial.

All that mattered was death to his enemies. Triumph, or else he was dead.

CHAPTER 5
EXCESSIVE WRECKAGE

The whole pier was coming apart, twisting as if alive. The entire spaceport seemed to have taken on a monstrous life of its own.

Vy clung to the tilting launchpad. Ummins went sliding toward one edge, scrabbling to hold on, catching supply packs and wincing from explosive gunfire. The whole streamship might topple at any second. When it did, it would either crush the refugees or knock them off the ledge. Probably both.

Only one person seemed unafraid.

Ariock stood on the crazily tipped launchpad, unmindful of the massive falling objects, the screaming Torth, the whirlwinds, the webs of lightning, the flying cables, snapped piers, explosions, and millions of broken things flying through the air.

He must be controlling the chaos.

Actually, Vy was unsure if *control* was the right word. Ariock stood amid the destruction like a colossus, the only steady thing in sight, his eyes practically glowing with intensity. When he raised his massive fists, lighting arced between his arm spikes and zigzagged off his fingers toward the guns.

Torth got knocked off their seats. They fell, screaming, clawing the air as they tumbled out of sight.

The air seemed to breathe, to gather itself into a whirlwind. Delia screamed something, but Vy could not hear her over the monstrous, inhuman roar that formed words.

DIIIE. TORRRRTH.

It rolled through the spaceport like thunder.

A scrap of metal whizzed past Vy and embedded itself into a supply pack instead of her body.

"I'm afraid for him." Delia clutched Vy, but she was busy staring at her son with terrified wonder. "Is he really controlling all this?"

Ariock stepped forward. Just a single step, but when his foot touched the floor, a long moan built, echoing up the endless walls, to the metal bridges and platforms above. Launchpads wrenched at crazy angles, spilling ships. Walkways ripped apart. Transports crushed each other. Debris flew, and another spinning chunk of shrapnel whizzed in front of Vy, missing her nose by inches.

She didn't see how they could possibly blast off in this chaos, especially considering the severely damaged launchpad and the teetering ship.

Did Thomas have a brilliant plan to get them out of this death zone? Vy risked a glance and saw him madly swiping icons on the console. Weptolyso held the hoverchair steady, shielding the boy with his pebbly body.

"He's out in the open. We need to protect him." Delia crawled toward her son.

"Are you crazy?" Vy wanted to grab Delia, to haul her back, but she dared not expose herself to the hailstorm of shrieking debris.

One of the massive walls began to slowly lean inward. All the bridges attached to it buckled, then snapped like twigs. Sunlight illuminated a world of dust and ruination.

"Delia!" Vy yelled. "Come back!"

Her shouts merged with deafening chaos.

"You can't expect him to protect you while he's doing this!" Vy yelled. As far as she could tell, Ariock must be holding the launchpad aloft through sheer force of will.

Ariock deliberately raised his palms, and steel struts broke with a sound like gigantic bones snapping. An avalanche of spacecrafts crashed into each other, then fell in a jumble of tortured metal. They took down the remaining transports.

A spinning metal scrap, as sharp as a circular saw blade, rocketed toward Delia from above. Vy saw what it would do. She had time to understand, but not enough time to shout a warning.

The metal disk whisked through Delia and stuck in the causeway platform.

It left Delia severed in two parts, connected by geysering blood. She was skewered in place. She tried to crawl forward, as if she had not even realized that her lower body was disconnected from the upper half.

The whole world seemed to be unraveling. Ships slid off the remaining launchpads, screeching. Thuds and clanks resounded as they landed. The bottom of the spaceport must be piled high with millions of tons of wreckage and crushed corpses.

Only one launchpad—theirs—remained attached to the wall.

It began to tilt downward, moving as the wall buckled. Refugees screamed as they clung to the edge. One tumbled into the abyss, screaming and flailing.

Vy threw herself toward Delia and hoped gravity still worked well enough to make her land in the right place.

She ended up next to the injured patient, and she wasted no time. She bunched up Delia's ragged shirt in an effort to stanch the blood geyser. The rags got soaked. Nothing she could do. This patient needed triage, but Vy lacked equipment or bandages or assistance.

"ARIOCK!" she bellowed.

The floor plummeted. For a sickening instant, Vy was sure they were all dead and nothing she did mattered.

Then the floor jerked flat.

Vy had no spare focus to wonder why or how. She took the opportunity to survey the damage to Delia and to try to mentally fit her back together again. Never mind cancer. This was critically severe. She had to figure out how to keep Delia alive long enough for a miracle.

"Ariock," she begged.

The colossal wreckage died down. Without explosions and demolition, Vy heard Delia's weak whisper. "...take care of him."

Vy was sticky with blood, but she made herself sound definite. "Stay with us."

She sensed the warmth of a large presence behind her. Ariock must be close by. Vy braced herself, half certain that his eyes would be glowing with power and devoid of humanity.

But no. He looked human, and horror-stricken as he stared at his impaled mother.

Something distant and huge collapsed. Its dying mutters haunted the ruined spaceport.

"Heal her!" Vy demanded.

"I..." Ariock sounded like he was having trouble thinking of adequate words. "I'm holding the platform together."

"Oh," Vy said, realizing how much strain he must be under.

Ariock eyed the twisted metal disk that had severed his mother in two halves. He seemed to consider it. Then he knelt, holding his hands over her in the healing pose. "Hang on to something."

The only thing close enough for Vy to hang on to was Ariock himself. She grabbed the metal spike jutting out from one of his colossal arms.

The launchpad plunged, tipping them over a gigantic mass grave. Vy lost her footing. She clung to the spike, which was shaped like a lightning bolt, giving her enough metal to clutch with both hands.

At the same time, the air beneath Ariock's hands shimmered, like a thousand invisible, writhing snakes.

The metal disk that bisected Delia wrenched itself out of the causeway. It fell into the abyss, bloodied, while Delia herself got sucked upward as if magnetized. The two halves of her broken body fit together.

But her skin was as white as her hair. She had lost too much blood.

Her head hung down, as if her neck was boneless.

Vy could see the valiant attempt that Ariock was making. He wanted to spur his mother's body to knit together, to heal the severed arteries and muscles and bones. But the damage was catastrophic. It was beyond his power, the same way he could not resurrect missing fingers or muscles that had never existed.

Delia was dead.

A refugee nearly plummeted off the edge of the precariously tilted launchpad. Another caught her and begged her to hold on.

The streamship slid. The crew—her friends—shouted in terror.

"Stop!" Vy shouted.

Ariock looked agonized. The launchpad tipped upright, wobbling in a drunken way.

But Ariock wasn't done. He held his hands out with a look of intense focus, fixated on his mother's broken corpse.

Everyone screamed as the platform dropped again.

"You can't save her!" Vy clung to Ariock's arm spike. She hated herself for being so blunt, for saying something so awful. But someone needed to make Ariock focus on the living.

"She's dead," Vy said.

Ariock's face was grim with superhuman focus. Invisible snakes writhed over Delia's remains.

"Ariock?" Vy begged. "I want to live. Please? Help?"

That seemed to stop him.

The causeway righted itself, although it remained warped and broken in many places. The ship settled on the launchpad, although it was off-kilter.

Ariock remained kneeling by his mother's broken corpse.

"I should have…" Ariock trailed off, then tried again. "I could have protected her, if I'd been better at…" He seemed at a loss.

"It wasn't your fault." Vy was afraid to loosen her grip on his arm spike, just in case the whole launchpad collapsed. She risked letting go with one hand so she could touch his massive arm. She wanted to remind him that he had protected most of the rest of them from certain death. He was still protecting them.

Dust sparkled in the sunlight that filtered down through the ruination.

But in the far distance, there was an ominous sound. It was like a lot of fast-moving airborne traffic.

"We can't linger here," Thomas called from the shadows. "The Torth will send a bigger army with better weapons. We need to take off."

"Another army?" Weptolyso sounded disbelieving.

"A fresh one," Thomas affirmed. "As fast as they can muster more Red Ranks. I don't want to find out what kind of weapons they'll try out."

Vy scrambled to Delia. She was still facedown. There was no time for a memorial service or a burial. No time to say goodbye, really.

She held her fingers to Delia's neck, as if to check for a pulse. It was a symbolic gesture.

"I'm sorry, Delia," Vy said. "You will be missed."

There was much more to say, but no time. Delia Dovanack had survived cancer, single motherhood, and slavery. She had done her best to protect her sole surviving family member. She had deserved a better ending—something less bloody and violent.

"I'm sorry," Thomas said.

Ariock was clearly undecided about how to handle his mother's body. He shrugged off the remaining shreds of the blanket wrapped around his huge shoulders and tried to use it to wrap her up.

"We have to leave," Vy urged him.

Ariock pushed himself to his feet. He was a towering colossus, impossible to ignore. Every line of his body seemed to droop, weighed down by sorrow.

"Do you need me to tear the hatch open?" Ariock asked.

"Nope!" Thomas looked terrified by the idea. "Nope, I got it."

Indeed, a curved platform unfurled from the underside of the ship. It must be some kind of high-tech elevator or lift.

The traffic sounds grew louder. That was the hum of many engines.

"Everyone aboard!" Thomas yelled. "Ariock, come on. And hold the launchpad in place. We'll need your power to blast off."

Vy wanted to help Ariock wrap up his mother's body, but there was no time for a dignified send-off. "I'm sorry." It was all she could think to say. She touched his arm.

Ariock hesitated, gazing down at his mother's body.

"We have to leave," Vy said.

Refugees crowded onto the lifter, shouldering the remaining supply packs. They disappeared into the ship in groups. Thomas went with them, and soon lights began to turn on inside the ship, reflected on the warped and cracked floor of the launchpad.

Sunlight dimmed as transports streamed into the ruined spaceport. They descended with enormous guns pointed downward.

At Ariock.

"The ship's hull is all that can protect you," Vy remembered. She pulled Ariock's arm. "Come on!"

Their launchpad would not survive another round of destruction. None of them would, except perhaps for Ariock.

He lingered, clearly torn about what to do.

"Do you want us to die?" Vy asked him.

Ariock gave her a look.

"We're dead unless you come with us." Vy emphasized each word. "We have to leave."

"Get in here, Ariock!" Thomas's shout came from inside the ship, full of urgency. "We can't take off without you!"

The lowered lifter was an invitation to climb aboard. Vy tugged Ariock, trying to make him move.

Ariock seemed to come to a decision. He abandoned his mother's body and strode toward the ship. The half-ruined launchpad trembled, and Vy knew that he must be having trouble holding it all together.

She hurried to catch up with him.

Ariock lifted Vy in both hands and placed her on the lifter platform. A fresh volley of blasts rocked the launchpad. Debris jumped. Explosions cratered the inert remains of Delia.

Vy thought that Ariock would quit and abandon the rest of them. "I'm sorry," she whispered.

But Ariock must have an inner reserve of strength. Despite the carnage, despite the accidental death of his mother, he understood that his living friends needed him. Perhaps he recalled his promise to protect them or die trying.

He joined Vy on the lifter, shielding her from shock waves.

They left his mother's covered body behind. The lifter brought Vy and Ariock into a tidy, glowing interior that was crowded with their refugee friends.

CHAPTER 6

BLAST OFF

Ariock found himself standing amid snow-white cushions and glass sculptures. The interior of the streamship was round, clean, and orderly. It was the opposite of the wreckage outside.

Refugees watched him, probably for signs of aggression. A few clung to each other. They knew that he did not belong amid delicate, breakable furniture. The domed ceiling was only tall enough for him near the center. Otherwise he had to tilt his head.

His mother might have asked him to sit down. But she was dead. He had sensed her utter absence of a life spark.

He just didn't have enough room in his thoughts for the shame of being too tall. Part of his awareness remained in the battered pier, where the launchpad was barely attached. He needed to keep the broken ground level. Otherwise the ship and everyone aboard would plunge into the abyss.

So he was partly steel. He did not dare think about the atrocity he had caused. Not yet. He had to remain strong.

"Ariock?" Thomas floated in front of an arc of holographic displays, selecting his way through glowing menus. "I'm going to need you to direct an electromagnetic pulse into our launchpad when I tell you to."

Ariock stared at the boy. Thomas should be afraid, like everyone else. Was he hiding his emotions? Probably.

At the very least, Thomas must sense how clueless Ariock was about electromagnetic pulses.

"Electromagnetic pulses are just a certain type of…" Thomas gave Ariock a resentful glance, as if he was an idiot. "Never mind." He tapped rapidly through menus. "Just get ready to generate electric energy. I know you're capable. We saw you tear those cables down and redirect their electricity."

Ariock noticed that a few of the refugees were bruised or bloody. One was tying makeshift bandages around another.

Had he caused that?

He remembered the metal scrap that had severed his mother in half. That was not how she'd deserved to die. If the Torth had accidentally blasted her to death, he might have understood. She had gotten too close to their main target—Ariock.

He should have noticed her. He should have used his powers to push her back to relative safety.

Instead, he had torn the spaceport apart with little regard for anyone else.

He had crushed vehicles and terraces and sent the scraps flying, and he had not even noticed the life sparks of his friends.

He had not even noticed when he accidentally killed his own mother.

What kind of monster—

Their ship plummeted. There was a mad scramble as refugees tried to protect each other. Ariock spiked his awareness outward, realizing that he had gotten distracted by his own thoughts.

He inhabited the ultrastrong hull. He ignored explosions against his hull self and reexamined his levitation of the launchpad. How long did he need to hold it up for?

"Keep us steady!" Thomas snapped.

It was far too easy for Ariock to get distracted. Every time his attention wavered even a little bit, he forgot exactly what he needed to hold, and where. A prolonged distraction would send them plummeting to the mountain of ruination below.

Perhaps he should pour even more of himself into the launchpad?

No. Nothing was worth the risk of losing control again. Next time he might kill Vy by accident, or Thomas.

He needed to stay at least somewhat small. He needed to remember who he was.

"I'm doing my best," Ariock said. His human voice sounded faraway to himself.

Thomas selected holographic icons as fast as his atrophied limbs would allow. "Vy? Hit that blue symbol for me."

He went on, commanding Vy as he worked. The adolescent ummin pilot, Varktezo, stood attentive on Thomas's other side. Soon Thomas gave orders to that one in the slave tongue.

The brassy wall flickered, then shifted to glassy transparency. The crew stared wildly at a fresh armada of transports outside.

"Oh, good." Thomas sounded pleased. "I wasn't sure where the setting for that was."

A fiery explosion hit the dome. It looked volcanic, but there was no heat, no shock wave. It felt almost like watching an explosion on TV.

The hull must have shielded them.

"We're taking damage." Thomas's fingers danced through geometric Torth glyphs. "They're trying to weaken our hull. It's fine for now, but we'll have a problem if they drop a nuke on us or anything of that caliber."

A nuke?

Ariock did not want to imagine fending off a nuclear bomb. He wasn't sure if he was that strong. It seemed unlikely.

He had failed when it mattered most.

He had tried to recreate the life spark in Delia, or at least to reignite an ember. But reversing death, or creating new life, might be impossible for him. He had limits.

And he was still a clumsy oaf.

He had accidentally killed her. His own mother.

"Ten seconds till launch," Thomas stated. "Ariock, energize the launchpad."

Ariock would have asked questions, but all his concentration was on holding the remnants of the pier together and bracing for each explosion.

"And clear a path overhead." Thomas's voice turned squeaky with panic. "Do it now! Right now!"

Ariock wanted to explain that his attention was already split and wavering. He had a lot on his mind. He didn't want to go titanic again and risk hurting his friends. He couldn't think how to describe how it felt to cradle the launchpad the way he had cradled his mother's dead body.

"Forget gentleness!" Thomas screamed at him. "Be a monster or we're all dead!"

So Ariock poured all his awareness into the platform below their ship.

It required all his concentration to refrain from spiraling farther outward. He sensed circuitry and wiring, and he overloaded it with as much power as he could give.

Thomas flipped a switch.

The padded floor gave Ariock such a hard shove, he completely lost his connection. He slammed entirely into his body, which now felt weirdly fragile. All he could do was brace himself as he flattened painfully against the floor.

Thomas wheezed. He began to speak.

And Ariock remembered that he was supposed to clear their path to freedom. A battalion of transports blocked the sky. He shoved his awareness upward and outward. He was the wind, the metal, the missiles, the vehicles...

Too many things to stay human.

Ariock narrowed his focus, horrified by how close he'd come to becoming a monstrous titan. He needed to stay cognizant of his friends.

Rather than shoving his awareness into everything within the vicinity of the spaceport, he closed his eyes and gently pushed aside the transports in their way.

Vehicles and chunks of debris tumbled into the mass grave.

Meanwhile, their streamship rocketed into daylight like a bullet streaking from a gun. The ship trembled from forces beyond Ariock's awareness.

Far below, ribbons of traffic looped around the city's outskirts. Clouds lay thick in one direction, like a blanket of cotton snug against the land.

It took Ariock a few moments to realize that he no longer needed to hold together a launchpad, or fend off explosions or microbullets, or energize anything, or shield people, or try to heal death.

At long last, Ariock allowed himself to be fully human.

He sank his head into his hands. His sinking feeling had nothing to do with the ship's speed.

He had failed in the worst way possible. During their sneaky trek along the mezzanine, he had inwardly vowed to not let any more innocent people die. Five minutes later? He had trashed that vow. Not only had he let his mother die, but he had nearly let all his friends slide into an abyss while he tore the spaceport apart.

The only reason he'd protected them at all was because of a vestigial instinct to protect his core self, his mortal body.

He could not trust himself with the power he had.

"Are we safe?" Kessa asked.

"Not until we get through the nearest temporal stream," Thomas said in a grim tone, swiping icons on the holograph. "We, uh, might be in for a rough ride."

The aqua emptiness of the sky overhead gradated into a summer blue.

Beyond that blueness was the rest of the galaxy. Countless worlds like this one, and like Earth, were surveilled or colonized by the Torth Empire.

Vy's soft voice filled the silence. "They said they're going to enslave Earth."

"We can't control the Torth Empire." Thomas spoke without looking away from his work. "Let's stay focused on our own problems."

Ariock inwardly agreed with Thomas. He had the power to murder a spaceport full of people—maybe even a city—but mass murder wasn't heroic.

And it didn't seem to really faze the Torth. Why should it? They had trillions of loyal citizens, and they probably owned quadrillions of dedicated slaves and guards.

He couldn't win a fight against all that.

Immense power just made him a useless danger to everyone. It seemed the Torth had been right to sentence him to death.

"Crap," Thomas said, staring down toward the hazy horizon, where a V formation of drone-like black shuttles rocketed toward them.

Missiles popped out from their hulls.

"Ariock," Thomas said in a tone that was almost conversational, "I'm going to need you to take care of those for us."

CHAPTER 7

A FLAME INSIDE THE SUN

Ariock knew that he could take control of wind currents and knock the incoming missiles aside. No problem. Except...

In order to do so, he would need to inhabit at least a mile of empty air.

He would have to become the size of a spaceport. Again.

Unlike rock or metal, air really encouraged his subconscious titanic self to expand. Air felt limitless. And then he might cause tornadoes just by breathing.

What if he lost track of his human core and forgot whom he was protecting?

"Ariock." Thomas sounded tense. He pointed upward. "They're coming at us from all directions."

Sure enough, distant objects marred the twilight sky above. They grew fast in apparent size. A hailstorm of missiles was coming.

"Didn't you say the Torth would try to take you alive?" Vy asked Thomas, staring at the barrage racing toward them.

"They're trying to wear down my protector," Thomas explained. "They want Ariock to deplete his power."

"Is that possible?" Vy asked worriedly.

"I guess," Thomas said, impatient. "At the very least, they can exhaust him to the point where he'll make mistakes. Or miss something. Ariock! We won't survive a collision!"

Ariock touched the invisible wall, a physical reminder of where he was. His fingertips might keep him tethered to his human self.

Outside, the daylight was a dusky indigo. It was almost too serene to be real.

During the spaceport battle, the Torth could have—maybe should have—obliterated Ariock with bombs. They probably had nuclear missiles. Instead, they had sent hundreds of Red Ranks to try to disable him with the inhibitor serum.

Deaths were just a game to the Torth Majority.

This was playtime.

The wrecked spaceport was barely visible anymore. Rare Moonrise MetroHub glinted like a splinter in the desert. But the mangled pieces of his mother were buried in that wreckage.

Ariock took a deep breath and tried to expel his fury at the Torth. He needed to stay in control of his emotions, not spike out in rage.

Cautiously, gently, he sent his awareness outward. He expanded into the hull. Then he passed it, sending focus into wind and vapor and sunlight.

He stretched farther. He became airy and vast. But not too vast. It seemed safest to be conservative and not too gigantic, even if that meant intercepting missiles at the last second.

Projectiles shrieked through his airy self. They were on a trajectory toward his core self.

Ariock knew from experience that he had trouble splitting his focus in too many ways. Could he get rid of the missiles in one massive sweep?

He rolled air together. If there had been any clouds in the cloudless sky, they would have roiled into a vortex. He compressed the air, forming what he suspected would be an immense thunderbolt.

He released his thunder.

Air exploded outward in a shock wave that batted missiles away from his core self. The air lit up with fiery explosions.

He would have liked to watch the destructive fireworks display, but it seemed prudent to shield the racing vessel that contained his core self. He rolled air pressure into a tube around the ship. He funneled air to push them higher.

They roared upward.

"Smart," Thomas said with warm approval. "Good job, Ariock."

Ariock withdrew his awareness back to the bubble of life support that contained his human body. Maybe he should feel proud.

But the loss of his mother weighed on his mind. His failure felt like a storm cloud sinking to engulf him.

How could anyone trust him? How could he trust himself?

Despite their escape velocity, he felt a dark certainty that they weren't racing toward safety. They might be heading into a trap. *Failure*, his inner mind whispered at him. *You are always a failure.*

Thomas glanced toward him, frowning with concern. "You're not a failure, Ariock," he said. "That's what the Torth Empire wants you to believe. They're trying to peel away your self-respect. Don't let them do it."

Brilliant electricity webbed across their faux-glass dome.

"It's not Ariock," Thomas said quickly, seeing the fearful refugees. "It's ionization caused by the friction of our speed in the upper atmosphere. We're heading into orbit."

Lightning scribbled afterimages into Ariock's vision. The streamship rattled alarmingly.

"Hold on to something," Thomas said, just as the floor dropped away.

Ariock couldn't figure out how he was both falling and hurtling upward at the same time. He puffed out his awareness to enfold their ship in an even more protective shield.

People shouted in fearful astonishment, floating.

The world of Umdalkdul spread out below them like a massive marble. It appeared to be rolling slowly away from them.

"I can see the edges of the world." Kessa gazed at her planet with a mixture of awe and sadness.

In the opposite direction, stars appeared like chips of ice. It had been a bright noonday, but now it was night.

Vy touched the dome. "How does the view look so real?"

"Think of it as high definition." Thomas waved through holographic menus as he half floated out of his hoverchair. "Crap. Can someone please— oh, never mind." He sounded relieved.

Ariock fell hard.

The gravity increased, until he worried that the floor might crack under his weight.

Abruptly, he was floating again. He searched for a way to anchor himself, but it turned out to be pointless, as he fell a second time.

"Oops." Thomas sounded embarrassed. "Artificial gravity needed calibration. Sorry about that."

Vy sat up. She looked disheveled, and Ariock had a stupid, shameful wish that she would have fallen on top of him instead of nearby.

"How many piloting experiences did you soak up?" Vy asked Thomas.

"Plenty," Thomas said with an acidic tone. "But there's a difference between firsthand experience and casual thirdhand absorption. Plus, there are hundreds of different models of streamship, and I only learned the rudiments of… Never mind." He seemed to give up on explaining. "You're going to have to be satisfied with an amateur. Be grateful that I can calculate hyperluminal vertices and orthogonal photometrics without aid from the Megacosm. Otherwise we'd be screwed."

Vy gave him a wary look.

Ariock inwardly felt wary around Thomas, too. The boy was not quite a teenager, not quite a Torth, but he seemed to be more than the sum of those parts.

"How is it nighttime?" Kessa asked with amazement.

Ariock saw wonderment on the face of every former slave. They had been told about space travel, but without the internet or books or films, they'd only had an abstract idea of what it entailed.

"It's always nighttime between worlds," Thomas said. "Cold and empty." He looked so grim, he might be talking about something more personal than the universe.

Kessa translated what he'd said to the slave tongue. The refugees listened with rapt attention.

"What are those?" Vy pointed.

Enormous industrial complexes floated in space. They looked like triangles melded into each other, all slick angles and stark shadows. Pipes and protrusions roughened their surfaces. Each detail looked crisp, no matter the distance, undistorted by any atmospheric haze.

"Industrial plantations," Thomas said. "With some military capabilities."

Ariock watched in dismay as missiles emerged from the plantations. Millions of missiles.

"At least they're far away." Vy was trying to be brave.

"Well, they might have time to catch up," Thomas said grimly. "And there's time to block us." He pointed ahead, to the enormity of the moons. Each moon was webbed with cities.

"Can we, uh, take a different route?" Vy asked.

"Our only chance of escape is to make it to the temporal stream." Thomas tapped icons on the control panel. "The entrance is like an invisible moving ribbon in deep space. They require precise calculations in order to enter without dying."

"What's a temporal stream?" Ariock asked. He thought he could guess. It sounded like a wormhole.

"It's a wormhole," Thomas said. "They're like unseen currents in spacetime, like underwater rivers in the ocean."

Their streamship seemed to be gaining speed. They traveled toward what looked like nothingness.

"It will take us six hours to get there," Thomas said. "At top speed." He swiped icons and selected from menus. "There. I've cloaked our ship. Unfortunately, that won't do us much good. The Torth have plenty of instrumentation to detect us."

Kessa stared at the urbanized moons. "They won't need instrumentation," she said. "Not if they can detect Ariock's sphere of influence." She gave Thomas a pointed look. "And yours."

"Not mine," Thomas said. "They can't detect me at all, as long as I'm within the same solar system as Ariock. He eclipses every lesser Yeresunsa inside his sphere." Thomas held his fingers an inch apart. "If I'm a flame, then Ariock is the sun." He spread his arms wide. "You can't see a flame when it's inside the sun."

The analogy made Ariock uncomfortable. Thomas seemed eager to erase his own power—almost happy about it.

But surely he didn't want his identity to be engulfed or erased? He was probably more powerful than he gave himself credit for.

"I don't have any power right now," Thomas said happily, perhaps responding to Ariock's thoughts. "I got hit with the inhibitor."

It took a moment for Ariock to process the implications. Thomas had been hit during the spaceport battle.

"Are you hurt?" Ariock scanned the boy for problems.

"Nah, I'm fine." Thomas held out his arm, displaying several pinprick dots of blood. "I just got dosed with about two dozen microdarts."

Ariock wished he had focused on shielding his friends rather than killing Torth. He should have made protection his priority.

"You couldn't have shielded me while doing everything else you were doing," Thomas told him. "It's all right. Anyway, a lot of those microdarts were aimed at me, not just you."

Ariock doubted that. Not if Thomas was a flame and he was the sun.

"If we can cloak our ship," Vy said, "can they?" She gazed at the distant ships, or drones, or whatever they were. The spiky ones had an ominous look.

"Of course," Thomas said. "The Torth excel in optics. They can turn their soldier ships invisible, more or less. There must be thousands of swarm shuttles we're not seeing."

Ariock hoped Thomas was exaggerating.

Vy eyed the control panel. "Can we detect them with radar or something?"

"No," Thomas said. "We're in a luxury vessel, not a military vessel. Loyal Torth who are plugged into the Megacosm get all the updates. We don't." He quirked a humorless grin. "They wouldn't want to give solo Torth too much individual power. That's why vessels like this are low on instrumentation. If every Torth had the capability to blast free of the Torth Empire, there might be more renegades. Like me."

Kessa looked interested.

Ariock had questions, but he was distracted. Ships were amassing in their route. The sight gave him a sense of dread.

"Ariock," Thomas said. "You're going to need to protect us for the next six hours." He nodded toward the enemy fleet. "Spread your awareness as much as you possibly can." He made a weak fist with his underdeveloped hand. "Kill any life sparks that you sense."

CHAPTER 8

GENTLE

No one else seemed to understand how frighteningly easy it was for Ariock to kill. Or how hard it could be to stop.

"What if those ships have slaves?" Ariock asked pointedly.

Thomas gave him a look. "They're mostly Red Ranks, I'm sure."

Mostly. Thomas didn't sound certain. And even if they were all murderous Torth, there must be more than a thousand—too many for Ariock to pay individual attention to.

He remembered Red Ranks flailing as they fell to their deaths. He suspected those military ranks had been coerced into battle, the same way Thomas had been coerced into torturing Cherise and sentencing Ariock to death.

"I've killed enough people today," Ariock decided.

Thomas gave him an incredulous, outraged look.

"I'll push them back." Ariock reached out with his awareness, skipping across miles of vacuum where nothing existed. He sensed microscopic puffs of dust, barely there. Nothing big. Nothing threatening.

Thomas's voice became insignificant as Ariock unraveled further. He contained miles. Millions of miles?

Billions of miles?

He had no way to measure the distance.

At last, his expanded awareness encountered tiny capsules. They seemed tiny, but he guessed that each one was actually as large as the streamship where his core self sat. They might as well be as minuscule and delicate as his skin cells. He barely felt them.

Life pulsed inside each tiny capsule.

He could not discern whether each electric spark was a bug, a Torth, a slave, or some other type of alien. They were so little. So fragile.

Insignificant voices chattered near his core self. Friends. Ariock heard snatches of conversation. He even considered joining in, to assure Vy and Thomas that gentleness would not wear him down or lead to power depletion. He felt fine.

His awareness drifted across space, vacuous and relaxed.

He rolled, collecting dust and vapors and heat and life sparks. His motion counteracted the tiny propulsion of the tiny capsules. Those ships were stronger than their puny size implied.

But Ariock was stronger.

He pushed them as gently as possible. If he shoved too hard, he might crush them by accident. He took his time, sweeping them aside until they were a great distance away.

Then he withdrew and drifted elsewhere, searching for more.

He found more within moments. He did it again. And again.

"Ariock?"

The voice sounded tentative and faraway. Ariock tuned her out. There were always more ships to push away.

But then she touched his arm.

He was so surprised, he slammed all the way back into his human body. That was as shocking as an unexpected fall. After engulfing endless miles of space, he felt vulnerable and fragile, downright tiny.

Everyone looked wary of him. Scared.

Only Vy stood nearby. Since Ariock sat on the floor, she was at his eye level, her gaze fixed on him as if no one else in the universe mattered.

"You were making things float." She gestured around. "By accident."

"Oh." Ariock's mouth felt dry. When he shifted, he felt like he was ungluing himself. His whole body was stiff and achy.

Vy offered him a gourd canteen. "Want a drink? You've been sitting in the same position for hours."

The view outside was different. They had left the industrial behemoths behind, and they had sailed past the moons.

"Thanks." Ariock sipped from the canteen. "How long was I…" He didn't know how to describe his power usage. "…in a Yeresunsa trance?"

"Six hours," she said.

He must have looked stunned, because Vy gave him a deeply concerned look. "Are you all right?"

Ariock flexed. His aches were fading fast.

Every fantasy novel he'd ever read put a painful price on using magic. But he had managed to stay upright and functional the whole time, and he felt…

"I'm fine," he said. "A little tired, I guess."

But he used to feel the same mental fatigue after staring out his sky-room window, watching the shadows under pine trees for signs of human movement. Protecting their ship wasn't any harder than that.

The depletion headache he'd experienced after his crucifixion must have been caused by the inhibitor serum.

"You saved us." Vy touched his arm again. "You've been protecting us, all this time."

Her touch was light, but somehow, it consumed all of Ariock's attention. He gazed down at her slender, pale hand. She must be forcing herself to touch him.

"Thank you," Vy said. "You're doing a better job than everyone expected. Even Thomas, I think."

It was painfully obvious that she was just being polite. She must be afraid to be blunt about his failure to protect his mother.

"It's all right." Ariock gently picked up her hand and moved it away.

Vy looked baffled for a moment. Then she looked offended. "You can't blame yourself for what happened in the spaceport. Those deaths weren't you. Those were the Torth."

Ariock met her gaze. "Did I kill anyone else, besides my mom?" he asked, in a blunt way that she couldn't possibly dodge or sugarcoat. "I see how the refugees keep looking at me. They're afraid."

He expected Vy to make excuses.

Instead, she gazed at him with fierce eyes. "Okay," she said in a tone of admission. "Two of our refugee friends fell in the spaceport battle. Your mom and two others. But none were your fault."

Did she honestly believe that?

Ariock inwardly decided to learn the names of the refugees who had died because of his clumsy battle lust. Those victims must have felt honored to travel with the so-called Bringer of Hope. Now? Their surviving friends probably wished that they had stayed in their doomed village.

The village that he had doomed.

"Ariock." Vy squeezed his arm. "You're the only reason we're not all dead or enslaved." She squeezed harder. "You realize that, right?"

She clearly expected an answer, but Ariock couldn't bring himself to agree. How could anyone forgive what he'd done?

"Kessa," Vy called. "Help me tell Ariock that he saved us."

The elderly ummin had been lounging on a couch, chatting with a few refugees. She excused herself and paced over to them.

Ariock expected her to give him a stiffly formal congratulations, hiding her unease and resentment.

"We owe you our lives." Kessa removed her head cover, a gesture of deep respect. "Everyone here agrees."

At least she didn't call him the Bringer of Hope.

"You have made it safe to have hope." Kessa's smile made her whole face crinkle. She put her head cover back on and included Vy in her gaze. "When I look at you, I see friends. I do not see Torth, even for an instant."

"Sorry to break up your little party," Thomas said, "but we're not free yet. Ariock, I still need your help."

Ariock shifted closer to Thomas, wary yet secretly relieved to escape from undeserved admiration.

"What do you need?" Vy asked Thomas. "We just have to get through the temporal stream. Right?"

"*Just.*" Thomas said with sarcastic scorn. "Here's the problem." He flicked icons along a pedestal. A cobweb holograph appeared above the pedestal, with sparkles flowing along its strands. "Temporal streams are a network. They connect the galaxy. Our goal is to get to a frontier that's less well monitored than the hub planets. Any way we go, we'll need to juke through a lot of streams."

He swiped the holograph, and a zigzag route lit up in the galactic cobweb, with what looked like thousands of stops.

"Can we go to another galaxy?" Vy interrupted.

"No," Thomas said. "The Torth never figured out how to create or modify temporal streams. They inherited the network, so to speak, from an extinct civilization."

A conquered civilization, Ariock suspected.

"It's confined to our galaxy," Thomas said. "So the Torth Empire is finite. But that's a problem, because there are only so many potential remote destinations for us to go. The Torth will have spent the last six hours beefing up security. There's a possible chance that we'll face an enemy force waiting on the other end." He gave Ariock a pitiless stare. "If so, you will need to kill them the instant we emerge at our destination."

That was a command, not a request.

"No," Ariock said.

Kessa blinked at him. Vy stared in surprise.

"I'll push them away," Ariock said.

"That's not good enough." Thomas bared his teeth in a snarl that could have looked threatening, if he weren't so young. "You can't push them away forever. You'll need to sleep sometime, or your power will get depleted. You don't have an endless amount. They'll shoot nuclear warheads at us."

Ariock gazed beyond Thomas, to where the globe of Umdalkdul slowly twisted away in the distance.

Millions of innocent people lived there. Billions, perhaps. The slaves were unaware that Ariock existed, unaware that he could engulf them in his awareness. It would be easy.

Mass murder should never be easy.

Ariock imagined that a Torth armada would be as populous as a city. Slaves would be aboard the starships, serving the Torth crew.

"There may be some innocent casualties," Thomas admitted. "But we don't have much choice. It's their lives or ours."

Vy gave Thomas an anguished look. She didn't say anything, but her objection was clear.

"I'll push them away," Ariock repeated. "And I'm sure you can help by outmaneuvering them. You can probably fly circles around an average spaceship pilot."

Thomas gave him an incredulous glare. "You see these hands?" He displayed his malformed arms. "I have the knowledge, but I do not have the strength or the reflexes. There's no way I can—"

"Then I'll drive." Vy plopped into a seat next to him.

Thomas gave her a level look. "The best pilot in the universe couldn't get us through a Torth armada."

"Can you use your supergenius brain to fool them?" Vy asked. "Or, I don't know, redirect some temporal streams?"

"No," Thomas said before she'd finished speaking. "Temporal streams were invented by a prior civilization. The actual science is outlawed and long forgotten. The Torth Majority forbids superluminal travel."

He saw their questioning looks.

"It's outlawed," he said in a pedantic tone, "because the Torth Majority doesn't want anyone going renegade and escaping. Like we're about to do."

Ariock wondered if the Torth Empire was ruled by a bunch of idiots. How could they believe that hobbling their own science was a good idea?

Kessa wore a look of amazed comprehension. "They gave up access to potential power," she mused, "because they fear what one person might be able to do with it?"

"Right," Thomas told her. "Any technology that can be commandeered by one individual and potentially used to harm the Torth Empire is against the law."

Kessa looked fascinated.

"That includes temporal stream technology," Thomas said, apparently answering Kessa's unspoken questions, "and related research. Other empowering technologies are likewise outlawed. Artificial intelligence, for instance. Bioengineering." He indicated his medicine case. "And Yeresunsa powers." He nodded toward Ariock. "They bent some laws for me. And now they're regretting it."

Distant ships seemed to watch them. The moons and industrial plantations all seemed as watchful as the silent audience in the prison arena.

"You're extremely lucky to have a supergenius pilot," Thomas said. "Since the only way to use a temporal stream, normally, is to access the Megacosm and ask for hyperluminal vertex calculations. Normal Torth cannot do what we're about to do."

Ariock was impressed.

"Anyway." Thomas tapped the pedestal, and the holograph winked out of existence. "If you want to survive, there's only one way." His gaze bored into Ariock. "Kill them."

Ariock hesitated, certain there must be another way.

"I would kill them, if I could," Thomas said. "I'd throw fireballs. I'd do whatever is necessary."

Ariock imagined Thomas roasting people alive with the same stony face he wore while teaching.

Maybe it was a good thing he'd been hit with the inhibitor serum.

Thomas stared at the control panel as if it might talk back. "Think of the innocent lives you'd save by killing a bunch of militarized Torth. If that's not enough reason for you? Then remember how easily you get distracted or overwhelmed. They can trip you up in a matter of seconds. Every little failure you have peels away your self-confidence, and they know that. They'll exploit your weakness."

Thomas seemed to be exploiting it himself. Had he just implied that Ariock's dead mother was a "little failure"?

A "little failure" described something trite and insignificant. Not what Ariock had done. Thomas must know that. He was using manipulative tactics, as ruthless as any Torth.

"Fail," Thomas said, "and you will trash every risk we took and every person we lost today. You would make it all meaningless."

He didn't call Ariock a negligent brute or a murderer, but the implication was plain.

Ariock reminded himself that Thomas probably had good intentions. But why couldn't he compromise? Why did he have to insist on getting his way, no matter what?

"I said I'd keep them away." Ariock tried to mitigate the anger in his tone. "I'll do my part. You do yours."

Supplies levitated, caught in his extended attention, raised along with his temper.

"I, um…" Thomas's voice squeaked with fear. "Okay!"

Ariock put all his focus into calming down. He inwardly vowed that if they ever got to a safe haven, he would never use his powers again.

Well, he might heal an injury or a sickness, when needed.

But otherwise? Ariock silently vowed to do everything possible to refrain from expanding his awareness. No more crushing storms. No more wreckage. No more killing, ever again.

He would stay small.

CHAPTER 9

A NEW ATMOSPHERE

Cherise sat against a curved wall that displayed an ever-changing starscape. The view changes happened faster than eye blinks. Each refresh showed a new configuration of unfamiliar constellations, stars that hung in the void of space without twinkling.

So many configurations.

If even a tiny fraction of those bright stars hosted worlds as populated as Earth, then the galactic Torth Empire must be incomprehensibly huge. Endless.

Inescapable.

Dugwon sat next to her, gazing outside with solemnity. Cherise couldn't guess what the adolescent villager thought of space travel, but she supposed it might be the same experience for both of them. They were on a mysterious journey through a universe of eternal night.

The rapid view changes stopped abruptly. They drifted.

Space looked ordinary here, but to Cherise, it was desolation. They were between worlds. This was no place. It had no name.

"I see no Torth," Kessa said cautiously.

They were apparently alone in outer space—but Cherise did not trust the view. Every slave knew that Torth habitats masked doors and control panels and all kinds of things. Windows often displayed false illusions.

"They could be cloaked," Thomas said. "It's now or never, Ariock. If there's anyone out there, you have to kill them."

Cherise hated how human he sounded. A telepathic supergenius could speak in any accent, in any language, using any slang, but Thomas purposely chose to sound like her friend from the Hollander home.

Was it just an old habit for him to sound like that? Did he have any idea how his voice affected her?

He must have some idea. It was clear that he just didn't care about filthy slaves like her. He seemed focused on just one thing: his promise to Ariock. He would make sure that Ariock survived.

Everyone else was just cargo.

Cherise remembered a different version of Thomas. That version would have couched his words to Ariock in an apologetic tone instead of making them a heartless command.

That version of Thomas would have made supreme efforts to rescue the villagers of Duin.

That version would have checked on Cherise to make sure she was all right.

She wondered if that version would ever reemerge.

"I don't sense anyone out there." Ariock wore a look of concentration.

The crew members who understood English relaxed a little bit. Weptolyso and Pung glanced at each other with cautious hope.

"Are you sure?" Thomas sounded surprised.

"I'm sure." Ariock gazed at the endless array of stars. "We're safe."

All the refugees understood that word. *Safe* and *free* had entered their vocabulary faster than Cherise could pick up alien words. Ummins seemed to be masters of foreign language learning.

Dugwon turned to her with excitement.

To Cherise, it seemed too soon to celebrate. Not after they'd watched Delia die. Not when the Torth had threatened to invade Earth. Billions of people were on the brink of losing their freedom.

Thomas's pleased look turned to suspicion. "This escape was too easy."

Ariock and Vy both gave him stares of incredulity. To call this escape "easy" seemed like a gross exaggeration. It meant trivializing Delia's death.

"I mean," Thomas quickly elaborated, "it doesn't make sense. Since they were unable to pursue us, I would think they'd throw all their resources into trying to blockade, or at least surveil, the vicinity of remote temporal streams."

"Maybe they're afraid of Ariock," Vy said, her tone full of secondhand pride. "They didn't expect him to kill, like, a thousand of them."

Ariock looked embarrassed. He actually blushed.

"Yes," Weptolyso thundered in the slave tongue. "The Torth fear Ariock, son of Jonathan Stead!"

Refugees heard that proclamation, and they seemed to agree. One refugee whooped. Two more babbled praise for the Bringer of Hope, the Son of Storms.

A few adolescents grabbed each other and bounced in a victory dance.

Then everyone surged to their feet, jumping and shouting at the top of their lungs.

Ummins, normally reserved, broke into supply packs and shared food. They ripped crystal sculptures off their magnetic pedestals and waved them like trophies, chasing each other around luxurious furniture like hyperactive children.

Cherise wanted to join the fervor. But she was all too aware that she resembled a Torth. Dugwon would probably recoil if she saw her human friend dance, as if Cherise had as much right to celebrate freedom as someone born on a slave farm. It would seem like an offensively bad joke.

Anyhow, attention was always bad. It didn't matter whether it came from a Torth or from a friendly adolescent ummin.

Cherise saw that Vy wasn't dancing, either. Happiness encircled Vy and Ariock, Thomas, and Kessa, walling them off from everyone else. Cherise sidled close enough to overhear their conversation.

"...I'm sure it's just leftover paranoia," Ariock was saying. He laughed in a way that sounded forced. "We're safe."

He didn't seem to fully believe that.

"I wouldn't discount your gut feeling," Thomas said. "You may have a touch of, uh, prophetic power."

Vy gave Thomas a warning look, unnoticed by Ariock. Cherise remembered that Delia had begged them to never tell Ariock about the prophetic nightmare he'd forgotten about. Just before his father had died in a plane crash, young Ariock had dreamed it. Delia hadn't wanted her son to torment himself with guilt over might-have-beens.

"There's no Torth out there," Vy pointed out. "So we're safe. Right?"

"In theory." Judging by Thomas's tone, he was racking his overdeveloped brain to figure out why he wasn't feeling joyful. "They can't track us. Superluminal technology is forbidden in the Torth Empire."

"So..."

"A few things aren't adding up for me," Thomas said. "My anticipated exit calculations were off."

Vy looked nonplussed. "Are you saying you made a math mistake?"

"I never make mistakes."

Vy looked extremely skeptical, and Cherise could have hugged her for that.

"Not with math," Thomas clarified.

"So what are you saying?" Vy asked. "Are we lost in space?" She made it sound like a joke, but Cherise saw the gravity in her eyes.

"We emerged where I expected to be," Thomas said. "It could be nothing. Hyperluminal matrices fluctuate, and I guess it's possible the difference was within normal parameters."

Vy sounded relieved. "So what's the problem?"

"I just don't like anomalous data." Thomas seemed annoyed at having to explain his reasoning. "Plus the fact that the Torth are not likely to just give up so easily."

"Maybe we're not important in the grand scheme of the galaxy," Ariock suggested.

Thomas gave him a level look. "Ariock, you're one of the most powerful Yeresunsa in history. You really think the Torth will be okay with you vanishing? Like you're not any sort of a threat?"

"I don't think I'm a threat," Ariock said in a stiff tone. "If they ever put their mind-reading powers to use, they would know that I never wanted to hurt anyone."

"Your intentions don't matter," Thomas said in a patient tone. "As far as they're concerned, you're ruled by emotions instead of logic. That makes you unpredictable."

Cherise figured, with reluctance, that Thomas had a point. Ariock had power like a nuclear bomb.

And the Torth were not known to be forgiving.

They had hunted Jonathan Stead until he'd crash-landed, faked his own death, and spent the rest of his life in hiding. Even then, the Torth hadn't given up. They had hunted him until they found the family he'd left behind.

It seemed certain they would do the same to Ariock.

"The Torth Majority never give up when they want something," Thomas said. "They'd sacrifice one half of the Empire to protect the other half." He stared distastefully at the celebrating ummins. "I don't believe they've given up."

The group fell silent amid the joy around them.

Kessa perched on a cushy chair. She looked like she belonged in luxury, despite her rags. "Would this be a good time to check the Megacosm?" she asked.

Thomas gave her a measuring look. "I was just going to suggest that."

"You said that you would not ascend until we are safe." Kessa sounded apologetic, perhaps afraid to remind him. "Are we—"

"Done." Thomas opened his eyes.

He had blinked. His sour expression smoothed out, and he looked almost blissful, as if he had sipped hot cocoa or luxuriated in a spa.

Cherise wondered if he had allowed a billion Torth to crawl through his secrets, like flies exploring a feast. Did he actually crave their attention?

Perhaps he had never truly escaped the Torth Empire.

Saddened, Cherise reached into the makeshift pocket of her outfit and touched the paper lion. An earlier version of Thomas had folded that origami symbol of courage for her, on another world.

Perhaps he needed some of the courage he had gifted to her?

His heroism seemed to be enough for Vy, for Ariock, and for Kessa. But Cherise saw a deadness in his eyes. Nothing much mattered to this version of Thomas. He wasn't invested in the future of escaped slaves. He wasn't invested in anyone's future—not even his own.

"The Megacosm is in an uproar," Thomas reported. "They're throwing around blame, because…well. We've escaped."

Ariock's huge shoulders lost tension. Vy broke into a joyful grin.

"They cannot guess where we are?" Kessa examined Thomas with her bright gray eyes. She must have noticed his hesitation.

"I don't see how they'd find us," Thomas said. "I juked so many times, our location is random from their perspective. And we haven't chosen our final destination."

"So..." Vy studied him. "We're safe?"

"I guess so," Thomas said. "Yeah. I guess we made it."

Vy squealed with joy and threw her arms around a very surprised Ariock. His face broke into a huge grin.

Thomas turned toward the control panel, shoulders hunched as if to defend himself.

Until Vy joined him. She gently embraced Thomas, radiating so much visible happiness, it must be overwhelming to a mind reader. Thomas looked shocked.

In that brief moment, Cherise saw a glimpse of her heroic friend. The coldness melted from his gaze. He looked human.

But it didn't last.

He regained his icy demeanor and indicated that Vy should move away. "I'm busy," he said. "There's still a lot to do."

He saw Cherise for a second. Then his iridescent yellow eyes flinched away.

The ummins chanted a song about freedom.

Cherise stood, taller than any ummin, her black hair swinging around her like an extralong head cover. Her home world seemed impossibly distant, like a dream. She would probably never see Earth again.

But did she need to keep clinging to an identity that had never quite fit her?

She did not need to be an abuse victim. She did not need to be a victim at all.

As she followed Dugwon into the midst of the dancers, she left her old self behind. Her friends were all orphans. Some of them had left parents behind in Duin, but they were like her. They were teenagers. Although they used to be victims of abuse or slavery, that was the past.

The universe was gloriously immense. There must be places untouched by the Torth Empire.

Behind them, Kessa interrogated Thomas in the language of paradise. Only Cherise could overhear and comprehend their conversation.

"Can Torth keep major secrets in the Megacosm?"

"If you had asked me a week ago, I would have said no. But I think it's theoretically possible, if they're a high enough rank. Low ranks would not dare to question Servants of All."

"So they might know something you do not?"

"It's possible."

"When you checked the Megacosm, were any notable Torth absent?"

A hesitation. Cherise glanced toward the control pedestal and saw Thomas reassessing Kessa.

"That's an insightful question," he admitted. "Yes. High ranks can drop out of the Megacosm for temporary privacy breaks, and they could keep a secret that way, for a short time." He paused. "My nemesis wasn't there."

Cherise caught her breath at the implication. She wondered if Thomas would fulfill his promise or die trying, even if he was no longer capable of feeling like a human.

"You suspect a trap," Kessa stated flatly. "Yet you did not warn Ariock."

"It might be nothing," Thomas said. "It's possible the Upward Governess was just asleep."

Cherise recalled the gigantic holograph of that powerful Blue Rank. She did not want that nemesis coming after them.

"Come on!" Dugwon grabbed both of Cherise's hands and yanked her into a dancing circle of adolescent refugees.

Soon Cherise was away from dour Thomas and his worries. She let ummins whirl her from one to another. The freedom filled her with so much joy, she began to laugh.

Threats were far away.

At least they were on their way to someplace new. They would make a home where freedom existed.

CHAPTER 10

SWEET SECRET

The Upward Governess commanded one of her bodyguards to fluff her pillows. After many sleepless hours, she couldn't find a comfortable position, no matter how many pillows she used or which way she reclined.

Uniformed slaves entered, bearing a tray of gourmet snacks. The Upward Governess bit into a berry tart. Her abstinence from the Megacosm made her both uncomfortable and ravenous. She couldn't imagine how the Betrayer had survived it for as long as he had. Entire days! Was he even sane anymore? He must have an astronomically high tolerance for austerity.

The door of her solarium slid open again. This time, an elderly Blue Rank stepped inside.

How did you get in? the Upward Governess demanded. Her nussian guards should have barred any lower ranks from entering her palatial suite.

Judging from the minds of her nearest bodyguards, they'd let this Blue Rank in because he had threatened to kill their loved ones if they continued to block his way.

Hm. Threats were always effective on slaves, even on loyal nussians.

That made her wonder why she bothered to own nussians. She ought to swap the lot of them for a few packs of well-trained Algypaean battlebeasts.

I did not intend to interrupt Your meal, the Blue Rank thought. *I apologize.* He bowed his head, which was encased in a hood to hide the misshapen ears he had been born with. *You (Superior One) are sorely missed. Local matters require Your attention.*

At least he was contrite. The Upward Governess nibbled on her tart and decided that if this man failed to leave within five seconds, she would have her mostly useless bodyguards escort him away.

The Blue Rank reprioritized his thoughts. *An aqueduct pipeline broke due to the disaster caused by the Giant. It will take days to repair the damage.*

The countdown in her mind concluded.

Wait! he thought. *Slaves in New GoodLife WaterGarden City are getting sick from dirty water.* He eyed the plentiful waterfalls of her open terrace. *Will You use Your governance tablet to reroute key aqueducts?*

The Upward Governess tapped her tablet, adjusting the flow of water throughout her city. The fountains and waterfalls in her solarium slowed to a trickle.

Thank You. The Blue Rank emanated relief.

For good measure, the Upward Governess dialed up the breeze turbines throughout the city. Maybe a good breeze would take people's minds off the lessened water flow.

The Blue Rank lingered within her telepathic range. He clearly still had concerns and had questions that he didn't dare to think about.

It occurs to Me, the Upward Governess thought, *that I have struggled for much of My (short) life with entirely too much responsibility upon My shoulders. Few supergeniuses (in history) have been so eager to contribute to Our majestic Empire. Perhaps My time is misspent?*

The Blue Rank's mind spiked with concern. *The Empire benefits greatly from Your contributions. In fact,* he hastened to add, *some research projects cannot be completed without You. The details of an estimated 680 theorems exist only in Your mind at this moment. It is important that We (the Empire) catalog Your vast knowledge before You die.* He lowered his gaze. *I would like to record some of Your knowledge, (if You approve), Great One.*

So he wasn't one of the many Torth who was hoping that she would die sooner rather than later.

I will continue to contribute, she assured him. *Right up until the hour of My death. But I suppose I have been neglectful of My duties.* She finished off the tart. *I want you to serve as an interim governor for My metropolis and province. Starting now.*

His mouth dropped open. *Me???* A savage emotion, shock, flashed through him. *You want Me to be a governor???*

It was a good thing that neither of them was in the Megacosm. Otherwise he might have been sentenced to death for such a rude emotional outburst.

Yes, she assured him calmly. *It is just a temporary position. Govern in My stead while I am indisposed.*

If he did a good job, she supposed the Servants of All were likely to promote him to her own lofty rank. Maybe they'd even raise him higher. Unlike her, he wasn't held back by a debilitating mutation, so it was possible for him to become a Servant of All.

The Blue Rank ducked his head under the weighty idea of such great honor heaped upon him. *With all due respect, governors and Servants tend to get promoted young. I am old. If I was meant to rise that high, surely the Servants of All would have promoted Me decades ago?*

There are exceptions, the Upward Governess thought. *Stranger things have happened.*

After she triumphed in capturing the Betrayer and getting the Giant killed, well, she might be able to get anything she desired. She would certainly get to choose her own replacement.

Now go and be My temporary governor. She removed the protective algorithms on her governance tablet and offered it to the Blue Rank. *Do not contact Me again. And do not allow anyone else to do so. I shall rejoin the Megacosm and resume My duties, but I must abstain for a while longer.*

The Blue Rank bowed in respect. He did not question her abstinence from the Megacosm, which meant he understood why it was necessary. He did not speculate on what enormous secret she must be keeping. Instead, he accepted the governance tablet and thought, *If only You could live long enough to become the Commander of All Living Things. You would be worthy of that grand position (unlike Our current Commander).*

The Upward Governess stopped eating for long enough to watch him go. Part of her longed to call him back, to make him stay and keep her company.

But no. That would undermine the security and success of the Torth Empire.

She could not allow herself to have companions. Other mind readers had to be off-limits to her for now. She could not predict when the Betrayer might ascend into the Megacosm or how much he would soak up.

She had to make sure that he would be utterly caught off guard when the jaws of her trap closed around him.

A nearby slave noticed a trace of a smile on her lips. He was so surprised, he fumbled with a nectar drink. He caught it before it could hit the floor.

The Upward Governess pretended not to notice. Punishments cost effort, and anyway, a slave in pain would sour her mood.

She could almost taste her upcoming triumph. The Majority would shower her with honors. They might even feel indebted enough to gift her with an endless supply of NAI-12 medicine…

Well, no. That was a fantasy.

No one wanted to help her live to adulthood.

But she knew exactly what reward the Majority would readily grant her. They would give it to her the instant she made the demand. It was something to look forward to, even better than a sweet dessert, even better than acquiring lovely, nurturing animals for her menagerie.

She would gain access to the clearest memory of the Betrayer's face in the exact moment when he understood the inescapable fate she had engineered for him.

Her smile widened, and she pushed another tart into her mouth.

AFTERWORD

When I outlined the Torth series, I figured that the best way to emphasize the heroism of my heroes was to make the bad guys extremely awful and overpowered. The best way to show why justice matters, I thought, was to show injustice on a grand scale. I stand by that decision.

At the same time, I acknowledge that I may have gone overboard with the injustices piled up in this first book, and a bit in the next one. I was surprised by the reactions from RoyalRoad readers calling for Cherise to die or begging for Thomas to go on a murder spree. I didn't understand why a contingent of readers expected major wins for Thomas at the outset (the major wins will come later in the series). Maybe I got desensitized to brutality as a reader, having grown up on horror, sci-fi, dark epic fantasy, historical nonfiction, and harrowing nonfiction memoirs.

If Cherise were to be extremely understanding and forgiving of Thomas while he is still acting like a slave master, superior to everyone else, that might be satisfying to some readers, but not to me. Cherise is learning what she wants in a partner and how she wants to be treated.

Likewise, if Thomas were to snap and totally abandon the friends who are being unfair to him, this would be a different story. Thomas is more interested in solving injustice on a grand scale than on addressing injustice toward himself. It's also one of his greatest qualities as a hero. He honors his word, and he gets s*** done, no matter who stands in his way, no matter what obstacles he faces.

I offer this promise: justice matters. There will be consequences for the wrongs committed by the Torth Empire, as well as for individuals who have mistreated Thomas. The really big wins happen later in the series. I say that with surety, because the Torth series is entirely prewritten.

It will come out in this order:

Torth Book 1: *Majority*
Torth Book 2: *Colossus Rising*
Torth Book 3: *World of Wreckage*
Torth Book 4: *Megacosmic Rift*

Torth Book 5: *Greater Than All*
Torth Book 6: *Empire Ender*

This first book was originally two books, but I combined them for a more complete experience.

Abby
March 2023

ACKNOWLEDGMENTS

This series was a magnum opus project. It would be a much poorer story if not for the advice, kindness, and incisive humor of the alpha reader whom I married, Adam Robert Thompson. He got me past the hardest parts of my life as well as the knots I encountered in storytelling!

Special thanks also go to my longtime readers on Wattpad. It means the world that strangers in various countries around the world were willing to stick with my series for six-plus years of weekly chapter posts. I especially loved comments from Ceilingfanenvy, Whiplash246, IceFireStarFire, _mehatepizza_, V6ct9r, and AGENT_88. Meaningful support from GOLIXTH, NoteOfE, and KarenSampson was extremely valuable to me. I don't want to skip others who showed up for every chapter, like micpanda, Yung_dnzel, lisadavis910, Joey-Jay_Spooner, CraigWalker7, kafui27, and really a lot of others.

I'm grateful for my readers on RoyalRoad as well, especially the ones who fought back on semi-abusive comments. Thank you, Cjenx, WalterD, General Peaceful, Shadow of Marethyu, Miss Nomer, Smoarville, EatMoreVegetables, and too many more to name!

Before I plunged into the online web serial world, I had friendly strangers and critique groups look over my series in progress. I particularly want to thank the people who devoted a lot of their time to the Torth series. I'm especially grateful to Brian Rappatta, Marc Geddes, Colleen Robbins, Sarah Kelderman, Vidya Gopalakrishna, Ellen Van Hensbergen, Leigh Berggren, Marissa Engel, Mike McCauley, Susan Shell Winston, Rebecca Shelley, Laurie Lemieux, Nicky Drayden, Marshall Ryan Maresca, K. G. Jewell, Katy Stauber, Ethan Reid, Caitlin Jennings, Tracy Berg, Susan Abel Sullivan, Damon DuBois, Larry Paul Holdaway, David Pardoe, Bob Cutchin, Rita Oakes, Luisa Prieto, Rebecca Roland, J. R. Murdock, Jeremy Whitted, Jackline Waye, Jan Wakelin, Amanda Hernandez, Steven Roy, Jon Arild Karlsen, Tore Rambøl, David Doyle, Elze Hamilton, Douglas Schwartz, Elinor Caiman Sands, Cécile Cristofari, and many others.

Further thanks go to Jeanne Cavelos and George R. R. Martin, who gave me wonderful personal feedback and encouragement at the Odyssey Fantasy Writing Workshop.

Thank you so much.

And my parents. They offered true support!

ABOUT THE AUTHOR

Abby Goldsmith is the author of the Torth series, originally released on Wattpad and Royal Road. Additionally, her work has been sold to Escape Pod and Writer's Digest Books. She is also a 2D and 3D animator with game credits. Goldsmith has lived on all three coasts of the United States and currently resides in Texas, where she is married to her favorite reader.

DISCOVER
STORIES UNBOUND

PodiumAudio.com

Printed in Great Britain
by Amazon

26849428R00335